The

Absolute

Book

ALSO BY ELIZABETH KNOX

After Z-Hour

Treasure

Glamour and the Sea

The Vintner's Luck

The High Jump: A New Zealand Childhood

Black Oxen

Billie's Kiss

Daylight

The Love School: Personal Essays

The Angel's Cut

Wake

FOR YOUNG ADULTS

Dreamhunter

Dreamquake

Mortal Fire

The

Absolute

Book

Elizabeth Knox

First published in New Zealand in a slightly different form
by Victoria University Press, Wellington, 2019
First Published in Great Britain by Michael Joseph, 2021

004

Grateful acknowledgment is made for permission to reprint the following:
Page 30: Excerpt from 'Armchair Traveller' by Bill Manhire, in *Wow*
(Victoria University Press, 2020), p. 16. Reproduced with kind permission.
Page 84: Excerpt from *Priestdaddy: A Memoir* by Patricia Lockwood, copyright © 2017
by Patricia Lockwood. Used by permission of Riverhead, an imprint of
Penguin Publishing Group, a division of Penguin Random House LLC. All rights reserved.
Pages 224–5: 'These Fevered Days— to take them to the Forest' by Emily Dickinson.
From *The Poems of Emily Dickinson*, edited by Thomas H. Johnson, Cambridge,
Mass.: The Belknap Press of Harvard University Press, Copyright © 1951, 1955 by the
President and Fellows of Harvard College. Copyright © renewed 1979, 1983 by the
President and Fellows of Harvard College. Copyright © 1914, 1918, 1919,
1924, 1929, 1930, 1932, 1935, 1937, 1942, by Martha Dickinson Bianchi.
Copyright © 1952, 1957, 1958, 1963, 1965, by Mary L. Hampson.
Page 458: Excerpt from 'Near the Wall of a House' by Yehuda Amichai,
in *The Selected Poetry of Yehuda Amichai*, translated by Chana Bloch and Stephen Mitchell
(Berkeley: University of California Press, 2013), p. 126. Reproduced with kind permission.

Printed and bound in Great Britain by Clays Ltd, Elcograf S.p.A.

The authorized representative in the EEA is Penguin Random House Ireland,
Morrison Chambers, 32 Nassau Street, Dublin D02 YH68

A CIP catalogue record for this book is available from the British Library

HARDBACK ISBN: 978–0–241–47392–4
TRADE PAPERBACK ISBN: 978–0–241–47393–1

www.greenpenguin.co.uk

MIX
Paper from
responsible sources
FSC
www.fsc.org   FSC® C018179

Penguin Random House is committed to a
sustainable future for our business, our readers
and our planet. This book is made from Forest
Stewardship Council® certified paper.

CONTENTS

PART ONE

Insects

1. A Book with a Light in Its Long Perspective   3
2. The Muleskinner   11

PART TWO

Fire

3. Matron of Honour   31
4. The Library at Princes Gate, 1995   49
5. Documentary Evidence   59
6. The Bibliothèque Méjanes   77

PART THREE

Light

7. The Island of Apples   85
8. Norfolk   111
9. Night in a Tree   123

10. The Firestarter   133

11. Nil by Mouth   143

12. Brutal   159

PART FOUR

Damp

13. Failing Kindness   171

14. The Pale Lady   183

15. The Summer Road   215

16. The Island of Women   235

17. Kernow's Story   247

18. Go to Your Gate   271

19. Questions from the Audience   287

20. Green Pressure   307

PART FIVE

Carelessness

21. Two Graves   313

22. Basil Cornick's Screen Test   355

23. Mimir's Well   367

24. A Torah Above the Torah   391

25. Taken Lightly   413

26. Quarry House   - 419

PART SIX
Uncaring

27. The Moot   459

28. Call and Response   481

29. Purgatory   491

30. Neve's Story   531

31. Tintern   547

32. The Folly   583

Epilogue One Hundred Years, Eighty with
          Good Behaviour   609

PART ONE

Insects

I am Envy, begotten of a chimney-sweeper and an oyster-wife. I cannot read, and therefore wish all books were burnt. I am lean with seeing others eat. O, that there would come a famine through all the world, that all might die, and I live alone! Then thou should'st see how fat I would be. But must thou sit and I stand? Come down, with a vengeance!

Christopher Marlowe, *Doctor Faustus*

One

A Book with a Light in Its Long Perspective

When Taryn Cornick's sister was killed, she was carrying a book. People don't usually take books when out on a run, but Beatrice must have planned to stop, perhaps at the Pale Lady, where she was often seen tucked in a corner, reading, a pencil behind her ear.

The book in the bag still strapped to Beatrice's body when Timothy Webber bundled her into the boot of his car was the blockbuster of that year, 2003, a novel about tantalising, epoch-spanning conspiracies. Beatrice enjoyed those books, perhaps because they were often set in libraries.

The Cornick girls loved libraries, most of all the one at Princes Gate, which belonged to their grandfather, James Northover. Beatrice was seventeen and Taryn thirteen when their grandfather died. The family had to give up the debt-encumbered house—though Grandma Ruth stayed on in the gatehouse while she continued at her vet's practice. It was Grandma Ruth whom Beatrice was visiting when Webber found her.

Beatrice and Taryn's parents were separated. Basil Cornick was in New Zealand, playing the bluff fellow in a fantasy epic. Addy Cornick had been struggling with illness and was dispiriting company. Taryn would spend some of her holidays with her mother, then stay with friends. She never went near Princes Gate, because she couldn't cope with the changes. A farm conglomerate had taken over the estate. The new owners left the last of the wetlands intact, and the plantation forest with its kernel, a copse of ancient oaks. But the stone walls were dismantled to make long fields with nothing to impede the big harvesting machines—not walls, or drainage ditches, or the hawthorn hedges the foxes had followed.

The library had already gone, broken up before the sale. James Northover's books passed into the hands of the owners of antiquarian bookshops, except a few long-coveted items that went to his collector friends, perhaps including the ancient scroll box known as 'The Firestarter', because it was said to have survived no fewer than five fires in famous libraries.

So, the book bumping against Beatrice's shoulder blades as she took her last steps was one of those set in old museums and libraries. A book with a light in its long perspective, like the light of a grail. A book with scholarly heroes and hidden treasure.

Beatrice was running in her baggy sweats and bouncing backpack. It was autumn, and there was a light mist. The road between St Cynog's Cross and the village of Princes Gate Magna was thickly covered in fallen leaves, its surface amber but for two black streaks where the leaves had been chewed up and tossed aside by the tyres of passing cars. The road was quiet. Beatrice wasn't wearing headphones. She moved off onto the verge when she heard the car. The mist began to sparkle, and the reflectors on Beatrice's shoes flashed as the headlights caught them.

Whenever a restless night summoned her sister—her grey sweats and swinging ponytail—Taryn never found herself on that road. She was always in the car. In the driver's seat. She was the murderer, Timothy Webber. Taryn thought this might have been because she had spent so much time wondering why Webber had done it. Wondering how anyone does a thing like that.

The trial was held a year after Beatrice died. Taryn attended and became familiar with every detail of what happened—or, at least, what was known.

Webber's car hadn't clipped Beatrice because she wasn't far enough off the road. The police photographs showed a curved tyre track in the black mud. They showed how far he had swerved to catch her. There were no skid marks, because he'd braked already, reducing speed not to pass safely but to hit Beatrice hard enough, he hoped, to subdue her. His car cracked Beatrice's pelvis, and a roadside oak her skull. He stopped, got out, and scooped Beatrice up from where she lay in the lap of some tree roots. He put her in his boot.

Webber's lawyers let him take the stand, perhaps hoping his fecklessness would convince the jury that his actions lacked malice. He told the kind of feeble story kids concoct when they're caught out. He said he put Ms Cornick in his trunk to take her to hospital. But—the prosecution asked—wouldn't most people place an injured person in the back seat, or not move her at all and wait to flag down the next car?

Webber said he'd been too afraid to wait for someone to come along. It was a quiet road. He wasn't carrying a phone. It would probably have all gone better for him, he said, if he'd just driven off and had to face a charge of hit-and-run instead of this one. 'But I couldn't do that.' He screwed up his mouth in an expression of apology. 'Why I put her in my trunk rather than my back seat must have been because she'd soiled herself and was a bit of a mess.'

The jury moaned in anger.

Timothy Webber had been charged with manslaughter, not murder, because, the prosecutor explained to Beatrice's family, it was very difficult to prove intent. The police didn't want to risk him getting off altogether. Webber wasn't a bad character on paper. He had a job. He was an honest and reliable worker. He had no criminal record. He had friends and family. He hadn't been equipped for an abduction, wasn't carrying rope or duct tape. He hadn't lined his boot with plastic. He made no attempt to conceal anything, leaving Beatrice's thrown shoe where it lay, on the road, pointing back the way she'd come. He ran her down, but it was difficult to prove conclusively that it wasn't an accident. He may have bundled her into his boot and driven off, but in the end, all he had done was take her another two miles in the direction he'd been going, before performing a U-turn to drive to his sister's house. His sister called an ambulance. She said to the paramedics, then to the police, 'Tim just isn't very bright.'

Beatrice was dead when the ambulance arrived.

Taryn wanted to know what it had been like for her sister, locked in the dark of Webber's car boot. After the trial, a medical intern friend took a copy of the coroner's report to his colleague and arranged a meeting so the neurologist could tell Taryn how it might have been.

'It's unlikely your sister regained consciousness after the impact,' said the neurologist. 'She had a skull fracture, compression fractures in two cervical vertebrae, and the crucial thing, a brain stem injury. It was the swelling in your sister's brain stem that killed her—through uncontrollable blood pressure and disruptions to the normal rhythms of her heart. If you're wondering whether she suffered, she almost certainly knew nothing from the moment the car ran into her.' The neurologist's look said it all—how he respected Taryn's need to know. How this was all he could tell her. How he knew it could never be enough.

What he said helped Taryn believe what the jury had believed—that Webber wasn't a killer with a plan. He hadn't stalked her sister, and he wasn't prepared. He'd only nurtured a fantasy, then surrendered to an impulse. He pulled the wheel to the left. He picked Beatrice up. But she'd soiled herself and wasn't what he had wanted—a woman thrown down, stunned and helpless. It all went wrong for Webber. He hadn't felt what he'd hoped to feel, or gotten to do what he'd dreamed of doing, and he couldn't cope with any of it. And, because he didn't follow through and rape the woman he'd injured and abducted, maybe that was why he was able to stubbornly insist on his innocence. He hadn't *meant* to hurt Beatrice and was indignant that anyone would suggest he had. He just ran into her, then panicked. 'I was upset,' he said—almost as if he expected the court to kiss him better.

Webber was convicted of the charge of manslaughter and sentenced to six years. Five with good behaviour.

I'll be twenty-five then, Taryn thought. She hoped five years would be long enough for her to move on—as people put it, not seeming to understand how she was always on the move, even in her dreams, driving along the amber road as the mist began to sparkle.

As it was it took most of that time for Taryn even to learn to hide her rage. She wanted to keep her friends—not that they were much use to her now, but she understood that they might be one day. In time she'd feel human again, and part of some civil world.

To starve her rage, Taryn stopped talking about Beatrice, not just about what had happened—everything. There were stories she would tell about her childhood where she and her mother and father, grandmother and grandfather would be there, in the room of the story, with a ghostly absence, the now unmentionable Beatrice. Taryn couldn't separate her sister from her death, from the mark on the oak at the fringe of the forest. In Taryn's memory, her sister was a tender wound, Beatrice's whole life stained with the blood she had shed inside her own head. Taryn was angry—burned and pitted by anger like acid. Other things came with the anger: fearlessness, recklessness, chilliness, insolence.

When Taryn met her husband, Alan Palfreyman, she wasn't after a man of any sort, let alone a rich one. She only wanted something to eat, a glass of wine, a comfortable place to sit. She'd been caught in Frankfurt Airport by a cancelled flight on a budget airline. She'd had a holiday in Greece, on a beach she went to only at dusk, because the sun was fierce and her skin very fair. She was on her way home—sea salt still powdering her faintly mauve-shaded white skin; salt in her hair too, so that it was curling and almost black in its thicknesses. Taryn was superficially tired and very hungry, so she staked out the first-class lounges and shamelessly followed one man, a self-contained individual whose passing glance had registered not exactly interest but passive admiration, as if she were a fine watch and he had enough watches. Taryn followed him up the escalator, and when he was showing his membership card to the woman at the front desk of a hushed and scented lounge, and that woman was saying, 'Good afternoon, Mr Palfreyman,' Taryn gently slipped her arm through his and said, 'Mr Palfreyman and *guest*.'

Alan looked at her in surprise but consented. 'And guest.' And they were through, arm in arm.

Taryn was twenty-three when she married, the same age Beatrice had been when she died. Webber had three years of his sentence left to run—if he was serving the full sentence. Taryn's mother had gone. Addy Cornick had been battling breast cancer for years and was in remission when Beatrice was killed. Shortly before Webber's trial Taryn's mother had one of her twice yearly check-ups. Taryn went with her mother for the follow-up appointment. When Addy Cornick's oncologist told her she was still in remission she wept, not with relief, but bitterly, like someone who has had the worst possible news. She wiped her eyes and shrank in her chair, saying to herself, over and over, 'Do I have to keep doing this?' Meaning, 'Must I go on living?' Then, once the trial was over, Addy lost ground. She gave up. She seemed to be in a hurry to leave the world before her daughter's killer returned to it.

For much of that period Taryn's father was in New Zealand. Basil Cornick had a role in what he invariably referred to as 'a juicy fantasy franchise'. It made him a lot of money, though the lonely interactions with imaginary friends and foes in front of a green screen almost robbed him of his lifelong joy in acting. Taryn's father returned for her wedding. He gave her away. He also gave a speech and got the guests to raise their glasses to Beatrice: 'My elder girl, who was tragically taken from us by violence, four years ago.'

Taryn carefully avoided looking at her husband. He knew she'd had a sister, and that Beatrice was dead. But she'd only told him that Bea was hit by a car. Perhaps, when her father was making his overly informative toast, she should have met Alan's eyes so he'd at least see her wondering what he might be thinking. Taryn had, after all, wanted to share her life. To at least have a roost, as if she were a solitary ocean-going bird looking for somewhere solid to set down, no matter how bare and exposed it might be.

On her wedding night Alan was still a little under the shadow of the loneliness he'd felt as he sat, his face stiff with shock, hearing his bride's rather off-putting actor father outline the appalling story of her sister's murder. The speech had been so strange, somewhere between sentimen-tal and perfunctory. Sitting with his bride on a splendid hotel bed, that loneliness wasn't a thing Alan could recall in its horrible purity. He re-fused it, because he loved Taryn, the mysterious woman with wounds so deep she hid them from him. He hadn't yet begun to think, *Who am I to her that she hides a thing like that from me?* Alan Palfreyman thought too well of himself for that.

Once they were finally alone, Alan took Taryn's face between his hands and looked into her eyes. 'You're so sad, Taryn, and haunted, and out of step with others.'

Even Taryn could see this was true. She was always studying the world, not rapt or curious, but patient and dutiful, as if the world was something she'd paid good money to see. She was studying it now too—in the shape of Alan's tender, troubled face. She was listening to the whisper of his smooth palm on the skin of her jaw, as he gazed at her and said, 'Who *are* you, Taryn?'

Two

The Muleskinner

The first thing the guide did when they met was explain himself. He had been talking to the hunting party, Alan and Alan's guests, but it was only when Taryn joined the group that he told them that as a master guide he was a hunter himself, but on this trip he was along only as a tracker and a muleskinner. 'A muleskinner's job is to make sure the trophies are properly preserved. I'll be tracking for the party, and I can give Mr Palfreyman advice about his new crossbow. But I won't be shooting any animals myself.'

This last remark he addressed to Taryn. The intensity of his regard confused her, so she knelt to strip the bear bells from her legs. She'd been for a walk, and there were bears, and it was best to let them know you were coming so they'd move on. She'd been up on Tunnel Mountain with the other wife of the party, who, like Taryn, was along for the scenery and the lodge's spa and five-star cuisine, but not for the hunt.

As Taryn stooped to unfasten her bells, she looked by degrees at the person before her, beginning with his Gore-Tex boots and thick oatmeal socks folded over their tops, proceeding to the old-fashioned corduroy trousers tucked into the boots, then to the belt with loops for shotgun shells, and stopping at his red-knuckled hands. The boots were in line with what the other hunters were wearing, but everything else was pioneer gentleman.

While Alan's party was at the lodge, Taryn saw very little of the Muleskinner. At dinner he was quiet and passed the dishes. One time another guide got him to tell them about the grizzly he'd bagged with his bow a year before. Where he'd found the bear, how long he'd tracked it. When he was speaking he sat almost entirely still, his hands folded, only his eyes moving between the faces of the men who'd got him talking, his fellow guide, and his client and host, Alan. And Taryn. She was sitting beside Alan, eating her kirsch-soaked blueberries one by one with her fingers. The Muleskinner's gaze was mild, but the back of Taryn's head got hot, as if he were throwing microwaves through her.

Taryn hadn't planned to go to the top camp—she just decided to at the last minute. Alan was a little piqued; after all, his colleague's wife had come along solely to keep Taryn company. Alan had wanted his wife of two years to come to Canada with him, but not to go hunting. Then, when it came to it, she complained about being left in Banff, and it had been a bit of a scramble to get her and the other wife included in the trip to the lodge. The top camp was miles beyond and higher up than the lodge. It had no comforts, and the men would be spending most of each day out in the woods. Alan said, 'You'll be on your own with just a cattle prod between you and the bears.'

'The cabin has a door, doesn't it?' Taryn said. 'I'll take paper and pens. I might write something.'

'Okay. This is new. This writing things.'

'The devil is making me,' Taryn said, and leaned against her husband. She slipped a foot out of her trainer and tried to poke it, toe pointed, down the side of Alan's nearest boot. He put an arm around her so she could maintain her balance. He said, 'The devil should write his own book.'

Left alone in the camp, Taryn meant to stay close to the buildings. But when she stepped outside she could see a patch of sunlit green in one of the few straight-through lines in the forest. She walked into the trees. Their thick trunks deadened every sound. Taryn half expected the green to be a sward—the English green of Marvell's 'green thought in a green shade'. But the mountain meadow she found was as botanically complicated as a garden. Many flowers among many grasses; the meadow a space that simply began and ended, trees coming right up to its every edge. A fallen tree made a walkway some hundred feet out from what Taryn wanted to call a shore—though a shore would be a transition between forest and meadow, and here there was no transition.

Taryn walked out along the log.

'And then came a young deer,' Taryn told the Muleskinner. It was late that night and she'd returned to the fire in her boots and long nightshirt. The Muleskinner was just sitting, nothing in his hands, no drink, no cigarette, no dismantled gun (he'd been oiling guns before dinner). He was alone and unoccupied.

Taryn told him about her day. 'She was a little deer, walking slowly, with her ears swivelling to all points of the compass, but her eyes on me. She made no sound. She didn't seem solid. I've seen at least one great ballerina, and I remember being stabbed through the heart by this thing she could do. She'd go en pointe, but incredibly slowly, with her arms up over her head. She'd rise onto the toe of one foot by straightening it really gradually. She looked weightless, as if she might just drift upward.

The deer was like that. If she had started floating, I wouldn't have been very surprised.'

'Was she a whitetail?'

'Yes.'

'And we were out after them.'

The men had bagged an elk and would try for moose the next day.

Taryn thought about how keenly she'd watched the deer and realised that she'd taught herself only to pay close attention to what was unlikely to suffer harm. The deer was young, so not fair game. She looked at the Muleskinner. 'This wasn't a fully grown animal. None of you would have shot her.'

'The young deer don't know,' the Muleskinner said.

'What?'

'Two ridges up that way a deer will take off if it even smells you. But down in the valley, say another five miles, they'll stop and stare. Because that's a national park and somehow they know it. But your deer wasn't in the national park.'

'It didn't have any reason to be scared of me.'

'She should at least have been wary.'

Taryn thought about this. She shuffled over to sit nearer.

He stretched a hand to the stack of split logs beside the wind shelter and put another in the fire. It was a tacit agreement. They were going to stay up and keep talking. He dusted the loose bark from his palms. 'I don't know how the deer learn where they're safe. How they develop expectations.'

'You mean without teaching one another?'

'Yes.'

'They must learn from one another,' she said. 'And even if the place wasn't safe, the deer could see I was.'

'Were you?'

'I wasn't going to hurt it. Or are you asking whether I was safe myself? I wasn't wearing my bear bells or checking over my shoulder for cougar.'

There was a pause, and Taryn heard the fire begin to busy itself.

She was thinking of a familiar road, and of feeling safe when you shouldn't. Then, 'I had a sister,' she said.

By the time the party left the top camp, the Muleskinner knew everything Taryn thought but never spoke about. He just listened, his eyes sometimes on her face but more often on the fire. He asked easy questions that first night—easy, factual questions—not the sort of try-hard ones that might make the person asking look concerned and interested, but which only had very simple answers, the kind of answers that, if Taryn gave them honestly, always made her feel she was somehow failing to live her life. 'You must be pretty angry,' someone would say. How could she respond to that except by admitting it? 'Yes. My eyes are always stinging from the smoke of it.' But no one was supposed to stay angry, especially not a woman. Anger was futile and exhausting—or at least that was the common wisdom.

The Muleskinner asked, 'What was Beatrice like?' He said, 'Beatrice', not 'your sister'. Saying 'your sister', if you knew her name, was like saying 'your wound' and not asking about Beatrice at all. Beatrice had an existence apart from Taryn's wound—just being dead didn't mean she'd stopped having an existence. When Taryn mentioned that Bea had a book in her bag, the Muleskinner even asked what book it was. Taryn knew a lot of people whom she thought of as intellectual snobs. What they were, in fact, were people incapable of relinquishing their sovereign sense that their identity was tied up with what they understood and enjoyed. And they liked to stay sure of themselves, so they never read or watched anything outside what they already approved as good or enjoyable for them. These were the people who, when Taryn told them what book Bea had been carrying, sometimes said, 'Oh, I couldn't finish that.' To which she'd reply, 'Neither could Beatrice.'

Taryn explained things to the Muleskinner that she hadn't been able to explain to anyone else. With Alan she hadn't even made the attempt, feeling unable to risk that much exposure to someone who was going to be a constant presence in her future. Also, Taryn wasn't ready for Alan to help her by being wiser and showing her a way out of her misery. By *squiring* her.

Taryn explained how she was plaited closely with Beatrice and how, once Beatrice had gone, she herself came loose from everything. Even her mother and father and grandmother. 'As if our lives *are* threads,' Taryn told the Muleskinner. 'In the hands of the Fates of legend. The one with the spindle, the one with the loom, and the one with the scissors. The thread of my life has come loose from the cloth. Right now I'm dragging, but maybe one day I'll be hooked in again somewhere.'

Taryn tucked her hair behind her ears. She could see the Muleskinner would like to touch her hair to tidy it. She could see him thinking how he had picked up her thread and would follow it, and they'd go on together, his colour by hers. She may be married to Alan, but it was him she was inviting to do something to anchor her.

'People come loose from their lives all the time,' she said. 'It's nothing special. I'm just putting it well.'

After that conversation the Muleskinner was attentive but unobtrusive. He carried an extra water bottle for her. He found a pink quartz crystal and gave it to her, with no ceremony. And when the party went back down the mountain for some fly-fishing, he taught her how to cast. Alan said, 'That guy has a crush on you.'

Taryn knew that in every important respect Alan was right—but she also felt the Muleskinner was less interested in enjoying her attention than figuring out what he could do for her. There were people who stole near to you, and you could sense their shadows touching you, darkening the air around you, and beginning to stretch out over your life. But it wasn't like that with the Muleskinner. Rather, it was as if Taryn's shadow had attached itself to him, and he wasn't going to feel right again until he had helped her change her life. Taryn sensed that she was dragging the Muleskinner's imagination around after her, and when she left, his thoughts would continue to follow her. He'd keep thinking, *What can I do for Taryn?*

On the day they were to fly out of the wilderness lodge, Alan was inside settling up and giving final instructions about the delivery of his trophies, which were going not in either his London or Norfolk home, but to his office, instead of artwork. (Though only the antlers, because he said the moose's head reminded him too much of an elderly bridge player.)

It was pouring. Water was cascading off the high canopy before the lodge entrance. The rain was supposed to pass over soon and let their helicopter come and go.

The Muleskinner came over to shake Taryn's hand and say goodbye. He had to raise his voice to be heard.

Taryn shouted, 'I liked the hunt despite myself,' and thought, *I should step back into the lobby and stop saying this shit after all the things we've shared.*

The Muleskinner was making all the usual polite noises, even—looking a bit desperate—'I really enjoyed our talks.' Then he swooped and drew her back from the rebounding rain. They were right by the lobby doors, which activated, letting out a cloud of warm air. Taryn glanced in and saw Alan. He gave her an I'll-only-be-a-minute wave.

The Muleskinner stepped close, ducked his head, and said, 'What do you want to happen, Taryn?' He looked calm and patient, his hands in his pockets.

Taryn was only ever to see this capacity for stillness in one other person she met—of all the extraordinary people who passed before her eyes in later years. And, because she'd known the Muleskinner, she was able to recognise the stillness as a poised, powerful intention, and only had to work out what the intention might possibly be. (She guessed, but she didn't believe it. Who would believe it?)

Taryn said to the Muleskinner, 'When a guy asks me what I want to happen, he's asking me to choose.'

'You *can* choose,' he said. But then Alan joined them, and that was—Taryn thought—the end of that.

Some months later Taryn was in her Audi, waiting at the turn from the driveway to Alan's Norfolk house, an 'architectural monsterpiece', as his friends called it. The house was a glass-and-concrete edifice that stood by the shore in its sandblasted, sculptural garden, screened every way but seaward by belts of dark pines.

Even after two years of marriage Taryn still thought of Alan's house and apartment as his and of herself as his guest. She was comfortable, but poised to move, and always finding reasons to go out, to see people she didn't particularly want to see. What she in fact wanted was to be between people and places, and on the road. She was off to an appointment now—a couple of hours driving for an hour at lunch. Which was perfect.

The coast road was quiet, but the turn from the driveway was a tricky one. Taryn was always careful to check the convex mirror opposite the gate. She peered at the mirror and saw a figure in the pines behind her, by the driveway entrance. A man stepped out of the trees. Taryn put her foot on the gas and accelerated away, spraying gravel. She pulled in further down the road and checked her rear-vision mirror. The man jumped over the shallow drainage ditch and came towards her. She recognised him by his grace, and waited. He got in beside her. She said his name. Taryn knew his name, of course. This was before she began purposely to forget him, to think of him—when he did force himself into her thoughts—only as 'the Muleskinner'.

The Muleskinner said, 'Sorry if I gave you a scare, Taryn. But I can only be of any use to you if we leave no trail and meet only in person.' He took a watch cap out of his pocket and pulled it on, then restored his sunglasses. 'We should go somewhere we won't be noticed. People around here must know this car.'

Taryn pulled out. They headed west. At the entrance to the village the Muleskinner tilted his seat all the way back and lay flat so he wouldn't be seen. When they were through he returned the seat to upright. He stayed quiet.

It was only when they were beyond Norwich on the A11 and settled into the middle lane that Taryn opened a discussion. 'I didn't ask you to come.'

'And yet here I am.'

'A demon I've summoned.'

'You're in charge here, Taryn. I came to see what you want. I do have other reasons to be in England. I have family in Southampton. I finished a guiding job in New Mexico and used some air points.'

'Am I before or after your family visit?'

'Before.'

'Where's your car?'

'I don't have one. I have warm clothes, waterproof matches, a knife, and this high-compression bivvy that is both tent and sleeping bag.' He kicked the roll at his feet.

'So you've come to have a look at the size of the job and give me a quote?'

He didn't answer. Instead he asked, 'Are you expected anywhere?'

'I should text my apologies,' she said. Then, 'You're scaring me.'

'I'm not going to impose on you in any way, Taryn. That's a promise.'

'Except to make something possible that wasn't before, no matter how much I wished it.'

'Yes.'

'For a price.'

'I don't want any money.'

'Okay. Now you're really scaring me.'

They passed into a rain shower, the car plunging through the big hard drops as if through a swarm of bees.

'Your story moved me,' the Muleskinner said, then frowned and corrected himself. 'Not your story. Your situation.'

'I have money and freedom and a husband who loves me.'

'Not your situation, then. Your predicament. You know what I mean.'

They passed beneath a wire-grilled footbridge, straddling the motorway and shedding mildew-infused rain in the first downpour in weeks.

The wipers came on again for a moment to clear blackened droplets from the windscreen.

Taryn glanced at the sprawl of tract housing. She thought of the occupants, with their view of the motorway. That, compared with the Rockies, where she'd last seen the Muleskinner. Taryn wanted to apologise to him for what they could see from the A11. England had too many people. Though, of course, people who talked about there being 'too many people' never meant themselves and their kind. She said, 'The somewhere quiet I'm taking you is five hours away. But at least it's beautiful.'

I t was a dull, turbulent summer of overcast days where noon could look like twilight, but it was still light at seven thirty when they got to that stretch of road and the green tunnel of oaks. Taryn wasn't certain she'd recognise the exact spot after nearly seven years. And if she didn't, if the sight didn't jump out at her like a savage animal, did that disqualify her desire for revenge?

Then she saw it, the crime scene, undressed now. Police photos from the trial had directional arrows, and those things that were like place cards at a banquet table, except with numbers instead of names. 1) The bloodstain on the tree trunk. 2) A dropped shoe.

Taryn pulled in. The road was narrow, but there'd be room to pass. What had Webber been thinking when he'd tried to make out that he'd just wandered a little off course?

The Muleskinner said, 'I didn't realise how close we were till we passed the monument.'

'St Cynog's Cross,' Taryn said. 'I thought you were asleep.'

They got out and shook off their stiffness.

Taryn said, 'How did you know Webber was about to be released?'

'You said six years, five with good behaviour. I picked a point between.' The Muleskinner's fists were in his pockets, though the evening was mild. 'Don't ask me for anything,' he said. 'Then you can truthfully say "I didn't ask anyone to . . ."'

'To,' she echoed, without a tone of query. It wasn't a prompt.

'You only have to say no, if that's what you'd prefer.'

Taryn didn't say anything. Instead she led him across the road to Beatrice's oak.

A breeze passed through the forest, and the leaves, still tender, made the sound of fluttering fairground pennants. The Muleskinner took one hand from his pocket and put it on the rough bark of the tree trunk. 'It can be accomplished without you knowing any details.'

'Even when?'

'Even that.'

'And then what?' She put a hand on the trunk too, beside his.

'Then nothing,' he said. 'This will only work if we've no further contact. So, I'm in England for family reasons, then I'm back in Canada. And you are the wife of a former client. And that's all.'

She removed her hand. 'I don't know that I believe you. I feel like you've started a count. I'm waiting to hear you call out, "Coming, ready or not."'

He shook his head. 'Do you have any idea what you're like?'

'What do you mean?'

'You're like a heroine,' he said.

She was about to respond, 'Then who is my hero?'—because she really should make him say it, because how could she trust him to want only that?—when they were both roused by the sound of hurrying footsteps. Someone was coming from the direction of Princes Gate Magna, walking with strange slapping footfalls.

The Muleskinner took Taryn by her arm and drew her off the road and into the forest. They leaned on a dry, moss-furred tree trunk, his arm about her waist.

The person came into sight. A barefoot young man wearing a shapeless, mushroom-brown, home-knitted jersey, too thick for even a chilly summer. His trousers were wool too, a tweed, fawn flecked with white. Homespun hippy clothes, in shades similar to his dark skin, which made him somehow difficult to see.

The young man had an armful of cardboard parcels. Books, by the look of them.

Barefoot-with-books hurried past their hiding place. His footfalls receded, then changed as he left the road. The undergrowth rustled.

The Muleskinner tilted his head to peer around the tree, his motion stealthy.

It was then that the young man lost control of his burden. Taryn heard a breathy curse and a series of thumps and crackles. One package tumbled through the bracken and landed near her, and Barefoot came to retrieve it. He bounded into view, stooped to seize the errant parcel, straightened, and they came eye to eye. He appeared surprised but not alarmed. 'I beg your pardon,' he said. He turned and walked away, leaving a palpable bristle of curiosity in his wake. It was disconcerting. If only she and the Muleskinner hadn't hidden, they wouldn't have looked furtive.

The Muleskinner moved away from her. He said, 'I'll follow him. Find out where he belongs.'

'But he's already seen us.'

'Not me. I turned my head.'

For an uncanny moment it was as if this taciturn woodsman became completely transparent to Taryn. She suddenly understood that he liked to stalk people more than animals because people had the habits of people, and he supposed that if he watched the right quarry closely, he might come to know what kind of animal he was. He couldn't get behind himself, but he could follow a civilised, book-buying, strangely camouflaged, creature-swift stranger, and that act of stalking would help to settle some of the things about himself he didn't understand.

The Muleskinner melted into the forest. He made less noise moving on his sturdy boots than the young man had unshod.

Taryn called after him. 'Why give the guy another opportunity to see you?'

He ignored her fierce whisper.

Taryn stayed put. The skin all over her body was stinging as if she were sunburnt. Was this shame? Why should she be ashamed? No passing stranger could read her intentions. And they were so far only intentions.

Taryn understood that her discomfort was only a small foretaste of what it would be like if the crime she incited with her silence was discovered. She was honest enough to see the trouble coming, but she still kept thinking about herself, what she felt and wanted. Not about the Muleskinner, her instrument. She was weighing up the cost to herself, the risk of terrible public shame, but it never crossed her mind that, by doing this, she would break the locks on all the doors to her soul. Taryn Cornick didn't know she had a soul.

She was tired and chilled. The bracken hadn't seen the sun, and its furred roots were silvered by last night's dew. She stepped back onto the road and shook her feet. In the treetop a bird ruffled its wings, as if in imitation. Taryn looked up, saw a serrated shadow folding back into the darkness of the thick branches of the wounded oak. Jet eyes caught the light. 'Crow.' Taryn named the bird, remembering her grandfather, pointing with his stick as they crossed a field hand in hand. 'Crow, *Corvus corone*.'

The bird shuffled along the branch and made itself visible against a shrinking valve of dark blue sky. It was huge—night in a tree. Taryn saw it was the rarer bird, not often found this far east. *Corvus corax*. Raven.

Taryn sat down between the tree roots that had once cradled her sister. She put her head in her hands.

'Och,' said the raven, in a regretful baritone. This made Taryn laugh, but when she looked up again, the raven was already halfway along the darkening tunnel of oaks. Just before it disappeared, a second raven flew out of the woods and joined it.

A moment later the Muleskinner arrived, soundless, beside her. 'I lost him.' He looked vexed. He handed Taryn a book. *Labyrinth*, a novel by Kate Mosse. 'He didn't spot me. He was dawdling. Kept arguing with himself, or with someone he could see and I couldn't. He threw one of the parcels at a tree. It burst open, and he just left it. I stopped to pick it up, and he vanished. I climbed an escarpment to look around. Apart from this stand of oaks, all the trees are the same height and in discernible rows. This is a plantation. There isn't a lot of undergrowth, but the guy still managed to disappear.'

'He must have been taking a shortcut.'

'I couldn't see where.'

Taryn said, 'There's a dry cave system near here. During the war, treasures from the British Museum were stored in the caves so that if England were invaded, they wouldn't fall into enemy hands. My grandfather was involved in the scheme. The cave entrance was on Grandad's land. This was once our land. Maybe that person is holed up in the cave.'

The idea that his quarry had literally gone underground seemed to console the Muleskinner, who was usually able to keep track of much shyer animals than fleet but noisy Barefoot.

They went back to Taryn's car. The Muleskinner held her hand to keep her steady. It was dusk, and the ground was difficult to see.

When they'd first arrived at the wounded oak, Taryn felt she was sleepwalking into an exceptional state of being—as if the leaves of the trees were the days and days between Beatrice and her, in the same place, almost the last place Beatrice ever was. Taryn had felt she was taking the Muleskinner not so much to the crime scene as to Beatrice herself. 'Beatrice, this is your avenger.' But the book-burdened young man had blundered along and ruined Taryn's great moment.

If Taryn was feeling discouraged and low, the Muleskinner was not. He was moving with his usual competent decision. He opened the passenger's door for Taryn and took the wheel himself. 'It's a long drive if we're heading straight back,' he said.

Taryn didn't hear the 'if'. She sat, mute, staring through the windscreen at the road that led on to Princes Gate Magna and the house her mother's family once owned.

He put a hand on her arm and said, 'You can leave it to me.'

What had felt like a symphonic play of fate now seemed faintly ridiculous. *Oh, God, let him*, she thought in disgust. *Just let him*. Nothing was ever accomplished by anyone with too keen a sense of the ridiculous. She must screw her courage to the sticking place. All she had to do, after all, was endure what she already knew—her own complicity—and what she imagined, Webber damaged and dying. After all, she'd endured her knowledge of what happened to Bea, and in time her true feelings about that would come back and sustain her through whatever else she had to endure. It was all only knowledge.

In the autumn of 2010, Webber was released from prison, six months shy of the full six-year sentence. A few weeks later, he was found dead in a street in Chepstow, drowned in the silty overflow from a flooded storm drain. He wasn't drunk and hadn't fallen. His face had grazes, but his knees and hands did not. It was a suspicious death, and of course the police checked the alibis of those closest to his victim—Beatrice's father, her sister, her former boyfriend, her close friends.

Basil Cornick was in New Zealand, and Beatrice's sister and friends were all miles away, together, celebrating the thirtieth birthday of that former boyfriend. This mass alibi was so convenient that the detectives became suspicious. The timing was too perfect, and it seemed plausible that one of them was the opportunist who saw his or her chance when the birthday invitation arrived.

The police called on Taryn at her London home. There were two of them, a detective inspector who had headed the investigation into Beatrice's death, and with her a young detective constable.

The police sat Taryn and Alan down for a quiet chat. It was all very civil, though Taryn was unnerved by the piercing intensity of the young DC's regard. Throughout the interview, Taryn held Alan's hand. She was drained and watery, wrapped in a mohair throw, a hot water bottle clutched to her abdomen and the small, still-tender wound from a laparoscopy. She was just out of hospital following an ectopic pregnancy.

Her trouble had begun as niggling discomfort that turned, by degrees, to side-clutching pain. In the emergency room Alan shouted at people. He wanted to see action and urgency. The staff asked him to leave. Then the thing in Taryn's side flexed its chain-mail body and her fallopian tube ruptured. She had lost herself in moments of mindless agony. There was a gap, and she woke up groggy. Alan was by her bed, his face white, listening to a doctor talk about 'removing the conceptus' and 'repairing the tube'.

The older detective put her questions very gingerly. 'You must have gone to hospital straight after the birthday party in Scotland.'

'I didn't know I was pregnant. I wish I hadn't gone to Scotland.'

'I was away on business.' Alan made his excuses, though neither detective had looked at him.

'When did you hear Webber was dead?'

'Only now, from you,' Taryn said. 'Our lawyer called some weeks ago to say he was out of prison. I've been trying not to think about it.'

'We'll check on the timing of that call,' said the younger detective, which earned a scowl from Alan.

Taryn then told them she wasn't ashamed to say that she was glad Webber was dead. 'It's the icing on the cake, the cake being five and a half years in prison. It's not as if I wished he'd die, but I'm not above celebrating a neat stroke of fate.'

When the police came away from the grand but virtually bookless Palfreyman apartment, the one who had known the family dusted her hands together and said, 'We're done, I reckon. That's Tim Webber's full ration of me giving a fuck.'

The young DC, Jacob Berger, who had no previous connection to the case, didn't contradict his colleague. He only thought of Taryn: *She's done it somehow.* It wasn't Taryn's admission of satisfaction that made Berger think it, or even the abashed happiness shining out of her face. It was that look, in the back of her eyes, of pride. *Devilish pride,* Berger thought. Not that it mattered much. Someone like Taryn Palfreyman only had one revenge. She'd only had one sister. The thing that did trouble Berger was the idea that, although it wasn't possible for Taryn Palfreyman to have accomplished a murder in person, she was more than rich enough to have paid someone. No self-respecting police officer should be comfortable closing the file on a possible contract killing.

PART TWO

Fire

Excuse me if I laugh.

The roads are dark and large books block our path.

The air we breathe is made of evening air.

The world is longer than the road that brings us here.

Bill Manhire, 'Armchair Traveller'

Three

Matron of Honour

The first of the two calls Taryn absolutely had to take was from a journalist writing a feature ahead of her appearance at the Sydney Writers' Festival. The ten-hour time difference was always going to be tricky, and she'd had to reschedule to an hour worse for him. 'Sorry. I'm in hospital,' she said. 'The ward has a rule about calls after nine p.m.'

Throughout her explanation the journalist maintained a disconcerting silence.

It was a blue evening turning black too soon. The hospital had begun to glow and the highway overpass to scintillate.

It turned out that the journalist's long pause was just him thinking how not to have to ask about her health. But there was no way around it. 'Nothing serious, I hope.' His voice was less expressive than a text-to-speech app.

What would count as serious? Taryn wondered. Her bloodwork was normal and her CAT scan clear. She was due for more tests once the anticonvulsants had cleared her system. But she had next to no memory of the ten hours preceding her collapse.

She did recall staring at the ghost of her reflection in a condensation-covered ice bucket, champagne in her mouth, bubbles tickling against her palate. She was in a hotel room with her oldest friend, Carol. It was Carol's wedding day. Taryn was matron of honour, about which she was uneasy since, strictly speaking, to be matron of honour she should still be married. She and Alan had parted ways seven years before, just a few months after Webber's death.

Carol had a few cherished ideas about weddings, one being the slow ceremonial preparation of herself, her matron of honour, and her brides-maids in a posh hotel. Hence the champagne—the bottle that was suddenly empty and upturned, the condensation halfway down the ice bucket, no longer a mist but dribbles.

Carol was still in her bathrobe but fully made up. She was staring at Taryn, perplexed. She said, 'Why are you asking me about the fire in the library at Princes Gate? It was before I knew you. I might be familiar with your family stories, including the fire, but this *scroll box* is new. I think I'd have remembered a "Firestarter" if you'd mentioned it before.'

Taryn had only two further memories from Carol's wedding day. In one she was standing at the mirror in the hotel bathroom—once more recalled to herself by the sight of her own face. She had her eyeliner in hand and had used it to draw a cat's whiskers on her cheeks. The bath-room stank of accretions of fermented soap and rotted human skin.

The last window of recollection opened onto the footpath outside the church, and the sight of the bridesmaids sitting on their heels to make adjustments to the drape of Carol's dress. Taryn was frozen, icy cold, though sweat was pouring in rivulets under her silk slip. She felt as if she'd dropped something and, were she to stoop to retrieve it, things would pass over her head. Things like Edgar Allan Poe's pendulum, the planes that flew into the Twin Towers, the howling Chelyabinsk meteor, and the angel of death. *Stop and tie your shoe, Taryn,* said a voice in her head. *You have work to do, Taryn. Walk away.* Taryn's shoes were closed-toe, open-waisted sandals with buckles, not laces, so the voice in her head couldn't see what was on her feet. She scanned the street and churchyard for the threat, for there must have been a threat, something she was being warned about.

Warned, as Beatrice wasn't.

The lychgate was covered in climbing roses, still only in bud. The lawn was closely mown and trimmed around the bases of the head-stones. The church was suburban, Victorian brick.

Then—impossibly—it came at her, the smell from *inside* the church, of beeswax polish, and incense, and prayer-book perfume. Taryn's spine arched as her body became a bent bow, full of pent-up power. Her tongue humped in her mouth, gagging her, and the world tilted downwards as if it meant to tip her off it.

'Let's just get on,' Taryn said to the Australian journalist at the other end of the phone.

They spent the first five minutes on the usual questions. Yes, *The Feverish Library* was her first book. She was thirty-three. Yes, her book had begun its life as a PhD dissertation.

It wasn't until they got on to the subject of the Reading Room in the State Library of New South Wales that the journalist came to life. The library was being refitted, he said, turned into a 'friendly and less bookish' space. 'The plans cite visitor figures. Because most people who visit don't do so to read books. They come in for the café or to use the internet.'

'Have the planners established that people don't want to do those things in the presence of the books?'

'Of course not. Anyway, the main bone of contention is the Reading Room. At the moment it's only for researchers. It houses Australian books, maps, manuscripts, newspapers, and magazines. They want to clear all that out and send it off-site and use the space as a kind of corporate shopfront, with the lovely architecture and furniture and the scholars sitting around like movie extras. Sending the materials off-site will mean that one newspaper or book won't send a researcher straight off to consult another. They'll have to put in an order. Fill out a form.'

'This is the other great conflagration of libraries,' Taryn said. 'Public libraries being closed or run down because the people with the purse strings don't understand that today doesn't always know what tomorrow will need.' Then, 'If there's a petition, I'll sign it.'

He said he'd send her a link. He went on to say that he found he'd quite liked her book. He hadn't expected to. 'I thought it might be a little academic.'

'I think I prefer the word "scholarly" to "academic".'

'Yes. You would.' He went on to tell her that he'd liked her book's anecdotes rather than its arguments.

They talked about the bear who broke into a priory in Jura, in the very cold winter of 1500, attracted by the aroma of fresh vellum, and ate a copy of the letters of St Jerome. They talked about the pope who ordered copies of Livy and Cicero burned because young Romans preferred them to reading scripture. They discussed the Mongol commander Hulagu Khan, who used books from the great library of Baghdad to build a road for his army through the swamps of the Tigris. Books in bellies, books burned, books trodden underfoot. The journalist then quoted Heine. People who read Taryn's book often quoted Heine: '"Where they have burned books at the end they will burn people."'

That's what your book is about,' he said. 'That's where its whole argument leads.'

Taryn reflected that it was where he wanted her argument to lead—the ultimate talking point in her publisher's Ten Talking Points for Book Clubs.

She said, 'Hulagu and the bear in Jura aren't just a preface to Nazi book burning.'

'No?'

'Let us think for a moment about Hulagu Khan. His sack of Baghdad's libraries wasn't just a gesture of hatred against Islamic culture and Syrian scholarship. He also destroyed the city's bridges. Hulagu understood the relationship between knowledge and communication, communication and commerce, commerce and power. It is as if he took Baghdad and knocked the teeth out of its head. Not just the teeth that bite, but the teeth that facilitate eating and speech. He crippled the city. Hulagu took treasure and slaves, but he wasn't a covetous conqueror; he didn't want to stay and enjoy anything. He just wanted to beat the city down and make sure it stayed down.'

'But the destruction of books is a gesture and a threat. It's like saying to the people of those books: You're next.'

Taryn was relieved that he'd finally decided to conduct his author interview at the level of her book. She wanted to please him enough to get a little warmth from their encounter. But she had no energy and couldn't keep up, and he'd already gone on to noticing parallels between her account of the botched efforts of manuscript preservation following the 1731 Cotton Library fire in the unfortunately named Ashburnham House and the 2004 fire in the Duchess Anna Amalia Library in Weimar, after which damaged books were freeze-dried to spare them from rotting.

The dinner trolley arrived at Taryn's door, wheels squeaking, steaming at all its seams. The woman pushing it carried Taryn's tray to her bedside table and checked the diet sheet. She mouthed at Taryn, 'Would you like a cup of tea?' And Taryn covered the mouthpiece to answer, 'That would be lovely.'

Her attention wasn't substantial enough to be divisible. She got that sensation again, the one she'd had in Carol's hotel room, of something scraping its yellow nails on the inside of her skull. She wanted to end the phone call but couldn't summon the right polite words. But, suddenly, he was asking his fluffy final questions. Would this be Taryn's first trip south of the equator? Then, angling, 'Your father spent a lot of time in New Zealand a few years back. You must have visited him.' Perhaps he hoped to work his way around to asking whether she had any insights on what would happen next in the mega hit TV series her father was now working on.

'I had planned back then to visit Dad in Wellington, but then my sister was killed.'

'Oh,' said the journalist. After that the interview came to an awkward close.

Taryn swung her bedside table over her legs, uncovered her meal, and let its steam wash her face. She ate as much as she could until she was overcome by tiredness. Then she reclined her bed, closed her eyes, and wished there wasn't a nurse coming soon, who would wake her up only to give her something to help her sleep.

Much to her surprise, Taryn's work of musing nonfiction had found its way onto the bestseller lists. *The Feverish Library* was about the threats to libraries, from silverfish to austerity measures. And it was about what libraries chose to keep. Books made to be treasured, and books made for use. And the things never intended for preservation, like letters. A letter once read might be twisted into a spill to carry flame from hearth to candle, or torn into strips for curl-papers to make ringlets in a child's hair. But such were the vagaries of value that a thing meant for the eyes of only one person, like a letter of apology or a declaration of love, would be stashed and cared for, along with public documents, peace treaties, royal proclamations, and papal bulls. A note scribbled on a table napkin by a famous jazz pianist, or an alphabet book made by a mother for her child, gathered together in the democracy of a library, might keep company with a papyrus scroll chronicling all that remained of the story of Gilgamesh and his visit to the underworld, or Ibn Hawqal's map of the world. All kept, and safe. Safe from the light that fades, speckling paper, ageing it as skin ages, with freckles and liver spots; from the insects that burrow, punctuating the middles of words, making merry hell of sentences and dust of reason; from the damp that brings mildew and makes books secretive, gluing their pages together and causing even gilded titles to fade into its grey-green mist. Light, insects, damp are the enemies of books. Light, insects, damp—and fire.

The Feverish Library concluded with library fires, a subject that intersected with that of book burning and censorship. It was Taryn's take on these matters that drew noisy notice to a work that might otherwise have had only a few thoughtful reviews.

Of library fires there was no end of stories. And that was the charm Taryn found in the history of burned libraries—no end of stories, and their sudden, accomplished end.

Light came rosy through Taryn's eyelids. She was drifting, a thing neither sunk nor floating. Someone was talking to her. Taryn identified her father's considering manner, his usual boisterous bonhomie turned down a notch.

Nowadays Taryn heard her father's hail-well-met mode as his most famous film character, a fun-loving, salt-of-the-earth fellow who tried to jolly the fate-bedevilled leads out of their grimness. A man always laughing, knitting his brow, and starting every sentence with 'Surely . . .', 'Surely we have time to . . .' To rest. To eat. To blow foam from the top of the tankard. The character whose rosy face, pale and fallen, let the audience know what they were supposed to feel when the worst calamity finally arrived. The face of a man looking on corpses whose gaze was made for the contemplation of cakes and ale. Between the release of the second and third films in the trilogy, Beatrice was killed. One review of the final instalment even went so far as to refer to 'the terrible gift of Basil Cornick's recent history'.

Taryn had never known what to think about her father's feelings or his expression of them. He was such a good actor.

But who was her father talking to? She had come awake in the middle of the exchange. Her back was glued to the bed by sweat, her head to the pillow. Her mouth was dry, and the linings of her cheeks clung to her teeth.

She managed to open her eyes. Her father was looking at her keenly. There was blue sky visible in the window behind him. It was daytime, maybe afternoon. 'That's an interesting question,' he said, as if continuing a conversation.

Taryn hadn't heard a question. Her jaw ached. Her nostrils felt stripped inside, as if she'd been snorting baking soda.

Her father went on. 'Well—your mother's family were all rather refined. I always had the sense that the son-in-law didn't quite cut it. It wasn't an attitude enforced by anyone in particular. Your grandad was an easy-going fellow. But Princes Gate wasn't welcoming. It was dilapidated. On its way down. So perhaps the general stiffness of the North-overs was just the shame of genteel poverty. Shame and prickly pride. But I always felt that the house itself was standing guard and trying to see me off. I swear your grandma's long hours weren't all about her love of horses, pigs, and cows, but also about escaping the clammy gloom of Princes Gate. Getting out to someone's nice cosy stable. So—I wasn't often there, and my memories of the place are sparse.'

He ran out of talk. Taryn looked around, saw they were alone, and tried to ask him who he was talking to. What had brought all this on. But she couldn't even grunt. Her eyes were open and her face turned his way, but she couldn't communicate. She began to panic. Then she heard the *other* person. A sly, dry, insinuating voice. 'There was a fire in the library,' it said. 'Do you remember?'

'Ninety-five, wasn't it? Your mother and I were on holiday in France. Beatrice received some slight burns. All sign of the fire had gone by the time we got back. Of course Addy wanted to rush home—but your grandma Ruth had everything well in hand.'

'Do you remember what was damaged in the fire? What was *un-damaged?*'

'The library lost a rug. The big rug with the bloodstain. You girls used to call it "Colonel Mustard in the library with a revolver". There was a good tale attached to it. Do you remember? You girls were always asking for the story. Let's see. It goes like this.

'One night Ruth, coming back late from her clinic, ran down a dog. A slender, long-haired cross-breed female; the most beautiful animal she ever saw. Ruth wrapped the dog in a coat and brought her home and into the only warm room, the library. She put her on the threadbare Turkestan—because the library tables were never clear. Ruth planned to check the animal over, give it a painkiller, then take it to the surgery. But then she and your grandad heard someone calling. They went out onto the terrace, and Ruth tinkled the little silver bell the dog had been wearing on her collar. A light came around the lake shore. A person holding a lantern. A hippy girl, with pale caramel-coloured hair, who came glimmering over the lawn.

'The girl pulled off her coat and wrapped the dog in it. And the animal came back to life—Ruth had mistaken canine stoicism for more serious trauma. The girl thanked your grandmother, gracious and formal, and carried the dog out of the house—leaving Ruth with its collar and bell.'

Taryn glared at her father—or, at least, she hoped she was glaring. He was looking right at her and seemed relaxed. His legs were crossed, and he was jiggling his ankle—something he did when he was in good spirits.

'A fine fairy tale,' the voice said. 'For those who can tolerate fairies. But tell me, apart from the bloodstained rug, do you recall whether anything else was damaged in the library fire?'

'A map of the estate and surrounding country. Linen paper, nineteenth century. Your grandfather felt its loss.'

'And what was *undamaged?*' said the voice, persistent and strained. A little bit robotic now.

'It was only a small fire, Taryn,' said her father, who seemed to think he was talking to her. 'You were there. Though I always thought we didn't get the full story. I know it started due to carelessness on the part of the man who was helping James with his papers. Jason Battle. Your grandfather sacked him.'

Taryn stopped trying to make herself heard and instead tried to stop speaking. She clenched her teeth until she felt her mandible muscles might shatter her jaw.

Her father half rose from his chair. 'Taryn? Are you all right?'

He didn't get an answer and hurried out of the room. Taryn could hear him calling for a nurse. She looked at the call button on the bed control, fumbled for it, suddenly free, but stiff and clumsy. She had it in her hand when the nurse came in, followed by her father. 'What's the matter, Ms Cornick?'

'Is this a seizure?' asked Taryn's father.

The nurse put a firm hand on Taryn's shoulder and pressed her onto the bed. 'I've paged Neuro. If you're going to seize that's what they want to see. I know it's alarming, but we've been waiting for this. The doctor can get a much better idea of what's going on with you. Taryn? Can you hear me?'

The EEG Taryn had the day before hadn't yielded any useful information. The neurologist said the seizures were a mystery. 'They're hiding,' he said.

The nurse released Taryn and hauled the monitors closer to her bed. She checked the sensor clipped to Taryn's finger, and all the other connections. She slipped her hand under Taryn's backside to see whether Taryn had wet the bed.

'No,' Taryn said. 'I'm with you now. I couldn't wake up properly. I could hear—talking'—she paused, then pressed on—'but Dad wasn't speaking to me.'

'I was,' he protested. 'You certainly spoke to me.'

'Do you think that maybe your daughter was talking in her sleep, Mr Cornick?'

Basil Cornick's frown was too expressive for normal use. 'She seemed relaxed and friendly.' Then, helpful, 'My other daughter had night terrors, when she was five or so. Bea would sit up in bed and point past her mother and me at the doorway as if she could see something we couldn't. She'd keep trying to look around us at whatever it was she could see. Something that scared her silly.'

'We have Taryn down for a sleep-related eating disorder,' the nurse said. 'Self-reported. Sleep-related eating disorders do have some connection to night terrors.'

Taryn had told the doctors that, for the past week or so, she would wake up to a trilling, like the last cicada of summer. It was her refrigerator. She'd go to shut its door and would find bloody crumbs of steak mince scattered on the fridge shelf next to an empty polystyrene meat tray. It was only when Taryn saw the empty tray that she'd feel the cold fat coating the roof of her mouth.

'I felt as if I couldn't move at all, but I was talking. And it wasn't me,' Taryn now insisted. This was the real problem—the heart of the whole thing.

'But we were talking about things that had happened to you, like the fire in the library,' her father said. 'So I can't see how it wasn't you. And—sorry—what is a sleep-related eating disorder?' He looked beseechingly at the nurse.

'It's where the patient experiences episodes of getting up in the night—still asleep—and bingeing, often on uncooked food.'

'But Taryn has always been so careful about her figure,' he said. Whenever matters of weight and appearance came up, Taryn's father immediately lost all tact and judgement.

Taryn groaned.

The nurse leaned over her and shot her a quick confiding look.

'Don't worry about him,' Taryn said.

Taryn's father realised he was out of line and tried to make amends, but all his panic buttons had been pushed—his daughter was going to make herself fat and unattractive—so he dug himself in deeper. 'You mustn't be guilty about it,' he said. 'That does no good.'

Taryn lost her temper. 'I'm not guilty about anything!'

It was a reflex disavowal, a hangover from her teenaged impatience with him. But of course she was guilty. And used to it—the queasy discomfort that came and went like regular flare-ups of a chronic illness. On the nights when she'd lie awake counting the flashes of the tiny light on the smoke alarm, she'd remind herself that was it *all done*. Webber and the Muleskinner. Done, and in the past. She'd had seven years of that—the remorse that wouldn't ever recede.

'I should go,' said her father. 'Though I hoped to talk to you about something Carol mentioned. The silent phone calls you've been getting.'

'Carol shouldn't have said anything.'

'It's a matter for the police, Taryn.' Her father looked uncomfortable, even guilty.

Taryn chose to ignore his particular concerns but otherwise took pity on him. She thanked him for coming and asked if he'd come again the next day, but to text first, in case she had tests. 'Or they discharge me.'

He squeezed her fingertips and went out.

A minute after that the neurologist arrived with more questions, and tests for some abnormality that *wasn't* just reported by the patient herself.

Taryn woke to find two people in her room.

A small woman with cheekbones as sharp as adze heads was sitting in the chair beside her bed. She wore a crisp trouser suit and had cornrow braids. The man standing against the light of the window had black hair, black jeans, and a black leather jacket.

There was a strip of sunlight on the room's windowsill. It was the morning of a new day, Taryn's third in hospital.

The woman turned to the man. 'She's awake.'

He came over, blocking the light.

'I'm Detective Sergeant Rosemary Hemms,' said the woman. 'And this is Detective Inspector Jacob Berger.'

Berger took out his badge and held it up. 'We've met, Ms Cornick,' he said. 'Seven years ago, when I came with my former boss to speak to you and your former husband about the death of Timothy Webber.' Berger sat himself on the edge of Taryn's bed, leaned forward, and met her eyes. His were blue. *Cold as the March wind*, thought the book-haunted Taryn.

'We're here to talk to you about your silent phone calls,' Hemms said. She looked concerned. Sympathetic.

Taryn heaved herself into a sitting position. She put her elbow on her IV line and gave the cannula a painful tug. Berger came to her aid. He took her weight for a moment and arranged the pillow behind her.

'Get off!' said Taryn.

Berger's spectacular widow's peak bristled.

'I haven't reported any calls,' Taryn said. She was close to tears.

Twice a day for ten days now her phone would ring and there'd be a silent presence at the other end, a presence to which she'd said the usual things, like, 'If you have something to say, just say it.' But she hadn't threatened to call the police. She knew she wasn't just imagining the calls, because sometimes he wouldn't hang up before the beep, and her voicemail would record a hungry, hissing gap, or a moment of muffled street noise. The calls were real and verifiable, unlike what she was now thinking of as her *figurative* silent phone calls. Those arrived like a self-annihilating, post-hypnotic trigger and caused her to do things she wasn't aware she was doing, like get up in the night to gorge herself on raw mincemeat.

'You told your friend Carol about the calls; she told your father. He sees the calls as a possible contributing cause of your troubles. It was he who got in touch with us.'

'Surely you don't expect me to believe someone sent a detective inspector about nuisance calls?'

Berger told Taryn that her father had reached out to his old boss, the detective who had led the investigations into both her sister's and Timothy Webber's deaths. 'She was someone your father knew and trusted. But she's retiring at the end of the month, so she called me.'

Taryn concentrated on Berger. 'How is this connected to my illness?'

'Well, as it turns out, that's an interesting question,' said Hemms. She looked excited. Then she glanced at Berger and dampened it down some.

He said, 'We had a talk with your doctor, and he's extended his brief. He's having your blood tested for exotic toxins.'

'Just in case,' said Hemms.

'Someone else will be in to speak to you about that,' said Berger.

'A doctor?'

They didn't respond to her question. Instead Berger said, 'We know you're still getting the phone calls. We know that someone rings you at the same time every morning and evening from public phones, progressing gradually up the country. The first call came from a payphone by the harbour at Chepstow—a spot very near where Webber died. The latest came from a phone outside Salisbury Cathedral. There are nearly two weeks between the first and last calls. Two weeks and one hundred plus kilometres, as if whoever is making the calls is travelling on foot.'

'Are you monitoring my phone? I didn't give permission for that. It wasn't me who put in a complaint; it was my father, without my knowledge or say-so.'

Hemms looked uncomfortable. Berger did not. He said, 'We aren't monitoring your phone.'

Taryn fumbled one hand free of the bedding to helplessly slap at the air before their dark bodies. 'You need my permission,' she said. 'Or a court order. Isn't that right?'

'Yes, that's right.' Hemms leaned in. 'But, as Berger says, we aren't monitoring your phone. Look—is someone threatening you, Taryn?'

Berger added, with heavy insinuation, 'Do you know of any reason why someone might threaten you?'

'No.'

'You've been in the papers,' Berger said. 'And on the radio. You've stepped into the light.'

'I need rest,' Taryn said, as feebly as she could. 'DS Hemms, DI Berger, I'm afraid I can't help you anymore.'

Hemms got up, decisively clicked her pen, and put it and her note-book back in her jacket.

Berger touched Taryn's hand. The hand that still had a cannula under tape, in a halo of bruising. His touch was light but hurt her. 'Per-haps you've attracted the wrong kind of attention,' he said, then stepped away from the bed.

Once the detectives had gone, Taryn reclined her bed and dimmed her light. She lay feeling as if she were shrinking from the inside out, flesh from her bones, skin from her hospital gown and chilly bedsheets. She thought about Princes Gate. Or, rather, she simply ached to go back there. But anything she might look for was long gone. Grandfather and grandmother, the punt in the reeds on the lake shore, Grandma's cats, the catastrophically leaky roof and green-streaked walls, the solid cold of the upstairs rooms with their smell of sour rugs and old board games. Beatrice. And Taryn herself, before events and errors without remedy.

Lightning flashed. Taryn looked out the window and saw only building windows and the parabola of lamps along the rail line and overpass. The lightning came again, a discharge not in the sky over the city but inside her head. A blue-white flash. And with it came the voice. The eerie, merry voice. 'Show me the box!' it cried, and coruscated, 'Show me the thing that didn't burn!'

Four

The Library at
Princes Gate, 1995

Taryn was curled up on cushions piled in the bay window. The day was dull, and for the past hour she had bent ever closer to her book while tilting its pages to the light.

Of the many stories Taryn had read about only children—lonely onlys, or plucky girls with odd ways of reasoning; about orphans in attics, or hidden demigods with the weight of the world on their shoulders—this book was the best. The girl in the book was the same age as Taryn, who was ten, and at the beginning the girl was doing the same thing she was, sitting on a window seat, in a fine old house, reading, while outside it rained and rained. Before Taryn got very far in, she pulled the curtains closed, exiling herself from the warm room, the library lamps and the fire her grandfather had laid, one of coal heaped over the white bricks that Taryn's Kiwi grandmother called 'little Lucifers', though the packet read 'Strike-a-Fire'.

Taryn was also hiding from her stack of books. Grandfather had found her reading *Tales of the Greek Heroes* and had fished out a book of Norse mythology, and one he insisted she must read—above all others— because the stories in it were the myths of *this place*. The sight of *The Mabinogion* weighed on Taryn, so she'd closed the curtain on it.

Wind joined the rain. Raindrops blew right in under the portico to hit the window, forming glassy freckles on its dust-powdered surface. It was the kind of weather that made Taryn think the sun wasn't shining anywhere, though her parents were probably right then sitting on a restaurant terrace above the sea in Antibes, drinking pink wine. Her father would be eyeing up anyone 'with a bit of vivacity', as he put it, from behind dark glasses to be sure, but always transparent to Taryn whenever she was around to monitor him. Taryn's father's looking didn't always lead to anything, but he was forever perusing the menu.

Taryn was cold behind the curtain. It was cold in her book too, in the locked room where the girl had been sent to think on her ingratitude. Taryn understood that the red room's cold was worse than that of her grandfather's house, though Princes Gate's upper floors were now only waterproof in four bedrooms.

Any moment now a ghost would appear. And a ghost would mean the whole story would be friendlier to wild girls than to stuffy adults.

Taryn raised her eyes from the page to savour the moment before the ghost arrived and changed the story. She saw the wind sweeping yellow leaves into the angle between the terrace and wall. She screwed up her eyes. How did one perform passionate weeping? She could ask her father, but then he might demonstrate rather than explain, and that was always embarrassing.

Then the curtain was pulled back and Taryn was discovered—not by John Reed, Jane Eyre's bullying cousin, but by her sister. Beatrice climbed onto the window seat and pinched the curtains closed. She met Taryn's eyes and put a finger to her lips.

Who were they hiding from? Grandma was at her veterinary practice, and Grandfather had taken a few of his many dozen notebooks away to the kitchen to review a chapter of his history of this house, leaving the girls the library.

The library was Princes Gate's most distinguished room. It was carpeted in old silk rugs pinned down by heavy oak furniture. Its shelves had sliding library ladders. There were glass-front cabinets full of faded butterflies, giant shells, and withered pufferfish. The huge globe labelled in gilt lettering no longer swivelled—hadn't since, years earlier, a schoolfriend of their mother's had rolled it down the lawn and into the lake. There were deep shelves full of scroll cases. And, of course, there were the books, many of them leather-bound classics, some welcoming to young readers, like *Kidnapped* and *Ivanhoe*, *The Black Arrow* and *Jane Eyre*.

Grandfather could get a little peace if, on their visits, he ceded the girls his library. He didn't mind disobliging himself, or the man he liked to call, in a lavish way, his secretary.

Jason Battle, a local youngster who'd read history at Oxford, was employed two days a week, bringing some order to the small museum in the nearby market town of Alnwinton. On the other days he helped Grandfather with the family history. Battle had been present now for several of the sisters' visits. Grandfather's history was going slowly, partly because he enjoyed Battle's company. Taryn liked Battle for his eagerness, his knowledgeability, and that he fitted in with everything else in the country. He drove an old Land Rover and wore green Wellingtons eight months out of twelve, and socks indoors. Battle could look at a Roman coin and tell you what emperor it was, or explain how the ancient Britons built their palisades of thorns.

Beatrice did not like Battle, who stammered whenever he spoke to her and made a clumsy show of getting out of her way. He'd gather up his sliding piles of papers and rush off, making Bea feel inconvenient and exceptional. Bea tried to explain her discomfort to Taryn, who, once it was explained, began to see the problem too.

Beatrice was beautiful, but only fourteen, a girl who liked books and playing with the cats in the cattery above her grandmother's surgery. She wasn't ready to be admired, or discompose anyone. She'd rather not be noticed at all.

This visit was worse. For a start it kept raining, and there was no getting out of the house. For the first days of their holiday Taryn and Bea put on their anoraks and walked up and down the gallery on the third floor, gazing at the rectangular marks on the wallpaper where ancestral portraits once hung until they'd had to be moved because the copper frame of the skylight corroded and rainwater came in and streaked the walls acid green. Bea would now and then pause before one of these phantom paintings to tell a story.

'This is Sir Secundus Northover, who dammed a brook to make the lake and built the folly on the island. He was an authority on Arthurian legends. He liked to dress up as the Lady of the Lake and play the harp on misty nights. He was sadly found drowned, clad in a white robe, white fur tippet, and jewelled slippers.'

Taryn would stare at the discoloured wallpaper, see the imaginary Sir Secundus, and want to know more. But Beatrice would just smile and move on to the next shadowy square.

Mid-morning Battle would arrive at the house, his Land Rover knocking and pinging. Bea would go to the windows to watch him come stumping in. Taryn would peer at her sister's tight face and know Bea wouldn't follow her downstairs until Battle had shut himself away with Grandfather. Or, if he appeared close to lunchtime, Bea would skip lunch, saying she wasn't hungry. If Grandma was home, she would put down her cutlery and head upstairs, only to reappear several minutes later without Bea. She'd say nothing, glare at Grandfather, and eat her cold soup.

This past week things with Battle had worsened. He'd stopped gulping, stammering, and dropping things. Instead it seemed he'd decided to give up washing. He began to emanate a stink, at first dank like standing water, then rank and goaty. He stank, but he was still shaving and his clothes looked clean. Taryn held her breath and tried not to giggle whenever she encountered him. Bea continued to melt away after a cool 'Good morning'. She didn't stay long enough to notice how Battle had altered. He no longer watched Bea. His eyes now passed blindly over everything, as if he were in pain or running a fever. He still paid attention to Grandfather, sometimes barely polite, like a bored kid in class, and sometimes with febrile expectancy.

That day Grandfather had said at lunch, 'Jason and I won't work in the library again until the weather has cleared and you girls can take your games outdoors.' Battle put his coffee mug on the kitchen table and folded his hands in his lap. It was a gesture of schooled patience. It looked to Taryn like something she'd do when trying hard to convince everyone she was behaving herself. She also registered that Grandfather might have said she and Bea *played games* to remind Battle that Bea was just a girl, something Grandfather had been doing, like this, sidelong, since the early days of that visit. A week earlier Battle might have blushed, because he had started to see the self-consciousness Bea suffered due to his untoward admiration. But Battle didn't blush; he only watched Grandfather in a way that reminded Taryn of one of those films where a prisoner is always keeping an eye on what the prison guard is doing with his keys.

Taryn heaved a sigh. Grandma and Grandfather looked at her;

Battle did not. Taryn wished that these comparisons she always made were more help in understanding things. What was the point of noticing things and understanding so little?

Bea climbed behind the curtains and put her finger to her lips. The rain rattled on the window like rice coming to a boil. Taryn couldn't hear anything else. She opened her mouth to ask, 'What is it?' But her sister scowled and shook her head.

Bea had been at the big table, poring over a local map, learning the names of vanished woods and checking the diminished boundaries of those still standing. It was Bea's whispered recitation of Lode Wood, Lower West Wood, Higher West Wood, St Cynog's Wood, Princes Gate Wood, Lower Field Wood that drove Taryn to the window seat.

Taryn returned her sister's scowl and only mouthed her question. Then she heard something, one word—her grandfather's indignant 'my'.

Grandfather was a frugal man who made do with mended things and always looked for ways to save. But he was generous, and the house, land, and chattels remained 'ours' in his speech to the family and often also to the other old families of the neighbourhood. Anyone who earned Grandfather's stern 'my' must somehow have pushed him.

Taryn poked her head through the curtains. Bea tugged at the back of her jersey, but Taryn fended her sister off. 'I'm watching to see if the door handle turns.'

Out in the passage Grandfather said, 'My Torah came from a scholar in Lodz, a gift to my venturesome ancestor William Northover. I've always kept it with due reverence, shawled, and shut away in its box.'

'Box,' said Battle.

Grandfather said, 'And why are you asking about my Torah, anyway?'

Battle said, 'My Torah, your Torah. The gross Torah, not the ghost Torah.'

'Is *that* what this is? You've converted? Isn't it usually Baha'i or veganism with you people?'

Battle said, 'Who are "you people"?'

'You *young* people.' Grandfather sounded exasperated. 'And if you have converted, Jason, why can't you do it in the normal way and make an announcement: "I've discovered a Jewish ancestor and decided to study Hebrew." Then I'd be saying "Good for you" and offering to show you my Torah.'

The handle turned. Taryn pulled her head back and pinched the folds of the curtains to stop them from swinging.

'They're not here,' said Grandfather. 'And my fire is going to waste.'

'Fire,' said Battle.

'I beg your pardon?' said Grandfather, who was a little hard of hearing. Then, 'It's time to knuckle down, Jason. We'd best fetch what we need and go. If the girls are up in the gallery, they'll soon be back. On a day like today it'll be positively Arctic up there. Except the polar regions at least have the virtue of being dry.'

Battle said, 'You take the estate manager's journal. I'll carry the map. Its case must be around here somewhere.' He now sounded businesslike and ordinary.

A library ladder trundled along its iron track. Its steps creaked. Volumes pulled from shelves and stacked made a solid, leathery thumping. It sounded to Taryn as if someone were putting a saddle on a horse.

The library door squeaked as one or both men went out. The girls didn't move. It was dusk outside; Bea's face was ghostly, bluish. Her brown eyes had lost all their warmth and were only alert. The girls listened for the sound of a map rolled and slipped into its case.

Instead the door closed and latched. Battle was still present, motionless, making no attempt to hunt for the map case. The flames in the fireplace were audible, fluttering. Then the girls heard the legs of the brass fire screen scraping on the hearth as Battle dragged it aside. There came a stealthy crackle. Bea put her hand over her mouth. The reflection in her eyes of light coming through the crack in the curtains turned from white-yellow to yellow-orange.

Battle said to himself, to the empty room: 'The new Torah will issue from me. The new Torah is the aspect of the Torah which is above, which is the aspect of the Tree of Life in actuality. And this is above our Torah, which is garbed in the Tree of Knowledge of Good and Evil.' His tone of voice was more that of someone telling a joke than intoning a sermon.

Taryn put her eye to the gap in the curtains. She saw Battle holding a burning twist of paper. He touched the flame to the edges of Grandfather's old map of Princes Gate and its surrounding countryside. The map was reluctant to burn, perhaps because of its linen backing, or something in the ink.

Taryn said to Bea, 'He's setting fire to Grandad's map!' She didn't bother to whisper.

Bea gasped and launched herself through the curtains. Taryn followed her.

Bea picked up *The Mabinogion* from Taryn's stack and threw it at Battle. The book clipped him on the elbow, but not before the map caught fire.

As it burned it curled up, rolling across the desk and setting other papers alight.

'To purify and to separate!' Battle yelled.

Bea shoved him aside. She stretched her jersey cuffs over her hands, grasped the as-yet-unlit edge of the map, and whipped it off the table and onto the Turkestan rug. She stamped on the flames.

Taryn opened the library door to shout for Grandfather. Fresh air rushed in past her, and Bea screamed. Taryn turned back to see her sister on fire. Flames streaked up Bea's favourite cotton clown pants. Bea rushed to the French doors and rammed through them. She dropped onto the waterlogged gravel of the terrace and rolled. The flames went out.

Taryn had an idea. The rug wasn't under the desk; in fact, the only piece of furniture on the rug was a heavy leather armchair. It was on casters. Taryn put her shoulder to the chair and bulldozed it out of the way. Then she grabbed a big art book, came back to the desk, and used the book's edge to scrape the rest of the burning papers off the desk and onto the rug. Then she ran around and seized the corner of the rug nearest the French doors and hauled with all her might.

Bea came back inside and joined her. Battle gave a mad cackle and came to stand on the far edge of the rug. The girls yelled at him, but he just stood, his face bright red and glaring challenge.

Grandfather arrived. He roared in horror, then took in the girls' problem and rushed at Battle, taking him by one arm and tugging him away. The girls gave a hard heave on the rug. Battle lost his footing and toppled backwards, his body rigid. His head slammed into the parquet floor.

Bea and Taryn dragged the rug out the French doors, across the terrace, and onto the lawn. They flipped it over, tipping out the fire and smothering it. For a moment they were making smoke signals, black smoke, then white.

Grandfather hurried down the steps. He eased himself onto his knees beside Bea to inspect her legs. Her pants hung in shrivelled tatters, and the skin on her calves looked as if it had been licked by a dog with its tongue coated in strawberry syrup. She shivered and wept.

'It doesn't look too bad, love,' Grandfather said. 'We'll get you to a doctor.'

From the corner of her eye Taryn saw movement in the library. Battle rose to his feet without using hands or arms; he levered himself up, knock-kneed, by standing on the inner edges of each foot. His face tilted towards the ceiling as if he were balancing a ball on his nose. Taryn fumbled for her grandfather's arm and tugged on it. She pointed—in her shock she'd lost her language, had gone as silent as a sole fledgling in a nest.

Battle swivelled his head, his eyes shut, scenting the air. He grinned and started for the hearth. His gait was peculiar, his legs lifting only from the hip. His ankles wouldn't lock to keep his feet in line.

Grandfather said sternly, 'Oh, no, you don't.' He got up with his granddaughters' help and hurried to interpose himself between his secretary and the fire, until, struck by another thought, he dodged sideways and embraced a vase of flowers on a plinth to one side of the French doors. Hugging the vase to him, Grandfather shuffled over to the fire and tipped its contents into the grate. The fireplace billowed steam, and the room filled with the horrible smell of burning lilies.

Battle turned his face to the grate. His nostrils vibrated, but he didn't open his eyes. Then he ran. Taryn couldn't remember ever having seen Battle move at anything faster than a pitched-forward, flat-footed walk. His running gait was loose, caroming. He tottered from the terrace and slithered across the lawn. He rounded the southwest tower and passed out of sight.

Five

Documentary Evidence

Taryn's literary agent, Angela, texted to ask if she was ready to be picked up. Taryn replied that she was waiting for her discharge papers. The ward was very busy, and she didn't want to nag.

Taryn had noticed how busy everyone was, but she'd been so low that she hadn't considered how remarkable it was that she had a room to herself. Of course her father had paid for one—and when he visited she'd shown him no gratitude, nor even much politeness.

After their mother's double mastectomy Taryn and Beatrice's visits were to a six-bed cubicle on the post-surgical ward. There were other women present, and their problems made Addy Cornick seem less isolated and exceptional. Once Beatrice had gone, and Addy's cancer came back, Taryn's father had the film money and, though he and his wife had been divorced for years, he made sure she had a private room. That room had a full-length mirror, angled to reflect a view of the corridor. But the door was often closed. Taryn would shut it whenever her mother began her quiet weeping. When the door was closed the mirror showed only

Addy's black cashmere robe hanging on the back of it. The robe looked like the shadowy shape of a third person present in the room.

Beatrice.

Taryn, in her private room, thought she should shed a tear—should be able to—for her father, who'd no doubt given the hospital his credit card the moment Carol called him. Who arrived soon afterwards, all the way from Lake Bled and the set of his television fantasy series, possibly causing the rearrangement of the whole shooting schedule.

A very well-turned-out man walked in to Taryn's room. She looked up from her phone, regarded him with a baleful expression, and wished she wasn't in a private room. She wished for more beds, and someone coughing, and someone else receiving a cellophane-wrapped fruit basket and the news of the day. There was of course some chance this man might be another specialist, brought in by the neurologist for a second opinion. He *was* holding a yellow envelope, though it looked too small for films of a scan. Taryn thought it more likely he was the 'someone' DI Berger had promised.

The man introduced himself as Raymond Price, inquired after her health, and then, without waiting for an answer, told her he wanted to ask a few questions about the two men she'd spoken to following her appearance at the Southbank Centre. 'Three and a half weeks ago. Faheem Khalef and Riad Tahan. The very odd circumstance is that it seems they were in the UK with the sole purpose of meeting you and visiting a single tech company. Had you had any previous contact with either of them?'

'No.'

'You do remember them? They approached you after your session, when you were at the signing table.'

Taryn remembered that she'd shared the signing table with a fantasy writer whose session had been scheduled opposite hers. Angela had been breezy about the clash. 'Different audiences. Don't worry yourself.'

The fantasy writer was a grandfatherly man who, when Taryn took her seat, was quick to ask her how it had gone. His first fans were there already, several with bulging book bags stuffed with thumbed and furry copies of every one of his titles from their personal libraries, or their secondhand bookshops. The one at the head of the line swayed from foot to foot like an eager owl moving to check focal distances on prey before it swooped. Taryn took in this agitation and kept what she wanted to say short and waited for her own line to form. It did. And when it petered out after a respectable thirty-five minutes, there was still a contour-snaking Great Wall of fans waiting for her tablemate.

It was then that the gentlemen appeared. There was really no other way to describe them. They wore beautifully cut suits. Their hands were manicured. She noticed the bright half-moons on the fingernails of the hand holding a copy of her book. They each had their own copy. They stood side by side and asked her a series of questions about the book, and then one of them gave her his card.

Taryn pointed at the bedside cabinet and asked Price if he'd please hand her the purse there.

He opened the drawer and regarded her pale green beaded purse with consternation.

'I was at a wedding,' Taryn explained. She found her wallet. The business card was still there. Taryn was always tardy about transferring things from her wallet.

Taryn remembered the men's dark faces. Their groomed beards. Their smooth, cultivated voices and flattering eagerness. She couldn't remember what they'd talked about. Probably the usual questions about deliberate book burnings. The Nazis. School boards in the Midwest banning and occasionally destroying gay and lesbian books. Or questions about Sappho and other famous manuscript losses and survivals.

Taryn got out her phone, opened Google, and typed in the name from the business card. Dr Abdul Alhazred. It seemed familiar. It had associations for her—something sickly, something pleasurable, something from the past she'd shared with Beatrice.

A Wikipedia entry topped the search results: 'Abdul Alhazred is a character created by American horror writer H. P. Lovecraft. He is the so-called mad Arab credited with authoring the fictional book the *Necronomicon*.'

Forbidden books were another thing Taryn's audiences asked about. Forbidden books, secret books, cursed books. Like *The Lesser Key of Solomon*—lost in 1608 and found again in two pieces, one in the British Library and the other in the Bodleian, back in the early twentieth century, about the time that Lovecraft came up with his terrible *Necronomicon*. Which probably meant that he had read about *The Lesser Key* in the newspapers of the day, and that gave him the idea.

Taryn told Price that one of the men had given her a business card in the name of a fictional character.

Price plucked the card from her fingers and studied it. 'We have their names from their credit cards. Faheem Khalef and Riad Tahan. We have no idea about their passports because there's no record of them entering any port in Europe.'

'But you know they left the UK?'

'After a fashion.'

'What does that mean?'

'At this point I'd rather not pollute your recollection with narrative. Let's just see what your memory turns up.'

'I'm having difficulties with my memory. Have you spoken to my doctors?'

Price waved the business card. 'Might I have this?'

'Of course. I'm not going to contact him. "Abdul Alhazred" is a character invented by H. P. Lovecraft. He's the author of a cursed book.'

Price looked displeased. His lips pursed. He produced his phone and showed Taryn a couple of photos. The enhanced beauty of the men's flattened-out faces and the soft-focus background told Taryn the photos were taken with a long lens.

'Yes. That's them,' she said. Then, 'You're MI5.'

'I'm a public servant.'

'Aren't you supposed to tell me if you're MI5?'

'I imagined it would declare itself.'

Taryn thought that MI5 would almost certainly be able to monitor her phone calls without the permission of a judge. And MI5 were helping Hemms and Berger. She also wondered how much information Price might give her in order to discover what she knew. She asked about the name of the company on the business card. 'Are Khalef and Tahan from Dynamic Systems? Does the company exist?'

'Yes. Dynamic Systems is a tech start-up specialising in the design of cluster computers. For the past months they've been buying PCs in the thousands and shipping them to Skardu, where they're building a server farm. They are also recruiting coders.'

'So this is cyberterrorism?' Taryn said.

'What do you know about cyberterrorism?'

'Only what I get from the *Guardian*. What did the tech company they visited here have to say?'

'They claim there was no visit—and indeed Khalef and Tahan didn't go through the gates and report at reception or show up on any of the internal security cameras.'

'You mean they showed up on the *external* security cameras?'

Price's smile might have been described as functionally warm.

'Is the British tech company another server farm?' Taryn asked.

'They make RPGs.'

'Rocket-propelled grenades?' Taryn was quite confused by then.

'Role-playing games. *The Blue Empire* is one. I'm told it's a little like *Dark Souls*. Which sheds no light, I might say.'

'All I remember about Khalef and Tahan was that I signed their copies of my book,' said Taryn. 'And answered questions that they were too shy or diffident to ask during my session's question time. I can't recall what those questions were—which almost certainly means it was stuff I always get asked. Though "always" is a bit pretentious since I'm new to this business.'

'What are the usual questions?'

'About deliberate book burnings. The Nazis and so forth.'

'Why would Khalef or Tahan use an alias?'

'What we'd call a pseudonym in my business. The *Necronomicon* is a fictional forbidden book, like M. R. James's "Tractate Middoth" or Robert Chambers's *The King in Yellow*. Someone handing me a card with "Abdul Alhazred" on it would mean to say: "I am the master of forbidden knowledge."'

All this was strangely like something in one of Beatrice's favourite books. In fact, Beatrice's love of those books had begun not with *The Da Vinci Code* or *The Shadow of the Wind* but with the book-haunted stories of old horror writers—James, Chambers, Lovecraft, Arthur Machen, and Algernon Blackwood.

Price stood, his face turned partly away, his eyes hooded, nodding slightly, more thoughtful than assenting. He kept turning and turning the yellow envelope he held.

Taryn said, 'I could make a case for a bookish person from a video games production company wanting to speak to me. But not cyber-terrorists.'

Price returned his mild and superficial gaze to her face. 'Who is it that calls you every day, in the morning around seven, and in the evening around ten? From public phones, moving closer to London each day.'

'How close now?' Taryn couldn't help herself.

'Answer and ye shall receive.'

'I'm not sure who it is.'

'So you're telling me you'll be faced with a complete stranger when this caller finally reaches your door?'

'It's a private matter,' said Taryn. MI5 was monitoring her calls because she had been approached by some suspicious Middle Eastern men. And MI5 were talking to Hemms and Berger. She couldn't even try to find out what the Muleskinner wanted. They wouldn't be able to have a conversation that wasn't overheard. 'A private matter that I'll deal with privately.'

'Another interesting detail,' Price said, 'is that the games company Khalef and Tahan visited has its headquarters in a country house near the Forest of Dean.'

Taryn's hair prickled.

'Princes Gate,' said Price. 'By the way, no one seems to know where the apostrophe goes. Whether it's one prince or several.'

'The locals say it's several, and that they were fairy princes.'

'How quaint,' said Price.

'My family had to give up Princes Gate in 1999. Though my grandmother stayed on in the gatehouse until 2005.'

'And in 2003, your sister died very near there. A man called Timothy Webber was tried and sent to prison. On his release in 2010, he met his death in suspicious circumstances.'

'All right—you know all about that,' Taryn said, furious. 'But it's 2017 now, and Webber has nothing to do with your bloody cyberterrorists.'

'Ms Cornick, because the men we've been watching spoke to you and visited a house your family once owned—and did nothing else of note—we are naturally very interested in whoever is putting pressure on you.'

'*You're* putting pressure on me. DI Berger and his partner are putting pressure on me.'

Price opened the yellow envelope and handed Taryn the photographs it held.

At first the shapes looked like a pile of clothes. But they were two corpses, garments tight on bloated torsos and puddled around fallen thighs and shins. One man had lost a shoe. His shin was still brown, but his foot looked like a lump of fatty wax. The other photos were close-ups of their faces.

Price said, 'A hiker discovered the bodies when he sought shelter from a rain shower in the holloway that runs through Lode Wood. You know Lode Wood?'

Taryn could almost hear her sister's recitation of the names of the woods on the map that burned. She nodded.

'Khalef and Tahan stopped at the post shop in Princes Gate Magna. They paid postage for a small package, then put their credit cards into it and dropped it in the mailbox. The proprietor watched them do it. Then he saw them walk off in the rain in their Savile Row suits, having left their rental car in a field proximate to Princes Gate. They must have hiked the nine kilometres to the holloway.'

Price stopped speaking. He just sat watching Taryn.

'What?' she said. 'I wasn't there.'

'No. You were being interviewed on BBC Radio 4 and signing books at Foyles. You seem to have a knack for alibis.'

Taryn ignored that last remark. 'Do you have any idea who killed them?'

'What appears to have happened is this: Khalef throttled Tahan, who seems to have offered no resistance. Then Khalef bashed his own brains out with a rock. He had two goes at it with several hours intervening. In the coroner's opinion, what happened was the man knocked himself senseless, woke up several hours later, and, despite all kinds of possible challenges of bodily coordination and the discouragement of pain, he finished the job. Poison would have been quicker, and pills kinder,' Price said. 'It's unlikely they were seeking to punish themselves for failing at something. That doesn't fit with what we know about these people.'

By 'these people' he meant Islamist terrorists. The deaths did seem too secretive, abject, intimate for terrorists—not that Taryn knew much more about terrorism than what films and the *Guardian* told her. She said, 'Are you sure that's what happened?'

'The coroner is sure. We are confounded,' Price said.

'And how did my silent caller coincide with Mr Khalef's and Mr Tahan's last hours?'

'So you're admitting a link?'

'I'm just working the angles, like you.'

'We can help each other,' he said.

'I want to help,' Taryn said. 'But I'm in the dark.'

Price put the photographs back in the envelope. Its yellow suddenly seemed miraculously clean. He said, 'I suppose we're just going to have to wait to see who comes knocking at your door. Good luck, Ms Cornick.'

'Give me your number.'

Price again favoured her with his mild, well-bred smile. 'DI Berger has my number. You have his.'

'I don't want to talk to DI Berger.'

'I'd put his number on speed dial if I were you,' said Price. 'He strikes me as a man who'd do his very best to get there in time.'

He left the room.

Angela insisted on accompanying Taryn into her flat, where Taryn went straight to her fridge and emptied it of perishables.

Angela sat down. 'When is your next break?'

'Tomorrow. It's why I was so keen for my discharge.' Taryn had a few days in Aix-en-Provence. A single, tax-deductible, professional commitment, then a drive to a restaurant with a view of Mont Sainte-Victoire and a long lunch in the sun.

The collections manager of the Bibliothèque Méjanes in Aix had written to Taryn after her book came out. He said that he was taken by a passage in the book concerning an eyewitness to the 1731 Cotton Library fire. It mentioned a particular scroll box. Did Ms Cornick know anything more about the box? And would Ms Cornick like to visit him at the Bibliothèque Méjanes—a model of state-of-the-art, climate-controlled manuscript storage?

The only passage in Taryn's book that fitted the librarian's description was in the endnotes. An eyewitness account of a smoke-stained collector and his servants carrying to safety the few things they could save after the conflagration in the central reading room of the library. The witness spoke of 'a gleaming black box'. Probably the silky black of charcoal.

Angela said, 'And when does your period of luxurious house-minding commence?'

Alan had offered Taryn the use of his Norfolk house. He and his Irish second wife had decided to move to County Cavan. The Norfolk house was on the market, but the market was slow.

Angela was looking a little self-conscious. She and Taryn had the house-minding down as a time when Taryn might give some thought to a next book. Angela was hoping Taryn would produce a proposal she could show to publishers.

Taryn said, 'Thank you so much for the lift. Can you do me another favour on your way out and drop this bin bag in the chute?'

Angela got up, accepted the bulging bag, and took her leave—with admonishments to Taryn that she stay in touch.

Taryn firmly closed her front door and sat down to check her messages. Two were business. People Angela hadn't managed to field. Three were moments of near silence—muffled traffic noise, a ball bouncing on pavement, and children yelling, or rain spattering on the reinforced glass of a phone booth.

Taryn upped the number of times the phone would ring before voicemail kicked in. That would give her more time to get somewhere private and talk to the Muleskinner, in a way that would warn him that someone might be listening. Would that stop him? Probably not. He'd want to talk, like their first talks, when everyone else had gone off to their bunks and she'd come back to the campfire to sit with him, discussing happiness, and loneliness, and loyalty.

Taryn packed for Provence in spring. She inscribed a copy of her book for Claude Pujol, the librarian at the Bibliothèque Méjanes. Before she put the book in her bag, she looked up the passages concerning the 1731 fire that destroyed much of the Cotton collection.

Taryn's own description used an account printed in *The Gentleman's Quarterly*, a report to Parliament on the losses sustained in the fire. That, and several private letters written at the time, and in subsequent years.

The chapter described the hurried removal first of the collection of Alexandrian manuscripts—some of which fire had stalked over several centuries. It spoke of burning presses broken open and books removed; the fire engines sent for but not coming 'so soon as could be wished'; of books thrown from the windows, books showering into the street, some shedding pages later carried away as souvenirs by the boys of the Westminster School. It described how Dr Bentley escaped the flames in nightgown and wig with the *Codex Alexandrinus* tucked under his arm. It described the immediate aftermath of the fire—streets full of charred books and loose scorched paper. The rescued manuscripts and vellum scrolls were stored in rooms at the boarding house of the nearby school. The condition of those treasures was terrible. The scrolls were shrunken and gluey—animal fat drawn out of the vellum by heat. Taryn wrote about sodden paper manuscripts, whose leaves someone was hired as soon as possible to turn over, moving back and forth through the book in front of a hearth fire. Unfortunately the people hired were unskilled and handled the damaged paper with their bare hands. Some of the books were pulled apart and hung up in bunches on lines to dry, then put back together later, pages not always in the correct order. Despite all speedy efforts at remedy, the fog of mildew settled on the paper, and the vellum dried brittle. Books with pages burnt on their edges could not be rebound, trimmed as they were by the flames. Taryn wrote about how, later, the committee charged with the recovery recommended that loose pages be collated and kept, stored in as near as possible the same order they were in before the fire. But much of this material was misplaced, tidied away by unskilled helpers who saw a flake of paper or shrivelled lump of vellum only as mess.

Taryn's book provided a list of the Cotton's great losses, with something about the provenance of each. Losses that were truly terrible: St Æthelwold's translation of *The Rule of St Benedict*; Asser's *Life of King Alfred* and his history of the Battle of Maldon; an eighth-century gospel from Northumbria—even two of the four surviving letters of patent where King John recorded the grant of Magna Carta, the text of one letter in some places a mere gleam of carbonated ink, a charred substance composed only a little differently from that of the carbonised surface it was inscribed upon. The king's great seals, though still attached to the letters, were reduced to shapeless blobs.

There was a particular note reference at the end of Taryn's passage describing the destroyed great seals. When she read its innocuous number—note 32 of 53 for that chapter—she knew at once that it was what Pujol was interested in.

Taryn turned to her book's appendix.

Note 32 quoted a letter by a master of Westminster School, who went from a description of the condition of the seal on King John's letters to that of another seal on a scroll box. The box was scorched itself, but its seal was somehow intact. The master reported marvelling over the strange appearance of fire-damaged box and untouched seal, and how one librarian told him that the box had already come through the fire in the library at Raglan Castle, set by Thomas Fairfax's parliamentary forces during the Civil War. And it was said to have come unscathed through two earlier fires: the burning of the Ravy Library in Persia, and of the Library of the Serapeum in Alexandria (that city's second great library conflagration). It was this schoolmaster who first called the box 'the Firestarter'.

There it was. Taryn had added her own gloss to note 32: 'From the Cotton, the scorched scroll box went to the British Museum, where it remained until, rather astonishingly in character, it survived a bombing raid in World War Two, though the material surrounding it was utterly incinerated. Subsequently evacuated, the box spent the remainder of the war in a dry cave system near the Welsh border, with other treasures.'

Taryn had written about the box, then somehow disregarded it and forgotten her own family's connection to it. That cave system had its entrance on Northover land, and, as a young man, her grandfather had helped the British Museum hide their treasures. Taryn knew all this.

But, as she read over her note, she could sense something in the story *eating* the story.

Or perhaps it was just the medications she was taking piling up on her.

She stowed the book in her bag and took herself off to bed.

She was on the escalator, ticket in hand, ready for the nominal checkpoint on the platform, when she saw DI Berger waiting for her. Or rather, she noticed a strikingly handsome man looking expectantly at her, had a little lift of pride and interest, and only then realised he was someone she didn't want to speak to.

Berger summarily removed her carry-on from her grip and led her back out of the stream of boarding passengers. Then he handed her bag back but stayed standing between her and the train.

He raised his voice above the booming of the concourse. 'Your silent phone calls?'

'Have been dealt with,' Taryn said. 'Sometimes you just need to talk to a person.'

'You're still getting them.'

'Please stop monitoring my phone.'

'We're not.'

'Stop talking to MI5, then.'

'Raymond Price came to see *me*. He asked about Webber, his crime and conviction, and his mysterious demise. Are you still maintaining that you don't know who your calls are from?'

Taryn decided to lie. 'I do know. It was an old boyfriend. Like I said, sometimes people just need to talk.'

'And I said the calls haven't stopped.'

They were going in circles. Taryn tried being more firm. 'I only talked to him yesterday, once the doctors cleared me. I had to have my head in the right space.'

'Does this "old boyfriend" have a name?'

'You don't need to know his name. He's not dangerous. He's said his piece now.'

'According to my information, he hasn't said anything.'

'Any business you ever had with me is all in the past,' Taryn said. She could feel herself flushing with indignation—as if she had a right to be indignant. 'As for MI5—my part in their investigation seems to hang entirely on something in my book, believe it or not. An endnote about my grandfather's involvement in a plan, during World War Two, to preserve treasures from the British Museum by storing them in King Offa's caves. My mother's family, the Northovers of Princes Gate, owned the wood where the cave entrance was. During the war various items came to the caves for safekeeping. The men Raymond Price asked about had questions relating to that.'

'Really?' Berger looked like someone who has been given ice to eat. 'Treasures from the British Museum are more present to you than Timothy Webber?'

Taryn glanced at the clock on the concourse. 'I have to go.'

Berger regarded her, his cold blue eyes not as cold as they should have been, given what he believed. 'And what about your seizures?'

'The doctors couldn't find anything wrong with me.' To have any hope of making the train, she'd have to get on the nearest carriage. 'Detective Inspector, what prompted you to turn up with all this now?'

'I read about you in the *Guardian*. It reminded me how I didn't like your answers back in 2010.'

'The woman you once looked at with a doubting gaze got your attention again by being *celebrated* for something. You thought, "That Taryn Cornick is doing well for herself."' Taryn paused, then added, 'That's the story I'm going to tell my famous father.'

Berger's face lost all expression. Then it showed a slight twitch of malice and pleasure. 'I wouldn't start broadcasting any stories with MI5 still on your case. They wouldn't like it.'

Taryn said, 'If you have any legal cause to stop me leaving the country, do so now.' She waited a moment, then grabbed her bag and stalked off.

From the Gare du Nord, Taryn caught a taxi to the Gare de Lyon and her train to Aix-en-Provence. When she was settled in the quiet carriage, surrounded by knitting women, she began to feel tender and ill. The smell of the hospital was still coming out of her pores. Her head had left a greasy mark on the train window. Her smell seemed to fill the carriage. But no one looked at her.

She took out her little makeup mirror and assessed herself in pieces. Her skin was pink on her shoulders and yellow at the top of her neck— like her grandfather's body when he was seventy-nine, old upholstery fading in places, blood and subcutaneous fat showing through. Her flesh was transparent and oleaginous. It was appalling. *She* was appalling.

It was as if she were assessing herself with someone else's hateful gaze. Perhaps Jacob Berger's.

Spring unspooled beyond the window: green poplars and black cypresses, a lime escarpment and a church with an attenuated teardrop dome.

Taryn closed her eyes on the view. She thought, *It's the box.* The scroll box stored in the dry cave system, whose entrance was on her grandfather's land. The box that, for some reason, hadn't gone back to the British Museum after the war. The box Battle had been asking about before he set fire to the library at Princes Gate.

The Firestarter. Where was it now?

Taryn's Grandma Ruth had James Northover's papers. Did any of them include a record of the disposition of the library after his death? Where all his books and manuscripts finally fetched up?

Six

The Bibliothèque Méjanes

The following morning Taryn set out from her hotel to the Bibliothèque Méjanes, near the margin of the old centre of Aix-en-Provence.

Her skull felt jarred by each step along the cobbled street, so she moved onto the flagstones that lined the shallow drain in the middle of the road. The soles of her sandals picked up a coating of silt, but the going was smoother.

The leaves on the plane trees sighed in puffs of sweet wind. She turned into the Avenue Camille Pelletan, which was sealed rather than cobbled. She stepped out bolder and stopped watching her feet.

Pujol had asked her to come at eight thirty, when he could find time for her. It was odd he spoke of 'finding time' when he was the one who had issued the invitation. Surely he wasn't on a clock—the senior librarian in charge of the Salle Peiresc, an aboveground display room that exhibited a constantly changing sample of the ancient treasures stored in the library's boasted ten kilometres of subterranean shelving. Perhaps the early start meant that, after her tour, he intended to take her across the road to the café she could see opposite the library entrance—not yet open, its chairs still stacked on its tables. Or maybe there'd be a proper morning tea, and he'd introduce her to all his colleagues. And after that she'd be free, unoccupied, under the saturated blue Provençal sky.

Taryn's phone vibrated. She took it out, swiped, and pressed it to her ear.

Silence.

'Listen,' she said. 'I know you're creeping up on me. But there are people listening in on us, and they're not the sort of people you'd want to disregard.'

Silence.

'You should just stop. Go back into the woodwork.'

She let the silence run on for another thirty seconds before ending the call.

The Bibliothèque Méjanes was a modern refit of a medieval building. What had once been an entrance with steps and tall doors was now a courtyard flanked by bicycle racks. Automatic doors opened from the courtyard into an atrium, with a cinema, public library, and the Salle Peiresc, with its ever-rotating sample of the subterranean collection. The glass doors were in two sections, interrupted by an artwork.

Three giant-sized books had been reproduced in enamelled steel. Two of them were severely upright, apparently held in place by to-scale bookends, which were in fact steel security gates, open and clipped back against the walls. One book leaned into the others, as if another volume had been removed from the shelf. The book in the middle of the three towered over the top of the building and was painted to imitate gilded leather. The other two had their famous illustrated dust jackets. In order they were *The Little Prince*, leaning; Molière's *Les Malades* in the middle; and Camus's *The Stranger*, which was nearest to Taryn.

Taryn didn't usually like giant replicas, but these were perfect, three beloved French books shelved in the building. She paused to appreciate them, the quiet street and the promising blue morning.

Before Taryn had turned into the street, the bus station had been before her. She could still hear the wheeze of air brakes and hydraulic doors. And the perky warning bell of a bicycle.

There was no one about. Only one parked car—a sizeable four-wheel-drive with tinted windows.

Taryn tapped the backs of her heels on the path to dislodge grit, and approached the building. She was only a little early. The librarian might have already been poised beyond the automatic doors, waiting to buzz her in.

He wasn't. So Taryn waited.

She took the opportunity to drum her knuckles on the dust jacket of the Camus, to test what it was made of. The steel rang. She got out her phone and stepped back out of the bay to take a photo of the sculpture. She framed her shot, horizontal, then vertical. Neither did it justice. It really needed a wide-angle lens. Perhaps she should try a pano.

That bicycle bell seemed to be going on and on.

Taryn crossed the road to try once again to get the books fully in shot, and spotted someone standing in the smaller of the two ingress points, between the wall of the building and the canted cover of *The Little Prince*. A person almost as wide as he was high. Despite the warm morning he was wearing a heavy coat and perspiring so much that his face seemed more sticky than wet with perspiration. His cheeks had the texture of boiled lollies that had been sucked, spat out, and left to liquify.

Taryn lowered her phone before Mr Sticky could decide he was being photographed, rather than just accidentally included in her shot. She made herself look away.

The chirping of the bicycle bell had changed to chiming—like tambourines, or the bell-sticks of Morris dancers.

Or like bear bells. Like the sound that had accompanied Taryn on her walks in the woods of the Rockies, all those years earlier.

She spun around, looking for the source of the sound and, at the same time, let each rotation carry her towards the doors. There was someone there now, behind the glass. A stooped figure in brown slacks and a beige jacket. Taryn put a brake on her agitation and raised a hand in greeting. Claude Pujol responded with a wave.

The tinkling was raining all around Taryn, as if she were standing in a shower of invisible coins.

The sticky person came out of the narrower entranceway. He gazed at Taryn and parted his lips. Threads of something like sugar syrup stretched and thinned before the dark cave of his mouth.

Nearby a car door slammed. Taryn heard running footsteps converging on her from two directions. Behind her, where the car was, and further along the street, where, beyond Mr Sticky a slight, dark-skinned young man was coming at a run. When Taryn looked at him, he sped up, as if aiming to take Mr Sticky in a flying tackle.

But it wasn't Mr Sticky who was tackled. Taryn was grabbed from behind. The person who seized her said her name. She flailed her arms and fought—because of the timing, the bear bells, because she was being stalked and terrorised, and this must be the Muleskinner, who wanted things from her, things she felt he might have a right to, and deserve. She yelled, 'Leave me alone!'

Taryn was clasped against her attacker, restrained, picked up, and hustled towards the automatic doors. She saw Pujol behind the glass, apparently frozen with indecision. She shouted for his help.

'Ms Cornick!' said her assailant again.

The Muleskinner would have used 'Taryn'.

Then he suddenly dropped her. She fell to her knees, jarring them painfully. He vaulted over her, landed deftly, surged forward.

Taryn saw that Mr Sticky had a long-barrelled gun concealed under his coat. He was lifting it free of the coat's skirts and bringing it to bear on the young man, who saw it but kept on at more or less the same pace, while putting up both arms and swivelling his shoulder against the coming blast. It was an insane thing to do.

Taryn's assailant—DI Berger—didn't hesitate either. Both men hit Mr Sticky simultaneously and drove him sideways and backwards towards the doors. Claude Pujol retreated. The doors began to slide shut. Mr Sticky kept his feet, as if he were made of heavier material than the two men bulldozing him.

Taryn staggered up and tried to dodge them and reach the doors and the safety of the atrium. The gun might be pointed that way, but Berger had hold of its barrel and was forcing it up, his arm trembling.

Then the gun went off. Taryn flinched down, and hot matter flew past her face. She smelled scorching hair.

There was a gouge in the cover of the Camus and, below that, three figures, still wrestling with the gun. One was the young man, blood-spattered, the only one in pale clothing—a loose and roughly woven shirt and pants, like a costume from some biblical epic.

Pujol was now signalling madly to Taryn, urging her his way. Berger still had hold of the gun and was trying to wrench it from Mr Sticky. His feet flew—shin gouge, foot stomp, a sharp precise kick to the back of the knee, then an elbow to Mr Sticky's nose.

The bridge of that nose caved in under the blow, collapsing in discernible layers, like a rice wafer biscuit, dry, without blood.

The blow finally knocked Mr Sticky off-balance. He, Berger, and the young man staggered sideways in a struggling mass and were abruptly behind Taryn. She pushed herself up onto her hands and feet, kept her head low, and scrambled towards the doors. There was a yell, and she glanced back under her arm and saw the gun barrel swing free and out, preparing for a clubbing blow. It was the young man who'd shouted. He let go of Mr Sticky and seized a handful of Berger's hair and hauled him backwards. Berger twisted to face his new attacker and simultaneously delivered a hard kick to Mr Sticky's hip. The gun barrel swept back incredibly fast and passed only an inch above Berger's right ear. The young man let go of Berger's hair. He darted towards Taryn, scooped her up, and stretched forward. He pointed his free hand at the doors— apparently making a highly choreographed appeal to Pujol.

His hand was gleaming, was gold, was claws.

Berger grabbed Taryn too. He pushed, and the young man pulled, and they all staggered at the doors, and through them.

But not into the atrium of the Bibliothèque Méjanes.

PART THREE

Light

When you are born, you walk on the ark. The ark is the earth. From there, the elephants go with the elephants, and the little gold mites with the little gold mites. It makes me long to see a different animal, from a different story. I wish Grendel would burst into the hall and eat us.

Patricia Lockwood, *Priestdaddy*

Seven

The Island of Apples

Dragged by Berger and supporting the young man, Taryn fell through the doors of the Bibliothèque Méjanes—and lost her balance when her feet passed from paving stones to grass, the kind of thick pasture that requires you to step high when you walk through it. She sprawled, and her body broke the young man's fall.

It was dark. The grass was damp, thick, scented. Taryn raised her head to see more, to sort in her mind how this outdoor room had been trundled into the atrium of the Bibliothèque Méjanes in time to catch her and close her off from danger. She was vaguely aware of Berger, somewhere off to her left, twisting this way and that, moving so rapidly that Taryn could hear the grass tearing. He was making hard exhalations, combat grunts, but was finding nothing to fight. Then he was on his feet and silent. Taryn could see his form, black against a dark blue, dusky sky. The whites of his eyes glimmered.

Taryn thought she could make out a body of water below them, a pond or lake. The stars in the zenith were reflected in the water. Taryn looked at the reflection, then up into the sky.

Constellations thundered silently down on her, and she thought of Dante. *We came forth and once more saw the stars.*

Then: *I was in Aix*, she thought. *It was morning.*

Berger stopped holding his breath and began to pant raggedly, as if he were wounded or caught in some unstoppable cascade of panic. Taryn thought she should say something to calm him. He was turning around and around again, as if seeking something to attack, some lever to move the world, the unyielding, impossible, absolute change in the world.

The horrible chiming had ceased. A soft wind brushed Taryn's ears, then dropped again.

She was alarmed and astonished—but she felt better, as if her heart had been fibrillating and had just been shocked back into its normal rhythm. She felt that she would *live*.

She dared a few steps and stumbled over her own bag. Before she even thought of her phone, Berger had his in his hand—its light shining blue into his face. Then he turned on the phone's flashlight and aimed it at the ground.

The young man was lying on his back, his face bloodless, his teeth clenched in pain, his hands pressed on the torn, bloody front of his shirt.

Berger said to Taryn, 'You hold the light while I check his wounds.'

Taryn took the phone and fumbled it—the light swung in a small arc, and she saw green grass and delicate flowers, pinched closed for the night.

'Hold it steady,' Berger said. With every word his voice sounded firmer and cooler. Just having something to do was helping him.

Taryn knelt beside the fallen man and shone her light on the blood.

The shirt was fastened with ties, not buttons. It resisted Berger's efforts to tear it. He was forced to pick at the knots with his shaking fingers.

'Iron,' said the young man. One word, uttered with what sounded like satisfaction and deep amusement.

Berger parted the shirt. The young man's chest was perforated by bloody holes and dappled with bruises. Taryn could see some shallowly embedded shot, but some of the holes were welling red.

'Have you got anything that would work as a bandage?' Berger asked.

Taryn stripped off her cardigan, then told Berger to wait a minute. She found her bag and the inscribed copy of her book that she'd brought for M. Pujol. She tore out a wad of pages. She passed them to Berger, who sat the young man up and pressed the pages against the thickest patch of holes. He got Taryn to hold the compress in place while he positioned her cardigan. He knotted its sleeves behind the young man's back and laid him carefully down again.

Berger tapped the young man's cheek to rouse him. 'Where do we go to get help? My phone has no signal.' He'd commenced speaking in a businesslike way and ended it almost choking with fear.

'My house is this side of the lake.' The young man pointed. 'See the patches of white? Those are my goats. They're beside the house.'

Berger slung the young man's left arm over his neck and helped him up. Taryn looped her bag across her body and took the other arm. She shone the flashlight at their feet.

They walked slowly downhill. The light found a way for them, and fragments of landscape: pasture, a rose bush covered in withered rose-hips and new shoots, a confined tangle of blackberries, various fruit trees. A goat bleated and leapt away. The goats weren't penned, and Taryn did take a moment to wonder how the new shoots and rosehips had been spared.

The young man's house was a hut with round walls and a domed roof. It appeared to be made of woven willow and mud daub. The door was low and had a stone sill. In the juddering light Taryn saw a round, raised fireplace with a large copper trivet over the dead coals. There was a smoke hole in the roof. Carved chests in assorted sizes were pushed up against the walls. There were two stools, one in use as a table. It had a plate and cup on it; the cup was made from horn, the plate was silver. Most of the space was occupied by a low, wide bed of heaped bracken covered with bearskins.

Berger lowered the young man onto the bed, then sat on the floor, which was laid with overlapping woven rush mats, like tatami. Berger's back was bowed, his head hanging. Taryn thought he was about to faint.

She shone the light on the bandage. The pages were rimmed by blood, but the rivulets on the young man's stomach were beginning to dry.

The young man was peering at her intently, frowning. Then, when she met his eyes, his face relaxed into an expression of expectancy.

'Who are you?' she demanded. 'Why were you following me?' She was sure she'd seen him before, but she couldn't think where.

'I was following the one who was lying in wait for you. The one who shot me.'

Berger jumped on this. 'Who was he? The man who shot us?'

'We prefer to use "one". It's more accurate. Also, it annoys them, because it's the singular, and they are legion.'

'Who is "we"?' Berger was in full, nervy interrogatory mode.

'It's not really "we" when I say it.'

'You're being rather obstructive in your answers.'

The injured man laughed.

Berger said, 'It's too dark in here for us to check your wounds.'

The man directed Taryn to one of the carved chests and a metal jar containing a black herbal paste. The metal was very heavy and bright.

Taryn thought it might be gold. A small fortune in gold. He also pointed to a copper caddy. Taryn removed its lid and found it full of greyish-white fibrous clots that clung to her fingers. It looked and felt like bundled spiderweb. Was she supposed to use spiderweb to stop the bleeding? 'Don't you have dressings?'

'I have nothing between primitive and miraculous. And the miracles are offline for now. Sorry.'

'You think apologies are going to buy you time?' Berger growled.

'Why was that man waiting for me?' Taryn said. 'Did he plan to shoot me?'

'The shot is iron. He was armed against the people of the place he'd been trespassing in. I don't think it was his intention to shoot anyone. But I startled him. And your hero here grabbed the gun.'

Taryn was puzzled. 'Trespassing where? I don't think he came out of the library.'

'Library?'

'The Bibliothèque Méjanes. That's where we all were.'

'Between *The Stranger* and *The Little Prince*,' Berger said. He sounded droll.

Taryn said, 'The librarian, M. Pujol, was standing on the other side of the doors. He was about to buzz me in.'

'The door opened,' Berger said. 'The librarian seemed to be phoning the police. That's what I saw, though I guess it's what I expected to see. When the door opened, I pushed you both through. Only suddenly it wasn't the library.' Then, 'Show him your book, Ms Cornick. It's the thing Khalef and Tahan asked about. And wasn't it your book that brought you to the Bibliothèque Méjanes?'

'Why would my book cause anyone to assault me?'

The young man said, 'Who are Khalef and Tahan?'

Taryn looked around. There was more light—a soft mushroom-coloured predawn glow coming in at the door. She found her bag and what was left of the book. She was surprised she'd had enough presence of mind to put it back. Its cover was tacky with blood. Taryn saw she had torn pages from the bibliography and index, not the main text. Her carefully cultivated stories and arguments were still intact. She said to Berger, 'And how can my book explain where we are now?'

'I'm trying to work on one thing at a time,' Berger said. 'Someone way-laid you. I'm starting by trying to determine what that person wanted.'

Berger's dedication to the process of an investigation was absurd, but it really did seem to be the only path to take—the rapidly disappearing path of some tidal causeway.

Taryn said, 'Khalef and Tahan are two men from a company called Dynamic Systems who are building a server farm in Pakistan. They came to speak to me about my book.' She duly proffered her book to the wounded stranger.

He took it in one hand. 'Thank you,' he said, grateful and reverent. He looked at its cover and registered deep, delighted surprise. 'Taryn Cornick of the Northovers,' he said.

Taryn had just noticed the teetering piles of books on and around all the hut's furniture. Hardback and paperback books, all recent editions. 'It's you,' she said in baffled wonder. 'Barefoot-with-books. Seven years ago. On the road between Princes Gate Magna and St Cynog's Cross.' Then, 'But it can't be you.'

He smiled at her. But his arm was quaking. He had to lay down her book.

'He's going into shock,' Berger said. He got up, his hair brushing the roof. He grabbed the bearskin blanket and dragged blanket and man off the bundles of sleek, fresh bracken. Berger hauled him outside, into the twilight. He got on his knees, pushed Taryn's book aside, untied the bandaging cardigan, and peeled away the gore-gummed compress of index and bibliography. 'I need water. Wet a cloth.'

Taryn ducked back into the hut and scrambled about, opening the boxes and peering in at clinking bottles, and smaller boxes, and jumbled objects made of copper and wood, gold and silver. The sight of so much gold made the hair on the back of her neck bristle, almost painfully, as if someone were plucking it. She found a stack of neatly folded shirts. She bunched one in her hands and helplessly showed it to Berger.

'It'll have to be the lake,' he said, and jerked his head at the water visible behind him.

Taryn hurried that way. The turf at the water's edge yielded, wheezing under her feet. Where the water began the shore was so thickly fenced with sedges that Taryn could only get at the lake in one place, a slim border of fawn sand. Taryn thrust the shirt under the water. The cloth silvered and bubbled but wouldn't soak through.

There was a fence of tufted trees along the brow of the hill above the far shore. Beyond the hill was only sky, the palest blue shading to soft lemon at the ridgeline. The ridge was a good way off but looked like a garden wall, abrupt, knife-edge thin, slightly crenellated. Perhaps it was the rim of an extinct volcano, and this was a crater lake.

'Taryn!' Berger shouted.

Taryn massaged the shirt, squeezing and wringing until the fabric darkened. Then she lifted it above her head and ran back to the hut. Water poured down her arms and under her clothes.

Berger took the shirt and swabbed the shot holes. Blood and water mixed and ran in rivulets over the young man's dark skin. Berger kept wiping and peering. He said he was checking for the skin discolouration that was a sign of internal bleeding. He didn't think any of the shot had gone deep; most of it was up in the guy's pectoral muscles and shoulder. 'It'll have to be removed, but . . .'

Berger paused and bent over. He subsided until his hair was dabbling in the welling blood. Taryn thought he was taking a very close look. Then she realised he'd simply folded over mid-sentence.

'Berger!' she yelled. Her shout didn't echo. It should have, given the bowl-like enclosure of the hills. She heard her own cry, its isolate perfection, as if she were in a studio lined with acoustic panels.

The wounded man put his hand in Berger's hair. It wasn't the wondering touch of someone feeling their way back to consciousness. It was a caress or a blessing. 'Is this the same man?'

'The same as what?'

His face was drained, his pupils huge, but he wasn't trembling anymore. 'The Valravn,' he said. Then looked irritated. 'The man standing with you at the edge of the wood.'

Taryn shook her head. She wanted to ask, 'What's a Valravn?' The word was vaguely familiar. And the way the stranger used it sounded informed. Flat on his back and bleeding, his whole manner was that of someone who knew many things.

But then, 'I can't make any sense of this,' he said, and pushed his fingers into Berger's hair and pulled them through, combing it. 'It's the iron. You are going to have to go get help. The nearest house is three miles downhill, along the stream.' He indicated with his chin. 'West.'

Taryn saw that it was west because that was the darkest place in a sky that was growing lighter by the minute. Birds were singing—a thick, chiming, burring, complicated music of bird calls she'd never heard before in actuality or on a soundtrack. 'Where are we?' she asked.

He let go of Berger and put his hand on hers. 'Don't you feel better?'

Taryn consulted her body. She was chilled from giving up her cardigan, from fear and confusion and cold lake water. Her hands were red from being immersed. She felt very alone. But as soon as she registered that, she realised she hadn't felt alone for weeks. She'd felt occupied, spied on, contaminated by some poisonous personality, not her own.

She began to cry. Throughout all the terrors and alarms and humiliations of those weeks she hadn't shed a single tear. These tears were like grace. Her throat was full and thick with sobbing. She gazed into the stranger's eyes and cried her own out. Because she was a rational adult, she was waiting for an explanation. But on some level that didn't matter at all—something had happened to her, and she understood that her life had been saved.

'Yes?' he said.

She nodded.

'As soon as I saw you I knew something had you. I decided to bring you here. But I was shot. You and your friend carried me through the gate. I didn't decide to admit your friend. It just happened.'

He had been momentarily unconscious. He'd been tugging at her, then he was falling. She and Berger picked him up between them and hauled him, feet dragging, towards the library atrium. Berger was a little behind her. He'd put his body between them and the man who was maybe reloading his gun. And then they found themselves on a grassy hillside.

'You had to come here,' the stranger said. 'It was an emergency.' He gazed at her, his eyes wide. He was apologising for something, but she couldn't see what.

'I'm here on purpose and Berger by accident?' Taryn said, to help him.

The rim of the sun had cleared the hidden horizon. The sky above the lake filled with light. Taryn looked up. She had never seen such a clear, lucent blue. The slopes around the hut were rich pasture, graduating to heath in softer colours: thyme yellow, sage green. There were flowers through all of it, blue, yellow, red and white, pink and purple. It looked by turns intensely cultivated and profoundly wild.

Taryn wiped her eyes with her blood-stiffened cardigan and returned her gaze to the stranger. She remembered his eyes—a clear hazel, shy, curious, very warm. She said, inanely, 'You're just a person.'

He laughed. 'Well, that's the thing. We are all just people. Even my goats and silly hens are persons.' He looked around. 'My silly hens who are hiding.'

The warm sawing noise of a clutch of broody hens was coming from a thicket of fuchsia bushes by the wall of the hut. The hut really was wattle and daub, like the replica of a traditional Irish bothy in the National Museum in Dublin.

Both the shirt Taryn had soaked and the torn one the stranger wore were handwoven and hand-stitched, a wool cloth, she thought. The hut and his clothes were weathered and thrown together, but he and the landscape seemed somehow polished to the point of perfection.

'I'm really scared,' Taryn said, whispering confidingly. 'But the dread has gone. It was like I was trapped deep inside myself and, at the same time, exiled to my very edges.'

'It doesn't usually work that way,' he said. He sounded baffled and concerned. Then, 'Hello,' to Berger, who had regained consciousness. 'I think you caught some shot too.' Again apologetic.

Berger lifted his head off the stranger's stomach and sat back on his haunches. He raised his arm. His leather jacket was perforated from his elbow to his armpit. 'I shoved the barrel down. It would have been better if I had knocked it up again, but I was levering off an elbow to his face. A shotgun ricochet only has force at close quarters. Most of the first blast came off the metal sculpture and got you only because you covered Ms Cornick. We'd be a lot worse off if it wasn't all ricochet. But, yes, I seem to have caught some.'

'Thank you,' Taryn said. 'Both of you.' Then, 'Jacob . . .' She decided that, under the circumstances, she was going to use his first name and adopt him as an ally, for the moment at least. 'I think this character was about to explain what was wrong with me.' She looked at the stranger. 'Before I go to get help, I need to know. I need to understand.'

'But I might be about to succumb to my injuries,' said the stranger.

'I don't think the buckshot hit anything vital,' Berger said. 'But if I'm wrong, perhaps, before you expire, you might explain what was the matter with her. We had her doctors investigating experimental neurotoxins. Various people were getting ghoulishly excited.'

'Who's "we"?' asked the stranger.

Berger said, 'I asked you the same question earlier and you didn't answer.'

'The police,' said Taryn. 'And MI5.'

The beautiful eyes lit up. 'Like George Smiley?'

'I think he gets everything from novels,' Taryn explained to Berger.

Berger was exasperated. 'Everyone gets everything from novels.'

'I do know that most fiction has things a little wrong,' said the stranger.

'You changed the subject,' Berger said. 'Again. And you're still bleeding.'

'It's the iron that's the problem, not the bleeding. The gun looked like an old fowling piece, so I expected lead.'

'It *was* an old fowling piece. Antique, a double-barrelled front loader.' Berger scowled. 'You know your guns.'

'Not like you do, and just the old ones. Everything else only from novels.'

'He's changed the subject again,' Taryn said. She was worried he'd pass out. Or that Berger would—though looking at him then she was sure that the detective was used to a bit of action and danger and was probably very fit. He had only fainted from the shock of finding himself somewhere very far away from Aix-en-Provence.

'Where are we?' she asked again.

'The Island of Apples. In the Land of the Pact. And before you do anything else—like collapse again, or go for help, can you take off my glove?' The young man lifted the hand that had been buried in the thick brown fur of the bearskin. Covering his fingers and thumb were gleaming, rose gold claws with finely interlocked plating. The glove left the back of his hand exposed, a bit like a driving glove. It wasn't armour, or if it was, it wouldn't have been very effective.

'See, it's just a pin and chain.' He showed them the underside of his wrist and the clasp.

Taryn picked the clasp apart and pulled off the glove. The gold was warm and heavy, and for a moment she imagined the object was radioactive because she could feel pressure emanating from it, as if it were shining through her flesh. She placed it beside him on the bearskin. Berger picked it up, weighed it, cupped the clawed fingers to close them, then shook them open again. The stranger watched this with an expression of cool assessment. 'And this is not that man? The Valravn,' he said again.

'No. That man was fair-haired and freckled—don't you remember?'

'It wasn't me who noticed him and judged him. I saw only you.'

'Because Taryn is beautiful,' Berger said.

Taryn started with surprise. That he should say it. Was he trying to draw something out of the stranger, who had after all moved himself between her and a gun? Was Berger trying to divine the stranger's motivations regarding her? But why would he start with something so unremarkable as her appearance? And how did Berger know she was beautiful? She had been oily and bloated and bruised and stinky and demented for weeks.

The stranger was blushing, so he couldn't be in any danger of bleeding out. The blush seemed to please Berger. Surely the detective wasn't performing triage by embarrassment?

'Answer Taryn's question,' Berger said. 'What was wrong with her?'

'She was possessed. Occupied by a considerable, intelligent, self-controlled demon. I've never encountered anything like it. Demons possess people to appal the faithful. They worm their way in and imprison the demoniac's soul and put on a big, flagrant, vile show to frighten loving families and ministers of religion. They are doing their duty in a war. And they're doing what they like to do. But as far as I could tell this one was being as quiet and covert and subtle as it possibly could.'

'People don't get possessed,' Berger said, indignant.

'No. Not often,' the stranger conceded mildly.

Berger made an abortive gesture of disgust—threw up his hands—which pulled his wounds. He subsided onto his back on the grass, gasping in pain.

'Some demons are bodies, and some are spirits,' the stranger said to Taryn, ignoring Berger. 'They are either. As opposed to you—who are both. Demons are a species of many different breeds. But they are the only indigenous fauna of their world, and their intelligence and characters are of a very narrow spectrum compared to the fauna of your world and mine, where there is, for example, a great difference between my intelligence and character and the intelligence and character of my hens.'

Taryn just gaped at him. He looked collected. But pale. His mouth was the soft peach shade of sard—the dark chalcedony in a cameo brooch. She could see him piecemeal, but the more she looked at him, the more he receded, dissolving mysteriously as though the sun were rising everywhere but on his face.

'I still know a little about demons,' he said, with the same mix of shamelessness and apology. Taryn could hear it now, the shade of pride and power in his contrition.

'You. Are. Both. Fucking. Baked,' Berger said from his bed of grass and pain.

Taryn looked at the notch in the far slope, where the lake water smoothed out in the tiny current of a very small outlet. 'Do I go that way?'

'Follow the stream. There is a path, and before too long you'll see my neighbour's house. Tell the people there I've been shot and that it's iron. If you mention iron, they'll bring someone who can get the shot out.'

She looked at Berger. 'Will you be all right?'

'Sure, sure.' He sounded a bit delirious.

'I'll take care of him,' the stranger reassured Taryn.

She didn't wait. She set off around the lake, stepping high through the thick pasture.

The heath hid tumbled stones, and Taryn had to go slowly to avoid turning an ankle. She didn't look up until she reached the place where the quiet lake turned into a stream, water flowing in a hushed wash across solid bedrock, then tumbling away in a white rush.

Though Taryn was now in the sun, she started to shiver again. She sagged onto her knees and dug her fingers into the loam.

The slope faced due west. A moon was at the horizon of what looked like another sky but was a far-off smoky silver sea. Above the moon the sky continued, clear, deepening to dark blue at the zenith, where the last stars showed in terrible transparency.

Below Taryn was a long fall of folded hills and valleys, each hilltop a little lower than the one before, a rolling country with the chalky line of a bare-earth path, visible here and there between copses and limestone escarpments, and not a wall, or hedge, or highway in sight. Not a church tower or town hanging under an exhalation of car exhaust.

The air was thin, cool, and sweet. A soft breeze blew up from the country. A country that was beautiful, unspoilt, and alien.

Taryn thought, *The Land of the Pact*. Then she picked herself up and followed the track down a series of long shallow steps that followed the stream, each a slab of green or grey shale. River valley rocks, not indigenous to that hillside, so transported there. What kind of world had the *time* to build a path like this in such a wild place?

After a long descent through heath and a belt of forest, Taryn came upon a house.

Beside the house was a waterwheel, whose sleek, flashing blades provided the only sign of life or activity in the dwelling. Beyond the waterwheel the stream dropped, making a dulcet music, to feed a deep green pool directly below the lowest of the house's five stepped levels. The water filled the pool then spilled in a wide, gentle rill over its lip and continued on again, white and wild beside another stepping-stone staircase.

The house was constructed of huge slabs of stone, evenly shaped but rough in texture and covered in lichen of many colours, from a soft green-grey to an orange as bright as rust. It had windows, but Taryn could see no glass in them. The pasture surrounding the house was full of flowers and browsing bees, but as she came close, she could see all the insects were passing around or over the building. Not one seemed to want or expect to be able to go in through the windows.

The nearest doorway was to the room with the waterwheel flush to its exterior wall. From within the room came a whir and clap and ratcheting, a noise a little like the combined sounds of a loom and a spinning wheel. Given everything she'd seen so far—the young man's homespun clothes, his horn cups, copper plates, gold and silver containers, his furniture, none of it mass-produced—Taryn expected to look into the room and find a weaver and a spinner. But what she saw first was a woman, wiry, with cropped grey hair and tanned, suede-soft skin.

The woman was wearing a calf-length linen dress, a leather apron, and wooden clogs. She stood holding up a sheet of paper to the light and eyeing it critically. Behind her a crankshaft came in through the wall. Attached to it was a waterwheel-powered printing press. The press was still moving, gently clapping the typeface to the paper tray, not quite touching, its movement arrested several inches from closure by some adjustment in the cogs and wheels of the machine. This movement was slow enough that two people working in coordination might have time to refresh the ink in the plate and position a sheet of paper.

The woman turned to Taryn, startled. Her eyes grew wide. Taryn realised that she had blood on her summer dress and streaking her bare legs.

'The blood isn't mine,' she said quickly. She hoped the woman spoke English. That seemed a very remote possibility, given everything.

'Whose is it?' the woman asked, in English, with what Taryn thought was an old Yankee accent—which is to say she sounded like Katharine Hepburn.

'It's the young man in the round hut, by the lake. He was shot. With an antique fowling piece loaded with iron pellets. I'm meant not to forget to say it's iron.' Taryn realised she'd passed over the matter of who had done the shooting. She wasn't ready to offer any explanations on matters she could barely comprehend herself. Her mind kept making periodic nervous darts at it. *Demons. Possession.* It was terrifying—but she felt so well now. She felt ten years younger than she had only a few hours before.

The woman let the page float to the floor. She seized Taryn's wrist, left the printing press doing its slow clap to the empty room, and hustled Taryn out the door and around the far side of the house. They climbed to the waist of the sprawling building and stepped up onto a shelving balcony.

This huge slab of stone was continuous with the floor of a very big room. It was all one; Taryn could see no joins. The room had unglazed windows on three sides and receded into a cave-like rear, in the gloom of which Taryn saw a tiled platform with copper vaults beneath it, one showing a small heap of live coals. A raised, heated floor. On the platform was one made-up bed, and stacks of flat and rolled futons and bolsters and blankets in a mixture of linen, wool, silk, and heavily furred animal skins.

A woman rose from the bed and came forward into the light. Her gait and gestures were languid.

A child sat up from a kind of nest at the foot of the bed and rubbed its knuckles into its eyes. It stayed back in the darkness, small, drooping, drugged by sleep.

The printer launched into a kind of report—facts *and* opinions, it seemed, from its length and the alteration partway through in the woman's expression. The printer was speaking a language unfamiliar to Taryn, only one word of which she recognised. *Shift.* The word occurred several times.

Shivers of heat and cold were trickling down through Taryn's frame, from the top of her skull to the soles of her feet, as if something were flowing out of her. She kept trying to take in the woman in parts, because the sum of her was too terrible. Her measured voice as she answered the printer—melodious, something quizzical in it, as if she were hearing something she hadn't heard said before, something she would have to think through before accepting. The reservation or doubt was deep in that voice, innate, as though everything might be in question. The woman was slender, and her skin was very smooth and seemed to have light added to its cells. Her hair was the colour of light caramel, and consistent in tone and texture through all its length and volume. Her eyes were round, with perfect half-round lids and high arching brows. They were dark olive and had too much confidence and ease in them, too much savvy, too little understanding and feeling.

Taryn stood stiffly in the middle of the room, like a small cat making a brave show before a much bigger one, with something like her life running out of her in wormy little shivers. She knew she was looking at a different species. At someone who only *looked* human.

The woman walked past Taryn and glanced into her eyes. The glance was amused. She called for others—for help or attendance; Taryn didn't know. Other people came into the room—but most of them weren't people.

The printer took Taryn's arm and directed her to a seat, a long bolster that, once Taryn sat, was like sinking into a thoughtful beanbag. Taryn sat knock-kneed. Her legs began to quake. She could only manage to look at the feet of the people in the room. The anklets and bejewelled toe-rings. The people were standing on one leg to pull on embroidered felt boots. Someone squatted on the floor to unwrap and check the inventory in a leather pouch filled with scissors and knives—surgical implements, none of them made of surgical steel. The scissors appeared to be silver, and the knives were stone—chert, the hard flakes of stone used by early hunters to make arrowheads. Taryn remembered reading that chert was as sharp as surgical steel if fractured skilfully. The pouch was passed to the printer, who thrust it into a sling bag. She swung the bag onto her shoulder. 'Come on,' she said to Taryn. 'There's no time to waste. And I'm afraid I can't offer you anything to eat or drink until I've talked to Shift.'

Shift was the young man's name, it seemed.

The printer had another thought, and frowned. 'You didn't drink from the stream on your way down, did you?'

'No. Drinking from wilderness streams isn't a habit I have. Because hikers are careless and giardia is everywhere.'

'I don't know what that is.'

'An amoebic infection.'

The printer shook her head. Taryn heard herself say, 'But I don't suppose you have those. No self-respecting microbe would come trying to peddle its pots and pans at the door of *this* house.'

The printer laughed. She drew Taryn to her and walked beside her out of the house.

In the end only three of the terrible people came with them. The tall woman moving at the head of the column, and two men following after. One carried a basket of provisions in stoneware bottles and bundles of white cloth. The other bore bandages and bedding—possibly—folded squares of linen and silk, mostly white, some soft green and amber.

Taryn only registered her tiredness and thirst once she reached the top of the shale steps. The sun was twenty degrees above the horizon and shining on the far slope of the hollow. It was hot. As they went around the lake the sunlight crept down towards the hut, touched its rough dun roof, and made the leaves of the orchard sparkle.

Berger came partway around the lake to meet them. Once he was close, he stalled, his face draining then filling with colour and consciousness. By the time the party reached his side he'd chosen to focus his gaze only on Taryn. She stopped beside him and let the others go on. The printer glanced at Berger and gave him a polite nod as she went by. But even she didn't do the expected thing and ask him for an update on the injured man.

'How are you holding up?' Taryn said. It seemed a ridiculously ordinary thing to ask.

Berger took her arm and encouraged her to sit for a moment. He said, 'If I had any hope of sterile instruments I'd wait my turn and ask someone to remove these few pellets.'

'Have you had anything to eat or drink?'

'Shift says I shouldn't. On pain of something. He's feigning suffering in order to have time to figure out what to tell people and what to keep to himself. I'm not taking it personally. I think possibly he is preparing for them.' He nodded in the direction of the receding party. Then, 'His name is Shift.'

'That older woman said I mustn't eat or drink until she's had a chance to consult Shift.' Taryn paused, then said, 'Who has a name like Shift?'

'Someone shifty.' Berger propped his arms on his knees, his head on his fists, and gazed out over the lake. The sun was illuminating the air above its surface. Dragonflies zipped and hovered, bright above the dark ruffled water.

'All right,' Berger said. 'What do we know about not partaking of food or drink offered by certain hosts?'

Taryn gazed at him, surprised he'd come so far.

He met her eyes and said, 'I mean—some things we've learnt might not make any kind of sense according to what we're used to seeing as sense, but they might work with the bits and pieces of knowledge we have. All the obscurities that have been driving me crazy. For instance, Shift got me to tell him everything I know about Khalef and Tahan—two polished conspirators who dispensed with themselves, with their *bodies*, like drug dealers ditching burner phones.'

Taryn thought about this.

'Which is not something people do,' Berger added.

'Their bodies weren't themselves,' Taryn said. 'The bodies were possessed too. Whoever they were.' She looked at Berger warily. 'Raymond Price is really keeping you informed, isn't he?'

Berger picked up a stone and threw it into the lake. The dragonflies jolted away as if the air in which they hung had fractured along a plane and, all of a piece, jumped neatly sideways.

There was activity beside the hut. The men had the bearskin blanket gathered like a sling. They carried Shift into the shade of a peach tree. The tall woman had tossed a filmy white silk awning up over its branches to filter and even out the light.

'I don't want to go over there,' Taryn said.

Berger was still chewing on the little he knew. 'If Khalef and Tahan were possessed, was there any sign in them of their human selves? You were possessed, and you still made your little sallies of independent thought.'

Taryn stared at him in blank tiredness.

'Big sallies, then,' he said, as if he thought he'd offended her. 'Mustang sallies.'

She laughed.

Berger went on. 'Were Khalef and Tahan possessed cyberterrorists? Or were they demons up to something that only *looks* like cyberterrorism to MI5?'

'Good luck trying to make that distinction to Price.'

Berger put his hands over his face and scrubbed vigorously. His voice was muffled. 'We have to hope Price loses interest in both of us.' He got up. 'Come on.'

Taryn was obliged to follow him. She didn't want to be alone with the landscape, looking at what was going on across the lake and trying to interpret it from a distance. But before they got within earshot of the others, she said, 'On the Welsh border, where my mother's family are from, they're called the Tylwyth Teg.' Then, in a fierce whisper, because they were too close now to the small gathering, 'I can't even *look* at her.'

The men were rolling Shift to the edge of the bearskin. They unfolded a white linen sheet under him, then eased him back onto it. The tall woman and the printer knelt on the ground to inspect his wounds. The printer wiped away the blood. It seemed that none of the holes was still bleeding. Some were scabbed over, some pouting, puffy and red.

The tall woman hadn't touched Shift. Her consultation didn't involve any physical contact.

The printer unwrapped her instruments and selected a pair of silver tweezers. She began to probe one of the more shallow wounds. The tweezers pecked and emerged with a bloody metal peppercorn. The tall woman covered her mouth, rose to her feet, and drew back. The printer dropped the pellet on the sheet. It rolled towards Shift's body, leaving a snail's trail of blood.

As soon as Taryn and Berger entered Shift's field of vision, he waved them over. 'You need to go home, Jacob,' he said. Then, to the tall woman, 'Neve, would you please take Jacob to the gate for me?'

Neve said something in her own language that caused Shift to blush and the printer to look at him sharply.

'Speak English,' said Berger. 'If we are the subject of your remark, please share it with us.'

'I said I thought Shift had got himself a breeding pair,' Neve said.

'Jacob is here by accident,' Shift said. He gritted his teeth, and air hissed through his nostrils as the printer fished and probed.

'Are they not a pair?' Neve said. 'They look like a pair.'

'DI Berger has me under investigation,' Taryn said. 'That's our only connection.'

Neve ignored Taryn completely.

'Don't you people use painkillers?' Berger was disgusted.

'Please remove him,' Shift said to Neve. 'And his pointless concern.'

'Come with me, little soldier,' Neve said to Berger.

Taryn seized Berger's hand again and stood hip to hip with him.

Shift shook his head at her. 'You have to stay. Your passenger would take at the most only days to find you again. And it wouldn't be the same as the first time it latched on. Its return would be much more brutal.'

'Passenger?' said Neve.

Shift grabbed the printer's hand. 'You've been probing in that place for ages.'

'I think you've one lodged in your rib,' she said.

'Leave it, then.'

'I can't leave it. It'll cripple you.'

'I'll have it seen to later. Elsewhere,' he said.

'Neve could take you to Quarry House,' said the printer.

'No,' said Neve.

And, 'No,' said Shift.

The printer wiped the blood away from the bruised, stretched, and ragged hole and went on to another wound. 'You have too few friends to be so choosy,' she said.

Taryn said, 'I'll just see Berger out. I won't go with him.'

Shift nodded. His eyes were glazed, and he was trembling with pain.

Neve smiled at him—or possibly with pleasure at his condition. She walked away uphill.

Taryn pulled Berger along after Neve.

'You can't stay here,' Berger whispered. 'I can't just leave you.'

'You have to. Just pick up where you left off with . . . whatever else you have on your plate.'

'I have my cold case. Timothy Webber,' Berger said pointedly. Then, a little wild, 'But that's just a fragment of a floor that has fallen away under me.'

'You'll have to pretend. It strikes me you're good at that.'

'My difficulties are nothing compared to yours. Sooner or later someone will offer you something to eat. If the stories are true, your soul becomes theirs. Or your life. Or something.'

'My life has been saved,' Taryn said. As to her soul—now that she understood she *had* a soul, she saw that she had already put it in peril. Not because she'd secured Webber's death but because she'd let someone else kill him for her. Khalef and Tahan, whomever they once had been, must have made the same kind of error. Sin must be a prerequisite for the attentions of a demon. But there were sinners everywhere and very few demoniacs, so it wasn't *just* that she had sinned. Her demon hadn't meant to 'appal the faithful'—Shift's words—it had meant to discover what she knew.

She squeezed Berger's arm and made him slow down a little more. Neve was well ahead of them, apparently not at all interested in anything they had to say to each other. When Taryn made Berger pause Neve continued at the same pace, stepping high through the pasture, her silky caramel-coloured hair rippling down her back.

Berger leaned close and whispered, 'I hope Price keeps copying me in on whatever information he can. Because Khalef and Tahan are related to this'—he gestured around them—'somehow. I don't know exactly what measures MI5 are taking, but Price mentioned they were waiting for some time on a drone. There were political considerations—Pakistan being a sovereign state whose government co-operates with ours. And Dynamic Systems being a tax-paying company with a portfolio and venture capital.'

'Price must like you,' Taryn said.

Neve had stopped. They were so engrossed in their conversation that they'd nearly walked into her. She looked surprised by this carelessness—to have been disregarded, if only for a moment.

They stared at her and fell still, like nestlings under the shadow of a bird of prey. They were at the end of the vestigial pathway they'd followed up the hill—the kind made by very little foot traffic over a very long time. A slot in the heath, of plants that didn't mind being trodden on. The path simply terminated. The heath went on beyond that termination to the rampart-like rim of encircling hills.

'This is the gate,' Neve said.

'Don't you need Shift's gold claws?' Taryn asked. She was determined to give Berger as much information as she could—even if it was only a useless torment to him afterwards. She was grateful to him just for *being there*. The information was a gift. She got the feeling information was something he valued and enjoyed.

'The Gatemaker's glove,' Neve said. 'I do have it.' She shook her sleeve, and it dropped onto her hand, then into place on her fingers, as if it knew where to go. 'Where were you when Shift took you?'

'Aix-en-Provence,' said Berger.

'The gate has swung back to where it belongs. It's always open in its usual place to anyone invited. I'll send you there. Put you through, and rescind your invitation.'

Taryn released Berger's arm, and Neve put out a hand to him.

'Don't touch me,' he said. His muscles seemed to grow dense. He bristled like an angry dog.

Neve said, 'Come on, then.' And, as he started forward, 'You'll want to hold your breath.'

Eight

Norfolk

Nearly a week later, Jacob Berger was on leave and at home nursing his arm and side when he got a call from Taryn. She told him she was safe. She thought he'd want to know.

'Where are you?'

'We're making our way to my former husband's house in Norfolk.'

We, thought Jacob, and asked, 'Where in Norfolk?'

'Goodness.' She sounded amused. 'Something you don't know.'

'I feel as if I know nothing.'

'Which is why you should step out now. Lack of result in the Webber case isn't a good enough reason for you to stay involved.'

'Is that something you think about, Taryn—what is enough? Because I think about that all the time.'

'I've had a hole in my world since I was nineteen and my sister was killed. I don't think about my life in terms of sufficiency and insufficiency.'

'I'm not going to give up any of this,' Jacob said. He wanted to say that this was the first thing that had happened in his life that felt *the right size* for him.

Taryn was quiet for an long time, then said, 'You didn't just wait for me at the station; you followed me to France.'

'I did. But my perspective has altered somewhat.'

There was another long silence, then she said, 'Alan's house is the last on Soult Head before the shore reserve.' She gave him the door code.

Jacob repeated the code back to her and promised he'd come at once.

Three hours later, past midnight, Jacob reached Alan Palfreyman's house on the Norfolk shore. He used the code and let himself in. He didn't know whether Taryn was close or still hours away. He wandered around the open-plan living area, peering at ceramic artworks and signatures on paintings. A mist rolled in off the Channel, slowly obliterating his view of the rampart of dune grasses and sand-blasted concrete. It bandaged and muffled the house until the only animated thing in his field of vision was a tiny red pulse on the sideboard under the stairs. A message alert on the landline phone. Beside the phone was a note, welcoming Taryn, giving her the password for the Wi-Fi, the PIN for the landline's voicemail, and letting her know the fridge was full. It was signed 'Alan'.

Jacob checked over his shoulder and saw nothing but milky, motionless vapour in all the room's expanses of glass. He picked up the receiver and used the PIN for the voicemail. The first message was from a realtor, who got partway through her update on a market appraisal, then said, 'You know what, Mr Palfreyman? I'll email the report.'

The second was Alan Palfreyman himself. 'Taryn. I tried your cell. I had a call from a Detective Sergeant Hemms, who is working with a Detective Inspector Berger. If you remember, Berger was with the Bristol Police CID—one of the two detectives who talked to us after Webber died. He's a DI in London now, which suggests he's a clever fellow. Hemms asked when I'd last seen you. I didn't tell her you were expected at Norfolk. I did tell her I'd sent you a congratulatory card after I finished reading your book, but hadn't seen you for months. Hemms then informed me you're missing.'

A short silence followed, then a placid question: 'Are you missing?'

Palfreyman didn't sound like a man who'd had the venom-tipped spear of worry plunged into his chest. He appeared to be prompting Taryn to pick up if she was present and auditing calls.

Jacob told himself to stop trying to work out how much Taryn's former husband still cared for her and just listen.

'Hemms said you booked for three nights at a hotel in Aix, arriving on the sixteenth of April. You had breakfast at your hotel on the seventeenth and might not have been missed until checkout on the nineteenth if the Aix police hadn't come looking for you in connection with a suicide. One Claude Pujol. But I should let Hemms tell you about that.' Another silence, then, 'Taryn?'

Eight seconds later, the message ended.

Jacob decided that Palfreyman was a cool customer but was probably still in love with his first wife.

A couple of hours after that, Jacob felt himself watched. He'd had his back to the big tilt windows that looked out over the shore. He turned and saw Taryn Cornick beyond the glass, wet to the bone, her red hair blackened by rain.

Jacob altered the clever window's axis of tilt and let her in. She set her fingers against his left cheek, rose on her toes, and kissed his right ear. Her mouth was cold too.

A *social kisser*, thought Jacob, who was not of that class.

Taryn wasn't alone. The unprepossessing, slight young man followed her in, and further in, and stood dripping on Alan Palfreyman's yakskin rug.

Taryn and Shift were wearing the same clothes, more or less. Oversized jerseys of rain-silvered wool a few shades darker than olive drab, pale suede trousers, and sodden embroidered wool felt boots. They both made squelching noises when they moved.

Shift seemed bewitched by Palfreyman's Stanley Spencer. It wasn't one of the grand allegorical paintings with British villagers as biblical personages. It was just a view out someone's window of cabbages and cauliflowers in allotments beside a railway line.

The air beyond the living room windows was fuming white. The sea was invisible. The fog would have helped Taryn and Shift with the security cameras. Jacob was concerned about the cameras. Palfreyman's home security system was no doubt monitored. Now that Taryn was here, she should call her ex-husband's security contractors and tell them that everything was fine.

He took out his phone and passed it to her.

Taryn frowned. 'Who am I calling?'

Jacob explained the benefit of reassuring certain people.

'Oh yes, Stuart,' said Taryn. 'Better to use the house phone.' She went to the machine, and Jacob watched her narrowly as she checked the messages. Partway through Palfreyman's she turned fully away from Jacob and leaned over the sideboard, the crown of her head pressed to the wall.

Jacob joined her and put his hand on her shoulder. She didn't react, other than to pause the message. Under Jacob's hand her wet jersey sizzled. 'You'll be wanting to get out of those clothes,' he said.

There was a splat as Shift stripped off his jersey and dropped it on the marble floor. He wasn't wearing anything under it. He gleamed like a young seal, sleek but for the stippling of bruises and scabbed wounds from the centre of his chest up to his right shoulder. He was lean and muscled but had an unfashionable farmer's tan, his dark skin darker on his face, neck, and forearms. The rose gold plate–mail claws of the Gatemaker's glove gleamed against his bruise-mottled chest. He was wearing them around his neck, strung on a leather thong. He stood on the backs of his boots and pulled his feet free with sucking noises, kicking one towards the hearth and the other under a sofa.

'Shift, you are not planning to take all your clothes off, are you?' Taryn said.

'I am.' Shift tilted his pelvis to wrestle with the soaked leather ties at the top of his baggy-seated pants. 'People used to think nothing of nudity. Well—even "nudity" is a late adoption, for politeness, of a word from the French. I'd say "bare", like Shakespeare's English "poor bare forked thing". British warriors would go into battle naked, which is of course why the Romans made such short work of them.'

Jacob met Taryn's eyes. She shook her head. He said he'd find them each a robe and then try to make coffee and see about some food. Something warm and hearty.

Taryn said that, after she had called Stuart, she'd find food. She knew her way around Alan's kitchen.

Shift paused in his knot-tackling and said, 'I don't eat meat.'

'I don't suppose you do,' said Jacob.

'Or grain,' Shift said.

'Naturally,' said Jacob.

'But I do eat fish.'

'I'll go bait my hook,' said Jacob, and went to find something for them to wear, leaving Shift's dietary demands to Taryn.

In the kitchen Taryn discovered a top-of-the-line Nespresso machine. She fired it up and located its bullets. She set cups on a tray, foraged for crackers, and cut a wedge off the big wheel of Brie in the refrigerator dedicated solely to cheeses. It was an updated model of the one they'd had when she lived here. Taryn wondered how much the kitchen's changes owed to Alan's second wife. The bench tops had been refitted in white granite. The floor was freshly resurfaced and looked like a Bakelite dance floor in a Fred Astaire and Ginger Rogers film: slick, but not quite smooth, so that Taryn's reflected form had the appearance of a shrouded body suspended upside down in light-splashed darkness.

Alan's Norfolk house had predated Taryn. She had brought nothing to it but clothes and toiletries, books and papers, and had taken everything away with her when she left, as if she had been Alan's tenant. It wasn't as if he hadn't asked her about additions and refurbishment. He had, but she would only say, 'The place is in such good nick, Alan. Why change it?' To which he'd reply fondly that she didn't understand the necessity of display. But he left things as they were, for her.

The Nespresso machine concluded its throat clearing. Taryn put everything on a tray and carried it back to the others. Jacob had found a robe for her, and she put it on over her damp clothes.

Shift ate the cheese and walnuts but gazed with distaste at the oat crackers and with perplexity at the coffee, which he left half finished. Then he went to sleep on the sofa farthest from the window and seemed to shrink, like a young animal in a nest of grass.

Taryn sat rubbing her own feet and trying to collect her thoughts. 'The next thing I should do is call Alan and persuade him to have Stuart find a doctor who can remove the remaining iron shot from him.' She waved a hand in the direction of the recumbent form on the far side of the cavernous room. 'But I do have work I need to get on with—for panels at writers' festivals—even while having to help with his stuff.' She heaved a sigh. 'Whatever his stuff is, and I'm not even sure he knows.'

'What is it with him? Vitamin B-twelve deficiency?'

'Come on, Jacob. Try "not human".'

He pulled a face, fastidious, as if reacting to a bad smell.

'Please don't disappoint me now. You're the only person who passed through that gate with me.' She needed him to talk to her about it. The dislocations—Aix, the roaring stars, dawn in a different world, people who moved with gentle deliberation and made her feel heavy, and clumsy, and provisional. And Shift, who wasn't as alarming as Neve and the others, wasn't whatever they were, but whom she somehow kept losing sight of, even when he was standing right beside her. 'We just caught a train and a bus and walked along a dyke across the fens all the way to the sea,' she told Jacob, to prompt him.

'You've come from the Wye Valley,' Jacob said.

'Yes.'

'When I went through that gate I came out under a body of water in the dark of night,' Jacob said. 'I surfaced and swam to shore, only to discover I was on a small island. An island with a folly—a mini marble pagan temple—in the middle of an ornamental lake. I got back in the water and swam in the direction of a lighted building I could see. I didn't know what I'd find there, so I decided to avoid it. I hiked across fields and into a forest. Eventually I hit a nettle-covered stone wall and a country lane.' He looked at Taryn. 'You know where that lane took me, don't you?'

'Either Alnwinton or Princes Gate Magna, depending on which way you turned where it met the road.'

Jacob continued. 'I walked right through Alnwinton and hitched a ride from Ross-on-Wye all the way to London. There I took myself to a Boots, got disinfectant, dressings, tweezers, and a good magnifying mirror. I went home, removed the buckshot myself, drank quite a bit of whisky, called in sick, and crashed.'

Taryn was wondering whether her grandfather had had any knowledge of the portal to fairyland beneath the lake at Princes Gate. She suspected he did. She should probably tell Jacob what she knew about those things—the Firestarter and fairy hounds. She wasn't ready to talk about Webber and the Muleskinner, but she should perhaps do that to explain her susceptibility to possession and how she knew that the Pakistani gentlemen, like her, had somehow fatally weakened their spiritual immune systems. Khalef and Tahan were dead now. For them, there was no avenue for atonement. But perhaps it was different for her. Perhaps she would be able to figure out what she could do for the Muleskinner. It might be possible to assist or appease him. Handing him over to the police would only be another injury.

God. She had been so careless.

She said, 'Even if I'd broken a leg, I'd probably still think I should make my scheduled appearances at those festivals in New Zealand and Australia.'

'Demonic possession is only as bad as a broken leg?'

'I'd like to continue with my bloody hard-won career.'

Jacob pointed at Shift. 'And him?'

'We have to get the iron out of his system before he can do anything effective. Whatever he means by "effective".'

'And my cold case?'

Taryn sat for a moment, feeling sad and inward, then glanced, as if for reassurance, at her strange protector.

Shift was awake and looking at her.

She asked him how he felt.

'Severely weakened.'

'You look in the pink to me,' Jacob said.

Taryn said, 'I'll arrange for a doctor to come and get the rest of the iron out.' Then she faced Jacob. 'Can your investigation wait for a time?'

'It can, if you're sure Hemms and I are the only ones interested in Webber's demise.'

Taryn didn't respond to that. She returned to the landline. There was no need for her to listen to the rest of Alan's message. Of course Jacob had listened to it, had thought nothing of her privacy or Alan's. She called her ex's personal number.

Shift stirred, stretched, and got up. He smiled at Jacob, made a big falsely prudish show of fastening his robe more firmly, and came over to Taryn.

She held up a finger. Alan had answered.

It was a matter of some twenty minutes to reassure Alan and inveigle him into finding a doctor and sending said doctor their way. Alan wanted to know more than she was prepared to tell him, but once she gave in to his reasonable request that she explain the nature of the medical problem, his can-do self took over. They'd need a surgeon. Maybe even a portable X-ray machine. Yes, that was all doable, he said, clearly enjoying his rich man's ability to ignore norms and bend the law.

'Thank you,' Taryn said, then, feeling she should reward him a little for his willingness to help, she asked what DS Hemms had said about Claude Pujol.

'Apparently, in the weeks prior to your visit, Pujol wasn't himself. He kept wandering off and had a minor car accident when he fell asleep at the wheel. He took some sick days but insisted on keeping your appointment.'

Taryn turned her face up to Shift's. He might have little idea what she and Alan were discussing, but he responded to her mute appeal. 'Once the iron is out I can ask questions in the right places.'

Taryn returned her attention to Alan. She asked him to get word to her father that she was okay. 'Tell him I'll meet him for lunch sometime soon and have a proper catch-up.'

'Of course,' Alan said, unconvinced but compliant. 'And if there's anything else you need.'

'Thank you for the place to stay. It's a lifesaver.'

She put down the phone. Jacob Berger was beside her, having replaced Shift. They were both horribly stealthy and inclined to stand too close. Jacob's eyes were bright, and tired, and searching.

Taryn raised her shoulder, slipped past him, and hurried upstairs. She got herself dressed in Alan's T-shirt, boxers, and thick cotton socks. She found Shift some of Alan's sweats. They fit perfectly. Alan was lean, mid-height, and Shift turned out to be less insubstantial than her estimate. His air of wispiness was personality-based.

Once he was dressed, Shift folded gracefully onto the yak-skin rug as if settling in for a yoga class.

'How is the buckshot?' Jacob asked.

'Ninety percent gone,' Shift said.

'And what does that mean?'

Shift's wispiness momentarily dissolved. He looked pleased and present. 'You've worked out that means something?'

'You're allergic to iron.'

'I am.'

'Because—' Jacob clenched his jaw, held his breath, and flushed.

'Never mind about that,' Taryn said. 'Where does Hemms think you are, Jacob? And what did she make of what happened in Aix?'

'But, Taryn, what Jacob has worked out isn't what you think. He's shrewder than that,' Shift said.

'You're trying to hoodwink someone,' Berger said to Shift.

'Are you sure he's not your Valravn, Taryn?' Shift said.

'That I looked up,' Jacob said. 'It's from Danish mythology. A Valravn is a bewitched man transformed into a hero by a sacrifice.'

'Traditionally of a child's heart,' Shift said. He was watching Taryn with keen attention.

Her ears started ringing. 'A child's heart?' she repeated. Then, 'A child's life?' She put her hands over her face. That was what had happened. Webber had died, and what would have been her and Alan's child never reached her womb, but grew in her fallopian tube until the tube ruptured. A tiny curled creature, its heart only a shadow. And the knight, the 'bewitched man', was the Muleskinner.

'Look,' Jacob said, 'Raymond Price of MI5 is chasing cyberterrorists—but that's not what this is.'

Taryn uncovered her face. 'We don't know what it is.' She glanced at Shift, moved closer to Jacob, and lowered her voice. 'He says he'll keep me safe. That the Land of the Pact is safe for me.'

Shift made a little avian clicking noise but didn't interrupt her.

She continued. 'I can't imagine why he's so stymied by the demon chasing me and the ones who were possessing Claude Pujol, Khalef, and Tahan. He says he hasn't any more idea what's going on than I have.'

Jacob said, 'And has he fully outlined what kind of safety his land offers? Its freedoms and its rules?'

Shift said softly, 'No one ever sees me straight.' It didn't sound like a complaint.

Jacob rolled his shoulders to loosen them and announced that he had better call Hemms again before she sounded any alarms. 'And it's highly likely Raymond Price knows about your request for a surgeon.'

'MI5 are bugging Alan?'

'Price may be watching me in the hopes of locating you. So I wouldn't be surprised. I spoke to him briefly yesterday and got the feeling the scope of his investigation has changed. Perhaps there was something on the drone footage that alarmed them.'

'Drone footage?' Shift said.

They both ignored him.

'But how can anyone see my dropping off the map as criminal?' Taryn said. 'It's just a *mystery*, Jacob.'

'A mystery with corpses and trespasses is a crime, Taryn.'

Nine

Night in a Tree

Jacob took his phone out the landward side of the building. It was around five, and the sky beyond the angles of Palfreyman's showy house was a soft yellow. There was dew on the lawn. Jacob halted at a pale patch of something on the grass and stooped to examine the evidence—fur, each strand flecked at its end and blue-grey at its roots. A halo of fur where an owl had stood on one foot, using the claws of the other, and its beak, to pluck the corpse of its prey—probably a squirrel. The centre of the halo was a coin-sized patch of clean grass. There was no blood, no skin, no bones, only fur. The squirrel had been plucked, then carried off or swallowed whole.

This discovery, and the black wall of pine trees on the boundary, the phone in his hands, and the absence of a viable script for a situation update, all filled Jacob with a vast sense of loneliness.

Jacob respected his colleague Hemms, but any warm feelings he had were for his principles, loyalties, and beliefs. Those beliefs, though, had become a problem. Only the week before he had known what to do with Taryn Cornick. He'd put pressure on her till she cracked. He was sure of her guilt and had been just as certain that she deserved no quarter. She had used her husband's money to buy a death. She had walked away from it and flourished. She'd threatened Jacob with her famous father. She was one of those people who get bad service in a restaurant and try to scare the staff with their thousands of Twitter followers. She was 'Taryn Cornick of the Northovers', whose name seemed to have currency in more than one world.

Jacob was tired and a little nostalgic for the surety of his own wounded pride. But wasn't what was happening to him now the kind of change he'd been waiting for his whole life?

As a child the only way Jacob Berger had of recognising anything as exceptional was by its effect on his parents. There were only ever faint clues. His family was as dedicated to switching off any 'upsetting news' as they were to keeping the property tidy. They wouldn't show concern at national or international events, only getting worked up when their local council made a section of the high street one-way or brought in 'those clattering bins' for kerbside recycling. All causes of excitement became alien to young Jacob. Either they were none of his business, or they were silly.

When he was twelve, a visiting aunt complained of Jacob that he had the smug air of having seen everything before. Jacob's problem was that he was unimpressed by what he could see—his provincial suburban existence, where unusual movements always counted as 'going too far', so that the neighbour who lost his licence after a drink-driving conviction was treated perfectly civilly, whereas the one whose unknown griefs drove him to get up in church and shout that God must be mad was shunned. Not coldly shunned, only helplessly. The drunk driver's failings were not an embarrassment; the other man's expression of torment was.

Teenage Jacob was bored, but he was not above it all.

He was never sufficiently at ease or firm on his emotional feet for that.

He did leave as soon as he was able. And at university he found things to admire, like other people's enthusiasms, especially in the fun first year, when none of them minded their debts and responsible adulthood seemed a long way off. By degrees Jacob arrived, an adult, in an already decided world, another occupier among many occupiers and few owners. A world where changes of government that caused various of his university friends to tear their hair out seemed to Jacob not much more than the seasonal differences in the taste of milk depending on the richness of pasture. Matters of governance and regulation were organised reasonably well, as far as he could see. And they might be much worse. Jacob was always able to imagine worse. His gifts were as limited as almost everyone else's. His strongest distinguishing trait was his lifelong restless disdain. He didn't have a calling, only a skill set. He was clever, and cool-headed, and prepared to do tough things so long as someone he trusted offered him a good enough reason.

Jacob's class and temperament pointed him to the police force. To the watchdogs, who were also hunting dogs and had more in common with the wolves they prevented than the flock they protected. It suited him to be in a line of work where he could reflexively relegate a vast majority of people to the status of dim innocents who needed looking after. He enjoyed the *game* of being a detective, the twists and turns of this target, that plot. The things that took a toll on others—like constantly seeing the worst of people, or encounter after encounter where the other person was badly frightened—left his temperature unchanged.

But lately Jacob had undergone a troubling alteration in attitude. Instead of enjoying the smug sense that he knew more than the civilians, Jacob found himself simply wanting the world to change. And then it did. He recalled how, a year earlier, the very erudite lawyer he regularly had a drink with had explained to him why the coming referendum wasn't going to devolve into the usual political point-scoring but instead produce something extraordinary. 'And it's not just Murdoch and immigrants and implied promises about what might be done to save the NHS by the very people dismantling it. It's not just memories of busy shipyards and Grandad's self-respect. No, it's an almost mythical yearning, as though, if only we can create the right conditions, a stranger might come out of the mist, thrust a sword into a stone, and say, "Whosoever draws forth this blade . . ."'

And now here he was, having returned from another world, with a much better understanding of the depth of his ignorance concerning what might be yearned for, and *not* be mythical.

Hemms picked up on the tenth ring. When he said hello, she said, 'Is that you, Jacob? This isn't your number.'

'It's a prepaid. My phone took a swim and is in a bag of rice. Rosemary—I've found Taryn Cornick.'

'You didn't think to tell me you were looking?'

'I'm telling you now. I'm at the Palfreyman house in Norfolk.'

'Okay. Since we're coming clean, I know about Palfreyman's request for a doctor. Is Ms Cornick ill?'

'God, that was quick,' Jacob said. MI5 was keeping Hemms not just up to date, but up to the minute.

'What is it with you and Taryn Cornick?' Hemms said.

Jacob ignored her question. The scope of Hemms's imaginings was useful to him. Let her get the wrong idea. He said, 'Ms Cornick's former husband is a man who can summon doctors to make house calls for what's going to turn out to be nothing more than a UTI.'

'Symptoms?'

'I said a UTI, didn't I? Those symptoms.'

'Jacob, you're not being coy about women's stuff, are you?'

Jacob grunted.

'Raymond Price tells me he encouraged you to follow Ms Cornick to France.'

Jacob had called Price from the platform of London St Pancras to report—needlessly—on Taryn Cornick's movements. Price said, 'Your DS tells me you've taken some leave. That makes you free to follow Ms Cornick, should you wish to.'

Jacob said yes, he had taken leave, but not of his senses.

'Please yourself,' Price said.

Jacob usually heard 'Please yourself' as 'Piss off'. But Price was asking him to indulge his instincts. It felt like an invitation to play. So Jacob did. He ended his call and stepped from platform to train—in good time, though three minutes after his punctilious prey. His badge got him over any difficulties he might have had boarding without a ticket. He'd never been to Provence. At the worst, he thought, he'd just be kicking around some pretty place and have to buy a few things he already owned, like shirts and jeans and swimming trunks.

'So it's true?' Hemms said.

'I followed Price's suggestion because he's been generous with information.'

'I don't like him, Jacob. I feel as if he's trying to cut you out from the herd.'

'Me especially?'

Hemms changed the subject. 'Did Palfreyman tell his ex-wife about Claude Pujol's suicide?'

'Yes, and she was naturally upset by the news.'

'And what does she have to say about her disappearance?'

'Nothing yet.'

'Price says his people thought her stalker followed her to France and got her. But then she was called at the usual evening time, yesterday, from a phone in the Red Lion in Chisenbury. We have a description from the proprietor. A male, fortyish, freckled complexion. He bought a beer. Paid cash. I'd very much like to run that by Taryn Cornick. *Myself.*'

'Where are you now, Rosemary?' Jacob said.

'At my desk.'

He didn't believe her. 'Should I not mention it to her, then? Your Chisenbury witness?'

'Suit yourself, Jacob. I know you will.'

Jacob wrapped up the call, stepped out of the halo of squirrel fur, and went back indoors.

Taryn was standing by the living room windows in the lemony dawn light, as motionless as a stone. The main door was open. The scoured concrete ramp that ran from the terrace to the beach was wet, its end invisible in the mist. Shift was out on the ramp, standing, his head bent. At his feet was a bird, huge, black, its head in a silver cowl of condensed water vapour. Shift gave a big demonstrative shiver and took several steps back towards the door. He came through it and turned to them. He said, 'Taryn, can the raven come in?'

Berger said he couldn't see why the raven would *want* to come in. Then they both just stared at Shift.

The raven struck the glass with its beak. A single, gentle tap.

Jacob said, 'I suppose it talks.'

'Yes,' Shift said. 'But only ever to the purpose.'

'Do you know what it wants?' Taryn said.

The bird was eyeing them all, turning its head one way, then the other.

'No, I don't.'

'Taryn?' Jacob said.

'All right. All right.' Taryn was trembling so badly she had to sit down.

Shift opened the door, and the raven hopped and ambled into the house. It flew up to perch on the back of the white leather sofa and shook its head, shedding drops of water, then settled the wet points of its feathers and looked around.

'I think I've seen you before,' Taryn said to the raven.

'That was my sister,' said the raven. Its voice was deep, but without resonance. Dry. The last word of the sentence was slightly curtailed. Its tone was uninflected but not robotic.

Shift said, 'Everyone supposes they're brothers, but any wise male god will have female advisors.' Then, to the raven, 'Have you been following Taryn since we first saw her?'

'*What?*' said Taryn.

'On and off,' said the raven.

Shift turned to the others. He said, with reverence, 'This is Munin.'

'Naturally,' said Jacob. He got out his phone, pressed voice record, and slid it across the coffee table nearer the bird.

Munin swooped on the phone and delivered a volley of sharp pecks with her big strong beak. Its screen shattered. She continued until its light was extinguished.

Jacob said, 'Look. I'm fighting for my dignity here.'

'You don't know what your dignity is,' the raven said.

'I know it's doing its job and keeping me from running screaming from the room.'

'When the godly wish to speak to human beings, we can't have them running away from us.'

Jacob was incensed. 'So you're controlling my response?'

'Your own instincts are. The same instincts that guide you to fight or flee a lion make you stand still and listen to a god.'

'You mean, now that the situation has arisen, I'm behaving in line with atavistic conditioning concerning gods?'

'Yes.'

'Munin,' Shift said, 'stop setting Jacob straight and tell me why you're here.'

'You, and Taryn Cornick of the Northovers, emerged from your gate and walked to Alnwinton. From there you rode in a car to Monmouth, where you caught a train and then a bus northwest. You got off the bus at Morston. From there you made your way to the coast along a dyke beside the fens.'

Jacob was impressed. The raven seemed to have followed Taryn's movements more comprehensively than MI5 were able to.

'Five days before that you turned your gate almost as far southeast as it goes. Do you know that every time you use your glove to move a gate to any extremity it wakes up more?'

Shift heaved a sigh and ran his hands through his hair, which was tangled and made tearing sounds. 'Fine. Since you're following me, I'll satisfy your curiosity. Demons are entering and crossing the Sidh. They go armed with shotguns loaded with iron.'

It seemed he'd decided to explain himself. Or perhaps with Munin it was impossible to be slippery and sidelong.

'As far as I can tell, they are only passing through the Sidh on their way here. Which is very odd. Up until now they've been content to come here only in spirit, to do the usual things: possess people, rap on tables, cover things in slime and shame. Now suddenly they're trespassing in their bodily forms. I've tried to corner one and ask it questions, like, "What the *hell* is Hell doing?" Bodies I can corner. I followed one to a library in Aix-en-Provence, where it was lying in wait for Taryn. Which didn't make sense because she already had a demon passenger. And so did the librarian she was on her way to meet.'

The raven set up a storm of flapping without moving from the spot. Jacob's ruined phone skidded off the table and an Arts and Crafts bowl followed, but Jacob snatched it out of the air before it hit the floor. Munin folded her wings, arched her neck, and, ruff raised, made a series of loud noises like a cat trying to cough up a furball. She shook her feathers flat and peered at Shift with one eye, then the other. 'What do you suppose Hell is doing?'

Shift said nothing.

'Help us out here,' Jacob said.

'Jacob's interest is earnest. He is a defender of the realm,' Shift explained to the raven.

'You're trying to change the subject by explaining everyone else's relation to matters. You do that,' Taryn said.

Munin croaked in pleasure. 'He's always done that. An expert in telling others how they fit into the scheme of things.'

'Very well.' Shift took a deep breath. 'For a while now I've been feeling that those of my people I take time to speak to, like Neve, have begun to treat me as if I'm only living with them on sufferance. I think they're planning to compel me to give up my Taken people at Hell's next Tithe.'

'Your Taken, or possibly yourself,' said the raven.

Shift ignored this. 'I didn't Take my people for the Tithe, so why should I let them go?'

'That has always been your position,' Munin agreed.

'It must mean something that Hell is suddenly sending demons across the Sidh.'

'And building server farms in Pakistan,' Jacob said.

Shift gave Jacob an appreciative glance. 'Yes, and that. That is very mysterious.'

'Hugin will know what a server farm is,' Munin said, making a mental note.

'Hell has always abided by the treaty of the Tithe,' Shift said. 'But now they're using the gates of the Sidh to go, in their own bodies, to

Earth. They're looking for something. If I can find that something first, perhaps it might be used to renegotiate the Treaty of the Tithe. As for Taryn, I Took her on the spur of the moment because I saw she had a passenger and, since exorcisms are often deadly, and spirits can't go into the Sidh without a body of their own, I hustled Taryn through my gate, which brushed the demon off her. I'd swung my gate around to Aix. I have the glove.' He pulled the gold claws from under his sweatshirt and waved them at the raven.

'Yes, Shift,' the raven said drily. 'It's only when you're carrying it that we can find you. You are very obscure in yourself, but the glove is a beacon of magic.'

'Oh yes, I forgot,' Shift said, not particularly convincing. Jacob had the impression he was telling himself to remember to stop carrying the glove.

'Did the defender of the realm have a demon too?'

'Jacob just got tangled up with us. I was injured, and he and Taryn helped me.'

The raven's head swivelled. After a time, her left eye settled on Taryn. 'Does Taryn Cornick have any idea how she came to pick up a demon?'

Taryn gestured for Shift and Jacob to sit. And, as skins formed on the remains in their coffee cups, and the wedge of Brie collapsed and began to exhale ammonia, Taryn told them all how, when she was ten years old, her grandfather's secretary, Jason Battle, went mad and tried to burn the library at Princes Gate. How Battle *wasn't himself* and seemed to be looking to destroy a Torah—a Torah above the Torah.

And then she went on, as the light beyond the windows brightened, to recount what happened directly after that.

Ten

The Firestarter

When her grandfather came to find Taryn, she was asleep, draped over the arm of a chair in a corridor of Monmouth Hospital. He shook her awake. 'On your feet. You're too big now for me to carry.'

She got up, rubbing her eyes.

'They want to keep Beatrice for tonight. Grandma is settled next to her in a comfy chair. You can continue your sleep in the car.' He offered her a blanket.

She hesitated. Bea had been wrapped in it on the drive to Monmouth. 'Is it crusty?'

'Taryn!' he scolded.

Taryn took the blanket.

Once she was in the back seat of the Land Rover, her grandfather stayed by the open door, his hand on the back of her neck. 'I expect you're worried about Mr Battle? He's in the hospital too. He came in a couple of hours ago with a skull fracture. You remember that he fell hard when you girls pulled the rug out from under him?'

'But he got up again after that. And ran off,' Taryn added. 'Is it a bad skull fracture?'

'I think skull fractures are always bad. He's in surgery.'

'We didn't mean to hurt him.'

He patted her. 'I know.' He got in, started the engine, and raised his voice over its clamour. 'We'll not see him up at the house again till he gets the help he needs.'

Taryn relaxed. She could go to sleep in her bed, and stay asleep until she was ready to wake up and think over what had happened. 'Did you call Mummy and Daddy?'

'Yes, and your mother talked to Bea.'

'They don't need to come home.' Taryn still wanted to stay the whole holidays at Princes Gate.

Her grandfather met her eyes in his mirror, smiled, and drove out of the hospital car park.

The lower floor of Princes Gate stank of fire, the nasty sweetness of lilies and a perfume that reminded Taryn of the smell on the back of the neck of Grandma's ginger cat when he'd been sleeping in the thyme patch and come running in to escape a sudden summer shower—a scent of herbs and ozone and clean animal.

Grandad sent Taryn to bed and came in a few minutes later with a hot water bottle that he tucked under the covers next to her feet. He said, 'I'll be awake, cleaning up.' He left her door open a crack so he could hear if she called.

Grandad was awake. She was safe.

But the fire had been so fast. Flakes of paper flew up like moths, as if the collectors' boxes had broken open and their long-stilled occupants had burst forth, bent on vengeance. Flames wrapped Bea and shrivelled her clothes. The map rolled up as if trying to contain the fire, and did for a moment, its tube full of it. The burning things kept their shapes as they burned. Battle bashed his head, then got up, not a person but a puppet. He kept his shape, but something irrevocable had happened to him.

It's difficult to get warm on a chilly night when you go to bed too late. Despite her hot water bottle, Taryn couldn't sleep. If her sister had been there, she'd have crawled into bed with her. Bea would ask, 'What's wrong?' and only stay awake for half of Taryn's answer if it took any longer than twenty seconds.

Taryn was reading her book when Grandfather appeared at the door. He was wearing an anorak.

Taryn sat up. 'Is it morning?'

'It's milking time, dear.' The estate had no cows, but Grandfather by habit offered little lessons on country living to his city granddaughters. Milking time was four a.m. 'Put on your coat and boots. I need your help.'

Taryn put on her wet-weather gear over her pyjamas. She followed her grandfather downstairs, out the kitchen door, and into the yard between the scullery wall and wash house. There was a lantern on the cobbles, surrounded by a globe of vaporous yellow light.

The mist was on the move. The arms of the outbuildings provided enough of a barrier so it mostly just passed over their roofs, dragging its fleecy belly.

Beside the lamp was a package. A rectangular object wrapped in canvas and cords. The wrapping looked like an old tent. Taryn ran through her memories of the house's things, measuring those memories against the package. She considered Grandma's sewing machine and Grandfather's old walnut wood valve radio, which made the kitchen sound as mellow as the polished copper jelly moulds made it look. The radio and sewing machine were the only right-sized objects that came to mind.

'Can you take the lamp, please?' Grandfather said. He stooped, wrapped his arms around the bundle, and lifted it. It looked heavy, which didn't eliminate either radio or sewing machine.

Taryn picked up the lamp. Grandad sent her off ahead of him. 'We're going to the lake.'

A former Baron Northover had dammed a brook to make an ornamental lake. The lake had an island in its centre, only accessible by boat. That same Baron Northover built a folly on the island—a circular building of white marble columns, with red marble pediments and a green marble cupola. Though it could usually only be appreciated as a spectacle from the far shore, the folly was finished in every detail, even its interior, which had flagstone floors and benches facing one another as if prepared for a gathering of Roman senators. The lake was surrounded on every side by reeds, except for the shore facing the house, where there was a landing stage, or at least the unstable remains of one.

Taryn and her grandfather emerged from between the outbuildings, and the mist engulfed them. The lamp turned more yellow and lost brightness. Taryn looked back. She saw her own footprints dark in the gravel, as if she were treading moisture out of the air and into the ground. Grandfather was a man-shaped blur, a figure with no volume.

After a minute a garden wall loomed in front of Taryn. She followed it away from the house until she reached an archway, beyond which was the main arterial path through the formal rose beds. The mist was full of the smell of their blooms, mixed with its own cool mineral scent. In the middle of the garden the walls disappeared. The only shapes were rose bushes, their foliage a thin shadow, their blooms stubborn wine stains on linen washed many times.

Taryn stopped walking. Her grandfather caught up and halted abruptly. And what he carried made a sound: a sliding noise and a hollow *tonk* as if something large and hard were shifting in a wooden container.

Grandma's sewing machine was clipped to its case. The radio was all of a piece. It couldn't be either.

'What is in there?' Taryn asked. Her question was followed by a blankness. The mist flowed through her head, and even her own curiosity was lost to her sight.

'Come on, Taryn, you know this path well,' Grandfather scolded. He thought she'd got herself turned around. He was being very gruff with her, as if he didn't want her there with him at all, and had only asked for her because he needed someone to carry the lamp.

Taryn walked on. The far wall of the rose garden appeared, one moment a hint of shadow, the next brick and mortar, and the rough cordage of a climbing rose. Taryn kept its wall in view. The southeast tower loomed and passed. She turned downhill, where the lake was, six hundred metres away. It was invisible, its waterfowl silenced in the pall of mist.

Grandfather's anorak was silvered by droplets. He looked as if he were about to turn into glass.

They left the bulk of the house behind. It was like pushing off from land with no far shore in sight.

By the time they reached the firm mud beach and landing stage, the mist was too thick for them to see even a shading of the sedges along the shore. Though they could hear wavelets in the reeds on either side of where they stood.

Grandad set the package on the ground. He asked Taryn to pass him the lamp. 'The boat is in the reeds. Let's hope I won't have to bail.'

'We put the cover back,' Taryn said. She and Bea had been for a chilly row on the day they arrived at Princes Gate. They had restored the oars and covered the boat and slid it back into the reeds, as the rules of the house dictated.

Grandfather lifted the lantern and walked away. His shape blurred and faded. Then the great lustrous pearl of light he moved inside lost its margins. A moment later all that Taryn could see was a glowing patch on the otherwise blank whiteness, as if the source of light had melted.

Taryn looked at the package. She pushed it with her toe. It was heavy and didn't budge.

Grandfather was pulling the mooring rope free of the reeds. The boat moved, its hull rasping on the roots of the sedges.

Taryn crouched and picked at the cord binding the package. It was tight, the knots hard and comprehensive.

Taryn's hands were small. She tried slipping one under the canvas. A metal eyelet scratched her, but she ignored the pain and pushed. Her fingertips found a wood surface, its texture smooth but wavering and very dry.

The bright patch in the mist gradually turned yellow, then the brightness flowed back into a circle and became a lantern.

Taryn wrenched her hand free and scrambled to her feet. She hid her hand behind her back and rubbed her fingers together. They were covered in silky dust.

Grandfather waded through the shallows, pulling the boat after him. He passed Taryn its slimed rope. He moved the lantern to the bow, picked up the package, and placed it on the back seat. 'I need the lamp, Taryn. You should go back to the house. It's a straight line up from here.'

'But isn't the front door locked?'

Grandfather looked taken aback. He clearly didn't want to row her out to the island with him.

'Do you not want me to see where you hide it?' Taryn nodded at the package.

'I don't know how long this will take.'

'You don't have any tools with you.'

'I was out on the island before you girls arrived, grubbing blackberry. My tools are still in the folly.'

'Oh.' Taryn was crestfallen. Her grandfather was more reluctant for her to see where he hid the package than he was to leave her. She pushed a little more. 'Can I wait for you on the beach of the island? Does it matter if I see where you put it, Grandad? I won't tell. Is it your Torah?'

Grandfather didn't respond. He put his hands on either side of her face. They gazed at each other. Taryn tried again with a general knowledge question. Her grandfather always had a hard time resisting those. 'What *is* a Torah?'

'The Torah is the holy book of the Hebrew faith. I wouldn't leave my Torah on a damp lake isle.'

'But it is something from the library.'

Grandfather said, impatient, 'I give in. Scramble aboard.'

Taryn stepped over the package and stowed oars and took the lantern's place. She put it between her feet. Its hot glass funnel warmed the sides of her Wellingtons.

Grandfather wrestled the rowlocks into their holes and ran out the oars. He pushed off the lake bottom, and the boat drifted into deeper water.

Partway across, when he wasn't looking, Taryn checked her fingertips. They were black with charcoal.

Taryn was left to wait. The mist magnified all sounds, though robbing them of any discernible direction. If her grandfather had only been digging, she wouldn't have guessed where his hole was. But she could hear the grinding noise of flagstones prised up and dragged one over the other.

The mist whitened as the sun came up. It didn't melt away but warmed and thickened.

Taryn heard a splash. A bird had startled out of its nest in the sedges and was airborne long enough to make a noise as it came down. Taryn watched for ripples. The mist pulsed and pushed at her. The more she strained to see, the faster the bubbles of light in the centre of her field of vision formed, and swelled, and broke.

From behind her came a scraping bump as a flagstone dropped back into its rightful place.

'Grandad!' Taryn shouted.

'I'll be along in a minute.'

A little later the mist blushed and grew golden, and once again the light poured out of it and back into the lamp.

Taryn and her grandfather got back in the boat, and he rowed them to the landing stage. She held the lamp for him while he fastened the mooring rope around one of its rotting posts. Then he took it from her and they retraced their steps. Taryn was reassured when she saw him produce his keys to unlock the front door. No one could have gotten inside without breaking a window. And there were no windows broken. The house was damp, but no more breezy than usual.

Grandad boiled a jug for tea and a fresh hot water bottle. He gave Taryn breakfast and sent her back to bed.

She climbed the stairs, clutching the bottle under her jumper. She thought she might read for a while. There was *Jane Eyre*. Jane was being questioned by Mr Brocklehurst. Taryn thought Jane's answers were very good, and even better because Mr Brocklehurst didn't like them.

Eleven

Nil by Mouth

Jacob had a question, the first of many. 'Do you think your grandfather's package is still in the grounds of Princes Gate? That would explain Khalef and Tahan's visit.'

'Those men were possessed, but their demons couldn't have known what happened after the fire, because Battle was unconscious in Monmouth Hospital and never saw the package.'

'You're positive Battle was possessed?'

'Yes,' Taryn said. 'Now that I know what that looks like.'

'I'll check the folly,' said Shift. 'After my operation.'

Taryn said, 'It's centuries between fires, if we count only the ones we know: the Ravy Library in Persia, the Library of the Serapeum in Alexandria, Raglan Castle, Ashburnham House, the British Museum, and Grandad's library. Hell is only back on the trail now because my book connects those fires and mentions the Firestarter. I don't, however, have any idea what Hell wants with it.'

Jacob dropped his chin onto his chest and considered the folly, the island, the lake, the gate. He glanced up and asked Shift if his gate was the one the demons were using.

Munin made a small indignant whiffling noise.

Shift said, 'No, they're using Hell's Gate, and the only thing guarding it is the Treaty of the Tithe, which they're failing to respect. Hell's Gate won't take them to Earth; it'll take them only to the Sidh. They do seem to be getting about with inexplicable speed, but of course there are many of them, setting off in all directions once they enter the Sidh. There are smaller gates called cut-throughs that simply go from the Sidh to Earth. Three cut-throughs lie close to Hell's Gate. One would put the demons on Orkney, another at Blakey Topping in North Yorkshire, the last beside the Higher Drift Menhirs in Cornwall.'

Munin mused aloud. 'Jason Battle's demon was asking about the box. The Firestarter. He set fire to the library, which would suggest he wanted to destroy it.'

'I'm not sure about that,' Jacob said. 'It sounds as if that thing has been repeatedly mislaid for centuries. Isn't lost just as good as destroyed?'

Taryn said, 'This is like one of those arcane thrillers my sister loved. When those books choose the thing at the heart of their plot—the forbidden book, the hidden cabal—they often go for something grand but puffed up. In *The Da Vinci Code*, it's the holy blood of a descendant of Christ and Mary Magdalene, which, diluted for a hundred generations, would be only a homeopathic holiness.'

'The blood in *The Da Vinci Code* isn't magical though, is it?' Jacob said. 'The point is that the bloodline is a secret that can undermine the Catholic Church. A scandal about the virginity of Christ. It's not supposed to be magic; it's supposed to be a problem. The book is about an ancient conspiracy of silence. The holy blood doesn't have to do anything. It's just the spooky idea of something people have taken trouble to hide for thousands of years.'

Shift said, 'A pact with the world that isn't part of the accepted historical record, but a steady referent, like a faraway star. The boat moves, and the star stays still. Time passes, generations rise and fall, but even with the changes something stays the same—truth and the conspiracy that keeps the truth hidden.'

Taryn said, 'People love the idea that there are things that matter which last and last, and *outlast* banks, businesses, and governments. Of course we wish the world was like that.'

'The world might be like that,' Shift said.

'Don't you know?' Jacob said. 'You of all people?'

Shift blinked. 'Who am I of all people? Do you suppose I have holy blood?'

'I've given up supposing,' Jacob said. 'However, I will interrupt the book group discussion with some practicalities.' He held up a hand and counted off on his fingers. 'One. I'm pretty sure my colleague Hemms is on her way here. Hemms knows you put your former husband on to finding a surgeon, Taryn. She's also very keen to hear what you have to say to the description we now have of the man stalking you.'

Munin turned her head this way and that, eyeing Taryn.

Taryn said to Shift and the raven, 'Jacob was the detective constable who came to question me seven years ago when Timothy Webber, the man who murdered my sister, was himself murdered after his release from prison. It's an unsolved crime.'

The raven made a deep, rubbery *crech* sound. She sounded satisfied and puffed up her feathers. 'I will ask my sister to find this Hemms and hamper her progress. Hugin will locate her easily if, like Jacob, she has a blood halo.'

'Two,' said Jacob, jabbing the air, 'there's a talking bird in the house. A talkative talking bird.' He was too alarmed to ask about his blood halo but suspected it might have to do with him once having to shoot an armed criminal, who then died of his wounds.

Shift went to the sliding door and opened it for Munin. 'Go and instruct your sister.'

Munin came to life, shook herself, and hopped across the room, pausing beside Taryn to cock her head and say one word: 'Sisters.' Then she flew out the open door and into the bright east. They watched her recede. All except Shift, who stood at the door letting in the cold air, his eyes on them and a smile on his face.

Munin's black shape stopped diminishing and seemed to set against the sky, as if the world out there had become two-dimensional.

Then the raven's wings flapped again and—without having turned— she was flying back towards them.

She flew in the door and caught herself on the back of the pristine white sofa, her talons puncturing the leather. 'Done,' she croaked. 'And I had to tell her everything. So now he'll know.'

Jacob's ears were ringing; he heard 'now' but ignored the raven's 'he'. Jacob had just seen a demonstration of 'now'. The raven flew away, across the world, had a long and involved conversation with her sister, then returned, all in an instant. Which was, of course, how it must work if, according to legend, Hugin and Munin flew around Midgard every day, collecting news for Odin.

Odin. Jacob arrived by accident at the 'he' he'd been trying to avoid.

Taryn announced she was hungry and went off to the kitchen.

Jacob was exasperated. He still had questions for Taryn and limited time in which to ask them, since Hemms would expect him to leave with her when she arrived, even if the other raven delayed her.

'Let us follow Taryn to the kitchen,' Munin said. 'I wonder if she has any macadamia nuts.'

In the kitchen Munin alighted in the largest of the three sinks, where she was immediately an impediment to Taryn's food preparation.

Jacob put his first question. 'Why do you suppose the demon inside your grandfather's secretary was talking about the Torah?'

'A Torah,' she said. She waved a bunch of spring onions at Munin. 'I want to wash these.'

Munin scrabbled her way out of the stainless steel pit and clicked across the marble countertop to the giant fruit bowl. She found walnuts and proceeded to split and eviscerate them. That sound, and running water, were driving Jacob wild. He wanted to shout at everyone to stop doing things and give him a situation update like competent people who know how to behave during a crisis. 'Torah, Taryn,' he said, insistent.

'I think the demon was being metaphorical. In its excitement it was quoting for effect.' She asked Jacob if he could please make more coffee. She fished around in the drawers under the kitchen island, produced a salad spinner, placed the wet spring onions in its basket, put on the lid, and pulled the cord. The spinner whirred. Jacob clenched his teeth so hard his ears whined. Then he turned to the Nespresso machine and the antique apothecary drawers full of its bullets. There were more than a dozen available flavours.

'I'm sorry, Jacob. It's difficult to explain,' Taryn said. 'The fire is a memory of a time Bea was in danger, and I guess once she died that recollection became a kind of forerunner of her murder and too painful to contemplate.' She paused and said, 'I never talk about this.'

The Nespresso made hatching-dragon sounds.

'On one occasion when I did think about the fire, I googled what I recalled of Battle's words. It turned out he was quoting Rabbi Nachman of Bratslav, who was a mystic and a writer of wonder tales. Nachman was riffing on his great-grandfather, the Hasidic teacher Ba'al Shem

Tov. Anyway, Nachman, at the end of his life, told his secretary to burn his writings. He thought people would die if they weren't burned. As if his papers were the makings of a cursed book.'

As she told this story, Taryn was smashing cloves of garlic with the flat of a knife, skinning and chopping them. Jacob filled two coffee cups. He kept one himself and handed the other to Taryn. Shift was watching Taryn closely. It turned out he was considering food, and his difficulties with it. He said, 'Remember what I can't eat.'

Taryn told Shift that she'd sauté a red onion and grill some zucchini and halloumi. She hoped that would suit him.

Jacob knocked back his tiny espresso and said to Taryn, 'Do you think we should consult works of Hebrew scholarship?' That would be a job for her, not him.

'The demon inside Battle wasn't recommending reading. I don't think it had its own words for its delight.' Taryn produced a packet of prosciutto from the capacious refrigerator. She peeled off a strip and offered it to Munin, who took it, threw her head back, and gulped. The ribbon of cured flesh flopped and whirled until the raven had swallowed it down.

Taryn offered the prosciutto to Jacob. As soon as the meat touched his tongue, his mouth flooded with saliva. He temporarily could not speak. He'd forgotten he was hungry.

Munin said, 'Did Battle's demon say "The new Torah will issue from me" because it was a *special* demon?'

'None of them is special,' Shift said. 'They are legion.'

Jacob swallowed. 'It thought it had captured the flag. It was crowing.' Then, 'No offence,' to Munin.

Shift said, 'The demon set fire to James Northover's library because it believed it held the box. Hell is chasing this object to destroy it. Because destroying it will bring something to pass. Some change in conditions desirable to Hell.'

'Well, that's a theory,' Jacob said. He thought Shift's take on the situation had firmed up far too early in the investigation.

Taryn turned on the flame under the grill and began slicing zucchini.

Jacob became very interested in what she was doing—and the result; an appetising salad. He liked watching the process itself, how graceful and competent her movements were, her fingertips reddened by cold tap water and shiny with oil—she had dressed then tossed some lettuce with her hands. Jacob could smell preserved meat, and the hot iron grill, and oil and garlic and lemon. The aroma was the most solid and real thing since the halo of squirrel fur. But inclusive, convivial, soothing—rather than lonely.

'But—' the raven said. The rest of her sentence was incomprehensible, as if she were just a bird, making bird noises.

'That's a good question,' Shift said, then pulled a face, backed off into the corner, and told Taryn he couldn't eat any vegetables she'd braised on *that*.

Taryn glanced at the iron grill, looked helpless for a moment, then went to the fridge to find more vegetables.

'A good question that we could judge for ourselves if it were put in a language we share,' Jacob muttered.

Shift looked at Jacob and spoke again. His expression was that of a person repeating another person's words. He stopped speaking and waited for a reaction.

'Would anyone drink wine if I opened a bottle?' Taryn asked. 'I was thinking a Sangiovese.'

Shift sounded frustrated. 'What Munin asked was—' He concluded his sentence in a string of nonsense. It wasn't even the same phrases he had used before, but another phonetically divergent language—equally incomprehensible.

Jacob was tired of Shift's opacity. 'Stop it,' he ordered.

'Yes,' the raven agreed. 'Best to.'

Shift regarded Jacob. His eyes grew dark. He flushed, only under his jaw at first, then the blush flashed across his lips as if it were a grass fire leaping from patch to patch. That Shift was offended and suppressing his anger was even more irritating.

Taryn had opened an airlock-like hatch in the corner of the kitchen and was now shoulders-deep in the floor, descending a tight spiral staircase into a wine cellar. She reappeared a moment later with a bottle, opened it, apologised for not leaving the wine to breathe, and poured a glass for everyone except the raven. Then she continued topping and tailing the green beans she'd found. She put them in the microwave and pressed buttons. The microwave's hum added itself to the sound of sizzling slices of zucchini.

Shift broke eye contact with Jacob and edged around the bench. He reached Munin and gathered her into his arms. Munin was surprised, and for a few moments there were talons and wings springing out around Shift like a splash of ink. Then Munin collected herself and settled in Shift's arms. 'I'm not one of your hens,' she reminded him.

Shift cuddled her as if she were. 'It's not a glamour,' he said.

'You can do better than that.'

'The box isn't even present, and it does this. It must be an enchantment.'

Munin said, 'I'm not sure we'd know if the box *was* present. That's how strong the spell is. Except it's more than a spell; it's a covenant.'

Shift said, 'How often have you encountered something like that?'

'In this world? A dozen times, maybe. *You're* a thing like that. One covenant built upon another.'

Taryn used tongs to lift grilled vegetables onto the plated lettuce. She drained the beans and cooled them with running water. She put them on a separate plate, laid grilled halloumi on the zucchini, shaved parmesan on Shift's beans, and spooned dressing over everything. She pushed the beans towards Shift and the grilled vegetables towards Jacob and kept a plate herself. She clearly wanted to make them eat standing at the bench. There was a lot of sense in that, Jacob thought, since anyone who arrived would do so from the road, not the shore. The kitchen overlooked a wind-break and had a staircase mounting to a gallery off which Jacob supposed there were bedrooms. Of course Taryn knew the house.

Jacob realised he was plotting avenues of escape and was watching Taryn do the same. But neither of them was thinking straight. And when Taryn spoke up again to say, 'They're talking about the box,' she sounded too calm, as if Shift and the raven's strange exchange had been all politeness, and her acknowledgement of it just civilised conversation.

Munin said, 'The box, which we will from now on dignify by calling "the Firestarter". The Firestarter has a kind of spell on it. You humans can consider it in some ways, but not others. You aren't able to formulate the obvious question about it, or even hear that question put to you. The Firestarter has been hidden here—Midgard—because the spell ensures you humans keep it hidden.'

'What is the obvious question?' Jacob asked.

'You won't hear me if I ask it.'

Taryn said, 'Can the demons ask?'

'Demons, sidhe, and the godly could get together and have a lively discussion about the Firestarter, covering all its known particulars,' Munin said.

'Not that they would.' Shift was whispering.

Jacob pointed his fork at Shift and asked the raven, 'Which is he? I need clarification because I think he's not playing straight about his al-lergies.'

'Sidhe,' Shift said. 'And human. The allergies to iron and grain and red meat apply, but not as strongly as they would to any full-blood.'

'But you're immune to this supposed spell?'

'I am.'

The raven jabbed Shift's hands a few times to persuade him to put her down. 'I wish you wouldn't do that,' she said, and Jacob decided she didn't mean she wished he wouldn't hold her.

'The Firestarter seems to frighten him.' Jacob's thoughts were coming back into focus now that he'd been given permission to steer them away from the maelstrom of the spell.

'It makes me sad,' Shift said. 'Magic is horrible.'

'No more than money,' Munin said. 'Money is truly horrible.' Then, sounding like someone's mother, 'Shift, eat the meal Taryn has made for you.'

Jacob grabbed Shift's plate and moved it out of his reach. 'I'm sure there'll be anaesthetic involved in the operation you're about to have. So—nil by mouth.'

The food, gastronomically exquisite though nutritionally sparse, seemed to restore everyone who ate. Even Munin had more, chasing several whey-slick bocconcini around the countertop before swallowing them whole. When she'd finished, she announced she was leaving. She took a short rocking walk to the end of the bench, flexed her wings, aimed at the door—then furled them again. 'Shift. You must continue to try to corner a demon and persuade it to speak to you.'

'I'm only pausing here to have the iron removed.'

'Very well,' the raven said. She flew from the kitchen, and they heard the noise of the latch as the door opened itself to let her out.

'We should try to rest,' Taryn said.

'Upstairs, out of sight,' Jacob said. 'I'll stay downstairs and watch for Hemms.'

'She won't come,' Shift said, but they both ignored him.

'Will I have to speak to her when she arrives?' Taryn asked.

'Yes. But feel free to be obstructive.'

J acob woke up when Alan Palfreyman's security contractor, Stuart, arrived with the doctor. They came in wheeling a portable X-ray machine on a sturdy handcart. Jacob got up to greet them. Taryn didn't reappear.

Jacob woke Shift, and between them they helped the doctor get everything set up. While that was going on, Stuart looked in on Taryn and had a talk with her, checking for his employer on her welfare.

Jacob stayed in the room throughout Shift's procedure. Then he gave Stuart and the doctor coffee. Stuart said, 'Since Ms Cornick is without her own car I'll leave her my Land Rover and ride back to London with the doctor. Mr Palfreyman would want that. And I've left a new phone in the glovebox.'

Stuart and the doctor departed in the late afternoon. Jacob lay down on a sofa and fell asleep again.

J acob's watch told him four hours had passed. Hemms had failed to turn up. The raven had talked about arranging a delay, not a deterrence, but Jacob was filled with a sick sense of worry.

Hemms's phone rang nine times before she answered. She said she was in Norwich Hospital waiting to see an orthopaedic surgeon. 'I don't think I'm going anywhere tonight.'

Her story was this: She was on her way at a good clip and had slowed at the intersection of A47 and Dunham Road when a large rock came through the windscreen. She tried to brake with her kneecap knocked out of place and couldn't do it. Her car swerved into a ditch, and her head bashed the doorpost hard enough to give her concussion. The car was wedged against a stone wall. Hemms hauled herself out the passenger's door. It was then she realised her leg wasn't operating properly. 'So I called an ambulance.'

'Where did the rock come from?' Jacob tried to put his question naturally. But what was natural? His history of regular dissembling hadn't equipped him to fake innocence on matters Hemms wouldn't believe anyway.

'Perhaps some idiot was playing with a catapult in a nearby field. How am I supposed to know? The Norwich police are investigating. If it turns out it was a space rock I'm shouting everyone in our section lottery tickets.' Hemms then got back on the case. 'How is Ms Cornick?'

'Sleeping. With a dose of antibiotics in her. I can't in all decency badger her until she is rested and the drugs kick in. She was feverish and wasn't making much sense. She ordered me out of the house—but I stayed.'

'All right.' Hemms was swallowing his story. Some or all of it.

'I'll come,' he said.

'Yes. Do,' she said.

'I'll leave a note and hit the road.'

'I'll see you soon. And, Jacob?'

'Yes?'

'Don't let me down.'

The only remaining medical equipment was a suspended bag of saline. Shift was on his back, bandaged, bare to the waist, with large expanses of his exposed flesh varnished with Betadine.

Jacob sat on the side of the bed. He tapped the back of Shift's hand, careful not to come into contact with the Gatemaker's glove, which was now fastened to Shift's wrist by both its pin clip and leather bindings.

Shift opened his eyes. He momentarily leapt into focus, as he never quite had before. It was as if their skin contact helped Jacob see him better—the dark-skinned young man with a raptor's nose and beautiful hazel eyes.

'I have to take off,' Jacob said. 'But I'm concerned for Taryn. She still seems determined to fulfil her professional obligations. To carry on as if she's not in danger. What can we do about that?'

'I'll stay with her. I too would like to have a look at the papers she tells me her New Zealand grandmother has. Papers about the dispersal of James Northover's library.'

'Are you well enough to travel?'

'The doctor told me that several pellets remain lodged behind my ribs, in positions too complicated for him to extract without a hospital and ultrasound.'

Jacob watched Shift's face and waited for a sign of self-consciousness, but his manner remained calm and confiding.

'How do you suppose the pellets got *behind* your ribs since everything that hit you was a ricochet?'

'I'm not a physicist, Jacob.'

'Well, that's what a plausible explanation would require, isn't it? Some fairly unusual physics.'

'People won't talk to me,' Shift said. 'They meet me without trust. Without appetite. Even when they're not wary they're never interested, as if to consider me would somehow rob them of consequence.'

Jacob remembered a friend from his university days, a musician who'd had a breakout album and a considerable career. She had worked very hard at maintaining her friendships. She confided to Jacob once that keeping her old relationships required her never to expect anyone to ask her about herself. 'It's my job to listen to them. I'm in the magazines, so they know everything they need to know about me. I get public attention, so I don't need their attention.'

Jacob thought what Shift was claiming for himself was something like that. He tried to put that together with the pellets of iron tucked in behind Shift's ribs where they couldn't be reached, so Shift couldn't be fixed, and couldn't be *himself*. He said, 'I'm not sure what you're trying to tell me.'

Shift waited, watching Jacob think.

'Are you saying that you're a person whom nobody would offer an advantage, even just information? Or are you telling me you don't inspire confidence?'

Shift seemed reluctant to give up trying to make Jacob guess. 'I need the people who I want to ask questions to tell me what they know, out of pride in what they know. I want them to pay me in coin they think I can't spend.'

Jacob kept his face still, hoping for further elaboration.

'I want a demon to boast to me, because I'm knowledgeable but ineffectual. I need the sidhe to feel bold enough to let on what their plans are for me.'

'So you've made sure you still have the iron sickness?'

Shift nodded.

'That's stupid,' Jacob said.

'I wasn't aware that *not* disappointing you was an option, so I'm afraid I haven't taken any steps to avoid it.'

Jacob got off the bed. 'Just don't fail Taryn.'

Shift smiled. 'I suppose that's one way of talking to me.'

Twelve

Brutal

Taryn woke to the sound of her own voice, pure and bodiless, a version of the mumbling internal self that would remind her to pay her car registration or buy toilet paper. A voluble and insistent voice that came to her when, for instance, she'd over-rehearsed a performance, like the oral defence of her thesis.

There are things you can't fix, said the voice, full of anxiety and self-reproach. *You have involved all these people—even Alan—in your dishonesty. And you keep lying. Why can't you just admit to them you're a murderer? A murderer by proxy. A great seductress of the sob story, who won a man over with her offer of intimacy. 'Be my hero,' you said, without being so crude as to actually say it. 'Do for me what no one else will do, and I'll hold you in the centre of my gaze forever.' And then what did you do once you had got your promise from him and he'd fulfilled it? You put him out of your mind, exiled him, willfully forgot his name . . .*

Taryn got up and went into the bathroom to splash cold water on her face. Her cheeks stung. She peered in the mirror. Her face was dripping.

She looked frightened. She pressed a towel to her wet skin, dropped it on the floor, and lay back down.

Must she always keep Shift on hand, as if she were an asthmatic and he her inhaler? She laughed at the thought. Then her inner voice came back. *You should go to Shift. Show your gratitude. It's all he wants. That wasn't what the Muleskinner wanted. He is coming for that. For your wet insides.*

Her cruel self would not be silenced. *You know what Jacob would like right now? To be unzipped and invited into your wet insides. He's a man who would enjoy a little fricative affection.*

Taryn wanted to cry out, but it was as if a thick Kevlar helmet had dropped onto her to cup and contain her head. All she was able to do was lick her lips as she was assaulted by the memory of how angular the rippled edge of Alan's glans felt when it stiffened in her mouth.

She lunged over the side of the bed and retched as if she could purge herself that way.

Jacob appeared in the doorway. He was wearing his coat, as if he'd just come back from somewhere or was about to leave. He hurried to her and scooped her hair back. When she'd finished he tried to put his arms around her. But Taryn didn't require comfort; she needed saving.

She fought free of his embrace and ran to find Shift. She crawled under the covers beside him. 'It's here,' she sobbed. 'I thought it was me.'

He took her face between his hands and gazed into her eyes.

'It's not afraid of you,' she said, desperate, and caught his fleeting look of satisfaction.

'We have to go,' he said, now talking over the top of her head to Jacob, who'd followed her.

'Stuart left his Land Rover. You can take that. I can't go with you. I have to get on the road to Norwich.'

Shift disengaged Taryn's arms. He rolled out of bed, steadied himself on the lowboy, and yanked the cannula out of his arm.

'Take it easy,' Jacob said. 'Can you drive?'

Shift said he could. Furthermore, he'd learned when there were no road signs.

Jacob snapped. 'Why, when I most need to feel okay about you, do you reach for the fakery? There were road signs before there were automobiles. I think even the Romans had road markers.'

'During the last war they removed the road signs so invading armies would wander the little lanes of England forever. Lovely idea. I learned to drive while hitching rides with lost American airmen on day jaunts, and men from ministries with sweaty foreheads and generous petrol rations.'

'Oh,' said Jacob.

Taryn moaned. The icy digitised voice was now making promises. *I will take you apart. Soften you up. Suck the marrow from your bones.* She smacked her lips. Or she didn't; *it* did.

Jacob, his confidence in Shift restored, asked whether sedation might help her. 'The doctor left lithium and codeine for you.'

'Giving Taryn drugs to subdue the demon would be an experiment. Everything I know about demons is secondhand. I don't remember ever having met one before. Please pick her up for me, Jacob. I don't want to tear my stitches.'

Taryn was grappled, lifted. The ceiling flowed by overhead as if she were on a gurney. She clenched her teeth and moaned. She was floating. The demon was holding her too and moving her away somewhere. Jacob and Shift's consultation continued around her. Jacob said, 'Go grab a couple of Palfreyman's sweaters. I'll find your boots.'

She felt Jacob's breath in her hair. He whispered that she'd be all right. Then she was wrestling inside herself while something energetic rifled through her life, gleefully pulling out every miserable thought or disgusting sensation and offering them to her. She lost some time. Then

Jacob was shaking her and almost shouting in her ear. 'Taryn! I found an OtterBox with Palfreyman's hunting gear. I put the phone Stuart left you in it. The phone will make it through the lake in the OtterBox.'

Your horrible encumbering bodies and feeble provisions against distance. Your phone calls and train tickets!

Then she was lying on a clammy padded surface, the back seat of a high headroom car. The demon was laughing. Jacob was at the window. Shift appeared beside him, opened the door, and raised her head to loop something around her neck. She touched it—his warm gold claws. She felt like a bird pulled out of an oil slick. Still poisoned and weighed down, but she didn't have to struggle anymore. The driver's door slammed, and the engine shivered. Jacob's face swam in starbursts of her tears. He pressed his palm on the glass and held it there, walking beside the Land Rover as it reversed. Then he stepped away and disappeared behind them.

The demon might be wary of the Gatemaker's glove, but it soon discovered the artefact wasn't going to make any judgements about whether two spirits belonged in one body. The glove was like a third person present in the tussle. It was a bystander, an impartial witness. It shone its aureate light on the demon's excavations. *Look at this*, said the demon to the glove. *Look at what I can do.*

Taryn was roused once or twice from her miserable struggle by the blast of an air horn as Shift cut between two trucks, and by a rapid deceleration at the site of an accident. Night came, and the sodium lamps flew by overhead. The dark patches between swinging bands of orange filled with bulbous forms, as if mushrooms were being cultivated in the black loam of shadow. By the light of the lamps the walls of buses and big rigs loomed and slid away, while the shadows remained a fixture and full of fleshy things, like the fists of babies, further forward than what appeared in the light, until the images that appeared finally receded to the size of very clear thumbnails and the hands of infants lunged in and pressed their sticky fingers to Taryn's face. She tried shutting her eyes. But the fingers commenced stroking her cheeks and picking at her lips as if trying to part them.

The Land Rover took a corner too fast. The top of Taryn's head banged the door panel, and the shadows emptied for a moment. Then it began all over again, a horrible creeping up. Taryn closed her eyes and kept them closed. The car slowed, time went away; the demon rooted in her body with its long tusks, turning up the bodies buried in her body. She tuned out the sound of delving and lamentation and finally heard the narrow lane—briars and nettles and sorrel and burdock and hollyhocks ticking against the sides of the car.

Taryn's face ached, her groin stung and throbbed, and her breasts prickled as if they'd been strapped down and recently unbound. Her arms were wrenched up over her head, and she couldn't lower them. Her fingers were swollen. There was an insistent, repeated pinging sound nearby that her brain eventually registered as the warning noise that accompanied a vehicle's hazard lights. These few impressions comprised almost the sum of her sensory input. But she could hear herself too, in full flight, her voice tight, divisive, smug—its tone explanatory, though she was only repeating, 'Two, two, two . . .' Then, 'I know you too.'

'If you mean to remark on my divided nature and the fact I'm both sidhe and human, yes, that's as remarkable as it ever was, given how few we are. But it's not something I keep secret, so your tone of sly disclosure is a little self-indulgent. Please make an effort to get unstuck, and communicate. We might find mutual benefit in that.'

'Whatever you are, you stink like a slaver,' said the demon. 'You can only care for this woman because you're trying to fan the shrunken flame of your human soul. You believe that tiny soul is worth more than your freedom to walk the roads of the Sidh.'

'Do you mean to remind yourself of your shortcomings? Anyone with a body, and the freedom of the Sidh, can go almost anywhere. When you lost Taryn all you could do—bodiless one—was waft about the world in the tides and traffic, shrinking and forgetting what you came here for. All you remembered was that Taryn alone was hospitable. And so here you are again. But can you even recall why you're here?'

'Are you trying to taunt me into frankness? Why don't you remove this . . . ornament . . . so we can converse, spirit to spirit.'

Silence.

'I made this miserable animal hurt herself while you were busy watching the road. You don't have eyes everywhere. You might as well be just a body.'

Silence.

'Why would you want her, anyway? She's well past her best. Her flesh is softening and growing sour.'

Silence.

'Tell me, how did this . . . ornament . . . come to be in your keeping?'

Shift laughed. 'You have no idea who I am, do you?'

The demon growled, which provoked Taryn into a coughing fit.

'I think you don't even know why Hell is looking for the Firestarter,' Shift said. 'You're not that important.'

'We know.' The demon was concentrating hard. It quenched Taryn's cough, and then she lost her body. Most of it. It still existed to her, but in a diagrammatic form, with its points of pain selected and highlighted. She was losing her sense of the position of her limbs. She knew that she still lay in the Land Rover's back seat, but she felt afloat, tethered by her hands but flapping in a wind.

'It is night and raining, and the wall is high here and covered by thorns and nettles,' the demon said. 'How do you suppose you will carry the woman and not have her claw you more? Believe me, she and I are both burning to lay our hands on you again.'

'Taryn is unconscious.'

'No, she's not. *Ah*. You seem concerned to hear that. Could it be that you don't want her overhearing what I say to you? What you say to me?'

Silence.

'I know more than you, fate-forsworn princeling. I *do* know who you are. And I know everything the woman knows. Soon I will kill her so that I can depart. Or you will try to drag me to the gate, the gate will brush me from her, and, this time, knowing more, I'll return to Hell.'

'You don't know what Taryn has forgotten, or discounted, or repressed. Or even what's temporarily slipped her mind. And where do you propose to go with your very partial information? Is it so easy to get to Hell? In this god-haunted world, you're a weak and addled thing. And alone, not legion.'

The demon let out a long shriek. It flinched away from Taryn's extremities and burrowed deeper into her brain. Taryn was once more able to sense her body, its aches, spasms, and injuries. She wanted to add her cry to the demon's, but it still had hold of her mouth and lungs. It screeched, and Taryn felt the hot wire jab of a blood vessel bursting in her left eye. That eye poured tears, but she could see, she could smell; she had got that much back.

Shift sat pressed against the door on the driver's side of the back seat. His hair clung to condensation on the window and made a spidery halo around his bloodied face. His cheeks and throat were striped by long, bloody gouges ending in dangling ribbons of skin.

The demon had done that, using her hands, when Shift had pulled over and climbed into the back seat to put a stop to whatever the demon was making her do to herself. Shift had tied her hands to the door behind her. He was peering at her now with an alert, guarded expression.

Drops of water ran on the insides of the car window. Water dripped from its ceiling and walls. The vehicle was a wet cave, its interior filling with steam.

The demon continued to wail until something gave way in Taryn's throat. The cry diminished and changed to a high rasping. In movies, demons had growling, layered voices representing the many beings clustered like parasitic cysts in one poor human body. But the spirit possessing Taryn was alone, forced to make do with her human vocal apparatus, and it was pushing that apparatus beyond its capabilities. 'Hell!' the demon shouted, articulate again. 'Hell is the Homeland!'

Taryn's legs flew wide. One of her feet thudded into Shift's shoulder, and the other stretched and pointed as if trying to perform a ballet pose. The demon seemed to be trying to use her muscles to dislocate her joints. It left her head free so that she could watch her body elongate and strain, her gaze leaping to each audible wrench and pop. She saw the tendons turning white below her hipbone. She threw back her head to see how her hands were tied. Shift had used the cotton cord from the hood of her sweatshirt and had looped it through the door handle. She was pulling against the cord, and her hands were swollen and purple. Her fingernails were rimmed with blood.

Through the window behind her head Taryn could see a flowering hawthorn hedge, its foliage lit from below by headlamps reflecting off the wet road. As she watched, drops on the inside of the window flattened as if there were a huge blow-dryer inside the car. The air got hotter and hotter.

Shift spoke. Taryn heard him begin, his words so slow and deliberate that they came out as separate sentences. 'That's. Enough. Of. That,' he said, his voice dropping octaves between each word. Then it wasn't a voice. It was the subharmonics of a volcano.

The door behind Taryn blasted out of its frame. A steely shrieking sounded around her, and she was dragged out of the car by her tied hands. Her breasts and thighs scraped and bashed across the door frame. She thought, *I'm going to die.*

And straight after dying she'd be in Hell, a place she now knew existed. She was unprepared. She remembered with cruel clarity her mother weeping after her cancer diagnosis. There was a lump, and Addy Cornick might have known about it if she'd had her scheduled mammogram, but she'd been depressed and careless—a late-twentieth-century woman putting her fate in her own self-examining hands, in superseded practices and blind chance, when there was that which, oracle-like, could see her future and could save her from it. Taryn's mother had blamed herself. Taryn was blaming herself. She was facing the blackness at the edges of her field of vision, and it was Hell, a sight-cancelling shadow in a sense-trammelled death.

The car's headlamps flew apart and were bowled along the lane, lighting it briefly as they faded then blinked out. For a moment Taryn dangled, the hawthorn tugging at her clothes and hair, her toes a few metres from the road. A storm of hot air swung her into the hedge, then away from it again. The demon relinquished her voice, and she screamed in terror.

Above her was a huge grey cloud. A grey glow like the billows of static electricity that filled Bea's favourite nightdress whenever Bea got up in the night, slid out of the polyester sheets of the creaky beds they occupied on their visits to Princes Gate. Taryn would urge Bea to roll around before getting up so there'd be more static. Bea would thrash about, then leap out of bed, her body haloed grey-white, crying, 'I'm the ghost of Princes Gate!'

Roiling plumes of luminescence surrounded Taryn. An icy object thumped against her chest: the Gatemaker's glove. When it touched her damp skin it stuck fast, as if it were a metal container straight out of the freezer.

The demon had scuttled to Taryn's interior, where it cowered in shock.

Taryn's arms dropped, her shoulders popping. Her hands were still tied to the door. She had only an instant to brace and take its weight on her spine. Then something hot, padded, and transparent closed around both her and the door. The thing holding her was filled with soft clouds of static. She heard the door panels popping with pressure. Her swollen fists jammed into her diaphragm, and she couldn't draw breath.

The last sensation Taryn had before losing consciousness was the demon doing something terrible to some essential part of her, like a clumsy brain surgeon, laser off by a millimetre, burning away an integral part of her. That, and the spine-compressing sensation of being in a poorly calibrated express elevator on its way up a very tall building with no one waiting for it on any floor.

PART FOUR

Damp

'No sight so sad as that of a naughty child,' he began, 'especially a naughty little girl. Do you know where the wicked go after death?'

'They go to hell,' was my ready and orthodox answer.

'And what is hell? Can you tell me that?'

'A pit full of fire.'

'And should you like to fall into that pit, and to be burning there for ever?'

'No, sir.'

'And what must you do to avoid it?'

I deliberated a moment; my answer, when it did come, was objectionable: 'I must keep in good health and not die.'

Charlotte Brontë, *Jane Eyre*

Thirteen

Failing Kindness

Taryn lay with the top of her head turned to the setting sun, her scalp saturated with the hot oil of its light. Her hands were bandaged, so she couldn't use her fingers to explore her injuries. Every breath pained her, but each was a continuation and promised consciousness.

But even semi-conscious, Taryn felt there was something she no longer owned. That when the demon left her, it had taken something of hers away with it.

Now and then she'd fumble for the call button. She'd try to summon a nurse. But there was no call button, and her carers came when they came. The water they gave her had a strange flavour. It wasn't town water or tank water. It tasted of washed rock dust, as fresh as some summer in a future with forests but without cities.

All day she was in the hut, her bed far from the low doorway. At dusk, when the light had gone, they'd carry her out into the fresh air. It was a routine. She and the bed covered in bearskins were at the centre of the routine. Anyone else at that centre and it would be a ritual. That was what she felt. They were all people of some size. She was not. She existed for routine, not ritual. She was smaller now.

Neve appeared once, at a fastidious distance. And the printer, whose name was Jane. Jane Aitken.

There was no sign of Shift until, some twilight along a succession of twilights, Taryn saw him standing on the beige sand of the pocket-sized beach of the little lake. She watched him crouch and scoop up water to wash his face.

'Was he hurt?' she asked Jane. 'Is he angry with me?'

'He's only out of sorts. He wants to get on with things. He has sent for a palanquin so you can be carried. We're going by way of the hot springs at Forsha to help you recover from your injuries.'

'If he's in a hurry we mustn't go out of our way,' Taryn said, then corrected herself. 'His way.'

Time was going by, and Taryn had somewhere else to be. But she couldn't even get up off the bed of bracken and bearskins when she needed to urinate. Several times a day Jane would slip a basin under her bottom. All she could manage to eat was a broth whose main ingredients seemed to be salt, honey, ginger, and bitter greens. The insides of her cheeks were lacerated, and eating hurt her. Her ribs were bound, but if she raised an arm or tried to turn over, she was reminded that some were broken.

'I don't know what happened.'

'Neither do I,' Jane said, but when she said it, she kept her face turned away.

The following day the palanquin arrived with a large party of sidhe. Two beautiful people, a man and a woman, carried Taryn out of Shift's hut. They put her down on the palanquin's platform, which was covered in white furs. They draped a cloudy silk eiderdown over her, closed the cream linen curtains, and slotted filigreed wood panels into place on all four sides. Then four people lifted the palanquin onto their padded shoulders and set off without ceremony. They didn't even pause to take refreshment at Shift's hut. Their haste wasn't an attempt to avoid him, because he came away with them, with Jane and Neve, who were waiting at the rim of the hollow.

Shift's goats trailed after them for a time but stopped at the belt of twisted trees. Their plaintive bleating followed the party as it set off around the side of the mountain.

The litter bearers high-stepped through tussock, they went along, careful but effortless. They admired the downhill view and lifted their faces to watch black hawks hovering on the wind. They sometimes spoke quietly among themselves, but they didn't look at Taryn. That was politeness, she decided. She wasn't being shunned. She wasn't beneath their notice. They were just leaving her in peace, letting her rest. They weren't a kind people, but they were enormously civil.

Taryn did rest. Once she'd got over imagining the bearers might take a tumble, she fell asleep and slept for most of the journey.

On the first night the party stopped at a level place, a platform cut into the hillside, with a sheltered firepit, a small stream dripping from a moss-covered channel into a pool overhung by ferns, and two stone slabs tilted together to make a shelter where dried wood was stored.

On the second night they halted by a mountain tarn, very similar to Shift's lake but with water stained tea-brown by the plant matter sifted to its bottom. The tarn was surrounded by tough alpine grasses and thorn bushes with berries of candy pink and cough-drop red. At that camp the party's fire looked choked and small. And when the moon came out its light shone on and through the blue ice cliffs fastened to the black rock faces of surrounding mountains. The night breeze came as an icy downdraught carrying a scent of hostile nothingness, as if it blew all the way from the stars.

On the third day Taryn sometimes pushed a curtain aside to watch the world go by. Or she dozed with her eyes open, hypnotised by the swinging cage that held the tea set.

Jane climbed into the litter with a copper kettle and filled the teapot with mint leaves and hot water. She let it steep for a time, then poured it into two jade cups. She helped Taryn to sit, settled the pillows behind her, and passed her the steaming tea. 'I wondered what your plans are. What you might do next.'

It seemed Jane had judged Taryn recovered enough to broach the subject of her future.

Taryn said, she hoped without self-pity, 'When I think of my future, I think of Hell.'

Jane took the cup from Taryn's grip and didn't give it back until Taryn's hands had stopped trembling. She said, 'You are one of Shift's people now. I think he means to let you fulfil your obligations in your world, as well as help him uncover things he's decided he needs to know.'

'That's something we're doing together. The uncovering. I'm not helping him. I'm not his servant, even if you are.' Taryn paused, studying Jane. 'Or perhaps you're Neve's?'

'I am one of Shift's people. As for Neve, she helped me build my printing press, and now houses it, and me whenever I'm printing. Neve wants to paper the walls of every house in the Tacit with copies of the great Sidh songs. I've printed those. And sometimes I print song sheets for choirs of Taken children, or new poems by the favoured Taken poets— Baudelaire, Emily Brontë. Wilfred Owen. You will know their names. They were after my time.' Jane smiled at Taryn's expression of numb astonishment. She refilled Taryn's cup and, her eyes lowered, said, 'That's how I occupy my time. Shift is less possessive of his Taken than the other sidhe. You might say he has me, but he didn't choose me, since I came with several hundred other women. My home is with them. You will stop there for a night on your way to the Horse Road, which is the route along which the demons have most often been seen. Shift and Neve hope to intercept and question one.'

Even battered and miserable, Taryn was keenly aware of her commitments. Of the career she'd earned and had to maintain.

All her life Taryn had loved books. She'd attended festivals, an eager member of their audiences. Now, finally, she got to be a guest at those festivals. She'd arrived. She had to do well by her book. Do well for Angela, for her publishers, and for her cherished subject, libraries—as if there were a god of libraries and she were that god's servant.

She needed to find out how long she'd lain in the wattle hut. 'When did Shift bring me here?'

'Seven nights ago,' Jane said. 'This detour will add several days to our journey. The Horse Road lies north. We'll go west, then north.'

'How many days altogether?'

Jane balanced her teacup on the box of the set and counted on her fingers. 'Four to the springs, and two or three nights at them. Four days down to the Summer Road. A week along the Summer Road to the Island of Women. One night on the isle. Or perhaps we will arrive and leave the same day—Shift doesn't like to stay there. I'll take leave of your party at the island. After the island you will cut straight across the great marsh to the Horse Road. That will take anywhere between two to four days, since I hear the boardwalk is under repair. You are ultimately headed to Hell's Gate—where the demons are coming through. Shift and Neve hope to encounter one on the road before the gate. Or, failing that, lie in wait at the gate.'

More than three weeks.

Jane said, 'All this could be accomplished more quickly if Shift would give the glove to Neve so she could call a gate. But I believe they both think it would be better if everything lay quiet until after they've cornered a demon. We have no idea if demons can feel the gates move, as the sidhe can.'

'Gods can. Munin said she and her sister could feel it when Shift moved a gate,' Taryn said. She felt as if she was name-dropping.

'Hugin knows everything that happens in your world that isn't purposely hidden from her.'

Taryn tried to take that in. She wanted to ask what kind of everything, and didn't the Raven of Knowledge have a point of view of her own? And were there things she knew but didn't understand?

Jane continued to lay out the course of Taryn's immediate future. 'After they have satisfied their curiosity, Neve will send you back to Earth through Hell's Gate. You can only use Princes Gate to come here, not go back through it. Shift left your demon trapped inside it. If you go out that way the demon can fasten onto you again. Shift believes the demon will fall into dormancy sooner or later, but for now you should regard Princes Gate as unhealthy.'

Taryn lay digesting this last bit of news, working her way around the oddity of Shift's gate having the same name as her grandfather's house. It was helpful anyway to have that report and forecast, baked firm by Jane's blithe telling.

'So I can go back to my life without the demon finding me?'

Jane nodded.

'I'm Taken, but I needn't stay?'

'You can go about your life. But my understanding is that you've somehow put your soul in peril. The demon might be foiled, but damnation can't be. If Hell is your future, fairyland makes that future much further off.'

'Yes,' Taryn agreed. 'But as I understand it Hell is the eventual fate of all who are Taken.'

'A fate that can be deferred for a very long time.'

Taryn waited.

'You can stay away if you want. Shift would let you. He would have let me—but I was an ailing, ageing woman, and under the hand of the law. For me the Sidh has meant health and freedom. Shift is not like the rest of them. He can't make anyone love him. But the Sidh itself can make you love it, so even if you go back to your life, sooner or later you'll start dreaming about it and waking up in tears.'

The hot springs emerged as a series of pools along a tumbling stream-bed of sculpted limestone. This warm waterway skirted the foot of a glacial terminal moraine, its slopes covered in alpine thorn bushes. A schist-stepped path climbed to a structure that took up the entire top of the moraine and overhung the slope on all sides like the brim of a trilby. The platform was supported by beams of squared tree trunks of some black timber. The decking was the same, only sun-silvered. But the long-house above the deck was like a piece of furniture from Thailand, a varnished table or tallboy or escritoire formed from sample inlays of various kinds of wood. It was like a museum piece made to a great scale.

Its interior was composed of only two rooms: a long hall, and a privy with box seats covering holes on the floor. The main room had a very high ceiling and pigeon-holed shelving on two sides. The deep oblong shelves mostly held rolled futon bedding, mattresses, and quilts of several thicknesses. None of these was the white, cream, amber, soft green palette of every textile Taryn had so far encountered. These were patterned, some by simple block prints of a single colour on white, others intricately, like Italian brocades. Faced with the privy on her first morning, Taryn peered through it and saw that the rock face forty feet below was wet but entirely clean. She sat, urinated, used a square of linen to mop herself dry, and placed it in the receptacle intended. The squares were obviously washed and reused. Then she glanced through the hole again to see something with the volume and transparency of a wash of clean water, but without water's liquescence, bubble across a slope and carry away the splashes of urine.

By the time Taryn finished and returned to the main room, full of questions, the beds—nine for her party, and five for the people already there when her party arrived—had been bundled and put away. Everyone was sitting on the deck, their legs dangling.

One of the litter bearers got up and collected cushions for Taryn. He piled them and help her recline. Breakfast appeared, carried in steaming copper containers in which food had been cooked by immersion in the hot springs. It was the usual Sidh food—a creamy porridge of sweet potato, with seeds, ground and whole; flakes of steamed fish; and a variety of slivered root vegetables, steamed in parcels of some large aromatic leaf and dressed with lemon juice. There was a bright green soup, and teas—mint, chamomile, chrysanthemum, and apple.

Taryn's hands were still bandaged, so Jane helped her. Everyone ate and admired the view. The sidhe talked quietly in their own language. Shift, who was farthest from Taryn, occasionally raised his head to listen, his eyes resting quietly on the speaker's face, his attention unwavering, as if he were a lip reader.

The sun was warm but the air cold. Snow lay between the tussocks on the slope below. Beyond one ridge, steam billowed up from hidden water, rose thick then melted in the breeze.

Neve was wearing fur boots and a fur tippet—white—but the interchangeably beautiful young men and women had bare feet and very good circulation, for their toes were rosy rather than puce.

Taryn bent her head towards Jane and whispered a question. 'There's something that cleans the rocks below the latrine. Something like sentient sago pudding. What is it?'

'The sidhe have three kinds of magic,' said Jane. 'There are glamours, which, contrary to folklore, are scarcely ever used to disguise their appearance. Rather, they might be used to conceal something, or pass one thing off as another. You won't encounter any of that in the Sidh—it's something the sidhe practice only on free human beings. Glamours aren't honest or respectful. Another magic is the gates. Gatemaking is now a lost art. Those that remain—the great gates, Princes, Hell's, Faul, Veya Lake and Inle Lake, Haar Island, and the Exiles' Gate, the oldest one, which can be moved anywhere but has nothing on the other side of it—all are solely for the purposes of travel. But gates could once do extraordinary things, like turn dirty water into clean. Only the sidhe can use them—others if invited and accompanied by a sidhe. Lady Neve's mother was the last Gatemaker.'

One of the bearers, listening in on Jane's explanation, muttered something in his own language, which Jane did not translate. She went on. 'The most common sidhe magic is that of mendings.' Jane touched her lips. 'How to explain?' Then she seemed to hit on it. 'So—the wind was blowing last night, wasn't it?'

It had been. At one point there had come a gust that made the whole building creak like a ship at sea. Taryn had poked her head out of her burrow of quilts to see rags of steam whipping past the wide-open end of the longhouse, and the stars shimmering as if the wind were shaking them. The room itself was quiet.

'The mendings make a kind of barrier that allows people to pass through it, and air, but not insects or air moving at any velocity. Once or twice I've seen people sweeping out rainwater and tree debris after a storm, because the storm continued too long and they had to let the mendings fail. The main purpose of mendings is as windows, and to keep everything clean and in good repair. You saw them at work on the slope below the privy. Sidhe wear them. You will never see Neve with a hair out of place, or a stray eyelash on her cheek, or a smear of food beside her mouth. Her clothes can be elaborate and stay perfectly neat even if she walks all day through high grass.'

Taryn glanced at Neve, who gave her what might in a human be a self-satisfied smirk. In fact it was, but it was also justified and persuasive. Taryn looked at the cup she held between her slightly grubby bandaged hands and the blackened blood blisters at the root of each tortured fingernail. Jane saw what Taryn was looking at and told her that the sidhe could have used mendings to help Taryn heal, but it wouldn't have been polite, because she was Shift's, not theirs.

'Can Shift make mendings?' Taryn asked.

'Shift can't do anything with the iron in him. That is why he just wiped his dripping nose on his already snot-stiffened sleeve,' Neve said, lightly contemptuous.

Shift scrambled to his feet. He gathered the chains of the copper vessels in one hand, picked them up, and said he'd go clean them. 'With grit and elbow grease—my snot-stiffened sleeves rolled up.'

As he walked away through the longhouse Neve made a bright-voiced remark in her own tongue to the assembly, and everyone but Jane laughed.

Taryn muttered, 'It's like high school.'

No one looked at her.

Over the next hour the sidhe went off, several carrying bows on their shoulders. They were going to cull wild goats and sheep, Jane said. The carcass of any animal they killed would be left for the eagles and ravens, since sidhe ate no red meat.

'Is it a religious restriction?'

'They can't digest it.'

Jane helped Taryn up off her cushions and led her indoors. She had Taryn remove her clothes and unwind her bandages. She wrapped her in a soft wool robe and gave her boots made of the pelts of long-haired goats. They looked like something an early seventies fashion model might have worn.

They went out the end of the longhouse that backed onto the slope and climbed a path over a sharp ridge, then descended through a forest of twisted white trees. Steam blew through the forest. That warmth must be what permitted the trees to flourish, since the springs were above the usual treeline.

The women emerged on the banks of the stream. It dropped, level to level, by smooth chutes of limestone, from pool to bubbling pool. In its higher reaches its channel was fringed with ice. But where the hot water emerged, the clean limestone gave way to pools with lips of white crystal, smooth accretions of mineral that made each level as tranquil and sculpted as the infinity pool in a posh resort. There were many springs, the earth giving up its thermal water in more than one place.

Jane and Taryn picked their way down steps beside the stream until they reached a pool of the right temperature. Jane removed Taryn's boots and robe and handed her into the water. Taryn settled herself on a rock shelf and rested her head on a slick dent in the crystal lip.

'I'll leave you to soak,' Jane said. She put the robe, boots, and a rolled linen towel within Taryn's reach. She unrolled the towel to show Taryn a copper bottle of water and a small silver bell. She shook the bell to demonstrate how its voice spiked through the burble of the stream. She assured Taryn that she would hear it. 'Stay in as long as you can. Keep drinking and let loose your water. No one is above or below you.'

Jane went off the way she'd come, and Taryn closed her eyes and let her arms float. The weight lifted from her shoulders. Her lacerations smarted, then after a time stopped. Now and then she let herself lose contact with the seat and bobbed up to cool her shoulders. Her skin turned rosy; her scabs softened and yellowed. Sometimes the steam-soaked bushes dripped blood-warm water on her head.

A small apricot-coloured bird came to bash a snail on the lip of the pool. It picked the meat—still whole and foaming with distress—from the crushed shell and dunked the shrinking, naked snail in the hot spring, held it underwater until it was tender, then gulped it down.

Taryn closed her eyes and dozed. Her hair escaped and slid over her shoulders and spread out on the water, caressing her breasts.

Fourteen

The Pale Lady

At Norwich Hospital, Jacob got as far as the nurses' station of the orthopaedics ward. There he was told that Hemms was still in surgery, and he might like to wait in the family room. It had couches with grease-blackened cracks in their vinyl armrests, a coffee machine with an Out of Order sign, a stainless steel bench frosted with spilled sugar, a window overlooking the city's skyline, and, at that window, Raymond Price.

Price's grip was weak and cold, his hand a bundle of sticks in a bag of eel skin. 'Jacob,' he said. It seemed they were now on a first-name basis.

Jacob said, 'Do we know anything more about Rosemary's accident?'

'Local police are asking around. It isn't a populous spot.'

'Did she tell you I talked to Taryn Cornick?'

Price looked amused. 'That's why I'm here. Rosemary phoned on her way up, before her accident but after she'd spoken to you. She wasn't able to tell me about the man who approached Ms Cornick outside the Bibliothèque Méjanes. But you can.'

Jacob kept his mouth shut.

'Ms Cornick, Claude Pujol, and a thickset individual appeared on security footage from the camera trained on the artwork at the front of the library.'

Jacob supposed he'd been recorded too—leaping out of his rental car and rushing to save Taryn. 'What did the camera show?'

'The thickset man approaches Ms Cornick. She backs off, then spots Pujol at the door to the library. She waves at him. Then there's fifty-one seconds of static.' Price regarded Jacob, his expression as neutral as that of a person waiting for an elevator. 'Has Ms Cornick mentioned the person who approached her?'

'She wasn't well, or talkative.'

'You were there, Jacob, in the Renault you rented in Avignon. You abandoned it outside the Bibliothèque Méjanes.'

Price had deduced Jacob's presence from the Renault, so perhaps the static on the security footage started before Jacob leapt out of it. 'I got to the library early, parked, then nodded off. I woke up when Taryn ran past. I followed her on foot, caught up, but she wasn't making sense. She refused to go back to the library, and by the time I'd got her settled and went back myself, the police were all over the place.'

'Got her settled where?'

'Her hotel,' Jacob said. 'When I returned they told me she'd gone out again, leaving her bags. I waited for her, but she didn't come back. She called me yesterday, mid-morning.'

'And you drove all the way to Soult Head to see her.'

'She's having some kind of crisis. Sooner or later she'll break down and come clean about Timothy Webber. That's what I'm waiting for.' Jacob took a seat. The couch huffed its sour breath at him. He said, 'I don't see how any of this helps you.'

'I'm interested to see what you make of the footage,' Price said.

Jacob leaned his head back and closed his eyes. He held out his hand and waited for Price to pass him a phone. A phone with the footage. While waiting, he fell asleep.

W hen Jacob woke the family room was hot, the sun glaring through its windows. Price was standing at the window but dabbing his mouth with a paper napkin. He saw Jacob was awake and gestured at the bench, where there was a plastic packet of sushi rolls.

The little bump the sushi gave Jacob's blood sugar cleared his head and raised his mood.

Price said, 'Right, you're coming with me.'

'I haven't seen Rosemary.'

'I saw her while you were snoring in your corner. She told me I must take you in hand. Besides, you're going to want to see this, since it concerns your main object of interest.'

'Or you could just tell me.'

'Seeing is believing, Jacob.'

'You're not talking about your footage, are you?'

'We'll get to that. This is even more interesting.'

A s they cruised out of the underground parking garage and passed his car, Jacob reflected on how he was always being denied the use of whatever kept him in touch. He had hurried to the hospital, concerned about

Hemms. Also, he wanted her not to be any more aware than she already was of his unreliable absences. He hadn't stopped to buy a phone to replace the one the raven destroyed.

Price took note of the direction of Jacob's gaze and said he'd send word for someone to return Jacob's car to his place of work.

As easy as that, Jacob thought, with real envy at the freedom and power Price enjoyed.

The car's engine was so quiet that he could hear the sticky sound made by Price's fingers as his grip shifted on the steering wheel. After a time Price said, 'Would you like me to tell you what the drone showed us in Skardu?'

'If you're at liberty to say.'

Price gave a small huff of mirth, and Jacob thought for the first time—and far too late—*Who exactly is this man?*

'Buildings without fences,' Price began. 'No gate, no checkpoint, no barrier arms. A partial barricade on three sides, made of thousand-watt baseload diesel generators, five to a row. A solar array on each of the larger permanent structures. Those buildings in an I-shaped configuration. All of them windowless and painted a highly reflective grey. What else? Water tanks. Enough water to keep everyone comfortable.'

'Would fifteen generators put out enough power to run the processors?' Jacob asked.

'Yes, but the compound is on the electrical grid. The generators are backup, it's to be presumed. However, taken altogether the generators and photovoltaic panels wouldn't put out enough power to cover a cooling system in the event of a power cut. I don't know if you know this, Jacob, but server farms are all about their cooling systems. It's the energy outlay of keeping processors at an optimal running temperature that has big data companies building all their new server farms nearer the Arctic Circle. Also—the compound isn't pulling enough power off the grid to run a cooling system. So we know that they haven't yet fired up their processors.'

'Then the place is still under construction?'

'Looks like it. No satellite array, or microwave tower, or cable.'

'Maybe they're just doing things arse backwards. Or maybe it's *not* cyberterrorism. They have all that processing power but aren't connected because it's super-secret and they're a games development company. That would explain their interest in the games company they visited here.'

'We tend to see the lion as a man-eater until we can examine the contents of its stomach,' Price said. 'We have shipping orders. We know they've completed their quota of processing hardware. We have manifests itemising post racks, perforated flooring, compressors, exhaust fans, all the peripheral arrangements of a cooling system. But no refrigerator units.' Price cleared his throat. 'Most of these people's activities have been conducted quite openly. They have records that aren't punishingly hard to obtain. They leave their *bodies* unburied, for Christ's sake. They might be lax about concealment, but nonsense and obscurity seem to being doing a far better job of confounding us than the most clandestine of operations.'

'Arse backward isn't "nonsense",' Jacob said.

'So you think we're all over-reading things?'

Jacob suppressed a shrug. Shrugging might be construed as lack of interest. He waited for Price to tell him whatever it was—the thing they'd discovered that seemed odd and uncanny.

But Price just looked at him, as unselfconscious as a predator peering through a parting in the grass.

'Just tell me,' Jacob said.

'We had the drone make two passes. One at a lower altitude, with infrared. Every eye in our room was trained to some degree and went at once to the blocks of heat, the generators, which were all in operation. The smaller buildings were softly green-blue, with blotches of orange showing the engine of an extractor fan. But the central building was blue-black.'

'Meaning what?'

'We jumped out of our skins. In Thames House. In Nevada, where the drone operator was.'

'You're going to have to help me.'

'Why would a building that's kept cold for the servers not be insulated?' Price said.

'It would be,' said Jacob. 'Wouldn't it?'

'You know what our technicians said? They said that the central building was too cold.'

'So that building holds the refrigeration units. They must be piping chilled air through to the other buildings, where the processors are,' Jacob proposed. He still couldn't see the problem.

Price said, 'It was the blue that mapmakers give the Mariana Trench on nautical charts. The deep blue sea. A temperature outside the operational temperature of almost all electronics. As one of our technicians put it: "I guess NASA knows how to deal with those temperatures."'

'What?' said Jacob.

'To recap, the compound is running banks of servers that require a cooling system. How they are powering their cooling system is a mystery, since they're not pulling the kind of power from the grid that could run industrial refrigeration. And there's a building that is too cold. Colder than the temperature at which scientists store ice cores from Antarctica.'

Jacob suggested liquid oxygen, and Price said it had been discussed and that the building would contain enough liquid oxygen for three

Saturn rockets. Price then asked Jacob to reach into the back seat and have a look at what was in the document folder he'd find there.

It was a report about the latest equipment sent to the server farm, including copies of shipping orders. Jacob scanned the pages, then looked up at Price, who glanced at him with amused expectancy.

Jacob turned another page. A moment later he understood what Price was waiting for. 'Snow machines,' he said, bemused.

'A rather novel approach, wouldn't you say?'

'Don't snow machines require refrigeration?'

'We know they *have* refrigeration.'

'You know it's cold in the compound's central building.'

'Cold equals refrigeration,' Price said. 'You seem to want to make a lateral leap, Jacob. A leap with no landing place.'

Jacob stared at the paper in his hand. Whisper Quiet Snow Machines, times ten. Thousands of gallons of evaporating snow fluid.

'This is the sort of stuff used on film sets. Or in the theatre.'

'*Slava's Snowshow*,' Price said.

Jacob had a disconcerting image of the man holding hands with two pink-cheeked children on their way into a matinée of that clown's icy extravaganza.

Price continued. 'Since you want to make a distinction between refrigeration and the building being cold, do you have any insights into the snow machines?'

Jacob stalled. In a minute he might have to stop stalling and try flannelling. Flannelling was foreign to Jacob. How often had he watched with chilly patience as various criminals did it? 'Snow guns on ski slopes only need a water supply,' he said, 'because ski slopes are already cold.'

'Stop chewing it over and just read on,' Price said. Then his phone burred and he took it out and glanced at it.

Jacob continued to read.

Bunk beds, bedding, towels. Big-screen televisions. Gaming consoles. Kitchen equipment. No sizeable quantities of food yet, so the recruited coders hadn't arrived. 'These restaurant-grade fridges must be for their kitchen. They wouldn't work for a film or theatre snow machine.'

'Our current thinking is that the very cold room must be an uninsulated structure containing industrial refrigeration units,' said Price. 'A criminally inefficient cooling system. And somehow we missed their purchase, arrival, and installation. And we can't see how they're being powered. And no one has any useful thoughts about the highly fantastical snow machines.'

'But hang on. You said the building was too cold.'

'It is.'

Was Price letting Jacob know that MI5's current thinking was delusional? 'I can't make head or tail of this,' Jacob said, trying to sound sincere, and not to think of scaly heads and pointed tails.

'Perhaps the coders were recruited with promises like, "Come to Skardu for some low-headroom snowboarding."' Price made a little stagey flourish with his hands.

'We have to stop somewhere,' Jacob told Price. 'I need a phone. I have a strong desire to find out the chemical composition of fluid snow.'

'Hydrocarbonated surfactants, water, and glycol,' Price said. 'Impossible to weaponise that.'

Jacob read everything over again. He found himself memorising dates and quantities, as if that would help. When he finally put the papers away, Price said, 'Since you left the Palfreyman house, Ms Cornick has moved. Or has been moved. We've lost her for now, but have the vehicle she was travelling in.'

Jacob's heart jumped. He parted his lips in an effort to relax his jaw.

'Palfreyman's security contractors shut off the camera feeds at the Norfolk house,' Price said. 'But something else scrambled traffic cameras along roads from Norfolk to the Wye Valley.' He picked up his phone, unlocked it, and passed it to Jacob. 'That *something else* is very interesting to us,' he said, then told Jacob to watch the video.

The footage showed the street outside the Bibliothèque Méjanes, the spines of the statuesque French classics, the sliding doors to the atrium. It also showed the roof of a dark blue Renault Koleos parked opposite those doors. A figure on a bicycle went by. Then a man carrying five trays of eggs. The slider measured twenty-six seconds of nothing, then a sudden thick flight of pigeons, birds and their shadows, black in the air and on the street.

A figure appeared moving left to right. Someone who, like the man with the eggs, may well have walked past the gendarmerie moments earlier. The person was clumsy, rough, ugly. A shape like raw dough poured into men's clothing.

Jacob suspended his breathing.

The unhealthy specimen stopped near the auto door, then tucked himself closer to the building, beside the bike rack.

A moment later Taryn appeared, walking in the shallow drain of the dry street, moving right to left. She wore a cotton tunic dress, white with a pale blue stripe, and a light cardigan. Her legs were bare, and her feet in strappy sandals. Her red hair was arranged in a loose, artfully messy bun. She paused adjacent to the library entrance, stamped her heels to clean her sandals, then lifted her phone—which she'd had in her hand—to frame a shot of the sculpture.

'I'd like to see Taryn's photos. She'd have a clear shot of that loitering person,' Jacob said. To sound helpful.

'Nothing yet uploaded to her cloud account,' Price said.

'I'm surprised you got a judge to sign off on that,' Jacob said.

'The year we're having, you shouldn't be surprised.'

Taryn Cornick lowered her phone. She averted her face. Then turned her whole body but tilted her face back. It looked like a competing compulsion—not to be caught staring, and to keep her eye on something that frightened her.

The stumping, solid figure started towards her.

The driver's door of the Koleos flew open, and Jacob Berger emerged. He hurried towards the lurker, meaning to intercept him before he got to Taryn. Behind the glass doors a pale, stooped man appeared. Taryn Cornick saw the man and waved.

'Claude Pujol,' said Price. 'And then we lose it for fifty-one seconds.'

Jacob fervently wished the video had stopped before his appearance. Why hadn't he waited to see it before telling his story? Okay. He'd watch it to its end and make adjustments.

The image dissolved into bands of violent static. It came in ripples and pulses and was not a lost signal but interference.

Jacob's scrubbing finger had moved towards the video's slider when the static came, but he didn't touch it.

There was a final burst of white, then the image of the street blinked back into existence.

A thin veil of gun smoke hung in the still morning air. Only Claude Pujol remained in the frame. He was pacing back and forth in front of the library. Several times he rushed back through the doors, waving his key card at the lock. He'd go in, stop, and come back out. It was as if he were looking for something immediately beyond the doors but was unable to find it.

There was blood on the cobbles. The enamelled steel of the statuesque book nearest the door had a starburst dent. The door to the Koleos remained open.

Pujol stopped pacing. For a moment he was absolutely motionless.

Then he began to claw at his own face. Not in the manner of one stricken by grief. There was no sense in which his violence was a gesture. His nails dug into his lower eyelids and dragged them down. On a third pass they tore. His hands moved repeatedly from the crown of his head downwards, drawing torn hair through the blood until his chin and neck were bearded with it. He staggered off to the left, still tearing at himself.

'God in Heaven!' said Jacob.

'Twelve minutes later, witnesses saw Pujol scale the barrier on the overbridge above the on-ramp to the autoroute,' Price said.

'I tried to get Taryn into my car,' Jacob said. 'She walked away from me, and I followed her.'

'It was the discharge of a shotgun that damaged the sculpture. Surely you heard it?'

Jacob shook his head.

'We have Ms Cornick on several cameras earlier, walking from her hotel to the library. But neither of you after that.'

'And the big guy?'

'He made off into a nearby parking garage, where the cameras lost him. We've checked the ownership of all the vehicles that left the garage in the next two hours. No leads.'

Jacob felt blank. He hoped he looked it. He moved the slider back to the moment before the eruption of static.

The shapeless man lumbered towards the poetically beautiful and uncertain Taryn Cornick. Jacob flung open the door of the Koleos. Claude Pujol appeared behind the glass, and Taryn waved to him. There was a flicker from the right. The body of a bird briefly between the camera and the road. Like the earlier pigeons, but closer to the camera. To be that big, it must have been close. Only another bird, fleet, moving into the field of view.

Jacob once again moved the slider a fraction back.

The man of proved but unbaked dough moved towards Taryn Cornick. She shrank back. The door of the SUV swung open, and Jacob moved to her rescue. Pujol reared whitely behind the glass, already a ghost of himself. Taryn Cornick collected herself and waved. A bird dropped to land on the street to the far left of the screen. It was too big to be that far from the camera, landing, but landing it was, because shadow and bird came together. Something flashed at its throat. A gleam of gold.

Static.

Jacob scrubbed back once more.

A bird much bigger than a pigeon came in to land. Bigger than a hawk. Some kind of raptor. Something bright haloed its head. Something hanging around its neck. It shook its wings and closed them.

Static.

Price said, 'I presume Palfreyman turned off his Norfolk security system because his wife asked him to. He is clearly still fond of wife number one. Positively uxorious. We've found a note on some of Mr Palfreyman's elegant personal stationery.' Price quoted from memory, and his memory was superb: '"Just to remind you that the uncomfortable object in your pocket is an OtterBox, containing a phone, fully charged, its charger and portable battery. Don't open the box—Box!—till you're on the other side. I know you won't be able to call until you come out again, but how about taking photos and video for me?"'

Jacob wished he'd put his note inside the OtterBox, rather than attaching it to the outside with a rubber band. He waited a moment, then said, 'Was this note found in the abandoned vehicle?'

'Yes. The Land Rover belonging to Palfreyman's head of security, Gavin Stuart. You wouldn't happen to have any idea what "other side" is being referred to in this friendly communication?'

'The other side of the English Channel?'

'And why the emphatic "Box"?'

'Pass,' said Jacob. He wondered how long it would be until Price figured out the handwriting was his. Price must have known Palfreyman was in Ireland. But Price had nothing further to say until they left the A11 just before Newmarket, when he told Jacob that there was also blood in the Land Rover. Then he was silent for the next three hours and 175 miles.

A couple of minutes after they went by the stone cross, they turned off from a road that ran along the edge of the Forest of Dean into a narrow lane. The lane took them between a hawthorn hedge and the nettle-clothed stone wall that bordered the grounds of Princes Gate. Jacob recognised the wall because he'd climbed over it in the dark and hadn't avoided the depredations of nettles.

Price drove faster than Jacob would have driven with such poor visibility and only very occasional passing bays. But of course Price knew the lane was closed. They eventually came to the fluorescent cones and police tape, to the constables in high-visibility gear holding glowsticks in their fists. Several squad cars filled the lane, and a police tow truck. Behind the tow truck was a fire appliance. It stood across an entrance to a field of rye, the grain showing bluish in the evening light.

The vegetation in the hedges on either side of the lane was shrunken and discoloured, not scorched, but wilted and darkened, like weeds that had had boiling water poured on them.

Price stopped behind the police vehicles, and they got out. Price paused to speak to an officer while Jacob walked on. He put out his hands to take the gloves someone offered. He stood still while someone else slipped paper booties on over his shoes.

It took Jacob a moment to recognise the remains of Stuart's Land Rover. The vehicle didn't even resemble a wreck. It was distorted, but not skewed or collapsed as cars are by crashes. The doors had come off, and the roof was bowed outwards, as if someone had *inflated* the whole car. Its tough automotive paint had crazed, like mud in a dry lakebed. The doorposts were bent, and the roof had separated from them. All the windows were missing, and the windscreen was lying in a single whitened piece on the road in front of the vehicle. The hood was depressed, the engine pushed out of its housing and down onto the road, as if something huge and heavy had stepped on it. The fog lights were cockeyed, and the headlights had popped right out of their sockets and were lying some distance up the lane.

Jacob walked around the car, keeping out of the way of the people taking photos and samples. Then he made another circuit, this time counting the doors.

'Yes,' said one of the police forensic team. 'There is one door missing.'

'Anything else?' Jacob asked.

'The driver and passenger. We have the passenger's identity, but not that of the driver.' The man paused. 'You'll be with MI5, like some of these other fellows.'

Jacob produced his ID, and the technician carried on in a more friendly manner. 'You see, Detective Inspector, there's what they're calling "the wave"—CCTV on the blink, in a kind of path passing through the country all the way from Norwich to here.'

Jacob nodded.

'If you don't mind me saying, you don't seem very surprised.'

'I've heard about it.'

'What did this, though?' said the man. 'Some kind of weapon?'

'A vehicle-bursting weapon?' Jacob said, and then, hearing the silence, looked at the technician and realised he was being taken at his word. 'Mate, seriously, what would anyone want with a vehicle-bursting weapon that wrecks the car but doesn't kill the occupants?'

'We don't know they're not dead. Only that they're missing.' The technician was defensive. 'And the fact remains I have never in my life seen a car that has come apart without a high-impact collision, or the assistance of explosives, or the jaws of life, or the equipment in a car wrecker's yard. And those wrecks look nothing like this. Also—when it comes to explosions—there's no chemical residue.'

'But that's not quite true, is it?' said Raymond Price, who had joined them. 'Other than the blood and tissue samples, there is something else you all agree is a "chemical residue" and also probably bodily.'

'Yes,' said the technician, all business again. 'There is silicone gel splattered about.'

'You wouldn't happen to know whether Ms Cornick had silicone breast implants, Jacob?'

Jacob shook his head.

'Are you sure? On close examination it's quite easy to tell.'

Jacob gritted his teeth.

'The driver might have had silicone implants, I suppose,' Price said, offhand.

'The car was at a standstill when the silicone—vessel—ruptured,' the technician said. 'Both the driver and Ms Cornick were in the back seat.'

Jacob said, 'Taryn was ill. Perhaps she had some kind of crisis, and the driver pulled over to see to her.'

'And her implants,' Price said.

'I mean, that's why the driver was in the back seat. He was trying to help her.'

'He?'

'It's Stuart's car.'

'We've accounted for Stuart. He returned to London with the doctor. The doctor who arrived when you were there.'

'Yes.'

'With his portable X-ray machine. For Taryn, who you told Rosemary had a urinary tract infection.'

'One so bad it was obstructive,' Jacob said, feeling proud of himself. 'The doctor was sent for discreetly because Alan Palfreyman thinks his ex-wife is a fugitive.'

'You're telling me that Palfreyman didn't know you were there? That the police had caught up with his ex?'

'He wouldn't have known till Stuart arrived and reported to him.'

'You must understand why I'm pushing you on what you know, Jacob. About Ms Cornick. About "the wave". You were with Ms Cornick for hours. Your movements are *peculiar*, Jacob, and your account of them is far from satisfactory. And now you're looking at this'—Price gestured at the wreck—'more close-mouthed than stumped. Plus, you flushed with annoyance when I implied that Ms Cornick might be doing the usual thing with her friend in the back seat of the Land Rover.'

The forensic team were all watching Jacob and Price with rapt attention. Price shot them an impatient glance. He grabbed the tender place on the inside of Jacob's elbow in a pinching grip and led him further along the hedgerow. Its plants were blanched and pasted to the stone walls like seaweed drying on a rocky shore.

Jacob dug in his heels and forcefully extracted his arm.

'I'm your ride, Jacob,' Price said sweetly.

Jacob tilted his head down to eye Price. He had a good four inches on the agent. 'And I'm surrounded by my fellow police officers. Are we finished here?'

Price looked around at the wilted vegetation, the forensic team in their bridal jumpsuits, and the clustered emergency vehicles.

Jacob said, 'I promised Rosemary I'd be there.'

'Rosemary knows you made the effort. Please, Jacob, spare me your indignation and explain this. Explain the wave. Explain how you know to say "he" of the driver.'

'I say "he" because it's generally men who carry off women. And because, unlike you, I hadn't established that it wasn't Stuart.'

'It wasn't. We've spoken to Stuart. He's not at all helpful. But from the little he said I gathered that you were still at the Norfolk house when he and the doctor departed.'

'Stuart might have come back after I left, for all I know. And why are we talking about an abduction anyway? We don't know that Ms Cornick was an unwilling passenger.'

'Safely back to "Ms Cornick", then?'

'I use her first name because I'm worried about her. Because she has a stalker, and now she's vanished.'

'And what about the snow machines? What's your take on them?'

'Haven't a clue. Low-headroom snowboarding sounds good to me. You people employ experts who spend all their time figuring out the innovations of cyberterrorists. So you tell *me* about the wave.'

Price gazed at Jacob, his head tilted back. Jacob felt as if he were being sniffed all over. 'What would you say if I told you that the twenty coders recruited by Dynamic Systems are, in fact, thirteen coders and seven cryptographers?'

At the word 'cryptographer' Jacob experienced an electric connection in his mind, a leap of intuition that spanned chasms and categories and felt almost physical. But Jacob's leap was aborted. His intuition came down somewhere spongy. He tried to retrace his mental steps. Cryptographers. Demons who were looking for a box—

'Jacob?' Price said.

Jacob blinked.

'You were in a bit of a fugue there.'

'I'm hungry,' Jacob said, but he thought, *The raven was right. There's a thing I literally cannot consider.* It was most annoying.

Price decided they must adjourn to a pub. They drove into the village of Princes Gate Magna and stopped at the Pale Lady. Jacob bought a pint and a pie with onion gravy and, on the side, a little furball of pea shoots in a pool of vinaigrette. He put on his listening face, which was pretty much identical to his I-don't-care-whether-you-live-or-die face.

Price was unperturbed or, Jacob suspected, pleased to have some company, anyone he could casually sharpen his claws on.

It began to rain after they arrived, and before long the pub stank of wet wool and damp shoes. The moisture activated all the other smells in the carpet—spilled beer, deodorising carpet cleaner, and dog. Jacob had mistaken the blurry pelt in front of the fire for a bearskin, but it was a Newfoundland, elderly, overweight, and determined to stay put. Jacob only identified it as a dog when it lifted its head to scan the room as if making a calculation like, 'Do we have enough salt and vinegar crisps for this lot?'

Price polished off his ploughman's sandwich and produced his phone. He looked at it, pursed his lips, and put it back. He got up abruptly and walked off through a set of brass-and-glass swing doors. They juddered closed. Jacob stared at their oscillating reflection of the bar: time-blackened oak, greasy red leather booths, old men in tweed caps and green Wellingtons. His fingers touched his jacket, itching for a phone.

He should just borrow one and make a call to Hemms at the hospital. He turned to the booth nearest his table and asked the young people sitting there if he could borrow a phone.

A girl with pink dreadlocks picked up hers and showed it to Jacob. 'We had bars before, but not for the last half hour.' She sounded aggrieved.

Jacob stiffened and made a more careful examination of the room. And the hard-to-see figure leapt into focus. Shift gave Jacob a dazzling, eager smile, picked up his glass, came over, and slipped into Price's seat.

Shift didn't look like someone who'd had an operation within the last thirty hours. He looked well. 'I was hanging about waiting for ravens,' he said. 'But then I saw you in the lane and followed you here. I thought you might want to know how Taryn is.' He didn't wait for a sign of assent. 'She's taken a battering. But soon we'll carry her to the hot springs at Forsha, where she can recuperate.'

'The demon harmed her?'

'I had hoped my presence would put a dampener on it,' Shift said.

'Why do I get the feeling you're lying to me?'

Shift was quiet a moment, then he beamed. 'Because you have a knack for knowing when I'm lying.' Then something else occurred to him, and he looked disappointed. 'Unless it's not especially me. You're just good at spotting the holes in a story.' He glanced up through his eyelashes and said, 'I was hoping it was especially me.'

Jacob ignored this. 'So Taryn is going to be all right?'

'She's injured because I underestimated the demon. But now it's trapped in my gate, which means I have to take Taryn to another gate so she can get to her speaking engagements. That suits me. I can try to catch and question one of the demons entering the Sidh through Hell's Gate. So, after the springs, I'll take Taryn there.'

'Is there a Heaven's Gate—like the movie?'

'I don't know the movie. Heaven is closed, I believe, though I have no idea for how long. What I do know is that The Great God of the Deserts, the God from the Void, sequestered himself many hundreds of years ago. His worshippers had too many competing views of his nature, and it unsettled his mind. That's a thing that can happen to gods. They're very impressionable.'

Jacob sat with his mouth open.

Price came back through the swing doors, pocketing his wallet. He slowed as he approached the table, then took up a position directly between Shift and Jacob, as if he were a tennis umpire. He put his car keys on the table. 'Jacob, I have just secured myself a room at this establishment. Their only available room, I'm afraid. You can go to the Holiday Inn at Monmouth. But we'll want an early start.'

Jacob put his hand over the keys.

'A local?' Price asked Jacob, while examining Shift.

'Your friend asked to borrow my phone,' Shift said, then produced his phone and set it on the table. The phone was, of course, in an Otter-Box, along with its charging cord and a portable power bank.

Jacob and Price just stared at the phone. Shift prodded the box with his forefinger, pushing it closer to Jacob.

'Is that an OtterBox?' Price's question was blithe, peaceable.

Shift twisted his neck to read the brand mark on the box. 'That's what it says on its catch,' he said.

'And where did you find such a useful thing?'

'Amazon,' said Shift. 'Same place as I get my books.'

'Do you reside in these parts?'

Shift gazed at Price, frowned, and gave an answer that followed on from the last thing he'd been saying. 'I'd support local custom, but the nearest booksellers these days are the two antiquarians in Tintern.' He looked behind him at the nearest of the old men, perhaps a native of

Tintern. The man, at once grave and wide awake, met Shift's gaze, gave a slight bow, and said, '*Mab tylwyth teg.*'

'Price' was a Welsh name. Was Price a Welsh national and a product of the Welsh education system's endorsement of the language?

He was. 'Son of the fairy,' Price said. 'That's fighting talk.'

'But the gentleman was very polite about it,' Shift said. 'So I don't think I need to feel that my father has been maligned.' Then, frowning at Jacob, 'Why is it a problem that my phone is in a plastic box?'

Jacob opened the box and removed the phone. 'It isn't a problem. Thank you for the loan. I only want to check on a friend who is in hospital.'

Shift, equally smooth: 'I'll give you your privacy. Return it when you're done.' He picked up the OtterBox and went back to his booth.

Jacob opened the contacts list and deleted his own number. Then he tried to connect in order to find the number for Norwich Hospital.

'Phones aren't working,' Price said. Then, 'Agreed?' to the fidgeting young people in the booth.

They nodded. Jacob could see they didn't like the look of Price, which made him notice the lethal malice beneath the man's waspishness.

Price said, 'Take the phone outside, Jacob, and its owner will follow you.'

'What are you planning?'

'I'd like to get him on his own so I can pat him down.'

'For what?'

'Whatever kills phones and CCTV.'

'You're joking.' Jacob managed to sound sceptical and astonished.

'Take that call outside—colleague.' And, softer, 'I'll need those car keys back.'

'You're going to abduct the guy because his phone is in an OtterBox?'

'And because no phones are working. And the television is on the fritz.'

'And he has a bit of an Arab look to him,' said Jacob. 'Let's not forget that.'

'Just do what I tell you, Berger.'

Jacob got up and ducked under the pub's low lintel. It was pouring outside. The streetlight across from the pub also seemed to have a troubled signal, shining as it was through a static of rain.

Jacob huddled in under the eaves. Nothing happened. No one followed him out.

He waited a good ten minutes.

Through the beaded curtain of water coming down from the thatch Jacob saw the lit blue square of a phone booth along the road, outside what once had been a village post office and was now a grocer, newsagent, and post shop.

Jacob made a dash for it. He would call a cab, find a hotel in Monmouth, book a room, then phone Norwich Hospital and ask after Rosemary. That was a plan. He would dance attendance on Price until Price was satisfied that he, Jacob, was no more or less mystified than anyone else.

The stretch of gravel around the phone booth was sodden. But Jacob's shoes were waterproof high-tops. He climbed into the booth, shook himself, and scraped back his dripping hair. Before he consulted the phonebook—which was in one piece, though fattened and yellowed—he checked the phone from the OtterBox. It still had no signal. That glove had quite a range. Unless Shift wasn't wearing it and had left it outside the pub somewhere.

Jacob was on the landline to the Holiday Inn, reading out his credit card number, when Price's car pulled up alongside. Jacob concluded his business, left the phone booth, and got in. 'I was about to call myself a taxi,' he said. 'Might I have the car?'

'That establishment'—Price nodded towards the Pale Lady—'serves breakfast at seven. Please be there on time.' Price put out his hand for Shift's cell phone. Jacob gave it to him and watched Price produce a laptop and connect the phone to it. Price sent Jacob to the boot to find a factory-fresh phone in the collection of models he had there. Price cloned Shift's phone. And as he waited for the operation to finish, he said in a conversational tone, 'This is the post shop from which Khalef and Tahan dispatched their credit cards before asking directions to the holloway.'

The shop's interior was lit by a blue security light, an urban colour, antithetical to the wet stonework and minimal signage. Jacob wondered what it would have been like for Taryn to have grown up with all this beauty. He'd grown up in a new housing tract, streets where there was nowhere to walk unobserved and the only interesting variety was supplied by people and cars.

Price returned the original phone to Jacob and, without further ceremony or instructions, reversed down the road and stopped outside the pub. He bade Jacob goodnight, pulled up his coat collar against the rain, and hurried indoors.

Jacob waited. He understood that Price expected him to return the phone to Shift, who, contrary to Price's wishes, had not followed Jacob out into the night and made himself vulnerable to Price's boundless— lawless—curiosity.

Jacob continued to wait, hoping Price wasn't hovering in the bar but had taken himself off to his nice, dry bed. When Jacob finally decided he'd waited long enough, the pub was preparing to close. There was a crowd of middle-aged locals by the till, in a full flood of brain-freezingly dull conversations about a football game they'd missed because the TV was playing up. The barmaid was at the door handing out umbrellas. The group of old men were in the porch, peering off into the gleaming darkness, wearing identical expressions of curiosity, pride, and soft wonder. Their eyes were fixed on Shift, who had somehow left the pub without being spotted by Price or Jacob and was waiting under the last streetlight by the gate to the churchyard.

Jacob ducked back into the parlour, put a pound coin on the bar, and took a packet from the rack of gum. He stuffed a stick in his mouth and chewed. His inattention to the type he'd grabbed rewarded him with a burning burst of cinnamon.

Jacob couldn't turn off the phone. He was suspicious of the power and range of its microphone and of what MI5 could do. He hoped it wouldn't be able to transmit near to the Gatemaker's glove, but the wads of gum he pasted over its microphone and cameras were an extra precaution.

The barmaid offered him an umbrella. He shook his head, thanked her, and pointed at Price's car.

'That was kind of your friend,' she said, clearly inviting him to tell her more about their high-handed, unpleasant guest. Jacob only wished her goodnight. He felt her eyes on him as he strode off through the rain. He went out under the dripping trees, heading towards the slick green cave where Shift waited.

Shift produced the OtterBox and held it out. He let Jacob place the phone in the box but didn't shut it away. 'I thought I should let them make their calls,' he said, tilting his chin at the pub patrons.

Price would love this admission of culpability.

Jacob folded Shift's hands in his own and pressed them together. The OtterBox clicked shut. 'Keep that phone dry. It's an electronic instrument.' He spoke as if to a child.

Shift pointed his nose at Jacob and scented the air. 'I'm hungry. You had a pie, and something cinnamon afterwards. I only had a half of cider.'

'The cinnamon is sugarless gum, and I'm sure aspartame is another of those things you can't eat.'

'I'll go into the churchyard and get a mouse,' Shift said.

Jacob realised he still had the box and Shift's strong-fingered hands between his own. He let go. 'Price knows the phone is for Taryn. The note I wrote her was with the OtterBox. It got left behind in the car. I'm not sure whether Price has guessed that it was me who wrote it. Thank God it was Stuart who supplied the phone.'

'Your note must've fallen out of Taryn's pocket.'

'On the drive, rather than the seam-splitting demolition of Stuart's vehicle?' Jacob said. He paused, waiting for Shift to explain what had happened. Shift let the pause run on. He turned his head to listen to something behind the sound of rain dripping from the trees.

Jacob said, 'I never did get to make my call to Norwich Hospital and ask after Hemms.'

'Let's walk on and you can do that,' Shift said. 'I gave my glove to this tree. The phone won't work till we're well away from it.'

Jacob glanced up at the green ceiling above them. He was glad that Price hadn't yet heard anything. He wondered what the glove's range was. It hadn't used to disrupt phones so dramatically. He'd been able to call Hemms from the back lawn of Palfreyman's house, but perhaps that was far enough off. The glove had disrupted the cameras around the Bibliothèque Méjanes, and presumably the glove caused the wave of interference that followed Shift from Norfolk. Or was that the demon? Or—and this seemed more likely—the glove roused by the proximity of a demon.

Jacob then wondered what giving the glove to a tree entailed. What language would a person use to get the attention and compliance of a tree? Did you simply ask the tree, 'Would you mind holding this for a minute?'

Jacob longed to ask many things but was afraid of being overheard (and sounding insane). He looked back at the hotel. The lights in the bar had gone out. There was a taxi beside his car, several people piling into it. Jacob checked for a twitching curtain, for Price, who'd be able to see his car, still parked and not, as it should be, partway to Monmouth.

'No one is walking,' Jacob said. 'I think you're going to be out of luck with your mouse.'

'What?'

'You wanted a "mouse" for money, right?'

Shift looked puzzled.

'Money for a meal?' Jacob prompted.

'The going rate for mice is very low,' Shift said, solemn.

Jacob's ears got hot. He had assumed that 'mouse' was some quaint term Shift had for a kerb crawler. He had imagined some very damp fumbling in the churchyard. 'You mean a real mouse,' he said.

Shift laughed. 'The ways in which you want to think badly of me are interesting.'

'Who eats mice?' Jacob muttered. He was now pretending not to know what Shift was talking about.

'Owls,' said Shift.

The phone in the OtterBox gave a shudder. 'Let me take this,' Jacob said. 'You go do whatever you're planning to do with mice.'

Shift returned the box to Jacob and walked back towards the splash of green.

The alert was just the phone connecting to its telco. So Jacob used it to call Norwich Hospital.

Hemms was recovering well, said the ward sister. She was resting. Jacob said he'd let her sleep and would call again the next day. He ended the call and walked back towards the pub and Price's car. He stopped by the churchyard and waited. By his reckoning he'd have only four hours in bed at the Holiday Inn. Less if he kept standing here.

Still, he waited.

Somewhere in the soft welter of rain and night a small animal screamed in pain and terror. Jacob stared into the black air between the tall stone gateposts. He got wet. He ignored his impatience, which was after all childish and unprofessional. He stood there holding the phone, which didn't vibrate again. And while he waited he changed many of his ideas. If he were a person who made plans he'd have changed those too. But Jacob Berger was someone without any real aims of his own, someone who gave himself over to the better judgement of others and let himself be aimed.

Eventually Shift reappeared, looking very wet but more lively. His mouth was rosy. He said he'd got a rat, which meant he didn't have to wait in owl to digest it. 'A rat is a meal for a man too. So that's good. I didn't keep you waiting long.'

'You were an owl?' Jacob said.

Shift nodded.

'And no one else but me knows you can be an owl?'

'They think I can't right now, because of the iron.'

'And why am I in on your secret?'

'Because you can keep secrets.'

'I'm paid to keep the details of investigations I'm working on close to my chest. I'm not paid to keep your secrets, Shift.'

'You don't keep secrets because you're paid to, Jacob. The secrets are your coin. If you ran out of them you'd feel impoverished.'

Jacob thought he'd been seeing Shift as an obscure, fey being. Whimsical, because of the things he'd say. But it was bluntness. Each bit of poetry was a statement of fact. He was sharing and showing himself. A tree was holding his glove for him, and he could eat as an owl and digest as a man. And he wanted Jacob to know what he could do, because they had an alliance.

But because Jacob didn't quite believe the owl part without seeing it, and because he was far too frightened to want to witness it, he asked the kind of question one earnest fantasy fan might ask another. The goal of such a question would be one-upmanship—one nerd wanting to demonstrate that the other hadn't thought through whatever marvel they meant to convince their listeners of. There'd been boys like that at Jacob's school. He'd sometimes eavesdrop on them with fascinated contempt. Everything they were interested in was immaterial; the content of their thoughts was, to Jacob's mind, a waste of time. But the structure of their thinking was another matter, and Jacob had listened because he was attracted by their relentless logic, even if it was only ever applied to nonsense.

What he said to Shift was: 'So—do you leave your clothes puddled on the ground and flap up into the boughs of a tree?'

'I would if these weren't my clothes.' Shift passed a hand over his lumpy woollen jersey and baggy tweed trousers. 'I made these myself. And out of myself. Someone else has to help me—shear the sheep who is me, clip the goat who is me. And, if I'm very determined, which I sometimes must be, skin alive the hindquarters of the bull who is me—for leather, for shoes. It can't be so much skinning that I die. I have to change once I feel myself in danger of dying. Whenever I change I'm not injured anymore, which is why I'm not wearing Taryn's scratches now.

'Anyway—once I've got the raw materials I have to cure and tan, or wash, card, dye, spin, weave, knit everything myself. Only then will my clothes change when I change. And none of the others—sheep, goat, bull, owl, eel—is any less me than this body, this mix of several species who is speaking to you now. I chose to be human. When I was little my mother had to coax me back out of the marsh—its water and air—with her love, and with berries dipped in honey, and with stories. I wanted her touch, her smell, her voice, her view of things more than I wanted to live in scales or fur or feathers. I had her long enough and loved her well enough to learn to be human and remain human.'

Shift stopped talking and gazed at Jacob with an expression of mild expectation.

Jacob had a stone in his throat.

Shift added, 'I wish I could make a better job of my clothes. My mother taught me about weather and tides, she taught me eight languages and how to make various medicines, but she never thought to teach me to spin and weave and sew, because I was a boy. It seems silly now. There were many days I'd be reluctant to stop being a falcon or a fish, but to my mother I was still a boy and not a girl.'

Jacob laughed because he was startled, but also in a kind of delighted pride at being party to something so strange and wonderful. Also he found it funny that Shift the owl wasn't on a strict diet. 'You do eat red meat,' Jacob said, still laughing.

'Yes. I do, and I'm not allergic to iron, or not very. I'm just maintaining a fiction. I want the sidhe to consider me one of them and overlook my other ancestry. Though I should say that grain does not agree with me, which is why I didn't have a pie.' Shift clasped Jacob's arm, adjusting his grip so his hand slid up Jacob's sleeve and his wet fingers found dry skin. He came over all brisk. 'You're going to drive your . . . master's . . . car away, and I'm going to retrieve my glove and return to Taryn.'

'Raymond Price is not my master,' Jacob said, deeply indignant, but let himself be led.

They reached the pub. Jacob paused with his hand on the driver's-door handle and, quickly, tried to think what Shift should know. Because Shift was his partner too, someone with whom he was working on an investigation.

Shift had the OtterBox under his jersey and was hugging it to himself. Between the lumpy knit, the box itself, and Jacob's wad of cinnamon gum pressed over the microphone, surely Price wouldn't be able to hear them. Though, if he was still awake and at his window, Price could see them, together in an empty village square, at the end of a long confabulation. Over breakfast Price might remark on how much Jacob and Shift had to say to each other. The safest response to that would be to say that he was sounding Shift out. 'And what have you discovered?' Price would ask. 'He's some kind of local,' Jacob would say. 'Or seasonal, maybe. I asked if he rented a holiday home, but he didn't answer me. He's a little simple, and I couldn't figure out which end to pick him up by.'

Jacob decided that Price couldn't overhear them. 'Look,' he said. 'I should pass this on—to you, Taryn, and the raven. The server farm is using ski resort and theatrical snow machines, without providing refrigeration. Possibly they're only acquiring what they need in the wrong order, but somehow I don't think so. Because they have some kind of refrigeration anyway. Or something doing the same job. There's one very cold building at the site. I'm just going to say it—a supernaturally cold building.'

'They're making snow for something that likes snow, but which comes with its own cold,' Shift said.

He was quick. Jacob really had underestimated him. He said, 'And they've recruited cryptographers as well as coders.'

'Ah!' Shift was excited. 'They want the Firestarter, and they must think that whatever—'

Jacob had stepped into a steam room. He was surrounded by white obscurity. It was inside him, stifling all his senses, cooking his brain.

He found himself leaning on the car. It was wet, and water had soaked all the way through his shirt front. Shift was shaking him. The OtterBox dropped from Shift's jersey onto the gravel, and Jacob saw the lozenge of gum come unstuck from the microphone.

Jacob held Shift off and set a finger against his own lips. He turned his eyes to the boxed phone and gazed at it meaningfully. Then looked back at Shift—who'd got it and was clearly wondering why Jacob had taken so long to tip him off about its having been tampered with. Shift's expression was inquiring, then abruptly furious. He didn't just release Jacob; he shoved him away, snatched up the box, and stalked off in his squelching felt shoes.

'And we were getting on so fucking swimmingly!' Jacob shouted after him, for no good reason and nobody's benefit. Then he got into Price's car, drove a mile down the road, and pulled over, marring the mossy edge of the forest not fifty feet from the tree where Beatrice Cornick had fallen. He ran the heater for a time, tilted the seat back, and closed his eyes.

Fifteen

The Summer Road

It was a much smaller party that set out from the springs. Taryn, Shift, Jane, Neve, and three other sidhe. They travelled without the litter. Taryn didn't have much stamina, but they made short days, with many rest stops. She and Jane kept to the path and took their time, while Shift and the sidhe ranged off after game—rabbits, wood pigeons, quail.

Three days' walk took them many miles along a high path incised in the flanks of the mountains. Game supplemented the food they carried—cakes made of nut flour and sweet bean paste, dried fruit and hard cheeses. Taryn fought her cravings for wine, sugar, and salt. And by the time the party had divided, and only Jane, Neve, Shift, and she remained on the downhill road, her cravings had gone.

On the long descent the views of the encircling mountains, and foothills of tussock and wildflowers, gradually packed themselves away. The landscape became beautiful in a more managed way. Days were warmer, and nights milder.

By the fourth day, the path they were on passed into an endless half-pipe of trees, a tunnel of overhanging shade that let the sun warm them for several hours before midday, and then descended into a gloom that kept them cool all afternoon. Some trees were coming into fruit—tart cherry and early plum—while others were still in blossom.

This was, Jane said, the Summer Road.

At intervals this continuous strip of orchard broadened around a stream or pond, where berry bushes grew, along with self-seeded bean vines and tomato plants—small yet—and the feathery tops of carrots, and radishes, chard and collards, beets and potatoes. These nodes of food-forest all had cooking sites. There were stone-lined earth ovens capable of feeding scores of people, and firepits covered by copper grilles, more suitable for a party their size. Copper pots were stacked by the source of water. Patches of flourishing fern could be cut to pad the ground under the bedrolls they carried (Shift was carrying Taryn's). There was aloe to wash with, or soapwort.

Shift, Neve, and Jane would unselfconsciously strip off to wash themselves and their clothes, then stand by the firepit, naked and steaming. They'd hang their laundered clothes in the tree branches—Neve twisting her overdress into a long rope that she then wound around the trunk of a tree. The dress would still be damp in the morning, evenly creased, and would mould itself to her body.

Each night Taryn closed her eyes on stars sparkling through fresh spring foliage. She would sleep deeply, not stirring until dawn. She slept, ate, drank, walked. There was little conversation between Neve and Shift, and what there was seemed polite and practical and was conducted in their language. Theirs was a comfortable silence, and Jane's, Taryn realised, was respectful of her need to recover.

Taryn was better every day, stronger than she had been in years. She grew lithe and light-footed. Her hair softened and brightened; her skin felt supple and smooth. She was full of a sense of well-being and, as she became more accustomed to the plain fresh food, she felt she had never tasted such sweet peppery radishes, succulent earthy potatoes, savoury sticky rabbit meat, and huge cherries that gave between her teeth with a hard *crack* followed by a flood of sharply perfumed juice. The wildflowers, the tender foliage of the trees, each sunset with its high, lucent skies and soft shoals of cloud, all of it wrapped Taryn in a perfect sense of safety and contentment. She was enchanted, wide-eyed with wonder at a marsh covered in tiny dark blue flowers, and the apricot and fox-coloured songbirds, and the shy deer, their hides creamy white and dappled grey. All animals of types unknown to her, like the sleek, coal-black bear that ambled away from Neve's warning gaze, and the herd of grey-and-chestnut-spotted horses streaming along a ridge, and the big lake eels with their plum-purple skins. Fairy animals, each poised and pacific but somehow passionately alive.

The party descended in ease by the shallow uphill and slightly less shallow downhill undulations of the Summer Road. Despite the changes in the landscape, Taryn felt herself cleaving to it as if it were somewhere she was intimate with and loved; the setting of some spectacular alteration in her circumstances, like that hunting camp in the Rockies where she bewitched the Muleskinner.

It was by this making of comparisons to analyse her feelings that Taryn returned from her period of healing to who she was, what mattered to her, and what was inescapable. Her troubles had pressed on her for weeks, not just ill health caused by the demon but the Muleskinner's slow approach and what she thought she owed him—or worried he'd think she owed him. And there were other failings: how she took her former husband's generosity for granted, and how little kindness she seemed able to show to her father. The rest of it—her book, the festivals, her agent's and publisher's expectations—receded. But what had taken the place of the pressures wasn't Taryn's own tranquillity; it was the land itself, the Sidh, promising always to be there, always to be the same. Promising also that it would be the same Taryn who stepped out with sound knees and clear eyes from this blue lake, or stone hearth, or apple shade. *Come again, be again*—that was its promise, a sense of permanence Taryn hadn't felt since she was under ten years old and only able to imagine that she would always stay at Princes Gate with her grandparents, always find the same old Monopoly set, quoits, croquet hoops and mallets, the familiar punt, the cats—only a little indifferent whenever she arrived—but all as it should be, the same, *permanent*. The Sidh was turning Taryn into a child again, a child who knew everything sustaining would last. It gave her back that knowledge beyond faith—what the faithful meant when they said 'faith'.

In the week they were on the Summer Road they twice passed small mixed parties of sidhe and Taken going the opposite direction. And at one encampment a single sidhe woman appeared on the grassy path near a stream and brought them a cake made of apple and walnuts and honey. She sat for a time with Neve and spoke only to her, a little deferent. She scarcely looked at Jane, Taryn, and Shift.

That evening, while Taryn and Jane were bathing in a pool downstream, Jane explained a few things about the Summer Road, its emptiness and long cultivation, and how and where the sidhe lived. She began by saying that Neve had her house near the Gate she guarded but didn't maintain a household in one dwelling. 'She moves around, with her usual retinue, and often leaves her more vulnerable dependents, like children, in places salubrious to them, often in human care. But never for long, because the children begin to pine without their daily ration of

Neve's attention. On this journey you will see a few dwellings. They're close to the roads, and most are guest houses, like the house at Forsha Springs. The roads move between gates and cut-throughs, or desirable places to visit: a lake, a river landing, hot springs, one of the ancient forests where certain kinds of wild food flourish, like truffles or pine nuts. Trails go to the coast, where the sidhe hunt seals for their skins, or up to mountain passes, where the white tigers and leopards and foxes live, or to faraway rivers full of alluvial gold. But most of the roads are arterial forests of fruiting trees.'

'They're nomads,' Taryn said.

Jane nodded. 'The only sizeable settlement is on the coast at the mouth of the River Seinisteigh, where they hold the Moot in late summer every ten years.'

In Europe, long before canals and railways were built, there were paths for packhorses and roads for carts and carriages. For a long time in Britain that had meant Roman roads, the remnants of a civilisation that understood that the control of a territory was a matter of getting armed men from one place to another at speed. Taryn had yet to see a fortress or watchtower in the Sidh. But what would these people have to watch out for, or defend themselves against? Certainly not one another, since they seemed to hold everything but their Taken in common. The recent incursion of demons appeared to astonish them, but their astonishment didn't seem to give them any sense of urgency about putting a stop to it.

What's so good, Taryn thought, *about a world touched so lightly by people?* She had always enjoyed cities, Paris and Berlin, Vancouver and Hong Kong. She loved living in London, though lately she'd felt disturbed by the ghostliness of Marble Arch and its surrounds at night, no lights on in the apartments, all of them owned but few of them occupied, while in the daytime the homeless—many of them refugees—washed their clothes in the fountains and slept beside them on the grass as they dried. And, even for her, enough money seemed to mean more money all the time. There was always something new to pay for the privilege of existence and participation in her city. If her father hadn't paid for the hospital, she'd be very careful with money now. It was two months until her next royalty cheque.

Taryn had a two-book contract; she had qualifications and no student debt, thanks to her father. She had no cause for complaint or fear about her future. And sooner or later she'd have time to settle on a plan for her next book and write her proposal for Angela.

In the months before Carol's wedding, Carol and Taryn had talked about their futures at length over good bistro lunches in restaurants near Carol's place of work. They'd sat at a window table to take stock of their lives. Taryn could still see her friend, champagne flute held high while, on the other side of the glass, cavalcades of lunchtime shoppers went by with their boutique bags. 'I've found someone I love and trust enough to marry,' Carol said. 'Your book is a success. Look at us, finally on our way.'

Now, bedded down under the black and blazing skies of the Sidh, Taryn thought, *Why is happiness so self-congratulatory?* Because surely that had been happiness.

One evening, when Taryn and Jane were by a stream scrubbing cooking pans, their seats damp and hands red with cold and stippled by grit, Taryn asked Jane whether this love she had for the landscape meant she was bewitched. 'Does it go on like this? Does the feeling eclipse everything?'

'No. You're not "Taken" in the traditional way. Shift only protects you. Do you remember the children at Neve's house?'

Taryn recalled one little figure, rosy with health but somehow sullen and dazed.

'If Neve told one of them to play, it would be like a hawk when the falconer pulls off its hood. It would take wing, so to speak, shout, and gambol, and produce childish fancies. And if Neve then told it to be peaceful, the child would lie about, suck its fingers, and sleep. If Neve instructed *you* to play, you'd only say, "Play what?"'

'True,' said Taryn.

'You're just falling in love with the Sidh. Anyone would.'

Taryn picked up another handful of grit and continued to scour the pan of its sticky residue of cooked duck egg.

'Like you I'm here without ever having been Taken in the usual sense,' Jane said. 'Let me tell you the story.

'I first laid eyes on Shift when he came into my printing shop, where I was sitting with my type trays and composing block trying to set what I thought would be my last piece of paying work—a small job for a small fee. My legs had been bothering me for months. They'd become ulcerated, and it had got to the stage where I wasn't able to stand to compose and was scarcely able to remain upright long enough to set up the press when each plate was done.

'Shift arrived carrying a copy of the Bible that I had printed for Mr Charles Thomson. It was a sweltering summer day, but he was wearing gloves and wouldn't take them off when he was showing me what he admired about my Bible. Of course, his sidhe ancestry meant he was having to defend himself from the holy book. He told me he thought my Bible was a fine piece of work, and he'd like to commission me to print something for him. He had eighty pages in manuscript, and he wasn't at all sure how many pages that would make in print. As to the print run, he was thinking two thousand copies.

'That was an unprecedented number. I was curious to know what the manuscript was that he thought he could sell in that quantity and how he planned to pay me. He was a gentleman, but—"

'Wait,' said Taryn. 'You're talking about Charles Thomson's Bible, 1808, Philadelphia?'

'Yes. I was a citizen of Philadelphia, having come at seven years of age from Scotland with my family,' Jane said.

Taryn's bibliographic mind suggested the rest: Jane Aitken, an early American printer, who died in the poorhouse.

Jane Aitken, no longer astonished by the facts of her own life, had failed to notice Taryn's suffused cheeks and continued to tell her story.

'Shift showed me his manuscript. The writing was in our alphabet, but a language I couldn't recognise. I tried sounding it out, but its phonetics were alien. He said some time ago he had tried to invent an alphabet for this language—one of its own, as St Cyril had for Russian, but had lost the manuscript written in that invented alphabet. Using an existing alphabet to approximate the phonetics of a wholly oral language was something his mother had worked at and encouraged him to try. "She was much better at it than I am, and I made this work to honour her. I used the Roman alphabet and was very careful to establish and maintain consistency with the rules of phonology and grammar."

'I said, "What language is this?"

'He said, "One of the few I've had time to learn again."

'I couldn't make any sense of his "again". And he hadn't answered my question. He went on to explain that the manuscript was a collection of songs. "Songs and poems," he said. "I didn't have the heart to begin again with an encyclopaedia, because the manuscript I lost was an encyclopaedia. It was a pretty piece of illustrated work, and I'm sure someone has it and is looking after it. Anyway, the people whose songs these are aren't scholarly, and only have a child's interest in taxonomy. So an encyclopaedia is pointless. I really have to stop trying to teach them anything."

'I was tired, so I passed over all my questions to explain how I'd had to sell my printing press to cover my debts. But that a good friend of mine had leased it back to me so I might keep making books. I told him I only had the means of printing his book because of the grace and favour of my friend. But I didn't tell him I was ill and that the poorhouse was looming. I only accepted his commission because he offered to pay part upfront. In Spanish gold. I didn't ask where it came from. In the Old World, Napoleon's war was only just over, and all sorts of people and monies were moving through the Americas. I took his commission, though I thought I'd go blind setting all those alien words. I used the money to buy back my press, as if by buying back my livelihood and freedom my health might follow.

'Only days after that my legs worsened, and my health collapsed. I kept my lodgings and hired a nurse, but I soon exhausted my funds and ended up in a charity hospital. Then, once I was strong enough to move, the hospital sent me to the poorhouse in Norristown, outside the city. People must work in the poorhouse, but I couldn't get out of bed. And once my fever left me and I began to regain some strength, it turned out that the ghost of the fever had got into my brain. I couldn't tell whether I was awake or asleep, and my dreams and nightmares kept creeping up on me in the daytime. I was mourning all my losses. But what grieved me most was that I'd misplaced that gentleman's manuscript of songs no doubt taught to him by the natives of some South Seas island. I would dream about that manuscript and cry out my apologies, like a madwoman convinced of her own strange sinfulness.'

Taryn interrupted Jane to ask what name Shift had given her.

'Mr Shaw is what I heard and what he wrote down for me on the order. But the name on the manuscript was the Gaelic, *Seaghdh*, which means "hawkish". Then Jane sighed. 'In time my disorderly shouting and weeping caused me to fall from the poorhouse into a madhouse. I was lost to all my friends. And unlucky, because I might have gone to the Quaker hospital, but was instead sent to a crueller, more remote place.

'But Mr Shaw found me. He greased palms so we might have an interview. The first I knew about it the asylum nurses carried me off to change me into clean clothes, wash my face, and tie back my hair. They always did that any time a visitor came.' Jane's normally serene smile wavered a little. 'I believe he only wanted to discover what I'd done with his manuscript. But I was a pitiful spectacle. I wept all over his starched shirt-cuffs, and he gave up inquiring after the manuscript and asked me the polite and kind things people ask, like how I fared, where I slept, and what my keepers fed me. I answered him truthfully—that we were served only stale bread and spoiled meat, that we washed with scraps of soap, all in the same water. That I had boils on my back after being dried with a towel smeared with blood from another woman's sores. That when we walked we were tied around our waists and roped together, and that we were out under the sky in that way only on Sundays, when we were herded to hear sermons in a freezing church. That every other day of the week we would sit for hours on hard forms lining the walls of a great, cold room, given nothing to do. That even ancient women had to sit all day, and would beg to lie down, even on the floor. Oh—I told him all of it. And that I'd seen women wild with grief trying to resist some hard treatment until subdued by beatings, smothered, or choked, or half drowned in cold baths. "I'm losing my teeth," I said. "I'm losing my hair, and my mind."

'Since he brought me here, he has been giving me books. Whatever he thinks I'd like. Best of all was Emily Dickinson.' She quoted, '"These

Fevered Days—to take them to the Forest / Where Waters cool around the mosses crawl— / And shade is all that devastates the coolness."

'When I think of what I saw in Mr Shaw's eyes as he sat across a table from me in the receiving room of that asylum, I think of Miss Dickinson's devastated coolness. I didn't see pain or anger or pity, just a green cooling. And I thought—again like a madwoman—that it wasn't a man sitting there listening to me, but a forest.

'Then he asked after his manuscript, and I cried, from guilt, and fear that once I told him what had happened to it he would just go away in disgust, leaving me where I was.

'"Is it lost?" he asked. And all I could do was nod. I was weeping so hard I couldn't see his face anymore. But he was sitting still, and that gave me hope. Then he said, "Never mind. I'm always losing books. I even lost a whole library." Then he set an orange on the table in front of me, got up, and left me where I was.

'I was taken back to the cold hall, where I shared my orange with the women nearest me on the form. I kept one segment, deciding that it would be the last morsel of food to ever pass my lips. And that night, once I was in my cot, I ate that piece of orange then lay straight, rehearsing for my coffin—though I knew I'd not have one, only a shroud, as yellow as my canvas day dress.

'At midnight all the nurses fell asleep at their stations, and the doors of the dormitories unlocked themselves, and the inmates woke up and were drawn into the great hall by the smell coming from a basket packed with warm cakes made of almonds and clementines. We crowded around the basket in our grubby nightgowns, stuffing our faces. Except for me; I'd made that promise to myself and wasn't busy eating, so I was the first to see the water at the other end of the hall. The flagstones were dark, not from a spill but covered by a sheet of water sparkling in the light of an unseen moon. Beyond the water was a shore; sedges silvered by moonlight. Some women grabbed more cakes, and others dropped the ones they held. We crept towards the water. We were fearful and amazed, but it was the open air. One by one we came to the end of the cold stone floor and stepped down into thigh-deep, cool lake water. There was a moon above us, and more stars than I'd ever seen. Beyond the reeds was the slope of a sweet meadow.

'But you know the place: the Island of Apples. They'd built a fire, and there were clean garments and blankets waiting for us. Neve, her followers, and Taken were there to help Shift with us. The sidhe were frightening but gentle. We had already eaten the cakes he had made from fairy almonds and honey and clementines—and some of us had shared a fairy orange. So we were his.

'It wasn't until 1918 that Neve discovered he didn't mean to gift us all two hundred years of safety and happiness then turn us over to Hell. She and others of the sidhe were, at that time, giving up the first of the sleek and happy innocents they rescued from ships lost on the Middle Passage. French soldiers had already been Taken in their thousands as replacements from that battlefield that France never returned to farmland, so that ploughing farmers haven't had to puzzle at turning up far fewer bones than missing men. The Africans Taken in the eighteenth century were given in the last Tithe. The remainder of them will go in the coming one, and the French soldiers in the Tithe after that. But Shift means to keep all the women from that miserable asylum. You'll meet them soon. You are going to Hell's Gate by way of the Island of Women.'

A few minutes passed before Taryn noticed that Jane had stopped speaking. The printer was watching her with a careful look. Taryn's face felt stiff, and not from the threads of new skin formed under her scabs, most of which had fallen off after the many baths of their journey. She was silent because she was shocked. There had been talk about 'Taken'—how she was one of them—but she hadn't imagined the scale or the husbandry of the enterprise.

According to folk tales, and later literary productions, the fairy took pretty children, like the boy Oberon and Titania squabble over in *A Midsummer Night's Dream*. They stole away bards like Yeats's Oisin, or beautiful knights like Tam Lin. They acquired those they admired. And they actually did do that. They'd done it long and often enough for those stories to survive. Taryn remembered reading a shrewd examination of tales of Changeling children. Its argument was this: The 'Changeling' was an infant who'd survived a disease that inflamed the brain. Survived *damaged*, the infant's grace gone clumsy, its bright eyes dulled, and childish prattle turned to mucosal grunting. The parents of that child, in their appalling grief, might find a little comfort in the belief that their rosy infant had only been replaced, and was in fact safe, caressed by some beautiful lady in a firelit hall under the wintery mountains.

But it seemed that those stories of the selective theft of humans by fairy only *used to be* true. The sidhe weren't cold-hearted seducers and accidental saviours; they were dealing in souls by bulk. They were snatching chained men and women from the holds of sinking slave ships, and soldiers from the putrid mud of trenches at the end of the Voie Sacrée, the road that carried a generation of young men to their deaths at Verdun. The sidhe saved those people, body and soul, fattened them on happiness for two hundred years, then sent them away to Hell. The Tithe wasn't a home kill; it was an abattoir.

It was Taryn's instinct to research her way to understanding, so she thought of a question she could ask. 'What is Hell's price for one sidhe life?'

'Five human souls each hundred years.'

That didn't help Taryn. They'd met next to no one on their journey. There were no towns or villages, just the road and camps provisioned by orchards and gardens. She had no idea how many sidhe there were. How many times five.

Jane said, 'In former times each one of them paid for him- or herself. They took who they wanted and, in time, surrendered people they loved. But now there are many of them who can't go to our world, endure its challenges, and summon enough presence to make any human love them. So the strong and energetic ones like Neve collect for others so that those others might go on living.'

'Can you give me numbers?' Taryn asked, as if she were a reporter at a press conference trying to wring facts out of the spokesperson on the podium. It was her way of managing her horror.

'The sidhe number in only thousands. A little over twenty thousand, I think. But that still means a hundred thousand humans souls paid out at each Tithe.'

Taryn said nothing.

'You're safe,' Jane said.

'I'm not thinking of myself. Who pays for Shift's life?'

'No one. He's not subject to the Tithe.'

Taryn remembered her demon's taunts about Shift's shrivelled little soul. 'Because he has a soul?'

'Yes. He has an immortal soul and a mortal body. The sidhe don't have souls and can live for a very, very long time, if they don't die by violence. But they aren't paying for their eternal youth, as some of the stories say. They're paying for their freedom and sovereignty. The Pact put an end to a war between the Sidh and Hell. A war that was costly to both sides, and one that the sidhe couldn't win even then, when they were stronger.'

'Shift is worried about the Tithe. He seems to think he'll be compelled to give you up,' Taryn said. 'But if his life has no price, how can they compel him?'

Jane frowned. 'Is he worried?'

'It's why he's so determined to discover what Hell is up to. At least that's what he says. He thinks that if Hell is doing something different, then maybe the terms of the Tithe can change.'

'Hell is trespassing in the Sidh very close to the time of the Tithe, as if the Tithe is a small ceremonial matter. I don't know if that points to a possible change in the Pact, but it is worth looking into.'

'Can the other sidhe compel him to give you up?'

'They see that he hasn't made us love him, so they can't understand why he wants to keep us. A parcel of old and broken women. Maybe they imagine his loyalty to us is a stubborn habit he'll outgrow. Something they can scold him out of, by reminding him of his kinship and their long hospitality towards him. But none of that adds up to compulsion.'

This seemed a spectacular failure of imagination by Neve and her people. But Taryn had the impression that imagination wasn't a strong characteristic of the sidhe, who were at once too preoccupied, placid, and self-satisfied for the curiosity and restlessness needed to look beyond themselves and what they knew.

'Do you love him?' Taryn asked Jane.

'He's been like a son to me.'

'Isn't he a bit old for that? Or, as you say, long-lived.'

'When we first met, his friends had just had to raise him again.'

'What do you mean?'

Jane frowned at Taryn. She was weighing things. She got up to set all the scoured pans on a sun-warmed stone to dry, and Taryn imagined the conversation was over. She'd been trusted so far and no further. But then Jane dried her hands on her dress and took a seat on the stone. She patted it. 'Come up here out of the damp.'

Taryn perched beside her. The seat was warm. She was surprised how cold she'd let herself get. The rock under her wet legs started to steam.

'Shift rescued me and the other inmates on an impulse, but it took organisation, labour, provisions, a wide swing of the Faul Gate to reach across the Atlantic. You, he took on the spur of the moment, to free you from a demon. He should have no plans for you. But he has told me he means to bring you to some of his old friends to learn their stories. Now you're telling me he's afraid of having to give people up. And I think surely he doesn't imagine he'll be made to surrender his *old* Taken, like Kernow, who knew him when he was a child, or Petrus, who has been here for nearly five hundred years.' Jane sounded perplexed and troubled.

'But why am I expected to learn people's stories rather than just hear them?'

'Shift's stories are his memories. We keep them for him. He forgets everything.'

Wait, Taryn thought. *He's vague because he's confabulating? Filling in gaps in his memory like an end-stage alcoholic with wet brain?* No. Shift was way too collected for that.

'The Tithe comes every hundred years, and is due this year,' Jane said, in the tone of someone setting out a proposition step by step.

Taryn nodded. Apart from the alarming imminence of the Tithe, she'd got this part of the contract.

'Quite unrelated to the Tithe, except they're near in date, there is another "taking" that comes around every two hundred years, and is now four years off. Shift's covenant acts every two hundred years to subtract some years from his age and make him forget everything.'

'Some years' worth of everything?' Taryn knew this wasn't what Jane meant, but the true state of things was too horrible to contemplate.

Jane put a hand on Taryn's arm. The hand was warm now. 'Two hundred years of everything. He's a few years younger, and he begins again. That's why I say he was a son to me. When I met him he was only a handful of years on from his hollowing out.' Jane surprised Taryn then by glancing nervously behind her, making sure they weren't overheard. She leaned closer. 'That's why Neve was so helpful about his wishes for me and the other women. It wasn't because she was thinking of the Tithe. It had just been and gone and the sidhe like to enjoy the lightness of some long decades before it looms again. No, it was because Neve is always tender to Shift when he comes back. His mother was her sister. Neve treats him harshly sometimes, but these cold-hearted people do love their kin.'

Jane had been checking that Neve wasn't there to overhear her revealing this relationship that, as far as Taryn could see, declared itself in nothing Neve did.

Except Neve was with them now. She was going with them all the way to Hell's Gate.

Jane was gazing at Taryn. 'You see?'

Taryn couldn't see the relationship. Neve was stony and unalterable. Shift was tentative and changeable. Shift was unprepossessing, quiet, shy. Neve was magnificent. 'I believe you,' Taryn said. 'But Neve seems to have a low opinion of him. And I can't see how he could have been transcribing sidhe songs and organising for them to be printed so soon after forgetting everything. And surely an adult returned to mental infancy would be like an infant, shitting themselves and throwing tantrums? Also, can someone go on caring about another person once they've forgotten what they knew about them? Surely if he knows nothing he can feel nothing.'

Jane scrubbed a hand through her hair. 'Come and ask him about it yourself.'

Taryn was taken aback. It would be like asking someone with a terminal illness to talk about their funeral plans. But Jane had picked up a load of air-dried pans and was heading uphill, into the small node of orchard and berry bushes just off the long green tunnel of the Summer Road. Taryn picked up the remaining pans and followed.

They found Neve scaling a fish she'd caught in the stream. Shift was building a fire. He had two flints, a pile of dried moss, and kindling ready beside him.

Taryn snatched at Jane and squeezed her arm. But Jane was already speaking. 'Taryn would like to know what you remember when you forget yourself. *How* you remember. How it works.'

Shift didn't respond until his efforts had produced a thread of smoke in the moss, then flame. He fed the flame, then scooped up the burning moss on a bit of bark and slipped the whole thing under the kindling in the firepit. He stooped and blew on the flames, then sat by the fire feeding it.

'Every two hundred years I grow younger and forget everything that's happened to me and all that I've learned. I've always been curious about the mechanisms of that. In the last fifty years neuroscience has offered me some new perspectives. This is what happens, I think. I lose the explicit or declarative parts of my long-term memory. That is, my memory is wiped of facts and events. Also I lose my autobiographical or episodic memory. I forget my life. Which is why I have my friends remember what happened to us—how we met, what we shared. For instance, how I came to Jane with a manuscript I wanted her to print. And how later I was able to help her in return.

'I don't lose my procedural memory. So I can still ride and groom a horse. I can cook. Catch a fish. Burp a baby. Turn the pages of a book without tearing them. I don't forget physical skills, or any of the things I was born able to do. Also I retain one part of my episodic memory. I might forget who I've loved or hated. But when I meet them again, though I know nothing about them'—he looked at Neve—'about *us*, I do remember how I felt. Anyone I felt warm about, I warm to. Anyone I've trusted, I trust.'

'What more can we ask?' Jane said, to console him.

'All that learning we can ask,' Neve said, 'more magic than anyone has ever possessed. And his memory of the face of my dead sister. All gone.'

There was a long silence in which the air seemed to tremble.

Shift continued to feed the fire.

Neve met Taryn's eyes and actually addressed her. 'The Tithe is a covenant we can challenge. We may not care that the Tithe's conditions foster treachery and cruelty, but the pact has an ugly shape, and its ugliness is a weakness. A weakness that offers hope it might be amended. But Shift's covenant is fair. It is shapely and asked for. It's without faults, and it can't be undone.'

Shift said, 'In the end I'll choose to become a raven. I'll go live with the sisters. They can keep me warm in their nest as my feathers change to down and skin grows over my eyes.'

He liked to read thrillers, bought his books online, and the post shop at Princes Gate Magna kept them for him. He preferred hard cheese to soft, drove with the spatial judgement of Schumacher, and insisted his hens were people. And he was even less human than his inhuman aunt.

Sixteen

The Island of Women

The island was accessible only by boat or barge. The barge was unattended, so Shift and Jane rolled up their sleeves and pulled it across the water, hand over hand, by its dripping rope. It bumped into the bank, and they climbed on.

As the ferry glided across the still lake, the island revealed itself. It wasn't another sidhe food forest, but a human settlement. Its large garden beds were sheltered on two sides by green walls of flowering tomato and cucumber frames, the rest of the space devoted to root and salad crops in neat rows, and the traditional Iroquois 'Three Sisters' planting of corn stalks with bean vines climbing them, surrounded by tumbled heaps of squash. The houses were stone, their turf roofs planted with herbs and flowers. The goats in a nearby meadow hadn't invaded the gardens, which suggested to Taryn that there was magic at work. She strained her eyes to see the blistered atmosphere of mendings but couldn't. Then she noticed that the small windows of the houses weren't open and protected by mendings, but shuttered, or covered with sheets of thick parchment soaked with beeswax.

Some distance from the settlement, on a spit of land and half hidden by trees, were two sidhe buildings—an airy and pleasingly asymmetrical dwelling, and a conical building with a low spire and blind walls. It looked like a tomb.

As soon as the barge connected with the silvered timber landing Neve leapt to shore and set off towards those buildings. Once she was out of the way a good number of the island's occupants came down to greet Jane.

The women were all in robust health, but no more restored to youth, beauty, and wholeness than Jane was. Some were missing teeth or had crooked limbs. Their hair was often grey, but the grey was lustrous. Most of the women were as collected as Jane herself, but Taryn noted some odd mannerisms, defensive stooping walks, tics, hand wringing. These would have been odd outsiders even in Taryn's world—a world that was kinder than the one in which they were locked up two hundred years ago. The women might be shy or odd, but they all looked happy. Happy to see Jane and overjoyed by a visit from their benefactor.

Shift let himself be absorbed by the crowd of the shy and strange. The women hugged and kissed him, all talking at once, telling him their news—about gardens, goats, poultry, choirs, card games, bad weather, how much honey and how many preserves they'd swapped to have their mendings refreshed by passing ladies and gentlemen. They said that the ladies and gentlemen had left some children in the care of the women. Kernow the Grandfather would come along this road any day now, and the ladies and gentlemen liked the little ones to spend time with the Grandfather as well as the hundred grandmothers of the Island of Women.

As Shift was carried off by the throng, Taryn heard him called by his name, also 'dear' and 'pet'.

A few of the women stayed behind with Jane. They relieved her of her bedding bundle and stood smiling at Taryn, waiting for an introduction.

'This is Taryn Cornick,' Jane said. 'Shift Took her to save her from a demon.'

The women exclaimed. Taryn heard only surprise and sympathy, no fear, or that other thing, which she'd noticed even in Berger, who, given his line of work, might sometime have been tempted to acts that would compromise the safety of his soul. The other thing was reproach. No matter how out of the ordinary demonic possession was, it was still somehow a smoker's lung cancer, a drunk's pancreatitis, a philanderer's STI—a thing she had brought upon herself by not behaving properly. But there was no reproach in the women's words and looks, and Taryn imagined they were pretty conversant with stern judgements made against the hapless or unlucky.

The women welcomed Taryn and said they'd find her a whole hut to herself. 'Don't let us wear you out, young one. Some of us are unstoppable once we get talking.'

Jane told them, 'Shift wants Taryn to learn Grandfather Kernow's stories, so the children won't have him all to themselves.'

'Why would Shift transfer a story?' one woman asked.

'Things are afoot,' Jane said.

The woman crossed herself. 'Demons are afoot.' She shot Taryn a glance that was a shade more wary and less sympathetic. 'A group of them passed by at the last full moon, along the Horse Road. Their party included a great manlike monster—yellow-skinned and dappled blue. When they came near the landing on the far shore, the Queen roused herself to go out and challenge them. She was so incensed by the trespass that she put on her veil, stuffed her ears with beeswax, and had us pull her across the lake. But as soon as the horrible creatures saw her and the sword she carried they fled—one on wings of smoke.'

Jane said to Taryn, 'If Shift wants to question a demon he'll have to catch one. I'm sure they'll flee from him too.'

Taryn might have said that the sticky monster outside the Bibliothèque Méjanes had shown no fear at the sight of Shift, and that was *before* Shift had been disabled by iron shot. But she didn't want to worry her hosts.

They climbed a path between burgeoning gardens. Chickens started away before them, then fell in behind and followed. They looked like Shift's chickens, and not at all like the graceful fairy fowl Taryn had spotted along the Summer Road. Taryn looked around with more attention at the goats, the sheep, the gentle-eyed white cow up to her hocks in clover. All of them were earthly animals.

Jane followed her gaze. 'The truly Taken are never homesick. But we have been. Shift fetched us the ancestors of these animals.'

'The Queen has kept to her house since her outing,' one of the women told Jane. 'She no longer lets us grind spices for her incense. She claims she can hear the rasp of the mortar and pestle as it burns.'

Jane looked solemn. 'If she's stopped eating smoke, then she's not long out of her tomb.'

'The lady Neve will be unhappy to discover that the Queen is falling away. The last of her mother's cohort.'

'Yes,' said Jane.

The group paused and looked over at the house in the trees. Neve was nearly there. A breeze caught her hair, and it rippled like a silk pennant.

Another woman added, 'The Queen says she can't even make her own mendings, and that birds fly through her house.'

Jane sighed. 'Neve will repair her mendings.'

'Here is your hut, Taryn,' said the woman who had crossed herself. 'I imagine you'll enjoy four walls and a roof after days under the stars.'

The woman was right. It had been lonely and eerie to wake up under the skeins of a galactic arm, with frost setting on the fur of her hooded bedroll, and the voices of the night birds naked and close.

Taryn ducked her head to pass under the lintel. She found a single room with a woollen futon mattress on a solid timber bed, an ewer and basin, and wood stacked on the hearth, with a tinderbox to light the fire. There was also a kettle and a fat beeswax candle on the mantelpiece.

Jane said she'd bring Taryn water. 'I'll be nearby.'

Another woman promised bread and soup. Then, in response to Taryn's look of surprise, 'Yes, we grow rye as well as corn. The lady burns incense when our bread is baking.'

Jane said, 'Get some rest, Taryn.'

Ten minutes later a loose-bellied beige cat came and plopped itself down on Taryn's doorstep in the sunlight and stayed there, blinking and purring, as if Taryn had caught and reeled it in on a thread of love she didn't even know was dangling from her tightly knitted adult soul. As if it had followed its nose to find the girl who had always rushed off to see her grandmother's cats as soon as her father's car rolled up at the door of Princes Gate.

Jane brought water and filled Taryn's ewer. A procession of children appeared from somewhere further inland and rushed down to a stream on the lakeshore to continue the game it seemed they'd been playing for some time. They'd made a rock dam and fashioned cities from sand— towns with curtain walls and castles with crenellated towers. Generic sandcastles, which made Taryn wonder how they remembered to build like that, and if the memory came with reminders of long-ago picnics and lost families. She wondered whether fairyland had any settlement large enough to be called a town, like the town the children were building. Somewhere with theatres and concert halls and art galleries and marketplaces and parliaments. Places where children might have richer experiences. Not just a visit from a surrogate grandfather, but a whole civil world.

Taryn wondered if they got to grow up.

The smell of baking filled the village, and Taryn saw Shift hurry away upwind, not stopping and settling till he was a good way off. After a time Neve came back around the shore and sat beside him. Taryn joined them.

The aunt and nephew were sitting hip to hip on an undercut bank on the lakeshore, their legs dangling, a long sword lying across their knees. The sword had a plain hilt of white metal and an ornate scabbard of knotted gold wire encrusted with amber and uncut sapphires.

Taryn took a seat beside Shift on the lip of the bank.

'This is the plan,' Shift said. 'Tomorrow we will set out for Hell's Gate. Along the way we'll meet Kernow, and you will hear his story. I've Taken no one in the past two hundred years but the women of the island and you. I'm choosing you to remember things for me. You're scholarly and have a great respect for the documentary sources of history. You won't be soggy about the details, or add a gloss, or interpret what you hear.'

'I'm sure she'll interpret *privately*,' Neve said.

'But, Shift—I don't want to stay in the Sidh. I'm not saying no, or making a bid for freedom. But there are things I have to fix and things I owe my father. And, more immediately, I hope my grandmother will come up with something about what happened to Grandad's library. She has most of his papers. I want to see to that. Then I need to spend the rest of my life doing something useful, like helping to save libraries. Not those full of rare books, but public libraries.'

'Surely you want to avoid Hell,' Neve said.

'Yes, but I don't just want to fix things to fix myself—I want to make amends.'

'My plan and yours can work together,' Shift said. 'Sometime within the next ten years someone will bring me to you—all ignorant and instinctual—and you can repeat whatever stories you've memorised. By then you'll be a happier person, one who got to fix things and who kept a few truths safe for me.'

'Why not just write them down?'

'At one time I destroyed all my own writings. At another I lost a whole library. I can't trust myself with my belongings.'

Taryn peered around Shift at Neve, who was caressing the hilt of the sword. She asked, 'Do you know where his library got to?'

'We haven't any interest in books. We don't write them or read them. We live forever, our memories are perfect, and we hold all knowledge in common.'

'Thank you for being frank with me,' Taryn said.

'You shouldn't express gratitude. It's an insult to them,' Shift said.

Neve waved at him. 'You deserve frankness, Taryn Cornick of the Northovers. Shift has chosen you.'

'Which suggests he's a person of more status than your treatment would seem to merit,' Taryn said, mischievous.

Neve gave a faint, chilly smile. 'Shift is a disappointment to us all.'

Shift said, 'So, Taryn, the plan is that we set out tomorrow on the road Kernow is travelling. We'll pause where we meet him, and he'll tell you one of his stories. Then we go on to Hell's Gate, which Neve can turn to send you to London. She'll drop you somewhere discreet, close to your home. We stay at the gate to wait for a demon. Once we've caught one—"

Neve said, 'I cut off its limbs, and we keep it prisoner until we get satisfactory answers.'

Shift said, 'Once we have some satisfactory answers, Neve can line up gates to send me to you in Australia.'

'New Zealand,' Taryn corrected him. 'I'm at Auckland before Sydney. Where you're sent will depend on how long the demon holds out. Remember, I'm in the Coromandel for five days between Auckland and Sydney, visiting my grandmother Ruth. She should know about the dispersal of Grandad's library.'

Shift frowned at the sword. 'When you were recuperating in my hut, I did come up with a better plan. I asked the sisters if Odin would help me catch and question a demon. The demons aren't afraid of me. And I suspect they'll not be particularly afraid of Neve either. A *god*, on the other hand.'

'Odin refused Shift,' Neve told Taryn.

'Munin is displeased,' Shift said.

'Which she expresses how?' Taryn asked.

'By scheming.'

'She might come up with something. She's a devious bird,' said Neve. 'Meanwhile, Shift and I will try our best to discover what these demons want with the Firestarter. If we find it before they do, we can offer it to Hell in exchange for better terms on the Tithe.'

Shift nodded. 'That's our plan.'

Taryn found it hard to believe that Neve cared about the terms of the Tithe. Neve, who'd stolen away thousands of slaves or soldiers and treated them with kindness, then treachery. Neve, who had no soul to harm with her cruelties. But she did seem loyal to Shift, so perhaps she had some kind of heart.

Taryn said, 'Okay. That sounds like a plan.'

Taryn's party met Kernow and his company in the middle of the great marsh. A camp of wicker-framed waxed linen tents had been erected on a vast platform of bundled reeds that rose a good metre and a half above the tops of the moulting bulrushes. The tents encircled a stone hearth heaped with live coals on which wrapped parcels of fish and eel and squash were baking for a mid-afternoon meal. Plenty for everyone, since their party had been spotted while still some distance off, from the top of the camp's single more permanent structure.

Rising metres above the marsh on four sturdy cross-braced poles, the structure was roofed with fresh cedar shingles. It was open-sided, apart from a single rail at waist height. To Taryn the building looked like a fire watchtower, but when she was invited there after the meal Shift called it 'the breeze house'.

He showed her up and left her there, returning some minutes later with Kernow. Shift crouched at the foot of the ladder, coaxed the old man onto his back, then piggybacked him up.

Taryn and Kernow had met over the meal, but Shift nervously repeated his introductions, then scampered back down the ladder, as if hastening to escape. However, he reappeared three more times, bearing cushions, fruit, and beverages. Then he left them alone.

Taryn and the old man stood for a time, leaning on the rail, facing south. Kernow pointed out the place, miles off, where the Builders were at work. She could just make out three triangle gantries, their shapes wavering in the afternoon air.

'In the past they've always carried their materials in skiffs along one of the channels that run from the cut-throughs at either side of the marsh,' Kernow explained. 'But these are extensive repairs. A sinkhole appeared last winter. The marsh water drained away into the earth for miles around it. The Builders are making a small hill on the dry area. They'll rebuild the boardwalk around it. You'll continue your journey on the temporary track of bundled reeds. It will be half a day's wet walking.'

Taryn listened to Kernow's account of the work, concentrating hard, and gradually acclimatised herself to his by turns lilting and hesitant English.

He pointed to the shadowy furrows following the Builders back to their worksite. It looked as if small invisible dogs were energetically forging a way through long grass. 'Those are the Builder's Hands. They are like mendings, only of much greater size.' He moved his purple-knuckled hand to indicate a place further away. 'And those three Builders are maintaining a forcebeast. They make them for this kind of work, repairing roads, and clearing rockfalls from mountain passes. Those Builders didn't break for a meal, so they must be making as much use of their beast as they can before having to let it go.'

Taryn peered at the three sidhe and the patch of turbulent air between them. She saw two logs lift into the air and hang, poised like a drummer's drumsticks at the opening of a song. The Builders moved off, the suspended timber drifting after them.

'The sidhe once used forcebeasts to defend themselves. I suppose if these unwelcome incursions continue they might make one to chase and punish the demons.'

After a time the old man left the rail and made himself comfortable on the cushions. Taryn joined him and poured the tea—nettle for him, ginger and honey for her—and he began to tell the story she was tasked to learn.

She wished she could take notes. Taryn had the habits of a good researcher. She always did her reading, thought through what she'd read, then went back to read again, and only then took notes. Her initial reading was always for the shape of the story. Notes were for the facts: places, dates, persons. In this case the Welsh border, somewhere near the Monnow, in the fourth century CE. Personages: a captain of the king's guards, a witch, an archer, a monk, a number of soldiers, an unhappy king, and a boy called Shift—who couldn't stomach red meat or grain and who, much to Taryn's surprise, was dead and in his grave at the beginning of the story.

Seventeen

Kernow's Story

My troubled and sleepless king summoned me and said, 'Kernow, you must take ten of your men and fetch the witch Adhan.' We set off seaward in the summer heat to do so.

The witch lived with her son at the edge of a great marsh. No one had ever seen her boy up close, for, whenever visitors approached, she'd tell him to run and hide. When he was small, he'd conceal himself in the whins near her hut. Later, she'd send him out into the waterways. I once glimpsed him making off, his arms flapping for balance as he jumped from one footing to the next. It looked as if he were playing at flight, and perhaps he was, since all he knew was eels, fish, and waterfowl.

Whenever the king's emissaries visited the witch, we'd always approach her hut by a detour along the last spur of elevated land. There we'd stop to be seen, for she was not someone you'd want to alarm or offend.

That hot evening, as our horses found the uphill path, I was saying a prayer under my breath. 'Great God in Heaven,' I prayed, 'let the witch be dead, as rumour says, let her hut be empty, and grass growing on her doorstep. Let us find no sign of her son.' For I had orders I could barely stomach, and an abandoned hut and empty-handed return would be a good outcome for me.

Our party paused in the place of vantage until we caught sight of the witch, moving between her outdoor oven and a goat skin she had spread on the ground. The skin was littered with objects that sparkled like lumps of coal. She spotted us and straightened, a hand shading her eyes, but for once she didn't call into the hut to send the boy running.

Of all of us, Geff the archer had the keenest eyesight. He pointed at a patch of garden near the margin of the marsh. The witch had never gardened. Like the sidhe, the people she was kin to by birth or marriage—no one was sure which it was—she gathered throughout her territory, from the long flats of eelgrass nearer the sea, up to land high and dry enough for fruit trees. She kept a goat, but it seemed the animal had respected the narrow flowerbed. The blooms in the bed were blue and yellow, spring irises, though it was late summer. These out-of-season flowers were a shocking demonstration of her famed power—if pointless, and purely for her own pleasure. I remember making a mental note to caution my men against carrying this sight back to court. Our king often sent for Adhan's help, because she made a particular potion that brought on a deep and dreamless sleep. But he was twitchingly afraid even of the idea of her. He might enjoy the fealty of a woman who could perform great feats of magic, but he wouldn't want to be reminded that her magic belonged to her, not to any king with the power to command her presence.

We followed a sheep track around the side at the hill. As we descended, a small wood hid our view. It was a willow wood, tangled, the blackberry bushes flanking it stripped of fruit between elbow and shoulder height. We leaned from our saddles to pick the higher berries.

We weren't in a hurry. Our king's problem was not one that could be remedied quickly, and we knew he had one more plan in place before he resorted to magic. But he was an impatient man and wanted the next remedy to hand. Our instructions were to return with the witch and her son. I was to tell Adhan that her presence was required to confirm that the king's builders' current solution was correct and that his troubles were not a curse, merely ill luck. I was to tell her that she and her son could bide awhile in comfortable seclusion at the court, and if the king's tower continued to crumble, and workmen kept being crushed, Adhan might then help the king find a magical solution.

But my king had a secret plan. His seer had told him he must sacrifice the orphan child of a virgin at the tower's foundations to make it stand. Everyone knew the witch's boy had no earthly father—so perhaps the child had not been conceived in the usual way. And a rumour had come to the ear of the king that the witch had died. 'There's no one left to protect the orphan,' the king said. 'No one to mourn him or avenge him. It can be done kindly. The child can join my court. We can pamper and entertain him. He'll not know he's in danger before he's dead.' I argued with the king: 'What if the rumour is false and we find the witch alive?' And he said, 'Bring them both. The witch might have a better plan than my engineers. It is said that her unearthly paramour built the bridge that floats on the Gwy above Cleddon Falls. And, if it turns out she has no useful magic, then the child can become an orphan if an orphan is what we really need.'

We ate our blackberries and licked our fingers. Young Anselm, a newly made monk, had filled his round felt hat with fruit. 'For later,' he said.

'Like heaven,' teased Geff. 'Later. Always later.'

We came around the far end of the wide water-meadow, and on to the goat-clipped grass that surrounded the hut. The witch's indoor fire was alight. We could see a patch of smokeless heat against the blue air above its roof. But since the weather was hot, the witch was cooking medicines at her open-air hearth, and the glitter on the skin was deer horn containers, filled with unguents and stoppered with beeswax. The witch's bees were wild—their hive in a dead tree at the edge of the wetlands. There was a hole in the hive, and honey was dripping out of it into a bark bowl.

Adhan stood straight and pulled her long hair in front of her, perhaps to preserve her modesty, since her linen dress was damp and clinging. She looked well—vital, bold, supple, and strong. I looked at her, then suddenly had to look away. I wasn't afraid the witch could read my intentions or that she'd be offended by my gaze. It was something else, something strange. Though striking, she was hard to look at, to fix on and contemplate, and I had to force my eyes to return to hers.

She stood wringing the rag between her long, lean hands. When I met her stare, one eyebrow kinked, and she glanced sidelong at her anomalous spring garden. I followed her gaze and saw that the garden was a grave mound.

My heart lifted and went soaring. Death had saved me from murder.

'I am alone now,' the witch said. Her voice was low and rough—the voice of one who weeps every hour she's idle. 'There was so little the boy could stomach. Neither red meat, nor grain.' She paused and added, 'Imagine a life without bread.'

I had had a younger sister who'd eaten every meal and only grown thinner until finally seeming to die of hunger and thirst, as if none of the food and drink the family gave her could quench or nourish her. I wondered if the boy's trouble was something similar.

'How old was he?' I asked.

'He would now be twelve years of age.' Adhan stooped to the skin, threaded a thong through the eyelets around its edge, and drew it closed. The containers rattled. 'That,' she said, 'is the last of that batch bottled.'

'It is good that your work is done,' I said, 'for the king wishes you to come with us. Though we should stop here for a night to rest the horses.' I was in no hurry to face the king's displeasure, desperation, and despair.

Adhan said she'd feed us and promised to instruct the midges to stay away.

'As I recall you have a potion for that.'

'The potion stinks. Better I persuade the midges to respect the rules of hospitality.' She laughed, either at her own joke or at her own power. Her laugh had changed. It was four years since I'd seen her. On my last visit I was not a captain, only a promising guard. On that occasion the king's men had come to collect a consignment of medicines crucial to the king—most of them sleeping draughts. I studied her face. Her skin was the brown of flaxseed, shades darker than most people I knew. She had only a shallow dip where the straight bridge of her narrow nose met her forehead. This, and her wide-set eyes and smooth brow, had the effect of making the top half of her face seem semi-human: half raptor, owl, or eagle. But only when it was in repose. And there was a tiny muscle above her left eyebrow that, contracted, made her look keenly interested and then by degrees questioning and sceptical. Her eyes were wonderful, a clear hazel. Hers was a friendly, open, fearless gaze. I saw no madness in her eyes, only sadness. I saw her clearly for a moment; then it was as if my own seeing forced me to turn away.

We dismounted, and the witch at once said, 'And you must be tired too, my brothers and sisters. Go into the meadow and eat your fill.'

She was speaking to the horses. And, quite naturally, the animals turned away and clip-clopped into the long grass. Their heads vanished, ears deep.

Young Anselm had produced his missal—a gift from a rich aunt. He clutched it, blushing, and said, 'Can I say a rosary for your son?'

'That would please him,' the witch said.

Anselm picked up his hem and made his way over to the flower-covered mound. The witch ducked into her wattle-and-daub hut and then emerged, dragging a bunch of hassocks. My soldiers hurried to help her. They arranged the hassocks around the fire. The witch pointed to her woodpile, and my men picked out kindling and larger logs.

I settled against a horsehide bolster. Once I was comfortable I looked around, over the heads of the men laying new wood on the smoking ashes. It was then I saw the other extraordinary thing. A miles-long path ran straight from the hut's door, through the marsh, to the sea. It was as if a giant had run a comb through the reeds, parting them and pressing them down. A notch of ocean was visible through the parting, the water sparkling, beige-lilac.

The witch came out of the hut again and sat to pull on boots—felted wool, stinking of goose grease. She said, 'I'll check my eel traps—there should be enough for a good feed.' She lay on her back to pull her boots up her legs. It wasn't something I had ever seen a woman do while surrounded by men. 'What does your king want?' she asked, sitting up again.

'Is he not also your king?' I asked.

'*Is* he my king?' The witch sounded more curious than quizzical.

I couldn't think how to reply. To whom could this wild power owe fealty? Not the haunted, sleepless man who'd sent me.

The witch got her feet under her and stood up in one graceful movement. She pointed at the strange timber column by the wall of the hut. 'There is the water barrel.' It wasn't a barrel made of staves, but a hollow log with a dipper balanced on its rim. I got up and took a drink, and when next I looked, the witch was moving away into the marsh, no doubt to some seaward channel where she'd laid her traps.

Over our meal, the witch asked again what the king wanted, and I told her that he was trying to rebuild the fortress below the Roman road but that the tower of the keep wouldn't stand. The ground shook sometimes, and the stones gave way. It was like standing on a headland hollowed out by the sea. Holes kept appearing, and a surf could be heard beating deep inside the hill.

'Nowhere near the sea,' Anselm said, and made the sign of the cross.

I said, 'The king has considered the People Under the Hill.'

'And rather than build elsewhere, he wants to treat with them?' The witch naturally supposed that the king wanted her as an envoy. She had a tie to those ladies and gentlemen, even if her unhappy child was now dead.

'The fortress commands several passes, the river, and the high Sarn,' I said. 'The king must rebuild the keep if he wishes to hold his kingdom against the Picts and Jutes, even if the Saxons choose to honour his treaty.'

'Is the treaty in question?' the witch asked, but didn't wait for a reply. Instead she turned to Anselm and asked to see his missal. She spread her shawl on her lap to receive the book and wiped her fingers clean before opening its boards. As the twilight turned a deeper blue, she tilted its pages to the firelight and bent close. When there was no longer enough light to read, she passed the missal back to its owner and remarked, 'My hut is no place for books. I will leave it soon and go somewhere where I can keep papers, and a pen and ink, and a table with candles.'

'Do you mean to become a scholar?' The monk could not hide his tone of disparagement.

'Adhan can be a wise woman, but not a scholar?'

Anselm blushed and stammered. He said the Abbess Monacella at Cwm Pennant was considered a fine scholar. Of course the fool didn't stop there, but added, 'In her own right.' This elicited another of the witch's hair-raising laughs. She got up and said goodnight.

I told her I'd post a sentry.

'I'm here every night without a guard.'

'Still,' I said.

'Tell your sentry I must venture out again before sunrise,' she warned. 'When the mist comes, I will go into the marsh to speak to my ghost. I must tell my ghost I will be going away for a time.'

I felt my whole scalp move, as if someone had run their fingers from my nape and up over the top of my head, tugging my hair.

'You will have noticed it's a new grave. It is too soon for any loving ghost to have left the one they love.'

I thought of the shaggy, sturdy brown boy. I couldn't imagine that boy's ghost. I thought of the privations of illness, and how the boy would have looked before he died, and how his body might look now, after weeks in the marsh's wet soil.

The east turned silver. The rim of a full moon appeared above the sea horizon and for a moment seemed to melt and pour its light into the ocean. Then, as it continued to climb, it gathered its silver back into it-self and its round reflection. I saw that the moon was rising directly above the miles-long parting in the rushes, as if it was the moon that had made the path by rolling across the sea and reeds to finally bump at the doorway of the witch's hut.

'Yes,' Adhan whispered, as if she'd caught my thought. 'The path is for the moon. It was moonrise when my dear one was dying and wished to see, one more time, the moon come up from the belly of the ocean. The reeds were tall, and I was afraid the moon would take its time while death would not. So I parted the reeds. Autumn storms will restore them. Then everyone will forget again what I can do, even when I can do nothing.' She wished me goodnight and disappeared into her hut. I posted my unnecessary sentry as per my gallant promise. Then I wrapped myself in my cloak and slept. I didn't see the witch walk out in the morning but, when the soldiers were bundling up their bedrolls and tightening their girth straps, the sentry of the second watch reported that Adhan had headed out along the path of the moon—a channel for rolling sea fog. She'd gone into the whiteness and not returned until sunrise.

When the horses were saddled, Adhan appeared, her dark skin reddened by a wash in night-chilled water. She'd dressed for the journey and for an audience with royalty. She wore a fine wool gown, the shade of ripe wheat. It was girdled by a belt of thick felted wool, in the shape of a wreath of oak leaves, spring green to autumn brown. Her cloak was roughly made and in several shades of undyed lambswool, and the way she kept twitching at it showed her consciousness that it didn't fit with her finery. Her dark hair was in a single braid. At her throat she wore five claws of rose gold, a glove made to fit the fingers and thumb of her right hand. The claws were in hinged sections, like armour. It was too rich and crafty to be anything other than the work of the sidhe.

Geff held the palfrey's bridle for her to mount and passed her the reins. She leaned forward to gently pull one of the horse's ears. 'Sister,' she murmured. 'You are my teacher. Teach me horse.' As she drew back she let one fingertip trail across the iron ring of the bridle's cheek strap. Her nostrils quivered.

On the second day of the journey, towards sundown, we noticed the smoke, an even brown film over the sky in the west. The sunset was fierce orange, and as the dusk deepened, the fire glow beyond the mountains became visible.

Adhan joined me at the head of our small column and asked if that was where we were going. I told her not to be afraid. It wasn't the king's camp on fire. It was the tower. The king's builders wanted to fuse the foundation stones. When we left they'd had men cutting timber and piling logs ten deep around the curtain wall.

'What kind of trees?' asked the witch.

'Just timber,' I said. 'Our king is clearing the forest to the east of the tower, to make everything visible from the keep to the river. The river is how attackers would come, since the forests are thick everywhere, except the tops of the mountains.'

'Alder and Elder, Ash and Beech, Gean and Whitebeam, Oak, Rowan and Yew, Black Poplar and Wych Elm. A host and a legion,' she said. Then, 'Sometimes attacks come from the sky above the tops of the mountains. And there's not a thing anyone can do.'

Sweat pricked cold at my hairline.

'The king has sent for me even though he already has a plan to make his walls stand?'

I was pleased to have a question I could answer. 'The builders have had several ideas. All so far proved unsatisfactory. Now they mean to melt and fuse the stones, like the walls of the Pictish forts in the far north. Walls without mortar. Heaps of stones in shells of green and black glass.'

'I'd like to see that,' said the witch.

At dusk, the wind picked up and turned to the west. Our party made camp. The night thickened. After we'd kicked earth over our cooking fire we could still smell smoke. The horses snorted and sidled and tugged at their picket-line. Adhan got up to see to them and stood, her hands on the muzzles of two animals, little finger and thumb curled around the edges of their quivering nostrils. I joined her. She glanced at me, then back over my shoulder, her face brightening. I turned and saw that the fire glow seemed wider, though the outline of the range of hills before it was no longer as clear.

'The king's fire has got into the forest,' the witch said, calm.

Our party had been in thick woods for part of that day's ride, on a winding trail that would be very difficult to retrace in the dark. I asked the witch if she could make a light. With the forest so dry and smoke in the air, I didn't trust torches.

Adhan tucked in her chin and began to spit air. A greyish phosphorescence appeared at her lips, sparkled along her jaw and down one side of her throat to pool along her collarbones. It ran down her arms, above her clothes, a cloud of gold and silver sparks floating a hair's breadth from her skin. She moved closer to me and touched my arm. Light poured around my body, heatless and intangible. Coated with this seething radiance, my booted feet provided enough illumination for me to see the ground where I stood, a softly lit circle. 'We should go back the way we came,' I said. 'Get to open country.'

We moved among the sleeping men. I shook them awake, and Adhan lit them up.

When the horses were saddled we set out carefully, walking them. Our bodies illuminated the path only a pace ahead. The horses showed no alarm at the sight of their now spectral handlers. They walked with their noses to the ground as if they meant any moment to stop and graze. The witch had put a spell on them.

As the night lightened, she let our halos of misty radiance fade. The forest filled with the wavering shadows of trees, backlit by fire and, minute by minute, a more intense black.

I put my fingers to my cheek and felt a film of warm ash. It was coming down through the foliage, pattering like snow. I ordered everyone to mount up—and hurried to help the witch into her saddle. She seemed mesmerised. She was gazing back the way we'd come. The pupils of her eyes, and the contours of the claw necklace, were painted with orange. She said, 'The fire is over the crest of the highest hill.'

'It must climb down the far side of that range and cross the valley before reaching these foothills,' I said.

'As if a forest fire is an army and needs to keep its feet on the ground.'

I made a stirrup of my hands and boosted her up onto her horse. Our party picked up its pace, though the path was too narrow and the light too confusing to risk giving the horses their heads.

We were not alone in our flight. On either side of the trail herds of deer flowed away ahead of us, floating over fallen logs and vanishing from sight. The deer were followed by wolves and lynx, skulking foxes and trotting badgers. Then the forest floor came to life with crawling shadows, small creatures, rats and mice, stoats, weasels and voles. Daytime birds were awake, blundering through the branches and their swinging shadows.

A roar could be heard in the west.

The path ahead rose to climb through a stand of tumbled, vine-covered pillars of limestone. At its highest point the party reined in and looked back.

I would never have dreamed that a fire could burn a green forest, even in late summer when the leaves were dull and edged with brown. If asked, I'd have made arguments about trying to light a hearth fire with unseasoned wood. I'd offer as evidence my observations about how timber would smoke and sulk and drool sap onto the flames, and go out as soon as your back was turned.

This fire would be hard to turn your back on. The flames were hundreds of feet in height, pushed forward by a westerly and pulled upwards by the wind generated by their own heat. As I watched, I saw that wall of fire flex and snap like a whip, throwing out a great, ragged mass of flame, which sailed right across the valley to ignite the treetops of the forest on the foothills.

The wind was full of smoke and sparks. It was storm-strong. It caught our cloaks and made the horses flinch and fidget in circles. The witch was urging her own horse to the head of the column, shoving a way between my men. Her hair had come loose and was blown upwards, floating on the hot air. She had taken off the claw necklace and was busy knotting it into the locks at her nape. She glanced at me, then swung one leg back over her palfrey's withers and jumped down—at the same time slapping the horse to send it galloping away. Then she was in the forest, her pale form now visible, now vanishing into the shadows. I lost sight of her. A moment later another horse broke from cover onto the path. A yearling, its coat rich brown. A colt, with something bright tangled in its long mane. It whirled and took off along the path, stretching out into a gallop, its flag of a tail leaving a trail of clear air in the smoke. The witch's palfrey hadn't fled. The docile animal had stayed just off the path under the trees. Geff urged his horse towards it and caught its bridle. 'Where is she?' he asked.

'She's left us,' I told him, then I foundered and fell silent. *The witch had turned herself into a horse.* The transformation was astonishing and unexpected and alarming. I'd heard stories about witches transforming themselves into animals but had always assumed that the rules of magic must obey the more obvious rules of nature. Adhan was a mother. If she changed herself into a horse, shouldn't that animal be a mare? But the horse that fled ahead of us through the forest wasn't a mare, or even a filly. It was a rangy, bay-coloured, black-tailed colt.

I signalled the party to ride on. We gave our horses their heads, and the wise animals stuck with one another and to the trail. Bits of burning foliage, twigs, and even sizeable branches were dropping from the sky. Small fires started up beside and before us and quickly grew. We were riding into the wind now, as if it had swung from west to east, or as if the fire were drawing a long breath and emptying the east of air.

At a canter it took our party a third of the time to reach the river as it had going the opposite direction. The path became sandy and dropped to the banks of the Monnow, where we found the witch up to her waist in the water. She faced us but gazed blind-eyed into the air above our heads.

Burning brands rained from the sky. Some fell harmless into the lush riverside grass; others dropped with fierce hisses into the water. Our horses plunged and wheeled. I jumped from the saddle and pulled off my cloak. I thrust it under the water and held it there until its wool was heavy and soaked. Then I forced my horse into the shallows and draped the wet cloak over its head. The animal quietened. My men followed my example.

The fire was ripping into the forest we'd passed through. Above the roar we heard crashes as oaks and elms fell and caught themselves on their spreading branches.

The witch paced backwards across the channel, towards the far bank. She was waist-deep, then shoulder-deep, then hip-deep again. She stopped in the shallows. She spread her arms. The flow of water upstream hastened. Downstream it slowed and eddied. The water climbed the witch's calves. We drew our cloaked horses further back.

The downstream eddying resolved itself into a ridged rip as the inland river behaved like a tidal one, turning to flow in the opposite direction. Then the witch threw up her arms and the water leapt from the riverbed, rising in a solid, continuous flow, like a waterfall in reverse. For a moment there was a straight wall of water between us and the oncoming fire, then that wall curved in at either end. The witch turned her eyes to take in my men and the horses, her face calm and calculating. She was making a measurement. She folded the wall of water around us all. Before it thickened and closed, I saw how the wall was pulling water from upstream and down, exposing the riverbed and waterweeds to the bottom of its deepest channel. Then the vortex sealed itself. The air in its lofty funnel filled with the scent of mud and algae.

It was a vortex without wind, only the small, twisting breeze generated by its rotations. And it wasn't just rotating. The surface of the wall was braided, as if a rope maker were twisting strands of water and dropping his newly made rope in a high hollow coil. It made water music, like a stream rushing over stones, but louder, and only audible because it was closer to us than that other source of sound, the howling of the fire.

Flame vomited through the yet-unconsumed trees on the water meadow before the river. The late-summer leaves caught fire, tore loose, and flew upwards. The grass and meadow flowers shrivelled, then turned to ash before ever having been on fire. I watched this through one thick smooth turn in the funnel—at the witch's eye level. In that glassiness, rushing past, were the silhouettes of fish and frogs, translucent silks of waterweed, and freckles of tiny stones.

The fire rolled through the trees and along the bare ground. The witch's window vanished, and the outside air turned red, then pink with inspissated steam. The walls of the funnel darkened with mud as the witch drew more water than there was to be drawn. Beyond the funnel the fire was making a sound I had often heard at a forge when a smith thrusted red-hot ironwork into his barrel—but magnified tenfold. The air in the funnel became hot and thin. I saw the witch turn her face upwards. Above us the muddy water reached like a candle flame, tapered at its top, and pinched shut. The sense of airlessness relented.

It was muggy in the enclosed cone. Our clothes and skin steamed. I tugged at the man beside me, drew him to the riverbed, and had him lie down in the gluey silt. The others followed, coaxing the horses to lie too. I stretched out. Mud trickled around me. The witch continued to pull what water she could reach into the vortex, at least to replenish what was burning away. The crown of the cone was boiling. It was like watching water simmer from inside a pot. Then I couldn't see it anymore. The cone filled with steam, and we were lost to one another, except by touch. The vapour was orange and sometimes bloomed brighter as fire pushed against the water walls. Condensation pattered down around us.

The witch came and lay down near me. I closed my eyes and thrust the top of my head into the warm silt and listened to the hot rainstorm and dry surf of the fire. Now and then I could hear snatches of Latin. Anselm was praying. I was unable to pray. I'd remembered that this river had a god. That all rivers did, and that I knew old people who'd remember the name of the god of the Monnow. But it was foolish to think of prayer to God or gods with this great earthly power lying beside me in the mud.

We cowered in the riverbed for a very long time. The mud grew hot, and the steam scalding. I feared for my eyes. Already scoured by smoke, they now felt poached.

The heat proved too much for one man, who suddenly struggled up, shouting. I rose to snatch at him but was left with only a handful of slime. He wrapped his arms around his head and staggered, slithering, to the wall of water and pushed into it. The torqueing flow lifted and turned him. I kept my eyes open long enough to follow his figure as it rose feet first up the cone. Before reaching the apex, his struggling body was expelled. The smoke thickened where he landed. He rose onto his knees, then clutched his throat and dropped face first onto the black ground. A moment later flames erupted from his hair and clothes.

A short while after that, the roar receded. Adhan picked herself up and approached the wall with unsteady, tottering steps. She peered at the dusky red glow beyond the water. Gradually the glow began to separate into distinct patches of fire. None very near the base of the cone. The witch waited a while longer, then, with no change of expression, no evidence she was letting go a sustained and effortful task of defence, she blew the cone apart, throwing its water out in a wide circle. There was a din of hissing from the drifts of burning coals that surrounded us, and the smoke rushed in, blinding and choking us. My face dried instantly. I rubbed my forehead in the hot mud. Hot wind wafted over us, drawing clearer air up along the trench of the empty riverbed. We coughed and hacked. The horses were wheezing but utterly still under their horse-shaped shells of mud-stiffened wool.

A trickle of cooler water washed over my hands. The river was filling again. I scooped out a hollow in the silt and cupped my hands to drink. The water was sour with ash and corrosive on my tongue. My men and the witch were making the same discovery, gagging and spitting. I was almost pleased to see Adhan fail at the experiment, pleased to discover she didn't know the water was spoilt. I'd supposed she was all knowledge, but perhaps she was more wit and instinct, because how could someone learn to compel a river, and shape it? Was it that she could call on the river god and air gods? But what special sympathy would those beings have for her? What *was* magic? If it was just knowledge, then surely Adhan would have known not to try to drink the water.

The front of the fire had moved on. It had come to the end of the forest and was making its way over the heath, half starved now, flames greatly diminished in stature and scope.

I watched the ragged line of orange crawl up the flank of a faraway hill. The air was less air than an even suspension of thin smoke. The great billows were above us, making the sun show as a shrunken purple ball near the horizon due east—it had risen an hour earlier, though under the low black sky the day was as dark as night.

Much of the forest was now only a mass of crisscrossing heaps of live coals. Some oaks still stood, shorn of all but their thickest limbs. Others leaned like fallen warriors on their branch arms, as if trying to get up again.

The river was filling in its main channel but was still as white as lye. I got up, gathered the leads of several horses, and led them out of the water so they wouldn't drink. I got as far as the mud of the shallows. There was nowhere to stand in all those seething, smoking miles. The riverbed stank of scorched waterweed.

We waited. The river filled, and we edged away from the corrosive water, which continued to run white, then turned to a porridge of ash.

The witch had fallen asleep, her head on the flank of one of the hunkered-down horses. She was as monstrously muddy as the rest of us. The only bright thing about her, or indeed that bit of the world, was the necklace. Its rose gold was spotless, unmarked by mud or water or even oily fingers—as if it were made so that every stain melted from it.

Noon passed. The pall of smoke drifted away east, dragging a long veil of stained sky after it. The sun dried our clothes, and the mud hardened. We still could not stir from that spot, because the coal heaps of the consumed forest were furred white only on top; underneath, they were still alive. We were tormented by thirst. But when the sun was once again declining, true clouds came, and it began to rain. We turned our faces to it and opened our mouths. The big fat drops came thick and fast. The hot ashes spat and steamed.

The witch continued to sleep, although her exposed ear filled with rain.

Geff said to me, 'It will be dark again soon. And the path is buried.'

'She can make her live light,' I said. But I didn't try to wake her.

The rain continued until we were quaking with cold. The horses had tossed off their covers and were lipping the river, which now flowed full and clear. I thought we should follow it upstream, where the clean water was coming from, until we had gone around the fire. Much of the river margin had been gently sloping pasture, smooth ground. It should be safe to ride, if we travelled slowly.

Besides, I thought, why should we hurry to the camp of a king whose crown was now surely nothing but a lump of melted metal?

The witch finally woke and was at once convulsed by shivering. She gave a small whine like a distressed animal, then began to cry. It was disconcerting. I wondered whether an offer of comfort would act in my favour. But how to comfort her? It couldn't be just a gesture. I croaked, 'You must be very tired after'—then I foundered, and finished—'after such an effort.'

The witch looked at me, her eyes smoke-reddened and blurry. She gave a hitching sob that ended in laughter.

'Adhan,' I said, to bring her back to herself.

She heard the reproach and straightened her face. She said she was freezing. Could someone creep out over the ashes and roll one of those smouldering logs this way?

Two of the men got up and made their way across the smoking

ground to the nearest movable log. They used their swords to lever it free of heaped ashes.

I tried to explain my plan to leave that night along the river, guided by her live light, but she just shook her head.

I said, 'I expect you'd prefer to return to your marsh?'

She said, 'I will see this king.'

'If he still lives,' I said. 'You have no ill intentions, I hope.'

'I will talk with him. And then I'll go to see the king of Mercia, and Duke Gwyrlais in Cornwall, and the king in Anglesey.'

'Do you need to inspect the Saxon king too?' I asked. I'd gathered that, for some reason, this disaster had prompted the witch to seek out and compare the royal personages of Britain. 'And the High King in Tara? And whichever Northman now counts himself supreme?'

She said, 'I'll start nearer home and see whether I need to cast a wider net.'

'For what? Your marsh is in *this* kingdom.'

The log arrived, bowled by swords and leaving a track of live coals. The witch scooted near the log, put up her hood, and drew her limbs in under her mud-crusted cloak.

'I can't bring you near my king if you wish him ill,' I said, sounding helpless even to myself. She didn't respond.

First we found the bodies whose mouths still grinned at what had overwhelmed them. Many of them had their heads twisted right back over their shoulders as if the fire had been a bear or wolf and they'd meant by instinct to turn their bodies to stand and fight, as men will when pursued by a predator, though the fire had overtaken them with more than predatory swiftness. Some distance beyond the bodies we found charred armour, helmets, breastplates, greaves, discarded by the fleeing soldiers. Further on still we found horses, piled together, fouled on a dragged picket line. They had freed themselves from the pickets, but not from the rope, or one another.

Our party came across one half-burnt horse, still on its feet. I cut its throat.

In time we reached the hill the river ran around, turning east to north. The forest on the far bank was still green. On the bare hill the fortress's fused ramparts gleamed black. There were tents on a shingle spit in the riverbed, and barges in the river's channel, the biggest one flying the colours of the king. It seemed the king's fire had travelled only eastward.

At the camp I summoned women and suggested Adhan might like to wash and change her clothes before she saw his majesty.

She said, 'Giving you time to carry your private views to him?'

'The king will need my report,' I said. 'And I'll be sure to tell him that you saved our lives.'

'And that I didn't save all of you?'

'I don't think anyone will reproach you for the loss of one man who couldn't be controlled.'

'Please wait until I'm ready to go with you, Kernow. You're speaking of a report, but when you came to fetch me from my marsh, your talk was all of honours and hospitality, treats and luxury.'

I frowned and shuffled. She was right. I hadn't been honest with her. She looked so uncertain, begrimed, youthful. I nodded to show her I agreed.

Adhan refused the women's offer of a tub of warm water. She only accepted fresh clothes and walked upstream to wash. When she returned, she looked completely restored, bright-eyed. Her hair was rinsed of mud but uncombed. She was wearing a long loose blue dress, cinched with her own felted foliage belt, turned inside out so that the mud stains were concealed. She had a brown jacket and her own singed and charcoal-blackened felt boots. And her sidhe necklace.

'I suppose you'll do,' I said.

She looked puzzled and examined herself, looking for whatever it was that hadn't quite met with my approval.

'Forgive me,' I said. 'I know you're unused to company. You look very fine—especially for one who has survived a great fire.'

She smiled, then touched the claws at her throat. 'I need to learn how to use this properly so I can run away with groups of people.'

I watched her caress the gold claws. I didn't understand what she meant, but I believed she was telling me that she meant to learn how to somehow pick up a whole party of men and spirit them away. Maybe fly them through the air.

She continued. 'I'll tell the king that I need to find a way in under his fortress. I'm sure there's a gate in the hill. When I was small I lived near a gate—this feels like the same one.'

I said, 'A way into the Land Under the Hill, the land of the sidhe? The king will want you to close it. To fill it in like a dry well.'

'Why would anyone want to do that?' She looked perplexed. 'The gate has been moved there. It can be moved away. It's making the ground shake because it's resisting movement. Something is stopping it going back where it belongs.'

I knew my king was very slow to change his ideas. He'd exhaust all his own plans before hearing another. How to warn her? I said, 'The court is decorous, even in an encampment. One thing the king intensely dislikes is the gluttony of women. Any offer of further refreshment—a second glass of wine, for example—will be a test. Don't take that second glass or fill your plate again. Eat what you're offered, and then parlay, and don't eat afterwards.' I was sure the witch would be safe from anything but attack by stealth—a sleeping draught, probably one of her own—and being bled on the keep's foundation stones without ever waking up.

Adhan frowned. Her brow rumpled strangely as if a diamond-shaped boss of bone suddenly showed above the place her eyebrows met. And I saw it again, the look of a bird of prey worn like a crown above her gentle eyes. 'I feel that I should do something to save you from this king, Kernow,' she said.

I said, 'That's not your place.'

'Oh, well—I don't really have a place,' she answered.

Eighteen

Go to Your Gate

That was where the story broke for me,' Kernow told Taryn. 'I delivered Adhan the witch to the king's pavilion and never saw her again. The following day the ground shook once more and the fused and still-cooling foundations slumped into a hollow in the hill. A spring appeared, Nant Newydd in the Welsh—new waterway. An ancestor of yours built a dam on that brook, Taryn Cornick of the Northovers, and made a lake.

'It was another thirty years before I heard the rest of it. What happened under the hill. By that time I had retired from soldiering and was living on charity at the court of the Chosen King. It was summer. A summer with the same hot and windy weather. Most of the court were away. The king had gone to fetch his bride and cement a great alliance. Effort and plenty had departed the castle with the king's progress. The bakehouse was closed because there were too few mouths to feed to justify anyone having to tend ovens in the terrible heat. Food was spoiling in the castle storehouses, and vegetables wilting in the ground.

'The weather made my eyes burn, as if there were smoke in the air. On the hottest day I sought relief in the wizard's orchard, a maze of walled gardens where the court's prized fruit trees grew. The fruit garden was an innovation of the king's wizard, patron, and teacher. I hadn't met the man, though I'd often seen him at a distance, in his homespun clothes, little, bent, brown, and many, many years my senior.

'I found a bench in the deepest shade. After a time the wizard turned up and sat beside me. When I offered my mannerly greeting, he gazed at me intently, then said, "Kernow. You won't know me, but we were together, up to our knees in the Monnow when the world was on fire, on a day just like this." He spoke, and at once I knew him. He was so changed, from a youth to an ancient, from woman to man, but no one who saw that spell twice—that spell on him—could mistake it for another thing. It disguised him as ordinary, but its strength and character were so distinct and unmistakable that, when encountered a second time, the spell itself identified him. There could be no two spells like that.

'We sat together in the hot shade, pensioner and powerful witch, and he—the old man whom I'd known as a young woman—told me the rest: what Adhan had said to the king, and then went on to do.

'Taryn Cornick of the Northovers,' said Kernow, 'my first tale will be enough for you to wash, card, spin, and spool for now. I'll tell you the rest when we next meet. Now I must bid you goodnight, and climb into my bed, to be ready for tomorrow's onslaught of children.'

Taryn wished Kernow goodnight and repaired to her bedroll. There, surrounded by the soft susurrations of her reed mattress, she switched on the phone from the OtterBox, opened its Notes app, and spent half an hour writing an outline of the tale.

A few days later Taryn was lying in a field, looking up at the sky, her view interrupted only by the occasional zigging black dot of a foraging bee. She was trying to remember when she'd last lain in long grass. She recalled stretching out on a bench at the hunting camp in the Rockies and gazing up at the forest canopy, its tessellated pattern of shy crowns. But when had she last let anything rob her of peripheral vision?

In her first year away from home Taryn was casual about locking the door of her dorm room in her university hall of residence. Then Bea was killed. After that Taryn would get up several times during the night to check she had locked her door. She didn't feel safe.

She dropped out and went to live with her mother, and before she'd even unpacked she bought a deadbolt for her bedroom door. For years she wouldn't lie down until she felt secure, either safe or in charge, as she had with Alan. She never went any lonely place alone. She wouldn't walk along the street wearing earbuds, and if a man approached her, to ask for directions or—more often—spare change, she'd give him as wide a berth as she could without provoking hostility. She never surrendered her situational awareness, didn't sit on a park bench, close her eyes, tip her head back, and bask. She kept her eyes open and always wore the bear bells of an unwelcoming stare, a look that said, *Stay well clear of me.*

Taryn stretched her arms up over her head. Her turf bed rustled and released more grassy perfume. She was full to the brim with a sense of contentment, an animal happiness that wasn't normal for her yet, but which she now felt she had a right to.

She'd have to move soon. When they'd arrived at Hell's Gate, Shift said he reckoned it was two hours till sunrise in London. He wasn't sure of the date. Either the tenth or eleventh of May. Taryn's flight was on the twelfth. But that was all right. She'd rather not have to shop for food or settle in. She had removed the perishables from her refrigerator before she'd left for Aix and hadn't been back to her flat since.

The clouds in one corner of her slot of blue had a rose tinge, and the browsing insects and nodding flowers were silhouettes. The sun had gone from this level stretch of the Horse Road.

Taryn sat up. The sun had vanished behind one range of hills but was still lighting a higher range, further off. The shaded hills were a smoky lavender, the open valley green, with a miles-wide circle around the gate of wildflowers: blue and orange, red, purple and white.

Shift and Neve were leaning on the stone pillars that flanked the gate. Shift was crumbling dry seed heads for a flock of those apricot-coloured songbirds. The birds happily pecked between the pillars, quite unperturbed. Neve wore the sword, and her right hand was covered by the claws of the Gatemaker's glove.

The Gatemaker, Shift's grandmother. Neve's mother. A person, not an emblematic thing. Then Taryn thought, *I must ask Shift if he knows where the apostrophe belongs in Princes Gate. Whether it's fairy princes, or a particular prince.*

Once it was light in London, Neve would send Taryn out onto one of those meadow trails in Hyde Park where strangers still met to canoodle (Taryn's father's word) on fine summer days. Taryn would head towards the bridle path—there'd be people there, even if it was very early or raining. Taryn would walk along the bridle path towards her street. Either that, or her phone would find its telco, give her the correct time, and she could sign in to her Uber and summon a ride.

She raised her phone and started filming Neve, Shift, the songbirds.

The birds exploded from the ground and scattered.

Shift and Neve came off the pillars. Neve drew her sword—it came out of its scabbard singing as if it were alive.

Taryn dropped her arm and backed off a few steps—but then she raised the phone again.

The air between the pillars turned dark, and a demon stepped through the gate.

Taryn was filled with dismay. She had absorbed Shift's explanation of demons—that they were either spirits or bodies. She was sure Neve and he were expecting a body. This thing might be physical, but it wasn't solid, and it had no limbs that Neve might lop off.

It was huge, a good ten foot in height, and of near equivalent circumference. It was bruise-black and fuming. It looked like dark pigment dropped into disturbed water, turbulent and tendrilled, as if at any moment it might mix all the way into the local atmosphere and make a stain in a lighter shade of its colour, like friar's balsam dropped in water, with a dash of gentian violet. Old-fashioned medicines.

Taryn retreated to what she hoped would be a safe distance. She didn't flee, because the monster stood between her and her life.

The demon noticed Shift and Neve. It shimmered: a single beat like a vibrating timpani.

Neve lunged forward and thrust the sword into the roiling mass. The demon emitted a bubbling squeal like red-hot metal plunged into water. Its body reshaped itself around the blade. It formed a vortex and pulled on the sword. Neve didn't let go. She put her head down and leapt through the demon. She landed, her clothes ripped and scuffed, her hands and face bleeding, grazed, as if she'd been licked by an orbital sander. She didn't seem to notice her injuries, but instantly spun and slashed at the mass, her eyes blazing. She danced around the edge of it, striking at it, disturbing it, and, Taryn thought, driving it away from the gate.

For a moment it seemed that was what was happening. Neve was ferocious in her attack, and the demon was retreating from her blows.

But then the demon rolled sideways and surged past Neve. It engulfed Shift and folded him into its boiling, oily body.

Neve lurched and stumbled as if she'd been leaning on something and it had collapsed beneath her. She regained her footing and straightened. Her cold gaze calculated what her next move might be.

The demon encased Shift but didn't touch him. He wasn't struggling, and the substance of his attacker seemed to be suspended everywhere a centimetre from his skin. Shift looked out at them through vortices of smoke and spinning grains of darkness. He was pale with shock, or pain, but his expression was composed. He was weathering it, whatever it was—stricture, maybe, or heat, for wherever the demon moved the grass had withered and blackened.

Shift met Neve's eyes, then gave her a slight nod. To Taryn it was more a look of calm resignation than *I've got this*.

Neve thought so too. She changed tactics from offensive to defensive. She lowered her sword, stepped forward, and pointed at the gate with her gloved hand.

The ground shook, and green rays of ionised air streamed up from between the stone pillars.

Neve collapsed onto her knees and dropped her fists into the grass to steady herself. The green aurora melted away, and the ground stopped shaking.

Neve raised her head and gazed at the gate. She looked puzzled.

The landscape was utterly silent. Even Taryn's ears had stopped ringing. There was only a faint whispering crackle from the hot turf where the demon stood, and Neve's harsh panting.

Then Taryn's skin came alive with a horrible sensation, as if she were being stroked by stiff quills in an upward motion. Her hair filled with static and lifted from her head. Taryn knew it had, because the same thing happened to Neve. The sidhe's shining mane flared and lifted.

The demon spoke. Its voice was like the sound made by sparks splattering from a welder's torch. 'Little god of the marshlands,' said the demon to Shift. 'Fate-forsworn princeling.' It was at once mocking and a formal address. The formality was some kind of feint, because as soon as it stopped speaking it darted across the grass, making for the gate. Shift's feet left the ground, and the demon folded him, his face to his knees, as it contracted itself and slipped back between the pillars.

Neve followed, her gloved hand pointed, some now discernible power pouring out of her.

Unmasked by the demon's sensory disturbances, Taryn felt a reach, a grasp, and a titanic alteration coming from the gate, from the glove, and from Neve's body.

Again the ground quivered, and the air ionised.

Taryn's nostrils filled with the scent of ozone. Cracks formed on the ground at the base of the pillars as they rocked in their sockets. The grove that surrounded the gate began to lose all its spring foliage. The leaves detached without drying and pelted down around Taryn and Neve. Neve gave a cry of rage and threw up her arms. Everything quietened.

The sun had gone. The cool evening breeze came and chilled the sweat on Taryn's breastbone and breathed flowers into her face. The Sidh flowed back into itself, all sweetness and calm life.

Neve sank to the ground, dropped the sword, and pulled off the glove. She used her shirt's hem to clean her face, then asked Taryn to bring her water. Her voice was hoarse.

Taryn went to the spring, filled a copper basin she found there, and carried it to Neve. She took off her lambswool scarf and dabbed at Neve's grazes. The scarf grew pink and stippled by flaxseed-sized grains of blackish metal.

Neve studied the grains between her wet fingers. Her gloved hand was unharmed; the knuckles of her other hand were skinned raw. She got up, stooped, and shook all the matter from her hair. 'The demon had added iron filings, I believe,' she said.

'Is it making you sick?'

'I can wipe most of it off. I'll walk along the stream and find a pool to bathe in.' Neve snapped her spine straight, and her hair whipped up over her head and fell into its usual shining waves. Taryn got a whiff of Neve's bodily perfume, which was exquisite, like good earth, moss, cold water, and fresh pine needles.

'But first I must put you through the gate.'

Taryn looked at the air between the pillars. The ground was glowing green there, carpeted with plucked leaves.

'The gate is intact and functional. Only the way to Hell is closed to me. I have no idea how.' Neve gave a sharp, furious bark of laughter.

'Maybe Shift blocked you.'

'Not without the glove.' Neve stopped brushing at her clothes and eyed Taryn. 'He didn't let himself be taken, if that's what you're thinking. That wouldn't serve anyone's purpose.'

'Hell wants him,' Taryn said.

'It wants him to volunteer, Taryn. Hell has promised us one thousand years free of the Tithe in exchange for Shift. A million Taken souls spared. But for Hell to take Shift, he must give himself.'

Taryn swallowed a few times, as if spit would help her digest this. Then she said, 'He was telling you something. Just now.'

'He was telling me not to risk my life.'

Taryn nodded.

'He's the last child of the blood, and grandson of a Gatemaker. That's always been his value to those of us who treasure him. Others of us would like to trade his valuable soul while it still has value. There has been a stalemate for a long time—the opportunists have waited to be sure he's no longer strong enough to defend himself against however many of them it would take to hustle him to Hell's Gate, and then nag him through it. They believe they can make him hate himself enough to go. Or he'll become so afraid of his future he'll decide to make the best use of his remaining time by offering himself and being honoured in our memory. That's why they treat him with contempt. They're hardening their hearts against him. He's planning to attend the Moot. At which they mean to prevail on his loneliness and misery and fear, and his sense that he owes us for our friendship and hospitality—as if he isn't one of us. If that doesn't produce the result they want, then they plan to take him by force.'

'He knows this?'

'I haven't told him they're planning to take him by force. I'd rather their treachery comes as a surprise, and he defends himself instinctively.'

Neve continued to dab at her face. Blood was still seeping to the surface, bright, as if purging itself of iron was its business before it clotted.

'My people think they can beguile and manipulate any mortal. And they think of Shift as mortal. The spell my sister Adhan put on him before she died makes everyone see him as slight, plain, insubstantial. As *no one special*. My people imagine they can inveigle him. Once he was too wise to fall for any of their tricks. Too knowledgeable. Now they think he's sufficiently diminished to give in.' Neve rinsed the cloth and wrung it out. Watery blood was flowing in pink rivulets on her face and throat. The bodice of her dress was stained. The silk thread of the embroidered flowers and vines was more thirsty than the plain linen and had taken the blood to show red on pink.

'Are you saying they think they can force him, and they can't?'

'He's almost as shifty now as he was when he was a child. Back then, when he wanted to whistle, he'd turn himself into a songbird. When he wanted to run, he'd be a deer or horse; swim, and he'd be an otter. There's that. And his bones still remember his formation in the womb when his grandmother took his mother from gate to gate for months, trying to make a Gatemaker of Adhan's unborn child, in the same way she'd tried to make Gatemakers of Adhan and me. Her efforts didn't pay off in the way she wanted, but when he has the glove, the gates answer him faster and move further. His only weakness is the sidhe susceptibility to iron.'

'You're saying he's too strong or slippery for your people to force him to do anything? That the only chance they have is to persuade him to show his love for them by sacrificing himself?'

'Or to be so sad and afraid of forgetting that he just gives up.'

Neve kept washing. Taryn watched tiny grains of iron rolling out of the wounds. There was no sign of swelling or bruising, and Taryn wondered whether these people swelled or bruised. Swelling would staunch the bleeding—but then the iron wouldn't wash away so readily.

'Does he know you're worried about him?'

'I think his attachment to you is a very good sign. And this business with the Firestarter seems to be holding his interest.'

Taryn wondered if the main reason Neve was involved in their search for the Firestarter was to oversee a therapeutic activity for her dangerously depressed relative. But she didn't dare ask.

Neve said, 'He seems to have decided to stay free and trust his friends to teach him about himself again. And next time his forgetting looms, as it is now, I can tell him that once he's a child again, I'll be a mother to him.'

Taryn thought of the dazed, bewitched human child she'd glimpsed at Neve's house and shivered.

Neve became practical. 'I'll send you to London, then go gather some worthies so we might approach Hell and demand Shift's immediate return.'

Taryn waited to hear her add 'Don't worry', or somesuch, but realised she'd be waiting forever for ordinary reassurances from this woman. She wrapped her arms around herself. 'Will I be safe?'

Neve actually scowled. It took a little of the edge off her beauty. 'I'll put you in Hyde Park, not Hell.'

'I mean safe from my demon. It won't find me?'

'It's trapped in Princes Gate.'

Taryn pressed her lips together and nodded.

Neve picked up the glove and fastened it on again. She sat for a moment, her head down, shoulders heaving. She took deep breaths, gathering herself.

Taryn got up and walked onto the gleaming leaf carpet and waited. After a moment Neve joined her, stood beside her, and stretched out her arm.

This time Taryn felt the gate as a lurch in the centre of her chest. A wind blew through her and filtered her life away with it, giving her in return sorrow and longing, with a lift of wonder at its end. Neve put a hand on Taryn's shoulder and propelled her forward into the park, a meadow surrounded by great trees and bathed in traffic fumes. Taryn stood breathing her world. Her throat and eyes prickled. She was alone.

And then her phone vibrated. The message welcomed her to British Telecom. The time was 7:13 a.m. The date was the eleventh of May.

After a shower and change, Taryn went right back out again to spend the day doing many more things than she'd bargained on. She visited her bank to order a new credit card, replaced her phone, transferring the number of her old one, which had drowned when she came through the gate under the lake on her first return from the Sidh. She decided to keep Stuart's phone, but she would not use it unless there was something she wanted MI5 to hear.

She finally thought of food but managed only a few mouthfuls of pot noodles before feeling the sodium and preservatives pinching the blood vessels in her legs. The noodles went in the rubbish.

Taryn switched on her new phone. There were 116 text messages, and her voicemail was full.

Fifteen of the voice messages were her agent, each message progressively more desperate, until, after ten, Angela's tone suddenly became careful and gentle. She said she'd heard from Taryn's friend Carol about the retreat. She hoped it was 'doing the trick'. She said she'd taken Carol's word for it that Taryn wouldn't want to cancel anything. 'So, I've fielded calls from your editor and the chair of your session in Auckland. Now is *your time*, Taryn—you have to seize these opportunities.'

When Taryn was two-thirds of the way through her voice messages she had a clear sense of the story her father and Carol had been telling to fend everyone off. No, Taryn wasn't in rehab. No, she hadn't had a breakdown. It was just that a police detective had upset her by stirring up matters around the murder of her sister, and she'd decided to go on a retreat.

The story appeared to have originated with her father, whose latest message was a series of statements, half boast and half reassurance, about how he'd 'set that copper straight'. Presumably Jacob. 'I'll call you when I land, darling. I'm flying out early. I have to make time for Peter. He's been in touch about a new project,' Basil confided, in gloating tones. He was also a guest at the Auckland and Sydney festivals, with his tell-all memoir of his years working on the fantasy epic.

Only six of the messages were silences, though the last was four days earlier.

Taryn got a cramp. She'd been sitting at the dining table for over an hour. She wasn't used to immobility. She did some stretches, then stayed on the floor answering emails. Then she sent a text to Carol: 'Thank you for fielding Angela. The "retreat" was a good idea. I'll call you tomorrow.'

And she would, from the airport.

Then Angela: 'I'm on deck. I've spoken to my Auckland chair.' She hadn't, but she would.

To her father: 'Thank you for being there for me. You're a lifesaver. I fly out tomorrow. It'll be great to see you.'

She got up, found her other phone, the one from the OtterBox, which offered her not a single communication other than Telecom's welcome. She located the few photos and videos she'd made, uploaded them to her Dropbox, and used her new phone to send Jacob the link. Shift claimed Stuart's phone was bugged—'bugged', he'd said, then, racking his brains for a term from his thrillers, *cloned*. If the phone was cloned, then let MI5 make something of icy blue mountains, a long tunnel of blossoming fruit trees, a dark blue pond fringed by yellow irises, Jane at the cooking fire, Shift—as difficult to photograph as he was hard to see—drying his boots, his bare feet curled upwards, toes underlit by the flames. Let them make something of the three white deer on a green hillside, a fishing eagle on a branch by a cascade, a village of peat sod huts with turf roofs, three old women in the foreground, smiling tooth-lessly. Let them make something of the vague, slender, dark-skinned young man—the same seen earlier drying his boots—leaning on one menhir while a heart-stoppingly beautiful woman inclined on its mate; both relaxed, one hard to see, the other impossible to miss. And then those same two in action, as if in a movie, which is what MI5 might sup-pose the footage to be—leaked images from the television fantasy, fool-ishly sent by Basil Cornick to his daughter, then even more foolishly passed on by her to her new friend the detective inspector. Someone she trusted, sure, but wasn't that always how leaked things got around? So, television, that was how MI5 would see the fighting figures facing a dark clot of something smoky, tattered, opaque. Though surely someone smart would ask how Basil Cornick could use his phone to produce a process shot with the FX monster *already in it?*

The flight was an ordeal. Thirteen hours from London to Singapore, and ten and a half from Singapore to Auckland. Taryn had booked a stopover on advice from her New Zealand hosts, but her hotel was over an hour from Changi in slow traffic, and from the motorway the view of ships in the white haze of the Singapore Strait wasn't wonderful, as it once would have been. There had been a catastrophic leak right outside her hotel room, and all night she could hear the roaring whine of a commercial carpet dryer even through her earplugs.

On the second leg of her journey, Taryn sat in the dimmed airliner cabin, scrolling back and forth through the scant notes she'd taken on the tale she'd been so ceremoniously given the keeping of—the story of a woman who seemed only able to ask of her life which king it would be best to serve. Taryn readjusted her headrest for the tenth time and reflected that the headrests in economy class were made for men with substantial back fat. Her demon hadn't caught her up at thirty thousand feet and going eight hundred kilometres an hour, but here was that impatient, critical eye again. And it was *her* eye. Her dyspeptic self.

Perhaps, in a world too full of people, *she* was the one too many.

Taryn put herself aside and returned to Kernow's tale.

The orphan child of a virgin, required by a tormented king as a sacrifice to stabilise the foundations of a tower.

This story is familiar, she thought, and ran the thread of it back through her hands.

The witch changed herself into a horse to get to the river in time to use its water to make a shield for herself and Kernow's men. Kernow had been puzzled that the horse the witch had changed into was a colt, not a filly or mare. So that meant *Adhan* was the one under the iris-covered grave mound. Her son had dressed in her clothes and used her name. He had presented himself as dead. The boy. The little god of the marshlands.

A tower, a stripling wizard, a cruel and troubled king. It was like a fairy tale. Familiar. But fairy tales were always familiar.

Taryn was tired. Her brain had snagged on the story's details, its deer horn medicine bottles, tree bark rain barrels, and the smell of scorched river weed. She knew the Monnow but couldn't think where Shift's marsh might be. Probably it had been ditched and drained in the eighteenth century and used for pasture and was now a grassy tract full of mobile homes, half of them inhabited by frugal retirees.

I have to sleep, Taryn thought. The jet's engines were only a little lower-pitched than the carpet-drying machine of the night before. Taryn was desperate to stop listening and making comparisons. Weighing matters. Thinking things through. She closed her eyes and remembered somewhere quiet and uncrowded, the gallery at the top of her grandparents' house. She was walking on the long runner of balding carpet. Rain was ticking on the skylight. And Beatrice was walking behind her, quiet only for a moment as she came up with another story about the blank spaces on the walls where there should be Northovers, those complete people, who were now almost completely gone.

Nineteen

Questions from the Audience

Auckland spread out along an isthmus. From the air it appeared less built than grown, like coral on the bones of a volcanic cone. It was green, wet, sunny, its atmosphere white with water vapour rather than with traffic fumes. The plane came in over throngs of mangroves, sunlight scintillating on the water between muddy leaves, and blunt suckers thumbs-up in silt. It crossed warehouses, part of a spreading low-built light industrial zone. A bulldozer was carving out a new footing from loose black earth, and James Northover's granddaughter, passing overhead, wondered whether all the soil sealed under roads and buildings and parking lots was as good as that. *What a waste.*

Taryn pulled her plait in front of her and, as she had used to when she was a child, pressed it to her nose and inhaled. The smell of her hair always turned back the clock. At school it held the scent of home. Now it smelled of the airliner's recycled air and the shampoo from her noise-besieged hotel room in Singapore. She had wanted it to smell, at least at its roots, of cold pond water.

Taryn was keen to get out in the sunlight to reset her body clock. She set out without directions from the concierge and took the easy down-hill, looking for coffee. She passed places where sugar was spilled on tables and the cups not cleared away, and internet cafés full of boys in big sling chairs facing screens.

She went back uphill and turned to walk along a ridge and over a viaduct with an inward-curving Perspex barrier mounted on its balustrade. Not a safety barrier, but suicide prevention. She thought, *This must be the place of impulses.* She remembered Pujol, whose family would still suppose he jumped, when he had in fact been pushed.

Taryn picked up her pace and hurried off the bridge.

She found a café to her liking and sat outside with the sun on her back. A diverse population ambled past. Most were young. Half of them were wearing T-shirts.

I'm in the South Pacific, Taryn thought with real delight.

Even after two coffees her eyes kept drifting shut. She gave in, returned to the hotel, closed her curtains, and set her phone to wake her in plenty of time for the gala opening, a 'true stories told live' event featuring, among others, the famous actor Basil Cornick.

Five minutes later she sat up and phoned reception to tell them she was expecting a guest sometime during the next few days. 'If Mr Shift arrives can you let me know at once—but otherwise not disturb me.' She said thank you, hung up, and returned the room to darkness.

The pillows, quilt, and mattress topper were down-filled and almost as talkative as a bracken bed.

The smoky demon had shrunk and shivered before it seized hold of Shift. It had grown in volume but thinned at its edges. And when it grabbed him and backed towards the gate, it was less a trapdoor spider seizing a mouse and withdrawing into its burrow than someone in a movie shootout taking hold of a bystander to use as a human shield.

Neve had injured it. It was retreating from her, or from the sword she carried. Shift was just an object it put between itself and its assailant. Shift hadn't put up a fight. Was his surrender a last-minute change in his plans or lifelong, temperamental curiosity? Was taking off the Gate-maker's glove like putting on a disguise? Like dressing in his mother's clothes and name so he could leave the marsh he was always being sent to hide in?

Fifteen minutes after the opening-night performance, festival guests, patrons, and people with swing passes returned to the stage for the party. They lined up at the long barrier of a bar covered in gleaming ranks of champagne flutes, wineglasses, tumblers, and dewy bottles of craft beer. The servers standing with their backs to the orchestra pit were the only ones in danger of a calamitous exit downstage.

Waiters appeared from the wings with platters held head-high, bringing them down to waist height at the first knot of people. Taryn was stuck in a press centre stage and ate whatever canapés managed to reach her: sliced roast beef curled on tiny toasts and dabbed with horseradish cream, porcelain spoons with chopped abalone in yuzu mayonnaise. This had to be her dinner. She was now short of cash, and her credit card hadn't arrived.

Taryn spotted the tall and imposing figure of her father. She took a glass from a tray and headed for him. She slipped under his arm and stood on tiptoes to kiss him. Delighted, he introduced her to his circle of admirers and made a point of mentioning the day and hour of her solo session. Taryn sipped her champagne and waved away a tray with processed meat. Her father noticed. He held her at arm's length, inspected her, and smiled approvingly. 'You must give me the details of that retreat. For when I next need some privacy and pampering.'

'It wasn't an actual retreat. I was just holed up at Alan's Norfolk house.'

Basil Cornick's face did something odd. It was a very expressive face, and whenever he was rethinking his first reaction, strange pauses were produced, like a glitch in a film. 'But Alan's still with Saoirse?'

'Yes, Dad. He's just let me use the house to write.'

'Of course,' said Basil. 'And there's that DI Berger.'

'And what do you know about that DI Berger?'

'When we spoke he seemed very confiding. Then I got off the phone and discovered I'd learned next to nothing.'

Taryn laughed.

'Whatever or whoever it is that's put the roses in your cheeks, I thank them. You look marvellous.'

Taryn had been restored by just one good sleep. She was very fit and enjoying her own skin, the air on her bare shoulders, and the sight of her fingers twined in the knotted fringe of her shawl. How strong and defined they were. Hands that had been shelling beans and scaling fish.

Basil Cornick kept hold of his daughter while accepting more compliments about his True Story—which was told against himself and involved a haughty and glamorous horse. People who had read his book wanted to discuss it. Those who hadn't wanted to pick his brain about what the future held for his mega-hit fantasy programme, now in its fifth season.

'The scriptwriter fellows like to keep us in the dark,' Basil said. 'But I think my character is the only one with enough goodwill in the bank to intervene to save the lives of various people the audience will want saved. So, my *prophecy* is that I'll live long enough to cry mercy for other men.'

A spotlight went on stage right, and the speeches began.

Taryn's father bent to her ear and whispered, 'And that's enough for one evening from the artists. Now let's hear from the actual arts sector. The people with salaries.' Then he straightened and favoured the first speaker with a sunny-natured smile.

The festival organiser was brief and gracious. The mayor of Auckland brief and boosterish. The minister for arts spoke at length, opening with vigour and certainty, then circling back to sniff at her own certainties as if to check that they were indeed her own and proof of her intestinal well-being.

Taryn's father winked at her. The great mimic handed a whole new routine. By the time he got to Sydney, he'd have the New Zealand minister for arts down to a T.

The speeches concluded; the audience changed partners. Taryn's chair bowled up to her and introduced himself, and she spent the next half hour talking about her book with him and various others who leaned in to hear her. After that, she persuaded her chair to introduce her to one of the two international guests she was most keen to meet— an American novelist, a tall man, lanky, yellow of complexion. They had a largely one-sided 'Where have you just come from?' conversation. The novelist was on the festival circuit and making the most of it with travel between gigs.

He told her that six weeks earlier he'd been snowshoeing in the hills above St John's. He'd had to get out of town because there was a dead whale trapped in the ice and, with the melt, it was spreading its stink, so that the shorefront cafés, which normally opened their outdoor seating in April—with heaters and fleece blankets on offer—had kept their patios closed as if it were still midwinter.

And then he told her how St John's was a bit depressed. Fisheries were declining. 'Low catches coming in now as a matter of course.'

Taryn thought of the photograph doing the rounds on Facebook, of a starving polar bear balanced on a pillar of melting sea ice, like a statue on a plinth, a memorial to itself. She thought of Shift, who might know the names of the gods of all the rivers, or at least all those in the south of England and Wales. Then she thought of a scene in Hayao Miyazaki's *Spirited Away*, a film she loved, where a river deity arrives at the heroine's bathhouse. Shuffling and reeking, it floods the tub and scrubbed timber rooms with oily mud, broken bicycles, and supermarket trolleys. All the rotten flotsam that coats the shores of rivers everywhere. Did rivers still have gods, hidden deep in their silt, like frogs hibernating in a dried lakebed?

The novelist had a hand on Taryn's arm. He was smiling at her with a particular sparkling warmth. Taryn was irritated. She'd wanted to ask questions about a recurring character in his dense, social, nuanced novels—and he was hitting on her. She said, 'I must refresh my glass,' and moved away.

She couldn't go on like this. The hostility she often felt towards the men who showed interest in her must not continue to go unexamined. She was a policed border, when she should be an innocent meadow. Nothing bad had ever happened to her. Not anything that counted. She'd experienced the usual low-grade sexual harassment, but no sexual assault.

But of course it was all about Beatrice.

Taryn had been ten the summer that Battle made Beatrice miserable with his naked admiration. Battle started out as a blight on their holiday; then he became extravagantly crazy. He hurt Beatrice and himself, then vanished from their lives. Battle's breakdown was never discussed or explained. But as far as the child Taryn could see, male desire was dangerous—as it sometimes was in cop shows. Nine years later, Webber followed Bea, ran her down, and bundled her into the car boot in which she died. After that Taryn had difficulty seeing any male interest that was directed her way as appealing. Carol's husband's admiration of Carol was sweet, and other men with crushes on her friends were inoffensive. But no one was to look at her that way. Or lay a hand on her, or try to squire her. Those she'd bewitched, like Alan or the Muleskinner, she had to turn herself off to do so. Turn off the dread and suspicion, fury and hatred, and with those emotions *herself*, and her own desire.

The crowd had thinned. Taryn's father spotted her again and gestured at her to stay. He excused himself from some well-dressed patrons—people with an oddly self-effacing air that Taryn was already identifying as a national characteristic. Was it self-effacing, or diffident? Taryn tried to remember what her father's memoir had said about this—something sharp but funny. He'd got away with it, whatever it was, because there he was, throwing his light about, as fluid as she was frozen. Her father, who was always cheating on her mother, Addy, the loneliest person Taryn had ever known.

Taryn's mother had read all the Moomin books to her. There was the part in *Moominpappa at Sea* where Moominmamma takes to spending her days in a room near the top of the lighthouse, painting a garden on its curved, white-washed walls. Day after day, Moominmamma makes more lilac and rose bushes, until she's able to grab hold of the trunk of an apple tree and disappear into her garden. Reading that section, Taryn's mother had started to cry. Taryn had put her hand on the page so that her mother couldn't close the book. Close it and put it away. Moominmamma missed the garden in Moominvalley. It was sad. But Taryn's mother *had* a garden, a nice one, with standard rose bushes and a clematis-covered pergola. What business did her mother have comparing herself to a Moomin in a lighthouse on an island?

Taryn remembered how she had kept the book open but had cried too, not because she understood her mother's sadness but because she was angry at being made to witness it.

Basil Cornick put his arm around his daughter and failed to notice how subdued she was. He launched into a story. A bit of news.

'It seems that Peter has overlooked my remarks about my misery acting with a green screen. Though he has to have his dig. He called me up on Skype . . . ' Basil was now talking through chuckles—he was one of those rare people who could speak clearly whilst laughing. 'And there's his voice coming out of an animatronic bird! A genius thing. There's a project he's working on that he says he knows I'll like. The film is going to be full of animatronic animals. Which means less green screen. And the animals will have operators capable of responding to a performance, reacting to an actor. Anyway, he's arranged an audition in Wellington in three days' time. Just to see how I like it, he says.'

Taryn was happy to hear her father's tell-all memoir hadn't alienated his powerful friends. But, she said, didn't Basil's TV series have two seasons left to run?

'Darling, you must be the only person on the planet in any doubt about how much more of it there is.' Basil kissed her cheek. Then he explained. 'This thing is still in development. I'm keen to see what I can deduce about it from the audition. Peter says I can expect pages tomorrow. They'll be rough, he says, and I'm not to take too much from them about the story's eventual shape. If it looks like a kids' movie in one scene, another will be all terse and gritty. He described it as "a film grounded in the mythical, with flights of nuanced observation about the world we know". I love it that he reversed the usual order of those things, so the mythical is grounding, and the everyday provides the "flights". He says his watchwords for the project are "elegance, intrigue, feeling, grandeur and wonder". Anyway, he insists I'm the man for the job. How nice it is to be the man for the job.'

Taryn's father, in his good humour, grabbed dessert from a passing tray, for him and her, tiny cups of crème brûlée with bamboo spoons. Apparently it was so nice to be wanted that tonight no one needed to be careful of their figure.

'Mind you'—Basil sucked his spoon to achieve the right beat of pause—'it's very hush-hush. Peter prefers I not mention it to anyone. He said, "Don't even mention it to me," with a big animatronic wink.' Basil winked in a mechanical way, then guffawed.

'Do you want me to keep it secret?'

'Well, darling, you don't really know anyone, do you?'

Taryn laughed.

'My library-haunting daughter. How convenient it is that film world gossip can stop with you.' Basil grinned at her in his smugly loving way. Then, 'And you? Have you made time to visit your grandmother?'

Ruth Cornick had intended to come to the festival. She'd wanted to see both Taryn and Basil onstage. She'd told Taryn that she'd enjoyed her former son-in-law's book and thought his 'A Few Remarks in Passing' chapter, which dealt with the death of his daughter and the trial of her killer, was tasteful, well-judged, and moving. Ruth and Basil had had their differences, but she'd been looking forward to seeing him, as well as her only remaining granddaughter. But five weeks before the festival Ruth had broken her ankle walking the Routeburn Track—at eighty.

'Grandma's still in her moon boot,' Taryn said. 'The greataunties and Mum's cousins are a diligent support crew. She's healing quickly. The doctors are astonished, she says.'

'Modestly,' said Basil.

'Yes. She's always talking about this or that "old lady", as if she wasn't one.'

'That's how she's survived. Always future-focussed,' Basil said.

'I'm not,' Taryn said.

Her father drew her close. 'So—you get to sit at Ruth's feet for a few days?'

'I was going to spend the time going over Grandad's papers. But Grandma got one of the cousins to scan them onto a flash drive. I'll print it all at my hotel in Sydney to read on the plane home.'

'Is your interest general, or is there something you're looking for?'

'A scroll box. The Firestarter.'

Basil shook his head. 'It doesn't ring any bells.'

'I'm pretty sure it was what Jason Battle was looking for when he set fire to the library. I used to think he must have meant to destroy it. But I've done a little more research—in my own screeds of scanned documents—and apparently legend has it the thing is nonflammable. It's like a rock in a field of tall grass. If you can't locate the rock, you set fire to the field.' This was Taryn's latest insight about the Firestarter, one she was keen to communicate to Shift. Hell setting fires to locate the Firestarter was very different from their wanting to destroy it.

'Wasn't Battle going on about a Torah?'

'He was doing that too.'

'I've never heard mention of this Firestarter.'

'It's slippery,' Taryn said. 'Grandad was a man who tended to call a spade a spade, but when I go through his papers, believe me, I'll be looking for mentions of shovels, trowels, and scoops as well.'

She had fed her father a line. He assumed an expression both gleeful and haughty and performed Oscar Wilde's Gwendolen: 'I am glad to say that I have never seen a spade. It is obvious that our social spheres have been widely different.'

Taryn's solo session was on her second full day on the ground. It was at eleven thirty, which people told her was a good time. Not too early, nor in the metabolic slump following lunch.

Taryn planned to leave her hotel at eight thirty and go to someone else's session before hers, in order to have something in her head other than how little she knew about her own subject. Her book felt like all she could call on—the sum of her knowledge only an inch of topsoil over clay. She'd just have to have faith in the occasion and her chair.

All my figurative language has turned to nature, she thought as she waited, tapping her key card on the black granite countertop of the hotel reception. *Polar bears. Topsoil.*

'Good morning, ma'am,' said the woman at the reception desk. 'What can I do for you today?'

Taryn adjusted her message from the day before. If her friend Mr Shift came asking after her, could they please give him this ticket to her session? 'Also this one, to Basil Cornick's, at four. Tell Mr Shift I expect to be at the Aotea Centre all day.'

The receptionist slipped the tickets into an envelope and filed it away.

Taryn walked down the hill to Queen Street. The road was steep and slippery. Fallen leaves were rotting on the pavement. She had gone from spring to autumn, and that day that seemed stranger than the transition from the Horse Road to Hyde Park, because it was spring in both those places, as it should be.

In the green room Taryn's chair went over the outline of proceedings they'd decided in their emails and their short conversation at the opening-night party. In fact, there'd been only one email Taryn had answered, late, and she'd agreed to everything he suggested. But at least this way he was still interested in how she'd answer his questions, since she hadn't already run her answers nervously past him. She did ask him if they might push the whole subject of Nazi book-burning to the end of the discussion—since it inevitably came up in questions from the floor. Then she said, 'And how about we allow only a little time for those?'

'Why?'

The sound technician's knuckles were warm on Taryn's neck as he adjusted the wire of the microphone looped over her ear. Its little flesh-coloured bud bumped her mouth. He pulled it away, his fingers brushing her lips.

'I don't want that,' she said, in rather too definite a way. Then, by way of explanation, she asked her chair if he had been in the first session that morning. 'In the big auditorium? The Irish poet?'

Her chair pulled a face. 'He was unlucky. It was his chair's fault. I'm not going to let you be bushwhacked, Taryn. I'll be the brute who says, "Excuse me, is there a question in your question?"'

The technician had finished. He gave Taryn's shoulder a gentle squeeze.

Taryn's reading went well, and so did the conversation component of her session. She had a good-sized audience, some of them having come as a way of browsing a book they hadn't read.

Taryn told her audience about Hulagu Khan—and talked about the predations of one faith against another, and books as a casualty of that. She talked about the deliberate or collateral destruction of libraries in preindustrial conflicts, dwelling on what happened to the library on Iona after the failure of William Wallace's rebellion. She spoke of the two noble libraries bought for forty shillings during the reign of Henry VIII and used as toilet paper—and duly inventoried as a supply that lasted ten years. She told of the libraries of Buda and Pest burned by Suleiman the Magnificent. As an example of collateral destruction she mentioned the library destroyed by Thomas Fairfax's army during the English Civil War. (And flushed, remembering how the Firestarter had passed through that calamity unscathed.) She acknowledged the ruin of the libraries of Strasbourg, Louvain, the Molsheim Charterhouse in Paris. 'And many more,' she said. 'And many more.'

She gave bare numbers for the casualties of aerial bombing in World War Two—books, with a correlation to buildings and human lives. Beauvais, forty-two thousand books; Tours, two hundred thousand; Douai, one hundred and ten thousand; Chartres, twenty-three thousand books and two thousand manuscripts—some of those, only carbonised by heat, had been preserved and, thanks to modern methods, would one day be transcribed again. Italy, two million books, thirty-nine thousand manuscripts. Great Britain during the Blitz, twenty million books. Germany, ten million in public collections, and the rest, twenty-seven cities' worth of books.

She talked about books as collectibles, of great price and, by contrast, people's cherished personal libraries of 'little or no resale value', as all estate agents know. Lastly, so that the subject could be managed, Taryn's chair asked her to speak about Nazi book burnings.

'First there was a list of books containing "inaccurate information"—or, if you will, "fake news".'

Laughter.

'These were banned,' she said. 'If a book is deemed a bad character and sent packing, it cannot, like a homeless person, go walking the roads looking for succour or pity. You don't have to feed books, but, whereas a hungry person can survive a night out in wet weather, a book will not. An unhoused book is doomed.'

'Why did librarians burn the books rather than tearing out the offending pages or crossing out the lines with supposed lies in them?' Taryn's chair asked.

She said, 'You can see librarians' failure to try even that as the start of German society's treachery towards itself. Yes, it's meaningful that books were piled on bonfires, and *what* books they were, and *who* had written them. But that librarians collaborated, and why they did, is more than a fact that bears remembering; it's a question we should keep asking. Why do we sometimes decide that the things our ancestors have made, and kept, and cared for are suddenly too many mouths to feed, or of bad character and a menace to society? Why, for instance, is it unremarkable that we have warehouses full of garden furniture and running shoes and bails of bubble wrap, while public libraries are "rationalising their collections" to make space? Why does that happen? Well, one thing I think is that it's related to the defunding of the humanities in our universities, a refusal of one of the great conditions of history: that today cannot know what tomorrow will need. It's always better to keep books. In the same way that it's better not to pollute waterways and cover arable land with asphalt.'

'So it's the principle of preservation,' her chair said. 'Of conservation.'

'Yes. And it's the practice of not being high-handed towards the past. Or the future.'

'Can't it also be said that, in a way, books have souls? Here, many of us believe our waterways do. Rivers have mauri: life force. Wairua: spirit.'

'I think we should act as if *we* have souls,' Taryn said. 'Immortal souls we might imperil by cruelty or bad faith or a serious lack of charity. And if imagining that books have souls helps us believe we do, then books absolutely have souls.'

'In your book.'

She laughed. 'In my book.'

'And rivers?'

Taryn said, 'I was talking to a Welshman a few days ago who spoke quite naturally about the god of a certain river. The Monnow. It flows into the Wye at Monmouth, where my mother's family are from. I'd very much like to think those two rivers—the rivers of my childhood—have protective spirits.'

Then, having steered the discussion around the Nazi book burnings to what they agreed was at least a less predictable place, Taryn's chair asked for the house lights to come up. 'Let's have questions from the floor.'

The audience became visible. They looked friendly and stimulated. Taryn relaxed and smiled at them. She waited for a question, hoping they had circumvented any dull or hostile ones.

A man stood up to put a question that Taryn at first found impossible to get a purchase on, even though she could hear every word, since he had a BBC version of a New Zealand accent. He said that, in all honesty, he had not read her book, but he'd like her to explain what, from her talk, he understood to be her position. He had an air of faintly indignant surprise. Taryn realised she was frowning at him, purely from the effort of trying to follow his question. He said he had listened to her radio interview; that was why he'd come along to her session. From the interview, and her talk that day, he got the sense that her book had the wrong emphasis on certain historical events.

A minute later Taryn had the gist of his problem, which was that facts he treasured, and considered undervalued, were known to some young woman, who had written a book and got to be onstage commanding the attention of an audience, talking about things he'd supposed only he knew and cared about.

What on earth could she say in response to that?

Taryn hitched up her eyebrows. She didn't mean to look quizzical, only to avoid staring at him narrow-eyed.

Her chair asked for some clarification so she might answer. He appeared to have forgotten his promise to be the brute. Perhaps he knew who the man was—someone who must be given a fair hearing. The man rephrased his question. It appeared he thought Taryn had taken an interest in the subject in the service of fashion. 'Library fires are suddenly fashionable,' he explained.

'Oh dear. Everybody's going to want one,' Taryn said.

The audience laughed.

The questioner looked furious. 'I'm making a serious point.'

Taryn regrouped. She set off in her most gracious manner. 'Well, of course my book isn't a work of scholarship. It's for the general reader. That means it's less inclined to be exhaustive with the evidence and more inclined to expand in what I hope is a thought-provoking way on its arguments. A book for the general reader on an esoteric subject has to argue for its own interestingness by being interesting. And never argue for its own importance, which a work of scholarship may do. I consider the balancing act of "being accessible" a discipline rather than a limitation. What I hope is that I'm inviting people to think about libraries and what they mean to us. To think about what's kept, what's lost, what's destroyed. My book has to be welcoming, like a public library, rather than an archival collection.'

The audience applauded.

Taryn smiled at the man, and he sat down, his jaw tight.

Another man was already waiting at by the microphone in the far aisle. He began, 'I have yet to hear you make a distinction between . . .'

He thought that her correlation of books, buildings, and human bodies meant she didn't put people first.

Two minutes later Taryn had sweat running down her back and was wondering if this third degree she was getting was because she was a woman, or English, or had red hair, or whether she had walked into some current public tussle about the worth of libraries, in which case someone should have filled her in.

Next, a woman approached the microphone to compliment Taryn, rather than ask a question. 'I love your way with stories,' she said. She was red in the face. 'I *enjoyed* your book. And I found your talk illuminating.' The woman retreated to her seat while everyone clapped.

Taryn thanked her. So, it wasn't the audience as an entity. It wasn't Auckland or New Zealand. It was just that man, and that man, and— oh, God—this one shambling along the aisle to the microphone, big, with a grey ponytail and a shapeless coat and, on his head, something like a stockman's hat.

His tone was not censorious, not accusatory or querulous. But he didn't like the microphone, and he whispered into it, his voice soft and deep.

'You have spoken of efforts to preserve precious books and manuscripts in times of trouble. But in answering a question you say, "What is kept, what is lost, what is destroyed."'

'You mean I forgot to say who *chooses* what's kept or destroyed?'

He shook his head.

'You mean I forgot to mention what is hidden?'

He nodded, the shadows flowing in and out of the hollows under his stark browbone. 'Things are not hidden, and are destroyed. And things are hidden and forgotten, so lost.'

This she could talk about. 'In times of trouble the decision to move a library often comes too late. Almost always because the librarians' sense of duty to scholars outweighs their caution. Even in settled times there's a tension between the necessity of making books available to researchers and of conserving them for the future. When someone gifts their collection to a library, the gift usually comes with conditions. Either because the material is sensitive, or because it's precious and fragile and shouldn't be put into the hands of the merely curious. The manuscripts must be like maidens in a parlour with librarians as their chaperones.'

More laughter.

'Of course, now many libraries with manuscripts are putting them online. The British Library has a wonderful blog about its medieval collection. I think that kind of curated availability is the future of collections. Instead of an archive being open to scholars, who bring their scholarship in, the archive comes to the public, mediated by the people who care for it.'

'Everything will be open and to hand?' her questioner said.

Taryn nodded. 'An idea strong in our culture is that information should be available and transparent. So is the opposite idea—that the Secret Services, or whoever, are concealing vital things from us, yet at the same time poking their noses into all our business. But if you mean whether the availability of precious materials online will make us forget the back room, the vault—yes, I think it will. There is a school of thought that claims that, because of the internet, we are awash in uncurated information, and that has made us lose our appetite and judgement. I'm not sure that's true. But I do think we forget what's not there. Which is a tautology. I mean, we forget what isn't on the internet. We even neglect the idea of what's not there. Or we acknowledge what's been destroyed, while not trying quite as hard as we might to find what's lost or misfiled.'

'What *is* lost? What is not there?'

'You want an example?'

Again he nodded, darkness sliding about like liquid in the hollows under his brow.

Taryn had a moment of light-hearted daring. She said, 'Well, for example, there is a scroll box known as "the Firestarter", since it survived at least six documented conflagrations, going back to antiquity. For a short time it resided in my grandfather's library at Princes Gate, a manor house in the Wye Valley, having found its way there accidentally, or illicitly, or perhaps even *superstitiously*, since it came through a bombing raid that damaged part of the British Museum, when other things in its vicinity did not come through. The curators might have superstitiously refused to take it back when the war was over, since it's certainly not in the British Museum now. That's my example. The Firestarter isn't anywhere. Or it's nowhere we can find it.'

The audience made a hum of awe and pleasure.

Her questioner thanked her with a nod, returned to his seat, and sat placidly—unlike those two other men, whom Taryn was trying not to look at, who had by then understood the extent to which they had been betrayed by their eagerness and egos.

The chair wound up by telling everyone that Taryn would be available at the signing table if people had further questions, and to 'put your hands together'. As the audience applauded, that last man continued to gaze at Taryn, looking like someone who had come down out of the bush just to hear her, untamed, weathered, with the rigours of a landscape she didn't understand shining in his eyes.

No. In his *eye*. His remaining eye. An eye of awful intelligence, the colour of thin ice over deep water.

Twenty

Green Pressure

On a day in late May, Jacob was walking to court to give testimony in a case he'd wrapped up eight months before. He cut into Kensington Gardens to escape the traffic fumes. He'd been back at work for two weeks and had heard nothing from Taryn Cornick or from Raymond Price. He was feeling left out of something he'd like to be part of. Sure, he'd been instrumental. Phones had passed through his hands. He'd got to read documents and listen in on discussions and even have his say. But he'd never get to see the whole shape of the story, or understand what was happening, or lend a hand, or even be touched by any of it. Gates would stay closed to him.

Jacob came to a standstill on the path, suddenly so dizzy with misery that he nearly fell over. A cyclist coming up behind him swore and swerved. Jacob was on the wrong side of the shared track. The cyclist's lean face and fly-eye shades turned back his way. The man mouthed more obscenities.

Jacob stood under the oaks in Hyde Park, reasoning with his sadness. But it went on in its own voice under his blandishments. His world was a fold filled with sheep, and he was only a sheep dressed in a wolfskin. His world was just one walled garden in a series of walled gardens, like that last Narnia book. *Higher up and deeper in.*

A little gaggle of women with strollers went by. Two of them were blond, two veiled. The configuration of these different people—one of civil accord—seemed to be part of Jacob's sadness. *My sadness*, he thought. *Which is stupid. Who am I to hope for a bird's-eye view of the walled gardens?*

The leaves on the trees were still, but the canopy was collapsing, pressing greenly on him. The trees shared his feelings and were trying to tell him so.

Jacob closed his eyes, balled his fists, and spent a minute pushing thoughts from his head and feelings from his body. It was time to leave the park and plunge back into the traffic fumes. And his own life.

Real life.

He'd been back beside the road for five minutes when a car pulled into the bus stop beside him and he heard his name called. It was Raymond Price. When Jacob got in beside him, Price said, 'Goodness—your face. What are you thinking, Jacob? I'm convinced you're thinking things I'd be interested to hear.'

'I'm thinking I'm due in court in forty minutes,' Jacob said. And thought, *Why must it be Price asking me what I'm thinking? Why not someone else?*

Price said that Taryn Cornick had returned from her trip down under.

'Thank you for letting me know.'

'Do you not expect to hear from Ms Cornick?'

'I expect to talk to her. I have unanswered questions,' Jacob said. Taryn was still a person of interest in his cold case, and that could be represented straightforwardly.

Price said, 'I'll drop you at court. The Old Bailey.'

Jacob thought, *He's tracking my new phone.* He buckled his seat belt.

Price didn't immediately pull out into the traffic. He said, 'When Ms Cornick gave her talk in New Zealand, she mentioned an item from her grandfather James Northover's collection. A scroll box known as the Firestarter. We know Khalef and Tahan asked her about it.'

'She told me they asked her about a footnote in her book.'

'A footnote in her book that concerned the Firestarter.'

Jacob kept his mouth shut.

'Khalef and Tahan visited a games company that is housed in the former seat of the Northovers, Ms Cornick's mother's people.'

'Those aren't leads, Price. Leads lead somewhere.'

A bus pulled up behind them and honked its horn. Price performed a U-turn in front of it, forcing the traffic in his own lane to reverse to make room for him. Or rather, Jacob made them by pulling out his ID, pressing it on the windshield, and eyeballing everyone with his most frosty, no-nonsense stare.

Price accelerated away through the traffic. He said, 'I'm making your workday easier so your evening will be free and you can catch up with Taryn Cornick.'

'How thoughtful.'

'And, Jacob, what of your other friend? Do you expect to see him sometime?'

'Who?'

'The person in the Pale Lady.'

'Oh,' Jacob said. Then, 'I couldn't think who you meant. He isn't my friend. And he wasn't memorable.'

'It's your reaction to him I'm finding hard to forget,' Price said.

'What reaction?'

'It was as if you'd found yourself onstage in a farce, and the script required you to shove him in a cupboard.'

Jacob laughed. 'What did the publican at the Pale Lady have to say when you made inquiries? I'm sure you made inquiries.'

Price said he'd spoken to the pub's proprietor over breakfast. The man had hemmed and hawed then squared his jaw and said the person Price was asking about was one of the Tilwith Teaig, who was often seen in Alnwinton and Princes Gate Magna and had been for more than a century.

'Huh,' said Jacob, with no expression.

Price glanced at him, clicked his tongue against his palate like a displeased old lady, and didn't say anything further before dropping Jacob at the Old Bailey.

That evening Taryn called. Could Jacob meet her at Alan's house in Norfolk? Could he get away? 'I can't give you a lift because, once I'm there, I should stay for a time and at least think about my bloody book proposal. But I have my grandfather's papers, Jacob. Including his unfinished history of Princes Gate. I thought you might like to help me go through them. And, you know, catch up.' She left that hanging. There might be people listening, and there wasn't any need to say more. They would catch up. They would exchange notes.

Taryn said, 'I should mention, before I go to Norfolk, my agent wants a personal debrief about my festival triumphs. It'll probably be a breakfast meeting tomorrow. I'll leave straight after. I can text you when I'm sure what time I'll be at Alan's.'

'I'll be there,' Jacob said.

PART FIVE

Carelessness

O happy the isle of the great sea
Which the flood reaches after the ebb!
As for me, I do not expect
Flood after ebb to come to me.

There is scarce a little place to-day
That I can recognize:
What was on the flood
Is all on ebb.

'The Lament of the Old Woman of Beare',
Anonymous, tenth century

Twenty-One

Two Graves

Taryn got to Alan's house at eleven the following morning. She pulled in behind a car she recognised as Jacob's. She was late—she'd spent most of that morning talking to a distraught Carol, whose husband's citizenship application had been refused. Taryn had texted Jacob to tell him she'd be late, and why, and that maybe Carol's troubles were something about which he could give her advice. He hadn't replied, but she figured he was on the road.

The morning was bright, and the east-facing windows of Alan's house were dazzling. Taryn stood at the heavy door and peered expectantly into the camera above her. The door did not open.

Taryn tried the code, but the door stayed locked. She should ring Stuart to get the changed code. But first she'd better find Jacob. She set off around the barbecue pit, cupped her hands to her mouth, and called up and down the beach.

A faint voice sounded somewhere nearby.

'Jacob?'

'I'm around the back,' came the answer. His voice sounded thin and tinny.

Taryn walked around the house to where its kitchen faced an expanse of groomed lawn that terminated in a stand of pines. The trees provided shelter not from the prevailing but the coldest wind, which came across an inlet, a miles-wide notch in the shallow bow of coastline. The inlet's sands were bare at every low tide and silvered over every high tide.

The top of the inlet was a bird sanctuary. It was too shallow for any boat with an engine and too rapidly filled and emptied for kayakers to have time to enjoy themselves exploring it. When Taryn had lived with Alan, she'd always preferred to go through the pines and walk on the inlet, away from the noise of the surf and the sight of the sea traffic, the big container ships slipping along the North Sea horizon, headed anywhere between the Baltic and the rest of the world. She had even asked Alan to cut down the pines. (It was one of only a very few things she asked for—before finally asking for the very big dispensation of a divorce.) The inlet had the most interesting view. Faraway ships didn't provide as much variety as a big tide every twelve hours. But the pines had stayed, since Alan wanted to be able to land a helicopter and needed their shelter as protection from crosswinds.

Jacob was standing at the fringe of the shelter belt, his back to her. His collar was up, his hands in his pockets, and a watch cap pulled down over his ears. He seemed to be looking intently at something on the ground.

Taryn's heart changed weight, growing lighter. She had no reason to associate Jacob's posture with unearthly mysteries, but she did. Taryn had been insistent about her obligations, her career, what she'd called her life. But now she understood that she didn't want to attend festivals or 'come up with another book project'. It was good to discover how she really felt and to do so right that minute, with Jacob, because he was someone she could talk to about everything. She could tell him about Forsha Springs, mendings, Hands and forcebeasts; the Summer Road, the Island of Women, Jane and Neve, and the sword Neve had used to wound a demon. She could tell him about the Tithe, and he'd probably have insights into its politics. And she could tell him how Odin had got up at her session in Auckland to ask a question, one that was maybe a clue to how they should think about the thing they were all looking for. *They*—the author, the cop, the sidhe, the wizard, the god, demigods, demons—all together, or in opposition, but still together inasmuch as they were all apart from the everyday world.

Taryn hurried to Jacob's side, registering his crooked posture and that he was wearing a Norfolk jacket in Norfolk—an unexpected cliché for him.

She came up beside him, and he swung his arm back, she thought to draw her to him. But his arm passed behind her head and then came back, accelerating, and struck her hard at the base of her skull.

Taryn fell forward but kept her feet. Her sunglasses flew off, and she heard them strike the boll of a pine. She stumbled to a stop and turned back, and the Muleskinner slapped her in the mouth, a backhanded blow that mashed her lips against her teeth.

He snatched her bag off her shoulder, seized her ponytail, turned her around, and marched her ahead of him into the darkness of the wood.

Taryn walked, harried by frequent shoving. They crossed a large patch of disturbed pine needles, scuffed all the way down to humus and white mould. There had been a struggle at that place.

They passed a half-buried bivouac, a bag lumpy with tin cans, and a pine needle–scattered sleeping bag that Taryn was sure was visible only because the Muleskinner wanted her to understand that he had been camped for some time in the pines behind Alan's house. As they went by the bivouac, he tossed her bag down among his things.

'What have you done with Jacob?' Taryn asked. She turned partway back to him so that when he shoved her again—extra hard—she lost her balance and came down on her hands and knees.

She didn't immediately scramble up again. For long seconds, before he dug his hand into her armpit and hauled her upright, she made herself stay in this undignified position. Once she was up, she went on, this time at the pace he set, and he stopped shoving her.

Taryn was thinking. He hadn't kicked her in the backside while she was down. She had been waiting for the kick. She hadn't planned to offer herself, but something inside her, some deep intelligence, told her to stay there and take the measure of his contempt.

At his trial, Webber had said of Beatrice that he put her in his boot rather than his back seat because—with a cringing snigger—she'd 'soiled herself' and was 'a bit of a mess'. Webber's fastidious disdain had rearranged things inside Taryn, permanently. It taught her something a forensic psychologist might learn by interviewing multiple murderous misogynists. The Muleskinner had none of Webber's fundamental contempt. He might only want to terrify her and take her somewhere where they could be uninterrupted in whatever turbulent intimacy he craved. He hadn't kicked her, so he might not kill her.

But where was Jacob?

They came out onto the shore of the inlet, a short slope of soft dry sand stitched with sea pinks. Taryn stumbled down the slope to the wet sand. The tide was near its lowest ebb.

The Muleskinner caught up to her and draped an arm across her shoulders. To most observers they'd be a strolling couple, the man perhaps a little domineering. He locked his forearm across her collarbones and held her close. She had to keep in step with him to prevent his grip from hurting her.

The sand was full of crab holes that bubbled with displaced water as the vibrations of their feet frightened the crabs further down their burrows. Mud had settled in every channel in the hole-stippled sand. Some patches were narrow enough to jump over; others they had to slog through, the treads of their shoes collecting a buildup they weren't able to shed.

A breeze blew from the north, cold and steady. It stung the fresh splits in Taryn's lips. She drew her lower lip into her mouth and nursed it for a time, then asked the Muleskinner what he'd done with Jacob. 'I know he's here somewhere. His car is in the driveway.'

'You'll see soon enough where I've put him. You can be patient. After all, you've expected me to be patient.'

'If you'd left a number I would have been in touch. You put me in the position of having no way of contacting you.'

The Muleskinner answered her by producing a phone from his pocket. 'You're all slaves to these things.' He pressed its screen. It spoke in Jacob's voice. 'I'm around the back.' Taryn was now able to hear how stilted Jacob sounded, how strangled and compelled.

'Is that Jacob's phone?'

The Muleskinner didn't answer her question. He returned the phone to his pocket. 'You disappeared off the face of the Earth,' he said—accusatory and almost admiring.

'I was ill. Then I was on the other side of the world.'

'You don't look ill. Far from it.'

'I got better and was able to make my festival appearances. Look—you wanted to talk to me.' Taryn tried to turn to see his face. 'So talk to me. Tell me what happened to you.'

But he wasn't interested in facing her, or in having her slow down, and forced her to hurry on.

Taryn's neck ached from his first blow. As she continued to speak, she could feel her saliva thickening with blood from cuts inside her mouth. 'Please,' she said. 'Say what you want to say.'

'Give you my story?'

'Yes.'

'Like you gave me yours all those years ago?'

'Hamish.' Taryn said his name. 'You claimed you only wanted to do something for me. Something big that I couldn't do for myself. You wanted to plan it all and be in charge. At the time it was convenient for me to take you at your word and think no further. That was wrong. But I was twenty-five. What did I know about anything?'

'It's so long ago,' he said, in a high, whiny, reasonable voice, a cruel imitation of her own.

'I'm sorry,' she said. 'I'm sorry for what we did.'

'*You* didn't do anything.'

'I didn't make you do anything.'

'No. You only let me.'

Taryn began to cry; she turned away to conceal her tears and peered through swimming rainbow lozenges at the sand flats. There was nothing vertical in sight. Nothing but the white blur of the triangular navigation mark on a small nub of greenery where the inlet narrowed into marshland more than a mile away. There were no other people out for a walk, no tilting masts of beached sailboats.

Taryn gritted her teeth and turned back to the Muleskinner. She let her tears spill and run cold down her cheeks until they reached her mouth and the lacerations on her lips. Her mouth ignited and burned. 'I damned myself,' she said, bleak and matter-of-fact.

He was dismissive. 'So—you've found God.'

'I found Hell,' she said. As she spoke she felt a forceful cleaving apart, as if something cruelly conscientious inside her wanted to do the work he maybe intended before he got to it. There was the usual division of her well self and her whole self—because they were different. There was

the whole and savage Taryn who had persuaded this obsessively roman-
tic man to kill for her, and a well Taryn who had been living Taryn's
life for the past seven years. This cleaving was a deeper digging down,
as if some clawed creature had alighted inside her and was scraping
away trees to make a clearing in the depths of a dark forest. She was
changing—and it was too late to change.

'That's a strange thing for someone to say who's turned herself into
an intellectual.'

'Ah,' she said. 'I made myself visible, did I? My new self. My mature,
erudite, intellectual self. Was that the provocation?'

'You vain bitch,' was all he answered.

But it was true, Taryn knew. One way or another, her book had invited all these troubles into her life, or *back* into her life: demons, police,
MI5, the Muleskinner. To stay safe, she'd have had to remain unseen.

It was mid-morning, and a haze was building out over the sea, a
whiteness as thin as milk mixed with water, but enough to throw a veil
over details at a distance, details like footprints that went out into the
sand flats but had no return or continuation.

A few minutes' more walking and they met another set of prints, the
tracks of two people heading out into the bay, as they were.

Taryn kept her head down, only glanced at the tracks. Both individuals' feet were bigger than her own.

She hoped the Muleskinner was making nothing of the prints. She
lifted her head now and then to keep them in sight. They veered away
and seemed to run together as a white painted centreline does on a long
stretch of highway. Taryn kept her eyes turned up painfully in their
sockets to trace those footsteps.

Another five minutes and she noticed, off to one side, a single track
of same-sized prints leading back towards the shore. These, like the

others, were blurred by water, as if all these traverses had been undertaken after the tide had turned but before it ebbed far enough to empty the sand.

Taryn suddenly understood what she was looking at. She stopped walking and began to weep. She turned on the Muleskinner and attacked him with her mud-cushioned feet and pummelling fists.

He seized her wrists and held her off.

The mud she kicked up spattered his face and throat and chest. Her head connected with his, hard enough that her vision filled with sparks. He swore and pushed her down onto the sand.

Let someone be looking now, she thought. She crawled and wallowed after his retreating legs, howling all the time like an animal.

The Muleskinner had taken Jacob out on the sands while they were still filmed with water, which filled their footprints. And then before too long—before the inlet had completely emptied—the Muleskinner had made his way back, alone, to wait for her.

Taryn got to her feet and for a time fruitlessly charged after him, flailing as he dodged and backed away. Her grieving voice sounded tiny to her. It had no more substance than her raw grasping. The silence of the inlet swallowed her sorrow, or diluted it and blended it with the cries of curlews and terns.

He wouldn't let her get ahold of him. She couldn't touch him. She would reach nothing with nothing for the remainder of her existence. The Muleskinner was leading her to Jacob's corpse, and she would lie down there, the work of her life accomplished.

After a while Taryn stopped staggering about after the nimble man. She fell to her knees. She cried without touching her face. She had sand in her eyes, and her tears served at least to rinse it out. Sand in her eyes was too much pain, even for someone who knew she was about to die.

The Muleskinner had been laughing at her as he dodged her attack. He'd taken no particular care to avoid her blows. He was unfazed and scornfully amused. And as she knelt with her eyes streaming, he said, in a tone of saddened reprimand, 'Look at you.' Then, 'You're not what you once were.'

Taryn gradually collected herself. She got up and waited, staring at him dumbly.

Something terrible had happened in his life to send him back to her looking for revenge. He believed she had been unlucky for him and was to be blamed for some calamity, some failure or loss. But he didn't want to tell her about it; he just wanted her to suffer and be reduced, in his imagination and her own.

There was no point in understanding any of this if she couldn't see a way through it.

He didn't say anything more, only circled her and compelled her to walk on.

Jacob's muscles were jumping with the impulse of his only plan. He was coming up to the moment when he'd have to make a decision and chance his arm. But until then, the only good he was able to do for himself was to rest, and stay as warm as he could, and keep his head still so it would stop spinning and he'd stay conscious.

While he had been out cold, Jacob's attacker had taken his hat and jacket and put them on. Later, once they were out on the sands, he'd removed Jacob's shoes and had tossed them well out of reach, upstream, into the shell-studded bed of the channel.

After that the man clambered up the steep, scalloped side of the channel and disappeared southeast, heading back towards the house.

The man hadn't had much to say to Jacob, apart from instructions and one offhand, not very reassuring reassurance: 'I haven't hit any major blood vessels. If you don't use that arm, the wound could seal, for now.'

Other than that, his only words had been 'Move', and 'Don't try that again', and 'Sit down'.

He meant: Sit down on the tractor tyre, a third buried in the sand, with more sand built up around it than in its wheel well and rim. The tractor tyre that was not coated with barnacles, or white with weather, so hadn't been found there by the man but *put* there.

Jacob was pretty sure the man was Canadian. He was strong, clever, stealthy, skilled with his knife.

The Canadian had used something—probably the long serrated blade he carried—to make two holes in the top side of the tyre. Through them he had threaded a length of galvanised steel chain. One end of that chain was now fastened in two loops around Jacob's neck, the deadlock resting on his shoulder under his right ear. The other end was gathered into three loose bunches, another lock threaded through the gathers to make a clinking flounce that could not be pulled through its hole.

Jacob had fought to stay free of the chain and had for his trouble a torn ear and slashed hands. He'd landed a few blows on his attacker, but the stab wound under his arm had hampered and weakened him, and he was sure the man was at best only bruised.

Jacob inspected the chain—the place where it crossed the wheel well. He had understood what the Canadian intended as soon as the man had vanished from sight. Once the problematic and fascinating knife was gone from view, Jacob was able to stop planning attacks and looking for openings. He could get a proper measure of the danger he was in.

The man had gone to lie in wait for Taryn, who had sent a text early that morning to say, 'I won't make it until eleven.'

The trap the Canadian had set wasn't a hastily thrown together one. It was possible the man had been lying in wait for some time—in his forest bivouac by night—some way further off by day, with his field glasses, foraging, not lighting fires. Perhaps he had serendipitously found the tractor tyre, seen its possibilities, and managed to get it into this deep, steep-sided arm of the inlet's main channel. He'd bought a chain and locks in a hardware store nearby and had otherwise made do, like the outdoorsman he seemed to be.

What had drawn Jacob from the safety of his car, and out of the range of the security cameras, was a loud impact on one of the windows on the far side of the house. He got out and went to take a look. He found a smear on the glass of the kitchen window, and a large seabird— a cormorant—wallowing and flopping on the terrace, its wings loose and incompetent. Once he was standing over the cormorant, Jacob saw two other birds, stilts, he thought. One was on the far side of the lawn, waving its serpentine head, more lively than the other, which hung motionless, its dark wings barely visible against the black pine boughs, looking like St Peter, crucified upside down.

Jacob could hear yet another bird, somewhere in the pines, honking in distress, a ringing cry that choked and softened, then came back deeper and more pained.

Anyone would have gone out to investigate and assess the damage, call a wildlife officer, find an explanation—a freak downdraught, or poisoning. Those things were in Jacob's mind, as well as unearthly visitations. He hadn't considered any danger to himself. He was just curious and concerned.

The Canadian had been waiting for him just inside the treeline.

The Muleskinner seemed delighted by the revelation of one of his captives to the other. It was a sudden appearance. Taryn saw the fissure in the sand and remembered it. It had always been there, visible as a dark scratch from the treeline of the windbreak, but hidden again from the level sands, until you were right on top of it.

One particularly hot summer, when Alan had gone to London and left Taryn idle in Norfolk, she got tired of the lap pool and waiting on the tide. She took to walking over the inlet when the sun, coming green across the Broads, shone right into the channel, turning crushed cockleshells in the sand into a cloud of stars. The water itself was braided with sunlight and shadow, and warm. It wasn't as salty as the sea because, even at low tide, the river at the back of the inlet ran into that channel. Taryn would slip into the water, face the setting sun, and swim to keep her place. Still she would be swept slowly towards a little beach on the seaward bend, where she'd climb out and walk back to begin all over again.

The moment she saw Jacob—battered but alive—she let out a cry of relief. The Muleskinner thrust a fist into her shoulder and knocked her down the bank. She rolled, then sat up at the foot of the bank with dry sand plastered from her muddy overshoes to the crown of her head.

Jacob's face and neck, hands and feet, were webbed purple with chilled blood. He was wearing jeans and a cashmere jersey, but the wind would be blowing right through them. He was chained, but his chain had plenty of play in it. He looked up when he saw her and came as far as he could towards her, as if to help her to her feet. He stretched out his hands. Taryn got up and went to him. His hands were icy. His cheeks clammy and mouth dry. He had bruises on his jaw and forehead, blood on his sweater, and crisscross slashes on the backs of his hands. She let go when she saw that the webbing of one of his thumbs had been cut all the way through.

Jacob put his mouth to her ear and said, 'Run, Taryn. He'll catch you, but try to get around the corner and take a good look at the banks.' Then he let her go.

Taryn brushed past him and clambered over the tractor tyre. She ran as fast as she could seawards. She didn't bother to listen for pursuit, or look over her shoulder, or brace for impact. She built up momentum and used her newly conditioned muscles to power away over the shells and the film of warm water. She closed on the corner and jumped over the deep step in the small beach she'd used to climb out on all those years earlier.

Then the Muleskinner slammed into her back and lifted her over his head, and instead of struggling, she wrenched herself around to look as far as she could see. The view swam before her eyes, the scalloped sand-bank of the channel, its height diminishing a little—or was that only distance? A dead tree, half buried and slimed green. Another bend, maybe a hundred and fifty metres on, which hid the sea. She could hear the waves.

The Muleskinner carried her for a few paces, then threw her down and waited for her to get up. He said, 'If you try that again I'll cut off his nose.'

Jacobs's nose, not hers.

The Muleskinner wouldn't kick her or cut off her nose, because of course those things didn't fit the story he was telling himself, a version of the old story he'd had about how he was her white knight. Her dark white knight.

But Taryn was pretty sure now that none of this fastidiousness meant that he wouldn't kill her. She'd changed her mind about that.

There was a way in which he'd planned for her to die, and he was going to stick to his plan.

Before she got up, she dandled her hands in water collected in one of the wave-shaped depressions in the sand. She rinsed them, taking her time. Then she stood and went obediently back to Jacob.

The Muleskinner had her sit on the side of the tyre opposite Jacob. He unlocked the flounced knot and wound the chain twice around her neck, threaded the lock through, snapped it shut, tested it with a sharp tug, then dropped it, cold and wet and heavy, against her décolletage. It swung, tapping her, like a hand making that gesture—*mea culpa, mea culpa*: the fault is mine. Taryn tried to meet the Muleskinner's eyes and was horrified when she did. How bright and dead they were. She wanted to ask him if he was hearing voices or losing time, but of course that wasn't it. She said, 'I wanted to talk to you once I realised that it *was* you, but you didn't give me any way to contact you. You have to see that. Later everything was complicated by my getting mixed up with MI5 because some Pakistanis came to speak to me about my book. MI5 was bugging my phone. How could I speak to you freely without causing you trouble?'

'It may sound farfetched, but it's true,' Jacob said, his voice as reasonable as she'd tried to make hers.

'Look at your feet,' said the Muleskinner.

They both looked at their feet. There were halos of water around each of Jacob's naked toes. When he lifted one foot, the sand went matte again. The tide was turning. The first sign of it in the channel was this slight liquefying of the sand as more water came into it by capillary action.

'Your boyfriend has worked everything out. He can fill you in—as the inlet fills in.'

Taryn caught the smirk, brief and ghastly on that hollow-cheeked face.

'I'm not Taryn's boyfriend,' Jacob said. 'I'm interested in someone else. Who won't miss me. And you know how *that* is. So you might consider taking pity on me.' He said all this as if explaining something quite routine, as if he supposed it might make more impact that way than if it were delivered with tears and pleas.

Taryn was crying. She did the pleading for Jacob. She begged for his release, his innocence of anything she was guilty of.

'You don't sound convinced, Taryn. Neither of you sounds at all convinced of anything you've said.'

'Well, that's a shame,' said Jacob. 'Because it's all true.'

'Please,' sobbed Taryn.

'Perhaps we don't believe you capable of hearing us,' Jacob said. 'So haven't the heart to muster true sincerity. So why don't you just piss off and give us our privacy.'

The Muleskinner's eyes narrowed as he gazed at Jacob with what looked like indignation. 'Don't you want to know,' he said, '*why* you are going to drown?' His eyes flickered back to Taryn, and he flinched, as if he were shocked by the sight of her. 'Drown like Webber drowned, desperate, face mashed into three inches of water in a drain, spraying water everywhere, struggling, rubbing his chin raw?'

Good, thought Taryn, savagely. Her old hatred and satisfaction were suddenly roaring through her, and she didn't regret and hadn't repented.

But Jacob was saying something about there never being sufficient reason for murder. He didn't sound sincere. He sounded as savagely sardonic as her demon had.

'We will listen to whatever you want to tell us,' Taryn said, still trying. 'I'll confess.' She turned to Jacob. 'Detective Inspector Berger, I confess to getting this man to kill Webber for me.'

'*I'm* not listening to him. He can just fuck off,' Jacob said to Taryn. He turned himself completely away from the Muleskinner. 'If he's disabled one of the cameras, Palfreyman's security people will be at the house already. So if he means to get away, he'd better move.'

'I didn't disable a camera. I didn't have to. I got you both to walk into the trees,' said the Muleskinner. 'Also, I've already pulled Taryn's phone apart. And I borked the SIM on yours before using it as a sound recorder.'

Taryn wondered which of her phones he'd found. He would only have known to look for one. She'd been carrying both her new one and the phone MI5 had cloned. Had she said anything to the Muleskinner between when he delivered the blow to the back of her head and when he threw her bag into his bivouac? Would the bugged phone have picked up anything more than her calling out to Jacob in order to locate him? She had planned to go to the bathroom as soon as she got in the house and leave the phone there—then retrieve it before she went, and be heard saying, 'It's okay, I found it,' like a person who has innocently mislaid a phone. And anyway, she had imagined talking to Jacob outside the house, taking him for a walk along the beach and telling him everything that had happened, all she knew, before they sat down and went through her grandfather's papers.

And here she was now, still running through precautionary measures against surveillance and wishing she *was* being watched, by cloned phones, or drones, or ravens, or even demons—though she supposed demons could just as easily depose her about the dissolution of her grandfather's library once she was dead and in Hell.

And then Taryn had a moment. *Wait. There's something in that. What's stopping the demons from just killing me and asking all the questions they want to ask once they have me in Hell?*

The Muleskinner interrupted her thought. 'I'll leave you to get on with it,' he said. 'Drowning.' He turned on his heel and trudged back up the bank, its sides collapsing behind his boots. He paused at the top, looked at them once more, and made a gun of his hand, cocked his thumb, and mimed firing on them. Then he walked away, passing quickly below the horizon of the lip of the bank.

'Let's wait a few minutes,' Jacob said. 'He's a sly shit and might nip back to check what we're up to.'

Taryn wondered whether there was anything they could be up to. She bundled up her length of chain and went to Jacob. She pressed her face into his chest and began to cry, half real, half fake—as much weeping as growling and grinding her teeth. Her mind rushed along in a sluice of acid, conductive thoughts. Jacob must have a plan. It might be an outside chance, but Jacob had decided that they stood no chance of reasoning with the Muleskinner or appealing to him. That was why he was so rude; so keen to get the man out of his sight. Taryn wouldn't have been able to *decide* as Jacob had. She wouldn't have given up one option even to take hold of another.

She kept up her yelps and wails and was glad that she was at least warming Jacob as he held her.

He began to speak when her crying grew quieter. 'I tried talking to him, as a cop to a misunderstood and misled perpetrator. But he wasn't interested in telling me his story. He's a man of few words who doesn't like to open his mouth unless he's put the person he's talking to in a position where they won't talk back. But I'll tell you what: I don't think he's at all sure of his motivations for murder. Or even what murder means. Though he's done it before and, by putting us here, he's trying for a second and third. I think he's someone who has driven himself over the edge by doing extreme things in order to have feelings.' He paused, then added, 'I can see how that might happen.'

A group of terns flew overhead, travelling seawards. Taryn matched their cries with a deeper sound, a real moaning. She was about to die at the hands of a fantasist who set himself to do things, involved people in his acts, and then slipped his moorings.

'However,' Jacob said, 'on the subject of the tides he positively shone.'

He sounded calmly disdainful but was shivering with, Taryn thought, as much anger as cold.

'Ah,' he breathed, and Taryn knew the Muleskinner had reappeared to take a peek at them—hopefully a final one. She bunched Jacob's soft sweater in her fists and pushed it into her hot eye sockets. She burrowed into him, her face burning with fury. She felt she might at any moment levitate with rage, bound to the tractor tyre by the chain, like a helium balloon anchored by a ribbon to the railing of a hospital bed—a get-well-soon Taryn, making a gesture of caring in the absence of presence. The fashionable *presence*, prescribed for everyone now, like a spiritual super-food. The thing she could never get right, being Taryn Cornick, who was never in the right place at the right time.

A few minutes later Jacob set her gently away from him. He got onto his knees and began to scoop handfuls of black silt from the tyre's rim, favouring the hand with the injured thumb. Taryn set to helping him. At first her pace was that of an idle child on a beach, wrapped up in a project, busy but not compelled; then Jacob tapped her arm and made a speed-up gesture. She began digging in earnest.

Jacob left the rim to her and started excavating around the tyre, making discouraged noises as the water flowed back into the hollow he was making, carrying more sand down with it. 'What's around the bend?' he asked.

'Same as here, except the bank flattens out a bit at the turn. Opposite to the side we came from. Also, there's mist over the sea, but I couldn't say where it was headed.'

She looked up to check the movement of the clouds. Wind came into the channel, but it was difficult to tell which direction it was blowing. The clouds seemed to indicate a north-easterly. The mist might flow into the inlet, or it might stay out from the coast, following the sea lanes, as if stalking ships.

Taryn had lost the feeling in her fingers. They were bright red, and her nails were black, fine sand jammed into the cuticles as well as under the nail. She'd nearly cleared the rim.

The bed of the channel had begun to sparkle. Stream water was no longer filtering far down in the sand, but welling up, coaxed by the pressure of the incoming tide.

Taryn drew Jacob's attention to the fluent water.

'If I undermine the tyre here, it should tilt into the depression I'm making,' Jacob said. He didn't mean it would by itself. They would have to lift it. She didn't know if that was possible. She could see what Jacob was trying to do—that if they could get the tyre up on its rim, they might roll it out of the channel and across the flats. That was why he'd wanted her to take a look at the banks downstream. She thought of the incline at the lowest place, where she used to climb out of the water, a series of sand steps formed by each retreating tide, steps the shape of sedimentary rock but as soft and powdery as dry rot.

It would be very difficult. And it might be impossible.

Jacob told her to get up and free the spare lengths of her chain from the tyre as much as possible.

She lifted and shook it until it crossed the well of the wheel and pooled at her feet.

Jacob said, 'I'll get under the tyre and push. You can pull from the side where the chains are fixed. You'll have to stop pulling when I say, and get your hands back on it to steady it. We don't want it going all the way over.'

Taryn saw she'd have to be low for her pulling to tilt the tyre and not just drag it a little way across the sand—though she doubted that any force she could assert could do that. She got onto her knees and wrapped the chain around her wrists.

Jacob squatted and told her, 'Now.'

She flung herself backwards, hauling. It was the wrong angle. Several links popped through the slit, and each time it happened the tension went off the chain.

'Stop,' Jacob said. He came around the tyre again and bent over his water-filled excavation and burrowed, as energetic as a dog. The blood from his thumb reddened the water. Taryn was about to say something about the problem of the play of the chain through the two slits when she suddenly saw what Jacob had already seen—exactly what the Muleskinner had in mind for them.

He hadn't just meant them to pick up their ends of the chain and, as the water rose, step from the sand onto the tyre and perch there shouting for help, in the great estuary, hidden in a sound-deadening channel. No, that wasn't enough for him. And he hadn't just wanted them to balance on top of the tyre, fighting to keep their footing in the currents as the tide flowed in, then losing their footing to swim, chained like boats to a mooring buoy, trying to stay afloat for however long the tide was full, and slack, and ebbing. He hadn't just planned for that, which would be impossible anyway, since the chains were too short, and their bodies weren't buoyant boats at the top of a tide. What the Muleskinner had planned and provided for was worse. Jacob and Taryn were tied at either end of one length of chain. It had some play through the slits in the tyre and could be pulled either way. The stronger of them—Jacob, even with his injuries—would have the choice, when it came to it, when the waves were at his lips, of keeping his head above water if he pulled Taryn under. Yes, it would be she who drowned. The Muleskinner's ideal scenario had been not two deaths but a desperate contest, and Taryn's death at the hands of someone she trusted.

'Again, Taryn!' Jacob yelled. 'Pull! Keep your angle as low as you can.'

Taryn pressed her chain-wrapped fists towards the sand and hauled down and back.

The tyre came up with a loud sucking noise. Jacob frantically delved under it and got a grip and a tiny bit of leverage. 'Go,' he grunted. He put his strength into it while Taryn leaned all her weight back and took a couple of quaking, skidding steps backwards. She heard the sucking noise again and felt the tyre's inertia change to weight.

'Stop, stop.' Jacob's voice was muffled.

She stopped and sat down, keeping the chain taut.

The tyre was tilted up a bit. Jacob had a leg jammed under it. He was resting before making another effort, and wriggling in further, as far as he could. His face was white with effort and pain.

'He wants you to drown me,' Taryn said, panting.

'Yes, and I will. You know I will. So we have to get out of this.'

He certainly knew how to make a motivational speech. But he wouldn't meet her eyes after saying it, and Taryn was forced to accept he was making a statement of plain fact, a prediction about himself, and that, when it came to this sort of situation, he'd know full well what he was capable of.

Taryn's hair clung to her neck. Her pants were soaked, the sand under them was now filmed with water. She was hot but shaking hard.

'All right,' Jacob said. 'Get ready.'

Taryn pulled back and got in position.

'On three.' He counted. Taryn threw herself backwards. The sky swung over her. Two herons flew by, up the channel, crying, harsh and dark. The sky went red. Taryn's shoulders and elbows popped. And then she fell back as the strain abruptly went off the chain. She didn't pause but rolled up and scurried back to help Jacob steady the tyre, which was on edge, vomiting sandy water from its interior and teetering, threatening to go all the way over.

Taryn clasped it. It came up to the top of her head.

Jacob said, 'We're going downstream, where it's more likely the banks of the channel will flatten out and let us roll this up out of it.'

Taryn nodded. She saw that while the blood on his dark grey sweater had been indistinguishable from water, it had flowed past his waist and was showing as a darker, shinier streak on the fabric of his jeans. She didn't ask about the wound, because it was best forgotten for now by both of them.

'Are you ready?' he asked. They set their hands on top of the tyre and began to roll it into a gradual U-turn to head downstream. Its tread was deeper than the film of water, so it rolled smoothly and didn't start to speed up under the influence of its own forward-falling weight. At one place, where the sand was uneven, it sped up a little and tilted, but Jacob jammed his foot under its front edge to slow and right it. It wobbled but didn't go over.

They went on that way—not looking any further than a few feet ahead of them—towards the incoming sea.

After a time Taryn noticed Jacob's walk was oddly flat-footed. She wasn't sure what it meant. She wasn't used to seeing him with bare feet. She wasn't used to seeing him at all. But she did think that earlier, when he'd been standing in stubborn confrontation with the Muleskinner, his feet had had a normal spring to them. Now he was lifting his legs from his hips. He was concentrating, as was she, but it seemed to cost him; his face was stark, clenched, and beaded with sweat.

'You look dreadful,' she said.

He didn't respond. He continued clumsily forward, though always taking pains to clear his length of the chain.

Taryn listened to his shallow panting. 'If you keel over, I'm gone too,' she said.

'The chain is long enough, and might be light enough, for you to tread water at high tide.'

Taryn risked a glance over her shoulder at the top of the bank. The Muleskinner really had gone—had made his getaway.

'If that's true, perhaps we could risk taking this a little more slowly,' she said.

'Not in the channel,' he added. 'In this channel, we'll both drown. Out of it, one of us might make it—and both of us if we can get someone's attention or reach the far shore.'

The tyre rolled over Taryn's foot, wobbled, and Jacob leaned in to steady it. He moved awkwardly, and the tyre began oscillating rapidly, then went over. Taryn threw herself onto her knees and let it land on her shoulders. It slid across her, heavy and gouging, before Jacob brought it to a halt.

Taryn locked her elbows and stayed still, trembling. Her neck and scalp smarted.

'Right,' Jacob said. 'On three, together.' He counted. Taryn tried to straighten. Jacob threw himself back, hauling hard. His feet slid in the sand. He sobbed, took the strain, and the weight on Taryn momentarily slackened. Then the tyre dropped back onto her.

Jacob collapsed on the sand, gasping in pain. 'I don't have the strength. It's my back. My legs are all pins and needles. My muscles aren't answering.'

'Can you get the tyre up just a little?' Taryn's voice was squeezed and high. Her diaphragm was severely constricted, and her own lower back was in spasm. 'I'm going to try to turn over and use my legs.'

Jacob got up again and wrapped the chain around both his wrists. He planted his feet and began to pull. Again the weight relented, and then the tyre was swinging slightly above her. She rolled over, the tyre gripping and tearing her wet clothes and skin. She put her back flat to the sand and set her feet on the higher side of the tyre. Then, while Jacob still had some of its weight, she pushed. She slowly straightened her knees, and the tyre lifted. Jacob wound the chain to control its rise, so that it would end up on its rim and not continue all the way over. Taryn kept her feet on it until Jacob had it steady and upright once more.

His face was grey. The long stripe of fresh blood oozing from the wound under his arm had reached his knee.

Taryn got to her feet. Her clothes and hair were soaked. The water in the channel was now several centimetres deep and coming in discernible pulses. She didn't say anything further, just took her place, and then, when Jacob gave her a nod, began carefully rolling the tyre onwards, towards the place where the bank shelved out into the channel and might prove a negotiable ramp.

It wasn't a ramp, but a tide-scalloped incline, like a staircase with deep and uneven risers. Jacob and Taryn ran the tyre up the first of these and held it, tilted against the next level, while they caught their breath. Where the tread bit the side of the next terrace the sand crumbled. Lower down it came away in damp clumps, but higher up it simply lost any shape and trickled down around them in soft streams.

Jacob explained that they'd have to get behind the tyre, grip its tread, and walk it up. 'It will mean some more lifting as well as pushing, Taryn.'

He watched her digest this. She was pink with exertion but not too much worse for wear, only showing bruises at the base of her neck. These were developing slowly as Jacob watched. It was as if something invisible were standing behind her and bearing down with a crushing grip.

He said, 'We have to do this now, before more water gets in the wheel well.'

He kept gently talking. Their efforts had to be coordinated to be effective, he said. They couldn't let up. They'd get no assistance from momentum. Any pressure must be even. As even as possible. The tyre mustn't slew around, topple, and slide down.

He counted again, and they began. The pain in his back soared. His muscles spasmed from his feet to his elbows. To keep moving he had to trick himself: ask nothing of his muscles, picture his bones—his dead bones—doing the job alone, picture his nerveless, hinged, hardwood limbs, his body a puppet his brain was making move. Brain and will. He *would* live. The future he was pushing towards held no certainties, nothing but everything he'd missed out on, things he wasn't born to: significant acts, important work, some better cause to which to pledge his life. Those things, and only one certainty: pain. After this pain, more pain; months of pain.

The tyre ground its way up the first shelf, gouging a trough in the damp sand. Once it was on the sloped top of the shelf they tried to pause to rest, but the sand kept falling back beneath their feet and they were forced to press on.

Behind them the floor of the channel had filled. The tide was rolling in. Increasing the channel's depth ripple by ripple.

The next rise took even greater effort. The sand wouldn't hold together, and the tyre only dug itself into the angle of the step and wedged there, resting on nothing downhill but Jacob's and Taryn's arms.

'We can't do this,' Taryn said.

Jacob turned from her and tucked his neck and shoulders against the tyre. 'It's miles to the back of the lagoon,' he said. 'The channel winds, so, in fact, it's even further than that. And I imagine it gets muddier the higher it goes. And it's filling up. This is the only thing we can try.'

'I know,' she said. 'But there's eel grass at the top of the lagoon holding the banks of the stream together. And they're not as steep. And the tyre will still roll once it's partly submerged.'

'What about mud?'

She shook her head. She said she couldn't make any guarantees about the mud one way or another.

'Once we reach the top here, we'll have more than an hour until the tide catches us, Taryn. And we'll be visible. Someone will see us and come to our aid.'

'We're only pushing it into the bank here,' Taryn cried in frustration.

'It's a greater effort for a better chance.' Jacob pushed back from the tyre and stood inclined and ready. He counted, and she leaned in and shoved again. They braced themselves against the tyre's inertia, and their stiff arms trembled. It wouldn't move even a centimetre.

They tried rocking it, and it worked its way several centimetres backwards.

Jacob sat down, braced the tyre with his body, and tried to rest. He tried to think. The agony in his back kept goading him to movement—as if there were some position he might find that would give him ease.

Pain had put a saddle on him and was going to ride him to death.

A flight of egrets passed overhead, calling to one another. Taryn put her arm around Jacob's shoulders. He twitched and told her not to touch him. She withdrew. The sun was burning the skin in the parting of her hair—it had been wet and was now almost dry again. She contemplated the tyre and the chain. 'Jacob,' she said, 'we have to lay it on its side and haul it. It won't dig in so much if we do that.'

He lifted his head, looked from her to the tyre. Then got his feet under him and stood, leaning on the tyre. 'Clear the chains, and we'll get it over.'

Taryn made sure as much chain as possible was free.

'Don't let it slip back,' Jacob said. Then, 'This is our last chance. You know that, don't you?'

She nodded. She asked him if he was ready.

'I'll stay behind it,' he said. 'Try to lay it down gently.'

He hunkered down and put a shoulder to the ring in the belly of the tyre. Taryn wrapped her end of the chain around one hand and Jacob's around the other and backed up the slope, pulling to the side on her right, like someone riding a plough and turning their team at the end of a furrow. The tyre tilted right. She pulled left to slow its fall, and Jacob braced his arms, his fists sinking into the sand. The tyre slumped over and only swivelled back a few centimetres. It was now straddling the trench it had made, and lying against the slope, not dug in anywhere.

Jacob retrieved his chain from Taryn, pulled it across his body and over one shoulder. He turned to face uphill and waited for her to follow him.

They hauled and tried to climb, their feet digging in and sliding sideways. The tyre came slowly upwards, recovering the ground they'd lost. It made a small bow wave of sand. Jacob doubled back and pushed the sand away; then they tried again. Up it went, until the sand it was pushing ahead was wholly dry.

A continuous effort wasn't much use. So Jacob counted, and they'd pull for five seconds or so, and gain maybe ten centimetres. Over and over they readied themselves, pulled, and cleared sand from the forward rim. When they were halfway up they stopped and rested. Jacob prostrated himself on the slope below the tyre to hold it in place. Taryn climbed as far as her chain allowed. She was able to look over the edge of the channel.

The sand of the inlet was steaming in the sun. The mist bank was sliding by the coast, out to sea. Taryn peered at the line of ochre and green that was the nearest land, a wetland reserve, visited by kayakers at high tide, but usually empty at low tide. She looked for kayakers, for fluorescent life jackets and helmets, but her eyes found no non-natural colours. She lay down and let the hot, dry sand trickle around her neck and shoulders. She could hear the channel flowing, a low-pitched wet clicking of water licking water.

Jacob roused himself to ask her if she could see anyone.

'It's a weekday,' she said, meaning no. Then, 'If I get out of this, I'll sit down with you and Hemms in an interview room and tell you everything.'

'No, you won't.'

'I mean to, Jacob. Enough is enough.'

'Do you think if you're promising me, you'll not renege? Do you think your promise will make a difference to what happens?'

'If McFadden doesn't manage to kill me this time, he'll try again. I'd rather the police had my back.'

'McFadden? That's his name?'

'Hamish McFadden. He was a hunting guide.'

Jacob made a small breathy noise of acceptance, perhaps consoled by the credentials of the opponent who'd bested him. Then he said, 'Our fairy friend has your back.'

Taryn snapped, 'Where is he?' Then she was raging. 'Odin gets up at my session and only makes hints—as if he has to hide any interest in our matters. As if he's being *watched*. As for those ravens—I thought a Valravn was something special, not just a person who fancies a little murder now and then if it comes with a flattering story about himself. A *grand* story. When I didn't say no to McFadden in the wood near Princes Gate Magna, something happened—I felt it happen. The twilight turned my head horrible. But McFadden wasn't transformed. He's the same lurking, soft-eyed, creepy fantasist he always was, and I couldn't see he was, because it didn't suit me to see it. I've been carrying around a phone that supposedly reports on everything I say to that spook Price, and that phone is just lying uselessly in my bag in Alan's windbreak. Where are the spies? Where are the ravens? Where is the great fucking river-raising witch? Or even the demons? If one of them was here, I'd say that, in exchange for unlocking these chains, I'd tell Hell who is most likely to know what happened to the Firestarter. Because I've worked *that* much out. I've worked out that my mother might know. Because it was my mother who helped Grandad with the Princes Gate library when he had to sell. My mother, Addy, who is dead, but catalogued and shelved, as I understand all souls are. If the tide catches us, we'll be shelved too. But what good is *that* for my father?' Taryn was crying now. 'If I die, Dad will have lost his whole family—Beatrice, Mum, and me. It will break his heart.'

Jacob drew his chain tight and got up. He kept it taut. 'Turn around and pull,' he said.

She obeyed him, still crying. Again she took the strain, lunging forward. The tyre moved, pushing a wave of dry sand before it. It slid gradually, steadily, upwards, drawn by his white-faced determination and her tearful fury.

Taryn was the first up onto the level sand. She was pulling ahead of

Jacob. Then he was out too and they reeled in the tyre, cursing and crying, until it tipped out among the crab holes and fell with a rubbery slap, wobbling for a moment, then lying still.

They dropped onto their knees. Jacob shook the blood back into his hands.

Taryn rolled over onto her back. The sky was pale blue and crisscrossed by contrails. Too full up high, and below too empty of birds. One day on the Summer Road geese had gone over in their thousands, flying inland.

Taryn was parched. She moved her tongue, trying to stir up some spit to swallow.

Jacob said, 'Taryn, I think you're the Valravn, not McFadden.'

Taryn flopped over to peer at him.

'Must the Valravn be a man?' he said. 'You and McFadden were standing together in that wood. One of you changed, and the ravens assumed the "knight", the "hero", must be him.'

Taryn frowned at him.

He said, 'Do you suppose they're more farsighted than that? Or because they're female, they're any less subject to sexist assumptions?'

Taryn ran the scene through her head without, for once, letting her thoughts fall into the darkness of shame. 'One of them was above me in Beatrice's oak. The other was following Shift. The Muleskinner had followed Shift. We weren't together the whole time. The ravens could tell us apart.'

'I don't know, Taryn. Maybe they only register a Valravn at the moment of its conception.'

Taryn remembered how Shift and Munin would keep asking, of every male of her acquaintance, 'Is this your Valravn?' So it was true that they didn't know one when they saw one.

'It was Hugin in the oak,' she said. 'Because for a moment, before

McFadden went off to stalk Shift, I knew what he was thinking. I believe I did. And I'm positive McFadden didn't have any reciprocal glimpse of my thoughts.'

'Maybe sudden insights are your brand of heroism.'

Taryn shook her head. Then held still when her neck and shoulders answered the movement with alarming rubbery noises. She pressed herself up. The blood drained from her head as she stood, swaying, looking at the marshy land miles away over the sand. She turned to check the nearest shore, looking for a figure in the shadows of Alan's windbreak, but nobody was there, or nobody showing himself.

Jacob clambered painfully to his feet, using the tyre for support. 'We have to get it on end again,' he said.

The water in the centre of the channel below them was now more than a foot deep. The stream seemed to come in pulses, each one washing closer to the bank.

This time they both tried pulling the tyre upright. Jacob stood close to it, bracing it with his foot. They hauled, and it came up slowly, then fast, and they rushed in to stop it going all the way over. Then Taryn edged around it and disentangled her chains, and once again they began rolling it towards the distant russet band of reeds where the sand flat became wetland.

The tide came in. Before long, the tyre was making a wake. But the sand was firm, and the water not yet up to the wheel well, and they made good time, bowling it on, like Victorian children with an iron barrel hoop.

Taryn was sweating with exertion, but her feet and hands were cold.

The mist remained offshore but seemed to be flanked by a stream of cold air, an aqueous wind. Scales of cloud had covered the sky. Not only were they closer to shore, but that shore was more visible. The topography of the very flat land rose up and became clearer as they approached the tideline, until Taryn was sure that the creamy smear she could see above the reed beds was the roof of a coach in a car park. She remembered that when she lived here, someone had been developing a boardwalk through the wetland sanctuary. It must be completed now.

She turned to Jacob to ask whether that was a car park over there, but he had his head down and was dragging his feet. She looked behind him at the bubbles their passage had pressed out of breached crab holes and saw their shadows stretching out. It was late afternoon. They'd been at this for hours.

They kept moving. The tyre was, all the time, more trouble to push. Water was partway up the wheel well now, sluicing about with every revolution. It wouldn't be long before the tyre was half submerged, and the water up to their waists. However, they both knew that they were already possibly close enough to the shore to have to balance on the tyre but not drown. Still they kept on, the goal now being to find people—to find a knife to saw the tyre and free the chain. Boltcutters. The police and police dogs. The Muleskinner caught, and that threat sorted for good.

Taryn spotted a splash of colour, far out on the spit, concealed and revealed by waving reeds. Fluorescent yellow. And then again, further on. As she watched, all the gaps in the reeds showed the same yellow, as if someone were drawing a brilliant ribbon through the vegetation beyond the first fringe of marshland.

She looked back at Jacob, whose head hung so low she could see a tiny star of white skin in the springing black hair on his crown. He had no elasticity in his ankles or his knees. Taryn understood then how badly he had damaged his back. That he had probably ruptured several discs and that the inflammation was already pressing on his nerves and making his gait leaden.

She turned to follow the progress of the yellow. She saw bobbing heads in black sunhats. She saw the three taller figures, also in yellow. The yellow was windbreakers, a uniform, and the ribbon was a crowd of schoolchildren trooping up the boardwalk towards the car park and their coach, at the end of a day visiting in the sanctuary. The children had backpacks and water bottles. Some were stumbling along with their heads down and hands out, engrossed in their phones.

Taryn grabbed Jacob. She reined in the tyre, and it stopped, rocking and making waves against their thighs.

Jacob looked too, then they both began to yell and wave, one-handed, because they couldn't risk the tyre falling over. Even with rescue in sight, it still seemed too soon to trust their fortunes to anything other than themselves.

The inlet and encroaching waves swallowed their voices, but they kept calling and, after a little while, several children paused and looked their way.

Taryn picked up her chain and waved it. Surely someone would notice the chain and divine something of their predicament.

One of the teachers began jumping up and down to get a better look. Then he rushed to catch up with another of the adults. They both gazed Taryn's way, then hurried on towards the car park, which was slightly elevated and would give them a better view.

The children streamed excitedly after them. The group reached the car park and looked down at them. Then, after a short consultation, one of the teachers climbed over the barrier and picked his way through the reeds and tangle of driftwood, to the shore.

Taryn rattled the chain once more. She tried to make it clear their trouble wasn't accidental. Surely the school party could see that she and Jacob were chained to the tyre?

Some of the children drifted down to the shore after the teacher who was heading their way—though the two other teachers were clearly warning them not to even think of going wading.

The school party was joined by a couple of grey-haired women in leggings and clutching Nordic walking poles.

The teacher took out his phone and dialled, talking as he walked through the reeds. He was gazing at them, no doubt describing what he saw.

Another man joined the group on the shore and listened as one of the teachers explained what they were looking at. He hurried back to his car and got out some tool. Taryn watched them nodding. All in agreement that, yes, that was a good idea. Yes, that might do the job. The man threw his backpack in the car, shut the door and, tool in hand, strode decisively towards the shore. He jumped the fence, trampled the sea pinks, and hurried to catch up with the teacher.

Taryn looked from him to his car. It was her car. He had removed Jacob's jacket and hat and was carrying his own knife. He had no doubt told the teacher and pupils and hikers he might be able to cut those two people free from that tyre.

Jacob had recognised the Muleskinner too. He started to shout, 'It's him! He did this!' His voice was hoarse and scarcely rose above the sound of the incoming tide.

Taryn began to yell too—and not just yell, but stoop defensively and back away to the length of her chain. The tyre subsided with a splash and went under, spouting trapped air.

Taryn thrust her arms under the water and her fingers into the sand, trying to scoop up something solid—a shellfish, a stone, something to throw at the Muleskinner. The shells were tiny, only fragments. The sand inches under them was mixed with black organic silt. Taryn retained her handfuls of this. Perhaps she could throw it in his eyes. She should straighten to throw, but instead she stayed stooped over her soft parts, face forward, gesturing at the Muleskinner with one clenched, oil-black fist.

Jacob had given up shouting. He climbed on top of the submerged tyre and gathered his chain into a loop. He began twirling his doubled length, crouched, and made ready.

The nearest teacher had caught on—but well after the Muleskinner had overtaken him. He was in pursuit now, running in the Muleskinner's muddy wake and yelling over his shoulder for someone to call the police. Again. *Get them to hurry.*

Another teacher and the two grey-haired hikers were in the water too, on their way, but not moving fast enough.

A black, late-model SUV pulled up right by the barrier, and two people jumped out, leaving its doors open. They scrambled down the bank. One of them took a tumble into the reeds and vanished from sight. This seemed to go unobserved by everyone but Taryn.

She saw the Muleskinner alter his course. He veered towards her, not Jacob.

She dropped her globs of mud and fumbled underwater for her chain, to arm herself as Jacob had. But her hands were too small to get a secure grip on the chain once it was doubled up.

Why hadn't the Muleskinner just stabbed her before if he meant to stab her now? Why had she had to go through all the last hours' fears and privations?

Jacob was moving to her side—white-faced, the water around him pink with his blood. He'd reopened his wound. He was clumsy, staggering. In his hurry to reach her, he turned his back on the Muleskinner.

'Jacob! No!' she yelled.

The Muleskinner was a scant fifty yards off and closing as fast as wading permitted. Jacob had relinquished his looped chain, had nothing in his hands, but he did turn, helpless, to put himself between Taryn and the Muleskinner.

Someone further off was roaring, 'Out of the way!'

Taryn located the voice. The man from the SUV who hadn't fallen was pelting through the trail of schoolchildren, past the second teacher and the two hikers, who were running too, waving their poles, silent, determined, comical, and brave. The first teacher was beyond them, pushing through the sea, but still too far off.

The man passed the hikers. He was running flat out, a gun up by one shoulder, the sea white around him, hampered only slightly by his elegant coat.

The Muleskinner went by Jacob with scarcely a pause. He took a quick step closer and slashed upwards with his knife. He didn't even look at Jacob. His eyes were locked on Taryn's.

Jacob lost his footing and fell back from the knife, but it still opened his sweater and the skin under it. The Muleskinner's stroke continued up and hit Jacob below his jaw, knocking his head back and opening a great red gash. Jacob fell, and the muddied water closed over him. Taryn saw him struggle to the surface, his face coming up in a halo of blood.

There was a flat retort, and the Muleskinner—who was almost at Taryn—lurched sideways as if his hip had locked. Then he recovered, crossed the last bit of distance between them with a quick lunge. He seized her and put his bloodied knife against her throat. He turned her body between him and the gun.

Raymond Price came to a stop, his gun pointed and steady. His beautiful camel-hair coat was sopping up seawater. He didn't take his eyes off the Muleskinner. Taryn could see he was looking for a shot. The Muleskinner knew it—with his different and equivalent capabilities.

He had pulled Taryn up against his body so that she was on tiptoe and her body shielded a greater area of his. She could feel his hot breath puffing against the back of her neck.

One of the grey-haired women was still edging forward, towards Jacob. 'Let me help him, please,' she said.

The Muleskinner's answer was to move the rippled edge of his blade very slightly against Taryn's skin. She gasped. A thread of warm blood joined the water dripping from her, and was cold too by the time it reached her collarbone.

The hiker stopped moving but stayed in her semi-crouched stance, her arms out, as if there were a balance beam underwater that her feet must keep to.

Jacob had got his feet under him. He stood, one hand cupping his jaw, blood dripping through his fingers. He looked at the hiker and told her he was all right. 'Thank you, but don't get any more involved.'

'Good advice,' said the Muleskinner. 'Involvement isn't nearly as nice as it looks.'

Taryn shifted her gaze from Jacob to Price, looking to him for some sign about what she might do—how to move, where to turn, what to say. His expression was icy, his eyes calculating, measuring.

'Ray,' Jacob said. 'Careful.'

'Always,' said Price.

The Muleskinner's breathing had calmed. That frightened Taryn. She wondered whether he had been waiting for an audience. Because there they were: the adults, all close at hand; the children, further off, a scattered mob close behind the second teacher, who kept gesturing at them to get back, and a dribble of the more timid or less rapacious children, extending all the way back to the car park. They were a sight. All those bright yellow jackets and astonished, frightened, rapt young faces.

The second teacher turned to her pupils and began to herd them.

And Taryn thought, *She's making sure none of them sees a woman get her throat cut.*

'Please, Ray,' Jacob said. 'Take the shot.'

Price ignored him, his whole being concentrated into alertness.

Many of the children obeyed their teacher, others drifted left or right of her and, while continuing to shore, went very slowly. Some stayed put. One got out her phone and held it up, gazing into its display, at the video she was making and might already be planning to share on YouTube. Only her classmates and Taryn noticed what she was doing.

'Please,' Jacob said to the Muleskinner. 'You don't need to hurt her.' There was blood all down the front of his sweater.

Taryn's gaze travelled from person to person. She wasn't looking for help—just company. But not Jacob's company. His condition and his distress were breaking her heart.

Time had dilated but was now shrinking again. Most of the Muleskinner's audience was being marshalled back towards the shore. The sea was up to Taryn's breasts. The tide was coming in fast; the few people left standing had themselves diminished by half.

And then everything changed.

Or not everything. A change happened, and kept on happening, but Jacob kept behaving naturally, as if nothing could alter his current state of mind.

It started with the girl making the video. Something she saw in the faithfully focussed image on her screen caused her to stiffen in shock, snatch the phone to her chest, and bolt.

The other children reacted a fraction of a second later, and then the nearest grey-haired hiker, quickly followed by the other. They all turned to flee, pushing through the water and craning their heads to look back over their shoulders.

They made sounds too, sharp cries of horror, so primal they might be described as chimp-like.

Price's eyes flicked sideways and widened. A moment later he too began to back away, but with his eyes and aim still locked on the Muleskinner. 'Jacob,' he said. It wasn't a question, an appeal, a heads-up, but all of those things at once, and profoundly uncertain.

Jacob began to back away then. His chain tightened, and he slipped over, then struggled up, wrestling with it. The wound on his jaw was gaping, his mouth also.

Price stopped again and stood his ground. He'd finished flinching. He kept his eyes on his target through the ruckus of splashing and cries of terror. He stayed rock steady until the children, teachers, and hikers variously decided they'd retreated far enough and all came to a pause, wary and ready to run again. The teacher who had been so careful of what the children might see seemed to have completely forgotten her pastoral duty. She, and all the people who'd fled, seemed to have lost their individuality. They were like a herd, their eyes on something very dangerous, watching without intelligent interest, only wanting to see which direction it might be safest to run.

'I don't know how you organised them all into that, but I'm not going to fall for it,' the Muleskinner said to Price.

Even with the blade against her throat—a very direct source of danger—Taryn could feel something, a perilous pressure of attention, coming from behind her, in the estuary. She looked again at Jacob. He was standing on the tyre, bleeding, staring at a point behind Taryn, and not distant. His gaze was moving, as if whatever he was watching was in motion and coming nearer.

There was a slight slackening in the Muleskinner's grip as he carefully turned his head to glance behind him.

While the Muleskinner was turned away, Price let go of his two-handed grip on his gun and made a quick gesture, tilting his head and sliding the flat blade of his hand upwards against his own neck. Taryn saw what he meant. *Get your hand behind his arm.*

Taryn slipped her fingers behind the wrist of the hand that held the knife.

And then suddenly and involuntarily she was toppling forward, the Muleskinner's weight fully on her as her face hit the water. A second later he jerked abruptly backwards and his knife jittered across Taryn's collarbone. His free hand grappled at her and seized hold of the waistband of her pants.

Taryn tried to get her face up, but she was moving rapidly backwards through the water. She opened her eyes and saw billows of mud in cloudy seawater, bubbles, a feathered thread of blood. She saw the chain and grabbed it before it went taut. She kicked at the Muleskinner, but he held on, not to retain her but because she was his last handhold.

There were huge noises in the sea; there was scraping and thrashing and one long, closed-mouthed squeal of pain and fear from the man who held her.

Then Taryn was spinning at the end of the chain, holding on desperately with both hands to keep it from breaking her neck. Her left shoulder popped out of its joint. She screamed, swallowed water, but kept hold.

Suddenly she was free of the Muleskinner. She surfaced, still fettered. The water she stood in was now chest high. Her left arm dangled uselessly. She was coughing violently. Price reached her, put a supportive arm around her waist, and began to check her over.

Taryn's eyes cleared. She watched the patch of churning water a little further out in the inlet. The Muleskinner's head and arm broke the surface. He flexed forward to stab at the mud-studded sea, the rough hummocks of waves where there were no waves, the yellow foam, the white teeth, the pale, plate-armoured belly and thick ridged tail. The crocodile went into a death roll. The Muleskinner's wide-eyed face, rigid arm, and knife went under, then came up and around once more, like a sped-up clock hand. The last time the arm came up it was flopping loosely at the elbow joint, and the knife had gone.

The crocodile curled in on itself to swim away, one of the Muleskinner's legs clamped in its huge jaws, his other leg stuck out at an odd angle, dislocated at the hip. The crocodile flicked its head until the Muleskinner's body was lying along its back; then, perhaps detecting a slight movement, it rolled again. The thoroughness of its violence nearly stopped Taryn's heart. Its terrible thick body, its armoured tail, its mud-filmed black-and-olive eyes—all were terrible. It came out of its roll with a sack of clothing filled with disjointed flesh and, dragging it, serenely swam off towards the open water.

Taryn felt the sea around her turn warmish as she emptied her bladder.

The children were screaming, loud and repetitive, until their screams lost all human expression and became as robotic as car alarms.

Price was beside Jacob now. He made a loop of Jacob's chain, pressed the muzzle of his pistol into the top of the loop, and fired. The chain parted. He stooped and picked up Jacob in a fireman's hold, leaving Taryn to free the rest of the chain from the cuts in the top of the tractor tyre. It was difficult; she could work with only one hand. As she struggled everyone receded. The teachers, hikers, children had all bolted and were standing at some distance, where the water came to just above the adults' knees. Their heads were in constant motion, scanning the sea. They looked like meerkats in the Serengeti, coordinated and hyper-alert.

Price was the only one with his back to the estuary. He was plodding shorewards, burdened, apparently indifferent to danger.

Taryn had been shivering on and off but wasn't anymore. She knew the water was cold, but it was as if her body had come to some accommodation with that. It was strange that no one was rushing to help her, that she was left to gather up the slippery length of chain and carry it herself, one-handed, in Price's wake. He was the only person with his back to her, but no one else moved to help. As if the object had never been her rescue, but Jacob's. As if they all somehow understood it was she who was to blame for everything, and she was all at once the pariah she'd imagined being—if only momentarily—all those years earlier, as she stood under Beatrice's oak and didn't say no to the Muleskinner.

The crowd backed away as she came on, then turned and streamed from her, the water turning into a muddy froth around their rushing legs.

From far off the thready sound of sirens announced that officialdom was on its way, travelling as fast as possible along the coast road.

Twenty-Two

Basil Cornick's
Screen Test

While Taryn was waiting for Jacob to come out of surgery, her father arrived. He minutely examined the sling on her arm, her bandaged cuts and salved bruises. He tried to get her to come with him to a hotel. 'Somewhere nearby. It might be hours yet.' Finally he convinced her at least to come down to the café for something to eat.

He escorted her from the ward, leaving a wake of electrified excitement as he went. Even the ambulant convalescents pushing their IVs along the corridors straightened their spines and turned to follow the progress of the famous actor. Taryn spotted DS Hemms, in a cast and on crutches, lurking near the main lifts with a group of constables from Norwich.

She grabbed her father's arm. 'Let's take another route.'

Her father was quick to catch on, and they glided back the way they'd come and took the stairs.

The café's location was a little too visible for Taryn's liking, but she and her father found a table in a group of four separated from the others by a living wall. There was only one other person there, an elderly woman with her head down over an empty teapot and nest of wet tissues.

It had been nearly twenty-four hours since Taryn had had anything to eat, so for a time, her attention was totally devoted to the filled roll in front of her. While she ate her father began a desultory lament. He started by saying how well she'd looked in New Zealand. 'You seemed better than you have in years. Since Beatrice died, really. You have no idea how frightened I've been for you on and off over the years. I've never wanted to hover or press you. It's been hard to know what to do.'

Taryn took his hand and squeezed it, and for a few minutes they both quietly shed some tears.

Finally Basil went on. 'It seemed to me that you collapsed after you parted ways with Alan. In slow motion and in two stages. I think you postponed falling apart while your mother was dying. And then you did. And I did at the same time and wasn't much use to you. Then you got yourself hitched to Alan and spent the next few years pampered and dashing around the planet. I relaxed for a bit. But that came to an end, and once Alan wasn't propping you up, you subsided again. I know you have the doctorate and the book, and they're good things. But— darling—*my* Taryn wasn't a sober, hardworking soul who lived for her work. She was shrewd and tart and sparky. You both were. My girls.' Basil teared up again and wiped his eyes on the backs of his hands, then sat swivelling his teacup in its saucer, his tea poured but not yet tasted.

'Dad,' she said, with love.

He got out his handkerchief and blew his nose. 'So what about this McFadden fellow? Is there any truth in what the detective with the moon boot was saying?'

'They think I persuaded McFadden to kill Webber when Webber got out of prison. And it's true, Dad. I did.'

Basil's tears ran again. For long moments he just wept and squeezed her hand. Then he simply said, 'Good on you.'

'Not so good for McFadden,' she said. *Or Jacob*, she thought.

'Can they prove it?'

'Not without Jacob's testimony. He heard the little McFadden had to say to me. But Jacob's changed his mind, I think.'

'And if he hasn't?'

'Let's deal with that when it happens.'

They sat in silence for a time, punctuated now and then by Basil's solid nose-blowing.

Taryn finally said that she'd decided the saltwater crocodile was an endorsement from the universe.

Her father laughed. '*I* would.'

Taryn wiped the grease from her fingers and dabbed her eyes again. Then, to calm them both, she got her father to talk about himself. Talking about himself always centred Basil Cornick. She asked about the screen test. 'There were animatronic animals?'

Basil Cornick was accustomed to everyone being interested in what he had done, was doing, or planned to do. He brightened and began to expand.

'The only disappointment for me in the Wellington side trip was that the timing meant no one was at home. No old friends. The bonus, however, was that the young manager they'd put in charge of the operation, who picked me up at the airport and took me to the Stone Street Studios and oversaw the whole thing was—oh goodness!—I want to say "the most beautiful animal I ever saw", like "the hippy girl" in your grandfather's fairy hound story. This unbelievably glorious creature picked me up and took me to a restaurant for a bang-up lunch. It was just ourselves, but she was utterly charming company. We went over the pages she'd sent me. Then she drove me to Stone Street—and I have to say I felt quite nostalgic. A group of very personable technicians met us and conducted us to a soundstage. It was an oddly compartmentalised place, which they explained as being about the technology.' Basil performed a wheezing silent laugh that made his shoulders heave. It was one of a whole repertoire of laughs. 'They're perpetually improving the bloody technology, when everything depends on the performances. Anyway, they blinded me with science. Past a point I always just nod and look impressed. While we were on our way to our set—a shadowy void with a single fibreglass rock—I had a glimpse of some extraordinary projects, about which I'd heard not a whisper. And, Taryn, I'm always hearing whispers. There were sets with astonishing lighting, indoors that looked and even sounded like outdoors. It made my head spin. At one point we were edging across a smooth ramp made to look like the walls of a lava tube. I don't suppose you've been to the Jenolan Caves in New South Wales? It was like that, but more multihued and crystalline. And the art department had been tinkering with some kind of light effect that made snow in the air. Honestly, the snowflakes looked solid. But they couldn't be, because the snowfall was streaming *upwards*, from below a ramp and up into the darkness that hid the ceiling. It was utterly eerie.

'We went from that place, through a couple of murky voids, and into what looked like the most exquisite art installation. A field of grey grass and white flowers. I swear I could almost smell the flowers. A powerfully nostalgic scent; something like crumbled carnations wrapped in old lace. I asked my lovely guide whether I was the object of some pretty effective showing off, and she said why yes, of course.

'Honestly, Taryn, I can't wait to tell Peter what I think. Because no one hits you with stuff like that without wanting your opinion.

'We ended up in a dark soundstage. Then someone turned on a key light. And someone else trundled in the rock, with the animatronic ravens already attached to it.'

Basil stopped speaking when he saw his daughter jolt. 'Are you all right?'

'I just keep having reactions. Please keep talking, it helps.' Then, 'Ravens?' she prompted.

'They looked like a first-class diorama display in a natural history museum—actual mounted specimens, but sleek, not dusty or faded. The camera crew came out of the dark to introduce themselves and shake my hand. Then my guide trotted me off into a roofless room where the makeup team spent about two hours giving me more hair, messing with my beard, adding a bit of greenish pallor. Then they dressed me in a long coat that hid my clothes, plus a pair of chewed-looking fingerless gloves like something they'd pinched off a hobo. They bandaged up my left eye, stuck a battered leather stockman's hat on my head, and I was done.'

'Who were you supposed to be?' Taryn asked, and patted her hair, which was prickling all over her head.

'Odin. Hence the ravens. Anyway—we went back to the rock where the ravens were being put through their paces by concealed controllers. They were so lifelike I felt they'd been replaced by real birds. But then some card of a controller got one to perform some actorly vocal exercises. Shortly after that Peter came online, in raven, as it were. It's quite disconcerting to hear the voice of someone you know well issuing from the mouth of a robot. Peter said he hoped I didn't mind all the mystery and that I wouldn't be shocked by several things being incomplete.

'"If you're not, why would I be?" I said. "Or perhaps I should say maybe too complete," said Peter, and had a bit of a laugh. Then he told me what he wanted from me in the way of the performance, and we rehearsed for a time.

'Then it turned out it wasn't going to be just me and the ravens. No, they had a whole magic door effect set up. It was like something from Disneyland. That water-vapour screen in the Pirates of the Caribbean ride? Another actor came through—kind of materialised in the frame. It wasn't anyone I knew. Not that there was much chance of penetrating his layers of latex. He was a stuntman, I'd say, one of those giants who play monsters. I don't know how they got the lighting on him to work the way it did. He looked digital. Latex, even when it's painted and covered in hair, still manages to look waxy. This person was convincingly monstrous and, for a stuntman, he had considerable presence.

'Perhaps the whole point of this was a show-offy riposte to my complaints about acting with green screen. Because the staging was more like cutting-edge theatre than film. It was just as well I was under strict instructions to stay in character, no matter what. Peter must have wanted me to do that, and still have some kind of reaction, because this fellow was vast, totally naked, and had a huge johnson—which I guess was what Peter meant by "too complete". Anyway, I was thinking that this was all very strange because it's been a long time since Peter has wandered—not very successfully, I might add—into Restricted territory. There was that early puppet movie. A great big dick is definitely an R. This one was probably a joke. That, and a directorial desire for me to have to make an effort to maintain my dignity. I was supposed to not react, but Pete must have wanted *something* to show in my eyes.

'So—I was iron. I just stood there being as grey-eyed as I could with just the one eye. I stared at this velvety, chrome, yellow-and-peacock-blue mottled monster with the hard-on.'

Basil Cornick paused, and his daughter gave him an encouraging nod. The movement hurt. Her neck was stiff with a mix of injury, anticipation, and outrage.

Basil continued. 'You can appreciate my difficulties. I had lines. But beyond my own lines I had no brief about the content of the scene. What was supposed to be happening between Odin and this monster. And though I knew what I was supposed to say, I didn't know what would be said *to* me. I imagine the aim was to have me improvise all my non-verbal reactions, rather than anticipate them. I'd been confronted by this . . . spectacle . . . in order to turn in some kind of spur-of-the-moment performance.

'The ravens were preening and turning their heads to give the monster one eye or the other. And my guide was still there, running the scene, but almost *in* it. I mean, I could swear she was standing in the live area. You remember what I mean by the live area? Basically she was in shot. The actor playing the monster kept looking at her, talking to her as well as to me and the birds, throughout the whole take. So it can't have been just my test, you see. I mean, I know it was meant to be, but then I had to wonder why it was necessary for the man playing the monster to have gone through what would have been a many-hours-long process in makeup just to run lines.'

'That's very unusual?'

'Yes. Well—I suppose they might have wanted a camera test on the makeup. But the whole thing was very irregular. I found myself opposite a character with lines that only corresponded with mine in a very few places. However, my background is theatre, so I improvised.

'The monster's opening salvo was to address me as "ancient one" and "failing god". I didn't have any thunder to throw, so I just stood there maintaining my dignity. Then the monster offered to pluck out my other eye and eat it. At that, one of the ravens piped up—in, I might say, a voice that would never be described as piping. More like a French horn sounding through steel wool. The raven declared that my eye was the finest thing it had ever tasted, a sentiment seconded by the other raven. They opened their beaks and curled their tongues and made this off-putting sound of remembered pleasure. It was brilliant. Then the first raven launched into a little speech about how when I, Odin, first came to Mimir's Well, asking to drink of its waters to obtain wisdom, there was a raven waiting with the Norn.

'At this point the monster started in with some subterranean laughter. The ravens did their silent head-swivelling for a moment, looking with one eye, then the other, then the one who was speaking went on. It said that the raven waiting with Mimir was "the raven of no good news. Noah's raven, who was released into the air at the rail of the Ark and flew away, out of myth, and into nothing. Nothing," it croaked. "The promise of land, but no land."

'"Odin asked for wisdom," said the second raven. "A god who wanted to be wise more than he wanted his full presence in the world of men, or in his heaven of heroes. It was eating Odin's eye, which changed that loneliest of birds into two birds, sisters; one raven to see and understand, and one to remember the fullness of the world lost to perfect vision, and that world's value, which is the value of *that which was once enough*." The voice talent behind the raven articulated exactly like that. Very emphatic.

'The other raven took up the tale again. It said, "We were once one bird. The raven who flew through a terrible suspended promise."

'And then the monster spoke. It said, "Let us not speak of that sick and sequestered god." A line that I recognised as my cue. I started in on the dialogue I'd learned. It commenced with some folderol politeness, then went, "Let us instead talk about that god's cruel mechanics and how we might help you find an antidote to their poison."

'I have to say, when I first got the pages, I'd been interested in that "mechanics". It wasn't an abstract "mechanics"—fancy talk for machinations. The mechanics of the script seemed to be *persons*. Poisonous persons. Cruel mechanics.

'The monster then said, "Do you know what it is we seek?" I was thinking so far so good, because I'd also wondered what the "it" in my lines was supposed to be, and now it was clear that the "it" was also the "antidote". Plus, the monster's line gave me my next. Which was: "We need to know what it is in order to find it." The monster began his reply: "Ancient rumour tells us . . ."

'And that's when I came over all weak. Years ago, when you were about four and Bea was eight, I had a gastric bleed. Which of course you girls were supposed to know nothing about. I lost about two pints of blood but didn't vomit, so I wasn't alerted to the fact I'd had a bleed. It was so sudden and catastrophic it felt as if I'd powered down. As if I was on full steam ahead and someone had ordered, "Cut all engines."

'The monster was saying something about a key. But he stopped abruptly and gave me a horrible stark stare. Up until then he had been on the other side of the magic mirror effect. A glossy plane of light, oval in shape and green at its edges. He stared, then took a step over the sill of the oval. A weird perfume filled my nose. I'd decided at this point I must be having a stroke. My head was swimming, and my ears were ringing. I remember feeling behind me for the rock—which felt very like rock, not fibreglass. I slid down its cold surface. There was a flurry of feathers above me, and then a moment of absolute silence, as if someone had shut me in a glass box.

'I came to surrounded by the camera crew and the lovely assistant. They'd moved me. I was outdoors. I was so grateful to be in full possession of my senses that everything seemed to be shining and musical and sweet-smelling. The sun, the birdsong, the grass, the flowers, the beautiful natural world. I was quite puzzled as to where I was, because it didn't look like Stone Street, or anywhere in Wellington. Central Otago maybe, but not Wellington.

'The assistant propped me up on her knee and gave me a drink and said soothing things about how the on-site doctor was on his way. And then I fell asleep. I woke up hours later in my hotel suite, with the lovely assistant on hand. She told me what the doctor had said, about heat exhaustion, and asked how hard the Auckland Writers Festival organisers had been working me. And then we had a room-service dinner. I felt in the pink by the time it turned up. We polished off a bottle of wine and she bade me goodnight and the following day put me on my plane to Sydney.' Basil laughed. 'In the past I have once or twice passed out while performing, but never during a screen test. They're not that strenuous. This one wasn't. Strange, yes. Strenuous, no.'

'Have you seen your own doctor since you've been home?' Taryn asked.

'Yes, I have. And I'm in very good shape, so you're not to worry. He just told me to call him if it happens again.'

Taryn asked, 'After you fainted, when your host gave you a drink, was it from a water bottle?'

'Yes. But why do you ask? Do you suppose someone slipped me a mickey and the water contained a remedy? Oh, Taryn, you've been spending far too much time with your police detective.'

Taryn was relieved to hear that Neve had thought to carry bottled water. She knew fairyland when she heard it described. The sun, the birdsong, the grass, the flowers, the beautiful natural world. She wondered if the demon that Neve and the ravens had summoned to a meeting with Odin had told the real sidhe and demigods and ersatz god what it was they were seeking. 'A key.' Did the box have a lock as well as seals? Whatever it was the demon said, Taryn's human father had not been able to hear. But the whole plan was so daring. Odin hadn't come to the party, so the ravens had asserted themselves. They'd sought Neve's assistance, then secured an imposing, grizzled, magnificently present character-actor, lent him dignity, opened a gate some dark place adjacent to the Sidh, and worked their con.

'Have you spoken to Peter since the screen test?'

'No. I thought he'd have called by now, at the very least concerned about my collapse. The lovely assistant followed through. She phoned me in Sydney to see how I was. I'm very surprised I haven't heard from Peter.' Basil looked a little uneasy.

'I'm sure you will soon,' Taryn said. Her problems were proliferating, but the flamboyant determination of the strange alliance of Neve and the sisters made her feel oddly hopeful about some of the things she cared about—not the nearest things, but hers nevertheless.

Twenty-Three

Mimir's Well

From the beginning they were involved in fog. But at least they were a they. A raven and a man, so Jacob wasn't alone. Water-logged, several shades lighter and degrees more diaphanous than his everyday self, Jacob felt that any company, even this strange attendant, was welcome. He knew Munin only a little. Nothing compelled her to bear with him or barrack at him, but she did. She made herself large and stalked behind him, fussing and flapping, a small black storm that couldn't clear the air. Sometimes her agitation swept the vapour from the ground and Jacob saw that he was creeping forward over wet rock, as smooth and bare as the bed of a swift river.

Once Munin judged that she'd got Jacob up to speed, she began to urge him with talk too. 'This is your chance,' she said. 'Men think the quality of being a hero belongs to them, like something they've purchased. When, in fact, any heroic action belongs to its moment, the short moment or the long. You're a man of modern times. A man who knows the price of things, material and immaterial, so you believe you have a purchase on your moment. But no one has a purchase on their moment. That is a fact for which we can be thankful. Unlucky are those whose moment pursues them, as Taryn Cornick's moment pursued her.

'Jacob Berger, you should look on this as an honour. For in many ways it works like honours as you understand them. If the Crown you serve were to offer you a knighthood and you turned it down, you could be sure the offer would never come again. I believe this very thing—a knighthood offered once and never again—has happened to Taryn Cornick's former husband, Alan Palfreyman. He probably has few, or possibly no, regrets. But I want you to notice that "never again". I want you to understand that this offer behaves like an honour. But it is better than any honour.'

'Go on, say it,' Jacob said. 'You said "never again"; say "never more".'

Munin made the noise that might be a laugh. 'Maybe you won't die.'

Jacob stopped shuffling on the slick slightly downhill surface. Once he was still, the cessation of sound was absolute. The raven had frozen as if she were a film running in his head. As if all of this, the wet hardness of rock and the damp flannel of fog on his face, were a thing he'd conjured. 'Am I dying?' he said. 'I thought I was already dead.'

'You are in a place between loss and longing where a soul might linger. I am hurrying you along.'

'Do you want me to die?'

'I thought I'd explained myself.' She hopped around him, placing herself between his faded, filmy body and the hint of light ahead of them.

'I gathered you were talking about a one-time-only offer,' said Jacob. 'But what exactly is it I should be afraid of missing out on?'

Munin didn't answer.

'You don't really want me to choose it, whatever it is. Really, you're advising against it.'

The raven made a deep, twanging noise, it was impossible to say whether of surprise, pleasure, or irritation.

'Shift would know,' Jacob said aloud, meaning Shift would know what kind of noise it was.

'In these circumstances Shift would carry on like Cathy in *Wuthering Heights* and enrage the angels with cries and struggles.'

'I didn't mean that,' Jacob said. 'I didn't mean if it were him dying and not me. And you're no angel.'

'However, I am offering you a place in one of the heavens. A place you've earned.'

'Special conditions apply,' said Jacob.

Munin folded her elegant, black, well-breached legs under her and roosted on the rock.

Jacob gazed at her, stubborn and stupid. He understood he was fading and that before the process was finished he should complete this damp, blind journey. He should close the deal. But somewhere behind him was his body, his friend Taryn, his duties, the badly managed world he loved, and Shift, whom he doubted he'd ever find in any kind of heaven.

There was a clean white mist before them. It was as if they sat at the edge of a cliff above the sea, and the sun was just clearing the horizon. A dab of colour appeared in the mist. Many colours, like the stationary rainbow in the spray of a waterfall.

Jacob heaved himself from his seat onto his knees and paused there, panting. He complained that this did seem to be his body. His damaged body. He raised his head to get his bearings. He would turn himself all the way around and go back. Everything he wanted was behind him. Ahead was a gate, or a bridge of beautiful refracted light, white light divided and revealed as all colours, many-not-one, like the many small chiefdoms of the heavens of these gods.

It was snowing. The snowflakes streamed upwards, silent, at the speed of any feathery snowfall in still air.

Jacob turned himself around and crept away from the light. After a time he saw the raven was ahead of him, walking, an awkward avian strut.

Jacob was too tired to follow her, even with his eyes. He dropped his gaze. His hands had made blue dents in the snow. The snow had substance, and so did he. It was cold, and he was heavy.

They came to a staircase, a spiral of solid stone between walls covered in tree roots. Each riser was deep in pure, feathery snow.

The raven flew ahead in a tight spiral until her wings turned into a black wheel hovering high above Jacob, who sank down onto a step and stayed there, his back propped against tree roots. Soon there was snow in his lap, snow on his shoulders, snow on the crown of his head. Munin returned, alighted beside him, and landed a sharp peck on the back of his right hand. Jacob opened his eyes and gazed around him at the white gloom. The air was full of ice crystals, sparkling like transparent confetti.

The raven climbed into his lap and settled down, then addressed him with a formality that didn't at all match the position she was in.

'Jacob Berger, son of Carl Berger, car detailer of Sandwell, you have come a long way in life, and this is the furthest you've come. You turned your back on the heaven of heroes but have found your way to the stair to Mimir's Well. I was meaning to tell you about it, but it seems instead we've taken each other there. What better place than this to tell you this story? The story I've kept for Shift.'

She began. 'When Shift found his way up these stairs to Mimir's Well, the Norn Mimir wasn't there. But Odin was. And we were.

'Shift stood watching us, listening to us, but we didn't see him. Even Odin failed to notice we were under observation. Shift made himself known by coming closer, a picture of eagerness and timidity combined, a slight youth, underdressed for the weather, his fingertips bloodless, suppressing shivers and panting steam. Odin took off his cloak and dropped it around the boy's shoulders. Shift braced himself to sustain the weight, shuffled closer, and set his hands on the coping of the well— supporting himself and the cloak's weight that way. I laughed at him, and he—who knew how a raven sounded when it laughed—looked at me with reproach.

'We didn't know what he was. The air was too cold to carry smells, and it wasn't until he came close that I caught the scent of sidhe, that and the marsh: hawk, eel, osprey. Too many mixed scents and nothing definite or decided. And there was a gap in the scents, as if half his substance was anosmic, that is, made to induce anosmia, a loss of the sense of smell. It was like an injunction: *"You shall not catch my scent."* Catch my scent, or follow my trail.

'My sister and I are not indifferent to human beauty, and all strange and strong humans have beauty of some sort. This boy had no sort. Or he was impossible to anatomise. He was slight and dark-skinned, and wore drab clothes, and moved like a patch of windblown sand. He was beneath notice. Imagine putting out an all-points bulletin on that.

'I was simultaneously shrugging at him and trying to fathom how he came to be there, a place a god might reach, at the end of a difficult pilgrimage, with fasting and ritual cleansing, with a will, followed by meditation and the abnegation of will. Or perhaps a soul wandering between loss and longing might reach that place, arrive and leave, having touched nothing and having been felt by no one.

'This boy wasn't a wandering soul. He had a body. His fingertips were melting small holes in the frost on the coping of the well. His hands were bare, his nails white—which is how I saw that his skin was dark. He was slight, he was brown. My mind kept trying to list his particulars as I attempted to inspect him in parts. This part, that part. It was only when my eyes lit on the rose gold claws hanging at his throat, and I observed how they were both there, nestled in his woollen clothes, and also other places, sparking out their presence far from where we were, that I understood the boy was under a powerful enchantment. An enchantment strong enough to partly disguise the consummate craft of the object he wore.

'The boy thrust his hands into his armpits to warm them, lifted his chin, looked Odin in the eye, and announced that he too felt the need of wisdom. "Before going any further," he said.

'"I should think this is far enough," my sister said.

'"This is the branch off a path between villages that climbs to a shrine. Or maybe only to a view. Or the place birds nest and you can steal their eggs to fortify yourself for your journey," said the boy, and I understood he was boasting of his power to go anywhere. But mind, he was talking to birds and testing us with a provocation. He was trying to be noticed, Hugin thought, and told me later.

'"Unremarkable child," my sister said to him. "People always have a first reason among reasons to request a gift from the gods."

'"I do," he said. "I find myself unable to discover what king it would be best to serve. The Saxons and the Northmen threaten the kingdoms of the Angles and Welsh. The Empire of Rome has shrunk back over the horizon. We are broken and bare-boned. We need a king both strong and wise."

'"You would make yourself that monarch?" Odin asked.

'"No one pays me any mind. Birds notice me, as if I'm a loving scarecrow. Shelter and shade when they need it. I could easily make a kingdom of badgers and foxes and wolves and birds, but *people* don't see me. Men, sidhe—all the people who call themselves 'people'. Even the dragons I freed from a sidhe gate didn't see me, though I came close enough to caress them."

'"That's the gap in your smell," I guessed. "Dragon."

'"I wouldn't know how they smelled. We were underwater. I wasn't breathing. The dragons were caught in my grandmother's gate, which goes from a lake on one world to a lake in another. A deep lake I swam through with a sky above me and a sky below." His face was shining as he spoke. It was like the momentary uncovering of a distant landmark in a shaft of light on a stormy day. He shone out, then the enchantment quenched him once more. "A king needs to be noticed," he said, practical and humble, "by all the considerable people."

'Odin said, "Mimir's Well requires a price. Even if the Norn isn't here to ask it."

'"I could stand to lose an eye," the boy said, though he looked doubtful. "I'd be losing half the world whenever I was a bird. I'd have to give up being birds."

'Listening to him, I was beginning to feel as if I were trying to keep small stones on a cairn in a hard rainfall. There was a hero my sister and I once had the charge of burying, stone by stone. It had rained, and the stones would keep rolling off his beautiful forehead. My gathering on this occasion was meant to uncover rather than cover something, to keep it in mind once it was in sight, to make a list of the facts so far. But it was very difficult. *He* was very slippery.

'What I gathered was this. That his grandmother was a Gatemaker of the sidhe. I had believed them all gone. The boy could be a bird, a badger, a fox—and probably a dragon if he'd detained them long enough to learn one, and had the ability to encompass that knowledge. The boy was an instinctual shapeshifter, which meant he only wore the boy shape because his kin were sidhe and human and he'd loved their faces and held their hands. Sustained contact was the only way he might have learned to be a dragon. Dragons don't belong in any of the worlds, Earth or the Sidh, the hells, the heavens, the uncertain others. They are made from stuff no other living thing is made of—microbes to redwoods, amoeba to whales. Nothing is like a dragon. There are only a handful of them; they come from who knows where and, having come, keep themselves to themselves. They are never met with, which is just as well, since even a god might only match but not master one. But this child had hung in the water beside dragons and caressed them.

'These things I'd managed to gather about him. And that he was not much more than a child, his ancestry was human and sidhe, and *something else* that gave him the blank bit that the unlikeness of dragons had so easily rubbed off on. I understood all that—and that he was putting himself aside, doing so because he was under an enchantment that instructed, "Do not look at me, or notice me. Do not count me in." He wasn't immune to that enchantment and was discounting himself.

'It seemed that this was what interested Odin also. "Child," he said, "you offer a sacrifice and ask for wisdom, but not to rule yourself, because, you say, men won't follow you. But what of birds and beasts? Once you are duly wise, perhaps the birds and beasts that see you now will cease to pay you mind."

'"It is mind, not homage. They give me nothing more than their attention. They're not my followers. Not my fiefdom. And, were I wise, why should they spurn me?"

'"You'd risk giving up even their notice?"

'"I don't consider that I am risking it. Unless you tell me that's to be my sacrifice."

'"The Well decides what to ask of you. Though I might instruct the Well, to help shape its ideas."

'The boy said, "Let the Well choose." He stood straight, braced and trembling under the weight of Odin's cloak.

'But Odin wasn't done. "The birds aren't already asking you to be their champion? You're sure of that? Why are you only willing to bargain with the Well?"

"'I do understand that I'm bargaining with you, All-Father. But I don't understand why you seem to want reassurances about birds and beasts. They can't give me more wisdom than they already have. I'm a bird, a bear, a salmon, an ox. I'm wise in their ways. But I need the wisdom of books. All the books I might read in a lifetime. I need the judgement of someone older than I am, a mother, a grandmother. But my mother is dead, and my grandmother is in retirement. So the wisdom I need must be my own."

"'You want books? Is wisdom human?'"

"'The sidhe are threatened by nothing but their own customs, and they won't change. The kingdom I see the need for is a human kingdom. One with a court, laws, an army, roads, written intelligence passed from person to person, and tools and engines. I have asked men ploughing the fields, and women milking cows and cutting turf, peddlers and boatman, weavers and shepherds, soldiers and monks, what kind of king they want. They say a wise king or a kind one. I asked each king I visited what kind of king he'd be if crowned the monarch of greater and more populous land. 'Wise, I hope,' they said. Or, 'Strong. Like a father to his children,' they said. Or 'Godly. Christian.' There was even one who said that he was content as he was. And all I could think to do for him was make his orchards double in size. I've read many books. I have them in my mind, complete, and can tell you what each one said. But the more I seek answers and examine candidates and learn what people in the past have written down, the less equal I am to the task of making the best choice.'"

'Odin was silent for a time. And then when he spoke again it was in his high, nasal bardic voice. "*He hurried to a place from which others were fleeing, and held his course directly into danger.*"

'There was a pause filled with the pattering of wet snow, then the boy said, "Pliny the Younger."

'"After that eruption at Pompei the world was without birds," Odin said.

'"I've seen birds flying and on fire," said the boy. "Why do you want me to imagine a world without birds?"

'"You should return to your marsh and grow into your small godhood," said Hugin, who by looking at the boy would know some of the things he'd done and guess some of the things he might do. "A boy who can scatter windfall apples in a field and call on the-time-of-trees to make them grow is a boy who should pursue his imagination in that direction. Not in the direction of the governance of men."

'Odin said, "And you want to be a kingmaker, though the level of wisdom you seek is more that of someone who'd like to speak to gods without causing offence?"

'"Enough of your one-eyed examination," said the boy, angry then, and quite prepared to cause offence. "You can't make me see as you do without first *taking my eye*."

'"That is for the Well to decide. The Well's sacrifices aren't simply a subtraction balanced against the addition of its gifts. My eye made my ravens. Without my ravens what I know and understand would be confined to what I witness myself."

'The boy shot us a look, eager, covetous, and I thought maybe he wanted company as much as he wanted wisdom. And company was something he'd never find with the very air around him whispering that he must be turned from, neglected, forgotten, and that doors should be closed in his face by people thinking only how the wind had got up, and that there was a chill in the air. Whatever this boy had come to Mimir's Well to ask, the prior and more powerful plea of that enchantment would drown him out. I understood this and spoke up to tell Odin how he should counsel the Well. He should explain in detail what the child wanted and why, so that his will would be served. "Let us make sure the child's desires at least direct the fulfilment of his wish. The spell on him will choose his sacrifice. We have no power over that."

'Odin agreed. He abandoned his strange quizzing about silence and birds. But later, in our sleep, in our dream, my sister and I were one raven again, flying over a drowned world in the silence of a promise. And the ark this time wasn't Noah's big-bellied cedar ship but that other ark of the Scriptures, that carved and gilded box that held fragments of the Great God of the Deserts's covenant with his people. In our dream that buoyant box was bobbing on the waves and riding on it was the boy's mother, the witch of the marshlands, whom we had never seen alive. Her face was ravaged by her final illness, an illness whose cause was having put her whole long half-sidhe life into a spell made to hide her son from his father's enemies.

'Odin turned to the Well, leaned into its milky light, and whispered in the language of the Norn, which sounds like the voice of a pressure ridge, where a plate of sea ice joins an ice shelf. Crisp subharmonics. Odin explained what the boy wanted, how simple and innocent a wish it was.

'And the Well just gave it. Wisdom and sacrifice all at once. Odin had to take the cloak by the shoulders and support its weight while keeping the bent-backed old man inside the warmth his young body had made.

'The old man was ancient, toothless, his eyes red-rimmed and lashless. He had long, phosphorescently white hair. His lustrous young skin was now parchment brown. Drops of spittle gleamed at the corners of his shrunken mouth. But his hazel eyes shone with the light of every book in every library from now back until then, the fifth century after the birth of Christ.

'Is wisdom a triumph or a calamity? I think it's both. We watched that old man go mad. No human, no sidhe, could hold all that knowledge in his head. He went insane, and then sanity—or some similar capacity for reason—came back, flowed into him as if he had some reservoir designed to level off his mind if it were accidentally flooded or emptied. And then the man we were looking at was only half mad—and wise beyond measure. Knowledgeable beyond measure.

'Odin helped that old man down the winding stair and back along the ridge between Asgard and Elysium. We passed the border of the poorest heaven, later named Purgatory, which was just beginning to show signs of its later character, the shapes of fishes scratched on the rocks, fishes without tails, drawn by failed Christian souls. We walked through maybe only a mile of the Sidh before the old man roused himself enough to use his glove and call a gate. It was his grandmother's gate, the newest and last, no longer stopped up with the dragons his grandmother had contrived to trap there in order to prevent his father's enemies pursuing his mother and her infant son into the Sidh. The gate came out in a lake under a slumped ruin. There's a cross on that spot now, and no lake, and the gate has moved a mile or so north and east— you know where. The gate that was made for Shift's father, the Prince, and is known to this day as the Prince's Gate.'

Munin fell quiet.

That damned apostrophe, thought Jacob. He was fading out, so cold now he couldn't raise a shiver. He'd lost his legs, his hips. He could see his knees poking out of accumulated snow, but he couldn't feel them.

Somewhere, water was falling into a quiet pool—though with the air so cold it was full of ice crystals, how could any water still be flowing? Jacob could hear it, though, that steady articulation—*plink, plink, plink*.

It was the beat of a heart monitor.

He heard his heart grow steadier. He struggled to focus on the raven. Her body was a hole in his field of vision, but one that fidgeted, and had spikes, a beak, pinions, claws. Jacob tried to tell Munin what he thought—about the thing above all of them. He tried to say that no one had a fate, not the man in the street, the world leader, the CEO of the tech company trying to solve the problem of a cost-efficient solar battery; not the young man wearing a bomb vest who believes that someone on Earth might know what God wants. *There was no fate.* There was what people tell others and those others believe. There was conspiracy and propaganda and inspiration, not fate. Fate was only someone else's idea of how the world worked, a story people inherit, a lie they're told. If he'd learned anything, Jacob thought, he'd learned that. That there was no thing that *should* be, that *must* be, even the world.

Jacob kept coming up and going down again. His bed was full of butter. There was quiet weeping nearby. He was in Intensive Care and sometime during the night when he was anywhere near the surface of himself the people in the beds on either side of him expired. He heard the flurry, the crash cart, the hawking sound of curtains yanked shut, and a voice full of tears calling a stranger's name.

Jacob tried to draw in his limbs and sink into his oily bed. But he couldn't move, wouldn't bend, was tied like the Titan to his rock with the eagle on its way. A nurse came and slipped the switch for his pain medication into his hand and held it until she was sure he had it firmly.

The first news Jacob received that he actually wanted came, strangely, from his parents. He hadn't expected them. It was sobering to see them, in their matching windbreakers. Jacob might just have been creeping around the roots of the World Tree in spirit form, but he only really understood how close to death he'd been when he saw Carl and Sandra.

They stood by his bed, desperately uncomfortable and grey around the gills. He thought they'd find it easier to say things to him if he'd died and this was a viewing. Carl looked more embarrassed than distressed by his predicament.

Jacob swung between feeling touched and feeling furious. These were the wrong people. He had information to impart, and these were the last people he wanted to see.

A woman who patrolled the corridors with a tea cart looked in and asked his parents if they wanted a cuppa. They said yes. The woman moved a second chair from the empty cubicle so they'd both have a seat. They sat, still in their coats, and Jacob had the impression his father wouldn't have managed to stay seated without the cup balanced on his knee.

They made little sallies of talk. His father said something about Jacob's brother-in-law's new job managing a garden centre. A niece Jacob hadn't seen in two years had broken her arm playing soccer. The high street at Sandwell was now one-way, and it hadn't solved the traffic problems at all.

They made small offerings of their lives and then there was a long pause before his father spoke up with the urgent things he had to say and, listening to him, Jacob realised that, though the distress was about how he had nearly died, their embarrassment was one part awe and one part astonishment.

'They had helicopters out over that estuary for as long as it was light,' his father said. 'Police helicopters, spotters with hunting rifles. Wildlife officers. Big-game hunters. They had no end of volunteers with guns. They had over a hundred witnesses, but no one could bring themselves to believe it. Especially when no one could find the bloody thing, which was, by all accounts, huge.'

'Didn't they find it?' Jacob asked.

'No. But.' Jacob's father hesitated and glanced at Jacob's mother.

'Don't upset him, Carl,' she warned.

Jacob thought, *Speak your piece, Carl, car detailer of Sandwell.* 'I don't get upset,' he said.

'You mean you don't show it.' His mother was tart.

'Everyone has to believe in the beast because they found the man's body stored under a bank at the top of the estuary,' Jacob's father said. 'Crocodiles do that.'

Jacob nodded.

'The body was missing one of its arms,' his father added.

'It's been so hot this summer, the beaches should be full,' his mother said. 'But apparently people from Margate to Scarborough are googling, "How fast can a saltwater crocodile swim?"'

Jacob laughed.

'Rosemary Hemms says you didn't even know the man.' His mother's face creased with anxiety.

'Hamish McFadden. No, I didn't know him.'

'Rosemary says he had something to do with your work.'

'He was stalking Taryn Cornick. She was helping us with our inquiries.'

'Rosemary says McFadden supposed you were Ms Cornick's boyfriend.'

Jacob closed his eyes. 'I think,' he said, 'I'm her friend.'

'Bad business,' his father said.

'Yes. But there's bad business everywhere, Dad.'

'But that's just the news, isn't it. They make their money out of having ordinary people on the edge of their seats all the time and fretting over every little thing.'

'But, Carl, that's why "See something, say something" works,' said Jacob's mother.

'Don't get all up in my ear, Sandra,' said Jacob's father. 'Jacob doesn't need to hear our naive opinions.'

'Oh, excuse me, should I come back later?' A voice from the doorway, running the words of the commonplace question together in a strange way.

'Not if you have tests to perform or medication to offer,' said Jacob's father. 'Don't mind us. We won't be staying long.'

'Unless we're wanted for longer,' said Jacob's mother, timid and hopeful.

Between them, as usual, they were making it impossible for Jacob to say what he wanted, what was enough and what too much. Everything hurt him, and he was lying in a cloud of a meaty smell, the redolence of a stranger's blood in his sweat. He'd had two transfusions.

'Or are you a reporter?' Jacob's father's voice was sharp. 'They're only letting family in. So if you've cheated and sneaked—'

'Shift,' Jacob said. 'Come in. These are my parents.'

'I hope you have permission to be here,' Jacob's father said.

'No one noticed me,' Shift said, reassuring Jacob. 'Nobody's going to rush in and throw me out.'

Jacob found the bed controls and made the head of the bed come up.

'That's better,' said his mother, and hitched his blanket a little further up his chest.

Jacob said to Shift, 'Have you seen Taryn?'

'She's been here almost the whole time. Three days. You have to tell them to let her in. She says she knows things you'll want to know and she's sure it's reciprocal.'

Jacob's father got up and offered his hand to Shift. 'I'm Jacob's father, Carl Berger, and this is his mother, Sandra.'

Shift took the hand. 'Shift,' he said. 'Like Prince or Madonna or Capucine or Colette.'

Jacob muttered, 'Your slider has slid too far down the twentieth century, buddy.'

Shift laughed. 'I won't interrupt you for long. I only wanted to remind Jacob that he'll need to ask for Taryn if he wants to see her. It's this ward's policy for non–family members.'

'You're going?' Jacob said.

'I'm taking Taryn away. Which is why I'm trying to expedite a meeting between you. She's coming with me to the Moot, and the Tacit, and Purgatory.'

Jacob gave a moan of frustration and misery.

'I think he's feverish,' said his mother, and leaned over him to dab at the skin above his eyebrows, not confident enough to simply lay her hand on his forehead.

Jacob tried to collect himself. There were things he needed to know, even though Shift was standing there, by his bed, safe. 'Taryn said—' Jacob glanced at his parents and adjusted what he wanted to say. 'She said you'd suffered the same fate as Don Giovanni in that opera's final act.'

The room was again silent for a beat. Then Jacob's father said, 'And what is that?' And began to huff and blow a little, as he did whenever he thought someone was purposely talking over the top of this head. It was difficult not to—the top of Carl's head always having been held so resolutely low.

'Do you like opera, dear?' Jacob's mother was eager to be surprised. Eager for anything, really.

Jacob opened his eyes and tried to catch hers. 'Mum,' he said, with as much affection as he could muster, which turned out to be more than he imagined he had. Tears filled his eyes.

Jacob looked back at Shift and recklessly decided to continue in the same vein and quote the lines that had been running in his head on and off for weeks. He half sang, in his breathy, ruined voice, 'Misterioso, Misterioso altero, croce, croce, e delizia.' And then, 'I do like opera.'

'And that was *La Traviata*,' Shift said.

'Feel free to respond with Violetta's part of the duet,' Jacob said.

His parents had flanked his bed. Shift was behind his mother's shoulder, standing stock-still, radiating alertness and resolution despite the usual obscurity surrounding him. He said, 'I'll come back for you, Jacob. But you know the rules. If you say, "Take me with you," you're asking to be subject to conditions that are far from satisfactory.'

'You can change them.'

'I don't know that I can. Right now it's looking unlikely. You have your freedom to consider.'

'I'm done with it.'

'All right. I'll be back within a fortnight.'

'I won't be here in a fortnight. This hospital will have me up and out.'

'I'll find you.'

Jacob lost his temper. He'd delayed pressing the button for his pain medication too long and was in agony. 'You're crap at finding people! You hang around waiting in places they might be expected. You're never where you're meant to be. You lurk. You hide. You *consent to be hidden*. You're bloody useless!' Jacob subsided, panting and moaning.

His father huffed, but his mother showed great presence of mind and only straightened his covers again, while looking apprehensively at Shift.

Shift kept a steady gaze on Jacob until Jacob met his eyes. 'And,' he said, 'I'm not yours. And you're not mine.'

'And nothing is your business,' Jacob replied. 'Yes, I get it.'

Then Shift gave a polite nod to Jacob's parents and left the room.

Taryn and Jacob had half an hour. Enough for each of them to give the other the bare bones but no time for the telling detail. Having to leave out the telling detail gave Taryn an insight into Shift's insistence on stories personal to the people telling them, and anchored in a hat full of blackberries, a miles-long parting in the marsh, water acidic with potash, a canvas dress, cakes made of almonds and clementines. She wanted to interrupt Jacob and ask about the tree roots on the walls of the snow-covered stairway—what did they look like? Exactly?—because that was the World Tree. And why had Odin been at the well anyway when the boy Shift came looking for wisdom? But because Jacob was weak and drugged, she let him waste minutes on his refutation of 'fate'. Yes, she wanted to hear what mattered to him, and she must listen to *him* rather than indulge herself with apologies.

She told him about Odin's appearance in her audience at Auckland. She told him about her father's screen test and the fight at Hell's Gate, and that, as of yet, Shift hadn't told her how he escaped. He'd said there would be time for that once they were away. They had to set out at once. Until they caught up with Neve and he retrieved the Gatemaker's glove, they were committed to crossing the many miles from the Island of Apples to the place where the Moot was held. Shift had allowed time for the longest journey, the one without the glove, from the Summer Road to the Horse Road and then a days-long voyage down a river by boat. But they had to go now. She touched the phone in her pocket. 'Alan has called me twice today. I haven't answered. I should call him before we go through the gate. I don't know how to explain it to him. McFadden. Webber. Any of it.'

Jacob's voice was a whisper. 'I wish you and I had talked properly in the time we had out on the estuary.'

'You were using all your strength just to move. I'm told you'd lost more than three litres of blood by the time they transfused you. Sorry,' she said again.

He took her hand in the one of his that was unencumbered. There was a line in the back of that hand, but it was capped off. His central line and the cannula in the crook of his other elbow were still in commission.

'I've got this right?' Taryn said. 'Munin was taking you to Asgard?'

'For me it would have been like arriving at a very exclusive resort with the wrong wardrobe and credentials. Besides, Munin was overselling her one-time-only offer. I got suspicious.'

'Why do you think she made the offer?'

'Out of the kindness of her heart. My suspicion was a matter of habit. I've thought it through now.'

'Any regrets?'

'Yes. I don't want to have to live with chronic pain. And there's going to be a lot of that. But it's not an impact injury. And I'm fit. I'm told my back should come right in a couple of years. Right for ordinary purposes.'

Taryn didn't say anything.

'I've got good health insurance. And people in my line of work accept the risk of injury.' Then he asked, 'Were you hurt yourself?'

Taryn didn't admit to her joint injury and the anti-inflammatories she was on. She didn't say that she couldn't sit for longer than forty minutes and was dreading the car journey to Princes Gate. She only touched the big patch of gauze on her neck. 'The cuts,' she said.

'My concussion helps. I just sleep,' Jacob said. 'I'm worried I'll forget what you've told me. Things make sense and then unravel. I keep having to close my eyes.' He paused. 'I've never known cold like that. There was ice in the air, like confetti.' Again he paused and watched her face, his attention deep but not keen. 'Did you see how the crocodile shook him? Every time he came around, the leg the crocodile wasn't gripping seemed to have more joints. He was being smashed against the seabed.'

Taryn nodded.

'What was Shift's dragon like?'

Taryn frowned, perplexed.

'The dragon that exploded out of Stuart's Land Rover and carried you and one of the car's doors off to the gate.'

Of course, Taryn thought.

'He only needs to have done it once. After that it's muscle memory. Or cellular,' Jacob said. 'It's one of the things he doesn't forget.'

Taryn had just listened to Jacob tell her about Shift as an owl in the churchyard at Princes Gate Magna. She was reassured that he hadn't seen the change. The change was *too much* to contemplate. She felt the same way about the saltwater crocodile. She wanted to think of the crocodile as something Shift had summoned. It wasn't him. How could it be?

She thought then of the wind on the crown of her head as she rocketed up through the air above that country lane. And how her feet were free and swinging. She used her memories to measure a hand, a clawed forepaw. 'The dragon was big. Its grip was between my shoulders and knees, and it was holding both me and the door.' She remembered the billows of grey radiance. 'It had a light moving inside it. Like static coming off a synthetic carpet. It was transparent. I think I could see muscles moving like currents in clear water. I think it stepped on the bonnet of the car to push off. I heard the engine grind on the road. The engine was still running.'

'Why do you think he avoids causing a stir?' Jacob said.

'You mean *more* of a stir?'

'A saltwater crocodile is a mystery, but it's not unfathomable. I think we could all do with a dose of the unfathomable right about now.'

Taryn was becoming very sensitive to the use of 'we'. Not sensitive like the people who monitor language use for offence to themselves or others, but sensitive to whom the speaker hoped to be. She realised that Jacob's 'we' and hers were even more different than they had been. Her 'we' included Shift. Even if it didn't include his cold, passionate aunt.

She said, 'The unfathomable would just be another bit of astonishing news. Lots of people might dream about aliens arriving, and powerful people being put on the spot, and the rules of politics and society changing instantly, like *The Day the Earth Stood Still*. But a dragon appearing in the skies of England would be like the Virgin of Srebrenica, a sign and portent. You can't approve of portents if you don't believe in destiny. You can't want other people to believe in portents—even just to shake them up.'

'Do you believe in destiny?'

'No. I believe that you and I are part of something that is only coincidentally to do with us. You less than me. My grandfather helped hide the Firestarter in a cave on his land during World War Two, and the British Museum didn't want to take it back, or forgot to take it back, since it makes people forget it. I don't think you and I will benefit from any of this. All that has happened to me is basically that I've found out I'm damned decades before I have to die and go to Hell. I get to postpone it. If I stay in the Sidh, I live a long life. That's a benefit. But you don't have any benefits, unless you count knowing how things work over and above, or maybe just around, our own earthly reality. You do love being in the know, so maybe that's enough for you.'

Jacob released her hand. He closed his eyes, and Taryn stood there, wavering between sternness and pity. He had done so much for her. Too much. He should bow out now. Shift should practise catch-and-release with Jacob, who didn't need to be saved from Hell. *Reject us*, she thought at the man in the hospital bed. *Let your 'we' continue to be humanity, or the British public, or whatever it's so far been when you say 'we'.*

Jacob opened his eyes. He said, 'The Firestarter has a spell on it that makes human beings disregard it. Shift has a spell on him that makes everyone—gods, demigods, sidhe, us—disregard him. Think about Munin's dream. That she and her sister were one raven again, flying over the flooded Earth, looking for land and finding only an ark, not Noah's, but the Ark of the Covenant from King David's story. In their dream, Shift's mother was riding on it.'

Jacob was right. It wasn't the same spell, but it was the same witch who cast it. 'The Firestarter is Shift's mother's work,' Taryn said.

Jacob frowned and seemed to tussle with something. Taryn felt a damp fog close around her too. She was waiting on the shore of the lake at Princes Gate. Her grandfather had gone to get the punt from its mooring in the reeds. Her hand was under the canvas he'd used to wrap the box—her fingers slipping smoothly over lubricating charcoal dust. She shook her head. 'All right. We know that's half the answer.'

'Do you think Shift knows?'

Taryn considered and quickly came to the conclusion that Shift must know. That was why he was so assiduous in his pursuit of the Fire-starter, and at such pains to make as few ripples as possible. 'He wants it because he's worked out it's his,' she said. 'It's something he was meant to have.'

'He doesn't care about the Tithe or the terms of the bargain,' Jacob said.

'I don't know what he cares about.'

Jacob's hand returned to hers, and they stayed like that, hand in hand, until it was time for her to go.

Twenty-Four

A Torah Above the Torah

For the first part of the drive Taryn tilted back the passenger seat and slept. She'd had four days when she'd sometimes dozed in the family room on the ward and had only gone back to Alan's once, very late, when she was so sleepy and vague with painkillers that she wasn't a safe driver. She'd seen Jacob now. They were both up to speed—and fully cognisant about how unequal they were to everything. She might as well be a baby Shift was carrying about. Something soft and helpless and dependent. All she had to offer him was a single story—about her father's 'screen test'. One story, so she hugged it to herself, didn't tell it, and spent the drive asleep.

After a toilet stop, once they were back on the road, Taryn asked Shift to tell her about Hell. How had he escaped?

He told her that the fuming demon had dropped him directly on the other side of Hell's Gate, in a long, shallowly sloping tunnel. A lava tube. There was a dim brownish light at the very end. It was too dark for Shift to see his attacker. He just lay quiet and listened to it hissing and flopping. He could feel Neve trying to open the gate, and then he felt the

Sidh swing away from where he was. 'I thought she'd moved it. I wondered whether you'd notice she had and what kind of act she was putting on. I was worried about you. But then I thought, *Why would Neve do that? No one is going to want to hand me over to Hell prematurely, without negotiations and justifications and ceremony and farewells.*

'I got up and tried to make calculations about the size of the lava tube. There wasn't enough light to measure it with my eyes. I couldn't gauge the distance to the dull illumination at its end. I couldn't tell whether that light was shining on the slick walls of a bend or was an opening to some very dimly lit place. I'd never been to Hell. I had no knowledge about it other than what stories provide. Hebrew and Christian stories, because this was *that* Hell. The one the sidhe have a pact with.

'There was heat coming up the tunnel. If I was going much further, I'd have to change myself into something heat-resistant. A dragon was the obvious choice. But my dragon was too big for the tunnel. I have many kinds of hawk, and dog, and horse, but only one kind of dragon. So I stood there in the dark and hoped the demon had forgotten me. Which wasn't much of a strategy. I listened to that sound, of something smoky, and sandy, flopping about in its death throes. Something essential to the demon's pattern had been wounded by Neve's attack. Her sword had disrupted it, and it couldn't pull itself together. I listened to its scrapes and whispers become slower, quieter. I listened to it swearing, and moaning, and weeping. And I wasn't thinking, *Die, my enemy!* I was thinking of it as a person. Because life is all people. All people everywhere.

'Once it was quiet I got up and made my way down the tube. I walked for maybe an hour. I got thirsty. The patch of light grew larger and rosier. And then everything became a little Plato's Cave, because I saw shadows against the light, a group of demons, coming up the lava tube.

The tunnel was still too narrow for a dragon. And demons weren't going to be impressed by a tiger, or a crocodile, or a taipan. I didn't even think it would do me much good to throw them around. And I could do that—I could shove them back down the tunnel and press them to the floor. Kernow told you his story, so you know I can do that.'

Taryn thought that raising a river from its bed and making a spiralling cone of it was rather more than 'throwing things around'. She asked, 'What did you do?'

'I just stood there and waited. I'd like to say calmly. The group came up on me, hurrying once they saw me. Eager. They were all different, all formidable and dreadful—or mostly dreadful.' Shift frowned, a little flicker of something like wonder passed over his face. 'One of them was tall and had velvety skin, yellow-webbed turquoise. The colours of a poisonous frog.'

Taryn laughed. 'And did it have a big stiffy?'

Shift looked startled.

'I have a story to tell you. But first you finish yours.'

'We just stood looking at one another. And then I said, "You will let me by. I'm on my way to speak to your rulers." This generated a certain amount of shuffling. They exchanged glances—like people.'

Taryn's ears started to ring.

'"Since I can't find a satisfactory answer to my questions," I said, "I'm forced to take up matters with someone above you."

'Demons don't seem to be very good at hiding their feelings. One of them was growling, and another one was filling the air with a smell like burning kumquats. "Or perhaps, after all, you *could* satisfy my curiosity," I said. "Why are demons trespassing in the Sidh?" I was pretending not to know they were looking for the Firestarter. One of them said, "You have Taryn Cornick." And I said, "Not about my person." And then the tall yellow-and-turquoise one began to get a hard-on. Which was disconcerting. I decided it was for the Firestarter. Not for you or me.'

Taryn laughed.

'Perhaps it was the excitement of having a secret. I'll say this: They're not a poker-faced people. Though I guess the big yellow-and-turquoise one was poker-something-else.'

'Would you just stop,' Taryn scolded. She sat up and rubbed the knotted muscle between her eyebrows and tried to collect her thoughts. Of course she wanted to know how he'd escaped and wanted him to tell her, but she had a notion about that, and her notion was unfolding itself around her, more kaleidoscope than flower, shining and symmetrical. 'Do you remember what my demon was shouting before you turned into a dragon and carried us off?'

Shift tilted his head. A gesture of birdlike attention.

'"Hell is the homeland,"' she quoted, and watched him think. She saw the spark catch, and his eyes go the green of a mythical first spring-time. 'It's not Hell that wants the Firestarter,' she said. 'It's the demons.'

'But why?'

'You said they have masters. Fallen angels, I presume. I imagine you and I are on the same page about how Hell is organised. According to the stories.'

'Yes.'

'The fallen angels arrived in Hell when they were thrown out of Heaven?'

'That's right.'

'They took over.'

'A small number of angels is stronger than a great number of demons. They're like the men with the guns. Except no one can take their guns.'

'Okay,' Taryn said. 'Then "Hell is the homeland" is the rallying cry of an independence movement.'

Taryn watched understanding and calculation cascading in Shift's eyes. Then he returned his attention to the road, slowed down, and turned into the lane that ran along the boundary of what remained of the Northover land. It was dusk, and very green beyond the car windows. But the green was in the car too, something sparkling and voiceless, and dark and unfathomable, like acres of old-growth forest. The spell had withdrawn and uncovered him. For one exultant moment she imagined she—Taryn Cornick—had broken the spell.

The great spell with the same character as the one on the Firestarter.

Taryn watched Shift as he peered ahead for oncoming cars and made mental notes about the passing bays. He said, 'It's not guns or brute strength that keeps the demons subdued. It's a language.'

He slowed and pulled in at the gate to the rye field. He got out and opened it. Then he got back in, drove bumping into the field, then reversed to tuck the car in against the hedge, facing the gate.

'How long are we leaving my car here?'

'You are going to send an email to your former husband's factotum, the useful Mr Stuart, and tell him it's here.'

Taryn got out her phone and spent a few minutes composing an email. She reflected that she must by then have burned up all of Alan's goodwill. There was no point her being worried about it, but she was. She frowned over the email and fretted about the consequences of sending it. Shift meanwhile had got out of the car and was leaning on its side, in the last of the light, looking up into a sky of browns and soft lavenders, darker than the usual summer south-eastern haze, for it was stained by the smoke of European forest fires. Taryn got out too and leaned on the warm metal. 'My mind wandered,' she said. 'You were telling me how you escaped from Hell.'

Shift looked at her curiously, then laughed. 'There was a brief stand-off. Then they seized me bodily—but not roughly, so I held off on any defensive action until I knew what they were doing. What they did was lift me over their heads and run me back up the tunnel. They charged the gate, and they threw me at it. And it was open. Neve must have moved it away from the Sidh and opened it.'

'She didn't seem to be able to open it onto Hell.'

Shift shrugged. 'We aren't going to know what she did until we ask her.'

'Where did you come out?'

'Lake Baikal, near the mouth of the Turka. Long hours of daylight. I couldn't be a dragon; too conspicuous. Besides, it's difficult to stop being a dragon, so I don't like to do it. Or rather, I do like to do it, very much, which is why it's difficult to stop.' He gave a little yelp of laughter. 'I am always dragon myself back.'

Taryn moaned. 'Please.'

'I considered setting out for Australia—'

'New Zealand.'

'New Zealand—but decided instead to become a high-flying goose and fly back to London, where I could hover around outside Jacob's place of work.'

'On the grounds that Jacob was more helpful to you than I was? More helpful than my grandfather's papers pertaining to the distribution of his library?'

'Papers are just papers, Taryn. They sit about mutely, waiting to be read.'

'Whereas Jacob . . . ?'

'Whereas Jacob could send you a message telling you I was safe.'

'Oh,' Taryn said.

'I was hovering around in human form when Raymond Price approached me and told me that you were back in the country but that your phone had been unmoving in Alan Palfreyman's windbreak for some hours. And that he couldn't locate Jacob. And that he presumed I was waiting to catch Jacob. He didn't ask me why I didn't have a phone or anyone's number. He didn't seem surprised that I got in his car. He didn't seem baffled by my trusting him. He was businesslike and helpful. He gave me a packet of peanuts to eat when I told him I was hungry. We were hours away, Taryn. I could have got there much faster as a dragon, but imagine the repercussions. There's no point in just providing a spectacle. There's no point in changing people's minds or even their world views, but not having the means to change the world. That's just acting in bad faith.'

Taryn was startled. She had never considered that Shift was thinking of changing the world. She asked, 'How would you change the world?'

'I wouldn't change it.'

It took a moment, but suddenly Taryn was furious. 'Why the hell are you always so careful?'

'What else should I be? Most of the good in the world is remedial. It's fixing things and caring for people. *Taking care.*'

'Right. And none of it is your business.'

Shift drooped a little. 'That's what Jacob said.'

'It's what *you* said! Jacob and I are only quoting you! And your people are preparing to send a hundred thousand souls off to Hell to buy another century of their beautiful civilised lives. Which is why I have a lot of sympathy for the demons. At least the demons want to change things.'

'I can see that,' Shift said. His tone wasn't any cooler. It wasn't tired, or patient, or riled, or defensive. It just had that formidable neutrality he often used when speaking to one of his people. Who didn't consider themselves to be his people.

Taryn sighed. What else could she expect of this person with very few attachments and only a small hoard of his past, a legacy consisting of a few stories, like boundary pegs around a bit of real estate he never meant to develop. She had a tiny part in that impoverished future. All she could do was refine her story, whittle her peg. She guessed she should approach it all as a puzzle, a conundrum, a bit of research. 'So,' she said, 'why do *you* think the demons want the Firestarter?'

'It's the Torah above the Torah.'

Taryn clapped her hands to her face and rubbed it hard. How sharp and angular her jaw was now. It felt like it had when she was twenty. Shift didn't take pity on her. Nor should he. After all, she was the one who'd had the wit to realise that the demons and Hell weren't the same thing. It hadn't occurred to him.

Taryn mused for a time and kept rubbing her face until her skin burned. Then she stopped and abruptly uncovered her eyes and gazed at Shift. His silhouette was haloed in a pink and green swarm of visual snow. He was facing her fully, and she had the impression he was smiling at her. She said, 'The Torah is the word of God. A Torah above the Torah would be the *language* of God.'

'That's right. And we're back here now, at the place you got lost before the birds flew into their nests in the hedgerow, before the first stars came out. But let's see how you do this time—Taryn Cornick of the Northovers, Valravn, Hero of Understanding. Because now I think you can ask the question you couldn't ask or even hear asked.'

Taryn struggled for a minute, with the graciousness and oddity of his address, and the half hour she'd just lost as if she'd been drugged—or possessed. And then her scalp caught fire. All over her body her superficial nerves heated up. She wanted to throw off her clothes. She pushed off the car where she was leaning and staggered a few paces into the thick of the rye. She had to stop herself from looking about for the wasp nest she must accidentally have disturbed. Her ears roared.

Shift came to her, set his hands on her hips, and held her steady.

It took her a minute, then she caught her breath and shouted it at him. The simple question. The *obvious* one. Birds burst from the hedge, and a weasel appeared from a gap in the wall and gazed at them solemnly for a moment before looping away into the pasture. And all the time Taryn kept shouting. 'What is in the box?' she shouted. 'What the bloody hell is *in* the box?'

Shift pushed them hard, and they traversed the Summer Road from its closest point, near the Island of Apples, to where it intersected the Horse Road at the Island of Women. Seven days altogether. They were going too fast to travel on with Jane, Kernow, and the few other women who'd chosen to accompany Shift to the Moot. Shift promised them that the moment he had the glove he'd stop and wait for them to catch up.

Taryn and Shift walked every day from an hour after sunup to noon, when they rested for two hours, then continued till sundown. It was the height of summer. Most of the trees were in fruit, and Taryn learned to follow Shift's example and eat as she walked, pausing to pull broad beans from the masses of tall feathery plants, or snap off gritty asparagus, or swing up into the branches of the plum tree to reach the higher, riper fruit. Now and then they'd come upon a covered basket fastened to the trunk of a tree, and someone's stash of hazelnuts, or windfall walnuts already stripped of their oily black skins. Once or twice the basket had run low and Shift would find the fruiting nut tree and pick up more windfall walnuts, or shake the hazel so that he and Taryn could gather up the fruit. They'd take a few meals with them in the felt sling bags they carried and stow the rest in the baskets for the next party that came along.

At pond or lakeside encampments, Shift would pick his way through the reeds and return with the eggs of ducks or blue-backed swamphens. He'd set a fish or eel trap in the stream or lake before they lay down to sleep on their beds of cut ferns, and they'd have a good meal of fish in the morning before setting out.

As they walked, Shift taught Taryn sidhe—a few polite phrases, and many nouns. He taught her the names of animals and trees and types of cloud and the times of the day. And while they sat warming their hands on their copper cups of lemon balm or chrysanthemum tea he taught her the names of various celestial bodies—planets and the larger stars.

How far away I am, Taryn thought—with a kind of transparent happiness, looking up at the strange constellations. Sometimes she worried she wouldn't see her father again, or her grandmother, who had a few more good years in her. But Taryn had been pierced and punctured and leaking life away into another universe since Beatrice was killed, and her sister was still the furthest thing from her.

Taryn tried asking questions. Like: Were they somewhere else in the galaxy? Did Shift know?

'Sidhe gates are made to find certain kinds of places. The worlds are a network of places possible for such as us to live. And there's convenience in the details of it, like matching the gates between the Sidh and Earth by season, not latitude, so travelling sidhe don't have to carry a change of clothes. The gates work by quantum entanglement. I've gathered that much, thanks to twentieth- and twenty-first-century physics. One day I was reading about quantum entanglement and thought, *Oh, yes, of course.* I never had to *learn* that about gates, as I learned magic lore. The gates and glove speak to my bones. Like being an owl or a fox or a fish, my feeling for gates is a potential of my body.'

Taryn made a little hollow in the grit by her bed and set her cup in it, the few mouthfuls left in case she was thirsty in the night. She sat up to fold the sleeping blanket over her feet and knot its ties to keep it in place. The sleeping blankets weren't designed for anyone wanting to get up in a hurry. Which spoke volumes. The sidhe weren't taken by sudden sickness in the night. They weren't called to the bedsides of crying children, and no one crept up to attack them.

She lay down and tucked her hands under the covers. She'd never felt so safe. On the last journey she'd been lonely on this road—even as part of a bigger group. Shift might have something dangerous planned for her, but that was later. Now, with the lake water lapping, the coals tinkling in the stone fireplace, and the distant chorus of frogs that Shift had persuaded to move to the far side of the lake, she was safe and happy. *Now* partook of forever. No matter what came, this was the Sidh—the same as ever.

They caught up with Neve at a landing where the Horse Road looped down to the Senisteingh, a very deep river with transparent turquoise water and a swift current. The landing was on a shingle beach, below a vast water meadow. The meadow was scattered with tents, campfires, and palanquins like the one Taryn had been carried in when she was injured. A group of these were set under a wide shade tree, separated from the rest of the meadow by a low fence. This encampment within the camp had no fireplace, though threads of bluish smoke came up from several palanquins, and the scent of spicy smoke, cleaner and more astringent than any incense Taryn had encountered.

A number of boats were moored in the shelter of the landing, or further along the stream, bound by strong ropes to the trunks of riverside trees, or to boulders with holes drilled all the way through them.

The boats had oiled timber hulls, the oil so fresh that Taryn could see the water beading at the waterline. They had simple rudders for a helmsman, or wheel houses. They had masts and furled sails. Some looked big enough to transport the palanquins and horses; some were more suited to taking only a few people. In any other place Taryn wouldn't call it a crowd—but it was as many people as she'd seen since the Island of Women, and many more sidhe than she had ever encountered. Both sidhe and human travellers were building fires, gathering firewood, picking over bowls of seeds and nuts. The only purely sidhe task belonged to a dozen or so men and women, who were standing thigh-deep in the river, their feet planted against the current, long fishing spears in hand.

Shift didn't join any group, only cast his eyes about. Once he'd spotted what he wanted, he retired under a tree near the fenced encampment.

Taryn followed him, slow and footsore.

The tree Shift sheltered under was an olive. The ground under it was littered with slippery dried olive pits.

'Not here,' Taryn said, glaring at the top of Shift's head. 'I'm not lying down on this.'

He had dropped his sleeping roll and was fossicking in his sling bag.

'If you want to avoid these people we could just rent a boat,' Taryn suggested. 'Rent. Buy. Or barter.'

'Barter with what, Taryn?' He didn't sound irritated, just resolutely educational, which made her want to kick him.

He'd found what he was after. He produced several sealed packets of dressings. He got up and waved them at her. 'I swiped these from a cart on Jacob's ward. You are going to affix them to my chest.' He handed her the pads, pulled off his lumpy vest, and loosened the ribbon lacing on his shirt. There was no sign at all of his former injuries, no scarring or discolouration. 'I'm going to tell Neve that I finally had all the iron removed.'

'Right.' She opened a package and got him to point to where he wanted the square of gauze. He of course chose a spot where the dressing would be visible in the open neck of the shirt.

Taryn smoothed her fingers over the tape. 'I think that'll do,' she said, and put the rest of the dressings back in his bag. 'We should grubby it up a bit.' She rubbed some dust into the gauze and a little around the edges of the adhesive until it darkened. The bandage now looked as though he'd been wearing it for days.

'Now Neve can't say the glove is no use to me.'

'Isn't it yours?'

'Yes, but it's too precious to be merely ornamental. And Neve's the only other person who can use it.'

'Did you give it to her to lull her into a false sense of security?'

'To lull everyone. I'd love to be able to say I gave it to her to see what she'd do with it. But I had no idea she'd throw in with the sisters and try to trick a demon into revealing things. I love your father's story. I love it that the sisters went around Odin, and that Neve infringed on her own dignity. That it happened at all makes me think all sorts of things are possible.' He was smiling, stuffing his unattractive hippy vest into his unmanly hippy bag. He had burrs in his hair. Taryn removed them, and he froze starkly still and stared at her.

'Don't look so nervous,' she said.

'No one grooms me,' he said.

'Is Neve here?'

'She's under the giant fig with the royalty.'

'You people *do* have hierarchies.'

'"Royalty" is respectful. They're older than everyone else. They don't travel regularly.' He moved off, said over his shoulder, 'You can wait for me at the fence.'

Taryn did. The fence was at the limit of the thicker shade. The ground had been swept, and as she peered into the cool, scented, silent zone, she understood that it had been cleared so that there was no chance anyone would step on a stick or send one stone knocking against another. The only royal personage Taryn could see from where she stood was sitting cross-legged on cushions, young and limber, his hair thickly curled, his black skin smooth. But he also had charcoal silk gauze tied around his eyes and gold ear ornaments that were in fact earplugs. He was stooped over a brazier of scented smoke, protected by it from the wild and various scents of the water meadow, as he was from the afternoon's unmitigated sights and sounds by his veil and earplugs.

Shift had instructed Taryn to stand completely motionless, and make no sound. She was doing that, and could hear the tiny clicks that one of her eyes made when she moved them. Her eyes were dry. She needed tea. She needed to sit down and be fed.

Shift stepped over the fence and glided up to the palanquins. He was intercepted by a dark-skinned woman with sleek mahogany-brown hair. A woman so covered in mendings that Taryn could actually see them at work, tiny volumes like glass beads moving to dislodge a sprinkling of dried herbs on the woman's sleeve and brush grass from the tops of her naked feet. It made Taryn's skin crawl.

The woman wrapped her hand around Shift's upper arm and marched him back to the fence. She was hissing at him in sidhe, then glanced at Taryn and swapped to English. How did the woman know that it should be English rather than French or German or Danish? As it turned out, the woman's change in language was the opposite of politeness, because she was being not firm but rude.

'No one here wants to speak to you,' she said to Shift. 'And you haven't even washed. You stink. Your woman is worse. Sour.'

'Send Neve out to me,' Shift whispered.

'Leave. Wash.'

'Get Neve for me now, or I'll go and stand upwind.'

The woman reared back, her eyes shining with wrath.

'You're moving too precipitously,' Shift said. 'You're shaking the air.'

The man at the brazier had gently averted his face, as if from something he couldn't bear to watch.

The woman released her grip and slowly, gracefully, turned herself around and went to the furthest of the palanquins. She stood at its open trellis doors and spoke in sign language, the motion of her fingers restrained and at half the speed Taryn expected.

Neve climbed down from the interior of the palanquin and drifted across the grass, gleaming, barefoot. When she came close, Taryn smelled the perfume of the smoke on her. Neve pressed them to move further off, and followed. When they had reached enough of a distance she asked, 'Why are you being so insistent? None of us will strike camp before sunup.'

'Hello, Neve,' Taryn whispered.

'Hello, Taryn Cornick,' Neve replied.

'I'm all better,' Shift said, and yanked his shirt aside and tilted his collarbones to Neve's face.

'I believe it has been conveyed to you that you are odoriferous?' Neve said.

'I never stink. I smell like what I am.'

'What you are isn't appetising to us. And therefore must be offensive to the old ones.'

'The baggage. The dead wood, husks, and cobwebs,' Shift said.

Neve looked at him silently for a minute, then took his hand, lifted it to her lips, and closed her teeth on the pad of his thumb. She bore down. They had a strange silent tussle. Neither of them wanted to make any noise. Even their feet remained planted. Taryn was debating whether to intervene when Neve let him go.

Shift reeled back, then froze and glanced sidelong at the man by the brazier. His hand dripped blood onto the ground. 'Why did you do that?' he whispered. He cradled his hand.

Neve drew her hand slowly across her lips, leaving a red smear on her cheek. 'Because you're alive. It's always been the same reason. You're alive.'

She lifted the thong of the Gatemaker's glove over her head and put the glove into Taryn's hands. She stepped back over the fence and returned to the palanquin, moving as smoothly as a camera on a dolly.

Shift turned and walked off upriver. Taryn hurried after him. The Gatemaker's glove was warm from Neve's skin, but as Taryn carried it, it lost its warmth. It cooled and then wouldn't take up the heat of her hands.

Taryn caught up with Shift beyond a turn in the river. She got him to stand still and used the remaining dressings on his bite.

'Couldn't you just turn yourself into an owl or eel or something so the bite will be gone?' she asked, then muttered, 'You and your fucking "I got the last of the iron out". As if I haven't swapped notes with Jacob.'

His flesh was puffing up around the puncture marks.

Taryn said, 'Why doesn't Neve want you alive?'

'Whenever anyone says something like that, it always means someone else is dead. There is always an equivalent someone.'

'Your mother?'

'I don't know. It's Neve's story to tell.'

'But is it one of the stories you count as yours?'

'It won't be if I'm not in it. But I can't see why my life would be counted against the life of someone else in a story I'm not part of.'

The table of water meadow had lifted beside them and was now a tree-covered escarpment. They were out of the sun, and it was chilly. Taryn looked at the shaded green water and told Shift she wasn't going to wash there.

'There are gardens and orchards all around the landing. You'll have no trouble collecting food. And you can find a place at one of the campfires.' He passed her his bedroll and hers, but kept his bag. 'The encampment will thin out in the morning when the flotilla embarks. Some will stay waiting for people they mean to join up with. You wait for Jane, Kernow, and the others. Be led by them. They have done the voyage before. Kernow many times. It's over a thousand miles, but the river is easy the whole way.'

Taryn seized his arm. He had the glove, and he was just going to rush off. 'You won't change yourself for five seconds to rid yourself of the inconvenience of an injury, but you'll spend days running us skinny just to get your glove, and then suddenly I'm an encumbrance?'

Shift gently laid a hand over hers. 'Right now you should go downriver to the sunny swimming hole. The water looks inviting, and I would love to slip into a fish and swim for a time and listen to the water brush the boulders. Every time I'm an animal, I'm just one thing. This'—he used his free hand to indicate himself—'this is never settled. My bones and nerves can feel the gates. Whenever I'm tired or discouraged I want to bind my eyes and stop my ears and live in the smoke or just climb inside a tree and go to sleep for decades, as I've done before. And the godly part of me is pressed to become what its worshippers want. And the human part of me wants a hearth and friends and a rational, progressive, day-bound existence. I don't become a fish or a horse or a dragon to shed a small injury, but because I'm happier as a fish or a horse or a dragon. I'm happier being any *decided* thing. As for abandoning you—'

'You have worshippers?'

'Not here.' He laughed. 'And "worshippers" isn't quite the right word. That's me trying to think how the attention and appeal work on me. What I have is the trees saying, "Save us." I'm surprised you can't feel it. The trees, the marsh, the hedgerow where we left your car, the dune grass outside your former husband's house. The mass of things that know without thinking what they want me to be.'

'The little god of the marshlands.'

'That's right. And, Taryn, I'm not abandoning you. You're necessary to me. I can't find the Firestarter without you, because without you I have no hope of finding your mother, who it seems might be the only one with any clue to its whereabouts.'

'So we're really doing that? Going to Purgatory?'

'We've gone through your grandfather's papers. We have no other leads. The thing isn't going to stop hiding itself just because we understand more about it. I mean, it isn't as if you can see me more clearly just because you understand me better.'

Taryn peered at him—his dusky face. Life was full of people who weren't particularly captivating or interesting to look at. She wanted to look at him, not just listen to his gentle, unexceptional voice and have him fall back into obscurity minute by minute, and more so if she tried to penetrate the obscurity.

'You'll be fine,' he said. 'Jane will be along shortly. And I'm only leaving you because I think it might be logistically difficult to find Jacob. He won't be in Norfolk anymore. I don't want even a short delay for you anywhere the police can find you.'

She let go of his arm. 'Of course you've thought it through,' she said, resentful. 'Of course you're going to get Jacob.'

'I thought you'd want me to get Jacob.' He sounded surprised. 'You waited at the hospital for days to see him. Don't you want him?'

Taryn pressed her lips together firmly. That was not a question she was going to answer.

Shift took the glove from her and dropped it onto his right hand, then looked at it, disconcerted. It was balanced on the dressing like a too-small hat on a too-big head. He stripped off the dressing, then fastened the glove over his bruised and swollen hand. He clipped the pin and chain closed and wrapped the thong around his wrist. Then he stepped away from Taryn and stretched out the gloved hand.

Taryn felt the vertiginous lurch and soundless roaring as the gate arrived. It was the third time she'd felt that: the other times were outside the Bibliothèque Méjanes, and when Neve put her through Hell's Gate into that quiet spot in Hyde Park several weeks earlier. Neve had stood straight and made a ceremonious gesture, like someone performing magic. Shift looked the same as he did when he was plucking fruit from a tree. Then he dropped his hand, took a few steps forward, and disappeared. Taryn felt the gate wheel away again—Hell's Gate—probably reverting to its fixed point, like the dial on an old-fashioned phone revolving on a spring.

Taryn shouldered Shift's bedroll as well as her own and went downriver. She found a stretch of water sheltered from the current by the landing and a shingle spit. The water was sparkling, and several other people were swimming. Taryn took off her clothes and walked into the river, which was fresh but not cold. She swam and rinsed herself and sat in the shallows. She even had a conversation with a middle-aged man whose face was stippled by white scars—it looked as if someone had been chipping away at him with a chisel. He spoke in sparse formal French, with much more fluent dialect mixed into it, and a little English. Enough for Taryn to tell him that she came from London and was a writer of books. And for him to tell her that when he was last on Earth he was a *poilu*—an infantryman—and before that a cobbler. He originally came from a village in Brittany. They managed that little, then sat companionably, the water hissing as it lapped against the thick mat of hair on his chest. She tried some of her sidhe on him and he taught her a little more, all of it related to the river, upstream and downstream, boat and sail, voyage and current.

The sun left the water. Everyone got out and picked up their clothes and followed the sunlight higher up the water meadow. They stood and dried in the air. No midges or mosquitoes came to molest them.

Taryn put on her sweaty garments and joined the soldier at his fire, where there were several more Frenchmen, as well as two joyful Vietnamese teenagers, who were making everyone pool their food for as much of a feast as they could muster. Taryn contributed her walnuts and fresh apricots. Someone came around with a crock full of a powerful juniper-flavoured clear spirit. The crock still had scabs of fresh dirt on its sides, as someone had only just dug it up. It was clearly a piece of human provisioning, because none of the sidhe at the fires near Taryn's accepted any.

Everyone at her fire ate and drank and got a little inebriated. They sang for a bit, and then tried to get Taryn to tell them, in her poor French, how the world fared. Was it possible yet to be poor and live decently? Were young men still sent to die in wars made by old men? Were the meek still waiting to inherit the Earth, as Scripture promised, though generations of them were already under the ground, and a grave wasn't an inheritance?

Not really, Taryn said of the first. Yes, of course, of the second. And of the third, no. It's not like that. They made us believe we're weaklings if we can't do everything for ourselves *by ourselves*. We all say, 'So, I've failed,' when mostly we've been failed. They made us afraid of one another, but of themselves they say, 'There is no "they."'

Taryn's French didn't let her down. These were simple things to express. The people around the fire all looked at her sadly and nodded sagely. She stared at their human faces, painted by the firelight, and thought how those they loved and served would eventually sell them into perpetual misery. She wanted to tell them to run away. What were they going to say of themselves when their souls were marched through Hell's Gate and their bodies were buried no doubt with flowers and music and fine ceremony? Were they going to say, 'So, I've failed. Such and such a lady or gentleman no longer loves me, and has laid me by'? Taryn understood that her existence was only of use or not of use to her society. She was a consumer contributing to economic growth, which was an unquestioned good. To exist, she must spend her life spending. But these people were going to be sold to buy more time for time-rich, heartless people. They were going to be literally damned by association, never mind the original state of their souls. Heaven would not intervene as it did in Yeats's *Countess Cathleen*, because, for a start, none of these people was a countess. They were the numberless others of history, counted only by the Tithe. They were marks in a ledger. Taryn wanted to say, 'I'm a consumer and a client, and you're property. We have value, but it has nothing to do with who we are.'

But she didn't say that. Because what good would it do when a true understanding of what was in store for them couldn't save them from any of it?

Twenty-Five

Taken Lightly

Jacob, in the pit of his last dose of painkiller, lay looking at the sky. A dawn sky, scarcely blue, with soft gold clouds.

He was lying in a flattened clearing in a meadow, on a mounded bed of sleek and greenish hay. The ground around his bed was carefully swept, the strokes of the broom most evident around the stone walls of the campfire. The smoking coals were uncovered and topped with fresh kindling. The sticks had recently caught and were crackling and blackening.

Jacob's bed was hard, and something firm supported his lumbar region. A belt that braced his back, but without any corresponding stricture on his abdomen. The brace was firm, warm, but somehow not fully solid.

He attempted to get up. He bent his legs and tilted his hip off the mound of grass. He swung his opposite arm over so he'd roll onto his knees. The pressure and heat in the small of his back increased. It felt almost as if four branching hands had spread their fingers up under his kidneys and down between his buttocks. Hands with improbably long fingers bolstered his tailbone and branched around his rectum.

Pain lanced down his right leg. It was his right sciatic nerve that was compressed. The doctors had told him that. As the pain arrived, the heat and pressure moved out across his right buttock and hip. His thigh was gripped and held. There was a kind of current in the touch, an electric tickle. The pain began to relent. It was squeezed and buzzed away.

Jacob got himself upright and limped over to a tree and leaned on it. He stared at the fire, the hay, the doeskin blanket, and a grimy white cotton sheet that he recognised as belonging to the hospital he had been in when last awake, a London hospital specialising in spinal injuries.

The standing grass rustled, and a fox appeared. It was carrying a bird, the fan of wings masking its muzzle. It trotted out onto the flattened grass of the clearing and looked at Jacob. It didn't hesitate, going to the fire and dropping the bird, which turned out to be two birds—fat quail. The fox sat back on its haunches and licked its paws to wash its face. It groomed the blood from its muzzle and chest, then met Jacob's eye and gave a small black-lipped smile.

Jacob set his hands behind him and dug his fingernails into the tree trunk.

The fox did not turn into a man. It wasn't a television or movie version of shifting, of CGI morphing an image of an animal into the image of a man. Instead the fox became a small cloud of matter, dense and rosy, the colour of sunlight shining through a baby's ear. The cloud thinned, grew in volume, as if its particles were dividing. Again it gathered morning light into itself and then made Shift—Shift, in his homespun and home-knit clothes.

The fox had been sitting on its haunches; Shift was cross-legged. He reached for one quail, drew it into his lap, and began plucking it.

'I think I remember you arriving at the hospital,' Jacob said. He had a dreamlike recollection of Shift clambering over the bottom board of the bed, where the chart hung, and the motor of the pressure-relieving mattress. Shift had stood wobbling on the wheezing, constantly adjust-ing mattress, his arms out for balance, one hand bare, the other gleaming rose gold.

Jacob looked about and saw the glove hanging like a Christmas ornament in the branches of the tree he was leaning against. 'Aren't you afraid someone will take it?'

Shift looked where Jacob was looking and shook his head. 'It was made for my mother. Her sister Neve can use it. Her son can use it. And no one else.'

'I mean for the value of the gold?'

'Gold isn't for hoarding here. It's for tools. That glove is already a tool. No one would think to refashion it.'

'You put it in an oak at Princes Gate Magna.'

'Momentarily.'

'Momentarily unless something happened to you.'

'Yes, but I can't go around thinking like that. *You* don't think like that.'

'I floss my teeth,' Jacob said. He didn't court danger; danger was just part of the deal of his life. Otherwise he was as careful as the next care-ful person, and he'd never had time for this wafty put-the-priceless-object-in-a-tree, or sneaky pretend-to-be-crippled stuff.

Shift said, 'You've lost me.'

'Do I have to explain dental floss?'

'I'm not sure what it is, though I seem to remember Jack Reacher making a tripwire with some. A strong line, easily obtainable in a stan-dard grocery store. Something for cleaning the gaps between teeth, I believe.'

'So you do know.'

'Only when I think it through. So—what do I need to know about dental floss?'

'I use it to look after my teeth because I'll need my teeth for the duration of my life. You presumably will need the Gatemaker's glove for the duration of yours.'

'It does represent the freedom to go almost anywhere.'

'Which is why I'm surprised Neve gave it up.'

'Neve doesn't want to go anywhere. She doesn't want much at all.'

'Lucky her.'

'She eats. Her eyes tolerate the light. She doesn't walk away from quarrels, dogfights, dance music being too loud. But she's not all that interested in anything.'

Jacob was now lost.

'So,' Shift said, which sounded like a final word and a powerful conjunction that might be followed by a reasoned argument. But he only put down the denuded quail, its still-feathered head lolling, and picked up the second.

Jacob realised his back had stopped hurting. He stayed where he was, as motionless as possible, and watched Shift finish plucking the second bird. Once it was featherless Shift fished in the felted bag he'd left by the fire while he was off in fox. He produced a stone knife with a rippled translucent blade. He used it to gut the quail, then to cut the twigs off some stakes. He pushed the stakes through the quail and propped them up over the flames to roast. After a time the morning filled with the sound of softly snapping kindling and the juice and grease from the birds dripping onto the coals.

Jacob asked what the thing was that had him in its grip, and Shift said, 'A hand. Or rather two of them. Like mendings, but stronger and more sustained. They're being guided by your muscles. They'll warm them, press out a spasm, and firm up if you start to tire. You can stop trying to protect your back. Let the hands be vigilant for you.'

'So I might sit to eat?'

Jacob hadn't sat in weeks. He couldn't imagine it. Then he saw that there wasn't anything to sit on but the ground.

In her quick sketch of the nomadic, hunter-gatherer but highly cultivated and accommodating sidhe, Taryn had mentioned caches of cooking equipment, comfortable encampments, stores of firewood, wild gardens, and landscaped walks down to the water. Shift and he must have been well off the beaten path.

'Or maybe I'll stay standing.' Jacob gestured at the bare ground.

'There aren't any proper stopping places at Hell's Gate,' Shift said, and pointed towards the rising sun. 'It's just over there.'

'The gate is on the main thoroughfare?'

'The Horse Road. No one stops at the gate because of the graves. They're all around us.'

Jacob looked about for signs but saw only the meadow covered in wildflowers and large but widely scattered trees.

'The newest graves are nearly a century old. The ground dips, but time and vegetation plump it out again.'

Jacob was determined not to ask whose graves they were. Besides, Shift had gone on to give an account of his short visit to Hell.

After a time Shift brought the quail—charred on its outside and still taut and pink by its bones. Jacob took a few bites, and his brain woke up enough to let him know that the graves must have been for the bodies of the human beings whose souls were offered to Hell at the time of the Tithe. Taryn had been here; she'd sent photos, and he had seen what she saw—a long tract of grassland and mountains, another paradisiacal place. The apricot-coloured birds and tree with bright green leaves. The stone pillars and smoky demon. No sign of graves. But Taryn wouldn't have thought of mass graves. Mass graves were an idea that came more readily to Jacob.

'I brought my gate to your hospital bed as soon as I discovered where you were. I even brought it up to the level of your bed so I could take the end of your sheet and drag you directly to this fireside. I had the fire built already. You passed out when I pulled you through. I removed all your cannulas. I made my hands and set them on you, rolled you onto the bed I'd made, and covered you with the sheet that came with you. I wanted a quiet place to get my hands on you. And for the ceremonial moment.' Shift was looking at Jacob steadily, sombrely.

'What ceremonial moment?'

'Which has passed,' Shift said. 'I have no idea what the state of your soul was, or what it would have been if I'd left you to live out your life. This way I can guarantee a good four hundred years before I'm too young to defend you.'

Jacob looked at his still ferociously steaming quail. 'Huh,' he said. 'I just got Took.'

Twenty-Six

Quarry House

There was time, so the party went by the river to the Moot. The boat carried eight comfortably, with four sleeping in the cabin below the waterline. The cabin had no windows—glass seemed unknown, or simply unused, in the Sidh. The doors down to it were open in the daytime, and at night Taryn would light the single gimbal-mounted oil lamp. The other four bedded down on deck, among cushions piled in an open-sided shelter. Jacob spent most of his time there, day and night, flat on his back, or sometimes propped up enough to watch the land slipping by.

They travelled as part of a flotilla. Most of the boats would moor in the same harbour each night. Sites established at tributary streams, or where a road joined the river. Each site a node of the food forest that followed all roads and waterways, thickening or thinning according to the quality of the soil, irrigation and drainage, the orientation to the sun, and frequency of use. The food forests along the Senisteingh thickened wherever a bend in the river created a large stretch of calm water.

But there were many other places where one or two vessels might moor, like the deep water beside a tree whose trunk was worn smooth by ropes—somewhere boats had tied up for years, barges whose passengers wouldn't want to join a thronged harbour campsite. Their boat, heading for the customary nightly harbour, often passed barges moored at these quiet spots. At dusk, their curtained palanquins floated, dreamy and pale, in their clouds of spice-scented smoke. On their boat a hush would fall. Nobody would hail the barge, and all boat-board activities would be suspended until it had passed out of sight.

The harbours never held all the same vessels. Some dropped behind or got ahead. Their boat caught up with those Taryn had watched set off from the harbour where the Horse Road first met the Senisteingh, during the time she was alone, the two days she waited for Jane and her companions, and then four more for Shift and Jacob.

None of the boats used their sails. Theirs had no form of propulsion, only a tiller and a couple of oars, the first usually managed by one of the three sturdy women who had arrived with Jane and Kernow—Susan, Henriette, and Blanche—and the second scarcely used.

In the tricky stretches Shift and Henriette took turns at the tiller, Shift sometimes getting Taryn to stand at it with him. He'd point out signs of submerged snags or shingle banks and, after several sessions, posted her on the bow to give him a bit more warning about the river's obstacles. Taryn didn't offer any diagnosis of the conditions she was on the lookout for, just called out 'Over there!' and turned to check that he was looking where she pointed. It gave her something to do apart from watch the passing landscape and wonder at what she saw.

The river flowed through forested hills, rich soil covered in oak, elm, ash, cherry, apple, peach, pear, plum, quince, and medlar. Poorer soils on bluffs above the river were covered in hazels.

They passed steep dry hills of olives and acacias, and the river hurried through gorges of different character—some with tall cataracts of tributary rivers, some with no vegetation, only great falls of broken rock. The river in those places flowed pale and murky with a strong cable of current at its centre and wicked whirlpools where it touched the cliffs. Shift and Henriette would steer together, leaning into or away from the tiller, using the oars to help hold the boat steady.

Further downstream the flotilla converged into a slow-moving mass. The Senisteingh broadened. A path appeared on both banks and went alongside the river for miles. People took the opportunity to get out and walk, because it was easy to keep their boat in view. Taryn gathered berries and watched the other vessels, the tall figures with bright hair and faces that glowed with health, and their human companions, often also lovely, and at ease in a deep, complacent way that made them like the sidhe, only not nearly as packed with unused moment and energy.

Taryn was glad that her boat had none of the sidhe aboard. But even with exposure to them at a distance she became more able to see how little Shift was like them.

At evening, in the harbours, just about everyone would go swimming. Even Jacob. In the water the strange fan of force that was attached to his lower back became visible, the Hands Shift would refresh every day, simply sitting behind Jacob with his palms spread in the small of Jacob's back, showing no sign of effort, or cost, only serene absorption.

They'd swim in the sunshine. Jane would tread water with her friends, face to face, talking about this and that. Kernow would sit in the shallows and pour water over his white crown. Shift would shadow Jacob, who would swim up and down, determined and diligent, always a bit looser and stronger when he got out afterwards.

One night Shift built two fires on the narrow beach where they were moored, a groyne of big boulders and wet shingle between looming cliff faces. The mooring was sheltered from the wind, but sunless. Shift made soup for everyone but only invited Taryn, Jacob, and Kernow to the smaller fire. He ensured the old man and the invalid were comfortably supported by cushions, and then he served the soup.

Taryn balanced hers on a stone so it could cool a little and fixed Shift with her gaze. 'You've been thinking,' she said.

'Kernow has a story to tell.'

'But first I'll eat while it's still hot,' Kernow said.

Taryn drew breath to ask something, but before she'd said a word, Shift put a finger to his lips. 'No questions,' he said. 'We don't want him stopped before he starts.'

'Why would I stop?' Kernow was bemused. 'I have told you this story. I offered it when you came back two hundred years ago. Almost as soon as you could speak I told you every one of my stories. And this time around, when I finished that particular one, at least you didn't say, as you have in the past, "I never want to hear that again!"' Kernow sounded irascible. 'It isn't my fault if it slipped your mind.'

'Eat your soup.'

Kernow supped and muttered and had Shift rearrange his wrappings because he was cold, and no wonder in this chilly spot. After a time he went on, in a tone of objection. 'I don't know why you didn't Take the abbess as well as me. It's the abbess's story, after all. It was entrusted to her.'

'Monacella of Cwm Pennant was too holy to Take. She was so holy that it was her baptism that saved me from my fate. I wouldn't get between that woman and Heaven.'

'This is Heaven,' Kernow said. He put down his bowl, wiped his lips, and licked his fingers. Then he simply began: 'That old man, the wizard of the chosen king, brought me to the abbess of Cwm Pennant so that I could learn what our mutual acquaintance, the witch of the Marshlands, had told her and given her.'

He paused, crossed himself, and continued.

In late summer the mud of Adhan's marsh was thick and warm, the groundsel in flower, and the sweet galingale spiked and brown. In the mornings the air was clear over miles of marshland, except near her hut, where it shimmered, hot above the withered sedges.

Adhan sat on a deerskin beside her outdoor hearth, waiting for a membrane to form on a glue of boiled rabbit skin and bones. It was the first use she had made all summer of her medicine pot. There'd been no balms for coughs, or powders to bind or loosen bowels, no painkillers or sleeping draughts. Just this work, which might be a remedy, or a poison.

It was a manuscript, ink of wood ash mixed with blood, inscribed on skin as fine as vellum but darker in shade. The ink had taken weeks to dry. Adhan had been vigilant about the weather, and at any hint of damp had brought the scroll into the hut, where it had dispossessed her son of his bearskin-covered bracken bed. The scroll was only now ready to be rolled. The glue would fasten it to its spindles. The spindles, which were upper arm bones. The skin, which couldn't be stitched in place, for it was impenetrable to any needle or knife.

Adhan wrapped her own arms around herself and looked over at her son.

Shift was sitting a little distance from the fire, cross-legged, sewing. He was using her whalebone needles, and being careful, putting each back in the pouch before selecting another. If it was the felting needle he was using he'd have his back to her. He'd been felting a strip of cloth he hid at the bottom of the bag that held his raw fleece. A piece of work that, whenever he put it aside, made him either droop with disappointment or glow with pride. Adhan believed it was a present for her.

That morning Shift was using one of the larger needles to join two pieces of knitting, the front and back of a pair of short trousers he'd made to go with the vest he was wearing. The garments were lumpy knits of uneven yarn he'd spun himself. He'd been busy for weeks, filling time he normally spent in play. Each day he'd still tap the wild hive for honey, gather apples and plums, peaches and blackberries, and check his eel traps. But he'd carried some of the traps back to the clearing, and all the fyke nets he usually set at the outfall of the river. Instead he was bringing them rabbits. He'd drop down out of the sky in all his tawny, feathered glory, land, and extract his talons from his prey—one foot, then the next, like someone who has accidentally stepped into a puddle. Ruff flaring, he'd gaze at the places where the rabbit's fur puckered up around his withdrawing claws. His mother, watching, would try to remember when he was last a rabbit and would wonder how much of this delicacy was pity.

Shift's trousers would not be a success. He hadn't known how to change the tension on the yarn to make a gusset. Adhan didn't know how either. She hadn't ever had to make her own clothes. But she could see that the inner seam of his trousers was too thick and would chafe.

Now that the manuscript was done she would have time to recover and attend to all the things she'd neglected. Watching her child busy at something that would make it easier for him to be human, she allowed herself a decision beyond her task. They would go to stay in the abbey at Cwm Pennant. If everything went to plan, it would finally be safe to let Shift be seen. At the abbey there would be people to teach him how to weave, and cut cloth, and sew a fine seam. He might get by with spindle, knitting needles and sewing needles, but a day would come when he'd want to look his best. Adhan had been so single-minded that she'd forgotten how important it was for a young person to look their best. The boy had eight languages and all her herb lore, but she hadn't understood that of course he'd want clothes that changed when he changed, made of the wool he'd had her clip from his own back. He'd thought it all through; a solution to a problem no one else had. A practical solution to a magical problem, which Adhan thought showed the mind of a great magician.

Shift reached the end of his seam and bit the thread to sever it. He jumped up, shucked off his linen trousers, and pulled the wool ones up over his hips. He'd made the trousers narrow enough to stay put without a drawstring, at least until they stretched. He stood, his spine radically bowed, to admire himself. He took a few steps, then stopped, grabbed handfuls of fabric, and hauled at the trousers to get their seam out of his crack. His expression was that of someone enraged by disappointment.

Adhan didn't offer him any comfort. When she was finished she would, and it would be practical: *I will find someone to teach you how.*

Shift jiggled, squatted, lunged, and tugged at the gripping garment. Then he did what he always did when vexed or troubled by any physical indisposition. He shifted. For a moment he was a cloud of matter that coalesced and hardened as a hawk, four and a half feet from the ground, the height of his own head. The hawk passed at a slant above Adhan. It flew inland. She followed it with her eyes until it found a thermal and began to climb in a long spiral, diminishing beyond visibility.

Adhan got up, located the needle he'd been using last, and restored it to the pouch. She carried the pouch and bag of yarn into the hut. She opened her chest and took out her finest dress, and Shift's best shirt and pants, which wouldn't fit over his homemade, truly-own clothes. She could already see the argument they were going to have. And she could see how she'd settle it: 'Do you want people to think you're my servant, not my son?'

When Shift reappeared in the late afternoon, the top and bottom edges of Adhan's manuscript were folded over the arm bones, and the glue under the folds was nearly dry. She had written her letter. It was just a few paragraphs in two languages: one that of the scroll, the other Latin. The scroll itself was a purely spoken language for which she'd had to invent a written form, based largely on the Latin alphabet.

When Shift reappeared, his mother hid her letter in her apron pocket. He mustn't see it.

She sent him into the hut to find a comb. 'I'll brush the tangles out of your hair. We're going to visit the abbess. You must be presentable.'

'You're taking me with you?' His mother had kept him from people. He had only ever spied on them. For a long time it had been just the two of them, out on the edge of the world, though in a place that counted as part of the kingdom of Ercing. They hadn't seen anything of her family for years, though years were nothing to Adhan's mother and sister. But Shift was growing up at the speed of any other child, and the years between two and ten were the foundation of a life, of love and kinship.

People did occasionally visit the witch of the marshland, famous for her potions. Shift would run and hide, because his mother had told him early, often, and fearfully that he must avoid being seen, and that had made him afraid. He would conceal himself and watch her talk to people, hear news, exchange views, enjoy her visitors. And he would call out to her from the marsh in the voices of his hidden self: the burp of a bullfrog, a bullcalf's bellow, a heron's sky-scraping cry.

Shift took his time fetching the comb. He arrived at her side with a bowl of halved peaches, honey pooled in the hollows where their pits had been. The fruit was sprinkled with chopped hazelnuts and blue borage flowers.

He was looking after her.

He watched her eat, then shuffled to sit between her knees so she could comb his hair.

Adhan pressed her nose to his neck. He smelled of grass, mud, perspiration. And of mountain air, or what she knew as mountain air, though it must be the smell of the upper reaches of the sky.

'Mother, did you see that I came back in my clothes?'

'Yes. You're very clever.'

He gave a wriggle of pleasure at her praise. She continued to work the comb through his hair, trying not to tear the knots. 'We could cut it,' she suggested.

'You said being taken as a girl might help me to hide.'

'That can only work till your beard comes in. And I have a better plan.'

He turned to look at her, and she gripped his head and averted his face. She was rough because she was talking about the one hope she had, and she was afraid he'd see her desperation. 'My plan concerns my manuscript,' she said.

She released his head when he tilted it to peer down at the scroll.

'Writing for a language without a written form. I matched the sounds to parts of words from Latin and Norse and made special marks so the reader will know where it changes.'

'I can see the marks,' he said. 'I can tell how they work.'

No idea was beyond him. Except for the idea beyond any ten-year-old—that his mother will leave him, and he'll be alone. He was a boy who would always be able to feed himself, but he was already the loneliest being his mother had ever known.

'How about you read a little bit of it out loud while I finish grooming you?'

He seemed uncertain. 'Are you sure?'

'I need to know you understand it.'

He was very reluctant and tried another excuse. 'It's got beautiful pictures, but it's a book about baby things.' He sounded sulky, as if she'd spent years on a finely embroidered shirt for a boy of five and was presenting it to a boy of eight.

'Come.' She ran her fingers down the one brown curl she'd managed to smooth from scalp to tip. 'It may be a book for a baby, but its purpose isn't in its words.'

'I'm afraid of it,' he said.

She rested her palm on his warm cheek and gazed into his eyes. 'Being afraid has to happen sometimes, darling.'

He gave in and began to read to her. A wind punched straight down and flattened the grass around them and parted their hair. The marsh fell silent. A moment later the bees left their hive, not even gathering before they swarmed. Finally, the badgers who lived in the blackberry-covered thicket crept out on their bellies to beg him to stop. When Shift saw the badgers he shut his mouth with a snap and crawled across to lie between them. He held them close and blew softly on their masked muzzles.

Adhan's ears rang for hours, a stridulation that went on while she washed herself and changed her clothes, while she packed his clothes and shoes—and the beeswax-stoppered deerhorn bottles full of cures for catarrh and skin complaints, gifts for her friend the abbess.

When the sun was halfway down the sky she asked Shift to please put the bees back in their hive. He had been walking around the fields and calling them to him, and he had returned, his cheeks pink and streaming sweat from the heat of the insects coating him everywhere but his hands, face, and feet. He shuffled slowly to the hive and raised one hand. The bees flowed from him to the adjacent branches and began to repopulate their hive. Before too long they were busy carrying out the tiny corpses of the larvae who had perished of cold in their cells in the hours they'd been abandoned.

He came over. 'So that's what the box was for.'

Adhan had made her manuscript a scroll box. It was rectangular, long, deep, polished, its pieces fitting together without glue or nails. It was a well-made object, and Shift had been coveting it. Adhan hadn't known before then that her son had any covetousness in him. After all, he'd shown no interest in the most beautiful thing his mother owned, the rose gold plate–armoured glove her mother had made for her. She was wearing the glove now, on a thong around her neck. She needed her hands free, but must have the glove in order to exert her fullest authority over the spell she was about to cast.

'The box is yours. All of it is yours,' she said.

'Is the scroll inside it already?'

'Yes.' The scroll and her letter.

He clapped his strong hands, stamped his strong feet, and stooped to embrace the box, as if the box were his brother. 'Box, you smell so good,' he said.

'Could you please take a seat on it now? I'm going to cast a spell to seal it.'

'Will it spring open if I don't sit on it?' he asked. Then, 'Will we still be able to open it after you've cast your spell?'

'You will, when you're older and wiser.' *I hope*, she thought. For her spell was less to seal the box than to hide it. To hide it, and to hide him.

Shift looked astonished. She was asking him to wait. Nothing had ever been kept from him. He didn't even know there were such things as locks. Locks would be something else to laugh at—the little mouse passing through the crack under a door.

He sat on the box and looked at her expectantly.

She cast her spell. The spell it had taken her years to build—because she first had to understand the language in which it was formulated. When she was done there was blood on her chin, and her teeth were loose in her head. She knew that if she looked into the dark water of their bathing pool she would see her irises ringed by bright red blood.

Adhan lay down where she was, her arm over the box. She could feel it, but when she tried to look at it, her eyes poured tears.

When she woke up it wasn't the same day. The sun was in the east and halfway up the sky. She looked for Shift but couldn't see him anywhere. He had covered her with his bearskin and left a cup of water near her hand. She noticed it when she knocked it over and it poured, silver, across the grass and into the hollow the box made.

The meadow at the edge of the marsh was empty—so empty of her child that Adhan felt it was void of all life. The grass was brown.

She shouted his name, remembering all the times she'd lost him before, when he was very young and would forget himself in fur or feathers or fins. 'Shift!'

He spoke up from right beside her. 'I'm here, Mother. Can you not see me?' His voice was rough with tiredness and grief and worry.

Adhan put out her hand, and he took it. Suddenly she could see him again. And she saw that she had ruined him. Her lovely, sleek, sturdy boy was standing under open skies but in deep obscurity. His smooth skin seemed smudged by bruises or ingrained dirt. He'd diminished into an innocuous, unremarkable child.

Adhan began to cry, despite the terrible pain in her eyes.

'I'm here,' he said. 'I've been keeping you warm. Your mouth won't stop bleeding.'

She pulled him towards her. It was as if she had drawn him from the mouth of a cave into the light. His eyes were the same as ever—shy, intelligent, lovely—and filled with concern.

'I'll be better soon,' she said. 'We must take this to the abbey. They can keep it till you come of age.'

'What is "this"?' he said, puzzled.

She guided his hand to the box, understanding already that her spell had worked, and to what degree.

Once he had his hand on the box, he smiled and stroked it, again admiring the way the different grains of timber contrasted around the edges of its lid. 'I forgot about it,' he said.

Adhan asked him to help her to her feet. She felt she was standing up out of her own vitality, as if the distance between prone and upright was some altitude where the air was thin. Standing proved too much for her. She hunkered down again. 'I haven't left enough of myself to fill my body.'

Shift told her she just needed to eat. He hurried away to light the fire and make a meal.

Adhan stayed where she was. When he brought her food she ate a little. He fetched her bag from the hut—the bag with the deerhorn bottles of medicine. He'd already changed into his good clothes, ready to do what she had promised him they'd be doing next.

'In a minute,' Adhan said. 'Just let me rest a little while more.'

When next she looked for him, he was feeding the old eels that came to the bathing pool every day. What he had to feed the eels was eel, but that was often the case. Neither he nor they seemed to mind.

The eels were long and thick and black and moved like the shadows of ripples in water that was running deep, clear, and swift. When they arrived it always seemed as if they'd brought a different river with them.

When all of Shift's offerings had gone the eels heaved themselves up onto the muddy bank to accept caresses. Adhan watched them take turns to lay their long, cannibal jaws in his palms. Watching the eels she could see him. He was the same as ever, a wild thing tamed by and taming wild things. A boy who knew eels as eels knew themselves.

She called, 'Come away from there. I'm ready to go now.'

He came, shaking water from his hands. He picked up the box. Inside it the bone spindles slid and made a hollow knocking noise. He said, 'I'll carry this. It's too heavy for you. You grab your bag.'

Adhan pulled the bag into her lap. There was no need for her to stand up to travel. She slipped her hand into the glove made by her mother, the last Gatemaker. She called the gate.

'I believe it was hearing that story after I last came back that inspired me to invent an alphabet for sidhe and transcribe their songs. The rest of it simply slipped my mind.'

'The Firestarter is your birthright,' Taryn said. 'A primer of the language of God.'

'It killed her.'

'So you don't want it?'

'I want it.' Shift's tone was blandly dismissive, either of the Firestarter or of his own desire. 'It has value. At least face value, like paper money.'

Taryn was exasperated. 'Money to buy what?'

Jacob made a noise of happy discovery. 'The demons are gathering their computers and coders and cryptographers in preparation to decipher the scroll once they have their hands on it. They want the machines to read it. Because it can't kill machines.'

'I wouldn't bet on it,' Shift said.

There was a long thoughtful silence, then Jacob said, 'You do realise that you don't need to find the Firestarter in order to renegotiate the treaty of the Tithe? All you need to do is figure out how to sell out the demons' plans. Make revealing their plans the price of a new treaty with the fallen angels.'

'I'm not going to do that,' Shift said. He picked up the soup bowls and went down to the water to rinse them.

On another night, a few hundred miles downriver, Taryn got up, crept on deck, hung out over the side of the boat to urinate. The sound of her piss hitting the water was loud. Even a distant soprano owl stopped to listen.

The other boats at the anchorage were dark and silent. Taryn could see prone shapes making walls around the hearths of campfires on the beach. All the fires were flameless and smokeless, their coals furred with ash and only softly orange.

A golden light appeared upstream and gradually assumed the form of the largest barge, the one that bore several palanquins, their silk-curtained pavilions aglow like paper lanterns. The barge bearing the oldest sidhe went past the flotilla and encampment midstream, silent. It took its light behind the reeds and low trees of the next bend, until it was a barely discernible patch of colour in the greys and blacks of the night, and then not even that.

That was the last time Taryn saw the barge before they reached the river mouth. Neve, aboard that vessel, was at the place of the Moot days before they were, talking to people, shaping her plans, stiffening her resolve.

They reached the sea two thousand miles from the Island of Apples. They were closer to the equator. Where the Senisteingh met the sea, there were wide branching channels of deep green water bordered by broadleaf trees dripping with flowering vines. The forest came right down to the water.

Shift used the tiller to work them into the entrance of one arm of the inlet, and Taryn caught a glimpse of a lake with an island in its middle. The island had the same vine tangles and blossoms but also seemed to have dwellings all the way up its steep, conical sides. Hundreds of houses, honey-coloured sandstone with copper roofs bright with verdigris. It wasn't a city, but it looked densely settled and permanent.

Shift let their boat brush through the hanging hibiscus bushes at the mouth of the channel. Branches bent and snapped back. Whole blooms plopped into the water. Jane and the other women put their hands across their mouths and stood very still, their eyes straining to look where Shift was looking. His lips were moving. He was counting. Taryn saw that the only thing he might be counting was the dozen or so flag-topped wands of bamboo planted in the sand of the small beach of the island. Flags of different colours, like livery.

Taryn picked herself a yellow hibiscus blossom and tucked its stalk behind her ear. Its petals rested satiny and cold on her cheek.

Shift finished counting and hauled back and forth on the tiller. The boat freed itself from the noisy foliage and began to move on a skewed course back into the main current of the river. The other people on the boat uncovered their mouths and relaxed, but not completely, for once the boat had worked its way nearer to the widely scattered flotilla, Taryn saw that on all the other vessels, near and far, the tall, poised people were standing and gazing their way. Their regard was palpable, a feeling close to hostile attention, but more concentrated than plain hostility.

Taryn sidled over to Jane. 'What was that island?'

'The Tacit,' Jane whispered. 'Shift seemed to want to see who was visiting there.'

'The flags?'

'The sidhe fly colours for some purposes. Many of the boats have them, you will have noticed.'

Taryn had thought the flags were decoration, but the colour combinations were different for each boat. Knowing that helped her recognize Neve's barge, which was anchored off the Tacit.

Jane was explaining that the flags were displayed at the landing place on the island as a kind of warning. 'Because adjacent houses don't allow visits at the same time. The flags show which house has visitors.'

'But they were all watching Shift like hawks. Why would they care that he checked the flags?'

'He doesn't visit the Tacit. It's always Neve who visits.'

But Taryn remembered that Shift had said that visiting the Tacit was one of their goals.

'He means to take me there,' she said.

Jane looked over at Shift, who was leaning on the tiller so that the boat was side-on to the current. If they kept going that way, they'd be putting themselves on a slow spinning course through the flotilla.

Jane said, 'They're not houses. They're tombs.'

Henriette rushed past Taryn and Jane and grabbed the gaff from its rack on the deckhouse wall. She strode back, hefting it, and said to Shift, 'This is no way to be sailing a boat.' She posted herself at the bow, ready to repel any other vessel that came too close.

The boat spun and lurched, vaguely seaward, vaguely towards the far shore of the inlet. The water beyond the channel was pure green over sand. Shift was going to put them aground and seemed not to care whether it was bow or stern on.

A boat loomed up, bigger than their own, bow sharp and braced with copper sheeting.

Henriette clambered to the port side and levelled her gaff. Shift swung the tiller the other way. Their boat straightened out, steered into the current, and slipped under the bow of the other boat with only inches to spare. Henriette was left facing empty water. She looked surprised, then incensed, and turned to glare at Shift, who was once again turning the boat side-on to the current to slow its forward progress. He seemed completely unfazed, and Taryn decided that what had happened was exactly what he thought would happen.

He did it twice more, slightly differently each time, once halting their spin, the second time reversing the spin altogether, so that the boat wasn't where it otherwise would have been. Taryn couldn't imagine how he knew when to start his turn or how much alteration he should make. The whole thing looked chaotic, almost comical. It reminded her of Buster Keaton's *The General*, and what that delicate, deadpan man could do with trains and carriages, tracks, trestles and cannons. And then she realised the sidhe were glaring not because they thought Shift was a danger to shipping but possibly because his solution of how to get across the channel was both unseemly and something none of them were able to do.

As they righted from their last near-miss Jacob gave a whoop of delight, and Shift started. Only then did he seem to realise he was being watched. He straightened his body, and the boat's course, and tipped droll salutes in several directions.

Henriette pursed her lips and went to restore the gaff to its rack.

The censorious sidhe all turned away and began as if by simultaneous assent to ignore him.

The beach they were aiming for had a strip of groomed grass above it—a sloped lawn covered in three rows of canoes, hull-down above the tideline.

Shift put them aground, and everyone got out of the boat by sliding down the tilting deck and wading to shore, carrying their belongings on top of their heads. The able-bodied carried Kernow and Jacob. Jacob was dead set against being carried. He turned sullen and tried to climb over the rail until Shift yelled at him. 'Jacob! You wouldn't be here if I hadn't thought you could be told what to do!'

Once they were onshore, Shift stalked off along the row of canoes to find two he liked.

Taryn whispered to Jacob, 'I guess he's chosen us for our opposite virtues. My demon-attracting intransigence and your ability to follow orders.'

Jacob didn't look at her, only reminded her, 'He didn't choose you.'

A half hour later Taryn was helping paddle the larger of the two canoes. Henriette was taking a break. She and Kernow were sitting in the middle, passengers. Taryn's canoe was following the smaller one, paddled solely and energetically by Shift, his paddle digging into the sea on one side and then the other to steer a course along the shore. Jacob was in Shift's canoe.

Taryn glared at the two ahead of them. Henriette watched her with sympathy. 'Your friend is like a new dog who thinks it must usurp the old one to earn its master's love. The master never cares which is the stronger dog; he only wants less snarling.'

'Jacob isn't really like that. He's not petty or irritable.'

Kernow said, 'People don't have patience when they're in pain. And your friend is afraid of where he's found himself.'

'You're more used to it, Taryn,' Jane said. She was breathless from paddling. 'Besides, the Sidh suits you.'

It was true. Even allowing for the pain Jacob did seem unnerved by the vast, sparsely populated spaces. The whole river journey had confronted even Taryn with a humbling surfeit of space. But Jacob was finding things outlandish. She could tell by the way he watched everyone: the easy nudity of the sidhe and humans, young and old; the mix of the ceremonial and free in everything sidhe. Even the peculiarity of choosing a canoe, tipping over the ones you liked to find their paddles stored underneath—all of them there to be taken, things made for everybody's use. The trust in that. The trust and generosity, the rigid rules of politeness, and different rules of privacy—the endless, unyielding foreignness of all of it. Jacob didn't seem whole and healthy enough to cope with it.

Shift led them into the chop at the river mouth. The main current carried them past the shore of a long sand spit covered in grassy dunes. As many as five hundred boats had anchored off the landward shore of the spit. There were encampments facing the lagoon, threads of dry smoke from campfires, tents with wide-open awnings erected on low timber platforms heaped with cushions and quilts. There were horses tethered to picket lines with their noses in heaped hay.

The party paddled out to sea until the river current let them go. They turned towards the setting sun. Taryn flinched away from the glare and saw the seaward shore of the spit. It too was crowded with tents, and large areas sheltered by walls and roofs of light and semi-transparent fabric, probably silk. Out in the low surf, figures perched on bamboo fishing platforms, a single sidhe on each, sitting like tennis umpires, but with long rods and lines.

Someone in Taryn's boat spoke to her sharply about keeping up, and she turned back and concentrated on her paddle digging into the water. She kept her head low and wished for sunglasses. Sweat trickled down her sides and back.

An intense clear orange light filled the sky. She looked at her hands, gold against the dark blue water, and the flicker of pallor nearby where seabirds were flying in to raft on the low swells, thousands of floating birds that made a bristle on the rolling sea.

She noticed that the setting sun was on her left hand. The Senisteingh emptied to the north. They had travelled downriver to warmer climes. So that meant that the Sidh she knew was in a southern hemisphere, and her world and it weren't mapped onto each other in any way with which she could orient herself. Even if she had the freedom of the gates, she could never know where on Earth any gate would take her. It was a deeply unsettling thought. She had ridden a river, she thought, as far as Greenland and this offshore evening breeze was wrapping her in the scent of a subtropical rainforest.

The sun went down. Taryn put up her head again and forged on after Shift's distant canoe.

The great bay in the Senisteingh emptied into was full of islands, the nearer misty blue silhouettes, the further cobalt blue.

They were now out of the wash of the river. Shift cut towards the shore. Taryn's boat followed Shift's past the westward headland—a high cliff face. Beyond the headland was a beach with four jetties, and above it cleared land, pasture, plantations of fruiting trees, and a little settlement of timber houses, with streets and a collection of bigger buildings that looked communal.

Taryn stopped paddling and had Kernow point out landmarks. 'Those are storehouses,' he said. 'That one is a corn silo. That's a cider house. That's a bathhouse. That's a meeting hall.'

As they came in to a jetty, Taryn saw that the waterfront and streets were populated by her people. Maybe thousands of them—none of them following a sidhe, or standing silently and expectantly alongside a sidhe, or in any way waiting on the notice of a sidhe.

Their canoe bumped against the jetty. Taryn climbed out onto its sun-blistered timber and stood idle while the others disembarked and tied up their canoes.

She could smell cornbread, and roasting meat, and a nutty aromatic baking scent she identified as socca, the Mediterranean chickpea flat-bread.

They made their way up to a paved square thronged with people and found the source of the cooking smells—several rows of beehive ovens. Taryn watched a woman pass a small bundle of flax yarn to a man at one oven and accept half a large round of socca. The woman wrapped it in a cloth and walked on. There were other exchanges. Fish for bread, avocados for bread.

'They're bartering,' Taryn said.

'There are informal agreed prices.'

'This is so strange. Almost normal,' Taryn said.

'There are too many of them to think of themselves as a family, or even a kind of religious community, which is what the Island of Women is, in effect. Bartering and the division of labour works for these people. This is the Human Colony.'

'But where are the sidhe who Took them?' Taryn kept running her gaze over the crowd, waiting for her eyes to snag on someone poised, beautiful, momentous. But there were just humans, and all of them seemed to be speaking the language Taryn had come to recognise as sidhe, but in a hasty, choppy, expressive manner, making it their own.

'Most of these people were born here,' Jane said.

Taryn abruptly remembered Neve's slighting dig at Shift about her and Jacob. *Are they a breeding pair?* Neve had said.

'But when were they born?' Taryn asked. The people seemed all to be adults, somewhere between youth and early middle age.

'Continually. And sometimes there will be as many as three generations, before the pregnancies end.'

Of course, it would be simpler to acquire souls for the Tithe by breeding people. Of course. Of course. Taryn was chilled with horror, then hot with rage. She stopped walking, and Jane did too, turning back with a concerned expression. But Taryn wasn't just going to stand here and have someone equally helpless explain to her once again that *things were just the way they were.* Even if Jane acknowledged the criminal cruelty of it all, she'd still be used to it and would have come to some accommodation with the situation a long time ago.

Taryn set her jaw and pushed past Jane. She pursued Shift, who was going at Jacob's pace. Jacob had been jostled by the canoe ride, although he had spent most of it lying down with his head on Shift's feet.

Shift was buying food. He'd acquired a basket to carry it in and was now paying for it, apparently by spitting over and over into his hands and pouring the spit into the palms of the fruit seller and the baker and the fishmonger. Taryn barely registered this. She had a spurt of disgust that felt like a slick of fuel on the fire of her fury. She reached Shift's side and grabbed hold of him. Jacob, despite his infirmity, lunged quickly forward and caught and righted the falling basket.

'You're not going to tell me there's nothing you can do!' Taryn shouted.

Shift shook off her hand, and she grabbed at him again with both hands. She tried to pull him close, but her fat sling bag got between them.

'Let's take this somewhere else,' Jacob said. He was treading on the spot, lifting his knees high, trying to ease a spasm in his back.

Shift stayed quiet. This only made Taryn more furious. She shoved him, and he flung out an arm for balance and it met the hot wall of the nearest oven. His spray-dampened sleeve immediately began to steam.

Jane and the others arrived. Kernow chopped his walking pole down between Taryn and Shift. 'Young woman,' he chided. The tip of the stick landed in the tapioca-like clot of spittle and scattered it. It was mendings. Shift was swapping mendings for food.

Silence spread through the market. Shift edged away from the oven, and the dark print of his wet sleeve vanished almost immediately.

'I don't know what's thrown her into this passion,' Jane said to Shift, apologetic.

Taryn said, 'The sidhe breed people and barter them away for their own lives at the Tithe.'

The silence became absolute—all that could be heard was the bleating voice of a child fruitlessly demanding something, the same word over and over. And then the child stopped and melted against its mother's skirts.

A child, thought Taryn. There are children here.

'Stop it,' Shift said. 'These are all free people, and this is their home.'

'Shift even has a wife here,' Kernow said.

Shift looked at him like one betrayed; then, pushing people roughly out of his way, he hurried away from all of them.

Gradually the market came back to life. The baker gave Taryn a wary look, then crouched at her feet to scoop up the mendings. He carefully poured them onto a small crack at the apex of his hive-shaped oven.

Someone said, in English, 'Hark at the woman and her biting ways.'

Someone else said, 'Take thyself hence, thou quarrelsome carrot top!'

'Come on, quarrelsome carrot top,' Jacob said. He handed the basket to Jane and took Taryn's arm. He didn't lean on her but insisted on walking fast. 'It hurts me to walk slowly,' he said. Then, 'Did you see which way he went?'

It was a while before the women caught up with them. Kernow was still behind, his stick thumping. 'Take the next right,' said Henriette, 'and go on to the top.'

The street went straight uphill and branched into two paths.

'Right again,' said Henriette.

The path they took climbed the slope in a series of switchbacks, passing through citrus groves and avocado orchards. It went all the way up the headland, a bare bluff overlooking the lagoon, the river mouth, and the spit bedecked with cooking fires. The sun had gone below the horizon, and lamplight showed in the flotilla and tents, and as a very faint glow beyond the bend in the river that hid the lagoon where the Tacit lay.

Smoke rose from two holes in the rock on top of the bluff. One plume was clean woodsmoke, the highly scented timber that had appeared in wayside camps once they left the mountains, prized for cooking since it flavoured whatever food was cooked on it. The other plume was blue-grey and astringently chemical.

The steps down from the bluff didn't reveal themselves until they were right upon them. A steep staircase cut into the rock. It was wide enough for a single person and had a rope rail bolted to one side of it and, on the other side, a drop of hundreds of feet to the canopy of the riverside forest. The risers were too deep for Kernow to go down comfortably or safely, so he sat and lowered himself from step to step. Taryn was now behind him, at the back of the group. Jacob didn't need her help, and no one else seemed to want to talk to her. She waited while Kernow plopped himself down the staircase. He let her hold his stick.

A great crowd of swallows made knots in the sky above the cliff.

They sometimes plunged together, celebrating the twilight, their glassy voices deafening when they flew close, a black mass foaming up the cliff face, streaking by only a few feet from Taryn.

The women had vanished into the cliff. Taryn, at the elbow of the stairs, could see a flat platform at a cave mouth. The western light striped the platform, as if it were coming through tall narrow windows cut into the westward face of the spur. Taryn spotted windows further down the cliff. It appeared that the top third of the bluff was hollow and inhabited.

Someone strode onto the platform, a swirl of a skirted coat, wide sleeves, unbound, curling, dark red hair, all colour and glitter. The man vaulted up the steps and gathered Kernow into his arms. For a moment, Taryn had her nose near the sidhe's red curls. The perfume of his body broke over her, and she wilted. The gentle invisible Hands surrounding the sidhe caught her and helped her down the last flight. But once she was on the platform, they let her go, and she saw the oily disturbance in the air as they rushed to their master's feet like small, voiceless dogs.

The sidhe placed Kernow back on his feet and turned to Taryn and held out his hand.

For the stick.

Taryn gave it to him.

The sidhe folded the old man's hand around its handle, and they went into the light-splashed interior of the bluff.

Taryn remained where she was, in the open air, until the stone she sat on was cold. She huddled with her hands in her armpits until the fires on the shore were glowing dim red. The flotilla began to disappear light by light, and the stars in the black were bigger than anything, that winking one that must be a planet, and that long bright wash of the arm of whatever galaxy it was, and no brilliant points of busy satellites passing over. Satellites that, even in the loneliest places on Earth, were visible signs of crowds talking to crowds.

None of Taryn's party came to fetch her. Not even Jacob. In the end it was the red-haired sidhe who appeared. He crouched beside her, his robes whispering, haloed in energy and the perfume of his perfection. 'Taryn Cornick of the Northovers,' he said. 'Come in. There is a bed for you. And tomorrow a bath and fresh clothes.'

'Why are you being kind when no one else is?' she muttered, petulant.

'It's politeness, not kindness,' he said, mildly amused.

She got up. She was stiff and sore all over. He led her in. The hallways were lamplit, but all the rooms they passed had windows, sheets of mendings disturbing the stars in some but not all of them.

They went by one closed room, its big oak door strapped and studded with iron. Taryn stopped and stared. The sidhe lingered but stayed well back from the iron, while his attendant fists of force pressed to his ankles like nervous puppies.

'It's a laboratory,' the sidhe said. 'The workroom of Shift's friend, Petrus Alamire.'

Petrus. Kernow had mentioned Petrus. Jane had almost promised him.

'What about the wife?' Taryn said.

'The wife of whom?'

'Of Shift.' She was impatient to the point of brusqueness.

'She lives in the colony with the children, grandchildren, and great-grandchildren of her second marriage. She never sees Shift, and he does not remember her.'

Taryn didn't say anything.

'The only way he would know he was in her presence is by the behaviour of others around them. It has always pained me to see him ashamed of things he doesn't remember.'

'I wouldn't worry about it too much,' Taryn said. 'I'm sure it's quite convenient for him.'

'His former wife has laid joys and pains and daily life, new love and timeworn love, over her old unhappiness. He remembers nothing but asks to be reminded of his failings every time he comes back to the world younger and almost empty. I don't want to watch him and that woman come face to face again, him seeing that she is someone who can never forgive him. Shift tells me you can *see* him. That sometimes you can. So you could see that. Your friend with cold eyes tells me Shift chose you.'

Taryn was silent, remembering the times when Jacob had reminded her that Shift didn't choose her.

'And Kernow tells me you are going to learn Petrus's story,' the sidhe said.

'And Kernow's, and Jane's. Shift is securing his stories against the possibility of having to hand people over. In a way, you might say he's saving his own life.'

The sidhe said nothing, only looked at her with careful attention.

Taryn said, 'I don't know you from a hole in the ground. So while I'm grateful for the hospitality of your . . . hole in the ground, I have no reason to explain to you Shift's and my history, or my reservations about his plans. Or anything.'

He was still watching her in that cool, alert, mannerly way they had, but Taryn sensed she had riled him a little. So she kept on jabbing. She was in pain and waiting for some retaliatory act that would hurt her enough to distract her from the confused hurt of Jacob and Jane leaving her out in the cold without comfort or any sign of softening. This person had only come to get her because he was the *host* and the rules of hospitality dictated he do so.

She said, 'Shift only needs me to help him find my mother in Purgatory. She might have leads to a thing he wants. A *thing*,' she repeated with contempt, and waited for the sidhe to ask her what kind of thing. A question she wouldn't answer, because she was far too sensible to do so, no matter how angry she was at the way her place in this quest had been secured by all the things she had cared about and lost—like Princes Gate, her grandfather's library, her grandfather, her mother, Beatrice. How horrible it was to be drawn by degrees into caring about something that wasn't going to save her or her world.

But all the sidhe said was, 'Again?'

'Again,' Taryn echoed, in a firm way, as if she knew about a first time Shift had been to Purgatory. *Fine*, she thought. *Purgatory—again.*

'He isn't here for the Moot?' The sidhe looked surprised. 'Only for Petrus's help?'

'Yes.' Taryn was lying now, because it was all she had.

'He went to Purgatory five hundred years ago with Petrus's help, to find the soul of his only child, who died well before her time. Petrus and he made her a new body. They helped her recovered soul shape their homunculus so it was just like the body she had lost—in appearance, at least. But, of course, it was fully human since it had been made of human bodies. It couldn't hold the magic it had held. But she was still a powerful woman, with the pride of Lucifer. Her second life was more careless and heartless than her first, and her second death sent her to Hell. There's more, but it's Petrus's story. One you'll no doubt hear in its full, gory, transgressive, devilish detail. But you must understand that the only reason Shift wants anyone to tell it to him is to be reminded never again to attempt to raise the dead. He doesn't want sympathy or understanding, just the reminder.'

Taryn stood speechless.

'You're not planning to raise the dead, are you?'

She shook her head. Something far back in her heart—a hope she hadn't known she cherished—died like an air-starved candle; turned blue and went out. Despite magic, gates and gods, she would never see her sister again.

In the morning Blanche arrived to escort Taryn to an open-air cavern on the landward side of the bluff. There, the woman handed Taryn a big crock of rose-scented aloe wash, a boar-bristle hairbrush, and a washcloth and towel. In the middle of the cave a small waterfall spilled from a chute in the roof. A channel cut into the rock floor carried the water away down the cliff.

Taryn brushed the tangles out of her hair, stood under the cool stream, stepped out to lather up, then rinsed. She used the towel to wrap her hair and went to stand in a patch of sun at the cave mouth. The rock was already giving off heat, and she was soon warm and dry.

Blanche reappeared with fresh clothes. A long white linen dress and an olive green over-dress with three-quarter sleeves, a wide collar, and a row of amber buttons. These garments came with a soft wool wrap, cream with a lemon yellow stripe. With the new clothes were Taryn's own brown walking boots, cleaned and with new laces. Everything fitted perfectly. There wasn't a mirror, but Taryn knew she looked good. She brushed out her drying hair, and it didn't behave. It formed a cloud rather than waves. Blanche returned once more with unguents—one she insisted Taryn use, because it would save her fair skin from the sun. 'The sidhe don't have that problem. This lotion is an invention of Petrus's. He didn't think to do it until he went out fishing one day, wearing a hat, but was badly burned by the sun's reflection. The underside of his jaw came out in blisters. He's the sort of man who can't see a problem until he has some personal experience of it. Can't be told. Even after all his years of life.'

Taryn was very grateful that Blanche was speaking to her. She resolved to ask only appropriate questions and accept without comment whatever answers she received. She asked for their host's name.

'Aeng,' Blanche said. 'He's a friend of Shift's, though it's rather one-sided now. Shift values Aeng's loyalty without desiring to understand their history.'

Because she wasn't able to think of a safe question to follow that confidence, Taryn was thrown back on memories of her own one-sided relationship and how she'd left a man who loved her because his love couldn't fix her—as if that were its purpose. She'd thought she was letting Alan go. That he wouldn't have to carry her around, a cloud that rained on him all the time. But really she just couldn't bear seeing him wait—with dignity and patience—for her to love him back. Taryn wondered how Aeng felt about the one-sidedness.

Blanche conducted Taryn to another east-facing open-air chamber for breakfast. Susan was there, but not their host, or the vaunted Petrus, or Jane and Henriette. Or Shift, or Jacob.

Susan explained that the women of the island were taking turns watching the Tacit. 'Blanche and I were out at first light. We came back when Jane and Henriette relieved us. It seems there will always be visitors at the tombs adjacent to the Gatemaker's.'

'It's just spite,' Blanche said.

Taryn asked if blocking a graveside visit was just the sidhe's habitual cruelty to Shift, or whether there was some result they wanted.

'We don't know,' Blanche said. 'But Petrus thinks Neve bit Shift to test for any residue of iron in his blood. To see whether he'd had the shot removed, as he claimed, or had lost it all at once in the usual way.'

'By shifting,' Susan said. 'But would there still be a residue in his blood if he'd had the iron removed?'

'Petrus believes so.'

'He's not able to change with iron in or on his body,' Blanche said. 'Or so we've always been led to believe. But Petrus says that Neve thinks Shift has always lied about that.'

Taryn thought of Kernow's story, and the witch of the marshlands experimentally stroking the iron bit in the mouth of his horse. The expression on the witch's face when she did that. The observation was a clue for any person who heard the story and took it as gospel. Every time Shift came back to the world, he was told about his allergy to iron and also offered little pieces of evidence that the allergy was, at the very least, exaggerated. And she knew for a fact that he'd changed into a dragon shortly after an operation that had supposedly failed to remove all the iron pellets.

Shift had treated his mother's protective lies as his true inheritance. And neither his mother, nor he, had taken his aunt into their confidence.

'Neve must be furious,' Blanche said. 'If we keep seeing the wrong flags at the beach of the Tacit, it's her doing.'

Taryn finished her mango and sweet potato porridge and wiped her mouth. 'Where has Jacob got to?'

Jacob wasn't in pain anymore. He felt strong, mobile, energetic—although something had happened that he supposed should disturb him. Even with everything that had already happened, this was so outside what he'd anticipated or wished for that he knew—intellectually—that every alarm in his shrewd, dubious self should have been tripped.

But if they had, they were silent alarms, sounding somewhere else, alerting someone else.

It had begun with there being no immediate remedy for the pain that came on him in the canoe, and which took a harder grip after Shift abandoned him in the market. The abandonment *had* seemed like the problem, prompted as it was by Shift's anger or hurt feelings or whatever. Jacob remembered being distressed about it. Now he was severed from all troubles. He was in clover. In paradise.

When the party reached Quarry House, Jacob had collapsed. He was down but couldn't stop moving, because it was only movement that gave him relief. He was carried off to a firm bed in a quiet cavernous room, where he lay stretching his legs, cracking his tendons, rolling from side to side, his eyes wet with tears of pain.

A man came into the room with their host, Aeng.

Aeng. Smooth Aeng; herbs and honey.

The man was Petrus. Middle-aged and grizzled, Petrus smelled of chemicals, and his clothes were spotted with acid burns. Petrus had tincture of opium. The colony grew opium poppies, the plants imported from Earth. Apparently the sidhe liked the look of poppies but were immune to opiates.

The tincture helped, and Aeng undertook to replace the Hands bracing Jacob's spine. And Aeng didn't suffer from the scruples or indifference Shift felt. Touching Jacob had meant something to Aeng. Aeng, laughing and affectionate Aeng. Aeng was more frank and open than anyone Jacob had ever met; he was without embarrassment or hesitation, and his hands and Hands had healed Jacob.

Aeng was infinitely reassuring. He told Jacob that he was bound to no one. 'Only to the Sidh itself, and you can choose to live anywhere in the Sidh. You can live with me, above the human colony, where you'll never want for the company of free people of your own kind.'

And so Jacob would. It was decided. There were only a few formalities.

'Simple politeness,' Aeng said. 'You will have gathered already how much we treasure good manners.'

'And condemn ill manners.'

Aeng had laughed and reassured Jacob that he, Aeng, wasn't one to condemn anything. 'But we must mind our manners, so as soon as we can we will tell the people you travelled with that you have chosen to remain here with me.'

Now it was morning and they'd showered. When Jacob stepped out of the waterfall, one of Taryn's shining, fiery hairs was wrapped around the long second toe of his left foot. Jacob realised he'd completely forgotten Taryn through all the hours of the night; first in pain, and then in joy. The light stricture of the hair felt like someone trying to lay a rope on him and lead him away to somewhere he didn't want to go. He sat on the warm rock and picked the hair from his toe. And while he and Aeng dried, sitting hip to hip, fully conscious of each other and, at the same time, unselfconscious, Jacob told him about Taryn and the Muleskinner, and how he was suffering now because Taryn had ruined a man's life in the course of seeking revenge. Revenge that she hadn't had the honesty or moral courage to take herself.

Aeng listened, then kissed Jacob's shoulder and said, 'But you're not suffering now, Jacob. So you can forgive your friend. Forgive her, but keep your distance.'

'Is she my friend?'

'I don't know,' Aeng said. Then he said it was nearly midday and they should eat and dress. The Moot commenced at sundown. There was much to discuss. There always was at the Moot, which was held every ten years, but in the year of the Tithe there were accounts to be drawn up, trades to make, a final tally, and, as usual, as much justice done as it was possible to do. Then Aeng said, smiling, 'Would you like to wear something beautiful? This is the very first time we'll be seen together.'

In the late afternoon, Taryn stood on the platform at the entrance of Quarry House—a hill of limestone with cavities originally formed by the removal of the marble-veined limestone from which the tombs of the Tacit were built. Taryn watched crowds gather on the seaward shore of the spit. The silk screens had been reconfigured to form a vast semicircular shelter on the sloped beach. As seating, smooth driftwood logs were apparently rolling themselves into place. Each log was followed by three or more sidhe, and Taryn guessed that what she was watching was the work of forcebeasts. She didn't for a minute imagine that the invisible, collaboratively created monsters had been made that day simply to perform heavy lifting. She could tell from the palpable tension everywhere on the river mouth—the beach, flotilla, colony, Quarry House—that the sidhe were about to discuss contentious matters; that they weren't all in accord, and each had a reason to protect his or her own. And that when it came to surrendering Taken, even the practical measure of Taking people en masse hadn't completely done away with the need for some sidhe to make sacrifices as a peacekeeping gesture.

Jane, Blanche, Susan, and Henriette were grimly quiet. They had dressed carefully, and all had new haircuts. They looked wholesome and tidy. Once they joined that crowd on the beach they'd be exceptional—healthy and full of purpose, but not dewy fresh and beautiful, or ablaze with sinister intelligence, as Petrus was.

Petrus had dressed and perfumed his brown beard. Diamonds were winking in the lacquered hair at his ears. His robe was richly embroidered and his hands crowded with rings of gold and precious stones.

Jacob was all in white and fawn and burnt orange. Each item of clothing—his loose trousers, shirt, and long light coat—was covered in finely stitched embroidery in a yarn the same colour as the cloth, the effect being that he somehow looked more densely present and three-dimensional than the rest of them. Them. The humans. He looked handsome. He also looked whole and healed and very happy.

Taryn went to his side and took his hand. He held hers for a moment, then let it go to caress his closely cropped hair.

'That suits you,' she said.

'Thanks.'

'How are you?'

He looked at her, his eyes no longer cold. 'I'm happier than I've ever been.'

Her heart rose right out of her body. She was very relieved. 'You're not in pain?'

'No. I'm cured. Aeng cured me.'

'I'm so pleased. I like Aeng.'

Aeng joined them then. 'We must be on our way. I sent someone ahead to secure us enough boats. We're on the wrong side of the river, and there's always a run on boats.'

Aeng waved everyone towards the steps. And then he wrapped a hand around the back of Jacob's neck. They walked away like that, Jacob in calm bliss because of that proprietary touch.

Taryn's heart dropped like a shot bird, passed right down through her body, and vanished through the soles of her feet.

She joined the women and Kernow and, as soon as they were on the track down to the Human Colony, she herded everyone into a faster walk. Kernow complained but fell quiet when Taryn said, 'We must prevent Shift from seeing that Aeng has Jacob. I don't know how it happened, but it has happened.'

Jane and Kernow glanced back, then turned to face the path again. Jane looked stricken. Kernow darkened and hardened.

'This Moot is absolutely vital for Shift. And all of us,' Taryn said.

'We should run ahead, take the first boat, and have Shift ride with us,' Jane said. 'You and me and Henriette. You can run, can't you, Hen, dear?'

Henriette nodded.

Jane said, 'I did wonder why Aeng said to your friend that he'd sent "someone" to secure the boats, when he sent Shift. He's making Shift disappear from Jacob's mind by not-naming him.'

'Is that possible?' Taryn said.

'Possible, but extremely difficult.' Jane looked uneasy.

'Take Shift to Neve,' Kernow told them. 'Aeng will never voluntarily put himself near Neve.'

It was then that Taryn remembered she'd heard of Aeng before, though not by name. In her first hours in the Sidh, when Shift was stricken with iron sickness, Jane had suggested to Neve that they take him to Quarry House. Without pause, he and Neve had answered, 'No.'

'What is Aeng doing?' Taryn asked Kernow. She was desperate to understand.

Kernow only said, 'Hard to say.'

Jane turned around and called out to Jacob and Aeng, 'We're going to scamper.' She waved cheerfully, grabbed Taryn's and Henriette's hands, and broke into a trot. Taryn tried to ask another question but was told to save her breath.

Shift was waiting by the last three canoes. The churned-up turf around them clearly showed the prints of clawed bear paws. He was mud-splashed and underdressed, still in his homespun. He had no shoes.

Jane, puffing, said, 'What happened here?'

'I saved some boats.'

'Aeng says we should go ahead. He's taking care with Kernow.'

Together they flipped over a canoe and ran it into the water. Henriette took one paddle, and Jane insisted on taking the other. 'You have to attend to all the talk,' she explained to Shift. 'And you have to speak. You need to be fresh.'

Taryn sat with her knees pressed to Shift's back. She curled over him and rested her chin on his shoulder. 'I'm sorry if I upset you yesterday.'

'It wasn't you who spoke,' he said.

'Still.'

'I have only four more years. Sometimes I panic. I don't want to be any younger.'

'Is that something you can change?'

He shook his head. 'There are things I thought were unchanging that I can see a way to change now. But not that. I asked for that.'

Taryn nodded. Her cheek brushed his ear.

'I'm not prepared for this Moot,' he said. 'They made sure I couldn't ask the question I needed an answer to before the meeting.'

'They can't make you give anyone up.'

'They can hurt me in ways I can't anticipate.'

Taryn felt heart-wrung, so she just kissed his damp, musky shoulder and said, 'I love you.'

He was quiet through the watery percussion of a dozen strokes, then he said, 'But you can't see me.'

'That's true. But the world wakes up when you're there. Especially my world. And *that* I can see.'

He turned to look at her. They were inches apart, and she could clearly see his beautiful hazel eyes. 'Thank you, Taryn,' he said.

PART SIX

Uncaring

And he who was lost like a dog

will be found like a human being

and brought back home again.

Love is not the last room: there are others

after it, the whole length of the corridor

that has no end.

Yehuda Amichai, 'Near the Wall of a House'

Twenty-Seven

The Moot

Jane spotted Neve's banner near the apex of the half-circle and took the most direct route there, along the waterline where shoals of small silver fish billowed in the low waves. They passed behind a hillock of mounded sand. 'Speakers address the assembly from that,' Jane told Taryn. 'The meeting can go on for a long time, but once the mound is trampled down or surrounded by the tide, the Moot must come to an end. Even with business unfinished.'

Taryn thought this was a recipe for filibusters. But she had never known the sidhe to talk at length.

Neve frowned at their approach but greeted each of them by name. Her small party of humans made room. Introductions were exchanged, and Taryn found herself sitting one place along from Franz Schubert.

It was a good half hour before she managed to quiet the clamour in her brain. A sidhe with teak-coloured skin and curling waist-length blue-black hair was pacing in front of the mound, gesturing for the gathering to quieten down. The hush came with a ragged edge but was absolute. Taryn heard oystercatchers crying, and the long, soft collapse of a wave clearly running from her left ear to her right, like one of those old test-your-stereo-system recordings that people used to put on ironically at the end of their student parties, as an alternative to compilations of horror movie creaks, screams, and fiendish laughter.

A sense of the concentration of the present moment filled the beach. So many sidhe. Such dense life force.

The first speaker proceeded in sidhe, and with the usual fluent coolness of manner. Taryn had no idea what was happening. Most of the other humans seemed to be following him, since they had the language. When he concluded Taryn was horrified to see a delegation of young Africans on the far westward arm of the gathering simultaneously pull their scarves up over their heads and against their faces to stifle tears. The sidhe with them lowered their faces also.

Behind Taryn, in the thick of the crowd, someone swore. 'Merde.' Taryn hoped it wasn't—and believed it was—one of the men Taken from Verdun, a hundred years earlier now, cursing because he had been brought along to witness what was in store for him a hundred years hence. The Africans must be representative of the people 'rescued' from ships in the Middle Passage after 1800. If they had been left where they were, on the slave ships, in the early nineteenth century, they'd have maybe made it to miserable lives on plantations, or maybe drowned and gone to whatever heaven was waiting for them. Instead they had two centuries in the beautiful Sidh, in the superb company of their rescuers, and then were sold for those rescuers' well-being.

Taryn realised that Jane, Blanche, Susan, and Henriette were a delegation representative of the Island of Women. The realisation made her want to stand up, take the mound, and shout at the crowd. But it wouldn't have made a blind bit of difference. She understood that the sidhe knew they were doing wrong, but their habit of living meant they just kept on living with it.

Jane gave Taryn a sharp look and clutched her hand. Hard. She said, 'They are our betters.'

'No one is anyone's better,' Taryn said. But who was she to talk? She, who had made another person her instrument.

Several other sidhe got up to argue for or against something. Maybe the fate of their dependents. Questions were put by people who came to stand at the foot of the mound to interrogate the speakers. This went on for some time—arguments, with small deadly ripples of feeling in their wake.

Just when Taryn had come to the conclusion that no humans would speak, there was a kind of gear change in the mood of the meeting. Petrus appeared from the westward end of the gathering. He climbed the mound and gave a demonstration of an invention, a vast chandelier of mirrors and floating, fuel-less flames, which he sent up into the air above the mound, and which lit the dusky beach and sent swarms of warm colour over the assembled faces.

Applause. Sighs of pleasure.

A woman took the mound and sang, her voice eerie and pure. It brought tears to Taryn's eyes.

Schubert played a composition on his viola, something new, Taryn imagined.

Human after human got up and gave something.

'The treasured Taken,' Jane whispered. 'Making their argument. I made mine ten years ago with a book of sidhe botany. It took an artist friend and me fifty years to produce. I'm afraid the sidhe won't remember it, though those with houses will all have a copy. But of course I shouldn't worry, because none of them need to be reminded of a thing that happened only ten years ago.'

'Are these treasured people earning their keep?'

'They're just ensuring for their patrons that there will be no argument about their remaining here. They're demonstrating why they should be permitted to continue their work.'

Lamps were illuminated behind the crowd. Taryn expected any moment to catch a whiff of cooking smells, because surely the Moot must conclude with a shared meal. Even funerals ended with meals. But the air remained empty of anything but sea salt and the heart-shredding perfume of many sidhe.

The treasured ones concluded their pitches for continued existence, and the meeting returned—so far as Taryn could tell—to its combination of negotiation, concession, tally. The tally she understood. As each sacrifice was agreed on—this sidhe promising this human, or group of humans—a list was being compiled. She got the sense that the process wasn't going completely to plan and some sidhe were digging in either to refuse this Taken or that, or to shame someone else who was refusing to give up what they must know they should give up.

Taryn had sometimes watched her friends' families trying to get one up on each other in a moral or emotional accounting. Who did what for Mother when she was dying. How much money was borrowed. Who took time to attend all the school plays. Who remembered birthdays. Taryn couldn't understand the language in which the sidhe spoke, but she understood the character of the interactions. Sidhe were saying to other sidhe, 'I've done my bit. It's *your* turn.'

Inevitably Shift's name was mentioned. Taryn heard it once or twice. Many looked his way. They might be looking at him or Neve. It was hard to say. Taryn had the impression Neve was being urged to get up and speak her piece.

Shift just listened, his face set. Petrus's chandelier illuminated the faces around his, but its light seemed to be pulling his face apart. It was as if he had three panes of glass in front of him and the splashes of magnified candlelight were refracted and couldn't fully reach and reveal him. Everyone on the beach was determined to pay attention to him, and the spell, instead of making him inconsiderable, was trying to make it look as if he wasn't present in the same space as everyone else. It was resorting to camouflage—and was making itself visible.

Neve got up. She faced her nephew and asked him to follow her. Taryn heard him say, 'Do you want me on the mound or at its foot?'

She didn't answer, only gave him her hand, pulled him up, and led him down the beach. Her bare feet seemed to glide over the swarm of lights. He trailed after her, a dim little figure.

She took his hand again at the mound, walked him up onto it, and left him there. She positioned herself at its foot, there to examine him, like the lead prosecutor representing the Crown, the crowd.

Shift lifted his chin, raised his voice, and declared that this part of the discussion would be conducted in English, in deference to the majority of those of his people present, the Women of the Island, Petrus, and his two new Taken. He paused and scanned the gathering. Taryn knew he was looking for Jacob. She saw him locate Jacob, the bright pleasure that appeared and disappeared a second later. A shadow fell over his face, then made a kind of halo around him. The spell seemed to double its efforts, as if it thought he was in danger. Even the glancing, reflected flames that streamed over him seemed to reach his form dimmed and greyish.

This shook Neve, and she glanced over her shoulder, at Jacob and Aeng, no doubt, though Taryn couldn't see them from where she was. Neve registered something—disappointment, then some kind of relief. Whatever Neve felt about Aeng's theft of Jacob, Taryn decided she wasn't in on it. It was Aeng's idea, or impulse—it wasn't a conspiracy or part of that common agreement they all seemed to have on the benefits of making Shift feel bad about himself.

Neve turned back to her nephew and raised her voice to address him.

'Son of my sister, last child of the Sidh, little god of the marshlands, for many centuries you have had a home and refuge here among your grandmother's people. You have sustained yourself on the sweetness and peace of this place. You have invited people you loved or pitied into its shelter. You have acted as one of us. But you have never paid your part of the Tithe.'

He interrupted her. 'Is there a part of the Tithe that's mine? My life has an end. Whatever I pay will only prolong your lives.'

'Do you not want to prolong my life?' Neve said.

He didn't answer.

'Shift, I am speaking for all my kind. You know what offer Hell has made for you. Hell's standing offer of a thousand years in which the Sidh would not have to pay a single human soul. A thousand years in which our lives would be unthreatened and free. You have never seen your way to make that sacrifice. You love your life and cling to it, while human souls are pushed out of their bodies and through Hell's Gate every hundred years. You preserve only your own Taken, while all this time you've had the power to spare millions. You never attend the Tithe itself, only sit stony-faced through each accounting, offer nothing, and then let what we must do be done. You don't watch the slaughter, but you continue to sit at the feast.'

'I hoped to live long enough to change things,' he said.

Neve stiffened. 'And have you?' she said. 'Lived long enough? Changed things?' Then, 'What is there to hope for? Only that the angel of death will pass over you and your Taken once again, and none of you will be disturbed by the sight of the corpses heaped at Hell's Gate.'

Taryn looked at the people in the crowd she had already identified as doomed. She was astonished at their composure. Some of them were in tears, but they wept silently.

'Listen,' Neve said, and fell silent. A long moment passed in which only the waves spoke. *Hush, hush*. Then, 'None of them are begging for their lives. Not one of these promised people.'

'No one ever does,' he said. 'So deep is their habit of gratitude.'

Neve took a long breath and let it out. 'At the gate they beg. Until the end they can never believe we'll be so cruel.'

Cold shivers were crawling up and down Taryn's torso. Jane took her hand again. Jane's hand was icy.

'It is on me to say all this,' Neve said. 'I am speaking for my kind.'

'You will let me know when you begin to speak only for yourself?' He was droll.

'Once you have become an infant your soul will be of no great value to Hell. We believe that Hell cannot accept as true that your wisdom hasn't accumulated, that you're not a wise immortal with a young face and more magic than anyone ever had. But even Hell will find you worthless when once again you pass the age of ten, going in the wrong direction. If you want to save lives and do your grandmother's people a great service, you must give yourself up at this Tithe.'

'Or maybe the next,' Shift said. 'I calculate I have another four centuries before I pass ten. Going, as you say, in the wrong direction. Why must you all be in such a hurry?'

'We mean to impress upon you that you have kept this extraordinary benefit from us. This respite. A time-limited good, which you have all but squandered. We want you to fully consider *that*, and that half of the humans present tonight will be gone before the next full moon.'

'Yes. I understand. But the Tithe is not my arrangement. All sidhe on this beach were party to that treaty. I wasn't born when you found yourself having to pay for your stolen land. Which, being thieves, you chose to pay for with stolen human souls.'

A ripple of indrawn breath went through the sidhe.

Neve said, 'It was the sole agreed price. And may I remind you that

that price was demanded by your father's people.' She spoke with cold finality. 'He the chief of them.'

Taryn had a moment when the other shoe dropped. Of course there had to be a reason Hell was able to threaten the Sidh. There must be a claim. A claim recognised by both parties. That was how all these immortals worked. The sidhe had arrived, a very long time ago, in a place inhabited by demons. They drove the demons off, partitioned and—Taryn guessed she could say—*terraformed* the land. It was why there was an Exiles' Gate with nothing on the other side of it. They'd come from somewhere else, exiles who arrived as colonists. Then, in time, someone more powerful than demons enslaved the dispossessed demons, occupied their remaining territory, and approached those who'd displaced the twice-conquered people, saying something like, 'We hear this place wasn't always yours. Nice place. *Shame if something happened to it.*' Fallen angels had run a centuries-long protection racket, having the sidhe collect the souls of humans who hadn't actually damned themselves, like black marketers recruiting poachers to hunt in a wild-life sanctuary. Taryn suddenly understood so much more than she had only moments before. Then she thought, *He the chief of them*, and, *Wait. What?*

'Nothing you can say or do will persuade me to hand myself over to Hell just because I'm rapidly losing value,' Shift said, his voice filled with contempt.

Neve nodded. 'Then we must pass on to your people. You have listened to the tally. Everyone has surrendered what they must—with sorrow.'

'I'm sure the pledged Taken are deeply touched by your sorrow,' Shift said.

Neve cut him off. 'And still it is not enough. The way I've heard you tell it, we are all old and losing our virtue and no longer have enough energy to charm, glamour, and push with love our way into human hearts. We're afraid of the human world, you say. We find it too busy and loud. We flinch and act fastidious and find we've fallen short in our tally for the Tithe. But the fact is, we don't have the appetite for this horrible project. This wholesale false rescue and delayed treachery. It's poisoning us. You must know it's poisoning us. So we fall short. Our only consolation is the small justice of our arrangements. That these people'—she pointed at the delegation of French soldiers—'and all their friends will enjoy two centuries of happiness and ease here in the Sidh. But, Shift, if you surrender none of your people, we will have to offer some of them, and they've only been here a scant hundred years.'

The horrible reasonableness of this argument.

'If you give up half of the Women of the Island, the Tithe will be complete,' Neve said. 'The Women of the Island have had their two centuries.'

Shift lowered his head and looked up at her under his brow. With that strange continuous bone structure from his forehead to his raptor's nose, he looked like an angry hawk. 'I will not,' he said.

Neve sighed. 'Then,' she said, '*for myself*. I've always supported your decision to keep your retinue. Every Moot before this I've spoken for you. I accepted that you should be allowed to live by different rules, even if they are not the rules of the Sidh, where you live too.' She looked down at the sand. Petrus's chandelier slowly danced and scintillated above her graceful form and that dark smear of person that was her bespelled relative. 'But I cannot support you anymore.'

What was Neve going to do? Taryn thought. Register a protest? Issue a stern reprimand?

'I'll give you up,' Neve said. 'I'll move my household from your mountain and I'll never speak to you again. And when in four short years you come back to us erased, I'll not make myself known to you. And while you're under the River Styx, I'll take the glove and keep it from you. You won't ever be able to feel your way back into your freedom and mastery. It is by my grace that you've lived so long, so well, so safely—and when my grace has gone, your life will be stupid and constrained. And you won't even know it. And if you hope your old friends and your new will tell you everything that happened here, mind that there will be a long period when you lose sight of them, during which they will disappear from all the worlds you can reach, because they'll be in Hell, to which their souls are already promised. And then there will be scarcely anyone left who can tell you who you are. And the rest of us—your grandmother's people—we will not tell you.'

'Stop,' said someone, a sidhe.

'Don't silence me,' Neve said, her voice ringing. 'Having appointed me to speak to him, how dare you. I'll take his glove and throw this whole assembly five hundred miles out to sea. I am the last of the Nine Queens this side of the grave. I am the Gatemaker's daughter. Don't try to silence me.'

Shift stood through all her hard threats and her ringing rage. But as soon as she stopped speaking, he walked off the mound and out of the light. Taryn got up and blundered through the people in front of her to run after him.

She didn't catch up, only followed, keeping him in sight as they passed out of the light of the chandelier, the lamps and fires. After a time she could only make out his figure against the foam where the waves broke and rushed up the beach. Now and then she looked over her shoulder, thinking they might be followed. But the patch of light slowly shrank, and no one came.

She lost him when he cut up into the dunes. She retraced her steps, found his footprints, and followed him onto the dry sand. If she kept blinking, she could make out a pale, narrow path that climbed and wandered from crest to crest. She had to use her hands to climb. The sand was soft and cold. The dune grass scraped her face and threatened her eyes.

She wouldn't have located him except he called out to her. She slid over humps of grass and into a hollow. The sound of the sea was muffled there.

Taryn sat beside him and reclined on the slope. Cold sand trickled down her collar and into the tops of her boots. 'No one gave me fresh socks,' she said. 'And I didn't get mine back. They'd been rinsed in river water into a state of stand-up stiffness, but they were the moisture-wicking sort and good for at least another hundred miles.'

'How very remiss of everyone,' he said.

'I like my dress and coat and shawl,' she said.

'It hadn't occurred to me to procure any nice clothes for you.'

'You weren't presenting me for sale or exchange.'

'No. I still might have laid my hands on something attractive and practical.'

'Next time.'

'Next Moot?'

'Yes,' she said. She lay back and looked at the stars. They were out in force, the skein of a galactic arm pouring down the sky towards the hidden horizon. She said, 'I've been expecting to see my sister again. I only realised last night that that's what I was hoping for. I used to be an atheist, so of course I believed I'd never see her again. But then Munin strutted in through Alan's door, and I decided that a universe with gods might allow me, given enough time, to find her. But Beatrice won't be in Purgatory or Hell, so I won't see her again.'

'No.'

'I should be happy for her.'

'Yes.'

'She was the one person I couldn't do without. She died, and afterwards I couldn't find myself.'

He didn't respond to that, but Taryn waited a moment before asking him if Neve was the one person he couldn't do without.

'Probably. I've never had to think about it before.'

'You're thinking about it?'

'I'm having feelings. I'm waiting to stop shaking. If I try to lead us across this headland in the dark and all atremble, one of us will probably break a bone.'

'Neve just threatened all our lives.'

'Yes.'

'Does she mean it?'

'She wouldn't say any of that as a bluff.'

'All right. But at least Jacob is safe.'

Shift laughed wildly.

'It's one less person to worry about,' Taryn said. She was doing her feeble best to find a bright side to all this.

Shift lay down too, his head next to hers. She told him not to point at anything because sand was clinging to his lumpy sleeves and the last thing they needed was sand in their eyes.

'You sound like somebody's mother,' he said.

Taryn was nobody's mother, probably never would be. She hoped Alan and his second wife would have another. She hoped Carol and her husband would, once the uncertainty of his citizenship was settled. Children were what the sidhe lacked. There were stolen ones—and as far as Taryn could tell they didn't do as well with it as adults. And there'd been a handful of normal children in the market of the Human Colony, swinging along above a safety net of watchful smiles.

'Aeng told me about your daughter.'

'No, he didn't. It's Petrus's story. I might have Petrus tell it while we prepare for Purgatory. If we even go to Purgatory.'

'Is there some doubt about that?'

'It depends.'

'It's what we have to do. You said.'

'It can't change the outcome of the Tithe.'

'What about changing Neve's mind? What can you do about that?'

'Do you remember what happened when I went to Hell?'

'You told me. And I told Jacob. We're holding everything in common, Jacob and me. I hope Neve doesn't know that.'

'She understands he's so far from himself now that none of what you shared matters to him anymore.'

Taryn just accepted this. She knew that—yes—sometimes people were just suddenly lost.

'After I was dragged through the gate, why do you suppose Neve couldn't open it?'

'She was only pretending to try? Had she already made a bargain with Hell? The swap-Shift-for-a-thousand-years'-respite bargain?'

Taryn heard his hair rasp on the sand as he shook his head. He hadn't brushed it since she'd met him, and she knew it was full of felted knots and picked-up twigs and grasses from wherever he lay down. When he shifted, his body healed itself, but his hair was like his clothes, shabby if left uncared for.

'That's a no?' she said. 'I can't see you.'

'That's a negative,' he said, like some military character in an American movie.

'I gather you're asking me because you have an answer? I mean, what do I know about gates, so why bother asking?'

'I have an idea.'

'Which is what?'

'Shall we go and see?'

He got up, and she quickly turned her head from the flurry of clotted sand that dropped from his hair and clothes. He helped her up. They scrambled out of the hollow. Once they were on top of the dune, Taryn saw that the east was promising a greenish dawn.

They picked their way across the spit and came down among the scattered campfires around the lagoon. Picketed horses whickered and stamped. Shift started down the beach towards a small clinker-built boat with oars stowed inside it. He grabbed its prow and began easing it down the beach. Taryn joined him and tried to coordinate her heaving with his.

'My idea is quite tenuous,' he said, as if he were responding to a question she'd asked or issuing one of those apologies of his where he wouldn't say what he was sorry for, only that he was sorry.

They hauled the boat until the water caught its bow and lifted it. Shift let it slip past them, then jumped in. Taryn had to wade out and scramble on. The water was dark and still. Shift rowed slowly across the lagoon and into the black reflection of the headland that hid the Tacit. The stars dripped and stammered below them.

As they crept around the headland, clear of its hanging foliage and flowers, those stars paled and a milky green grew in the east. But before the sun came up, the green light lost its colour, then its luminosity, and a coverlet of clouds slid over the sky, moving seaward. The air grew cold. Drizzle began to fall. The water was speckled from above by raindrops and from below by fish rising to feed.

The boat cleared the headland, and for a time Shift had to row against the current. They passed into the Tacit's arm of the inlet, the current relented, and the boat sped on where it was aimed.

A wall of rain ran at them, falling drops and fizzing splashes. Water fell from the sky into the boat, and rain landing on the sea beside it splashed up, so even more water found its way in. Taryn's linen clothes clung to her back and sides, heavy and clammy. Her hair hung in her field of vision, curling tendrils stretched almost straight, not just wet, but channelling water.

The boat hit the beach before Taryn saw they'd reached the island. She struggled out and helped Shift rock it back and forth until it tipped far enough to empty itself. It was too heavy for just the two of them to turn over. They would have to let it fill again. They struggled to drag it up the beach till Taryn shouted at Shift to give up. 'We don't need it. You can use your glove to get us somewhere dry.'

She could see his reluctance, his inhibitions about losing a communal boat. 'Come on,' she said, and clutched his arm.

They hurried up the beach and onto a stone staircase, which plunged into a tunnel under thickly vined trees. The angle of each step was crammed with fallen leaves. They climbed blind, the downpour reaching them as soft drips and dribbles, the exposed forest above deafeningly loud.

The steps leveled out and became a single-file track covered in drifts of black leaf mulch. They started uphill, their feet slithering on mud and pulped plant matter.

Sometimes they crossed drains that flowed from open channels of squared stone, passed under the track, and continued as natural streams. After they had wound their way uphill for fifteen minutes Taryn saw that the water was now confined in these channels both above and below the path. She followed one gushing stream with her eyes to where it flowed under the walls of a building hidden in the trees below them. A building with blind walls. A tomb.

This was strange. Were the tombs only shelters for show, and did it not matter if they weren't weathertight and water ran under their walls?

The path coiled its way around the island, always climbing, and gradually less gloomy and more open to the sky. The uneven paving became level flagstones with mats of kikuyu between them. The rain fell quieter.

Soon they were passing rows of tombs that weren't built close together, right on the path, as mausoleums in the cemeteries Taryn was most familiar with were: Highgate's tiny Georgian terraces, Montparnasse's fin-de-siècle streets in miniature. Each of these tombs had a space the same size as itself between it and its neighbour. They were set back from the path, towered over by trees but elevated on well-groomed stone footings. Their tiled roofs of clean copper were steeply pitched. They had guttering but no downpipes. Instead there were rain chains. Taryn had seen rain chains on old buildings in Japan. The water ran down the chains with no splatter or gurgling, only a gentle trickling.

Shift turned back to Taryn and set a finger to his lips. He made the gesture of zipping, locking, and casting away the key.

She nodded and tried to stop her teeth from chattering.

Shift turned off the path and stepped onto pedestal porch of the nearest tomb. He drew Taryn close and put his mouth against her ear. 'You're a second set of eyes and ears,' he said.

She nodded. She thought of her visits to the oncologist with her mother. Once Beatrice was dead, there was only her to do it. She would take notes so that however overwhelmed her mother was by information, she'd have an account to consider later and help her make decisions.

The tomb's door didn't have a lock or latch, was only hung in such a way that its own weight held it shut. Shift pushed it, and it opened inwards. He went inside, pulling Taryn after him. He set her at one side of the door and closed it again.

The grey light diminished. They stood still and let their eyes adjust. There were vents in several places up under the eaves of the roof.

Horizontal slats of filigreed stonework through which an aqueous light gleamed and wavered. The room was dry. Taryn could hear water running under it, muffled by stone. Then she saw the coping of a covered well. Fixed to its wall was a golden cup on a silver chain.

A small stone bench stood against the wall opposite the vents that let in the light. On the bench was a pile of neatly folded fine linen. Lemon yellow, pale blue, pure white, and bone white—Neve's colours.

The room was swept clean. It had thick walls, and the sound of the storm came in, muffled and faint. There was a platform at the back of the room. It was the height and size of a bed, not a bier. There was a woman on the bed. Or, she was lying suspended maybe three centimetres from the scrubbed sandstone platform, on nothing at all. Taryn peered and saw the bubble tea texture of the air. The woman, curled up facing the wall, was lying on a mattress of mendings. She occupied half the mattress; the rest was covered by her hair. It trailed upwards from her head and lay piled above her in heaped waves the colour and lustre of a creamy pearl.

Shift crept towards the bed. He knelt and bent his head. He cupped his hands and after a time began to spit into them. He spat until they were full, then emptied what he held onto the bed. He kept it up for a long time, until his lips were pale and his arms had begun to shake.

Taryn moved her weight from foot to foot. She wished she could sit down, but she didn't even dare lean on the wall. She continued to shiver.

The woman on the bed stirred. She slowly rolled face up and straightened her legs. Shift drew back, careful not to come into contact with her.

The woman's body was wasted, but she was smooth-skinned and youthful. The branching blue veins in the hollows of her temples were clearly visible. Her bony arms were softly threaded blue. Her eyes were clear, and her eyelashes were glossy and black. She looked like a very young person who had been deathly ill and was convalescing. Except for her improbable doll-like mass of hair, which was too sleek to seem slept on. But when she did sit up Taryn saw the dead leaves caught in the hair at her nape, and how it was a little ropey and tangled there—felted and faded.

The woman held herself upright, straight-backed. The crumpled but clean collar of her dress slipped from one bony shoulder, revealing a round bone with the gleam of clean gristle, though it was taut skin over gristle. She put out her hand. It hovered, seeming to summon Shift closer. Her eyes were dreamy and bright black. They were fixed not on him but on the glove. When he came close she wrapped her hand around it. The tomb filled with a thick fur of power, as if an invisible animal had slipped through its walls and was turning and turning, treading down the silence, and making a nest for itself.

The woman was of course his grandmother, the Gatemaker. And when the sidhe said one of them was 'in their tomb', they hadn't meant dead. They meant retired, permanently sequestered, visited and served by friends and family, who moved deliberately, hushed, while tending the tombs, inside and out. Friends and family who plumped the mattress with mendings and brought fresh clothes.

There was nothing else in the room. This woman was sustaining herself on water alone and had been for more than two hundred years. Taryn wondered how long it took for a sidhe to devolve into a skin-covered skeleton with a brain. If they slept until they stopped waking. If all efforts never to disturb them became redundant. If finally they wouldn't rouse even for a lightning strike at the door of their tomb.

The grandmother and grandson sat unmoving; Shift hunched, his body making a space for her hand so that she didn't touch him, her straight-backed and musing on the glove. Then she looked up at Shift, gave him a weak, tremulous smile, and whispered, 'Shahen.'

'No. It's Shift.' He answered her in English, and she simply took his lead and spoke English too. 'You look like Shahen.'

'Yes, I look Syrian. It's recently caused me a bit of bother.'

She blinked and passed her arm over her face as if wiping off dust. Taryn looked for signs of grime, but the Gatemaker's sleeve was clean.

The Gatemaker's gaze returned to the glove. 'Adhan's,' she said.

'Yes, my mother's,' Shift answered. Then, very casual and careful, 'Did you make one for my father too?'

'I did,' said the Gatemaker. 'It never reached him. It was left with his body, and the baby, and lost.'

'I was the baby,' Shift said.

'No. The other baby. Neve's,' said the Gatemaker.

Shift grimaced. Taryn recognised the expression as the one people got when their eyes teared up so suddenly and violently it caused them pain. He turned to the wall. His jaw clenched and trembled, and the tears splashed onto the end of his grandmother's bed, from which they were coaxed away by the fastidious mendings, until they spilled and made dark splashes on the limestone wall of the platform. He didn't attempt to say anything further, and she didn't seem to expect him to, or to be at all conscious of the effect her words had had on him. She stayed where she was and continued to admire her own handiwork, with no sign of alarm, or regret, or anticipation, or longing. After a stretch of minutes she dropped the glove. She kept her hand in the air and seemed to call some intention into it from very far away; not from inside her present self, but perhaps her past self. She cupped his cheek and said, deliberate, but without feeling, 'That baby, Emesa, was Shahen's grandchild, but not mine.'

He nodded.

'You are mine,' she added. She removed her hand, sighed like a breeze stirring dead leaves, and lay down.

Shift got up and came back to Taryn. He quietly opened the door, let her through it, followed her, and pulled it closed.

Taryn trailed after him back the way they'd come. She let him collect himself.

But he didn't. He continued to cry, liberally and unselfconsciously—though very quietly. He was still weeping when they reached the beach. He sat on the sand above their boat, gripped his hair, and wept with a tumult of feeling, of which sorrow and exhaustion were only a part. Taryn sat beside him and gradually shuffled nearer until she was pressed against him. Her teeth chattered. They were both soaked through, but that join of warmth kept her from hypothermia.

It continued to rain on them, big drops that made pockmarks in the sand and turned the glossy sea matte. It rained harder. The world boiled around them.

Finally Taryn got up. She shouted, 'We can't just sit in the rain!' She shook him, trying to get him up too. She grabbed one of his hands and put it on the glove. 'Get us out of here,' she pleaded.

He pulled the glove off over his head, taking some hair with it. He tried to put it on, and she had to get behind him and clamp his arm under hers to hold it still while she fought with the cold gold claws, its ties, and chain, and pin. His hand was icy, hers numb and clumsy.

She tied a last knot and let go of his arm. His head was down, his face dripping. The rain was so hard it was carving channels in the sand. Pebbles and sticks were being washed out of the forest and were floating and rolling in the water rushing down the beach. Sand was piling up against the stern of the boat.

'Shift!' Taryn shouted.

His hand wavered up, and a somewhere else roared towards them; Taryn saw the rain bend and be swallowed. Gravity altered. There was a moment of darkness as the force that held them met another force and pulled them. Taryn thought she might be crushed or torn apart. Shift had passed them from gate to gate, without a pause.

They were standing on icy rocks in clouds of thick white steam through which soft, even whiter snowflakes drifted down. Taryn smelled sulphur and the spice of alpine thorn trees. They were on the flagstone staircase beside one of the hot pools at Forsha Springs.

Taryn crept to the water and dipped one foot in. It was cold. Or her nerves were so confused they expected to get colder. She sat down and gradually slipped her legs into the pool. It was snowing on her head and shoulders. But the water was hot.

She lowered herself into the pool. Once she could trust her limbs to move in a coordinated way she pushed off from her side and floated to the other to make room for Shift. He followed her. He was quaking with cold and emotion and was so clumsy that he slipped and fell in. He surfaced gasping, his skin flushed red. He wiped his hair out of his eyes, and Taryn heard the glove grate against his teeth.

They both settled, her with only her head out of the water. They stared at each other. Taryn shivered until it seemed she'd shaken the wakefulness out of her body. She fell asleep and possibly avoided drowning only because, at some point, Shift crossed the pool and wrapped his arm under hers to hold her up. He had more to recover from, but recovered first. When she did wake up, she found it had stopped snowing. He was gazing into the mist. His eyelids were a little red and swollen, but his eyes were clear, and he was thinking.

He was thinking, and it was like feeling a gate move. Or a hundred gates, like gears in a great clock. He was very still, and Taryn could sense it: the powerful intention, a plan forming inside him.

Twenty-Eight

Call and Response

Three days later Taryn found herself she didn't know where, in the grimly busy company of Shift and the magician Petrus Alamire.

Shift came and went, fetching things from Petrus's several lists—arcane objects and ingredients for potions. This was human magic, magic as Taryn had always understood it, with procedures, things done in the proper order, simmered but not boiled, a pinch of this and that, and words whispered at a confiding closeness to a copper pot, its contents tan in colour with globs of purplish oil. The smells were astonishing and the sense of concentration intense, but Taryn, idle now, kept feeling she was watching a performance. It had none of the directness of a Hand forming under Shift's hands, the air plump and solid and full of animation; or the gates moving like monsters further inside or outside the real. This looked like knowledge. It looked like an art, a practice, something *humans* did.

Earlier, Taryn had been asked to plait a lock of her own hair. Once she'd plaited it, Shift cut it several centimetres from her scalp. It was a substantial piece, and Taryn hated to think what her highly opinionated hairdresser would have to say when she next went in. She'd made the plait tight and neat. Shift gave it back to her and had her trim any loose strands with a pair of tiny silver scissors Petrus had among his equipment. Then, after threading it with a number of beads made of white gold—each one bright, but with the soft patina of wear—Shift crimped its ends with wire made of the same. He attached a hook to one end of the plait and an eye to the other, and tried it on himself, looping it double around his wrist. It was a little loose, but that seemed to satisfy him.

When Taryn asked him what it was for, he handed her a pen and some creamy parchment paper and told her to write a note to her father. 'Tell him you're off the grid again. You made this for him, and would he please wear it to bring both of you good luck.'

Taryn wrote what Shift asked. Then he folded the plait into her note and made a package of it, using sealing wax.

'Does the gold do anything magical?' Taryn asked.

'It's a sweetener,' Shift said. 'I'm sure your father will wear it, given everything you've been through lately. But we want to make it as attractive as we can.' Then, 'Where can I find him?'

The fantasy TV series had recommenced shooting, so her father could be found on the shores of Lake Bled, at a villa he shared with several other cast members. Taryn had visited the previous summer and was able to give directions—all the way to Basil Cornick's room. She asked, 'What does the bracelet do?'

Petrus said, 'Worn by someone who loves you it helps your soul find its way home.'

She looked at Shift, 'Who will you give your hair to?'

Petrus laughed. 'His hair is everywhere. It's in his apparel—his hair, his wool, his skin. His bone buttons.'

Taryn glanced at the brownish bugle bead at the neck of Shift's stretched and sloppy jersey. She shuddered.

'No one in their right mind would try to use *his* hair in magic,' Petrus said. He handed Shift another long list of materials, including an item that made Shift grimace with distaste and reluctance. But he didn't object, just left, walking off along the curved margin of the low wood they were camped near, a wood that had over it a mist which hadn't moved the whole time they'd been there.

The air pressure seemed to alter again, as it kept doing, and Taryn was overcome by dizziness. Petrus told her to lie down. She didn't want to. She'd be vulnerable. It wasn't that she didn't trust him. She knew he wouldn't hurt her. Not before she'd done what she was meant to do. But she didn't like him—his dry, dispassionate manner, his oiled hair and ornate clothes.

She lay down.

'He'll be gone for some time, so you should sleep,' Petrus said.

'Shouldn't you tell me your story?'

'Better to wait until you've returned,' Petrus said. 'The thoughts foremost in your mind should concern only what you have to accomplish in Purgatory.'

She thought, *He doesn't want to frighten me.*

Taryn woke and stretched, then went and stood over Shift and Petrus as they worked. After a time she addressed the crowns of their preoccupied heads. 'Will what I'm wearing make any difference?'

'You'll likely find yourself in a favourite outfit, or you'll change according to what's happening and how you feel,' Petrus said. 'When I went, I was sometimes so sure I was dreaming I'd find myself in night attire.'

'Taryn's not thinking of how she'll look. She's thinking of the cold, or of moisture-wicking socks good for another hundred miles.'

Shift really was a bowerbird of things people said, always overburdening his arguments with evidence.

Petrus said, 'It's all immaterial, because you'll be immaterial.'

'I'm trying to think of any safety measures I might take.'

Shift looked up. 'Petrus will issue instructions to both of us right before we go. Anything we want to bear in mind has to be bundled up with our death energy.'

Taryn became afraid then, as afraid as she'd been when, compelled, she had allowed McFadden to wrap the chain around her neck and shut its lock. On that occasion she'd been thinking ahead. Thinking that once McFadden had gone, Jacob would tell her his plan for escape. Or someone would happen along. When the lock snapped shut, Taryn hadn't had enough time to consider how little chance there was of someone happening along. So little that McFadden hadn't felt the need to go a step further and tape their mouths or tie their hands. He'd left their mouths and hands free to let them share their hope, and whatever else followed, like tears and recriminations.

She and Jacob had escaped, but none of it had been without consequences. And as soon as Jacob was able to collect himself, his resentment against her had ignited. She was to blame, and he blamed her. That had separated them and made him vulnerable to Aeng. And that was her loss and Shift's. Jacob himself was happy. And even if Neve made good on her threats, Jacob would be safe.

Shift and this magician with oiled curls were going to winkle her out of her body. Taryn had only ever been in her body. It was where she lived.

She couldn't think what precautions she could take against what was about to happen, and her thoughts began to circle familiar threats, like being cold to her core, as she had been on the beach of the Tacit.

Shift said, 'It would be convenient if we could stay in costume, like the ghosts in stories. The phantom monk in his cowl. The Lady of the West Walk in her bloodstained farthingale. Because if we had costumes we could write the rules on them.'

'They're not really rules,' Petrus said.

'Considerations.'

Petrus measured out equal portions of a pale medicine and gave one to Shift and the other to Taryn. Shift knocked his back, which was the right idea because the taste was terrible—only briefly on her tongue, but it took up residence in her sinus cavities.

Petrus kept taking the temperature of his second concoction. He used his pinkie. Taryn had the impression his touch was as finely tuned as a thermometer. Every now and then he looked up and around, as if he was worried about being intruded on or was expecting someone. This gave Taryn another concern. 'Will our bodies be safe while we're away from them?'

'The cut-through to Purgatory is an out-of-the-way spot,' Shift said. 'About as out of the way as it gets. The sidhe can't use it. It only admits those with souls.'

'I will watch over you,' said Petrus. 'Shift can't waste time waiting for ravens.'

'Taryn, forget your body for now.'

'This seems a very dangerous thing for us to be doing,' she said. 'I've been in danger, but so far I haven't walked into it with my eyes open.'

'I've done this before,' Shift said.

'I went with him and remember doing it,' Petrus said. 'Which is more than he does. So believe me when I tell you it can be done.'

'Will we be too late to save anyone this Tithe?' Taryn said.

Shift hesitated, then told the truth. 'Too late for a renegotiation, yes. Our Pact is with the government of Hell and will only be dissolved if there's a change of regime. There can be no blundering in with just the hopes we have. It would be very bad if the demons' plan was discovered. So we have to let the Tithe go ahead as usual.'

'The players are otherworldly, but the principles are ones we're familiar with, Taryn Cornick,' Petrus added. 'Shift is betting on the Tudors, not the Plantagenets, but the Tudors are still short of funds and allies.'

Shift smiled. 'Petrus bet on the Plantagenets.'

Taryn had expected magic to be *magical* and produce instant results. 'I have to wait another hundred years to benefit from this?' she said. 'That's too far off for me.'

Shift stood up. He reeled slightly, and Petrus jumped up and took his arm. 'Easy.'

Shift freed himself and grabbed Taryn's hands. 'What do you want, Taryn?'

She thought, *To be let off the hook. Not to be in the middle of all this. To go back and undo my mistakes and not owe anyone.*

'The truth, Taryn. And think it through. What is it you most want?'

Selfishly or unselfishly? She was only able to summon selfish desires. 'I want not to have made the mistakes I've made. Not to have inveigled McFadden into killing Webber. Not to have sought revenge. Not exchanged my unspoiled memories of my sister for my revenge, because that's what it feels like I did. I want Beatrice to be alive. I want Webber to have driven on past. I want my sister and me to have continued into our adulthood together and for her to have been at my side at our mother's funeral. Our mother might have lived if Bea had. I want the stone rolled away from the door of the tomb.' She started to cry and couldn't speak.

After several minutes Shift said, 'What else do you want?'

'Because all that's impossible?'

'Yes.'

'I want to see Beatrice again. And don't tell me *that's* impossible.'

'It will depend on what you do.'

'I have to do something extraordinary and heroic?'

'Yes. And the right ones have to notice. That's something we can't calculate or engineer. The citadels and prisons and quarantines of the Great God of the Deserts have all broken down.'

Heaven was the citadel, Hell the prison, Purgatory the quarantine. Taryn could figure that one out. She mopped her wet eyes on her still-material sleeve and tried to collect herself. 'All right,' she said, 'I want there to be libraries in the future. I want today to give up being so smugly sure about what tomorrow won't need.'

'For there to be libraries in the future, what would be required?'

'People to care about the transmission of knowledge from generation to generation, and about keeping what isn't immediately necessary because it might be vital one day. Or simply intriguing, or beautiful.'

'And?' Shift said.

Taryn lost her temper. 'Oh, God. Of course you have an "and". Of course you have an endpoint to your interrogation or homily or whatever.'

'Civilisation would help,' Petrus said, offering Taryn a clue to assist with his friend's inquisitorial nonsense.

She took a deep breath. 'Thanks. Yes. Of course I want civilisation. Cities are a necessary condition of libraries. I made that point in my book. The monastery on the spur of rock that people can only reach by being winched up in a basket is still a city—since each church is a house among houses.'

'Yes, you wrote that,' Petrus said. He had hunkered down again, his pinkie denting the surface of the second potion. He was interested in the argument but could divide his attention without being distracted.

Taryn was startled. 'Have you read my book?'

'Yes. I thought it quite wonderful.'

Taryn blushed.

Shift said, 'And what if the hillsides your houses are on slip into the valleys, and everything is buried in mud? What if the wind flattens your houses, or floods wash them off their foundations? What if you're all like too many mound-building birds in the same forest—you get so tired of stealing each other's twigs and sticks that no nests are finished, and no chicks hatch? You can't keep doing everything over, so you sit down in the ruins and starve. What if that? What if the floods sweep the soil into the sea, and the sea seeps up through the land and turns it sour? What if the conditions for civilisation are gone?'

Taryn stared at him, speechless.

Petrus said, 'This potion is ready. I would like you both to prepare by lying down.'

Taryn wasn't ready. She was furious. Speeches had been made at her. And that couldn't be Shift's endgame. No one could save the world.

'Lie down,' Petrus said.

The potion was cooling. It was yellow, with a chalky pinkish skin.

'You're crazy,' Taryn said to Shift, meaning it.

'I haven't got ahead of myself. I know everything depends on a few things,' he said.

'He's mad,' Taryn said to Petrus, in a tone of wonder, but it was an appeal.

'Lie down,' Petrus said again.

Taryn lay down and then had to sit up to accept her measure of potion. She looked at it. Steam still puffed out from under the twitching lid of its viscous skin.

Shift sat beside her.

'I'm going to tie your hands together. It will help.'

Petrus didn't mean her hands—she wouldn't have let anyone tie her hands now. He meant to tie her left hand to Shift's right.

Petrus hovered over them with a scarf. 'Move a little nearer Taryn, please, Shift.'

The gate swelled quietly towards them and moved the three of them away from the vials and baskets, the crucible and alembic, the beakers, glass tubes, and hearth. Taryn found herself sitting in dust as soft as face powder and close to the same colour. They were among rocks velvety with it. Water was running somewhere nearby, a stream with an odd muffled chuckle, as if it were hot milk rather than cold water.

There were carvings on the rocks.

The sign of a fish was what Christians used to mark the lintels of their meeting houses in the time of the Apostle Paul. Before they began to use crosses, there were fishes. These fishes had eyes and scales but no tails. Their tails were severed from them. These fishes were souls that couldn't swim all the way to Heaven. This was the border to the place where bodies couldn't go.

Petrus fastened Taryn's hand to Shift's. He said to them both, 'I'll tell you when to drink that.'

'It's too hot,' Taryn said—a small objection and postponement.

'These are the things you must consider and hold in mind. First, you will be souls. Souls can't be injured or killed, but they can get lost. Shift, you will have to follow Taryn. Prompt her, then follow her. She will be more forgetful than you. She will want to be helped. Don't let anyone help her or seek assistance yourself. Remember that almost no one in Purgatory is hostile or dishonest. They are only trying to pull themselves together. They try to provide guidance, because guidance is what they crave. But when in Rome, *do not do* as the Romans do. Taryn can find the shortest distance to her mother. Remember, Taryn, you are looking for your mother. You are not looking for your sister. Do not part ways with Shift—he belongs there even less than you. Purgatory is not a place prepared for the likes of him—so it will want him to leave. If you stick with him, you will get out, whether or not you've found what you're seeking, because Purgatory will expel him. Shift, do not try to change yourself. You will only be there by the virtue of your human soul, which does not comprise half of your living self, as Taryn's does. Your human soul is a passport, under which you can smuggle in your godhood and not be in any danger of forgetting what you're there to do. But you have to remember you can't *make* Taryn find her mother. Don't either of you look around for anyone else. If you are followed, remember: *Jesus saith unto her, "Woman, what have I to do with thee? Mine hour is not yet come."'*

Petrus guided the beakers to both their mouths. Taryn considered casting hers aside. She had no idea what her life would be like if she did. Would doing it be like saying no to McFadden when he laid out his offer to kill Webber? Or would it be like what she did do? Would it be like staying silent?

She drank down the mixture. She hoped her silence was a refusal of refusal.

Her gullet went numb, her face, her fingers. Petrus laid her down gently, then did the same for Shift. Petrus was saying to him again, 'Don't change, you'll ruin everything if you change.'

A yeasty silence flowered in Taryn's ears, spilled out, and fastened her head to the ground. The tailless, elliptical fish were eyes, not fish; and they weren't going anywhere themselves, just seeing her off.

Twenty-Nine

Purgatory

The light was even and dim, mid-afternoon of a thickly over-cast day. Wide-eyed or squinting, nothing improved visibility. Shift was a little ahead of Taryn. He was following a stream, but almost seemed to lead it. The trickle of water fingered out into the dust before him, cutting a channel in the powdery ground, flowing like a measure of water into flour, making a bed of batter.

There were a few trees, stunted olives. Shift wended his way to each, and the water followed him.

He wasn't wearing his homespun anymore. He was mantled in an unconnected cloud of matter, a bristle of air in which was suspended feathers and fur, seed heads, dead leaves, tufted grass, sparkling drops of rainwater, the wings of moths and butterflies, or their whole bodies, beetles, glistening skeins of frogspawn, and myriad tiny bones. The mantle of matter extended a good foot over his head, the detritus thin-ning so that if he looked behind him he'd be able to see through it. The mantle was thickest between his shoulders and knees, then sparse again below that. Taryn could see his bare feet through the floating objects and their faint shadows. In fact, Taryn could see him more clearly than she had before—a handsome young man of Arab descent with eyes too widely spaced, and something oddly raptor-like happening between his nose and forehead. That oddness was as disconcerting as the mantle; it was as alien and, for some reason, more alarming.

Taryn finished her examination of Shift, then stopped walking. He went on ahead, winding from tree to tree, the stream turning to come to heel each time he changed course. He continued on. It was all downhill from where Taryn stood. To either side the slope extended in a shallow curved contour into the distance or into the bad light. Down was a way to go, in lieu of a path, or any track other than the watercourse coming into existence as it nosed after that person she was thinking better of following.

She would just wait here until he was out of sight.

Taryn considered sitting down, and only then noticed she was wearing her favourite skirt, the turquoise one with geese on it. The skirt had pockets—pockets were rare and desirable in women's clothes. Taryn had got the skirt at a shop in Seven Dials the summer before she went to university the first time. With her skirt she was wearing a cropped T-shirt and a pair of walking sandals she'd bought in Paris while shopping with Alan. Everything Taryn wore went together, but her sense of satisfaction was mixed with one of incongruity, and she didn't know why.

The air pressure altered. The person in a nature-spirit mantle was standing in front of her. He'd crept up on her while she was admiring her clothes. He said, 'Have you already forgotten why you're here?'

'No, I'm meeting my sister. She'll be along in a minute. We're going to the movies. If it's any of your business.'

'What film will you see?'

'Beatrice wants to go to *Donnie Darko*.'

'And what film did you end up seeing?'

Taryn frowned at the question. Then she remembered how she had argued for *A Beautiful Mind* and they'd both been disappointed. Taryn watched *Donnie Darko* only last winter, in a hotel in Liverpool the night before some bookshop gig. She was very moved by how the hero let everything happen again so that it was he who died, not his sister.

Taryn looked down at her skirt. She'd bought it in 2001, on her eighteenth birthday. The skirt that was still hanging in her wardrobe, its waistband a little too tight. She'd got the crop top at fifteen. The sandals she'd owned for ten years.

Beatrice wasn't there, but their mother might be.

'Sorry,' she said. 'You look a little alarming.'

Shift gave her his hand, and they set off, straight down the hill. They passed the place where the thread of running water had doubled back on itself when he had turned around to fetch her. He said, 'I'm sorry too. I had no business watering the trees. We have to be careful. Right now we're pretty much only our propensities.'

Taryn tightened her grip. She kept hold of his hand because it wasn't a thing she'd do.

They'd been walking for hours but had gained no landmarks, or even level ground. Their shadows had reappeared, eight or so each, fanning out around their feet. They were moving through pasture of a sort, grass that was stiff and as glossy as tufts of raw asbestos.

They had been going downhill, but the land behind them wasn't uphill. The horizon was too close back the way they'd come, as if it were the edge of a cliff.

Taryn wasn't footsore or hungry, only hollow, as if her innards were spooling out of her the further she went.

Again Shift came back for her. She had stopped in order to listen. She thought she could hear a distant horn, sounding long and low. A train, she thought.

'This place is easier for me,' he said. 'Easier to keep my place. No one I remember is missing. No one I might expect to find here.'

'Shift.' She said his name just to remind herself who he was. 'Why do I look like a ghost while you look like the Wendigo?'

'You look like your twenty-year-old self on her way to a party,' he said.

'Eighteen-year-old. Before Bea was killed.'

He peered ahead, across the now undulating grassland. 'There's some sort of pull here for me. Something in this place likes the plan I've been carrying around.'

'Is your plan full of dried flowers and dead bees?'

The train horn sounded once more.

'The dried flowers and dead bees are just as far as I've got,' Shift said. He took her hand again.

The undulations became a plain, ground balding, grass malnourished. A little way out from the station they met a path. They followed it up onto the platform, which was ferrous-brown concrete. The rails in the track bed were bright, so used often.

Four men and three women were waiting under the station's high canopy. All were youngish, and their clothes were mismatched in both type and time period: dress shoes with a boiler suit, a fox stole with silk pyjamas.

When Shift and Taryn arrived, the people shuffled closer together in the patch of nominal shade. They moved as if they were troubled by arthritis. One of the women had what looked like osteoporosis of the spine, though by her face Taryn would have put her at twenty-five. Her mouth was covered in blisters.

Taryn asked when the next train was.

'The last one that went by didn't stop,' said a man, which wasn't much of an answer.

'The last I managed to catch took me all the way to the pool,' said a woman.

Taryn asked, 'What is the pool?'

'Wading pool,' said the woman. Or maybe it was 'waiting pool'.

'Before you get on, make sure it stops at the records office,' said another woman, more cogent. Then she unzipped the cracked leather document folder she was carrying and produced a file. 'When I came away from there I didn't realise they'd given me only half of what I needed.'

Taryn peered at the folder. Its cover was furry with age. She read out its label. 'Denise, 348. How did you find out which Denise you are?'

'You have to take a ticket and wait to be called.'

'Three hundred and forty-eight was your ticket number? Does that mean you're filed by just "Denise"?'

The third woman limped over to Shift and took hold of him. She said, 'When you go, will you take me with you?'

He pushed her hand from his arm. It wasn't easy, and his skin and hers together made a waxy, whimpering sound. 'What are you to me?' he said.

The woman fell back, glowered, then lunged at him and snatched a handful of bones and feathers from his mantle. She hurried out from under the canopy and into the glare.

The sun had come out. Its white force was making the dry shingles of the station roof creek and crackle. Heat sliced up from the stripe of platform outside the pool of shade.

Taryn said to the woman with the file, 'My name is Taryn. How many of us can there be?'

The railway line thumped and twanged. Half a minute later a train blasted through the station without stopping. Once it had gone, so had three of the people, including the woman with the file. The dilapidated carriage parked on the siding opposite the station now had people sitting in its windowless darkness, relaxed, their elbows resting on the windowsills. Had they always been there?

Taryn ventured out of the shade to take a closer look. She checked the line. There was no sign of another train. Back the way they'd come, the Uphill, a figure had appeared. It was creeping across the balding pasture. It was human, but there was something badly wrong with it. Something worse than stiff joints.

Taryn shaded her eyes.

Behind her, Shift's mantle made a faint hissing and bamboo wind chime clatter as he came towards her. 'We're waiting for a train in order to cover some distance,' he said. 'But we might as well just stay here. Distance doesn't figure. There isn't a deeper in.'

'But we've made progress. That's where we were.' Taryn pointed in the direction of the creeping shape.

The person was now up on its elbows, clawing its way forward, one leg dragging behind, the other extended straight upwards like the mast of a yacht.

The railway line sang, the pounding slower than it was before.

'This one will stop,' Shift said. 'We should get on.'

Taryn wasn't terribly surprised that he'd changed his mind. She was just as content to go as to stay. No place was crowded. The station wasn't. The train wouldn't be. Perhaps she could sit for a time.

The train slid into the station. It was without doors but did have glass in its windows. Everyone climbed into the same carriage, Taryn pushing the others until she was safely clear of the open doorway. The others seemed to be old hands at train travel. No sooner were they were on board than they turned either direction, one going towards the engine and the other towards the back of the train.

The train started up, jerking, carriage shunting carriage so that the floor swung. Taryn held on to the back of a seat. The man in the seat, dapper, strictly upright, turned to her, savage, and wiped her hand off his headrest. The cracked leather gave the same waxy creak that Shift's skin had, as if the sounds in this country were few and recycled unmodified.

Shift took Taryn's arm and led her forward. They went into the next carriage, passing through a slightly too long tunnel of black concertinaed rubber. Taryn used the hot, perishing smell to stabilise herself. In this country there were so few scents that the rubber stink acted on her like smelling salts. She said to Shift, 'You told me we shouldn't get on the train and that we didn't need to go any further. Then you suddenly changed your mind.'

They'd reached the next carriage. Shift ducked his head to look back at the station and the bald hills. The tunnel between the carriages was like a corridor in a space station. A portion of Shift's bones, seed heads, moth wings had detached from his orbit and was floating in the tunnel's zero gravity.

'You're shedding,' Taryn told him.

He gave the tunnel a sombre appraisal, then asked her if she'd please collect the seed heads for him.

She did. Her pockets were capacious enough for fistfuls of dried seed heads.

Taryn was walking on the road between St Cynog's Cross and Princes Gate on an overcast autumn day. The road had a long right-hand curve, but it went on for longer than she remembered. She was too tired to hurry. Her tiredness felt more like anaemia than a couple of skipped meals. The bend went on, without recognisable landmarks, no oak close to the road with the place she always laid a hand when she passed. The spot no higher up than when Bea's head had hit it. When Taryn was old, that spot might be a couple of centimetres higher, or maybe five. Oaks were slow. This roadway worse than slow, not swinging into a left-hand curve as it should, showing her the oak. Why had she undertaken this pilgrimage? What was there to say to the tree that killed your sister?

I should have killed you too. Drilled into your roots. Ring-barked you.

The swinging train had soothed Taryn into something like sleep. Something like a dream. When she opened her eyes, she was looking through a screen of tiny suspended shadows. The wings of a dead moth brushed her browbone and sprinkled its powder on her eyelid. Her head was resting on Shift's shoulder.

Beyond the train windows it was night. The train was travelling along an embankment. They were coming up on lighted buildings. A town, apparently one street in depth, in a strip below the embankment. Buildings maybe five storeys high, the third storey level with the railway line.

As the lighted windows came up, everyone sitting on the opposite side of the carriage crowded to Taryn's side and crammed up to the windows to peer intently at the buildings. It was possible to see straight into the third-floor windows and down into the second. Many of the rooms were illuminated. Taryn saw beige plastic furniture, neutral grey-green walls, narrow beds with guardrails and waffled cotton blankets. She saw a hospital. The whole strip was a hospital.

The train had slowed, until there were more than glimpses. A child sat in a wheelchair at a window. A man lay tucked up in bed, the twin tubes of an oxygen line in his nostrils. A figure of indeterminate sex, completely swathed in bandages, stood in the centre of the room with their back to the train.

At the sight of the figure in bandages the people pressed around Taryn and Shift made sounds of discovery, as if this might be someone known to all or any of them. The noises they made were of relief, or jubilation. They fought their way out of the press and rushed to either end of the carriage and the open doors.

The same thing was happening all over the train. Taryn could see figures rolling down the embankment, raising dust. She returned her gaze to the windows just in time to see a room whose every surface was loaded with vases of flowers, mostly white roses and peonies, daisies and baby's breath. Taryn's mother was in the bed. Taryn herself was already there, standing at the window, looking out. And there was a black-clad figure against the room's closed door, head down and hands clasped in prayer.

Taryn reeled back against Shift and was engulfed in his mantle of dead matter. A bird bone tapped on the side of her nose like a knowing finger. He caught her and helped her back through the bodies clustered at the windows. They hurried to an open door. She baulked and braced herself in its frame. The ground slipped past. In the squares of light cast on the bank by the hospital windows she could see bushes and sizeable stones and several winded or wounded jumpers struggling to pick themselves up at the foot of the slope. She glimpsed one maimed, knotted figure pushing himself to move between a roll and a crawl.

Shift seized her wrists, ripped her grip off the frame, wrapped her arms across her chest and himself around her. He propelled them out of the train. They hit the slope inside the dust devil of his mantle. Then he let her go and she slid free of it. Momentum carried her to the foot of the slope, where she lay coughing. Dust coated her teeth. She hawked and spat. It was some time till her tears had rinsed the dust from her eyes. Once she could see, she looked for Shift and found him combing the slope for what had been knocked out of his mantle when he fell. After a few minutes he seemed satisfied he'd recovered enough. He scrambled over to her and deposited his handfuls in her pockets. He helped her up, and the fat, light lumps of collected matter bumped against her thighs.

'You're spoiling the drape of my skirt,' she said. 'And I can't see why my good appearance should be sacrificed for yours.'

He said, 'Perhaps you will allow that for a time?' Then, 'Who was it you saw?'

'Beatrice, visiting my mother.' Once Taryn said it, she knew it was true. The woman in her mother's hospital room couldn't be herself, because here she was, outside, covered in dust.

'But Beatrice wasn't any kind of sinner,' he said. 'Why would she be here?'

'Maybe she was and we didn't know,' Taryn said. 'Bea was a terrible shoplifter at fourteen. Terrible as in very active. She was mean to her friends sometimes.' Taryn was reaching. She remembered Bea blowing marijuana smoke in the face of one of Grandma's cats and giving the stoned animal a spin on an office chair. That was some kind of cruel. A silly, careless kind. She remembered Bea picking all the banana slices off the top of a big bowl of jelly meant for Christmas dinner; Bea stacking books covered in Moroccan leather to stand on them and reach for something; Bea spending one wet Saturday afternoon making prank calls: 'Is your fridge running? Because it's just passed our house.' Bea pinching her when she had too effective a comeback in one of their arguments. But all that was just naughty or thoughtless, not sinful.

Shift interrupted her thoughts by asking her which building it was.

From the train, the room had been exactly like Addy Cornick's last, though that room was on floor nine, elevator D. *D for doomed* was what Taryn used to think each time she left, at the end of a long day. *D for die already why don't you.*

'Bea was never at that hospital. She'd been dead for two years,' Taryn said, again giving her sister up.

The wall beside her was mudbrick. The windows had no glass, though there was a gentle orange illumination spilling into the black air beyond each.

'If we're all dead, why would there be a hospital?' Now that she'd surrendered the possibility of Beatrice, Taryn had returned to logic.

'You and I aren't dead. Please bear that in mind. The people of this country built the hospital, I think. It's a real material building housing a ghost for everyone. Ghost beds. Ghost oxygen outlets and call buttons. Ghost electricity making a beacon for passengers on the ghost train. But these bricks are real.'

'I think the building we want is two back,' Taryn said. 'About five hundred metres.' She turned that way and made her jarred limbs move.

Many of the other jumpers had sorted themselves out and were making their way in already. On the railway line side there was a single doorless entrance to each building, and handsomely uneven mudbrick stairs going straight up.

'They built a hospital because they think people who are sick might be healed,' Shift said. 'They think themselves in need of healing. And that a hospital might attract healers.'

It seemed that each person there was telling a story about themselves and, if their stories matched up, then enough people might get together and make something—the shared memory of a train, a train for going places, or a building fashioned with the materials to hand, like mud, straw, and water.

Taryn and Shift had just about reached the single entranceway in the block they wanted when he stopped abruptly and she ran into him. She was momentarily submerged in the bristle of energy and objects, soft and hard, and drops of water, still cold, as if they'd just been shaken out of a chilled water bottle. She backed away, then further away as he retreated too, his hand groping for her, though he seemed unwilling to turn his head.

She peered around him and stopped cold.

At their feet and in their way was the crawling man. He was lying face up to drag himself along. His arms were twisted a full hundred-and-eighty degrees, shoulders out of their joints, the bone of the ball and socket making lumps in his armpits, his muscles stretched stringy and bruised deeply purple. One of his hands was paralysed but not flaccid. It was clenched, fingers as rigid as a garden weed-grubbing tool. The other hand was in motion and making some kind of signal at them. His hips were twisted sideways. One leg worked a little, and he was digging it in to help drag himself between them and the doorway. His other leg was a mast, dislocated at the hip and knee, sticking straight up.

His face was scoured by sand. Grains of sand made a black lacework around the edges of his grazes. The grit wasn't the soft yellow soil of the embankment but the grey of a tidal inlet.

Shift grabbed Taryn under her ribs, hoisted her, and tossed her over the Muleskinner. She banged against the wall just inside the stairway and dropped to the steps. A cold, wet hand brushed her ankle.

She scrambled upwards as fast as she could, though she was suddenly weighed down, her neck and shoulders pressed towards the steps. Where the stairs turned she stopped, checking whether Shift was behind her.

He was in the doorway, his back to her. He was stooped over the Muleskinner, talking or listening—Taryn couldn't tell which. He looked like the kindly stranger who stops to check on a child who has skinned its knee.

Another train roared past, the lights from its window strobing over the maimed man and igniting every glistening drop of water suspended in Shift's mantle.

The heaviness on Taryn was a chain. Once again, it was wrapped around her neck. Its length trailed behind her down the stairs, its end just out of reach of the Muleskinner's one good, groping hand.

Taryn reeled in the dangling chain. It rattled and danced up the stairs. She wrapped it around herself, making a thick bandolier.

Shift turned, came up to her, and encouraged her to go on.

Taryn went but kept turning to him to ask questions to which she already knew the answers. Why is he here? *More sinned against than sinning.* How did he find us? *The same way you're going to find your mother. The gravity of things unfinished.*

It took them some time to locate the room, and they found it empty. All that remained were dry, yellowed flowers and glass vases with greenish tidelines of evaporated water.

The black robe hanging on the back of the door—the only door in that hospital, a door to discourage visitors because there was someone who could never visit—was what Taryn had taken for the penitential figure of a third person in the room. She removed the robe from its hook and put it on over her looped chain and her favourite skirt with its bulging pockets.

'We'll look for another exit,' Shift said. 'We can hide between buildings and jump on the next slow train.'

If it was necessary to hide, Shift must believe the Muleskinner hadn't finished with her.

They wandered around the building's ground floor. They saw many people searching for friends and relatives, but all the rooms were empty. Eventually they climbed out a window. It was then they discovered that the buildings were linked by a single corridor at ground level, concertinaed rubber tubes like those between the train carriages.

The hospital had a frontage on the side opposite the railway, a large forecourt and canopy, a place ambulances might pull up. But the forecourt was beaten earth, and there was no road leading to it.

The tunnels prevented Shift and Taryn from concealing themselves between the buildings, so they made their way to the wall at the very end of the row, where they found several other souls clustered who were taking turns to peer around the corner, on the lookout for slow trains or for people they meant to avoid.

The wall was still warm from the day's sun. Taryn leaned against it while Shift went to the corner. Peering around it, he immediately spotted their pursuer. He pointed out the Muleskinner to the other people and asked their advice. 'If I straighten him out, will that help?'

'Help to what?' said one.

'Will helping him help you?' asked another.

'No one here can help us,' said yet another.

Shift said, 'I thought he wanted my friend to hear his story. But he seems to have no interest in that. It was me who twisted him up like that. He remembers most of what happened. But he doesn't know to lay the blame at my feet. His one good arm is the arm he lost. It works because he doesn't remember what happened to it.'

'Why do you say "friend"?' said the first speaker. 'How can you have a friend here with you?'

'By the most extraordinary luck.'

The third speaker asked, 'What happened to the man's arm?'

'I ate it,' Shift answered, and looked perplexed and alarmed, as if he hadn't meant to respond truthfully, or at all.

'He must have already been dead when you ate it, or you'd be in the Nearest Place,' the second speaker intoned in a singsong chant. 'You must have had a good reason to kill him, or you'd be in the Nearest Place. You must have had a good reason to eat him, or you'd be in the Nearest Place.'

Taryn gathered that the Nearest Place was Hell.

The first said, 'I've been looking for my friend up and down all the roads. In and out of all the parishes.'

The souls were clustered around Shift now, almost encroaching on his cloud of matter.

'Your friend is in Heaven,' Shift said. 'My friend is here.' He pointed at Taryn.

Everyone turned and gazed at her. Then the third speaker said, with polite censoriousness, 'No one has a friend here.'

The only one who hadn't yet spoken, but who had been examining Shift closely the whole time, said, 'What are you?'

'I'm a soul, like you.'

'We are people.'

'A person, like you. The soul of a person.'

'You are not a person.'

Taryn thought this was probably the direst insult she'd heard directed at Shift, who counted everyone as people.

Through the bricks at her back she felt the faint vibration of a train's wheels over joins in the tracks. She went to Shift and told him she thought a slow train was on its way. Everyone lost interest in them. They streamed away from their hiding place and up the embankment.

Taryn hauled on Shift, and they followed. They sprinted across the short stretch of level ground and up the embankment. The engine went by them, and they began running alongside the train. But it was gaining on them.

Shift stopped running so he'd be the first to reach the open door at the front of coach number three. He jumped on, then leaned out and snatched at Taryn as the train carried him past her.

His hand slid off her.

He vanished from the doorway, and Taryn understood that he was running back down the length of the train to catch her at another door. She looked behind her. The next door was nearly on her. She must try herself, but the bandolier of chain was weighing her down, and she couldn't vault, could barely run. There was nothing to grab on to. Her hands fumbled on the rear doorway of carriage three as it went past, and she tripped and tumbled against the moving carriage and then desperately pushed herself clear. She came down in the dust, and several souls trampled over her as they chased the receding doorway.

Once they passed, Taryn raised her head to look back along the line and count doors; count the chances she had left. Six. Five, for she'd not be on her feet quickly enough for the first of them.

She had been seen. The Muleskinner had left his post by the door to the third building and was hurrying her way, rolling like a spinifex seed barrelling along wet sand on a windy day.

Taryn screamed. A door sailed past over her head, and there was a thump as Shift landed behind her. He picked her up, lifted her over his head, and threw her into the next passing doorway. She tumbled between the legs of the people in what turned out to be a very crowded carriage.

She got to her feet and leaned out the door. Shift was still chasing the train, lining up with the last door. The ragged star of the Muleskinner bowled up behind him.

Shift jumped and made the door. The Muleskinner stretched and stamped his straight leg in behind Shift. He seemed to lodge there, like a thrown shuriken. The train picked him up and carried him along. Shift seized the Muleskinner's anchored leg, batted away the good hand, and flung the man out into the black air.

The hospital had illuminated the empty land around it, but they were now well past the hospital and everything was dark.

Taryn saw the Muleskinner drop away and become shadow. He fell lightly, like a dry plant, not a solid body, but as he fell, he grappled away a streamer of bones and leaves, moths and butterflies, seedpods, frogspawn. The matter scattered beside the track. Shift leaned from the doorway, looking back. Then he turned Taryn's way, shouted something she couldn't hear over the thump and squeal of the wheels, and jumped.

The remaining windows of the last carriage flashed their way over him, counting down from four to zero. Then he was lost in the darkness.

The train went on, submerged in the desert night.

Taryn remained by the door of the packed carriage. Hours went by, and very gradually the countryside reappeared. Blue-grey, then dun. The sun came up unseen, perhaps somewhere behind the train.

Desert and the odd dwelling; that was all there was. But then, after the train passed what looked like an artificial hill—narrow at its ends, with wide ramps facing up and down the line and some kind of lookout on top—the crowd in the carriage seemed to perk up. They began to peer expectantly out the windows.

How many of these passengers had made this journey before? Taryn wondered. They all seemed to know what came next.

The train slowed. It had entered some kind of suburb.

A billboard glided by, on it a man with his finger to his lips, except his finger was an unlit candle. Another billboard showed one of those tailless fish, up on end, its smiling mouth and single eye pointed skywards, and its sickle-shaped tail balanced on its head, like horns.

The billboards were painted, not printed. The only things in the settlement that looked mass-produced were the clothes people wore in the streets. Taryn saw Levi's and Reeboks and Yankees caps, Doc Martens, Lacoste shirts, Adidas sportswear. She saw bits and pieces of uniforms from various wars. Taryn understood that the clothes were all remembered—ghost objects. But the billboards were like the hospital, made there, with an idea in mind and an agreed-upon understanding. They were material and indigenous.

This was the sort of thinking she had to do in order to become someone who could settle here. She could stay. She could start a library: build a small house and fill it with the books she remembered. A real house, with ghost books. But when Taryn tried to remember books, the only one that came to mind was her own. Was her own book the only one she'd ever really needed?

She thought of the thing she and Shift were looking for—a cipher key to a language capable of commanding nature, a kind of absolute book, one they had dreamed up out of their different personal needs, and which was probably no more real than the fictional absolute books she had written about in *The Feverish Library*: Casaubon's *Key to All the Mythologies*; Lovecraft's *Necronomicon*; and the 'catalogue of catalogues' Borges's librarian wandered in search of in his youth.

And then she thought, *I will get off wherever this train stops, and I will wait right there until Shift finds me.* She could feel a tugging on the ends of that short, chopped-off lock at the back of her head. Her father was wearing a bracelet made of her hair. She had a body waiting for her. And it was her mother she must find, not her sister, not an occupation.

Taryn stayed at the station for two days and a night. She watched people disembark from trains that stopped, replaced by those who'd waited, often for most of a day. There was no timetable. But no one settled in on the platform and made themselves comfortable, as people normally would in the case of unreliable transport. With services like these you would expect to see folding chairs, thermoses, and sleeping bags. Everyone seemed to have remembered the form of waiting, but not the form of resting while waiting.

There were very few benches on the platform, so the throng simply stood, looking up the line. The trains only ran in one direction. It made Taryn worry about how she'd get back. She could walk, of course; follow the line, recognise where she'd been, orient herself to an uphill and an out. But walking would be slow, and Taryn had a vague sense that time mattered, that there was something she had to be back for—a talk to give, a celebration to witness. Perhaps it was Carol's wedding. She couldn't remember discharging her matron of honour duties at the ceremony or celebration, so the wedding must still be before her.

The people on the station didn't talk to one another, but Taryn was approached twice by individuals asking if she'd let them have her chain. What they wanted it for they didn't say. Taryn explained that she couldn't remove it, and they looked at her with uncertainty bordering on dread, and she intuited that few people came there so encumbered. Her chain didn't fit the usual picture.

Passengers came and went. Everyone flowing through the station seemed preoccupied, holding themselves in readiness for the next thing. Some had sheaves of documents in folders or envelopes. They would stand perusing their papers as they waited, some absorbed, some agitated. 'This is not my file,' one might declare, to no one in particular. 'I asked for mine, but this is the file of that dreadful woman who left me in the lurch.'

Many of them voiced complaints. But no one seemed to listen to anything anyone else had to say.

Even witnessing the dissatisfaction of others with their files, Taryn felt that if she were to visit the records office she'd be able to locate her own. She was an experienced researcher. She could read her file and make some sense of her situation. She hadn't forgotten that she wasn't dead, wasn't finished, was in fact a visitor in this great hospital's visiting hours, not herself someone in need of a cure. But the urge to go looking for some news about herself, some orienting information, possibly flattering, was exactly like the one she'd get when her Facebook stream presented her with a quiz: *Which of the four temperament types are you? Which philosopher are you? Which Star Wars character? Which endangered British bird?*

'Excuse me,' Taryn said to the person nearest her. 'How far is it to the records office?'

'If you go by the riverbed, you will reach its landing in an hour,' came the answer.

'But the riverbed is powdery, and with that chain you'll be sinking up to your ankles at every step,' said another.

Both of the people who spoke looked pleased with themselves, puffed up with importance.

'Oh, I wish I'd thought of helping her,' said someone else. 'That's a candle.'

The woman who'd voiced this thought was abruptly chastised, in a noisy chorus, like a fuss in a henhouse. People shouted at her in several languages. The only thing Taryn was able to pick out was, 'Do you imagine *she* can give you a candle? Where would she get a candle?' They seemed to be arguing about whether it was possible to earn enough points—candles—to escape this country. About a contractual arrangement that some seemed to believe in and others did not. It was either worth showing consideration to others as a general display of good form to the invisible powers who must surely be paying attention, or it was not, because no one here who helped another would, by doing so, help themselves.

Taryn wanted to say that the general habit of being helpful would make life easier for everyone, whether or not it was noticed. That human kindness was heartwarming, and didn't they need their hearts warmed? But it was pointless. They were here legitimately, while she was an illegal. They got to argue about the rules by which they lived, and to disagree on the spirit of the rules, while she got to stand by saddened and frightened by it all, clinging to a distinction that, as an illegal, she'd been able to make: Purgatory wasn't forever living with your mistakes; it was forever defending your decisions.

Taryn's chain got heavier by the hour. If it gained any more weight she wouldn't be able to get about even dragging herself. If she was going to make a move and explore the records office—not to look up her records or anyone else's, but to see what it was like, in case it was in any way like the Borges' library—she should move. Before another night arrived, she should wade along the river of powder, looking for some place imposing enough to be the focus of pilgrimages and hope. But then she remembered the hospital, real from afar, ruinous close to, and she kept her seat. After all, she was very lucky to have a seat. *It's the small things*, Taryn thought, and a few minutes later that minutes were small things, and that she was herself only minute by minute, and the chatter in her head was like a machine breathing for her.

T he weight was lifted from her kilo by kilo as someone unwound the chain. It was night, and there were no lights that side of the station. The ghost electricity in the city on the other side of the station only threw the building's shadow over the platform.

'Thank you,' Taryn murmured.

The last loop was lifted over her head, and the chain went taut. She was pulled up out of her seat. She stumbled where she was led and saw that it was the Muleskinner—standing straight now—his back to her as he drew her along.

Taryn grabbed her end of the chain to take the strain off her neck and hurried to catch up. She overtook the chain. Its slack loop fidgeted and rattled after them.

'I'm glad to see that you're more yourself,' Taryn said. She was glad; he was less frightening to look at and, she hoped, not as fast now that he was on his feet.

'As if you care.'

'To care I'd have to have known you were in trouble.'

'I wasn't in trouble. Your boyfriend broke me, and he straightened me out again.'

Taryn craned this way and that, but there was no other person in sight. The chain was making a hell of a noise. You'd think someone might look out a window.

She asked, 'Where is he?'

'He stopped to pick up his shit.'

Taryn was furious. Shift had said something about how they were mostly just their propensities here, and she'd managed to resist throwing herself at an archive, but he'd kept preening, which wasn't even a propensity he had. Either that, or he was putting himself back together, which might, she thought, be expressive of his forgetting everything every second century. But he had more power, more presence of mind, even under all his camouflage, than she could muster. He shouldn't be going to pieces.

The Muleskinner led Taryn off the platform and across the lines—there was a barrier arm, down when it should be up. They had to edge around it.

'What happened to you?' Taryn said.

'You happened to me.'

'No, Hamish, you weren't in love with me. I refuse to believe that.'

'What would you know? You've never been in love.' He waved the rectangular something he was carrying.

'Is that my file?'

'Yes.'

'Does it say I've never been in love?'

'That's right.'

Taryn absorbed this. She didn't ask for her file or for insights into whatever else it might contain. She kept meekly following him, making sure the chain didn't tighten and hurt her—though this wasn't her body and couldn't be damaged. She bore that in mind, and otherwise just followed where he led.

It was in the nature of that country that you either found what you looked for, or conjured it. And if you found what you looked for, it wasn't what you hoped for. It was either a dream of a thing—like the trains—or a dreamcatcher, like the mudbrick building that housed a remembered hospital. Accordingly, sometime after it got light and the streets filled with the usual resolutely occupied people, the Muleskinner found a kind of bar—a dark room, dusty bottles on one wall, a mirror so smeared it was just glassy vagueness, a few customers perched on stools, the bar before them empty. Perhaps the place wasn't yet serving, or perhaps it never did. The air in the room had no scent—not even stale alcohol—and no promise of flavour.

The tavern had a garden bar. Tables and benches under a pergola covered in vines. The vines had died back for winter—or were dead. Taryn thought they were dormant. She had seen grass and trees in this country, so plants could grow. Perhaps there was a season when grass and vines flowered. There was water—there'd been a stream they crossed over. Water had been used to make the hospital's bricks. The tavern's rough-hewn timber furniture was real, like the hospital building. They were things like the enduring part of a coral reef, the hard honeycomb in which tendrilled animals lived. The reef animals being all the ghost stuff—remembered window glass, bedding, oxygen tanks, call buttons, railway lines, train carriages, train whistles, barstools, and bottles of liquor. Taryn wanted to ask the Muleskinner whether he'd brought any remembered money so they could buy a drink. It was tempting to talk back to his silence.

Men and their silences, Taryn thought. Shift told her so little that her sense of why it was worthwhile being there was as thin as she was. She wasn't even making anything with her thoughts—as the Muleskinner had. He'd dreamed up a lock and chain. Couldn't she at least dream up a key for the lock?

Taryn considered the man across the table. 'So,' she said. 'McFadden. Here we are, in a social setting. When the bar opens for business, we can hash out our differences over a drink.'

He didn't respond, only gazed at her.

Taryn waited for something expressive to happen. Maybe he'd weep tears of blood. 'If you wanted what we'd had, the connection of our conspiracy, or more than that, you would have *talked* to me,' she said. 'You act as if I wouldn't have listened to you when you called me, but it was you who wouldn't talk.'

'I was waiting for you to say my name.'

'Like a magic word? Perhaps you've been telling yourself that, but I know what you really wanted was to scare me.'

'Are you saying you don't have to listen to me now because I didn't approach you in the right way?' He was scornful.

'Essentially, yes,' Taryn said.

'You think very highly of yourself.'

'This isn't a matter of my thinking highly of myself. It's common politeness that when someone asks, "What do you want?" you make some attempt at a frank answer. If you want your needs met, you say what those needs are. But what you wanted was to scare me.'

He stared at her, sullen and thwarted. A small spirit seeking a large experience—that was what he was. Taryn leaned across the table and said, very deliberately, 'What have I to do with you? My time has not yet come.'

The chain around her neck unlocked itself, slithered off her shoulder and landed heavily on the bench behind her. She got up and didn't even check to see whether he would pursue her. She walked between the tables towards the back of the garden, as if she were off to look for a toilet.

The pergola climbed overhead, receding until it was the canopy of a forest, trees just coming into leaf, each branch a tile in a tessellated pattern. *Crown shyness*, Taryn thought, as she had when she saw it the first time.

The forest was smudged grey and filled with a deep, smothering silence. Taryn stood in that ghostly place for as long as she could stand it, and then turned around and went back the way she'd come. McFadden had gone. The chain was still lying half on and half off the seat. Taryn hoped that the chain was there to offer her the gesture of walking away from her old bond, as the Muleskinner apparently had. But nothing here was that designed. She could summon things that were meaningful to her, but there wasn't any meaning in the things themselves; the chain didn't know to stay there so she could leave it. Nothing was that tidy, and no soul stuck in this supremely suggestive and unhelpful place could feel its way out of its errors.

Taryn wandered all day. She made an effort to do what she should and kept her mother in mind at every street she chose to enter. She let her feet demonstrate her faith, and walked and walked.

At dusk she could walk no more, which is to say she sat down for a short space and then found herself unable to get up again. It wasn't weakness, but a lack of communication between her volition and her spirit's limbs. She had been too long away from her body.

She felt fairly calm about being stuck. After all, the souls around her were still going places, moving in an intent way, motivated by things they needed, to find places they thought would be better for them than where they were. Souls didn't die, so if hers was losing vitality wouldn't it just fade out of this world and return to where it belonged? That made sense. But then Taryn remembered the precautions they'd taken before they left, the careful ways in which their bodies had been arranged, the hair she'd sent her father, Petrus's instructions and injunctions.

She sat in a state of doubt, able only to wait for whatever would happen. She thought of all the times when there were things she might have done, acts she could have performed and hadn't. She had stuck to habits, like the habit of being careless with her father, the habit of giving her friends only what they asked for, habits of secrecy and solitariness, of 'good working relationships' and postponed connections. She was as bad as Shift, and if she ever saw him again, she'd ask him not what his plan was but why he wouldn't tell her what his plan was.

'I'm glad you've got rid of that chain.'

It wasn't dusk anymore, but night. Shift was standing before her, taking up too much space, his mantle all bristle and shine. The air was tepid and smelled of rain. The low clouds reflected the town lights—such as they were, a yellow like the electric lamps in a painting by Edward Hopper.

Shift pulled her to her feet. Her legs wouldn't support her. He held her upright and frowned into her face, disconcerted.

'I think I'm now reduced to a kind of poseable figure. So you had better figure out what pose you want me in.'

He laughed. It was the only laugh she'd heard all day, and all the night before, and all the day before that.

Shift picked her up. Bundled her under his mantle. The matter tapped and tickled her. It seemed very little reduced, as if he'd taken the time to pick up as much of what he'd dropped as he could.

'Being purposeful is the mistake people make here,' she said. 'And it seems you've got stuck on keeping yourself decently clothed.'

'My mother would always say that the dead have no new ideas,' he said. 'And decency isn't a thing I've considered before.'

'We're not dead. And you've formed habits.'

'Yes, Taryn.'

She glowered at him. He wasn't agreeing with her. He was acknowledging how like her this remark was. She could tell by his smile—which wasn't directed at her, because he was watching where he was going.

Taryn was too limp to nestle. She was a dead weight. But he carried her easily. She was a sylphlike eighteen-year-old who fitted the skirt with the geese.

'Where are we going?'

'I'm walking you about.'

This wasn't a reassuring answer. She had walked herself about all day and got nowhere.

The hardpacked ground, the mudbrick walls, the parched border-town look of the place seemed more real every minute, thickening around them as Taryn grew thinner. She felt she didn't have long left, to herself, as herself. He wouldn't be able to tell she was going—she wouldn't grow lighter; she'd just lose substance all of a sudden. She should say something. Something real. Maybe goodbye.

Now and then they passed a lighted window. All of the windows were well above their heads, set into walls between dark, enclosed court-yards. There were timber gates and wickerwork gates, all material, not imagined. Sometimes they caught the scent of the oil people were burning in their lamps—something faintly camphor.

'Wait,' Taryn said. 'Go back.'

Shift took several backward paces and raised his head to look where she was looking.

Taryn was peering at the top of a wall and a wedge of ceiling visible through the window of an upper room. The room was illuminated by more lamps than most. The roughcast surfaces had been whitewashed, and the wall was decorated in a muted palette—dark olive for the outlines of vines, leaves, and flowers, and the outlines filled in with dull but softer greens, some mustard yellows, greys, mushroom browns. The mural looked like a pattern on 1960s Scandinavian crockery.

Shift didn't ask Taryn what she wanted. He just pushed open the gate with his foot and crossed the courtyard, which was bare but not completely featureless. It contained a large rock, not meant as a seat, since it was set nowhere convenient. It had probably simply been enclosed when the courtyard was built.

Shift carried Taryn upstairs to a single, sizeable room. There, small against her frescoes, mixing paint, was Taryn's mother. Not her jaundiced dying mother, or ailing, parchment-pale mother, nor even the smartly dressed, nervy woman Taryn the teenager would often look at with irritation. No, this was the mother of Taryn's childhood—slender, her red hair short on the sides and long on top, wearing a too-big shirt, sleeves rolled up, and cotton tights, baggy at the knees.

Shift kicked a battered cushion to Addy Cornick's feet—moving her worktable out of the way with one hip. He put Taryn down on the cushion and leaned her against her mother's legs.

Addy Cornick thanked Shift politely, put down her palette and brush, and placed her paint-freckled hand on Taryn's cheek. 'So good of you to visit me,' she said, and her daughter heard in that one sentence all the things she'd forgotten: the manor house, the private school, the riding lessons—everything short of a debut, since Addy came of age in the late seventies and wouldn't have had a bar of that old nonsense. Taryn heard and saw the poise, the breeding, the signs of class she'd never really noticed in her grandfather, and which Kiwi Ruth never demonstrated.

'Adelaide Cornick of the Northovers,' Shift said, in formal greeting. He rested his hand momentarily on Taryn's hair, then left her with her mother.

'How thoughtful that you came.' Addy Cornick's reiteration of her gratitude said a great deal. Taryn now understood how little her mother had expected of anyone in the final years of her life.

'But, dear, I would have thought you'd done better for yourself,' Addy said.

Taryn didn't want to say she was only in Purgatory temporarily. All its permanent residents had let themselves or others down, and it seemed irrevocable. Anyway, anything she said would sound like an excuse. Like the remark offered by Ruth Northover's friend when she introduced her daughter to Taryn in a café in Whitianga. 'Justine is only here for a visit. She lives in San Francisco.' Justine, a crab who had climbed out of the bucket of crabs. Taryn had nodded but felt a kind of baffled pain. She'd just spent an hour sitting on the stone pier on the far side of the harbour mouth, lulled by the sound the water made pulling and purling against the structure as the tide turned; listening to the water and dropping deeper into the self that didn't need to make decisions. No one with the option to walk to that pier every day needed excuses made for them.

Taryn didn't tell her mother she wasn't stuck in Purgatory. She just said, 'Ma, I'm satisfied with what I have.'

'I often am too,' Addy said, and looked around at her handiwork. 'Honestly, Taryn, if this wasn't difficult I wouldn't enjoy it. It's such a challenge to find pigments. I don't like to roam too far—you know how the roads and trains can carry you away with no guarantee they'll bring you back again?'

'I noticed,' Taryn said.

'I've made do with what I can source locally. But I have recruited a few people to bring back anything they imagine might work. That's how I acquired that almost yellow.' Addy pointed at the washed-out ochre trefoil flowers on the painted vine that reached the top of the wall and crept across the ceiling.

'How do you get up that high?'

'I put a chair on a table. There's no one here to scold me. And I've taken no harm on the occasions I have fallen off.' She stroked Taryn's hair. 'You could help me mix paint if your arms worked.'

'They don't.'

'That must have been dreadful for you when you were alive. Was it like your uncle Taylor and his motor neurone disease?'

Taryn barely remembered Taylor—a non-familial 'uncle', and her godfather. She was eight when he died. She remembered only his wheelchair and cyborg-like array of tubes.

'This paralysis happened since I arrived.'

'Well, dear, that means it *didn't* happen,' Addy said sternly. 'It's only your mind imposing on your soul.'

Taryn asked her mother to tell her about Taylor. 'My memories of Taylor are sketchy. How did you meet? What did he do? How long was he sick before he died?'

As Addy told Taylor's story, it began to rain. Taryn gazed at the sparks of silver dropping past the window and the sill darkening as the rain seeped inside. There were flowers painted under the window, piles of loose and battered blossom. Taryn saw they'd been designed to look as if the seepage had washed them down to collect against the floor. This made the mural less purely decorative than a 1960s Scandinavian crockery pattern.

But of course that wasn't what it really reminded Taryn of. Really it was Moominmamma's painted garden in the lighthouse. The one Moominmamma vanished into, leaving her handbag sitting on a kitchen chair.

Addy broke off to remark, of the rain, 'That's good. I was just about out of water.' Then she asked whether Taryn minded if she finished this batch of paint. 'It'll be a waste if I don't get it on the wall.'

'That's fine.'

'You can talk to me as I work,' Addy said.

Taryn's mother had always put whatever she was doing aside as soon as her daughters walked in the door. Daughters, or husband. She gave them her undivided attention. It drove Taryn crazy. She had never been able to see where Addy had got the habit. Addy's parents were always busy. Ruth tended to leave the vetting at her practice, but she always had a book on the go and wouldn't look up from it if she was at a vital part. And James Northover was involved with local committees, his Historical Society projects, and bookmen all over the British Isles. He busied himself ineffectually with the farm, and hopefully with the rewilding group he joined late in life. Addy's habit of abandoning herself to pay attention to others had often looked to her daughter like a mute demand: *I'm paying attention to you, so you must pay attention to me.*

And there she was, with her back to Taryn, dabbing moss green paint on a wall.

The rain had stopped. The dripping and gurgling gradually quieted down, and the night seemed to fall asleep. The lamplight steadied. Addy worked on.

Taryn wondered whether she should catch her mother up on news. Talk about Grandma Ruth, how she had gone back to New Zealand to be near her sisters. Or she could say, 'Dad is so famous these days that it's very odd going anywhere with him. When I was in hospital recently, I swear the whole nursing staff stopped by to gawp at him. And—Ma— that whole business with the saltwater crocodile was always going to be the big news of its cycle, but with Basil Cornick's daughter the author Taryn Cornick involved it was everywhere. Writ large!'

Where to start?

Taryn didn't offer news. Instead she thought of more questions. Her mother was responding cogently. Telling stories. Expanding on things.

She had metabolised her friend Taylor's death long before she had died herself. *That* she could talk about. There were other things Taryn wanted to hear about. Her mother's miserable year at Girton. Her months-long trip around India in a battered Jeep with friends. Tents. Scorpions. Trains. Tiffins. How her friend Toby kept going barefoot and picked up hookworms.

Taryn knew that if she mentioned Basil or Beatrice her mother's flow of talk would break up, like phone reception in a tunnel under a river.

Taryn listened and responded with the right gentle urging interest and kept thinking, dazed, *It's Ma's voice. This is a story I haven't heard. Or it's one told differently—to an adult listener.*

She slumped against her mother's chair, watching Addy sidelong; Taryn herself was utterly inert and largely silent, but her head was singing. *This is her, her voice, her stories, her mural, her work she has found to do, her new idea, which the dead are said not to have, or an old idea, Moominmamma's garden, which made her cry from her own unhappiness, an idea renewed and now making her happy, or content, since in this dry, dim, directionless country, happiness might be impossible.*

Addy Cornick was now telling Taryn how she and Wally—another friend whose name Taryn had scarcely deigned to notice before—had prised the globe in the library out of its cradle and rolled it down the lawn into the lake.

Taryn remembered the story, then the library. She let her mother finish—'Well, of course Wally was never invited back'—and said, 'Ma?'

'Yes?'

'I believe you helped Grandad, before he died, figure out who Grandma might sell his books to?'

'I did. It wasn't going to happen until he was gone. He didn't want to see the sale of his books. He was very clear on that.'

'Once he was gone, did the sales go according to his plans?'

'More or less, as I remember. He knew who had made inquiries about various items. He made a list for me, and I just had to contact people and ask if they were still interested. It was a few weeks' work. Phoning around and comparing offers, because there were usually several interested parties, and your grandfather wanted to get as much as he could from the library, for your grandma.'

Taryn waited for more. Addy was talking as she had been, comfortable, and with some spirit, and Taryn thought it better not to interrupt.

'He carefully set aside a few gifts for his antiquarian friends. Like that globe Wally and I nearly ruined. It went, as I recall, to Jack Small in Liverpool. Mr Small had always admired the globe because it had trade routes. Do you remember? Sugar and spices, porcelain and so forth—everything but slavery. That was the glaring absence.'

The glaring absence wasn't something Taryn had noticed about the globe. Glaring absences were a sense people didn't tend to get until adulthood—if ever.

'Ma, do you remember an old scroll box? Very old. Maybe fourth century?'

'You mean the Firestarter,' Addy said, and continued, her wrist cocked with an orchestra conductor's expressiveness, to dab her tiny vine leaves on the wall.

'Yes, the Firestarter,' Taryn said.

'I don't recall ever asking its age. It was very old. If memory serves I'd say its decoration was late Romano-British. It was quite badly charred. I tried picking it up once. It lurched in my arms because there was something heavy sliding around inside it. It didn't feel like paper. It felt like another box inside the first one.'

Taryn's hearing was doing something strange, as if the pressure in the room kept changing. She could take in everything she was being told, but the fact that she was still alive was having some effect on her experience of hearing about the Firestarter. Taryn wished Shift had not left them alone. It was considerate of him, but beside the point.

'Did Grandad sell the Firestarter?' Taryn asked—though she already knew no such sale was recorded in the papers she had from Ruth.

'Heavens, no!' Addy said. 'It wasn't his to sell. He wasn't ever easy in his mind about it. I remember him telling me that he'd written a number of times, over a number of years—whenever he remembered he had the bloody thing—to its owners, the British Museum. You see, they'd left the Firestarter behind in the caves after the war. Along with steel shelving and sandbags. Your grandfather said he didn't find it until he went into the caves to store clover seed after the roof of the feed barn caved in. That would be 1953, the year he met your grandma.'

The feed-barn roof had been caved in for Taryn's entire childhood, the mildew-spotted tarpaulin covering the hole needing readjustment after every storm.

'He'd write to the British Museum and not get an answer, and between times the thing slipped his mind. It wasn't as if curators were coming from London and waving admonishing fingers at him.'

'What happened to it?'

Addy paused and put down her brush. She wiped her hands and stepped back to examine the effects of the latest plant. 'There were quite a few things your grandad packed up himself. With personal notes. Everything intended for his bookmen friends. The books or items they'd admired or that he thought they'd like. And there were one or two large crated consignments of books, like his whole set of Gibbon. The Firestarter would have gone among those, probably.'

'And those aren't on the record of sales, because they weren't sold.'

'That's right, they were gifts. The packages were all addressed and ready to go. He made sure of that. All I had to do was ship them.'

'How many packages, more or less?'

'At least a dozen. Your grandfather had warm friendships with book-men all around Britain.' Addy picked up her palette and knelt on the floor to resume painting.

'But, Ma, if the Firestarter wasn't Grandad's to sell, it wasn't his to give away either.'

'That's true,' Addy mused. 'But I don't remember shipping anything to the British Museum.'

There was a long silence. A moth flew in the window and began to circle the chimney of the lamp. Taryn stared at it, mesmerised. There was something novel about this very ordinary apparition.

'Also, he hated it,' Addy said. 'It's rather strange to think about it now. How uncomfortable he was about having the care of that box. I suppose I didn't think too much about that at the time, because he seemed to be so good at putting it out of his mind.'

Taryn tore her eyes away from the circling moth and stared at her mother's back. 'Would he have given something he hated to any of his friends?'

'No,' Addy said. 'That doesn't seem likely.'

The moth found its way into the chimney and disappeared with a hiss in a wisp of black smoke. The flame flared and wavered and showed up more moths fluttering around the room. It was as if the shadows had clotted.

Taryn's mother laughed. It made Taryn jump. 'He might have given it to someone he *didn't* like,' Addy said. 'Do you remember that detestable fellow in Tintern who was always trying to buy your grandfather's treasures? Dad used to say: "That man is like a bloody seagull at a beach picnic."' Addy put on a deep, plummy voice to imitate the detestable fellow. '"You're keeping them all out of circulation, James!" The man was harmless, really, and if he hadn't been practically on our doorstep Dad probably would have had a perfectly cordial relationship with him. It was a case of familiarity breeding contempt.'

Taryn did remember then how her grandfather disliked the antiquarian in Tintern. She said, 'Do you think Grandad gave the Firestarter to that man?'

'Ross Belkin,' Addy said. 'Esquire. I don't know, Taryn. But your grandfather didn't like either of them—Belkin or the Firestarter.'

Taryn wanted to move. To make some gesture. To get up and embrace her mother. But she stayed slumped and watched the night come inside in fluttering fragments. After a while, something else came into the room. She had been able to smell the wet, but now she could smell foliage and flowers.

Her mother noticed. The hand holding the brush sank slowly until its bristles were dabbing the floorboards. 'The things you remember,' Addy said, in a tone of soft wonder. Then she got up, went to the window, and leaned out. She stayed that way, her body quite still, her head swivelling slowly this way and that. When she turned back to the room her face was glowing with joy. She came to Taryn and hoisted her to her feet. She dragged her to the door and down the stairs.

Halfway down—galvanised by the shame of having her small, ill mother supporting her—Taryn's toes and heels found the steps. Her ankles and knees locked, then their hinges began to work, and she was walking.

At the foot of the stairs Addy released Taryn and hurried out into the courtyard. Taryn followed her into a damp night garden.

A small singing frog on the tree by the door stopped chirping and shuffled around the far side of the trunk. The walls were dripping with vines. There was a fur of moss on the large stone, thickest and greenest around the pool of water in the hollow on its top. There were soft herbs underfoot, and flowers everywhere. Something was humming in a high corner on the far wall, in the shelter of the lintel above the gate. Taryn knew where Shift had got the bees but couldn't think how he'd managed to restore them to life. She didn't know how the vines were so thick, or the trees so tall, or how the frogspawn had hatched into tadpoles then grown to frogs overnight. The seeds and spawn had been dormant. But the bees had been dead. How could they be alive?

Shift was standing in the middle of it all, completely naked, his dark skin slick and shining with rain, his hair plastered to his head and shoulders.

Addy wandered enchanted around the garden. She glanced at Shift. 'It'll have to rain often enough to keep this alive.'

'It will.'

'How? How?' Taryn demanded. 'What *is* this? Is this a *reward?*' She was so astonished it felt like fury—as if the miracle were something she had to fight.

'I think it might one day be a gate,' he said. 'Given time. And other things even time can't provide.'

'We don't have time,' Taryn said.

'I don't,' he agreed. 'But let's just see.'

'It'll do nicely just as a garden,' Addy said. Then, 'Thank you.'

Shift smiled at her, then said to Taryn, 'Do we have any leads on the Firestarter?'

'The Firestarter wasn't Grandad's to sell, and he wouldn't encumber anyone he liked with it, since he hated it, so he might've sent it to someone he really didn't like. The man who still runs the antiquarian bookshop in Tintern qualifies.'

'But why do you want that thing?' Addy said, puzzled. 'No one ever seemed to want it.'

'It's mine,' Shift said. 'I'm going to sell it.'

'Are you from the British Museum?' Addy said, pointedly looking him up and down. Then she added, 'It's so hard to tell with people here where they're from and whether they are respectable.'

'Ma!' Taryn said, amused and embarrassed.

'But, dear, he clearly doesn't belong here.'

Taryn went to her mother and hugged her. 'No. And we have to go.'

'Everyone is going to want to come and look at my garden.'

'Give them seeds or cuttings and send them off,' Shift said. 'Tell them the Little God of the Marshlands says they should grow their own gardens.'

'That's good,' Addy said. 'People here respect gods.'

They left at dawn, just as the browsing bees were crawling out of their hive, resting on its doorstep, and tapping their feelers. Shift pulled the wicker gate shut behind them. He picked up Taryn and walked towards the river—a vague downhill.

Two streets away from Taryn's mother's house there was no sign that it had rained—and perhaps it hadn't rained anywhere but in that street.

Thirty

Neve's Story

Visible beyond the few trees around Hell's Gate were the thick bamboo poles and pennants Taryn had seen at the Moot. The poles were now painted white, and flying streamers in the colours of the ladies and gentlemen—as it seemed everyone but Taryn had learned to call them.

Petrus hung back by the gate. He was being passed along to the Human Colony through the relay of gates that swivelled to meet one another: Princes, Hell's, Senisteingh Mouth. He remained by the gate to wait for his ride, but also to avoid what surrounded each snapping banner.

The grave mounds were already covered in wildflowers, not cut but growing. The same flowers Taryn had admired when she was last in this grassland. She had thought nothing of the flowers heaped to the horizon so that the view was coloured all the way to the sunlit slopes of faraway hills. The flank of that range was now mauve with some sun-loving, late-summer plant. Against the soft colour the white poles and streamers burned.

Shift stopped walking. Taryn turned back and tried, as she kept trying, with variable success, to read his face, his body. Shift had found Neve among the mounds. It was Neve he aimed to speak to. They'd interrupted Petrus's homecoming to seek her here—administering the aftermath of the Tithe. Taryn had lost track of time and so had forgotten that the Tithe was why Neve might be sought here.

Shift continued walking; Taryn fell in behind him.

The graves grouped around Neve's colours numbered around thirty. They were beside a bigger grouping, a hundred or more, under Shift's colours. Taryn saw Jane, Henriette, Susan, and several other women sitting, apart from one another, at the heads of a handful of those mounds.

Taryn saw what had happened. She grabbed Shift's arm. 'Don't kill her,' she said.

He glanced at her, his eyes calm and pacific. This wasn't enough of a refutation of murderous intent for Taryn, and she kept hold of his arm again until they were among the graves and she couldn't walk beside him without putting her feet places she shouldn't.

Jane ran at Shift. She was howling. She beat her fists on his chest. He put his arms up to block her blows but didn't evade her or catch her hands.

'Where were you?' Jane shouted. 'Why didn't you protect us? Why didn't you believe your aunt when she said they meant to use us to make up their numbers?'

Neve came over to them, and Jane, in her rage, turned and attacked her too.

Furrows streaked through the meadow to Neve's feet, parting the grass and even uprooting some of the flowers, as a half dozen invisible Hands rushed to her aid. These knots of twisted air fastened onto Jane's arms and ankles and hauled her off.

Neve said to Jane, 'Be careful. You have your life.'

'What do I care? I'm not like you, heartless and self-centred and able to stomach mass murder.' Jane turned back to Shift, her face polished by tears. 'Your aunt came to our island and asked us to choose who would go.'

'So that you could keep your leaders and more productive members,' Neve said. 'Or whom you most loved, which is the usual form.'

'We refused to choose,' Jane said. 'Then, when they came to take us, some of us volunteered to go instead.'

'We didn't take anyone who made that offer,' Neve said, as if explaining a reasonable and possibly even admirable act.

'They wouldn't let us accompany the people they took. They sank our ferry. Those who were able swam across the lake to follow on foot. Of course the sidhe had horses. We only reached the gate just in time to help bury the bodies of our friends.'

There were thousands upon thousands of fresh graves. The older mounds—further from the gate—had lower profiles and fewer flowers. The new ones were high and freshly planted, with flower seeds coaxed into full, flourishing life by some kind of sidhe magic, perhaps the same kind that had raised Addy Cornick's courtyard garden.

Jane's friends had joined her, their faces tearstained and tight with fury. They faced Shift and put their backs to Neve.

Neve shrugged and walked off.

Shift called out after her, 'It's you I'm here to see.'

'Make your peace with your women,' Neve called back.

Shift touched Jane's arm. Jane jerked it away. He looked at her levelly, then followed Neve.

'Sorry,' Taryn said to Jane. 'I was always getting lost. It was me who kept him away so long.'

There was some truth in this, but essentially Taryn was lying for Shift, to make peace.

Jane shook her head. 'He's putting us behind him. In preparation for his forgetting. He's put your friend Jacob from his mind. And one day soon he'll do the same to you.'

'Sorry,' Taryn said again, and hurried after Shift.

She caught up in time to hear Neve telling him that her remaining people loved her too much to carry on in that way. 'They mourn with dignity and composure and without violent reproaches. I don't know why you don't make more effort to manage your people properly.'

'Never mind about that,' Shift said.

This got Neve's attention. She gave him a wary, assessing look. 'Oh, come on!' She was suddenly impatient. 'You're all talk. So start talking. Tell me off so that I can explain why handing over a hundred of your women is better for you than my withdrawing my patronage. Because, believe me, if one thing or the other didn't happen, you'd be in danger.'

'Let us walk out from among these graves,' Shift said. He led the way, and Neve and Taryn followed. The graves were so close together that they had to go single file. Picking her way through them reminded Taryn of a game she and Bea would play on flagstone paths and plazas, walking on the cracks instead of avoiding them, which was the traditional game of 'Step on a crack and marry a rat'. Bea had walked a zigzag tightrope across various public spaces, shouting, 'Bring on the rats!'— her little sister bumbling after her.

'Bring on the rats,' Taryn muttered to herself until they were through the patchwork of blooming grave mounds and out onto the meadow proper, where the flowers were thinner, no doubt hundreds of wind-blown generations from plants first propagated by these gracefully mourning murderers.

Shift led them to a shade tree near a ring of fire-blackened stones. Neve folded her legs under her and floated gracefully to the ground like a ballerina. Taryn found a seat a little further off and discovered that the rumpled dirt under her was a large piece of fabric. She got up again, carried it downwind and shook the dirt off it. It was a formerly white waffle cotton blanket, stamped 'St Stephens Hospital'. Taryn folded it, carried it back to her spot, and used it as a cushion.

'Taryn Cornick of the Northovers,' Neve said, finally acknowledging Taryn in her usual formal manner.

'Valravn. Hero of understanding,' Shift said. This apparently was the title Taryn had earned, and Shift was informing his aunt.

'Neve, daughter of the last Gatemaker, and last of the Nine Queens,' Taryn attempted. She was sure there was more, and that she hadn't got the phrasing right.

Neve inclined her head graciously.

Shift said, 'Neve. I need you to tell me the story you haven't told me.'

'It is my understanding that the stories you have people keep for you are meant to remind you of yourself, your acts, your errors, your losses and gains. My story might only help you to understand me, your mother, and your grandmother. It isn't really about you.'

'Please tell it,' he said, 'even if it pains you.'

'It's very late in your life for this,' Neve said.

'This is something I should already know.'

Neve sighed. 'You were always a problem,' she said. 'Blameless, and a problem.'

He nodded.

'I'll be brief,' Neve said.

'The Gatemaker was never grasping about love. Her one unshakeable desire was to replace herself for her people. When she was a child there were still some of them alive, the exiles, the settlers, the people who carved the hub, a world between other worlds, out of territory stolen from those worlds, and tied together by gates. Not only had the exiles made every gate, but some of them even carried personal gates, a defensive weapon as much as anything else. That knowledge hadn't wholly disappeared. But it was never like the learning of a magician, like the mastery of a Petrus Alamire or a forgetful Merlin. It was innate, experiential, like your shifting.

'A body can teach another body how things work, but only sometimes. No one can watch a gate made. There's nothing to see. The exiles had many years of life left and, having made a home for their people, they didn't see the necessity of passing on the mastery they had never enjoyed, since they had earned it fighting for their lives. They'd lost loved ones and given things up. They'd made terrible decisions for a better future. They were the parents who wanted their children and grandchildren to have easier lives. In order to do that, they'd had to accept harsh conditions. There were terms to the exile. The Land of the Pact is called that not because of the Tithe, as many assume, but because of those conditions.

'Everything the exiles were allowed to take with them to use—water and microbes, seeds, eggs, animals, rhizomes—everything they needed to make the Sidh had been altered so that while it could multiply, the sidhe could not. The flourishing world would put limits on sidhe lives; not their duration, but their ability to reproduce. Anyone of our kind, or enough like our kind—like humans—would flourish in the Sidh, but the longer they lived, drinking the water, eating the fruit, the less able to reproduce they'd become. That was the bargain the exiles made to be able to leave and make a new place to live. They'd accepted those terms and counted themselves lucky. For their descendants, it was different. It defied the imagination. The imagination of our bodies. When you are young and you love someone, you often think the feeling will translate into a child. And of course, at first, there were children. My mother was the granddaughter of an exile, and I am my mother's child. My mother's expectations were met. But very few of her generation had children, even those who tried to have children with humans.

'My much younger half-human sister was my mother's only other child. I was childless, so Adhan served also as my child. My sister, and a child I helped to raise.

'Your grandmother had tried to make a gatemaker of me. She had carried me in utero through every gate and spent time inside the gates, which is not an easy thing to do. You spent several hours in that watery place inside Princes Gate, learning the trapped dragons, before setting them free. You don't remember it, but Kernow can remind you of what you told him about surviving inside a gate.'

'Princes Gate was water to water then,' Shift said. 'I can be amphibious, but not at the same time as learning how to be a dragon. Kernow knows the story, but my body remembers.'

'Which is why you're better with the glove than I am,' Neve said. 'Your body-memory.

'Mother dedicated years to Adhan's education, trying to make a gatemaker of her too. It didn't work with either of us.

'Because Mother both loved and respected Adhan's father, Shahen, she let him go back to his earthly life. Shahen had been a slave, but his Roman master was so delighted to see him again that he freed Shahen and employed him as an honoured musician and maker of musical instruments. Shahen took a wife in late middle-age and fathered another daughter and son—Hestia and Marcus. Those children met their half-sister, Adhan, and our mother, and me. They grew up understanding that their family had powerful protectors. But when their time of need arrived, we, the powerful protectors, were very busy trying to secure our own safety. We were being inventive and energetic—and inattentive. And we didn't understand that we were in a fight for our lives.

'Sidhe were often abroad on Earth at that time, and it was easy for a human who could get themselves recognised by a lady or gentleman to have a message carried to one of us. Marcus's message was an appointed place and time where he'd be waiting with Hestia's youngest child, a baby boy. The child was one too many dependents now that Hestia had died and Marcus was moving his family, his wife, their children, and his dead sister's older children to the big settlement on the Thames. He thought we might like to raise the youngest.

'I met Marcus and took charge of the baby, Emesa. I wanted a baby. My sister had just given birth, and we thought it would be a happy thing to raise children together. Hestia's boy was Adhan's nephew, and, through her blood, my kin. He looked like Adhan. He looked like Adhan's infant son—only more human.

'Adhan at that time had a house in a dip between bluffs beside the Wye, across from a small marshland in an elbow of that river. There was a pontoon bridge from one bank to the other, and so she had, in easy reach, all the fruits of the forest and marsh, fish and eels and birds' eggs, mushrooms and hazelnuts. The pontoon bridge was not a structure that would disappear in a flood—and indeed it remained in place for another two hundred years, and that bend in the Wye was known as Prince's Bridge for a long time after it was gone. The bridge was bolted onto the rock with great chains. It was made of non-ferrous metal, copper, zinc, titanium. It was made by your father, Shift. Adhan had accepted his gift. She'd accepted his love, but she wouldn't leave her river or her marsh. Our mother had made a gate—her last—and put it right there, a quarter-mile from the house, up on the ridge where a horse track ran on from the Roman Road. The place where St Cynog later erected his cross. That was the place the gate swung back to then. Now it swings to the lake that was a brook, where the first Baron Northover built a manor house in the reign of the first Stuart king.

'Prince's Gate was made for your father, the Prince. It is the only gate to the Sidh that will admit anyone fully godly. That's why I live near it. I'm guarding it. Prince's Gate was made illicitly, because the godly were to be excluded from the Sidh. We'd been at war with the godly already, after your father's people enslaved Hell and decided that they'd rather not accept their banishment from Heaven and their task of punishing human souls, that instead they'd much rather retake the Sidh, the land we stole from the demons. Angels weren't able to come through Hell's Gate, but demons were. Demons were, because we had rounded them up from the territory we took and herded them through the gate into their remaining territory. The vulnerability of Hell's Gate was our ancestors' shortsighted expedience. Demons could pass through the gate, so the rulers of Hell sent armies of them against us. We couldn't bribe our attackers by welcoming them and giving them refuge. For a start, the Sidh was no longer salubrious to them. As far as they were concerned, we had spoiled it. Also, they were attacking under the compulsion of that language, the Language of Command, invented by the Great God of the Deserts and given to all his servant angels, so still retained by the exiled rulers of Hell.'

'Yes, a language!' Taryn choked out.

Neve looked astonished and incensed.

'Sorry,' Taryn said. 'Please go on.'

Shift said, 'Tell Taryn how the sidhe won that battle.'

'We didn't win. We made a treaty. The only term of which was the Tithe. The angels who ruled Hell had no respect for the lives of demons, and they had those lives in infinite supply. And they had absolute control of them. We had to sue for peace and pay a price. It is interesting that subsequent generations of demons seem to have more resistance to that language. The compulsion needs more frequent reinforcement. That's the enviable resilience of any natural order: that creatures can *breed themselves* out of weakness, bad memories, bad faith. Taryn, your people say "churn" when you want to describe how stories that matter are buried by more stories that might matter less. But nature is stability *and* flux. What flows and shifts and breeds is a glory.'

This is a tragedy, Taryn thought. *The tragedy of a people that was the tragedy of a family, and of one person, the woman telling the story.*

Neve continued. 'My mother made the Prince's Gate so that your father and mother could easily retreat into the Sidh. Your mother already had her glove. Adhan couldn't use a gate without one. We sidhe can go through any gate, but not call them, or carry them, as a gate-maker can. With the glove those borne through many gates in the womb can move gates. I can, you can, Adhan could.

'But the proximity of the gate to Adhan's house wasn't enough for our mother. She decided to make another glove for your father, so that he could come to Adhan's side and aid as quickly as possible. It was a challenge—a glove for someone with no sidhe blood—and she went to work not knowing whether she'd succeed. She worked carefully, but with a sense of urgency, because, although Hell wasn't at war anymore, your father was still in some danger from his heavenly brothers. Because of you—*"the beast that was, and is not, and yet is."* Because of the prophecy about a son of that father. That hateful prophecy belonging to the horrible *plan* of the God of the Deserts.

'We all thought it would be enough to retreat to the Sidh. Your grandmother was confident that her people could fight off any attackers, could defend that vulnerable gate. For a start, the angels were too grand to carry iron weapons. And, for another thing, three of the exiles were still out of their tombs, carrying around personal gates and able to displace attackers. You and I can do that with the glove if we're able to call a gate. They could do it willy-nilly, anywhere. And even creatures who can fly are greatly inconvenienced by being transported hundreds of miles out to sea.

'We weren't sure there was any danger from Heaven. Your father had a son, so surely Heaven would be happy that its prophecy about the end of days was closer to fulfilment. It was our idea that they could think what they liked, if it gave us time to find a way to circumvent the prophecy. After all, why should the world end just because that great monster from the void, the God of the Deserts, said it should? Personally I think that God was mad before his later worshippers drove him mad. He was already splitting, already a God who promised an afterlife and a God who didn't.

'We of the Sidh respect the forms and contracts of stories more than anyone, but we believed that particular story would change. We were people who'd made a world and how could people who have made a world have any hope of understanding those whose aim is to destroy one? We only knew one angel. He'd been that God's servant and soldier, but not his *believer*. We couldn't imagine the minds of the believers. We thought the prophecy would be rescinded since this particular son of the devil was so unsuitable for the prophecy.

'And you were unsuitable. You were a problem. Not sidhe, not human, not angelic. You were an abomination to your father's kind and a thorn in our hearts.

'We were so close, Adhan and I, that when you were born and she was nursing you, I began to produce milk. I nursed you too. It was a thing that seemed loving and wise. We all wanted you to be, as much as possible, a son of the Sidh. Your father did too. He said that his was a servant's birthright. Being the grandson of a gatemaker was a far finer inheritance.

'I nursed you, and it was a very happy thing that I had milk for Hestia's baby boy, Emesa. Hestia had wanted him named for the city where her father, Shahen, was born—Emesa, the home of the Hittites.

'We were a household. Adhan, myself, you, Emesa. Your father and grandmother came and went. We were all happy. Before you were walking, when it was summer, Adhan and I would spend our time by the river—either side of it—bathing, foraging, sunning ourselves, sleeping beside each other, playing with you both, singing, playing word games, gazing into your lovely faces. We were safe, and happy, and free.

'And then my sister lost her freedom. You began to shift. Humans don't shift. The sidhe don't. Angels certainly do not. Gods shift, but only a few of them.

'Adhan would spend her days and nights walking through the marsh and forest, and up and down the river, calling your name—your baby name, Gwy, after the river. What we called you before we chose a name to describe you. All day and night Adhan would be walking, weeping from her eyes and her breasts. Sometimes she'd find you and you'd be a fox kit suckling with other kits at the teat of a vixen in her set. You'd be the slow worm you'd found on the grass while you were playing—and the slow worm didn't need to suckle. You began hiding yourself before you could even speak. I tried to help Adhan, but Emesa couldn't be dragged all over the place, at all hours, especially as the days became cooler. So my sister was often alone. I would put Emesa down for the night and hear Adhan out on the marsh, calling and crying.

'The obvious solution was for your father to give up his half-hearted governorship of Hell and spend all his time with his family. He would have done so earlier, but his presence had been noticed by local people— the prince in his mantle of smoke—and a powerful holy man had heard about it and had already visited our house with his holy books, and iron-shod sandals, and other things offensive to us.

'My mother finished your father's glove and gave it to us, then sent word to your father to come and take possession of it. With the glove he'd be able to swing Hell's Gate to meet Prince's Gate and be with us instantly. He'd have freedom of movement, and his freedom would be a blessing to all of us.

'The appointed time arrived during the week of the Tithe. I had given up all of my people. It didn't feel like a terrible personal sacrifice because I had Emesa, and I didn't need lovers or beguiled children. I didn't need anyone beguiled. But the pain and shame of letting my people go were the same as ever, and I was feeling angry with your father for managing to secure his freedom and his family's safety before trying, while he still had any influence, to argue his followers out of their strict adherence to the terms of our treaty.

'So. The day came, and you had slipped away in fish the night before while your mother was trying to wash your muddy little legs. Adhan was out looking for you. I tied Emesa to my back with a shawl and set off up the hill to the gate, with the new glove, in a bad mood, and bad grace.

'I was almost at the gate when the angels attacked. They came down out of the air, out of the sun and clouds. One stooped on me and drove his sword through my back, below my left shoulder blade, and pinned me face down to the rock. The sword went right through Emesa too, as it had been aimed. I listened to my child crying and gasping and gurgling as he vomited blood. I felt his struggles, and the heat flooding out of him. I wasn't able to reach the hilt, because the sword was jammed right into the red sandstone. And I couldn't force myself up without causing my child more pain.

'Emesa was still alive and moving when your father arrived. He threw himself over us and tried to pull the sword out. He defended us with his body, instead of doing battle with them. If he had stayed airborne he might have lived. He and I would have survived. But he died. He pulled the sword out and freed us while they cut him to pieces.

'And I mean that literally. They used their swords like cleavers on his back and legs. They cut his head from his body. Then they lifted his body off me and carried it to a clear piece of ground and cut it up, jointed it, boned it. They cut his torso into two sections between his ribs and hips. And while doing that another of them pulled Emesa from my arms, shook him hard to make sure he was dead, then dropped his body back onto me. That same one picked up the glove that had fallen from my hands—and out of my reach—when the sword went through me. He fastened it around his throat by its pin and chain and flew with the others back into the sun, back into the clouds.'

Neve adjusted one hip so that she could reach behind her. She pulled her sword from its shoulder scabbard and laid it across her knees. 'And this is the sword. The sword of an angel, the only sword that wasn't used to kill your father. The sword that I gave to your chosen king. The sword that cannot be broken. The sword that demons fear. The sword that killed my child.'

Neve gazed at the sword. She said quietly, 'We've always talked about this. But my always isn't your always. You only ever give me two hundred years at a time.' She laughed. 'Which will seem more than long enough to Taryn. But Taryn has to try to understand what your life is like, and it might help if she understands a bit about mine.'

Taryn was crying from pity. No one said, *Don't cry, Taryn*. No one ever said, *Don't cry, Taryn*.

'After that, Adhan and I took our dead and buried them. I took to my bed to let my wound heal. And Adhan stopped crying and calling for you. Instead she just sat down in the place she supposed you might be and said, to the reeds and the water, "Shall I tell you a story?" She told stories about wise kings and brave heroes. She read from books. And one day there you were, standing behind her on your fat little legs, trying to turn the pages with your wet fingers.

'Your grandmother wore herself out trying to make her family safe. Then your mother wore herself out with study—trying to write down everything she had learned from your father and using that knowledge to make a spell to conceal you, the most powerful spell she ever cast. It took all her magic and most of her vitality. It brought on her illness, so that she was gone by the time you were twelve, when she should have had at least a thousand years of life.

'I saw very little of her in her last years. I didn't understand that she was mortally ill, not simply exhausted. I stayed away. She had her child, but mine was gone. The God of the Deserts had sent his angels to kill you, and Emesa died instead. They were looking for a sidhe woman with a child running to meet their enemy.'

Neve sat quiet for a time, then went on, speaking softly. 'I wish I'd visited my sister. I wish I'd known when she died. I wish I'd taken my orphaned nephew in hand before he decided that solving what seemed to be his most pressing problem meant he should make a bargain with a Norn and get himself turned into an old man. I lost you. I didn't find you again until I recognised the old man asleep in an oak. It was'—Neve shook her head—'very confusing. You always have been a challenge to sidhe sense, and human sense.'

She looked up at Shift and blushed, very faintly. 'Which might be why it's taken me this long to work out that, though those angels came out of the clouds and sun, they hadn't come from Heaven. They were your father's followers. Of course they were. They must've wanted to thwart the prophecy by killing you. They were buying themselves more time, suspending the promise of their permanent exile. I know this now

545

because when that smoky demon wrapped itself around you and carried you through Hell's Gate, and I tried to go after you, I could feel the gate blocked to me. I could feel the seesawing balance of that contest. I remembered the glove intended for your father. And I decided that some mysteriously capable demon—and you have to wonder about its ancestry—was using that glove.'

Thirty-One

Tintern

Jacob didn't want to stir himself. When Aeng left the bed, he put his head under the covers, inhaled Aeng's clean smell, nestled into the island of warmth their bodies had made, and relaxed into the *enough* of it—enough of life, enough for now. He stretched until his tendons cracked. Nothing hurt. He ran his checking hands over the jut of his hipbones, the trenches of his Adonis belt, the hard quilting of his abdominal muscles, satisfied with himself, wrapped in Aeng's atmosphere, the moment, his own happy being.

But Aeng was telling him he must get up.

Neve had arrived in the night. Aeng hadn't thought it necessary to wake Jacob with the news. She was requesting Aeng's help. 'I told her I won't be separated from you. So you must make ready to come with me.'

Jacob emerged from the covers. He sat straight up, with no twinge in his back.

Aeng placed clothes on the end of their bed. Light woollen trousers, linen shirt, leather boots with proper structured soles.

'If you get up and bring those with you, I'll help you wash,' Aeng promised.

Jacob got up. He gathered the clothes and led the way to the water-fall, turning all the way around now and then to watch Aeng following him.

They washed, then got each other dirty, then washed again and stood in the sunlight on the open balcony of the cave and watched eagles fishing at the river's mouth. They put their clothes on and went to find breakfast—which always appeared as if by magic. Jacob never saw the people who prepared the food. No one dusted, swept, washed floors. Aeng's mendings performed those jobs. The people who washed their clothes and prepared and laid out their meals always retreated ahead of Aeng and Jacob, were always just gone from the room, so that it was just them in Quarry House, the lovers, in the comfort and seclusion of their lamplit rooms, with only the remote and tranquil company of the sunlit or moonlit sea below, in a paradise of privacy.

Jacob ate his sweet potato porridge and watched Neve. He recalled how her presence had once alarmed him, and how being unnerved had filled him with stubborn resistance to her beauty. Now he felt only a little shy, mostly because she was another person and, for weeks, he'd not spoken to anyone but his lover.

Neve was wearing the Gatemaker's glove around her neck. She had threaded its thong through the plate armour of its fingers so that they sat against her throat like a throttling hand.

If Neve had the glove, that must mean they were being asked to go somewhere far away from Quarry House, far away from the bedroom and the bed.

Aeng and Neve spoke together briefly in their own tongue; he apparently proposing something she found offensive, she objecting, he standing his ground. Then Aeng looked at Jacob and said to Neve, in English, in a tone of mild censure, 'But we must not exclude Jacob this way. After all, he's been asked for too.'

Neve turned to Jacob. 'If any of us is being monitored by demons, it's Taryn Cornick. I have therefore been asked to go to the place she believes the Firestarter is hidden, to look for it, while she remains at some distance. Taryn has suggested you assist me, Jacob, because you will know how to speak appropriately to the locals.'

Jacob nodded.

'If we find what we're looking for, we will arrange a meeting with the demons and make a bargain. Exchange the Firestarter for what we want.'

'Which is . . . ?' Aeng said.

'Better terms for the Tithe, of course. Fewer souls. More time between tributes.'

'How strange to be considering a renegotiation of the Tithe when the full price has only just been paid,' Aeng said. 'Couldn't you manage to be in time for the one just past? And, since you weren't, why not wait longer to negotiate? We are a hundred years away from the next Tithe.'

'It was poor timing,' Neve said. 'Only now do we have the opportunity to put our hands on the Firestarter. It's an elusive object whose existence we only learned about while trying to discover why demons were trespassing in the Sidh. We need to act while the trail is fresh and find the thing before the demons do.'

Aeng seemed satisfied by this. Jacob thought Aeng might ask more questions. But of course Aeng must know as much as he knew—because they were inseparable.

Neve returned her dark-eyed gaze to Jacob. 'Aeng is required to help us make a forcebeast.'

'Neve and I have always had well-matched energies,' Aeng said. 'She is almost as alive as I am.'

Neve continued as if Aeng hadn't spoken. Jacob's ears got hot. He was offended on Aeng's behalf by her blank rebuff of the warm teasing. Neve clearly hadn't any sense of humour.

'We need a forcebeast because it is wiser to have some protection when meeting with demons,' Neve added. She was all business.

'Have you not yet managed to parlay with the demons?' Aeng asked, still teasing in tone.

'I've tried,' she said. 'Twice.'

The plan seemed straightforward to Jacob, although it meant leaving his only refuge from pain. But if Aeng was going, Jacob must go with him. It was a simple decision. Why then did he feel there was some obscurity in the plan, a darker patch in the dazzling surface of a frozen river where the ice was thin?

Aeng popped a last slice of pawpaw in his mouth, licked his fingers, and shuffled around the low table to sit behind Jacob. He spread his palms on the small of Jacob's back and began to conjure Hands. 'These will be more preventative than remedial,' he assured Jacob. Then, to Neve, 'Jacob has virtually healed.'

'I'm sure Taryn Cornick will be relieved to see her friend has taken no lasting harm,' said Neve.

They passed through three gates in a relay. The final one disgorged them not into the lake in the grounds of Princes Gate but onto a broad path in a forest. Jacob stepped out of the ankle-deep drift of beech mast he'd fetched up in. And Aeng climbed off the top of a stacked stone ramp. Aeng had had his hand wrapped around the back of Jacob's neck, but for some reason, the final gate had separated them.

Jacob had no idea where he was, and no interest in asking.

Neve set off uphill ahead of them, her hair gleaming as she crossed patches of sunlight. After a time they reached a weathered sign. One arm pointed to Tintern—one kilometre below them, across the Wye. The other arms pointed along Offa's Dyke Path in the direction they'd come from and the one they were headed.

In a further few minutes they reached a limestone outcrop overlooking the river and the ruined abbey. Taryn was waiting for them, sitting in the sun, her legs folded beneath her. 'Jacob!' she cried, and scrambled up.

Beside Jacob, Aeng said to Neve, 'Please inform Taryn Cornick of my conditions.'

Neve nodded agreement.

Taryn picked her way across the canted rock. The Devil's Pulpit. The name came to Jacob.

Taryn jumped onto the path and embraced him. She smelled of sweat and laundry soap—not strongly, but humanly. Her touch encountered the invisible Hands, and her face clenched.

'The Hands are just in case,' Jacob said.

She didn't seem reassured. Her eyes kept searching his face, then glancing away. It almost looked as if she were waiting for the nearest tree to offer its opinion on Jacob's situation. She only gave up her strange miming when Neve took her arm, drew her aside, and leaned in to confide—what?—Aeng's conditions?

Jacob turned his attention to the view. He had never seen the abbey. It stood on the far side of the river below them. Its grass-floored broken rooms looked like livestock pens. Vaults and end walls rose above the green squares. It looked not like a remnant, but a planned thing, as if it had been built to be ruined.

'No!' Taryn burst out, loud and indignant.

Neve continued to speak, her words inaudible, her voice low and quelling.

Aeng came to stand beside Jacob. He said the village of Tintern Parva was a little further along the road. Could Jacob smell the diesel fumes from the tour buses?

'Do you remember the abbey when it was still intact?' Jacob asked.

'Yes. I often sat here in the evening listening to the plainchant.'

Taryn joined them. Her face was tight with tension and repressed anger. She said, 'We'll accompany you downhill, Jacob, and leave you this side of the river. Remember there are two bookshops. One sells rare and out-of-print editions of children's books. The one we want is a little further along, and smaller. My grandfather used to hurry me and Bea past Stella's so we wouldn't have time to spot a book we just had to have—and couldn't, since it'd be a first edition. And past the other shop so "that shabby fellow Belkin" wouldn't see Grandad and pop out to ask about books Grandad didn't want to sell.'

Aeng and Jacob just looked at her.

She sighed. 'But you don't know any of this,' she said.

'You could fill me in,' said Jacob.

'No, I couldn't, there's too much I'd have to leave out.' She glared at Aeng.

Aeng leaned close until his breath warmed Jacob's ear. He said, caressingly, 'Best, and most adored.'

Taryn made a strangled noise. The leaf shadows bent around the nearest tree as if the sun had twitched sideways in the sky. Jacob felt dizzy. He pressed against Aeng to remain upright and waited for everything to fall back into its natural and proper place.

Taryn said, 'Google Maps tells me that, at this time of year, the antiquarian bookshop closes at six. Even so, you should get on.'

Jacob steadied himself and climbed back off the Devil's Pulpit. He waited for Aeng, and they walked on, hip to hip in perfect step, as they were always able to.

Neve took the lead. Taryn walked alone between Neve and them.

Taryn was using Google Maps, so she must have her phone. She'd know things that might help Jacob feel a little less disoriented. He called out, 'What month is it, Taryn?'

'September,' she called back. 'Season of mist and mellow fruitfulness. And hurricanes, floods, and threats of annihilation.'

Jacob asked her what she meant.

'Hurricane after hurricane in the Caribbean. People waving their nukes at each other.'

'I don't live here anymore,' Jacob said.

'Yes, I can see that,' Taryn answered, and hurried to catch up with Neve.

Jacob was less disquieted by Taryn's digest of news than by the fact she was angry with him. Angry or disappointed. It gave him the queasy feeling he got when he'd misplaced something and forgotten what the something was—an anxious urge to search, the anxiety threatening to blow away any system of searching. It reminded him of when he was four and lost his mother in a supermarket car park. She was wheeling a laden trolley, and he had run ahead in the wrong direction, then he couldn't see her between the cars. He had howled for her, and she had appeared, out of breath, the trolley dragged clattering behind her.

Jacob felt like howling now. He had lost something. His human unease, perhaps. But why should a failure to feel uneasy be distressing to him? Something *else* was missing. He looked around, peering past the eclipsing cloud of Aeng's perfumed red curls.

Great trees, a flagstone-edged path, Neve and Taryn up ahead, and, behind, a sunlit green tunnel, which appeared somehow to be singing, like Aeng's remembered plainchant. A green prayer was pouring down after them, on either side of the path, its light surrounding an obscurity that refused to be illuminated.

Jacob faced forward again.

'Think of what you have to do, Jacob,' Aeng said. 'Shape your mind to it.'

'I believe I'm just here to fill in any gaps in plausibility while Neve dazzles the antiquarian.'

'Still,' said Aeng. And Jacob began obediently to think of the task ahead of him rather than the puzzle behind.

Neve and Jacob left the others at the forest edge and walked to the road and over the bridge. The Wye was summer-shallow and full of waving waterweed.

Neve didn't speak to Jacob, not even to discuss what their strategy should be. He eventually asked, 'Have we already decided how we do this?'

'You are to provide the civilities. I'm to make sure he's motivated to help us.'

'Taryn is angry with me.'

'That isn't a thing we can discuss.'

'Fine,' said Jacob. 'I don't really care.'

'"Really" is the only salient word in that sentence,' Neve answered. Jacob couldn't imagine what she was getting at.

'Gwy,' Neve said, 'Gwy is the name of this river.' She said it, then looked both sad and satisfied.

I'll never understand the sidhe, Jacob thought, then realised that this wasn't right since he understood Aeng and was more in sympathy with him than he had ever been with anyone. 'So,' he said, 'you and Aeng are going to make a forcebeast to protect us in a meeting with demons?'

'It's good to see you taking an interest, Jacob. However, two sidhe cannot make a forcebeast.' Her look was cool, full of contempt it seemed he'd earned by being human.

'All right. I misunderstood,' he said. 'Has no one thought to enlist the ravens?'

Neve turned left along the high street. The footpath was narrow beside the houses. The great wall of a bus glided by, so close Jacob imagined himself being flattened. Once the bus had gone Neve replied, 'We're hoping the sisters will turn up. We can't summon them without maybe also summoning the god. Odin is best left out of this. We're not sure what his intentions are. He's not himself these days. His head has been turned by many new worshippers. Of the wrong kind.'

Jacob thought about that for a bit. The wrong worshippers for Odin. 'You mean white supremacists with valknuts tattooed on their man boobs?'

'I do,' she said. 'Your wits seem intact in some matters.'

The high street was a channel. The stone walls across the road banked up steep gardens reached by steps beyond trellised arches covered in climbing roses. The shops commenced a little further along the road. Jacob spotted the one with big windows full of bright book covers. 'I feel I need to further my education,' he told Neve, 'about how gods can be changed by the nature of their worshippers.'

'You were enrolled in a good school. You dropped out. But we are not to speak of that.'

'But you are speaking of it. And neither of us is carrying a cloned phone.'

'I'm carrying every promise I ever made,' Neve said. 'And I can scarcely support the weight of those I broke.'

Taryn had been using her cloned phone. To look up the closing time of the bookshop and read about hurricanes. Taryn's phone was a worry.

She wouldn't want the police turning up. And Jacob didn't want Price to appear. He didn't want his former life to. And then it did, like a blister on his thoughts. His ID left behind in the hospital. His unlovable apartment. His bank account. His parents. Hemms. Not broken promises, but neglected duties.

Jacob swore and stopped walking. Neve came back, came close, and the hot air radiating off the stone houses got between their bodies and made some kind of bond. Neve gripped his chin with her bony fingertips and shook him. 'Don't let me down,' she said.

Jacob saw she was no longer wearing the Gatemaker's glove. 'Where's the glove?' he asked, anxious.

'You know where,' she said, her eyes oil-bright and oil-hot. Then she said it again, 'Don't let me down.' She released him, checked for traffic, and crossed the road.

He followed her.

A bell above the shop door announced their entry. The shop smelled of camphor wood and Morocco leather. The shelves were as high as the low ceiling permitted. The space between them was wide enough for one person, but not two. Anyone tall would have to squat with their legs at an angle to read the spines of the books on the bottom shelves. The only clear spaces were behind the narrow counter, and directly before it, where there was an Oriental rug, a small table with a round top, and a single chair.

A voice from the back said, 'I'll be with you in just a minute.'

'What is this man's name?' Jacob whispered.

'Ross Belkin.'

When he emerged from behind a curtain, Ross Belkin was younger than Jacob had anticipated. He'd imagined an old man, a near contemporary of Taryn's grandfather. This man was fiftyish, a drinker, his cheeks and nose covered with a net of spore-like red veins. His eyes were blue and bloodshot.

The man only glanced at Jacob, and then he couldn't take his eyes off Neve. This was a little disconcerting, and Jacob realised that whenever Hemms and he had gone together to ask questions, most of the men they interviewed had directed their answers to him. All of the usual prejudices about whom to take seriously went out the window with Neve. Neve was royalty. She was a tiger—you watched her.

'Ross Belkin?' Jacob said.

'No. Sorry. My uncle is off on his holidays. I'm Jason Battle.'

The name clearly meant nothing to Neve, who hadn't been there when Taryn told that story. But this was James Northover's secretary, the local young man who had read history at Oxford, the man who had come closer than any other to smoking out the Firestarter.

Jacob gripped Neve's arm. He said something to Battle about browsing and hauled Neve off between the shelves. It wasn't easy to move her; she was slighter than Jacob but much stronger.

She planted her feet, her face almost against his, her eyes blazing. 'How dare you manhandle me!'

'That's James Northover's secretary,' Jacob said. 'He was possessed by a demon and set fire to Princes Gate's library, trying to find the Firestarter. This was when Taryn was a ten-year-old.'

'You don't imagine he's still possessed?' Neve said. 'Demoniacs die of their possessions.'

'Repossessed?' Jacob suggested, and glanced at Battle, who was still gazing at Neve. 'Anyway, the Firestarter will have very bad associations for him.'

'He might not remember anything,' Neve said. 'Humans seem terribly susceptible to forgetting some of their most important encounters. And he isn't possessed. If he was, I'd be able to see it.'

Jacob accepted that. 'I think we need Taryn. I think I should fetch her while you keep Battle occupied.'

'*Taryn* might be distressing for him,' Neve said. She put both her hands on Jacob to steady him. 'We don't need Taryn. We'll just approach Battle in an honest fashion and hope he remembers nothing about his ordeal.' She squeezed Jacob's arms. 'Follow my lead.'

Neve sauntered back to the counter, no doubt beaming. Battle's expression as she approached was rapt and tremulous. Jacob followed Neve and peered at Battle for any sign of another entity. He had heard it described—two souls in one body. He'd seen it in Taryn when her demon fastened on to her again in Norfolk—a poisonous calculation in her eyes. He remembered the look but, for some reason, not the events around what he'd seen. Who else had been there? Wasn't someone else there? Not the entity inside Taryn, but someone else. His mind strained against forgetfulness as if forgetfulness were physical, and its mist a barrier to movement as well as visibility.

'Good afternoon,' Neve said to Battle. 'My friend may be content to browse, but I'm here with something in mind.'

'How can I help you, Ms . . . ?'

'Gatewatch,' said Neve. 'Neve Gatewatch.'

'Ms Gatewatch—how may I be of assistance?'

'I am looking for an antique box. The sort of thing in which one might store a scroll.'

'A half-cylinder scroll case?'

'Something a bit wider and deeper in its dimensions, but yes, long enough to hold a manuscript on its spindle.'

'I can but look. My uncle keeps some things below decks, as it were.

But if I go downstairs I'm afraid I'll have to lock the shop. You won't mind?'

'With us in or out?' Jacob said.

'That's entirely your preference, sir.'

'May I come with you to your uncle's storeroom?' Neve asked sweetly. 'I do love an Aladdin's cave.'

Battle blushed, and beads of sweat popped out on his forehead, so large and so rapid in their appearance that Jacob expected them to be accompanied by some kind of sound effect.

'If you like,' Battle said. He lifted the hinged countertop, and Neve slipped through. Battle did a little dance out of her way and came through the gap himself to lock the door. 'I do apologise for appearing untrusting,' he said to Jacob. 'But my uncle has me under strict instructions.'

'So am I just now,' Neve said confidingly. 'And I might say "under strict instructions" is a very odd place for me to find myself.'

'Then you're not shopping for yourself?'

'I'm not a collector.'

'Except of people,' Jacob muttered. Battle was close enough to hear and looked at first alarmed, then eager. He hurried back behind the counter, dropped the leaf, and made obsequious motions to let Neve know she should proceed ahead of him. They went through the curtain.

Jacob stood where he'd been left. He was aware of his reflection in a security mirror opposite the counter, his stretched, silvered figure against the bamboo forest of book spines. Neve and Battle had passed beyond his hearing. What he could hear was the air brakes of a bus turning into the visitor centre at the abbey, and hooting laughter from the terrace of the pub across the road.

Jacob waited.

Fifteen minutes later he heard cries of protest, thumps, objects knocked over. Before Jacob could lift the flap and hurry to investigate, Jason Battle staggered back through the curtain. The man was sobbing and nursing one hand, which Jacob saw had a broken thumb. Battle dived behind the counter and emerged with a phone in his good hand. Jacob lunged forward and slammed his hand over Battle's and pushed the phone flat on the counter. He leaned all his weight on the hand and pinned Battle in place.

Somewhere behind the curtain came the sound of a window breaking—a bright smash and tinkle of falling glass. The atmosphere stirred; sun-warmed air flowed out of the shop and cool air breezed in, with smoke on its breath.

Neve came through the curtain. She was holding a fire extinguisher. Its seal was broken. It was armed, but Neve had taken it from Battle before he was able to use it—breaking his thumb in the process.

'What the hell have you done?'

'Expedited matters.'

Jacob leaned right across the counter, flung one arm behind Battle's back and hauled him across its surface. The invisible Hands bracing his spine hardened completely to help him. Jacob felt no pain, no weakness. He pulled Battle hard against his body and clapped a hand over the man's mouth. 'We have to get out of here,' he said. 'And we have to take him with us.'

'We can come back later to rake over the ashes,' Neve said.

'How is this going to help?' Jacob shouted. 'The ashes might be hot for days. And the crime scene will be crawling with firefighters and fire inspectors and insurance investigators and police. And sooner or later the antiquarian uncle. I'm here for my local knowledge. *That* is all "local knowledge".'

'The Firestarter is merely charred after its passage through many fires over many centuries. Its seals will hold.'

'And that's the only problem you can foresee?'

'The only one that might matter.'

'And how will the heat not ruin what's inside the box?'

'It won't,' Neve said, with blunt certainty. 'It's not possible. Come on, Jacob, we can decamp for now. If the box is here, let the fire find it for us.'

'Right,' Jacob said. Then to Battle, 'You will go with us quietly or I will break your neck.'

Neve fished in a pocket of her soft peach-coloured linen overdress and produced a cape gooseberry. Its lacy paper casing was split and crumpled, but the dark gold fruit within was perfect. She held the berry up to Battle's eyes. 'You will eat this,' she said. Then to Jacob, 'Please uncover his mouth.'

Jacob did so.

Neve broke the berry out of its sheath, asked Battle to open wide, and popped it into his mouth. Then she leaned against him, so that the man's faintly musty body was pressed between her and Jacob. She stroked Battle's sparse hair, his cheek, his neck, all the while examining him on the flavour of the berry. 'More perfume than any other fruit,' she said. 'Do you like it?'

'Yes,' Battle answered, his voice mushy.

'Are you refreshed by it?'

'Yes.'

'Are you nourished by it?'

'Yes, thank you.'

'Will you come along with me now?'

'Yes.'

She took Battle's hand and led him to the door. He stood stupidly for a moment, then, prompted, unlocked the door. The three of them emerged onto the street.

Jacob's desire to run was urgent, but his training stood him in good stead; that, Neve's brazenness, and Battle's bewitchment. They sauntered back the way they'd come, crossed the road, and were all the way to the bridge before the fire was discovered.

'That shop shared its end walls with two other buildings,' Jacob said. 'People could get hurt.'

'It's broad daylight. The village is full of sightseers. The houses are so squat that their windows are less than twenty feet from the ground.'

'So you class it as a calculated risk?' Jacob said, unconvinced.

B y the time they rejoined the others on Offa's Dyke Path the fire engines had arrived and were blocking Tintern Parva's narrow high street. A clatter of high-pressure water hitting slate roofs, and the roar of the pumping appliances were audible all the way across the river. Smoke rose above the trees.

Taryn ran to meet them. 'What have you done?'

'Neve did it,' Jacob said.

Neve leaned Battle against the tree, as stiff as a ladder until the trance relented and permitted him to sit. Neve kept her hand on him.

Aeng said mildly that he failed to see how destroying what they were trying to find would gain them anything. 'But I suspect I don't have the whole story.'

'What about the books?' Taryn shouted. 'Precious, irreplaceable books!'

'Jacob was concerned for the occupants of adjacent houses,' Neve said, in a censorious way.

Taryn began to cry. 'I rode the rails in Purgatory for this,' she said. 'I never wanted to be party to book burning. I hate you people. You don't have souls.'

'Souls may be endemic to this part of the universe,' Aeng said, 'but so are flies. Flies far out at sea. Flies on mountaintops.'

Taryn drew her sleeves up over her fists and dabbed her eyes. Then she properly looked at Battle, and blinked.

'It's Jason Battle,' Jacob said.

Taryn shot Battle a look of horror and walked away. She separated herself from them and went to sit in a deep patch of shade just off the path. She seemed to gather a length of shadow around her, like a shawl.

Neve gave Battle two more cape gooseberries, a mother doling out sweets to keep a child quiet.

'We will need a forcebeast to turn over the burnt brands,' Aeng said to Neve. 'We should sequester ourselves in the forest and make one.'

Neve raised her voice to ask, 'Did you sleep?'

There was no response to her question. She didn't seem to be asking Aeng, and Jacob couldn't see why Neve would want to know whether Taryn had slept. Besides, Taryn wasn't about to be coaxed out of her sulk.

Neve acted as if she'd had an answer. She nodded again. 'All right.'

'Your fire really took,' Aeng said, in a congratulatory way.

'There was a bottle of methylated spirits under the sink in the shop's little kitchen. Battle didn't even notice me pick it up. I pulled books out of the storeroom shelves and stood them on their ears so the fire could get right into them.'

'Ears?'

'Legs,' Neve said. 'I don't really know all the words for parts of books.' She returned her attention to Battle and took his face between her hands. 'Come a little way into the forest with me. I'll find a nice dry mossy place for you to lie down and perhaps have a little sleep.'

Jacob was left with the sulking Taryn. Her personal shade had retreated, as if the sun were hurrying down the sky. Eventually she joined him on the Devil's Pulpit, and they watched the fire, the smoke become steam, then the steam diminish. The windows in the shop proper were broken, but the upper floor of the building and its roof were still intact, and the houses beside it unharmed.

The visitor centre at the abbey had closed, but cars remained in the car park. Jacob assumed people were being waived a late fee since the fire had jammed up the traffic. They'd had to stick around. Jacob could see that the terraces of the café and pub were crowded.

They had to climb back off their vantage point whenever sightseers arrived and wanted to take photos, of the fire or of themselves with the view. Jacob even obliged some of them by taking a photo for them. Whenever they were displaced, Taryn would walk a little way downhill. It seemed she didn't have anything to say to him.

The light mellowed and turned gold. The trickle of hikers dried up, and the sixth time Jacob and Taryn returned to the roost he asked her if she had any idea how long it took to make a forcebeast.

'What I know about forcebeasts is that it takes three or more sidhe to make one. Three is the lower limit, and those individuals must be very strong. And I know the makers have to stay awake to keep the beast in existence. Forcebeasts are an emergency measure. They're heavy machinery, or weapons.'

'There aren't three sidhe here.'

Taryn looked at him, solemn. Her eyes were a little sunken, a little bruised. 'Oh, Jacob,' she said sadly.

He went back to watching the fire appliances. They were detaching their hoses from the fire plugs and restoring the yellow-painted metal plates that covered them. Taryn said, 'Tell me what you know about Aeng.'

Jacob did willingly. Eagerly. After all, Aeng was his favourite topic, the matter uppermost in his mind. First he sang Aeng's praises—his beauty, his tenderness and grace. His unfailing interest. How he was always wholly present, whether passionate or companionable. How he looked while he slept. The colour of his hair by moonlight. Jacob told Taryn how Aeng lived in Quarry House in the summer, and in the winter had a number of residences, some of them hunting camps. There were some sidhe who loved to hunt. It was practical—kept them supplied with dried white meat—but that wasn't the purpose of it. They hunted to cull animals whose populations weren't quite managed by the predators at the top of the food chain. Rightly the sidhe should be at the top of the food chain, but owing to their dietary restrictions, they didn't eat whole classes of herd animals. Culling was practical, but Aeng and his fellows hunted for the thrill of the chase. They stalked their prey on foot or pursued it on horseback. Some had eagles trained to bring down deer or even wolves. They hunted in the high mountain passes for the white foxes and wolves and rabbits whose fur was prized. They walked or rode horses or travelled by boat between gates, and used the gates to go far and wide. 'You know that, don't you? How they all use the gates, though only the glove can swing them around?'

'The glove and who?' Taryn asked. She was trembling.

Her question puzzled Jacob.

'I promised Neve,' Taryn said. 'She made me promise.'

'No one can compel a promise, Taryn. There's persuasion and extortion, and the latter isn't much different from knocking someone on the head and locking them in a room.'

'Or chaining them to a tractor tyre with the tide rising,' said Taryn. 'But there's other kinds of compulsion.'

'There are better choices,' Jacob said. 'Can't you see how happy I am?'

Taryn dropped her head until her hair hid her face.

'By the end of autumn I'll be hardy enough to join Aeng in his winter hunting. He says it'll be an occupation equal to my nerve and suited to all my skills.'

'What a flatterer he is.'

'It's honest praise, Taryn. We are incapable of honest praise.'

'We humans?'

'We British. We can't offer straightforward compliments on anything of substance. We operate on the meanest band of enthusiasm and—if we're of *your* class—remind people that too much fervour is vulgar. While my class just josh people out of their enthusiasms, make mock, burst the bubble of anybody giving themselves airs—anyone who has made a bubble just to be able to breathe.'

'Okay,' Taryn said. 'I actually agree with most of that.' She looked a little happier. Pleased he'd lost his temper. She put a hand on his arm, not to placate him but because she was about to be serious.

'Your plans with Aeng sound—well—they sound like a life. Like a future. But they make me think of the afterword in movies based on real events. The paragraph or two that appear to tell you what happened afterwards. How so-and-so lived many years, or emigrated to Australia, or invented this or that, or won the Nobel Prize, or finally saw justice in the next millennium. What came to pass. Your plans remind me of all that's left to say when the story is over.'

'Oh, you mean *this* is the story?' Jacob gestured around him. 'Are you saying I don't care about finding the bloody Firestarter? I do. And I think we will find it. Then there is an afterwards, and I mean mine to be fulfilling. You can't seriously expect me to go back to London, my apartment, the CID?—who wouldn't have me anyway, the constantly absent Jacob Berger.'

'You said it.' Taryn began to cry.

Jacob watched her, feeling helpless and guilty. He told her she was overtaxed. He'd seen this before. 'You mentioned Purgatory. That must have been tough. And you were at the Moot.'

'*You* were at the Moot.'

Jacob had a moment of bafflement. Another moment of bafflement. He remembered being at the Moot, on the beach, nestled in cushions and bolsters in the shade of a silk awning. He remembered the residual heat in the sand, the soft evening breeze on his face, and Aeng's proprietorial hand sometimes cupping the back of his neck, sometimes resting on his thigh. He'd been stupefied by the aftermath of lovemaking, the cessation of pain, Petrus's tincture of opium, all of it washing and backwashing from his brain to his muscles. He remembered the long negotiations in the language of which he still had only fragments. People sang and played musical instruments. People like him. Petrus floated candles and crystals and mirrors in the air. Jacob lay back, and Aeng gently wiped a soft palm down his face, closing his eyes.

Jacob stared at Taryn. Her face was dim—the sun had gone down and, though the September sky was still a crucible melting light of different colours and densities, the forest was dark. It was as if they were standing in a cool shadowy interior and the Devil's Pulpit was a window.

Jacob glanced away at the lights of the emergency vehicles splashing the stone walls of the narrow village on the terrace by the river. He could still feel Aeng's palm passing down his face, but what he remembered as a caress and a release came to him as a terrible draining away. It was similar to the feeling he'd had when McFadden slashed him the second time, after he and Taryn had dragged and lifted and rolled that tractor tyre for hours, when they were in sight of safety and suddenly found themselves in danger again. It was the same sensation. Jacob felt his life leaving him. Or his afterlife.

'Taryn,' he said, 'am I under a spell?'

She nodded. She looked hopeful and sympathetic. 'It's very strong.' She was trying to tell him he must not feel ashamed about it.

'What kind of spell?'

'I'm not sure. A glamour of some sort. One that's altering the appearance of reality in a very precise way. It's piggybacking on another spell that is much stronger, but similar.'

'Is it Aeng?'

'I promised not to tell.'

'I doubt you've promised anyone whom you owe more than you owe me.'

'True,' she said. Then she looked away and noticed something that caused her to jolt, then freeze. He looked too and saw the bright beams of flashlights coming along Offa's Dyke Path. He didn't imagine they were day walkers any more than Taryn did. He seized her hand and hurried her into the forest. They crashed through ferns and barked their ankles on tree roots. Jacob pulled Taryn down into a thick pile of leaves in the hollow between the roots of a giant beech tree. They stifled their panting to listen.

There was something in the voices, the urging, repetitious tone of everything that was audible. Jacob thought, *Police dog handlers, encouraging their dogs.*

It was a tranquil dusk; the ground between the trees was obscure, the tree trunks black on grey. There would be enough light for a little while for him and Taryn to make their way. But the dog handlers had torches.

'Where exactly are they?' Jacob asked. 'Aeng and Neve.'

'Christ,' Taryn said, in rage and frustration. 'I would have thought that you, having eyes only for Aeng, took note of which direction he went. Anyway, is it wise to disturb them?'

'Is it wise to let ourselves be apprehended?'

Taryn snatched her hand out of Jacob's grasp. She hissed, 'Honestly, I don't think it makes much difference.' She stood and waded out of the sink of dead leaves and went towards the lights. Or not exactly towards. The angle she took might bring her to the path along Offa's Dyke before she was intercepted by the dogs. She didn't hurry, wasn't furtive, just careful of her footing.

A moment passed, then Jacob saw Taryn's body outlined by light, the halo of her red hair. She'd lit up the torch on her phone. She directed its light at the ground and walked faster.

Jacob jumped up and sprinted after her. He got to her the same time as the most eager of the dogs, which was nose down and hauling with its shoulders as if trying to climb out of its harness. Of course the dog was still on its lead, since its handler wouldn't release it until he'd made an identification, or someone was foolish enough to flee before them.

Taryn came to a halt and tucked her hands into her armpits. 'Hey,' she said to the handler. 'You better keep a hold of him.'

Jacob called out, 'Taryn! Are you okay?' All anxious boyfriend. He bustled up and put himself between her and the dog. 'Go easy, okay?' he said to the dog handler.

The second handler arrived, followed by two constables. They were all wearing stab-proof vests and carrying heavy-duty torches. Jacob enviously eyed their boots. He'd rather not be wearing his hard-heeled sidhe walking boots, and the man farthest from him seemed to have the right-sized feet.

An officer asked them where they'd come from.

'This morning? Chepstow. Our friends were supposed to join us at the Rose and Crown in Tintern, but they say there's a traffic delay. Instead we're going to meet them at the brewery in Brockweir. But that's a further forty-minute hike, and I'm the only one with a torch.' Taryn waved her phone. Excited by this gesture, the nearest dog lunged and dragged its handler several staggering steps forward. Taryn stepped back. 'Hey, boy,' she said to the dog.

'You're travelling light,' said a constable.

'We've eaten our sandwiches.'

Not too glib, thought Jacob.

'And you are?' The man produced a small spiral-bound notebook.

'Taryn Cornick. This is Jacob Berger.'

The man asked for some ID. The other one spoke into his radio.

'I have my passport,' Taryn said. She fished an oilcloth pouch from her felt bag, opened it, and produced her passport, which was inspected.

One of the handlers responded to some urgency from his dog and let it lead him back through the fringe of the forest—where it discovered Battle, asleep under a tree. The handler called out, and the man with the notebook went over.

After a few minutes they managed to wake Battle, who cried out like a lost child. The constable spoke soothingly to him. In a minute Battle would offer his name and his relationship to the antiquarian bookshop in Tintern. *What can I do?* Jacob thought.

The radio clipped on the vest of the constable still with them coughed and began with questions and information. Before whoever was talking had got far, the officer shot Taryn and Jacob a galvanised glance, swapped a meaningful look with the dog handler who'd stayed by them, and went a short way off to listen to his brief without being overheard.

Battle was speaking now between sniffles, spilling everything.

Taryn took Jacob's hand.

The handler told his dog to sit. It sat. 'Don't worry about the time,' the handler said. 'Someone can light you down to our vehicles and run you to the Kingstone in Brockweir.'

Jacob's shoulders kept wanting to twitch upwards. He made an effort to relax. It must have worked because the dog put its ears forward and its tongue out.

'That would be kind of you,' Taryn said to the handler.

The man with the notebook joined the one on the radio. Jacob heard him report that the man on the ground was the antiquarian bookshop owner's nephew, who was in the shop when the fire started. 'He's not very helpful on how he got up here.'

The one with the radio still had his hand on the call switch, his elbow cocked upwards. He was waiting on something further.

I'm a missing person, Jacob thought.

The radio came alive; the voice on the other end rose and surged with excitement. The officer asked a few questions, then came back to Jacob and Taryn.

'You're the couple who were attacked at Scolt Head,' he said. 'When everyone saw the crocodile.'

'That's right,' Taryn said. '*I* saw the crocodile.'

'I'm told you took yourselves off before satisfying all inquiries.'

'I've had my phone with me the whole time.' Taryn waved it again.

'Is there an inquiry?' Jacob said—foolishly, before realising that the degree of naivety he was putting on was completely out of character with who the police knew him to be. If he had to play a part, he must play *himself.*

'You weren't supposed to be mobile, sir.' The officer looked Jacob up and down.

The other dog handler joined in. 'That was some crocodile. I saw it on YouTube.'

His dog's head abruptly snapped around. It rose to its feet and slowly dropped its nose to the ground, its eyes on the forest. Its shoulders sharpened inside round bristling bosses of raised hair. The hair on the ridge of its spine stood up. It laid its ears back, bared its teeth, and began to growl.

The other dog was doing the same, while also stepping sideways to edge away from its handler and closer to its canine companion. Its handler was remonstrating with it. The dog glanced at him, twitched back to duty, its job, its loyalties—but only for a second. For the rest of the time it trod stiffly sideways until it was as close to the other dog as it could get.

Something was moving through the forest. A rustling, crackling progress coming their way.

The police turned the beams of their torches on the trees.

The dogs simultaneously stopped growling and creeping backwards, and lunged out to the end of their leads, barking madly, drool dropping from their wholly bared black gums.

There was nothing at all to see until it emerged from the trees above the path, on the raised wall of King Offa's Dyke. A green branch ten feet up the trunk of an oak bent forward then whipped back as if it had been held and then released. Dead leaves billowed up and stayed suspended in the air within the thing that ploughed, and sometimes bounced, and sometimes floated, towards them all. Heavy and weightless, leaves and bark spinning in turbulence near its surface, its centre clear like a lens through which the two beautiful people following it appeared, pale and graceful; Neve with her long caramel-coloured hair, and Aeng, his curls the colour of blood in the dusk, his many rings scintillating in the beams of the police torches.

The dogs broke and fled, one pulling the lead from its handler's grip, the other practically airborne at the end of its harness until it rounded on its handler and bit his arm. The man let go.

The dogs ran straight down the hill. By the sounds, one went over the bluff, while the other doubled back to the path and continued to run silently, as fast and far as it could go.

The forcebeast spilled onto the path. It stopped, rocking in the six-foot-wide depression it made in the ground, a depression filled with tree roots, the soil brushed off them and tamped down around them by a pressure so finely calibrated that it cleaned the roots as it pressed the soil.

'Get their radios,' Jacob said.

Aeng made a gesture at the beast, which floated forward, leaves rolling inside it, and seized the police by the radios clipped to their vests. It closed tiny, inexorable fists around each radio and crushed it, then pulled away, bearing a collection of shattered black plastic and bent circuit boards.

Neve helped Battle to his feet. She fed him another few cape gooseberries, letting his wet lips linger on her slender fingertips.

'Taryn, you should ditch that phone,' Jacob said.

Taryn looked at her phone, then threw it in the direction of the river. It clipped the edge of the Devil's Pulpit and spun out of sight.

Neve joined them, leading Battle, his hand in hers.

'Sorry,' Jacob said to the police, who stood frozen, or crouched cowering, their legs refusing to let them straighten up.

'Best to put these men up a tree,' Aeng said. 'A tall tree.'

Neve made a gesture—this one more complicated than Aeng's.

The forcebeast drifted forward and seemed to lick the men. Their turned cheeks flattened, their clothes were pushed up, shirts coming loose from belts, trousers raised to expose vulnerable ankles above their boot tops. The forcebeast first wiped the men upward, then lifted them into the air. It left the ground with all four men. They struggled furiously until, twenty feet up, two of them managed to calm themselves, or at least decide that, at this height, passive acceptance might be the better option.

They floated out of sight above the crowns of the nearer trees.

Jacob knew when the forcebeast had left the police, because the men immediately began to shout for help—from a place some distance off and upwards.

Neve said to Taryn, 'The beast doesn't have to wait for the ashes to cool.'

To Jacob's surprise, Taryn seemed near to tears. 'I was going to call my friends and my father when all this was over. Now you've given me things I can't explain.'

'You'll have to rethink your plans,' Neve said.

Aeng picked up one of the dropped torches. 'Let us be quick, before the loose dogs or the men in the trees attract notice.' Then, 'Jacob, Taryn, it is safer for you behind the beast.' He came right up to Jacob, held him close, and kissed him.

Aeng's mouth tasted of blue borage honey and the ozone of a fresh rainfall. 'Soon you'll be able to sleep in my arms. Even if I must remain awake for as long as we need this beast.'

Jacob closed his eyes and leaned his face against Aeng's neck. He felt his own body grow steady and calm.

Aeng kissed him once more, a lingering gentle kiss, then walked ahead.

They came across the bridge into Tintern, Aeng and Neve flanking the beast, which had no more or less forest matter roiling inside it. From thirty feet behind it, where Jacob walked, it looked like a strangely sustained dust devil. Jacob kept trying to find its top—its *head*—but the thing seemed to have no agreed-upon dimensions or form. Jacob thought he'd worked out where it ended. Then as they crossed the bridge it brushed a streetlight high on its pole, cracking the plastic casing around the lamp and causing the light to arc, with a jolt of blue electricity.

In the village Neve kept to the narrow footpath while Aeng walked on the far side of the road, where there was no footpath. The forcebeast made its way along the stone channel of Tintern's high street, flipping the hanging signs as it went. It plucked the petals from the white climbing roses on an arched gate and carried them off. The petals quickly grew transparent, crushed, as if the barometric pressure inside the forcebeast exceeded even that in a decompression chamber set to its highest atmosphere. The beast crushed the white out of the petals, made them wet, and rolled them into a mass, as if it hated flowers.

The side of the beast slapping the signs so that they spun on their poles was Neve's; the side crushing the colour out of the flowers was Aeng's.

The fire appliances had gone. The road was open, but the traffic was very sparse, no doubt discouraged by the problems earlier. The one car that came along the road drove into the beast and was upended, turned to lie on its roof, and dragged a little way along the road as the beast shook itself free. Jacob crouched to check on the driver, who was hanging in his seat belt looking astonished. His airbag hadn't even deployed. Jacob helped the man out of his car and sat him down on the kerb, out of the way of any further traffic. Then he hurried to catch up with the others. When he reached Taryn, she was asking a question. 'Was the whirlwind that raised the River Monnow during the forest fire a forcebeast?'

Jacob said, 'I have no idea what you're talking about.'

Taryn shook her head at him. No one answered her question.

They reached the antiquarian bookshop. The already narrow road was halved by a cordon of heavy plastic interlocking barriers. The cordon blocked off the small gabled house. The bookshop's door and lovely mullioned windows had gone, replaced by sheets of hardboard. The stonework around the door was stained by a flaring corona of soot.

Aeng raised his hand and pushed the air.

The beast parted the barrier. It made a gap three sections wide. Enough for it to stand in. The hardboard on the door creaked, cracked, then exploded inwards.

A little way down the road, headlights and the blue-and-white bars on a police vehicle lit up. The police car bumped down off the high kerb, where it had been parked, and rolled the short distance to stop beside them.

Aeng and Neve dropped into a crouch. They were making small motions with their hands, as if parting long grass. They looked poised and preoccupied and, lit up by the headlights, they resembled people performing a dance on a stage.

Soot billowed out of the doorway as the greatly compressed forcebeast pushed its way into the shop. It passed all the way in, sucking an ash-filled bubble of itself after it.

Three officers emerged from the car and stood staring at the crouching figures, who seemed oblivious to their presence.

'What the hell are you people playing at?' demanded a voice behind the headlights.

Neve turned her head a fraction and said, 'Don't tiger, dragon, crocodile, or anything else, no matter what they do. Remember, we'll drop the forcebeast if you do.'

'Jacob,' Taryn said, 'I think it might be wise for us to kneel and put our hands behind our heads.'

It was a shrewd suggestion, and Jacob followed it. His back gave a twinge as his knees settled on the hard road. For a moment he was wholly engulfed in his fear of pain. Pain for weeks, months, and, if he wasn't careful, years.

He said, 'Aeng, I want to go home.'

'Yes, so do I, my love,' Aeng answered.

'I hope this won't take too long. But we can't teach the beast to recognise the Firestarter any more than we can recognise it ourselves when it's right under our noses,' Neve said. 'Instead we've instructed it to retrieve, and present to us, anything in the shop's downstairs that is loose and intact.'

'If we just said "intact" it would bring us the stones from the walls,' said Aeng.

'It looks like they're praying,' opined one of the police.

Neve and Aeng glanced at each other and brought their palms together in a pious attitude. Neve's lips were touching her fingertips. She whispered over the top of them, 'They'll get really excited when it starts bringing out charred shelving.'

As if on cue the forcebeast emerged with a blackened oil-fin heater, an electric kettle, and a two-drawer filing cabinet. It deposited all three objects on the road before the dark doorway.

Aeng and Neve made discreet opening motions.

The filing cabinet doors creaked, then burst open, spilling paper, brittle and browned by heat, plus some leather cases containing coins and medals.

Neve made a motion as if she were stuffing a thick quilt into a small cupboard. The now clear bubble of air that was the beast pushed itself back into the black haze of the antiquarian bookshop.

From behind the headlights there was complete silence. It was as if the three police officers had vanished. Then a light went on inside the car, as someone had got in to use the radio. The headlights were too bright for Jacob to see where the officers were. Perhaps they were sitting in the front seat or perhaps they were ducked down, hands on the dashboard, bracing themselves.

The forcebeast returned with a large square object, which proved to be a book so voluminous and dense that it had resisted the fire. That, and the bottom half of an antique swivel chair, and a whole antique page press—the sort of thing a Victorian botanist might have used to preserve specimens of leaves and flowers.

Another police vehicle pulled up next to them on the bridge side of the village. The two cars were now blinding each other, so both dipped their lights.

Hundreds of moths had come, their bodies and shadows a whirling flurry in the cones of light.

Someone called out, 'Is that Taryn Cornick?'

'Yes,' Taryn said, and gave a little wave, making shadow antlers above her own head.

'Taryn Cornick of the Northovers,' Neve said. 'Valravn. Hero of Understanding.'

'Thank you, madam,' said the voice. 'And you are?'

'None of your business,' said Neve.

The forcebeast returned with a mesh wastepaper basket, a cash box, and two bronze bookends shaped like winged sphinxes.

'How the hell are you doing that?' someone asked, sounding on the verge of hysteria.

The forcebeast went back into the shop.

The much more collected man from the first car said, 'Is that Jason Battle I see there? Are you all right, Mr Battle?'

'Jason. You must get up and go quietly to those men and stay with them for the time being,' Neve said.

Jason Battle had been lying face down on the road. He rose, shook his head dumbly for a time, then continued from all fours onto his feet and went unsteadily towards the first police car.

The forcebeast returned with some pots and pans, and the cash register. It was now at work on the upper level—kitchenette and shop proper, it seemed.

'Neve,' said Jacob. 'Do you want it to search the whole premises or only the basement?'

'Anywhere burnt,' Neve answered.

'What say the Firestarter is somewhere unburnt, like upstairs?' Taryn said.

'Is that Jacob Berger?' asked the collected voice.

Jacob didn't answer.

'What did you do with our officers? They called you and Ms Cornick and Jason Battle in, and then we lost them.'

'They are in the treetops,' Aeng said. 'And perfectly safe if they stay put until rescued.'

'Fuck this.' It was an officer in the car nearest the bridge. There came a small series of highly specific clicks that Jacob knew very well. He shouted, 'Gun!'

The forcebeast erupted through the shop doorway, blasting bits of stonework out into the street. One large piece thumped into Neve's shoulder; several small pieces stung Jacob's face and neck. Neve reeled back and caught herself on one hand. She came upright again and shouted, 'No!'

Then she and Aeng flung out their arms, fingers at full stretch, as if they'd been pulled roughly into that position rather than assuming it voluntarily. Jacob watched blood well up in the beds of Aeng's fingernails.

The forcebeast tore in two. The divided volumes of roiling air swelled, filled with static electricity, like the light in a plasma ball. The sizzling masses fell on both cars. The headlights died. The cars rocked several feet backwards as if in a shock wave, and two of the four men and one woman behind the lights were ripped up into the air by the guns they wouldn't let go of.

The forcebeast pulled one man and his gun apart. The gun's trigger guard completely ungloved the man's thumb. The other man let go of his. The forcebeast released the men; one fell onto the hood of his car, while the other landed on the road. The beast then drifted broodily back into one mass and shrank into a dense ball of electrical shorts and ballistic explosions as it fired every bullet from the guns and held the explosions inside itself.

Neve was down on all fours, her head hanging and hair sweeping the road. Aeng was still on his knees, but his arms were slack and his chin sagged to his breastbone. Both sidhe seemed to be fighting to stay conscious.

Taryn crawled over to Neve and helped her to sit up. She brushed Neve's hair off her face.

Jacob went to help Aeng. The guns had been disposed of. He didn't need to stay down. Aeng straightened and thereafter leaned on Jacob. He was trembling with exhaustion—Jacob didn't think it could be fear.

The forcebeast had gone back to the building. The sounds of rummaging came from within, things smashed and, continually, the squeak of charcoal ground underfoot. It returned and disgorged dozens of metal bookends, a charred leather horse collar with smoke-stained brasses, a bronze bust of William Wordsworth, a lectern shaped like an eagle, and a long, rectangular, silky black box.

Jacob heard Taryn make a noise of pain, of joy.

Neve slumped again. Taryn had forgotten to hold her up.

The forcebeast put everything down, gently, then it seemed to stand back and stretch up, until its clear turbulence was disturbing the stars above the roof of the antiquarian bookshop.

Aeng got to his feet. He gripped Jacob's hand, turned to him, and whispered, his breath warm on Jacob's ear, 'I'll need your help for the next little while. Your help, company, and love.'

Jacob's mouth sought and found Aeng's—agreeing, promising, happy to be asked. For a long moment they were locked together, and all Jacob could see was Aeng's blue eyes, and all he could hear was the soft sizzling noise of his own blood in his ears. Then, since he habitually held on to his situational awareness, he checked on the police—because Aeng was vulnerable, and because these were a bunch of stubborn bastards.

But it seemed the police had decided they were only witnesses. They, and the people who had come from the two pubs when the police car alarms went off then died. Some of the patrons had their phones out and were filming—that faithful new instinct—while others had pints in hand. The townspeople of Tintern were witnesses too, like the family of the terraced garden whose gate had lost its roses; and the woman belonging to the children's bookshop, who was still wearing her work smock and a kooky Dr Seuss hat. And there were holidaymakers and day-trippers, tourists, all watching from a safe distance. All of them waiting for the next spectacle. Or, like the forcebeast, for the next instruction.

Then the darkness shifted, and the available light shifted—one not ousting the other—and he lifted the box and stood cradling it in his arms.

Jacob could see that the box was heavy and that there was maybe something slippery about it, more than *everything* about it, but that it knew it could lie still in those arms, the lithe arms in the lumpy, grubby, home-knit jersey. Shift. Suddenly apparent to everyone, not just to Jacob, who had all but forgotten him.

The great spells of concealment, each with the same author, had come together and neutralised one another. The Firestarter lay quiet and was plainly there, and Shift was too, a dark-skinned, dark-haired young man with a sweet smile, and something disturbingly alien about his browbone, and with his human soul visible in his irresistibly lovely sidhe eyes.

Jacob shuddered and, without looking at Aeng, let go and stepped away.

Neve spoke up, her voice rasping. 'Call your gate.'

Shift looked up at her, and without touching the gold claws hanging at his throat, he summoned his gate. It came quickly, moving only a fraction of the diameter of its smallest possible circle. It picked them all up—all except the dozens of witnesses and poor Jason Battle—and carried them away.

Thirty-Two

The Folly

Shift brought them to Neve's house. The autumn sun was pouring, dazzling and syrupy, over the top of the building, none of it getting past the deep eaves of the great west-facing room.

Aeng left them and climbed down to the pool to wash, though the sun wasn't on the water. The forcebeast flowed after him, an anxious attendant.

Taryn sat on the floor and let clamour drain from her body. She was exhausted.

Shift took himself out onto the cantilevered balcony and put down the Firestarter. He sat beside it, his legs dangling over the drop.

Jacob subsided onto the tile platform at the back of the room and covered his face with his hands. Taryn told herself she should join him and offer some comfort, but she didn't move.

The house felt abandoned, the only sign of life the stream falling from level to level beside the building. The waterway was much smaller and quieter than Taryn remembered. But the last time she was there it had been early spring.

Neve crouched beside her. 'I broke up my household. The absences are too cruel. I sent my remaining people to the Human Colony for the time being. There's no one to serve us. You and I should go gather mushrooms before the sun spoils them.'

Neve led Taryn up to the forest of twisted pale trees. She went slowly, in deference to Taryn's exhaustion. Between the goat-clipped turf and leaf litter under the trees at the edge of the forest, they found mushrooms of all kinds. Taryn recognised ceps, field mushrooms, shitake, and wood ear, but Neve also instructed her to pick the firm puffballs.

'It's good that we've left the others back at the house,' Taryn said. 'They can sort themselves out.'

Neve shook her skirt to settle its load of mushrooms and gazed at Taryn, curious. 'Which of them? Jacob and Aeng? Jacob and Shift?'

'I presume Aeng and Shift were once lovers?' Taryn said. 'And that's what this is about.'

'For a very long time. And their relationship was sustained through one of Shift's forgettings. But the last time Shift returned not remembering he'd ever loved Aeng. I believe he feigned his regard in the last years of the relationship, to keep Aeng's patronage through his forgetting. He woke to his renewed self, feeling nothing for Aeng. And the insult added to that injury was that when he encountered his wife—an earlier relationship—he remembered loving her. Not that she'll have anything to do with him now.'

'Why did you choose Aeng to help us?'

'Aeng was Shift's choice, not mine. Very few of us can make a force-beast. I wanted to ask the Builders, but all of them are busy clearing a blocked mountain pass before winter sets in. Shift was impatient. Also, it was better to involve as few people as possible. The Firestarter is family business, no matter how altruistic Shift's plans are for it. So—Aeng was Shift's expedience. I agreed because I knew Aeng would bring Jacob with him, to taunt Shift. I hoped that once Jacob was with Shift and you, he'd be able to break Aeng's glamour.'

'He nearly had before the police arrived with their dogs.'

'Nearly isn't enough,' Neve said. 'Not for me. But Shift will forgive Jacob anything—for your sake.'

'He's not an unforgiving person.'

'That's true,' Neve said, then set off downhill.

Taryn followed, going carefully, clutching her laden shirt, a soft morning breeze caressing her bared midriff.

Shift was knee-deep in the tussock at the edge of the stream. He now had the forcebeast and was picking up large lumps of shale and throwing them into it. It caught them and kept them. The shale clattered like rocks rolling in the rapids of a river. Once the beast was grey and loud with stones Shift took the Firestarter and, with several swinging heaves, tossed it in. The racket of grinding and crashing increased. The stones grew black with soot. The box kept disappearing and reappearing, knocking the stones this way and that like a big asteroid dropped into a field of smaller ones.

Shift and the beast showed no sign of desisting, so Neve continued up to the house. Taryn trailed after her.

Neve lit a fire in the tiled stove. She put a large pot on to heat and sat down cross-legged to clean the mushrooms with a damp cloth. She sent Taryn out to the herb garden for parsley and thyme.

The herbs were watered by a tiny diverted rill of the stream. Taryn imagined Neve—and several of those Builders—camping at the site of the house many years earlier, watching what the stream did and mathematically planning what it could be made to do. She thought of the wealth of time in everything around her, the architecture of the house, the relationships of seasons in two worlds—as if gates were gears of synchronised watches. She thought of revenges nursed for centuries.

She used her fragrant bouquet to shade her eyes. Downhill, a figure was moving steadily away from the house—another in pursuit, leaping from step to step.

Aeng walking away, with Jacob chasing him.

Jacob had to call out several times before Aeng deigned to stop. Jacob was limping the last few steps. His back was jarred and felt weakened. It seemed better to let Aeng's beauty come on him by slow degrees. It intensified the closer he came; any possible flaws, lines, discolouration, roughness, dullness, all ruled out. Aeng's face and form were faultless and unique—nothing ordinary, nothing out of place.

'Take your time, Jacob. We are at seven thousand feet, and the air is thin.'

'You can't leave,' Jacob said, breathless.

'You're the only one who has noticed my departure. The others are carelessly trying to break into that box. A ruinous plan. Scarcely even a plan.'

'Why can't you say his name?'

'I never particularly cared for the name he's now known by.'

Jacob wouldn't ask. Aliases were a problem for him. They always meant someone was dealing dishonestly with either their present or their past. Instead he said, 'I love you.'

'You love me so you've pursued me seeking justice for your Taker?'

'It was you who Took me, Aeng, not him.'

'I believe he observed the correct formalities. He has your right of disposal. But that's at least a hundred years away.'

'He hasn't disposed of anyone.'

'He absented himself and let his aunt do it for him. Now he is smashing the thing he spent the last little while trying to find. He's like a child who asks and asks for something and in the end is only interested in the triumph of attainment, not the thing itself. I suspect it was the same with you once he had you.'

'He took me out of a sense of responsibility, because he wasn't there when I was injured.'

'He's never there.'

This was true except in one respect, but Jacob was sure that that was something only he could see. And he didn't know how to begin explaining it. But he tried. 'He's listening to something else. There's an appeal, a kind of prayer.'

'I have no idea what you're talking about.'

'The green prayer,' Jacob said. 'The green pressure.'

'All the changeable and loveless gods!' Aeng cursed. 'For seventeen hundred years we have tried to keep him sidhe. Now he means to embrace his godhood and betray us.'

'That's not my take-home from the evidence,' Jacob said, sounding like himself.

'I'm leaving,' Aeng said. 'You can find yourselves another bodyguard for your insincere parley with demons.' He stepped close, and Jacob was immersed in his rainstorm scent. 'If you have a change of heart, Jacob, or if you in any other way return to your senses—*senses*, which, after all, are where we all live—you can find me at Quarry House.' Aeng put his fingers on Jacob's throat and leaned into him chastely, only his face, not his body. He kissed Jacob. 'When trouble comes, please return to me.'

Jacob couldn't speak. His throat was tight with tears. His mouth would wear the ghost of that kiss for who knew how long. He stood and watched Aeng recede down the path.

Five minutes later the thrashing rattle of stones and hollow timber ceased, the stones and box thumping into the rough tussock as the force-beast disappeared.

Jacob didn't show any interest in Neve's cooking. He went up through the house and found a higher balcony. When Taryn finished her own mushroom broth she took some to him. She put down the bowl beside him and told him she thought he was being hopelessly impractical. And how out-of-character that was. Then she spotted the diminishing figure moving along a ridge several miles away. Aeng was setting a pace that even the former Jacob would have found hard to match. Taryn asked, 'Are you in pain?'

'Not really,' Jacob said. 'The weeks without it did the trick. I managed to haul Battle over his counter without taking any harm.' He picked up the bowl and tasted the broth. Taryn saw a tiny flicker of pleasure. He tore his eyes away from the far-off figure before it passed completely out of sight. He looked at Taryn. 'So what is the plan?'

'We get some sleep. Neve takes the glove, finds the sisters, and tells them to take a message to Hell. All the hells are adjacent to one another, including the Norse one. The message simply requests that any demon still near Hell's Gate steps into the Sidh to talk to the Queen who is waiting there. Neve thinks that, the Tithe being over, the only demons having any reason to hang around Hell's Gate will be the Homeland faction. When a demon shows up, Neve will tell them we have the Firestarter. She'll suggest a meeting, stating a time and place—nowhere near a gate they can use. We can't risk them snatching the Firestarter and disappearing with it.' Taryn paused, then ventured on. 'Jacob, I think before you sleep you should talk to Shift. You can find him grazing blackberries in the hollow over there.' She pointed.

Jacob said he didn't want to talk to Shift. 'I don't want to seem to be asking for anything.'

Taryn put her hand on his arm. 'What would you be asking for?'

'I've been existing in a vacuum. Proud of my strength without being alive in my own body. I can't unlearn what Aeng taught me. All Shift will do is give me tasks—it's the only kind of sharing he understands. But for my whole life the only gift I've been given is the gift of a place in other people's plans. Aeng gave me the gift of belonging. With him, and with myself.'

Taryn shook her head. 'Remember how reluctant you were to leave me here the first time we came to the Sidh? You didn't see gifts and kindnesses; you saw contracts and conditions. They're a conditional people. Please don't forget what you knew then.'

Early the next day, at dawn, Jacob went down to the pool to swim. Aeng's Hands had dissolved in the same moment the forcebeast collapsed. No one had offered to make more, and Jacob's back felt both weak and in need of loosening.

When he got close to the pool Jacob saw Shift was there already, standing thigh-deep in the water, washing blood from his arms and legs. His clothes lay on the flagstones in blood-tinged puddles.

Shift noticed he was being watched. He stood dripping and gazed at Jacob, his face indistinguishable in the twilight. A dark-eyed blur. Jacob didn't approach him, or speak, and after a minute broke away and retreated back to the house.

The house was quiet. Neve had gone about her business. The three who remained kept to separate rooms. Shift followed the sun around when he was awake. He carried the Firestarter wherever he went, a fact that added fuel to the suspicions Jacob was nursing, since the Firestarter had been nowhere in sight when Shift was at the pool, which must mean that Shift had been somewhere further off in the form of some animal incapable of carrying the box.

Jacob walked up to the Island of Apples to swim in the lake by Shift's wattle-and-daub hut. Shift's goats and chickens followed him about, complaining of their abandonment. While he was there, Jacob climbed the worn slot of track that led to the gate and found a dented car door, the one from Stuart's Land Rover, discarded by the dragon who had carried Taryn to safety before changing into a person. A person who wasn't a person, or anything, really.

Taryn altered for herself a dress and overdress of Neve's, careful to choose nothing too grand or too worn—either might be a favourite. She foraged and cooked for the others as a way of showing them she wasn't shunning them. She was giving Jacob time to come back to himself and his self-interest. And helping Shift keep quiet and gather his strength. Also, she hoped if they didn't have her ready ear they might get around to talking to each other. Even if they began with reproaches, it would be something.

Her hope was futile. Jacob watched Shift whenever they were in the same room, but his expression was cold and sceptical.

Taryn warned both of them, 'If you go on like this, you're going to lose him. If you want to keep someone, they have to believe you love them.' She didn't say, *You have to love them*, because she kept thinking of

Alan, whom she hadn't loved and who had eventually understood that he wasn't loved.

Jacob told Taryn, 'It turns out I need the people around me to be *good*.'

Shift told her, 'I only have four years, Taryn, and I've just had a reminder from Aeng of how badly it hurts those who love me that I forget them.'

Taryn had spent some time reckoning the sentence she might expect to receive after a guilty plea at trial. It would be more than four years.

Jacob finally told Taryn about the blood at the pool.

'But, Jacob,' she reasoned, 'if Shift had flown off to find Aeng and they had had an altercation, any injury he received would've vanished when he turned himself back into a bird to return. He'd come back clean. According to you, that's how it works. So it can't have been his blood, or Aeng's.'

Jacob told her she was being naive. And she told him he was being irrational, and then stopped speaking to him.

It was a relief when Neve returned. She had secured an agreement on the appointed time and place. 'There are usually plenty of people burning the midnight oil at the games company, but it's five weeks after their last big release, and many of the workers are off on holiday. That information is all courtesy of Hugin. She said Jacob would understand what it all meant.'

They emerged in the tangle of camomile, tansy, and old lilac bushes around the folly. It was a mellow sunset and the lake was stippled with feeding sprat and pond skimmers on their pontoons of thready legs.

The view from the folly shook Taryn's heart. The smooth lake, reed margin, and long lawn up to the house were the same as ever. The stone-work of the house had been cleaned. And two freshly painted punts were tied up at the new jetty, which extended far enough out into the deep water for swimmers to dive off it.

The ravens perched on the balustrade of the folly, sunning themselves. They were indistinguishable from each other but discernibly larger than earthly ravens. Munin soon made herself known by hopping in a circuit right around the balustrade to make a pecking pass at Shift as he came up the steps. 'No bodyguard,' she scolded. Then, 'No brass band either.'

The folly *was* reminiscent of a band rotunda but had a central table fixed to the floor right where any musicians would sit.

The table was a good place to lay the Firestarter. Shift put it down, and the ravens alighted beside it on the tabletop and tried what everyone had to try at least once. They attacked the seal with their beaks. They took turns to peck at it, and then worked in concert. Hugin desisted first and stood preening her feathers, like someone flattening their hair when something hair-raising has happened.

'It's hours until midnight,' Jacob complained. 'And it's not as if we needed to come early to case the joint. I for one do not want to sit twiddling my thumbs.'

Munin offered to twiddle Jacob's thumbs for him but said she'd have to remove them first.

He ignored her. 'We have time to hike to Princes Gate Magna, have a pint, use the payphone, and be back well before midnight.'

Taryn said, 'I *would* like to speak to my father. He'll have had the police and press all over him about Tintern.'

No one responded.

Taryn said, 'I'm sure the sisters can be trusted to mind the Firestarter.'

'I'll bring you a boat,' Munin said, and swooped across the lake, her pinions almost brushing their reflection on the water. She lifted the mooring line of one punt off its post and stretched it out, flapping strongly until the bow came around. The punt drifted slowly after the furious feathered black star of the raven.

'It is best to have a boat on either shore.' Having articulated her practical thought, Neve looked frowning from face to face. 'We're not under an enchantment, are we?'

'I think you're all feeling the way I normally feel,' Shift said. 'It's the Firestarter's field of influence. You've entered the realm of the unseen. Welcome.'

Neve went down to the shore and took the rope from Munin. She tied up the punt.

Jacob asked whether Neve's sword was the only weapon they had.

Hugin spat like an angry cat. 'I can stop time by flying around this building.'

'But then nothing happens,' Shift said.

'True. But it does give me time to think.'

'But time starts again from where it left off,' Shift said. 'Stopping it only makes a difference to you. Same with Munin and her dispensing with intervening time. To us it just looks like she never goes anywhere, and you're heroically decisive.'

Both ravens took off, and then the next instant landed in front of Shift. And so did a sizeable pile of snails, several of whom were already putting out exploratory horns. 'Have some snails,' Munin said to Shift. 'You've earned them.'

'I didn't mean to offend you. All I have right now is intervening time,' Shift said.

'And the Firestarter.' Hugin speared a snail and smashed its shell to pulp around its distressed foaming flesh. She ate it, and several more, leaving dark smears on the tabletop's chequerboard green and white marble. The other snails made off slowly around the fragments of their fellows.

Taryn asked Jacob to come and sit with her for a while by the water. They went down to the shore, climbed into the punt, and let it drift to the limit of its rope. Taryn turned her gaze to the house, the walled rose garden, the long slope of lawn. It was all so familiar that she kept expecting to look down and see her summer shorts and grass-stained childish knees.

The bushes on the island were browning and mildewed in some places, and jewelled with rosehips in others.

'I'm going to have this land restored to my family,' Taryn told Jacob.

'Is that before or after you confess to your crime, stand trial, and serve time?'

'Is that what you want me to do?'

'You know it isn't.'

'The house will be my reward,' Taryn said. 'I'm going to ask for a reward.'

'Great. You can live in anticipation, and I can live in nostalgia.'

Taryn lost her temper. 'You think the blood on Shift's clothes was Aeng's because *you'd* like to attack Aeng!'

'I was *happy* with Aeng.'

'With Aeng and without responsibilities.' Surely Jacob must understand that Aeng's only requirement of him had been that he believed the story he was being told.

Jacob didn't answer her.

'You shouldn't just nurse suspicions,' she said. 'And that's my last word on the subject.'

The sun had gone. Mosquitoes were biting. The twilit blue sky was grainy with them.

Someone had illuminated the camping lantern in the folly.

Taryn grabbed the rope and pulled the punt back into shore. They got out and picked their way over tree roots back up the slope.

Everyone was where they'd been when Taryn and Jacob left, sitting still in the greenish light. There were no snails left. Broken shells and smears of flesh and foam covered the table.

Taryn took off her boots and dried her legs with her skirt. The mosquitoes had followed them, but Taryn could see the swarming transparencies of mendings zipping through the air, hunting them.

Jacob sat down next to Shift and immediately said, 'Whose blood was it?'

'Mine,' Shift said. 'While you were all asleep I took Neve's sword, planted my feet on the box, and tried to lever off the seal. I got very enthusiastic. The sword slipped, and I sliced myself. It didn't hurt much, so I took my trousers off to have a look. That's when the calf muscle sagged off my left leg. I shifted. When I changed back I picked up my blood-soaked trousers and went to the pool to wash. Then you came along. I had no idea what you were thinking.'

'If you'd passed out you might have bled to death,' Neve said.

'I know. It was incredibly stupid. I feel shaky every time I think about it.'

Jacob laughed. 'That would have been a pretty ludicrous end to all this.'

Neve muttered that *she'd* still have managed to secure a bargain about the Tithe.

They sat in silence for a long time until, around eleven, perhaps meaning to be there first and check the lie of the land, the demons arrived on the island. Flew in after a journey from some cut-through. Two of them had wings. A third was supported by a cloud of smoke. These three arrived from above, alighting like waterfowl. They were followed by a fourth who dropped out of a steep parabola as if it travelled by great bounds rather than flew. Two of the demons were tall and looked as if they were at death's door from starvation. One was suede-skinned and pallid, the other covered in suppurating boils and blisters. The one in smoke was shapely and human-looking but had no arms. The last was Basil Cornick's yellow-and-turquoise monster, but without any sign of genitalia, erect or otherwise.

They crowded into the folly. One of the thin demons immediately took a seat on a bench by the wall. It looked exhausted. The vivid one swelled its muscles and folded its arms like a bouncer at the door of a nightclub. The smoky one darted at Neve, faster than Taryn's eyes could register. It snatched the sword off her and thrust it into the stone table-top. The sword stuck with only a foot of blade showing beneath its hilt. It quivered and shimmered.

'Not a good start,' Neve said.

The demons blinked at her, three with stony expressions and the fourth pulling faces, the changes between each inhumanly rapid.

'We will conduct this meeting in English,' Shift said, 'out of deference to—"

'—the people of the land,' Taryn supplied, thinking of the opening ceremony at the Auckland Writers Festival. *She* was the people of this land.

'I'm sure it's all the same to you what language we speak,' Shift added.

'We will not bargain,' said the demon in smoke. 'We revile all who are not ourselves.'

'Why are you here, then? Do you imagine you can just take the Firestarter from us?' Neve said.

'I took your sword.'

Shift said, 'If you took the Firestarter, you couldn't open it. If you burned everything around it to ashes of ashes, it would still be intact. The box was made using the power it contains.'

'And if we can't open it, what use is it to us?' the leader said, the one whose dark face had a diamond-shaped boss of bone above his nose and whose mantle of smoke stood in place of arms. Taryn didn't like to look at him too long. She thought his question must be meant to divine how much they knew about the contents of the box. Her eyes slid away from the group. There was a light on in the room that once housed her grandfather's library. The intervening time disappeared again. She wished, and almost believed, that her sister would come out through the doors onto the terrace and run down the lawn.

Shift said, 'Will you strike a deal with me if I promise to put what the box contains into your hands?'

'Sidhe trickery,' said the mottled one. 'You don't say you'll *leave* it in our hands after putting it there.'

'Very well,' said Shift. 'I will leave what the box contains in your hands.'

'We don't trade promises,' the pallid demon said, continuing to be obdurate. He looked around, jeering at the ravens, the humans, Neve. 'He has no solidarity. He says "I", not "we".'

'We don't hate everything that isn't us,' Neve said. 'We don't need to say or think "we" all the time.'

The turquoise-and-yellow monster spoke up. 'Do you know what the box contains?'

'A thing that won't burn.'

'And what good would such a thing be to us?' said the smoke-wrapped demon, resolute in his scorn.

Shift's tone when he answered was matter-of-fact. 'It is a scroll made from the skin of an angel. The skin is tattooed with words, in an ink made of the angel's own blood. The scroll is a primer of the tongues of angels, otherwise known as the Language of Command. A language that, like the language of the sidhe, has no written form. The primer is in the Roman alphabet, with the phonetics of Latin used to approximate the sounds of the words of the Language of Command.'

The demons had become very still. One finally asked, 'How do you know that?'

'Giving a purely spoken language the silent but visible voice of a written form is something my mother taught me. I enjoyed it enough to try again as a scholarly pastime, even after I'd forgotten being taught, and forgotten the small pieces of my mother's own great project that she showed me when I was a child. I invented an alphabet for the sidhe—who didn't have any use for it.'

'You've done it three times,' Neve said. 'Solving the challenges the same way each time. No one tells you you're repeating yourself because we don't like to spoil your enjoyment. Also it's interesting and instructive to see the character of an intellect assert itself like any other habit of temperament. It has helped us understand you a little better. Now, of course, Jane Aitken has printed books in your written sidhe, and you will inherit your own work as a fait accompli.'

Jacob looked at Taryn and rolled his eyes. He seemed almost cheerful. She suspected that Neve's sidhe indolence about achievements helped him feel a little superior to them—at least in some respects. He may have been jilted, but he would never be so complacent about an effort in futility.

The suppurating demon spoke up in a grating whisper, as if it were ulcerated through and through. 'Why would you give up your birthright?'

The pallid one said, 'How do you mean to open the box?'

'I have another birthright. It's one of the two things I'm bargaining for.'

'State your conditions,' said the mottled monster. It was getting excited. Its genitalia had appeared, a growing protuberance more like a snail's horn than a tumescent penis. The sight filled Taryn with queasy horror. She leaned against Jacob, who was trembling.

Shift stretched, and his elbows cracked. 'I should say first that you won't need your cryptographers at the server farm and that getting them to figure out the language would likely have killed them or driven them mad.'

'They don't care about that,' Jacob said.

'No. But nevertheless they won't need cryptographers. My mother's primer will lay it all out for them.'

'If that's what it is,' said Jacob.

'I can't see what else it would be.'

The mottled demon said, 'We meant to programme the machines to formulate the sentences we require. We would each learn parts of a Battle Speech. Each—one—of—us,' it said, clearly having some cognitive difficulty with even making a pass at personal pronouns in the singular.

'You'll all have understudies, I hope,' said Hugin. 'Redundancies.'

The demon ignored her. It asked Shift, 'Is that a condition? That the cryptographers be given their freedom?'

'Let to live,' said Jacob.

'Yes, we will grant that,' said the smoky one, with transparently insincere magnanimity.

'That wasn't a condition. That was one of the two things I must say first.'

'Hurry up, then. What else must you first say, little princeling?'

Demons didn't do diplomacy.

'I want you to understand that the language is lethal with short exposure to humans, and with only a little longer to sidhe. You are not your masters. The language doesn't just cause you pain because they use it to compel you. It compels you because it causes you pain.'

'We know that full well,' said the mottled one. 'We will master it. We are legion.'

The demon meant they'd spend as many lives as it took, Taryn thought.

It went on. 'You have satisfied your conscience. Now—what are your conditions?'

'When you win your freedom,' Shift said, and glowed at them with sympathy and encouragement, 'there must still be a treaty of peace between the Sidh and Hell. But without a Tithe.'

'Done,' said the smoky demon.

'And two,' Shift said, 'I want my father's glove.'

The demons became, if possible, even more still.

Shift said to the smoke-wrapped one, 'With it you can use the gates like a sidhe, because the glove was made for an angel, and you have an angel ancestor.'

'He has angel wings,' Neve added helpfully. 'That mantle of smoke. And the angel sign above his eyes is like yours.'

'And why shouldn't we keep the glove and take the Firestarter?' said the demon.

'Because you can use a gate and block a gate—but you can't move a gate or make a gate. Even with both gloves. It's sidhe magic, and you have no sidhe blood.'

A large moth thumped into the lamp, and Hugin hopped over and ate it. She continued to pace restlessly as if the moth were a stimulant.

Taryn thought, *She's ahead of us. Whatever she's worked out is making her anxious.*

Shift went on, his voice warm and reasonable. 'I need both gloves to make a gate into the box to remove the primer.'

'The putative primer,' said Jacob.

'Not possible,' said the demon. 'We know we can't put a hand through a gate to take anything. That's not how gates work. Our whole selves must pass through. It's the same for you. That's the way gates work. That box is too small for you.'

'That wasn't my plan.'

'Were you planning to *ask* me at some point?' Munin said. 'And to think I believed I was here to fulfil the role of bodyguard and generally add dignity to the proceedings.'

'No point in asking if I didn't have the glove,' Shift said. 'Besides, you won't say no.'

'No,' Hugin said. 'No.'

'We're not the same raven,' her sister reminded her.

'Apart from sending the Raven of Memory into the box to fetch for us the thing we want, what else would you do with the glove?' said the smoky one.

'Make it mine,' Shift said. 'And Neve's.'

'Pure symbolism and ceremony,' said the demon. 'What would you do with it in a *material* way?'

'Nothing to harm Hell.'

'Once you've tamed the language, and you're ready to rise, Shift and I will use the gloves to go to battle at your side and help you dispose of your masters,' Neve said. 'It would be an honour and a pleasure to help you with that.'

'But more immediately,' the mottled demon said, insistent and un-impressed by Neve's offer.

'I'd like to free that young frost giant you're using as a cooling system in your compound in Pakistan. Make a gate to get it straight back to its people. Who I hope will show their gratitude by lending me a few years of their time.'

'What for?'

'There are places that could do with being a little more cold,' Shift said, mild and ingenuous.

Taryn felt light-headed. *He's going to do it,* she thought. *God help us all. He really does mean to save the world.*

'You'd give up the language?'

'I believe that mastering it in order to make a primer for me is what killed my mother. I'm my mother's son.'

'And your grandmother's grandson,' Neve said. She, too, seemed to value the second glove more than the tongues of angels.

'Shift is sincere about helping you,' Hugin said. 'He says "people" of everyone. It isn't your "we", but he is a true egalitarian.'

'I do desire your freedom,' Shift said to the demons.

'But not the whole of our homeland in our hands,' said the suppurating one, in sly tones.

Neve lowered her eyelids and said, 'You wouldn't like what we've done with it.'

Taryn had looked away again at the house, her eyes drawn by the swoop of headlights, some visitor or security sweep well after midnight. When she looked back, she was just in time to see the smoke-wrapped demon float the glove into Shift's hands.

It was twice the size of the other and was made of white gold, stainless, very plain. It also had the late addition of an iron chain.

Shift put it down quickly. The ravens ambled over and set to work on the links. Under their blows the iron smoked, grew cherry red, and flew apart in molten sparks. Munin dragged the remainder of the chain away across the table, down the steps, and right out of the folly.

Neve picked up the glove and draped it over Shift's left hand. The fingers overlapped his by inches.

Shift said, 'Now why couldn't I have inherited some of his imposing size?'

'Oh, no, he was just a little fellow with giant hands,' Neve said. She removed the other glove from her throat and tied it onto Shift's right hand.

Hugin began her demented hopping again.

Shift laughed with delight, not at the raven but at whatever sensation he got from wearing both gloves.

Neve swivelled the Firestarter until one of its narrow ends faced him.

Jacob said, 'Do you think there's a box inside the box? The way Taryn remembered?'

'No. The noise it makes will be the spindles at the ends of the scroll knocking on the wood. Bone spindles,' Shift said. 'The entire thing is indestructible. Angel-bone spindles, angel-skin scroll, angel-blood ink. My father's killers left his body, and my mother used it to make something that would last. She knew what she was doing.'

'I don't think she knew it would kill her,' Neve said.

Shift looked at the demons. 'Do we have a bargain?'

'Yes,' said the leader.

Taryn seriously doubted that; now Shift had his hands on the gloves, or rather the gloves on his hands, the demons could take anything from him without a long period of planning and stealth.

'Will you go in the box?' Shift said to Munin. 'Please?'

'What's in it for us?' Hugin said.

'I'm hoping the sidhe will like having something new to do. Something really difficult. After all, they are the descendants of people who did something formidably difficult. They made a world out of pieces of other very different worlds. Any people who once built a house for themselves can certainly repair someone else's house. Do you think you and your sister might like to help with that too?'

Hugin spat and fluffed up.

'Odin is our second god,' Munin said to her sister. 'Perhaps Shift might be our third.'

'I'll forget my way out of any godhood.'

'True, true,' Munin said. Then, to her sister, 'I want to do it. I want to see how they all go on. Him, and all his *people people people*.'

Shift knelt and set his elbows on the snail-smeared, sword-pierced table. He eyed the short end of the rectangular box and edged both hands towards it, twisting and picking. His gestures were like those he, Aeng, and Neve used to direct their forcebeast.

The end of the larger glove clicked against the charred, stone-pummelled timber.

Taryn had a brief sensation of something hollowing out. It was like a barometric change, but wasn't. The chatter of late crickets and summer frogs dropped into silence—a silence that spread from the folly, across the lake, and through all the remnant woods of the Northover's former and future estate. It was like a birth. Something began to breathe, a child born with language already in its mind, not crying, not asking, just alive.

Shift withdrew his hands. The air beside the box sparkled with something.

'Gwy,' Neve said. 'I can smell the marsh. Mud, peat smoke, the honey from the wild hive. Adhan's house, her hands, her hair.'

'Yes. I smell those things too, but it doesn't remind me of anything.'

Munin trotted across the table and thrust her beak at the square end of the box. Then she put her head into it.

Hugin made a noise like someone snapping Christmas candy canes.

Munin walked into the box. Her tail feathers disappeared.

'No intervening time,' Jacob said, and Taryn recognised it as a very short prayer.

A few seconds later the tail feathers reappeared. Hugin snatched at them but managed to refrain from pulling her sister back out of the box.

Munin shuffled out, slowly dragging a scroll. Soft vellum, dark in colour, and wound onto polished white arm bones. She shook it from side to side as she went, as if having trouble freeing it. But before long it was out of the box, in one piece.

Shift reached for the box, to clear the table or close his gate, Taryn wasn't sure which.

Munin seemed to know. 'No, leave it be,' she chided. 'It's your first gate. We should celebrate its birthday with some ceremony.'

The demons crowded around the table. The mottled one unrolled the scroll.

Taryn felt as if something were pushing her head down. She wanted to get onto her knees and drag herself away. From the corner of one eye she saw Neve and three of the demons jostling as they retreated. They ended up on the steps, clustered together, enmity forgotten, staring in the direction of the scroll, too far away now to read anything accidentally.

Taryn was aware that Jacob was completely outside the folly. He had taken himself over the rail and was fighting his way free of the shrubbery.

Only Shift, the ravens, and the smoky demon remained at the table.

Shift said to the ravens, 'Does it make any sense to you?'

'It's all grebes and egrets, curlews and eels,' Hugin said. 'Though I suppose there is an "A" for "apple" there.'

Munin said, 'Your mother wrote this for you. It's all the things you first knew.'

The smoky demon said, 'In time we will make sense of it.'

Taryn heard the scroll roll up again, the clack of the ball joints knocking together.

'Thank you, and goodbye,' Shift said. 'Would you like me to put you as close to your place in Pakistan as the existing gates can go?'

'If you would,' said the demon politely. 'Little god of the marshlands, fate-forsworn princeling, Gatemaker.'

The demon joined its fellows on the steps. Neve stepped swiftly out of their way. Princes Gate jumped off the bottom of the lake and swallowed the four demons. Shift laughed as he swung all the gates into place and set his passengers somewhere near the server farm.

'So wide?' Neve breathed. 'Why did you use eight gates?'

'To let our people know they have a gatemaker again,' Shift said.

'Two gatemakers,' Neve said, gazing eagerly at the gloves.

Shift hurried out of the folly and helped Jacob from the lilac, which was covered in powdery mildew and had made a mess of his last fine Aeng outfit. They came back to the others. Neve was trying and failing to pull her sword out of the table. She complained, 'How did you make it work for Arthur?'

'I don't remember,' Shift said.

She gave up.

Hugin suddenly burst out into squawks of horror. Munin was once again venturing into the box. She disappeared completely. The chorus of insects and amphibians, which had only tentatively recommenced once the demons and primer vanished, dropped away again.

Munin backed out with a single sheet of vellum. Once again, everyone but Shift and the ravens quickly averted their eyes.

For a time no one said anything, then Shift said, in a carefully controlled voice, 'It's in Latin as well as the tongues of angels.' Further silence, then in the same careful voice, 'It's a letter from my mother. She apologises for all the deceptions she practised on me. And for hiding me.'

'By virtue of its being the same text written in two languages, it is also a cipher key,' Hugin said. 'It will be useful to you, Shift.'

'Yes,' Shift said. He wasn't replying to Hugin, but to the woman who wrote the letter. 'Being hidden has been difficult for me.'

Epilogue

Intreat me not to leave thee, or to return from following after thee: for wither thou goest, I will go; and where thou lodgest, I will lodge: thy people shall be my people . . .

Ruth 1:16

One Hundred Years, Eighty with Good Behaviour

Taryn was puzzled as to who her visitor might be, five days from Christmas and three before her release date. She was expecting her father, but not yet. She'd had a letter: 'I'm already near at hand and will be there on the dot to deliver you.' His play had wrapped till the roads were more passable. Its eighteen-month run had so far covered most of the island, from Land's End to York. The play was a theatrical adaptation of the final four episodes of the television fantasy series—never aired, never filmed—with large-scale puppetry supplying the action scenes. The four-hour production had retained a third of the show's cast and had altered its projected storylines to give all those people more to do. There had been a few unavoidable substitutions, accepted by the audience because of the faithful way the already familiar actors accommodated the newcomers. Besides, it was theatre, so there were no close-ups, and that helped.

The cast and company worked tirelessly, had fun, and proved that things didn't all have to wind down just because, as Basil Cornick liked to say, 'bloody elves have called time on us'.

Basil had rehearsed his opinions in a letter to Taryn, who'd written back to say he must know it wasn't the ladies and gentlemen calling time—more the exaggerated expectations of profit by various industries, like telcos. All the businesses that clambered over one another's bodies running down the mooring rope before the ship that may or may not sink even left the port. 'Governments should have nationalised things,' Taryn wrote. 'But I guess that since for years everything's been about returns to shareholders, and they're all shareholders, they couldn't get their heads around what's worth having and why.'

Basil replied, 'I accept your argument, but can you tell me why *that woman* looks like the person who received me at Stone Street and oversaw a screen test Peter insisted never happened?'

Basil meant the more visible of the two people who, throughout a year, five years before, had halved nine rivers from surface to bed, and bank to bank. There was a famous picture of the woman, posed as if holding one end of an invisible rope that stretched all the way to the far shore of the Ganges. Her feet were sudsy, ashy. She'd just walked right through people soaping clothes on the stone steps directly downstream of Manikarnika Ghat. There was a patch of sweat on the silk at the small of her back and a sheen on her bare arms and face. She stood directly before her handiwork—and his, her partner on the far side of the river, the man who was never successfully photographed. It looked as if a pane of glass had been dropped into the river, from shallows to depths, covering every contour of the riverbed all the way from one bank to the other. A brown wall just sat there, like water in a fish tank when the oxygen pump has failed, the whole thing left so long that only anaerobic algae hadn't stifled. Below the woman on the sticky riverbed were charred bones, a whole bail of construction site safety mesh, a blackly bleeding car battery, and a mattress-thick carpet of shredded plastic bags. The photograph had been taken only moments before another river appeared from an inlet in exactly the same dimensions as the outlet. A blue-green wall that sat flush against the brown, so that the river was continuous.

Taryn's father had visited the first of those refreshed rivers and had taken a tour boat that cruised across the line where brown became green, and opaque became translucent. He had marvelled at how the boat slipped serenely over the division, maybe hastening a little on the second river.

Taryn wanted to tell her father how it worked. That where the line appeared there were three gates, always open. The first, upstream gate removed all flotsam, but nothing living, and dropped it all beyond the Exiles' Gate and into interstellar space. The second gate took the water away and poured it into the wetlands at the mouth of a river in the Sidh. A river that, in turn, flowed through the third gate in the sequence—effectively replacing the Ganges. The 'blue line' in each of the nine changed rivers was always the continuation of one of the Sidh's great, clean waterways, now pouring themselves into the Indian Ocean, the China Sea, the Mekong Delta.

Taryn longed to tell her father everything. But she couldn't be sure she wasn't monitored.

She had however been able to write down much of what she'd like to tell her father. The history that was hers, and History's. She'd asked the ravens for pencils and notebooks. Munin would arrive with one notebook at a time, an hour before sunrise, when there was enough light coming through the window of the cell to illuminate a page. Several hours later, the raven would carry the filled notebook away with her.

By that time, Taryn had a cell to herself. Inmates were two to a cell when she came to the prison, but with pressure on lines of supply and communications, and budgets evaporating, the populations of women's prisons had begun to thin out by year two. Women's prisons first. Men's now too. Sentences were reduced. There were fewer incarcerations. And there were fewer crimes, or various authorities had adjusted their ideas about what was criminal. It was the creep of pragmatism more than compassion—the authorities were rethinking many matters around incarceration and, finally, putting sane solutions in place.

While Taryn wrote, Munin would nestle into the curve of her body. Hours would pass, and the noise would increase from the motorway across the valley. Later, when petrol consumption was curtailed, it was quieter. That pervasive longshore sound of a stream of traffic became a rarity everywhere.

By year four, two-thirds of the world's oil fields had turned into aquifers. It would occur without warning—apart from statistical probability, as it kept on occurring. One minute a well would be pumping oil; the next water and oil, and then water.

There was no territory where every field was transubstantiated, a fact that prompted intelligent observers to think that she—the constantly identified woman who cleaned rivers—was leaving each oil-producing region some fuel for the time being. 'It's a period of grace,' said the intelligent observers. 'It has to be.' Meanwhile, former desert places were using the aquifers to irrigate groves of young olives and date palms, and gardens of tomato, squash, cucumber, eggplant. In places where winter was irremediably cold, and people relied on oil for heating, and suddenly no one was interested in selling it to them, those people simply disappeared. Many of them came back in spring with packets of seed and bundles of cuttings and garden tools, bursting with good health and stubbornly refusing to elaborate on where they had been and what they had learned. The mayor of one such town produced what came to be the rote response to questions. 'I will only talk to whomever helps me build a glasshouse.' Bullying officials didn't roll up their sleeves. Reporters occasionally would. 'We were on an island,' explained the mayor, once the glasshouse door was hung and its interior swept out. 'With blue sea all around it. It wasn't as hot as a Greek isle, but it was otherwise quite similar. A group of people were ready and waiting for us when we arrived. They fed us, housed us, and put us to work. Only five of them had any Russian, and it was antique Russian. But we got by, and between the bouts of hard work had a pleasant time.' He grinned at the reporter. 'We're nomads now. We'll go back there when winter comes again. This is now our Summer Town.'

The motorway across the valley from the prison became quieter by degrees. Then, almost overnight, it fell completely silent.

It was the first stretch of road replaced by forest. A 'taking gate' soundlessly consumed the bitumen, crash barriers, cat's eyes, giant curettes of LEDs, the pre-cast concrete sound screens, and the manky road reserve. Forty miles in thirty-six hours. The disappearance left a trench all the way down to clay and gravel. The trench lay naked for a week, watered by rain, then was filled with a forest, shade trees and fruit trees, nut trees and little pools of potager-style gardens, with vegetables, mature seedlings, dormant seeds, and tubers, all flourishing according to the season, which was early spring. The forest arrived glistening with rain, under rain, walked into the world by that woman (and her generally neglected confederate).

These ready-lawn food forests—the temperate one that replaced the motorway near Taryn's prison; tropical ones with pawpaw and mango, banana, taro, cassava, and cocoa trees; or desert ones with olives, lemons, dates, tamarind, and pomegranates—always replaced roadways, always came with water if there wasn't any, bringing a series of small springs that flowed as if from underground. The ready-lawn forests were few and didn't have the dramatic impact on human lives that the cleaned rivers and stolen oil had. But they were as suggestive a gift as the unasked-for cookware or power tools spouses give each other at Christmas as a heavy hint. Hint or encouragement. (Yes. We have to learn to fix things, not throw them away. And no, we can't keep eating out.)

For the past year Taryn had enjoyed her twilight writing sprints to the sounds of owls, foxes, and badgers, and birdsong draining down into the world as sunrise touched the tops of the trees.

Munin was a frequent visitor. Between her visits, Taryn would be expecting her while never quite able to recall how it was the raven would arrive. Then, at five a.m. in winter or two a.m. in summer, there would be a stealthy rustle from under Taryn's bed as Munin emerged from the box Taryn kept forgetting was there. The box that no cell-inspector ever found. The Firestarter was now a two-way gate, raven-sized, its other end located in a very windy spot on the summit of Ben Nevis. It was Hugin's idea to make the gate two-way and send it to Taryn. 'I knew something had slipped my mind, and since it wasn't Shift, it had to be the Firestarter. Shift had left it just lying around in his hut, under things.'

Sometimes Taryn would sit on her bed swinging her foot so that it knocked on the box. *Tonk*. The Firestarter.

Sometimes another bird would come through, often surging into human form so fast he'd end up with his nose pressed to the closed hatch in Taryn's cell door, frozen in wariness, one eye rolled back to regard her.

But he hadn't come for two years, and the last time she saw him, he'd cried all night in her arms. Wept as he had on the beach of the Tacit. But this time there was nowhere she could ask him to take her. Nowhere he could run to.

Taryn's visitor wasn't her father, overeager and early. It wasn't Carol, who would visit, but not at this season, and whom Taryn would see very soon, since they planned to live together for part of every year. Carol, Carol's husband, and their three-year-old son were at Princes Gate with Angela, Angela's partner, Taryn's editor and her family, Jane Aitken and several other women of the island. They all worked in Princes Gate's extensive vegetable gardens and published informational booklets about preserving and smoking, making compost, caring for fruit trees and raising poultry and goats. The booklets were for barter, as were the packets of seeds they distributed at the local libraries in an eighty-mile radius of Princes Gate. (Libraries were becoming real centres of community everywhere. It was where people knew they'd find some often elderly gardener who'd been deputised by 'the ladies and gentlemen' to hand out seed, seedlings, and advice.)

The visitor wasn't Basil or Carol. It wasn't Jacob—who had been largely absent for the past two years, though Munin still delivered his short and unsatisfying letters. Taryn's visitor was Raymond Price.

Price was not dressed with his usual sartorial elegance—something Taryn had noticed and Jacob had made much of, with a mix of envy and admiration, every time he talked about the man. Price was wearing a woollen hat, Gore-Tex walking boots, and a duck-down body warmer. Taryn wouldn't have recognised him, except he had visited her a number of times in her first years of incarceration. Other people like him had visited also—and the three who threatened violence later suffered deaths of fairy-tale cruelty, after which she was left in peace.

Price sat at a table in the empty visitors' room. Taryn's guard turned up the heat pump. She settled on the other side of the room and got out her knitting.

Taryn took a seat opposite Price.

'I thought I'd drop in before you leave,' Price said. 'I'm surprised you refused early release.'

Taryn shrugged. She wasn't going to explain anything so near to her heart. There were days she'd find herself looking about for that length of chain—the one from Scolt Head, and Purgatory.

Price imitated her shrug and managed to make it look pubescent.

Taryn smiled. 'I will only speak to whomever helps me build a glass-house.'

Price pursed his lips. 'It's cold out there. The wrong season for glass-houses.'

'But not as cold as it was some years ago when the Arctic vortex kept collapsing.'

'Yes. It is properly cold in the Arctic now,' he conceded. 'So you might say we're beginning to see the point.'

'You still say "we".'

'I'm still working for the government. In a slightly different capacity.'

Taryn looked over at the guard. She could feel herself tensing up—a sense of peril in her throat and chest. 'Don't try anything,' she warned.

'You mean in a spiteful spirit of revenge? Surely you understand our cause for resentment?'

'Of course I do.'

'Really?'

Taryn didn't respond. A condensation of deeper silence began to rain down from the ceiling. Taryn's clothes were sticking to her. It was sweat, but it felt like cold and damp. She understood that she was isolated and indefensible, in every sense of the word. 'I have friends,' she reminded him, and herself.

'How nice for you. And none of your friends has been a casualty of the changes so far?'

Taryn considered the insinuation of 'so far' and wondered if sharing what she knew would help her. *Some* of what she knew, so he'd gather there was more, and might therefore value her more.

'I hope you don't imagine there haven't been casualties,' Price said. 'Great suffering. And where's the end of it?'

There was, it turned out, a line of inquiry he wanted to open. Things had been much quieter for two years. There were fewer notable events. Yes, groups of people in real strife would still vanish, and some of them would come back in better shape and equipped with know-how and new loyalties. But Price wanted to know whether this was it. A tapering off. He wanted to know whether there was a clock running on what people like him, and those he served, were expected to do in return. He wanted to know how long they had and what was negotiable. He wanted to negotiate.

'What do you have to say about the falling birth rates along those rivers?' he said.

Taryn sighed. 'You know, there were always people who found cause for complaint about falling birth rates whenever women in developing nations got educations and the means of supporting themselves.'

'I'm genuinely interested in what you think about it.'

'No, you're making a case. Look. There were too few sources of clean water. Those gates are now all running at twenty per cent, effectively only filtering these days. The sidhe couldn't keep poisoning their wetlands with our shitty water. And it wouldn't have done any good to—say—use the Lethe instead of their own rivers. Imagine the problems *that* would have brought with it.'

Price looked away, imagining. The dial of his indolent but somehow intense attention turned, and Taryn could almost hear the otherworldly voices come into his head.

'That's right,' she said. 'The glaciers of Jotunheim couldn't be persuaded to melt. And the frost giants have already given us more than enough. Once the upstream polluters stop, once the trash mountains have all been removed—then the rivers can become wholly themselves again. Wholly and holy in the case of the Ganges. They've been given a chance.'

The trash mountains were being dealt with very slowly. Neve had been picking away at the task on her own, so everything went at half speed. And there wasn't any useful gravity in interstellar space, and it turned out the Exiles' Gate was generating its own gravity, so the displaced pollution was being spun into a planetoid of frozen water, rubbish, and flotsam right on the other side of it.

Taryn said, 'We have to find something other than financial incentive for civilisation. At least for the time being.'

'So there is an end to this?'

'A hundred years, maybe. Eighty with good behaviour.'

Price leaned forward. The gentle clacking of knitting needles paused as the guard eyed him.

'Is there something about that particular period? One hundred years?'

'Yes. But we don't talk about it.'

'You have two kinds of "we", Ms Cornick. Humanity, and that other "we" of your inner circle.'

'Life is mostly Venn diagrams. Even a person can be. A quarter this, a quarter that, half something completely different.'

Price leaned back. His jaw muscles rippled. 'Why don't you people just give us a timetable? Conditions? Demands?'

'You must realise none of this is about us. It's not being done for us or against us. This isn't *The Day the Earth Stood Still*. We aren't being warned. We're being treated as kindly as possible while other interests are served. And if you haven't yet worked out whose interests, then you're not as smart as Jacob thinks you are.'

Price brightened. 'Berger is still in circulation?'

'He's liaising about. His joke. He gets to explain things when people are overexcited and the ladies and gentlemen can't make themselves understood. Or can't be bothered making themselves understood.'

'Do you not understand,' Price began with sudden evangelical fervour, 'that the interests mostly likely to be served by everything that's happened will be those of the brutal among us? Thugs. Warlords. Lawless people.'

Taryn laughed. 'Those people are easy to find. They have blood halos. They won't even get to finish sowing the wind before the whirlwind plucks out their eyes. And, Ray—may I call you Ray?—have you really not worked out who benefits? Who is meant to benefit? Tell me, what do you hear if you stop listening for the answers you anticipate? What would you hear if we opened the window?'

'You are not opening a window, Taryn,' the guard said. 'It's brass monkey balls today.'

They ignored her.

'You can't be serious,' Price said.

'That's what I used to say. "You can't really mean to save the world," I said, because I couldn't imagine anyone pulling the thread that would make so much of what I loved unravel. But we are not being saved. We didn't know which god to pray to.'

Price looked so alarmed, and so pleased underneath it—pleased to be proven right, somehow—that Taryn realised she'd have to clarify. 'We are being saved, by the by. Maybe not all, but most of us. But our salvation is a side effect of someone else's. The fossil fuels, the plastics and insecticides, the droughts and floods and hurricanes were going to kill us in our millions. This is better. This will be better.'

'But we don't have a choice!' Price shouted. Then blinked. His vehemence had surprised him.

'Most of us didn't, anyway.'

'They're dictating our futures.'

'They aren't. Only one of them made a decision. The rest went along with him because it gets them out of the house, while they're waiting for their own salvation to arrive from another quarter, pretending very hard that they don't really care about it anyway. We're very lucky they were charmed by his plans. Without the ladies and gentlemen, it wouldn't be possible to shoulder us aside quite so gently. Everything that's happening is a flow-on effect. This people and that people and *us* people. Changes. A shift in how things stand.'

The knitting hadn't resumed. The guard asked, 'What would we hear if we opened the window?'

'Birds. The creak of icy branches. *The forest.*'

'Brrr,' said the guard, with a shiver. She picked up a bag of yellow wool. It was time to start on a new stripe.

'It's all horribly high-handed,' Price said.

'Yes. So how does that feel?' Taryn was acid.

There was only the clack of knitting needles. Then another guard came in with a cup of tea for Taryn's guard, and another visitor.

Taryn's guard said, 'Okay, Mr Price, it's one visitor at a time, so you are going to have to leave.' She put her knitting aside, got up, and adjusted her belt, which was too loose now with all the walking she was doing—was having to do—these days.

'Hello, Berger,' said Price.

'You had the same idea we did,' Jacob said.

'A final interview?'

'I'd be careful about using the word "final",' Jacob said. Then, 'Taryn. It feels unnatural not to give you a kiss.'

'You're just going to have to feel unnatural,' said the guard.

'I frequently do,' said Jacob.

'Mr Price, you're really going to have to say your goodbyes.'

Price produced some credentials. Taryn craned over the table to get a look at them. 'The Ministry of *what?*' she said.

'Very well, Mr Price,' said the guard. 'But I'll have you know I thought it was very unfair of you people to make Ms Cornick serve a whole six years when most of our other inmates were being sent home.'

Taryn was perplexed. 'I chose to.'

'If you hadn't chosen, they meant to make you.' The guard was genuinely indignant. 'Everyone had instructions.'

Price said to Jacob, 'So, you thought to get in early and spirit Ms Cornick away before she answers any questions?'

'She's not going to answer any questions.'

'I've just about answered all the important ones,' Taryn said.

'Taryn!'

'What difference does it make? Munin has been carrying my notebooks out of here for months. A whole book's worth of writing. My next book, the one my agent wanted. Title: *The Absolute Book*. A history of how this all came to pass. It begins with two sisters raising their babies in a house beside the Wye, hands on through two sisters hiding behind a curtain while a man possessed by a demon sets fire to a library, and ends with the sisters who visit me in prison and bring me notebooks. My history, intimate at every point, right up to where I try to set Price straight, and it doesn't sound like a fairy tale anymore.'

Everyone stared at Taryn. She folded her hands, which were shaking.

Price recovered first. He said to Jacob, 'We have tried to keep track of your parents, Jacob. I don't suppose you ever see them.'

'Drop dead,' said Jacob.

'And you're here to make sure your friend doesn't talk to me?'

'No, Ray, I'm here to paint the target.' Jacob frowned and patted his pockets. He produced a note and read it out. '"Jacob—don't forget the Firestarter in Taryn's cell."' He laughed and looked over at the guard. 'Do you think you might be persuaded to let Taryn fetch something from her cell?'

The guard said she didn't like the sound of painting the target. Taryn reassured her that everyone was just being theatrical. Jacob was an actor friend of her father's. The thing they were talking about was a little prop from one of his films. She'd kept it as a comfort.

'Are you telling fibs?' said the guard. 'Whenever this man is in the room'—she gestured at Price—'you start making up all sorts of stuff.'

'Yes, I'm lying. The thing I want to fetch is a scroll box that once belonged to my grandfather. An antique.'

'All right. I'll take you,' the guard said.

They were gone for fifteen minutes. Taryn changed her shoes—she had a pair of walking shoes she was determined to hang on to, given the wide-open spaces waiting for her and the primitive and insufficient sidhe footwear. She carried the Firestarter back to her visitors and found them ignoring each other, like cats in the middle of a slow-burning territorial dispute. She put the Firestarter on the table but didn't sit down again. She could see her guard wanted her to. And Jacob also. But they remained standing, and the guard gave up.

Taryn touched Jacob's arm. 'How is he?'

Jacob stayed still for a time, then decided to talk. His expression became unguarded. 'He's a good-natured animal. I had to stay on him to keep him human. Or human and sidhe. For my part, it didn't feel quite right, even though he came back understanding our relationship and embracing it. But it was hard not to think, *Here is someone utterly helpless.* Since then, I've been watching him learn. Hugin is taking time to teach him. I mean that literally. She *takes time* to do it. I think they've crammed twenty years into two. He's always dizzily delighted to see me, as if we've been apart for weeks, when it's only hours for me. And he never sleeps. No one suggested to him that it's a thing he should do, that other people always do and he's just like them. No one told him he doesn't eat red meat, so he mostly shifts and hunts. He says he's only hungry for what he kills. He'll be out after deer and elk. He carries all the leftovers into the new human colonies. He can be a wolf one week, and the next an eagle hunting wolves. He doesn't really have any sense of contradiction. And that means you can see what he really is.

'We've only recently put the gloves back into his hands. Neve thought he'd have some kind of cataclysmic accident if he got them too early. He tells us he can feel all the gates, the newest ones cleaning the rivers, and filling the aquifers, and some he says are very old and very far away— Neve thinks they must be in the place their ancestors were exiled from.

'He found his library when he located the gate it was hidden behind. A gate of his grandmother's. She must have made it for him at some point. The library is inside a mountain in one of the wildernesses. One that's not quite so wild now, because there's a colony there. The people are pretty much all from Chongqing. The library has windows but no door and looks out over the new houses, the river landing, the river traffic.'

'You're going to like it very much, Taryn,' said the person who had been in the room for who knew how long. Even the guard had failed to notice him arrive.

He came to the table and put his hand on the box, and truly appeared.

He was too young. Maybe the wrong side of twenty. Taryn understood Jacob's scruples. She stayed very still and quietly fought tears.

Shift smiled at her in an anxious and eager way, then he frowned and looked at Price. 'This man has something about his person that has busier atoms than anything else for miles around.'

Jacob threw his arms around Price, pinning him. 'Search him,' he said to Shift.

Shift went straight to the right pocket and found a heavy tube, metal, matte black.

Jacob let Price go. 'So now you're an assassin?'

Shift peered at the tube, as if he could see through it. Strapped to his wrist was his father's glove, the fingers laced through his, all fastened tight across his palm with fresh sidhe metalwork in plain gold. Shift met Price's eyes and said, almost apologetic, 'This couldn't kill me. I can dissolve and re-form myself, and in the process rid myself of whatever isn't me.'

It shocked Taryn, this plain statement of what his shifting was. He'd always been secretive about it. She watched him toss the tube at his own face. It vanished before hitting him. He was carrying a personal gate.

'Nothing was ever on the table,' Price said. His face was white with fury. 'You mean to take our sovereignty. You have no respect for the rule of law.'

'Look,' Taryn said. 'I'm going to try this one more time. It's like that thing in *Star Trek*. The Starfleet regulation that says the doctor can relieve the captain of his duties. The writers probably got it from the real-life navy. Anyway, human beings are the captain. The doctor is the trees and the grasses and the marshes, and the beasts of the field and birds of the air. We humans were declared unfit for command.'

Jacob leaned towards her and kissed her on the cheek. 'Well done.'

She turned back to Shift. She found she was trembling. 'Do you remember me at all?'

'I remember feeling afraid for you,' he said. Then he *glowed* at her. 'I've been reading your notebooks. They've been very helpful. I can't wait to show you my library. And to talk to you about books. Jacob isn't much of a reader.'

She smiled at him, but he discerned the sadness. 'I won't be sorry for forgetting, Taryn. I love meeting people I know I love—it's like the sun coming out. Bigger and bigger skies inside me. Neve says this time I'll be welcomed by everyone. You welcome me, don't you?'

'Yes. You're the person I most wanted to see,' Taryn said. And it was true. She had longed to see him. Him, not Beatrice. Someone new had finally climbed into the throne of her heart.

She put her hand in his free one. It felt absolutely familiar. 'You have calluses.'

'I've been rowing.'

'So you haven't shifted recently. What are you eating?'

'Our friends at Princes Gate have introduced me to the joy of buttery cornbread.'

'If you move away from the Firestarter, will I still be able to see you properly?'

'You will. This extreme vagueness is temporary. The spell hides me when it supposes I'm vulnerable, Neve says. We're waiting for it to catch up.' He laughed.

'There's some ceremony to all this, Taryn,' Jacob said. 'A plan. We've come to collect you—Taryn Cornick of the Northovers, Valravn, Hero of Understanding.'

'Though the sisters couldn't be here,' Shift said. 'They've been trying to master the Language of Command and their flight feathers fell out.'

Jacob said, 'Come to the window.' Then, to the guard, 'Can you open one?'

Snow was falling in the sunlight, soft, insidious, scorchingly cold. The horses were stamping their hooves. Neve lifted her hand—the gold glove flashed like a star. Neve was smiling, and it was a warm smile. Beside her, on a larger horse because he was a big man, was Taryn's father. His face was pink with pleasure. He was pleased to be by the side of the enchanting woman from his strange screen test adventure, and pleased finally to have been told some things he deserved to know.

'Oh,' said Shift to Price. 'Neve says she wants the sword returned. You can take it and the marble tabletop back to the island in the lake at Princes Gate. There's no point you people hanging onto it. No king is going to come.'

Birdsong, the creek of icy branches, the stamp of hooves.

Shift said to Taryn, 'You haven't asked where you're going.'

Taryn said, 'I'm going with you.'

ACKNOWLEDGMENTS

This book has its roots in my lifelong interest in stories about the 'others' of mythology, folklore, fantasy, and science fiction—angels, aliens, golems, and, in this instance, a whole society of the other. My wondering and enthusiasm hadn't suggested an actual book to me until a conversation I had in the Lady Norwood Rose Garden with Danyl McLauchlan about arcane thrillers—what we liked about the genre and what we found frustrating. So, thanks, Danyl—our conversation set my scholarly hero, Taryn, off on a search for an arcane object that really is something, not just a cause for a search.

Taryn's own book, *The Feverish Library*, was inspired principally by Lucien X. Polastron's magnificent *Books on Fire*; also by *The Library: A Catalogue of Wonders* by Stuart Kells and Alberto Manguel's *The Library at Night*. My other key reading was Katharine Briggs's comprehensive *The Fairies in Tradition and Literature*.

Thank you to early readers of this novel: David Larsen, Francis Spufford, Sara Knox, and Holly Hunter.

Thank you to Claire McAlpine for scoping out the Bibliothèque Méjanes.

And, as ever, the wonderful team at Victoria University Press: my editor Ashleigh Young, Kirsten McDougall, Craig Gamble, Jasmine Sargent, Kyleigh Hodgson, and my husband, Fergus Barrowman.

Thank you to the guides of this novel's next life, my agent Scott Miller, and my three wonderful editors, Brian Tart, Gretchen Schmid, and Jillian Taylor.

Lastly, thank you, Jack Barrowman, for the late-night mutual story-doctoring sessions.